Prologue

His mother had always been able to surprise him. It had been
her way. But she had never surprised him as much as this. He
lifted the huge diamond out of the dark blue velvet socket of
her jewellery box, and held it up in the curtained dimness of
her bedroom with a sensation of sudden vertigo. It was a
brilliant, fiery, rectangular-cut stone, larger than a man could
comfortably swallow, and it was still unmounted; untouched
and untampered-with since the brilliandeer had buffed it up to
its final dazzling polish.

He had no exact idea of how much diamonds were worth,
although he had heard that if they were monstrously large, as
this one was, they could no longer be valued carat for carat: that
would put them beyond the reach of even the world's richest
men. But even at auction, this diamond would have to be valued
at hundreds of thousands of pounds, perhaps millions.

'I'm a millionaire,' he thought to himself. It was like
emerging from a wine-cellar into the open air and discovering
that he was drunk.

He had no doubt at all that the stone was real. He remembered as he turned it around and around in his fingers what his
mother had whispered to him only five weekends ago on the
wisteria-wrapped verandah of the Reverend Ponsford's house
at Herne Hill, when everybody else had been playing croquet
on the sun-blinded lawns.

'Your father made sure you were taken care of,' she had said.
'Your real father, that is. He provided for you, and for your
children, but secretly; so that when I go, you shall never want.'

'You're not going to *go*,' he had smiled at her, and taken her
hand between his. In its white summer glove, it had felt like
a dead starling, all bones and feathers.

I

But whether she had experienced a premonition or not, a kind of Tarot-reading from the weather, and the clouds, and the postures of the reverend gentlemen who were playing croquet, she *had* gone, within three weeks of the croquet party, of a summer cold that turned to pneumonia. At the age of thirty-three, Peter Ransome found himself to be an orphan.

The effect had caught him off-balance. He had not been prepared for the abrupt loneliness of it; nor for the pain that he would suffer as he tidied up his mother's affairs with Messrs Winchell & Golightly, Solicitors and Commissioners for Oaths, of Croydon; and as he cleared up his mother's house in Kennington, in South London, not far from the Oval cricket ground. As he came across photographs and memorabilia from his mother's past: a sepia print of his stepfather with the Bishop of Woolwich, another of his mother arm-in-arm in some scrubby landscape with Cecil Rhodes, a lion's-tooth necklet, a silver snuffbox with an embossed view of Victoria Falls, he began to feel as if he no longer knew who he was, or why he was here. He had inherited all of these fragments from other people's lives, but there was no longer anybody in the whole world to whom he was directly related.

His stepfather, the Reverend Hugh Ransome, had died of a seizure the day before Queen Victoria's Jubilee celebrations, on 21 June 1897. The excitement of arranging a party for Kennington's children and old folks had been too much for him: that, and the heat.

His real father had died a year before that, drowned, after a well-publicised incident on the cruise liner *Andromeda*, off Madagascar. One witness had insisted that Mr Blitz had 'recklessly and with aforethought' hurled himself over the rail of the quoits deck into the Indian Ocean, and had swallowed enough water to sink himself before the ship could be brought about. But Mrs Blitz had strenuously denied any suggestions of suicide. Her husband had been 'in bustling health', she had told the coroner, prettily, and he had been eager to start up a new property business in Cape Town.

But now Peter was here, in the big redbrick house in Montacute Road, overlooking a tired triangle of grass and plane trees, with his mother's jewellery case open in front of him, and a diamond between his fingers that was bigger than he would have thought possible. It *had* to be real, he was convinced of it, even though he had no expertise in diamonds, and no means of testing the stone, apart from using it to scratch his name on the bedroom window, which somehow did not seem like a very reverent idea. In the five years since his stepfather had died, Peter had gradually become aware that the love between his mother and his real father had been something intense, and very special, and that even their eventual separation had not been able to extinguish it.

If the love between his mother and his real father had been only half as fierce as his mother had described it (and being a modest woman, a vicar's widow, it had probably been twice as passionate, and twice as jealous as she had told him), then this diamond which symbolised it just *had* to be authentic, and flawless, too.

His mother's maid Olive came into the bedroom, with a japanned carpet sweeper, her hair a chaos of henna-stained curls and tortoise-shell combs. 'It wouldn't be disrespectful to open the curtains, do you think, sir?' she suggested. 'I would hate to think of you straining your eyes. My 'enry strained his eyes, fighting in the dark at Nicholson's Nek.'

Peter clasped the diamond protectively in both hands, and turned around in a way that was stiffer and more mannered than he would have liked. 'By all means draw them,' he said. 'I don't think Mother would have wanted to see the house so gloomy in any case, do you?'

Olive drew back the thick brocade drapes with a rattle of brass rings. The London sunlight fell across the patterned rug, and on to the white-covered bed on which only a fortnight ago his mother had closed her eyes for the last time, as if asleep. On the wall beside the bed hung a plain wooden crucifix: his mother used to tell Peter that she had been given it by a missionary in South Africa, when she was still a young girl – before she could even speak English.

'You'd like some tea, sir?' enquired Olive.

Peter kept his hands clasped tight together. 'Yes, tea,' he said. 'I shall be down directly.'

'Very good, sir.'

3

When Olive had gone, he left the dressing-table and walked across to the oval cheval-glass by the window. In it, he saw a dark, shy-looking young man in a plainly-tailored grey suit; a young man whose complexion was too dusky to be English, and yet whose short straight nose and sharply-defined forehead were too European to be those of a pure-blooded African. Racially, he was a thrice-cut cake: a third Dutch, a third Hottentot, and a third German-Jewish.

He was used to the difficulties of having tinted skin. He was an automobile mechanic, working for the Vulcan motor car company in Southport, Cheshire, but he knew that for all of his talent with a spanner he would never make chief engineer. He raced, too, a little, whenever there was a spare 10-hp car and enough ethyl. But he would never be allowed to make the grade as a first-class driver. This was an England which tolerated half-castes as the inevitable outcome of a far-flung colonial empire, but which scarcely ever admitted a 'fuzzy-wuzzy' to the inner circles of society.

It had helped Peter that his stepfather had been the Reverend Hugh Ransome, much respected for his work amongst the poor of south London, and amongst the heathen in South Africa. His stepfather had taught him manners, and proper dress, and all the niceties of small conversation. But none of these graces had really been enough to whiten his face, and he had known ever since he was at school that only an Act of God could win him admission to the prizewinner's enclosure of Edwardian society.

Perhaps this diamond was it. The one miracle which could change everything. He opened his hand, and the huge stone was warm, already infused with his own heat. The sun caught it, just the tip of it, and it flared up with brilliant rainbows and shatteringly bright triangles of reflected and re-reflected light, a spangled hall-of-mirrors in miniature.

'Your father made sure you were taken care of,' his mother had whispered, and the words fell on his memory like sheets of soft tissue paper.

He recalled sitting by his mother's knee almost twenty years ago on a winter's night in the old vicarage, toasting muffins on the end of a fork, his cheeks hot as baked apples, and he remembered his mother saying, 'Did I ever tell you the story

4

of the man who gave up everything he had, all his possessions, even the estates that he adored so much, just to buy his secret love the most precious stone in the whole world?'

He had said no, tell me. But she had simply smiled in an absent-minded sort of way, and tousled his hair, and told him to be careful not to drop his muffin into the coals. Now, however, he knew what she had meant.

He looked through the drawers of his mother's dressing-table until he found a silk drawstring sachet that had been used for carrying a gold powder compact. He dropped the diamond into the sachet, tightened the string, and slipped it into his pocket. Then he straightened his necktie in the looking-glass, and went downstairs to the front parlour, where Olive was setting out the tea things. There was a large Rockingham pot of fragrant Ceylon, and a small plate of rather stale rock cakes.

'You're looking pale, sir, if you don't mind my saying,' said Olive. 'You're not considering going down with the fever?'

'I didn't have it in mind,' said Peter. 'Would you pour?'

Olive poured, and the steam from the cup twisted up into the sunlight like the Indian rope-trick. 'I keep dwelling on your mother, sir,' said Olive, sadly. 'Such a lovely woman, you know; and even lovelier when she was younger.'

'Yes,' said Peter, sipping his scalding tea. He didn't really want to share his memories with Olive. 'I miss her very much.'

He finished his tea alone. He tried one of the buns, but they were too dry and somehow they tasted of death. At last, at three o'clock, he left the house and walked down to the end of the road, to wait for the horse-drawn omnibus to take him over the river into London. Across the street, as he waited, two barefoot street Arabs were trying to shin up the gas-lamp on the corner, watched in awe by another boy in a boater hat and a sailor suit, whose nanny had paused to gossip on the pavement with a postman.

The omnibus arrived late. Because it was a fine summer's day, Peter sat up on the roof, and smoked a cigarette. There was a traffic jam on Blackfriars Bridge, and the omnibus had to wait there for almost ten minutes, while a cool breeze blew up the Thames from the docks, fragrant with spices and

5

peppers from unloading ships and warehouses. Peter took out another cigarette, but tossed it half-smoked on to the road.

He arrived at a small jeweller's shop just opposite Holborn Circus a few minutes before five o'clock. The late afternoon was crowded with carriages and cabs and horse-drawn drays, and the noise of horseshoes and iron-bound wheels grinding on the wooden road-blocks was almost deafening. A bell jangled as he stepped into the door, and then there was silence as he closed it behind him.

The shop was very small. There were mahogany-and-glass showcases on all sides, crammed with rings and pendants and silver perfume-holders – lower middle-class jewellery, the kind of jewellery that a jobbing clerk might give to his lady-love at Christmas, or a shopkeeper buy for his wife on their wedding anniversary. There was a smell of dust and silver polish and jeweller's rouge.

From a door at the back of the shop came a man as lanky as a tailor, with blond hair which flopped over his right eye. 'My dear fellow!' he said, as soon as he saw it was Peter. 'What a complete surprise!'

Peter held out his hand. 'How are you, Samuel? You're not getting any plumper.'

'Not for want of eating, though,' said Samuel. 'Business has never been so brisk. Have you come down for anything special, or just for a jaw?'

Samuel Kellogg had been a schoolfriend of Peter's in Kennington, although when Samuel's father had died of consumption he had moved to Bloomsbury to live with his Uncle Max, and help in the family jewellery business. Still, the friends had kept in touch from time to time, even when Peter went to Southport, and only last summer they had met for supper in Oxford Street, at Runcorn's Chop House.

'My mother passed away,' said Peter. 'I've been down in Kennington clearing up the house.'

'My dear chap,' said Samuel, sympathetically.

'She was frailer than I thought,' Peter told him. 'I suppose she never really was cut out for the British climate. She always used to suffer from colds, and the influenza.'

'All the same, I'm very sorry,' said Samuel.

6

'Thanks,' said Peter, trying to brighten up.

'Won't you come through to the back?' asked Samuel. 'I have some tea left in the pot, and some capital veal pie.'

He lifted the mahogany flap of the counter, and Peter followed him through into a dark back room, where there was a badly dilapidated sofa, a fireplace still clogged with last winter's ashes, and a jeweller's workbench, cluttered with silver wire and forceps and soldering irons. On the wall was a saucy calendar of a naked theatre girl with plumes of ostrich feathers in her hair and strings of pearls around her ankles.

'I don't suppose you've seen anything of Walter,' said Samuel, taking the lid off the teapot and peering into it suspiciously.

'Not a peek. I heard he went off to Malaya to plant rubber.'

'He always did have the look of a rubber-planter, I must admit.'

Peter moved four or five tattered copies of *The London Illustrated News* from the sofa, and sat down. 'I don't know. What does a rubber-planter look like?'

Samuel shrugged. '*Rubbery*, I suppose. Shall I brew some fresh?'

'Don't bother. What I really came about was more in the line of business.'

'I see,' said Samuel, sitting down. He cut a piece of veal pie off a twenty-one pound slab, and pushed it into his mouth. 'I suppose your poor mama left you quite a bit of disposable jewellery?'

'I haven't been through it all yet,' Peter told him. 'But I was mainly concerned about *this*,' and he produced from his pocket the small drawstring purse, which he loosened, and then turned upside-down over Samuel's workbench.

The diamond rolled out on to the bench, and lay on its side, sparkling in the gaslight. Samuel, his mouth still stuffed with pie, stared at it as if God had just dropped a third tablet of commandments from the heavens above.

'What on earth...?' he asked. 'You're not telling me that's a real stone?'

Peter nodded. 'I'm pretty well convinced of it.'

'But that's a *diamond*,' said Samuel. 'You don't find diamonds in that sort of size. That's as big as the Regent. Bigger. It can't be real. Where on earth did you get it?'

'My mother's jewellery box.'

'Not even in a safe? It can't be real. My dear chap, if that were a real diamond, it would be worth ... a million pounds. Maybe more. You wouldn't keep it in a jewellery box. You'd have it locked up, in Coutts.'

'Maybe you would, and maybe you wouldn't. What burglar would ever suspect that a vicar's wife would have a million-pound diamond in her jewellery box? A couple of rings, maybe; a pinchbeck pendant. But not a million-pound diamond.'

Samuel picked the diamond up and frowned at it. Then he reached for his jeweller's loupe, his 10 × magnifying lens, and peered at it even more closely.

'It's difficult to tell in gaslight,' he said. 'But if it *is* a real diamond, it's magnificent. A slight pinkish tinge to it, don't you see? Very slight, but enough to make it a "fancy" diamond, and increase its value four to five times over, if you can find anyone to pay that sort of money.'

'Then you think it's genuine?'

'My dear chap, I couldn't tell you for certain. This is the whole illusion of the diamond business. Not even quite re-putable dealers are capable of telling whether some diamonds are real diamonds or not. There are plenty of very capable fakes around these days: and if they're mounted, they're even harder to detect. Some tricksters set inferior diamonds in a fine gold or silver setting, you see, and paint the back of the gems so that they reflect more light. There was the famous rainbow necklace of the Romanoffs, for instance. George Kunz, an American gemologist, and a very sceptical fellow, discovered by scratch-ing the backs of the diamonds with his finger-nail that they were nothing but second-rate stones with paint on them.'

'But this stone isn't mounted,' said Peter.

'No,' replied Samuel. 'But it could be topaz, or strass, which is high-density lead glass, or even quartz; although I doubt that it's quartz, because it appears too brilliant.'

Peter was silent for a moment, watching his friend examine the stone through his loupe, but then he said, 'I have to tell you something which may make you change your opinion.'

8

'Well, do,' said Samuel, 'because if this is a real diamond, then you're in the money for the rest of your life, and I'm not joking.'

'The Reverend Ransome wasn't my real father,' said Peter. 'I know that I always pretended he was, when I was at school, but that was only because I was embarrassed about it. My real father was Barney Blitz.'

Samuel put down the diamond and looked at his schoolfriend in astonishment. 'Now, you're really having me on toast. This is just a practical joke, isn't it? You're going to go back to all the fellows at Kennington and tell them how Samuel Kellogg thought a piece of glass from a Christmas cracker was worth millions of pounds.'

'Samuel, I'm telling you the truth. I swear it. When my mother was in South Africa, she lived with Barney Blitz for years. He was my real father.'

'Well, you could knock me down with a feather,' said Samuel.

Peter pointed to the diamond. 'That's why I'm quite sure that the diamond is real. And that's why I have to know where I can take it to sell it. I don't want to be sold short. My father gave that stone to my mother so that my future would be secure. I wouldn't want to let him down by giving it to the first diamond dealer I meet for only a quarter of what it's worth.'

Samuel looked at the stone for a long time. 'You'll excuse me,' he said, 'but I've never seen a diamond like this before, and I never will again. I want to make sure that I remember this moment. So, Barney Blitz was your father, was he? You could knock me down with a feather.'

'The point is,' said Peter, 'where can I go with such a diamond?'

Samuel laid the diamond carefully back on his workbench. 'There's only one man that I know of. Garth Steinman. I don't know whether you've ever heard of him or not, but he's a dealer in unusual and speciality jewels only. Quite an eccentric, but a very rich eccentric. He acquired the Montfort emeralds for the late Queen. He's a friend of the Rothschilds, and of J. P. Morgan. He has a house in St John's Wood, although he may

9

not be there now. He winters in Italy, and spends his summers in Switzerland.'

Peter took back the diamond and slipped it into the drawstring sachet. 'I can only try. Do you think you can find me his address?'

'My dear chap,' said Samuel, 'for the sake of a diamond like that, I'll even *take* you there.'

Samuel closed the jeweller's shop early, and the two of them hailed a hansom from the corner of Gray's Inn Road. The rush-hour traffic was easing off now, and the early evening sunlight filled the interior of the cab with gilded motes of dust. Neither of the friends spoke very much as they turned westwards towards Euston station. Peter felt as if the whole of his world had altered, as if he were now involved in a theatrical performance of his own life, rather than the real thing.

It took them a little over twenty minutes to reach the quiet sidestreet in St John's Wood where Garth Steinman's residence stood. The Steinman house was only one of a whole row of huge, expensive mansions, each with a high wall and hedges. In those days, St John's Wood, although it was only a mile or so north of Marylebone, was a quiet secluded village of its own, and the air was noticeably fresher than it had been in Holborn. Peter and Samuel alighted from the cab and paid the cabbie 1s 3d, with 3d tip.

Samuel rang at the bell-pull on the gate. But it was almost five minutes before a gardener, who was trundling a wheelbarrow of dug-up daffodil bulbs, came past the front of the house and noticed them. A little while later, a footman in a green coat and stockings came out to enquire what they wanted.

'Mr Steinman, if he's at home,' said Peter.

'You have an appointment, sir?'

'I have something better than an appointment.'

'Sir?'

'I have the largest diamond he's ever seen in his life.'

The footman said, 'I'm afraid Mr Steinman is seeing nobody today. He has a headache.'

Peter took the diamond out of his pocket, and held it up. It flashed in the sunshine as brilliantly as if it had actually caught fire. The footman could not keep his eyes off it.

'Tell Mr Steinman that you've seen the diamond for yourself,' said Peter, quietly. 'Tell him that it will be more than worth his while to forget his headache for five minutes.'

'Yes, sir,' said the footman, and retreated towards the house. Peter glanced at Samuel and gave him a teeth-gritted grin, half optimistic and half fearful.

Another five minutes passed before the footman returned. Without a word, he unlocked the gates, and beckoned them inside. He locked the gates behind them as they walked up the sloping gravelled driveway towards the pillared portico of the house. The flowerbeds all the way along the drive were clustered with white and yellow roses, and the fragrance was almost nauseating. Peter was reminded that he had not eaten anything all day, except for one desultory nibble at his rock cake.

The footman opened the black-painted front doors, and led the friends into a wide, high-ceilinged hallway which had been decorated in a style which Peter could only think of as over-extravagant Byzantine. There were arches everywhere, decorated with gold and peacock-blue mosaics, and a fountain of nude entwined mermaids splashed water into the cool echoing silence.

'You'll come through to the afternoon room, sir?' asked the footman, and ushered them into a sunny yellow-carpeted library at the far side of the hall.

At a wide leather-topped desk, smoking a Turkish cigarette in a long holder, sat a small rotund man with shiny brushed-back hair, and a monocle. He was wearing a yellow silk dressing-gown which matched the colour of the carpet, and yellow silk slippers.

On a chaise-longue at the opposite end of the room, next to a wall of gilded and leather-bound books, lay a very pretty girl who looked no more than sixteen or seventeen years old, with an embroidered silk headband around her blonde, upswept hair, and dressed in a multi-layered negligée of such fine laon and lace that Peter could distinguish the rosy pink of her nipples.

'You'd better introduce yourselves,' said the fat man behind the desk.

'My name's Peter Ransome,' said Peter. 'And this is Mr Samuel Kellogg, my friend. Mr Kellogg is a jeweller.'

'I see,' said Garth Steinman. 'And what are you?'

'I am an automobile mechanic,' said Peter.

Garth Steinman jotted a few notes on to the diary that was open in front of him. Then he closed it up, and said, 'What is an automobile mechanic doing with a large diamond, that's what I ask myself.'

'I came by it legitimately, Mr Steinman. It was a bequest from my late mother. My ... *recently* late mother.'

'My condolences,' said Garth Steinman. 'Your mother was a wealthy woman? Should I know her name?'

'She was not wealthy in any other respect, save this diamond,' Peter told him, quietly.

Garth Steinman looked up, one eye closed, the other eye staring through his monocle like a freshly opened clam. 'I see. Well, a diamond's provenance is not too difficult to check, if you know the right people to ask. My man told me that the stone was exceptional, by all appearances.'

Peter took the diamond out of his pocket again and set it precisely in the centre of Garth Steinman's closed diary. Garth Steinman kept his eyes on Peter for more than ten seconds before he turned his attention to the stone.

'Well, then,' he said. On the other side of the room, the pretty blonde girl had sat up and taken notice.

While Peter and Samuel stood and watched him in silence, Garth Steinman laid the diamond on a sheet of white paper, and examined it closely. His cigarette now burned unnoticed in the ashtray, and the only sound in the room, apart from the faint splashing of the fountain in the hallway, was Steinmen's hoarse breathing, in and out of his open mouth.

Now Steinman took out a 20 × loupe, and scrutinised the diamond for brilliance and fire, and also to check whether it contained any 'clouds', which are small clusters of bubbles; and 'butterflies', which are cleavage cracks; or 'naats', which are the knotty flaws that sometimes appear at the interface between twinned crystals.

After long minutes of study, he eventually put the diamond down again, and tucked his loupe into the breast pocket of his dressing-gown.

'I am very seldom taken by surprise,' he said, thickly. 'I

know the value and the whereabouts of almost every major gemstone in the world. I have friends in the Russian court; in Vienna; and in Berlin. I was a close friend of Cecil Rhodes before he died last year, and Mr Ernest Oppenheimer regularly sends me cables from De Beers, and dines with me whenever he comes to London, or to Berne.'

Garth Steinman paused, and then lifted up the diamond in his right hand. 'This, however, has taken me by surprise. It is genuine, I can assure you of that. No paste diamond could be made to this size without its falsity being immediately obvious. And who would attempt to fake a stone of this immensity? It would be absurd. Mr Ransome – that is your name? – this diamond I believe to be the famous Rio Diamond, which was sold at auction in 1888 to a New York diamond dealer called Greenberg. I don't remember how much it fetched, about two millions, I think. But its size, and its cut, and its colour – all correspond with what I know of the Rio.'

The blonde girl had now got up from the chaise-longue and crossed the room, the lacy train of her negligée dragging across the canary-yellow carpet. She stood a little way away from Garth Steinman's desk, and stared at the diamond as if it were a hypnotic eye. Peter gave her a quick, friendly smile, but she did not return it.

'How much do you think the diamond is worth now?' asked Samuel.

Garth Steinman puffed out his cheeks. 'It depends on its history. If Mr Ransome here can establish that it is rightfully his, then we can make some enquiries right away, of dealers and collectors, and of royal courts, and we may be lucky enough to be able to close a private sale, which usually fetches more than an open auction. The market price is quite steady at the moment – so we may get three to four millions, if we play things right. I'd expect a commission, of course, of thirty per cent.'

'That seems excessive,' said Peter.

Garth Steinman smiled tightly. 'Seventy per cent of three millions, which is what you'll be left with, is rather more than seventy per cent of nothing. There aren't many men on earth who can sell this diamond for you, I assure you. Well – you must

13

know that, or you wouldn't have brought it here to begin with.'

'He's right, Peter,' said Samuel.

Peter thought for a moment, and then nodded. 'Very well, Mr Steinman, I'll leave the sale to you. I shall require a receipt, of course, to the effect that you're holding the diamond. And I shall also require you to seek my approval before you close the sale.'

'Naturally,' said Garth Steinman. 'Can I offer you a brandy?'

It was more than a month before Peter heard from Garth Steinman again. Then, when he was back at the Vulcan motor works at Southport, on a sullen August day, he received a telegram saying, '*Entrain for London at once. I have a sale –* Steinman.' He told his chief engineer that he was feeling sick, and took an omnibus back to his small walk-up flat on the outskirts of Southport to pack, hurriedly, a portmanteau. By tea-time, his train was pulling out of Northampton on its way to London, and the first flickers of lightning were lighting up the eastern horizon, over towards the flatlands of East Anglia. He arrived in St John's Wood at six.

Garth Steinman met him at the door. This time, Steinman was dressed in a consummately-tailored afternoon suit, with a wing collar, which gave his head the appearance of a pale Christmas pudding on a white dish.

'You've been remarkably prompt,' he said, and showed Peter inside. 'Do you like nudes?' he asked, as they passed the fountain in the hallway.

Peter glanced at him. 'In moderation,' he replied. 'There's a time and a place for everything.'

Garth Steinman cackled out loud. 'I like your style, Mr Ransome. But then a man of your potential wealth can afford to have style.'

They went through to the library. There was no sign of the blonde girl who had been there before. Instead, by the window, smoking a cigar, stood a broad-shouldered man of about fifty, wearing a black tailcoat and striped trousers. He had a permanently amused expression on his ape-like face, and a very bushy moustache.

'Mr Ransome,' said Garth Steinman, 'I'd like you to meet Herr Albert Ballin. You might have heard of Herr Ballin – he is the managing director of the Hamburg-Amerika Line. He is also a close personal friend of the Kaiser, and that is why he has come here today.'

Herr Ballin stepped forward, one hand thrust into the pocket of his trousers, the other around his cigar. He looked at Peter for a while, his eyes half-closed against the smoke, and then he said, 'I have inspected your diamond, Mr Ransome, and I have made Mr Steinman an offer. My intention is to present it to the Kaiser as a gift on his next birthday.'

'Well, I'm sure the Kaiser will like it,' said Peter, hesitantly. 'Is the offer fair, Mr Steinman?'

'Three millions, seven hundred and fifty thousand,' smiled Garth Steinman. 'Three millions to be paid in two instalments in cash, in a London bank. The remainder in Hamburg-Amerika securities.'

Albert Ballin sat down in a small armchair, and crossed his podgy legs. 'You will not refuse me, Mr Ransome? I have a reputation for getting everything I want. My enemies call it *ballinismus*.'

'I can recommend that you accept the offer,' said Steinman. 'I doubt if anybody else is in a position to be more generous than Herr Ballin.'

Peter thought for a moment, and then shrugged. 'The arrangement seems fair to me. As long as Herr Ballin is satisfied.'

Albert Ballin nodded. 'I am *more* than satisfied. This is one of the great treasures of the earth.'

'You want to have it tested first?' asked Steinman.

Ballin laughed. 'I think I trust you. Mind you, I could always drop it into a glass of clear crème-de-menthe, couldn't I? That's supposed to be an infallible test for diamonds.'

Garth Steinman said, 'You can drop it into whatever you want. But I should warn you that the old crème-de-menthe test is something of a romantic fallacy. The theory behind it is that, in crème-de-menthe, a diamond will show up clearly, because of its high refractive qualities, whereas a synthetic stone will disappear. The trouble is, plenty of up-to-date synthetics have high refractive indices, too. I would hate you to fool yourself.'

'Very well,' said Herr Ballin. 'I will forego the test. If you are content with the price, Mr Ransome, I will talk to my bankers in the morning.'

'The price is fine,' said Peter. 'I'm just wondering if the destiny is right.'

'The *destiny*?' asked Herr Ballin.

'I'm wondering if this diamond was really meant to be the personal property of the Kaiser, and to be inherited by the German monarchy.'

Garth Steinman walked across to his desk, where the diamond was lying on a small cushion of white velvet, and picked it up. 'You should understand, Mr Ransome, that diamonds, even more than people, have their own destiny. Whatever their owners do, they will always find their place in history. If this diamond is not happy with the Kaiser, then it will not stay with the Kaiser. In any case, why should you worry? You are a rich man now, and you can do whatever you wish. Racing those motor cars of yours, I shouldn't be surprised?'

Peter said, slowly, 'Yes.' But he found himself looking at the diamond, and the way it sparkled, and he was suddenly reluctant to lose it. Garth Steinman recognised the expression on his face, however, and heartily grasped his shoulder. 'You will never get a better price, old fellow. And, believe me, diamonds are better off in the hands of those who can really afford them. To everyone else, they bring nothing but grief and despair.'

'*Sehr philosophisch,*' smiled Herr Ballin.

Peter took the diamond in his hand one last time. It meant so much more than Herr Ballin or Garth Steinman could ever understand. It was the crystallisation of the love between his mother and his father, the last adamant reminder of the passion that had created him, and of private fears and ambitions that he could only guess at.

'Very well,' he said, at last, and laid the diamond down again. He shook hands with Herr Ballin, and with Garth Steinman, and left the house quickly, without saying another word.

Later that day, he stood by the Thames at Chelsea embankment, as the sun sank behind the cluttered rooftops of World's

End. He tossed pennies into the river because now he could afford to; and each penny that splashed into the water created for one split second a sun-glittered diamond of its own.

He had never felt so lonely in his life.

ONE

From inside the apartment, as he reached the top of the stairs, Barney could hear his mother arguing, and sobbing, and banging her ladle. It was the same as always. A jumble of rage, entreaty, tears, and stunning absurdities. Enough to turn a good son's loyalty head-over-heels. 'If your father should walk in now! What would he say?' 'Why didn't I have sons like other women – sons who respect their mother?' 'Don't you know how much I suffered, giving birth to two *schlimazels* like you?' 'Is this the reward I get?'

Barney took the brass latchkey out of his dark vest pocket, on its long fine chain, and held it up for a moment. Then, with resignation, he unlocked the door. At the far end of the landing, rain still spattered against the frosted-glass window, like a pessimistic Romeo throwing up occasional handfuls of gravel. Barney hesitated, and then pushed the door wide. The scorched-tomato smell of burned goulash blew out of the apartment on the damp evening draught. He touched the *mezuzah* which hung on the doorframe, and stepped inside.

On the wall, beside the peg where he hung up his coat, there was a steel engraving of Drensteinfürt, in Westfalen, Germany. The picture was grimy and foxed. Barney touched that too, the same way his father used to.

Mrs Blitz was in the kitchen, a one-woman band, racketing her ladle against the sink, the cupboards, against the iron pans that hung above the range. Her hair was wiry and wild, as if she had just come in out of a hurricane. The goulash pot was smoking furiously on the hotplate, and there were half-chopped vegetables strewn everywhere.

'You wait!' she was screeching. 'You wait until you run out of friends, and out of money, and out of love!' And she beat

19

against the colander, and the door, and the tin bowl in the sink. 'You talk of gratitude! Duty, you talk of! Is this gratitude? Is this what you call duty? *Riboyne Shel O'lem!*'

Barney closed the apartment door behind him. And even though his mother was screaming, 'Don't come crawling back to me! Don't you ever come crying for money!' she stopped in mid-sentence at the almost inaudible click of the lock – silent, aghast, frozen, in case it was actually *him*, *Tateh* himself, Barney's father, returned from the cemetery with his smile and his moustache and his best broadcloth suit.

'Mama,' said Barney, gently.

Slowly, like a woman in a theatrical production of her own personal tragedy, Mrs Blitz came towards him, her arms out-stretched, and she clutched him so tight around the chest that he could feel her bony ribs through the thick fabric of his vest, her terrible scarecrow thinness, and it was all he could do to embrace her like a son, and consolingly stroke her frayed black hair, and whisper, 'Mama ... another *tarrarom*? ... now what for?'

Joel, his older brother, appeared at the far end of the kitchen. Joel was slighter than Barney, with his mother's dark hair and his mother's thin, intense face. His shirtsleeves were rolled up tight, and there was a purple marking-pencil behind his ear. He looked at Barney, and then across at the range, and then he walked over and took off the burning goulash pot.

'Well, it's a good think the neighbourhood wasn't hungry tonight,' he remarked, fanning away the smoke with his hand. 'Mama just burned enough goulash to feed everyone from here to Cherry Street.'

'What's wrong?' asked Barney, still holding his mother close, but more stiffly now.

His mother raised her head. It was difficult for Barney to believe that she was the same bright, fierce woman who had brought up the Blitz family – the same woman who had fed them with meatballs and clothed them in flannels and sung them songs of Münster, in 'the good old days'. It was even harder to associate her with the pretty girl who laughed from the pinchbeck photograph frame in the parlour, the girl who clung with pride and delight to the arm of that smiling, puff-chested man who stood beside her, all top hat and well-brushed moustaches.

But four years ago, on the seventh day of Tishri, that man had died of consumption in his upstairs bedroom; and while she waited outside his door, listening to the mumbling of the rabbi and the doctor, Feigel Blitz had slowly come apart, not just mentally, but physically as well, so that her eyes no longer seemed to fit her face, and her mouth appeared to speak without her forehead realising what she was saying. She could look elated, and say something moody and odd. She could look unhappy, and say something cheerful. The woman who stared up at Barney now was a scrambled jigsaw of the mother he had once loved dearly. The neighbours upstairs called her a *meshuggeneh*, a crazy woman. The rabbi, when he visited, would always take Barney's hand, and squeeze it, as if to say, I understand your problems, but, *nu-nu*, she's your mother, after all.

Barney repeated, 'What's wrong, Joel? What's happening here?'

Joel shrugged. Mrs Blitz said, 'He's leaving. He's packing his trunks.'

'You're *leaving*?' asked Barney.

'That's right,' said Joel. 'And if it hadn't been for the Great Fire of '45 here, and all this shouting and screaming, I would have had the chance to tell you decently.'

'I don't believe it,' said Barney. 'You mean you're packing now?'

'He's packing now,' put in Mrs Blitz. 'Shirts, shoes, even his pants!'

'You want I should leave my pants behind?' retorted Joel.

'Barney, you tell him,' wept Mrs Blitz. But, just as abruptly, she turned around and screamed at Joel, 'You're just like your father! That's what your father did – he left me! He went! Right when I needed him most of all!'

Barney held his mother's shoulders tight. 'Mama,' he said, 'yelling isn't going to get us any place at all.'

'No more is whispering!' cried Mrs Blitz. 'Yell, cry, what's the difference? Maybe I should sing him a song! *Ein Knabchen sah' ein Röselein steh'n ... Röselein auf der Heide ...* You remember that? But what's the difference? He's still going to walk out ... a first son walking out on his own mother, on his own brother! God should bring down a curse on you, Joel!'

'God already did!' Joel shouted, and banged the door so hard that dry plaster showered down from the laths around the frame.

Feigel Blitz clutched Barney's wrist. She did not say anything, but her face twitched as if she could feel something crawling up her back. Then she released him, and suddenly turned away.

'You're hungry?' she asked Barney. She picked the goulash pot out of the sink, lifted the lid, and inspected its charred contents.

'I can eat out,' said Barney.

'No, no ... I can easily make you meatballs ... maybe some sauerkraut?'

'Mama –'

'Well,' she said, replacing the lid on the pot. 'I know what you're thinking. He's a big boy now, he has a right to do whatever he chooses. But he has a family. Now his father's gone, he's the head of the table. You don't think that's a responsibility?'

Barney took a breath. He said, 'Yes, Mama, that's part of it.' Beside him, on the kitchen wall, was a calendar for 1868, a gift from Mrs Jana across the landing. There was a Polish quotation from the Bible for today's date: *'Badźcie nasladowcami moini, tak jak ja jestem naśladowca Chrystusa'*.

'I have herring, too,' suggested Barney's mother.

Barney stood in the kitchen for a moment, watching his mother dither from the scratched deal table to the sink, and back again, and smile at him with that infectious, dotty, frighteningly vacant smile. 'You'd like a herring?' she asked.

'I have to talk to Joel,' Barney told her. 'Now, please – promise you'll wait here, and make me some supper – and don't start yelling again. Will you, please?' He was very conscious, in his mother's home, of how American he sounded.

'Well, what do you think?' she asked him, in that ambiguous way that always infuriated him.

He opened the door at the far end of the kitchen, and walked along the dark narrow corridor to Joel's bedroom. The door to his mother's room was open, and he glimpsed as he passed the high sawn-oak bed, the stolid dressing-table, the pictures of the old country. There was the smell, too, of stale violets and powder, of a middle-aged woman sleeping on her own. He felt a wince of pain. *She's your mother, after all.*

Joel had the larger of the two other bedrooms. Its grimy window looked out over Clinton Street, where the gaslamps were already lit, although it was only seven o'clock, and late in April; and the rain was rattling in the gutters. Joel's two trunks were laid open on his iron-frame bed, and he had almost finished packing. His striped nightshirts, his books on geology and sailing, his best brown boots.

Barney stood in the doorway and watched him. Barney was tall for his age, nineteen, and meaty across the shoulders. Everybody in the family said he took after his *elter zayde*, his great-grandfather, Yussel Blitz. It had been Yussel who had first started the coat-cutting business by making winter jackets for the farmers and butchers in his home village of Drenstein-fürt, near Münster, on the grey Westphalian plain. Not that Yussel had looked much like a tailor: he had been strong, and husky, from a poor but respected *mishpocheh*. Barney had been told over and over again that he had inherited Yussel's brown curly hair, and wedge-shaped forehead, and that nose of Yussel's which looked more like the nose of a prize-fighter than a Jewish *schnoz*.

All Barney had inherited from his mother were his eyes – deep-set, and bright, and brown, as shiny as the toes of Joel's best boots.

'You didn't warn me,' Barney told Joel, quietly.

'Well – it was sudden,' Joel replied, rolling up a last pair of hand-knitted socks. 'I didn't even decide myself until last night. I was having tea with Moishe last night . . . and I just suddenly decided. But what's the difference? You know the business as well as I do. Now, it's yours.'

'What's the *difference*?' Barney demanded. 'The difference is that you've left me stuck with the whole thing, and nobody to help me. That's the difference!'

'Moishe will help.'

Barney rubbed his eyes. He was exhausted after a long day over his desk, and walking around the stores. 'Why didn't you tell me you wanted out?' he asked. 'We could have talked about it, found some kind of solution.'

'There wasn't anything to talk about, and the solution is that I'm going,' said Joel, flatly. 'Barney, I'm sorry. If you don't want to carry on with the business, then sell it. Buy Mama a home uptown. Let the *kuzinehs* look after her.'

'Ruchel and Rivke? Those two old crows? They'd kill her in six months. And, besides, what about everybody who works for us? Ten people, including David. What are *they* going to do if I sell?'

Joel closed the lids of his trunks, and began to buckle up the leather straps. 'Barney,' he said, controlling his voice. 'The simple truth is that I don't care. I know how it sounds. I know you think I'm letting everybody down, you included. But I've been choking for years, and if I don't get out now, then I'm going to end up like Father before I'm thirty. I'm *choking*, Barney. On chalk, on barathea, on thread. I'm choking on Clinton Street. And more than anything else, I'm choking on Mama's –'

He paused, ashamed of what he was going to say. 'I'm choking on Mama's love, and Mama's temper. I can't be a stand-in for *tateh* for the rest of my life. I can't measure up. I don't even want to measure up.'

Joel stood silent, his hands on top of one of his trunks as if it were a piano, and he was going to pick out some lost, sentimental tune.

Barney said, 'What are you going to do?'

'I've signed on to a passenger steamer, the *Stockdale*. She sails tonight, from the Cunard Liverpool Steamship Wharf, in Jersey. She's bound for England, and then for South Africa.'

Barney walked across the green and yellow linoleum floor to the window. There was hardly anybody around now. It was supper-time, and still raining hard, one of those wet New York nights when it seems as if the whole city is out at sea. Across the street, on the opposite sidewalk, a bagel-seller stood by his smoking cart, his shoulders hunched, water cascading from the brim of his hat.

'I'm going to miss you,' Barney told Joel. 'Soixow, I always thought we were going to stay together for the rest of our lives. You know, partners.'

Joel attempted a smile. 'I'm not going away for ever,' he said. 'I just want to breathe for a whila, that's all. I've had ten years of vests and linings and lapels. Come on, Barney, you know what it's like.'

'Sure,' said Barney, without turning away from the window. 'It's all sweat and toil and not much money. It's Moishe, and David. It's trying to cope with Mama's tantrums, trying to eat your way through a meal that was cooked for six people, just so you won't upset her. But what would *Tateh* think, if he knew?'

'*Tateh*'s dead,' said Joel, emphatically. He looked up at Barney, and then he reached out his arms for him, and the two brothers gripped each other close, cheek against cheek. Barney, in spite of his disappointment in Joel, or maybe because of it, found that his eyes were sticky with tears.

'Joel,' he said hoarsely.

'I have co go, Barney,' said Joel. 'I'm going to miss you ... I'm even going to miss Mama ... but I have to.'

Barney stood up straight. He wiped his eyes with his hand-kerchief, and blew his nose. 'Sure,' he said. 'I know.'

Joel said: 'Hey ... you remember the time we sewed up the cuffs of *Tateh*'s best pants?'

'I remember,' said Barney. 'He got straight out of bed, pulled them on, and fell flat on his face. Laugh?'

Joel gripped his younger brother's shoulder. 'He belted us, remember? "A *shtik* like that you should try on your father!"'

They didn't know what else to say to each other. Barney knew Joel well enough to realise that, whatever he said, Joel was going to leave. Joel had always been that way. Quiet, determined, and stubborn. Maybe he had too much of his mother in him.

'South Africa, huh?' he said. He tried to sound conversational. 'The land of the *schwarzers*?'

Joel smiled, and then laughed. 'You'll manage without me. When I'm sitting in a grass hut, stuffing myself with elephant-flavoured bialys, you'll be turning out broadcloth pants by the dozen!'

Barney said, 'Yes. I guess so.' He felt sadder than he could possibly explain.

Mrs Blitz appeared in the bedroom doorway, clutching her hands together. Barney glanced at Joel, and then said, 'Mama?'

'It's ready,' she nodded. Her eyes darted from side to side like tropical fish.

'Okay, then, we're coming,' said Barney. 'Joel – you're going to join us at the table?'

Joel looked at his strapped-up trunks. 'I can't be too late. The ship leaves at ten.'

'You've got time for a last meal,' said Barney.

They went into the kitchen, still smoky, where bread and meatballs and cold gefilte fish were laid out for them on heaped-up plates, enough to feed ten ravenous men. Joel pulled out Mrs Blitz's chair for her, and she sat down primly at the end of the table.

'Well,' she said, serving out meatballs. 'Have you decided what you're going to do?'

Joel picked up his fork and eyed his mother carefully. 'I'm leaving, Mama. I told you.'

'Didn't you listen to what Barney told you?'

'Barney didn't tell me anything. Barney knows what I feel. Anyway, it's a chance for Barney to run the business. It's good experience.'

Feigel Blitz looked from one of her sons to the other. 'I hope you're not trying to tell me you're both in this together?'

Barney, chewing meatball, said, 'I can't persuade him to stay, Mama. He's my older brother. He wants to go, and that's it.'

'You're really leaving?' snapped Mrs Blitz.

Joel put down his fork again, and pushed away his plate. 'I told you, Mama. I'm going. And I really think it's better if I do it right now.'

'Sit down,' ordered his mother, coldly. Her face was white, and set.

'Mama, I'm going. There's nothing in this whole world that can –'

'*Shah!*' shrieked Mrs Blitz. 'You think I made you this supper for nothing – that you should eat it, and then leave me?

26

What kind of son are you? What's your father going to say? Are you crazy, leaving the business? Blitz, Tailors? How can you turn your back on it?'

'Mama, please,' pleaded Barney. 'He's going to leave, whatever you say. Can't we just eat and say Shema and let him go with a blessing? Mama?'

Mrs Blitz swept her arm across the table, hurtling plates and meatballs and gefilte fish all over the kitchen floor. Then she seized the long sharp knife she used for slicing bread, and stabbed wildly at Joel's hands. Joel jumped back, lost his footing, and stumbled over his chair. Mrs Blitz got up from the table and went for him, the knife held over her head in both hands.

Barney was quicker. He overturned the deal table with one hefty thrust, so that it fell on top of his sprawling brother. Then he lunged for the knife in his mother's hands, yelling, 'Mama! What are you doing? *Mama!*'

He was too late to stop her first downward stab. The blackbladed knife, worn thin and keen from years of constant whetting, sliced right through the skin between Barney's thumb and index finger, and into the raw muscle. Blood spattered everywhere, scarlet exclamation points. Barney gripped his wrist in pain, and sank sideways on to his knees.

There was a hideous silence. Mrs Blitz stared at her sons in shock. Joel eased the overturned table off his legs, and stood up, brushing egg and fish and breadcrumbs from his trousers. Barney, bleeding, crouched on the floor amongst the chairs and the meatballs, his teeth gritted and his face grey like newspaper.

From another apartment, they could hear an unsteady violin playing a *mazel tov* dance. Young Leib Ginzberg, practising for his sister's wedding. It sounded ludicrously jolly.

Joel, without a word, tore a long strip from the tablecloth, knelt down beside Barney, and wrapped it around his thumb. Mrs Blitz stayed where she was, swaying slightly, as if she were on the deck of a ferry, the knife still clutched in her hand.

'I'll get you round to the doctor,' Joel told Barney. 'That's going to need stitching.'

Barney shook his head. 'You'll miss your ship. It's eight o'clock already.'

'You're my brother,' argued Joel.

Barney shook his head even more decisively. 'I can go to the doctor by myself. I want you to catch that ship. If you don't leave now, you never will.'

Joel looked towards his mother.

'*Leave,*' insisted Barney. 'Isn't this exactly why you're going, this kind of scene? Isn't this exactly what you want to leave behind?'

Joel stood up. He was flustered now, undecided. He wiped sweat from his forehead with the back of his hand. His mother looked at him with an expression that could have been resignation, or regret, or just plain contempt for everything and everyone, including herself.

Joel said, 'Mama –?'

But Mrs Blitz simply turned away, and walked off towards her bedroom. They heard her close the door behind her, and turn the key in the lock. The brothers looked at each other in silence.

'If you're not careful, she'll kill you one of these days, *chas vesholem,*' said Joel.

Barney said, 'No. She'll kill herself first.'

'I'd better say goodbye,' Joel told him, without any enthusiasm at all.

He went to his mother's bedroom door, and knocked. There was no answer. He made a face at Barney, shrugged, and shouted: 'Goodbye, Mama!'

'Go!' Mrs Blitz screeched back at him. 'And a *choleria* on you!'

Joel hesitated, then sighed. 'I'd better go fetch my trunks,' he said to Barney. 'I'll take them down to the street, and call a cab. You go straight round to the doctor. Don't wait.'

The two brothers stood in the shadowy hallway. 'This is goodbye, then,' said Joel.

'You're not going to touch the *mezuzah*?' asked Barney.

Joel smiled, and shook his head. 'It was never anything more than superstition, as far as I was concerned. I only did it because Father did it. And, remember, this isn't my home any more.'

28

They embraced tightly. 'I love you,' said Joel. 'I'm sorry I've left you with everything, the whole burden.'

'I'll manage,' Barney told him.

'I guess you will,' said Joel. 'But you wait – one day, when I'm rich, I'll come back. That's a promise. And I'll make *you* rich, too.'

Barney held his injured hand close against his chest. The tablecloth bandage was already dark crimson.

'Goodbye, Joel,' he said. 'God bless you.' Then he walked off quickly along the landing, and down the stiars.

They had snow early that year, in the third week of October. Barney was walking back from a long sales meeting with the men's-wear buyer of B. Meyberg & Co., on Broadway, and the afternoon streets were suddenly furious with white flakes. He tugged up the collar of his black wool coat, and straightened his hat, and hurried along Hester Street with his hands deep in his pockets. The snow did not settle. It was soon trodden into slush by the horsedrawn cabs and streetcars, and swept up by the rascally, emaciated men who had appeared with brooms at every intersection, tipping their caps and holding out their grimy mittens for nickels. But, as Barney trudged up the staircase of *Blitz, Tailors*, brushing the snow from his shoulders, and knocking it off the top of his hat, he felt as if the year which had only just begun was already half over, and he wondered how many more times he would climb this narrow wooden flight, brushing the snow from his coat, growing older and greyer with each successive climb.

He stopped on the landing and looked back towards the street, where the soft snow still pattered on to the sidewalk. He frowned.

In the little glazed cubicle by the tailor's shop door, David was warming his feet by a smoky oil fire, and sewing a silk braid edging to a detached sleeve. Barney opened the door, stepped in, and hung up his hat on the bentwood stand.

'Is Moishe back yet?' he asked.

David nodded. 'Ten minutes. Is it snowing? Itzik said it might snow.'

'It's snowing. Did you sweep up yet? It's getting late. I don't want this place looking like a rubbish-dump all through *Shabbes*.'

'Moishe asked me to finish the braid. It's the Military Academy order.'

Barney, picking up a sheaf of bills and invoices from the upright desk in the corner, said, 'Okay. If Moishe says so.'

David went on sewing. He started to hum, a monotonous tune without a beginning and without an end. Barney glanced at him in irritation as he read through the bills, but he did not say anything. David was a simpleton, a *golem*, and if Barney had told him to shut up he would not have understood. He might even have burst into tears.

It had been Barney's father who had taken David into the business, as a favour to one of the *kuzinehs*. Tall, big-nosed, with a pear-shaped body and soft dangling hands, David was the third child of Rivke's eminent and illustrious stepbrother, Dr Abraham Stein, the gynaecologist. Dr Stein, who lived on Fifth Avenue, albeit in one of the more modest mansions, had fathered three big-nosed daughters, and eventually David. For all his parents' early pride, David's mind had suddenly stopped developing at the age of thirteen, and after three grotesque incidents of exposing himself to the downstairs maids, and to one of Dr Stein's most genteel lady patients, Dr Stein had uncomfortably asked Rivke to persuade Barney's father to find the boy a place at Blitz's. To keep him out of harm's way, you understand? To keep his mind off – well, *things*.

That Rivke woman, with her barbed-wire hair and her ostentatious garnets – that Rivke woman could talk anyone into doing anything. Barney's father used to say that she could crawl into your bones. 'She crawls into my bones,' he used to say, gritting his teeth, and crunching up his face.

So David went on humming, with his simple future assured; and Barney, tired, tugged at the curls around his ears and tried to work out whether today's mail had brought him a profit or a loss. Usually, these days, it was a small profit, but it was hard, running the business without Joel. Moishe was a help when it came to rushing out orders, or to estimating how much broadcloth to buy; but Moishe did not want responsibility. He did not want to worry himself with cash flows, with profit margins, with rates of interest. He thought – and maybe quite rightly – that only the Lord had control over such things, and who was he to interfere in the works of the Lord?

Through the dusty glass of the cubicle where he was standing, Barney could see part of the cluttered, low-ceilinged workroom, lit with so many gas jets that it looked almost like a holy place during *Chanukah*, the Festival of Light, illuminated with dozens of *menorahs*. Under the lights, their heads bent over their work, his cutters and basters and seamstresses toiled away at the last few military coats for the academy; and although the sky outside their window was as dark as corroded copper, and still whirling with snow, they never raised their eyes once. They had an order to finish before the Sabbath.

Barney glanced back at David. 'Are you going back to your parents' house for *Shabbes*?' he asked him. 'Back to Fifth Avenue?'

David, still humming, shrugged.

'Maybe you'd like to come spend *Shabbes* with me, and my mother?' suggested Barney.

He didn't try to sound too encouraging. In fact, to his own restless shame, he was praying that David had already promised to spend the Sabbath with his own family. He tried not to think how often his father had brought home an *oyrech auf Shabbes*, even a filthy street musician once, with an oboe; and, one *Shabbes*, an extraordinary and eccentric prize-fighter, who had insisted on bending spoons and straightening them out again. 'At least he straightened them out again,' Barney's father had told his mother. But somehow, because of his own sparkling character, Barney's father had always been able to transform awkwardness into joy, embarrassment into laughter, and every one of those Sabbath days had been glowing with family love, and devotion, and affection for their guests. At least, they had always seemed that way.

Barney knew that he was different from his father. Warier, quicker to lose his temper, and more critical of weakness. Maybe it was New York that had made him harder, and less tolerant of those whining *shlemiels* who lived off their friends. More likely, he had been soured by the difficulty of running Blitz, Tailors, all by himself, and the violently changeable moods of his mother. Since Joel had left, Mrs Blitz's mind seemed to have tilted even further askew, and one morning last week he had caught her ripping at Joel's mattress with a knife, panting, convinced that Joel was hiding inside it just to tease her, just to play a malicious joke on his dear mad mother.

David finished sewing his braid, bit the thread between the teeth, and then looked up at Barney almost primly. 'Yes,' he said. 'I'd like that.'

'Fine,' said Barney, unenthusiastically, in his most American voice. 'I just have to talk to Moishe, find out what's going on, and then we can go.'

He stepped out of the cubicle into the workroom, and walked along between the benches to the far end. Usually, the loft was noisy with laughter and conversation. Blitz's was not a sweatshop. But this afternoon, with only two hours to go to sundown, and the room still heaped with work, it was almost silent, except for the crisp cutting of scissors through cloth, and the hiss of gas.

Over in the corner, where dozens of bolts of worsted and tweed and broadcloth were stacked, Irving and Hyman were cutting out the last of the uniform pockets; and beside them, on a stool, thin and studious, young Benjamin was busy threading needles. Irving and Hyman, both silver-haired, were Blitz's two best cutters. 'Cut!' Barney's father used to say. 'Those two could cut tarpaper, and make you a coat to be proud of.' They looked like brothers, Irving and Hyman, although they were not. Irving, with magnifying spectacles perched on the end of his nose, and a concentrated expression like a barn-owl, had immigrated from Munich. Hyman, whose black vest was always forested with glittering needles, had brought his family to New York from Zamosc, in Poland. But they were inseparable. They spent feast days together, and went fishing together off the Stanton Street pier, and shared a ridiculous sense of humour which had Barney laughing for hours at a time.

'You sold Meyberg's those overcoats?' called Irving, without looking up, as Barney approached them.

'They're taking half a dozen on trial.'

'On *trial*?' put in Hyman. 'The cloth we used for those, a

shmatte! They should know those coats are guilty, without a trial.'

Barney grinned. One of his seamstresses glanced up, the soft and docile Sarah Feinberg, and he touched her on the shoulder as he passed.

He found Moishe by the window, folding up tunics and inspecting them closely for uneven stitching or loose buttons. He was short, Moishe, and hugely fat, with hanging jowls, and a bald pate that lay in the chaotic nest of his gingery hair like a speckled roc's egg. His belly, swollen by years of gorging himself with *matzo* dumplings and bread pudding, had a bouncing animated life of its own; and on several occasions, Irving had peered down the front of Moishe's bottle-green vest, and called, 'How are you doing in there, *bubeleh*?'

'Well, Barney,' said Moishe, spreading a fresh sheet of tissue-paper over another folded tunic. He wiped a finger under his left eye, a sign of tiredness.

'You're almost through?' asked Barney. 'I want to close up in twenty minutes.'

'An hour maybe should do it,' Moishe told him, reaching past him to take another completed tunic from Benjamin.

Barney looked beyond Moishe, out of the window, where the snow had suddenly dwindled into thin, spiralling flakes, and the clouds that had banked themselves over the Jersey shore were dramatically brightening up, like the *Ecstasy of St Theresa*, by Bernini. Sunlight glistened briefly on the rooftops across the street, and the rattling of horse-drawn carriages began to grow busier and louder.

'Listen, you don't have to finish this order today,' Barney said, looking around at all the uncompleted tunics. 'Monday morning's going to be fine. You can send the uniforms out by carrier.'

Moishe, almost imperceptibly, shook his head, and folded the tunic's sleeve.

'Moishe,' insisted Barney, 'it won't *matter*. By the time you've packed up this order, everybody at the Military Academy will have gone home for the weekend anyway. They may be *goyim*, but they've got families, just like us. You think they're going to wait around, biting their nails, for tunics?'

33

'We told them we'd deliver,' said Moishe, dogmatically. He fixed Barney with tiny, uncompromising eyes, beady as raisins in a loaf. 'At Blitz's, when we say today, we mean today. Not tomorrow, nor the seventeenth day of Tammuz next year. *Today!*'

Barney, suppressing a smile, watched with proprietorial interest as Moishe folded one more sleeve, and brushed away a speck of lint with an exaggerated sweep of his podgy hand. Then he said, 'I seem to remember, Moishe, that your name is Teitelbaum, not Blitz. I'm Blitz, and what we say at Blitz's, that's my *medina*, not yours. Now, in twenty minutes, we close, whether you've finished this order, or not.'

Moishe reared his head up, like a surfacing walrus. 'You think your father would have let a two-hundred-dollar order go out two days late?' he demanded. 'Your father would have taken off his coat, and rolled up his sleeves, and helped me to pack – not stood there like a *fonfer* and told me to finish up! We have pride here, at Blitz's! A reputation! Even your brother Joel would have helped, and what Joel knew from tailoring you could have written on the head of a pin!'

Barney grinned, and appreciatively threw his arm around Moishe's fat shoulders. 'Just wrap it up for the day, Moishe. I appreciate your loyalty to Blitz's. I love your hard work. I love you. But it really won't make any difference at all, whether you finish this today, or Monday. Come on, Moishe, it's almost *Shabbes*.'

Moishe dragged a handkerchief from his pants pocket, and dabbed at his jowls. 'Your father should have seen you,' he said. 'You're an American now, you know that? All talk, all big ideas, and no work. A *shlepper*.'

'Sure, sure,' said Barney. 'So much of a *shlepper* I've persuaded Meyberg's to take six of those tweed overcoats on approval, and give me ten firm orders for shooting-jackets. You know the ones with the leather patches?'

Moishe looked down at the tunic he had been folding, and then at Barney. 'Ten, huh? Well, they could have taken fifteen.'

Barney raised his hands in mock-surrender. 'Moishe, with you, I'll never win. But meanwhile, we're not doing so bad, are we? Turnover's good, profits are steady. Maybe in a month

34

or two we can think about paying everybody a little more.'

Moishe sniffed. 'We're doing all right, I suppose. I guess I remember the old days too clearly, when your father was here.'

'Well, of course you do. How can I blame you for that? I'm young, and I'm different. But I'm not too young to understand how you feel.'

Moishe laid his hand on Barney's shoulder. 'Barney, let me ask you something. Something personal, serious.'

'Sure,' said Barney. He turned his head around, and called, 'Irving, Hyman – you want to clear up now? We're closing the shop in twenty minutes.'

'Listen to me,' said Moishe, gently. 'I'm not being critical. Simply truthful. I've been watching you for six months, ever since Joel left, and working with you. You don't like this business, do you? This tailoring. You're doing your best – as far as profit's concerned, you're doing good. But your heart's not in it, is it?'

Barney frowned at Moishe warily. 'What makes you say that?'

'Oh, come on, Barney, I'm not a blind man. Look how you've changed everything here since Joel left. All this ready-to-wear stuff we're making, for stores, and colleges, even for postal catalogues. Thirty tunics for the New York Military Academy? We never had an order like that in the whole of our fifteen years.'

Barney did not say anything. While Moishe had been talking, Irving had come across the room, and now he was standing two or three feet behind them, listening.

'Moishe's right, Barney,' Irving said. There was tenderness in his voice, understanding, but also regret. 'Blitz's was always bespoke before. High quality suits, made to measure. Some of the best in New York. We've still got the regulars, sure, the customers who know what they want, and won't change their tailor for anything. But these days, when you say Blitz's, most people think of ready-made. The trade does, for sure, and it won't be long before the customers do, too.'

'Another thing,' put in Hyman. 'David tells me you've been turning customers away.'

Barney let out a breath, took out his pocket-watch, and checked the time. 'Well,' he said, 'I can't deny it.'

'Deny what?' asked Irving.

'Any of it,' said Barney. 'I can't deny that my heart isn't really in tailoring. Nor can I deny that I've been trying to change Blitz's from a gentleman's personal tailors into a house with a good name for ready-mades. I can't even deny that I've been turning personal customers away. The truth is, it's a business, as far as I'm concerned, and that's it. And how can it make any business sense at all for Irving to spend two days cutting out one suit, for which we're going to change ten dollars forty-three cents the piece, when he could be cutting out *six* suits, for which we're going to charge six dollars and twenty-two cents the piece? It seems like it's to *your* advantage, and to *my* advantage, and especially to the advantage of the families and children who depend on us.'

Moishe looked uncomfortable. 'You're right, Barney, in a kind of a fashion. But Irving here, and Hyman ... they're artists. They can make a suit like it's magic, the way the coat hangs on the shoulders, the way the lapels roll over.'

'I know,' said Barney. 'Moishe, I *know*. But that's why the stores like their ready-mades so much. As far as ready-mades go, they're superb.'

'But, Barney. Understand me. You're asking Michaelangelo to put up wallpaper.'

Barney was about to snap back at Moishe, but then he stopped himself. These men were family, old friends of his father, and what was more, craftsmen. He was sensitive enough to know what Moishe was talking about and to know that if he didn't check himself, he'd be liable to let his anger and his impatience go hurtling off like a pair of ill-trained dogs. Whatever his father had given him – humour, and warmth, and balance – he still had his mother's hair-trigger temper. He lifted his hands, as if to show Moishe and Irving that he had understood them, as if he was suing them for peace.

'Listen,' he said, softly. 'I know that I've been asking you to undertake work that's way beneath your skills. But try to see it from my point of view, too. I've been building up some capital so that Blitz's can grow, and strengthen itself. Maybe

I've been overhasty. I'm young, I know that. Maybe I've been overdoing the profit motive, and not paying enough attention to the heart of the business. But, if the profits improve, everything's going to change. When we're solidly back into credit, we can set up a real quality tailoring department like you've never seen. Better than ever. All I'm asking you to realise is that we can't go from *peklech* to Lord & Taylor in six days. Not even in six months.'

Hyman slowly nodded. 'Spoken like an American,' he said, turning away, and his intonation was as bland as only a Yiddisher could make it – so bland that Barney could not tell if it was an insult or a compliment, or simply a resigned and accurate comment.

Moishe went to find his coat, and everybody else began to pack up, folding bolts of fabric, sticking pins and needles back in their pin-cushions, clearing away paper patterns, sweeping up scraps of basting and snarls of thread. One by one, the gas jets were turned down low, until the twilit workroom was beaded with scores of tiny blue flames.

'I expect you're looking forward to going home tonight,' said Moishe, brushing his hat.

Barney, who was helping to scoop up buttons, said, 'No more than usual. Why?'

'Such an *oyrech auf Shabbes* you've got,' winked Moishe.

'You mean David?' asked Barney, hefting up a bolt of navy blue union cassimere.

'David?' said Moishe. 'I don't mean David, I mean Leah Ginzburg. You didn't know she was coming? Her *bubbe's* sick, and so her mother's had to go to Front Street to take care of her, and her father's still in Jersey, so she's spending the Sabbath with you. Maybe Sunday, too.'

'Who told you?'

'Your mama. Who else? She came up here this afternoon while you were round at Meyberg's.'

'Leah Ginzburg?' Barney demanded, throwing down the cloth. 'How come you wait until *now* to tell me? *Oy gevalt*! If I'd known, I would never have invited David. David I asked, with Leah coming! Why didn't *David* tell me, for the love of God? He must have known!'

Moishe, buttoning up his coat, gave Barney a fat, sympathetic grin. 'Maybe David likes Leah as much as you do. Maybe he likes your mother's *knaydel*. Maybe he forgot.'

'Forgot? That *nebech* never forgets anything.'

'Well, you should be grateful,' said Moishe. 'It isn't every *Shabbes* you get the opportunity to do such a good deed. You should thank the Lord.'

Barney looked at him fiercely for a moment, and then relaxed, and laughed. 'I guess you're right. Thank you, Lord, for giving me this opportunity to show charity to my fellow man! But with Leah Ginzburg around, I should have David Stein, too?'

Irving came over, wrapping his long grey woollen scarf around his neck like a failed snake-charmer taking home his exhausted python. His wife always made him wear a scarf, even in summer, in case of what she called 'wind stiffness'. 'Listen, Barney,' he said, hoarsely, 'I don't want you to think that I'm *kvetching*. But we're family here, right? We can say what's on our minds. No secrets. Maybe next week we should talk over the whole business, all this ready-made work you've been asking Hyman and me to do. It's not our kind of work. I'm unhappy, for one; and I know that Hyman's unhappy. And, worst of all, Sussman knows we're unhappy, too.'

Barney said: 'Sussman?' The amusement faded from his face as rapidly as sensitised silver darkening in sunlight. 'They've made you an offer at Sussman?'

'I can't tell a lie,' said Irving.

'Well, then,' said Barney. 'If Sussman's made you an offer, and you're not happy here, you'd better leave. I wouldn't want to keep you here against your will. And the same goes for Hyman. Him, neither.'

Moishe looked at both of them uneasily. 'Come on, Barney,' he said, 'we're all tired. Let's leave it till Monday.'

Barney, without taking his eyes off Irving, nodded slowly. 'Sure,' he said. 'And maybe, during the Sabbath, we can all read what the *Talmud* has to say about loyalty.'

There was an embarrassed silence. Then Irving went off without a word, closely followed by Hyman. Barney watched the two of them walk between the glowing blue spots of light, their heads bowed; and then he turned to Moishe and said, 'Well?'

Moishe shrugged. 'They'll come around. But they're old men, remember, set in their ways. Joel they could accept. He knew how to cut, he knew how to make up, he was his father's elder boy. He didn't try to turn the business on its head. You, they're not sure of.'

Barney stood with his hands on his hips. The door of the workroom closed behind Irving and Hyman with a vivid squeal, and then a shudder of badly fitting wood. He saw their silhouettes through the glass of the cubicle as they went slowly downstairs.

'All right,' he said, 'let's leave it till Monday. But don't let's forget who's the *baleboss* at Blitz's, huh?'

Moishe put his arm around Barney's waist. 'Take some advice, will you? Rest, pray, and remember that everybody's got one love in their life, outside of their family. Yours may be money. Irving and Hyman's, it's cutting a perfect suit.'

David was waiting for Barney in the cubicle, wrapped up in a bright brown coat that Irving had once caustically described as 'the camel's feedbag'. His near-together eyes were bright with anticipation. 'Are you ready?' asked Barney, testily, and David waggled his head up and down with enthusiasm. What a lunatic, thought Barney. And what an *oyrech*.

'You go ahead, I'll lock everything up,' said Moishe, producing a fat jangling ring of keys. 'You have your guests to take care of.'

'Sure,' said Barney, and clattered quickly down the stairs to the wet street, without looking back to see if David was following. Of course David was following – so closely that when Barney reached the sidewalk, which was jostling with last-minute shoppers and tailors and trimmers on their way to the Turkish baths, and creaking pushcarts, and scampering children, David was right behind him, and bumped into him.

'*Shalom aleichem*, Moishe!' Barney called back, up the stairs, although his eyes were on David.

'*Aleichem shalom*,' came down the echoing response.

Barney took David's arm as unwillingly and impatiently as if it were the handle of a valise crammed with filthy laundry,

39

and tugged him through the evening crowds of Clinton Street to the flat-fronted tenement on the corner of Monroe Street, No. 121, where his mother would already be laying out his clean clothes for the synagogue.

It began to snow again, in wet, fitful whirls.

The neighbourhood was quiet when they returned home from the synagogue; enchanted with the particular stillness, that deep sense of rest, that always used to fall over the crowded homes of New York's Lower East Side at sundown on Fridays. In almost every house and tenement, even in basements where damp marked the walls and the cupboards rustled with rats, wives and mothers and daughters were dressed in the finest clothes they owned, and were lighting up the *Shabbes* candles.

'Blessed art Thou, O Lord our God, King of the Universe, Who has sanctified us by Thy commandments, and has commanded us to kindle the Sabbath lights.'

The sky above Clinton Street was smudged with clouds; umber ink on wet cartridge paper. It was too warm for snow now, but a thin drizzle slanted between the row houses and the shuttered stores, and the sidewalks shone with wet. In the windows all around, candles flickered; and through the streets the husbands and fathers walked silently home from the synagogue, each of them invisibly accompanied by the hosts of Sabbath angels they had brought back from their prayers. Their footsteps echoed all about them.

This was slumland, dirty and broken and uncompromising. The garbage from the day's trading lay sodden in the gutters – cabbage leaves, screwed-up wrapping paper, scraps of bloody meat, fish guts. Even a plateful of noodles, trodden into the filthy slush. Barney stopped on the corner of Monroe Street, opposite the old Rutgers mansion, and for a moment or two he looked around at the rain and the trash and the lighted windows, and he felt a coldness that brought him close to tears.

David said, 'What are you waiting for?'

Barney dabbed at his eye with the handkerchief pinned to his lapel. 'You wouldn't understand. Let's go.'

David kept pace with him as he crossed the street. 'You could try me,' he said.

'Try you?' asked Barney.

'Well, you're sad, aren't you?' David remarked.

'Isn't everybody? Tell me what there is to be happy about.'

'Most of the time, you seem like you're happy,' said David.

'Most of the time isn't *Shabbes*. Most of the time I'm too busy trying to keep the business afloat, too busy arguing with buyers in dry goods stores and department houses, too busy fighting with Irving and Hyman and everybody else. I don't have a moment to myself; and it's only when you have a moment to yourself that you feel anything at all. Tonight, it's sad. So what?'

'So why are you sad?' David wanted to know. Barney was striding along so quickly now that he was panting to keep up.

'I don't know,' Barney told him. 'If I knew, I don't suppose I'd tell *you* about it, anyway.'

David clutched at his sleeve, slowing him down. 'Do you really hate me that much?' he asked.

'I don't hate you. Why should I hate you?'

'You hate me because I'm dumb.'

'Listen, David, I don't hate you.'

'Then why don't you tell me why you're sad?'

'Because –' Barney hesitated, and stopped. They were standing outside his tenement building now. All along the street, the drizzle had turned the gaslamps into sow-thistles. Barney looked down at the six steps which led up to the black-painted front door, and across at the wet iron railings. David waited beside him, shivering, as if he had travelled a thousand miles to hear the secret of the universe from a renowned rabbi.

'I'm sad because I can never be what my father was,' said Barney, more to himself than to David. 'My father came here to New York when he was fifteen, with my grandfather. He brought some of the old ways along with him, he remembers what the old country was like. But I'm an American. I can't *help* being an American. But I can't carry on the old traditions the way my father did. Do you understand what I'm saying? I know what the old ways are. I study whenever I can, even on the streetcar. But they're not part of me, and I'm not really part of them.'

He wiped rain from his eyelashes with the back of his hand. 'I feel like I don't belong. I'm not really one of the *Deutsche Jehudim* any more, and I'm not really an American. I feel, I don't know, shut out.'

David silently chewed his lips. It was impossible to tell if he understood any of what Barney was saying or not.

Eventually, in a curiously childish lisp, he said, 'Remember thou wast a prisoner in the land of Egypt.' And without explaining himself any further, he climbed the steps to the front door. Barney stayed where he was for a while, feeling the drizzle on his face as if it were some kind of uncomfortable penance for doubting his Orthodox beliefs. Then he took out his keys and followed David inside.

Leah Ginzburg was standing in the hallway when Barney opened the door of the apartment. There was a rich aroma of roasted chicken and soup, mingled with the musty, penetrating smell of spices. 'You're soaked,' she said gently.

David grinned at her. 'It's God's tears,' he said, and then turned back towards Barney and grinned at him, too. Barney gave him a quick, embarrassed smile.

'Your mama was afraid you were going to be late,' Leah told Barney.

Barney did not say anything. He did not want to be uncharitable to his mother on the Sabbath, and tell Leah that his mama's usual terror was that he was not going to come home at all.

'She's in the parlour?'

Leah nodded. Barney had known Leah, and had a crush on her, ever since he was seven years old. The Ginzburgs used to live across the street, on the third floor of No. 129. In the dusty summers of his childhood, Barney had played with Leah on the front stoop, or round the wheels of the pushcarts where Polish and Armenian Jews with their beards and their kaftans sold fish, and sewing notions, and fruit. Those had been hot crowded days, those early days on Clinton Street and Hester Street, and all that had mattered in Barney's world had been his parents' doting affection, and a whipping-top that hummed, and a six-year-old girl with a pretty, heart-shaped face, and curls that strayed out from under her scarf.

Leah's father had started out with a pushcart, selling second-hand clothes. Then he had rented a small store on Hester Street, and started a dry goods business. Because of the poverty of his customers, the dry goods business had soon expanded into a pawnbroker's business; and before long, Mr Ginzburg had invested enough money to be able to move out of Clinton Street and buy a modest house further uptown. These days, he was a senior partner in Loeb & Landis, the finance company. But he had never forgotten his friends from the Tenth Ward; Moishe Teitelbaum, and Irving Finkelstein, and – while he was still alive – Barney's father, his old *chevra* who had helped him when he was freshly bewildered off the boat, the fellow Jews who had fed him with soup and given him places to sleep when he first arrived.

Barney's mother did not know it, and Barney himself had only discovered it when he had gone through Blitz's books after Joel had left, but Nathan Ginzburg had lent Blitz's over a thousand dollars, interest-free, just to keep going through the slump of 1857. The money had never been paid back.

But here was Leah, a guest for the Sabbath, in a simple white dress with a white lace overlay, and a white silk scarf over her head, dark-skinned and beautiful, with those brown eyes that looked like the eyes of an Eastern European gypsy. There was something wild about Leah. Barney had always been able to imagine her mouth stained in berry-juice, and gold rings on her toes; and, on some nights, in dreams, he had imagined her naked – small, only an inch over five feet, but big-breasted for her height, with skin so soft that it electrified his fingertips – and on those nights he had woken up sweaty and confused and ashamed.

'This is David Stein,' said Barney. Leah had been dressing when they had first come home to wash and to change their clothes. Barney's mother, fidgety but reasonably friendly, had not wanted to disturb her.

Leah curtsied to David, and David grinned again. Barney

expected that his mother had already told Leah that David was retarded. Or maybe she had not. She was so abstracted these days, so unpredictable; her mind was like a smashed mirror.

Mrs Blitz came out of the parlour. 'What's happening?' she asked. 'You're saying your prayers in the hallway?'

Barney said, 'I'm sorry, we're coming.' But the sight of his mother had given him a sharp, unpleasant thrill. For the first time in years, she was wearing her wedding-dress. It was yellowed, and part of the hem had come loose, but it was the same extravagant white dress of silk and Dresden lace which she had worn in Germany on the day that she had married Barney's father. It looked dated and almost macabre. It was tight as a sausage-skin around her waist, and under the armpits it was already stained with nervous perspiration. Barney could feel something off-key, something unpleasant, in the way his mother waved him into the parlour. *Her wedding-dress? Why?*

The parlour was small, but it was their best room. The walls were papered with flower baskets on a dark red background, and the drapes were best red velour. There was a cheap rosewood chiffonier on which the *Shabbes* candles burned, and a dining-table which Barney's father had brought all the way from the Pig-Market on his back. It smelled stale, as if every Sabbath past had been celebrated here and breathed here and the window had never been opened – as if Barney's mother had tried to entrap in this room all the ghosts of her vanished happiness.

Barney took his place at the head of the table. Leah, sitting on his right, smiled at him shyly. He did not want to look at David, whose lacquered, toy-soldier grin had not left his face since he had walked into the apartment. Nor could he look for long at his mother.

With a dry throat, he said, 'Thus the heavens and the earth were finished, and all the host of them. And on the seventh day God ended his work which he had made; and he rested on the seventh day from all his work which he had made. And God blessed the seventh day, and sanctified it . . .'

He blessed the wine, and made the *broche* for the Creation of the Sabbath, and for the departure out of Egypt. He had already silently said a *broche* to himself when he had seen Leah in her Sabbath dress; that special *broche* reserved for seeing beautiful people. He sipped the wine from the Kiddush cup, and he was aware when he lifted his eyes that Leah was watching him carefully. In a whisper, she sang the prayer to welcome the ministering angels which had returned home with him from the synagogue.

'May your coming be in peace, may you bless us with peace, and may you depart in peace ...'

Barney's mother, even before Leah had finished, began to spoon chopped chicken livers and olives on to their plates. Leah's voice faltered, but Barney raised his eyes to her in encouragement, and she finished the prayer just as Barney's mother pushed in front of her a mounded plateful of liver that would have stopped Moishe Teitelbaum in his tracks.

'Sabbath feasts are not what they were,' complained Feigel Blitz. 'When your father was alive, Barney, he made it holy! The whole family gathered round the table, Joel and Barney, and whichever *oyrech* Barney's father had brought home with him from the gutter! Holy, that's what they were! And a family! So where's my family now?'

Leah reached across the white linen tablecloth and held Mrs Blitz's hand. 'Mrs Blitz,' she said softly, 'we're your family now. Nobody's forgotten you.'

David was staring down at his plate of liver in bewilderment, as if he could not work out where it had come from. Then, fastidiously, he picked up his fork and began to nibble away at the edges of it.

'All the reverence, that's gone,' Feigel Blitz was saying loudly, to nobody in particular. 'Father would sit where Barney's sitting now, and describe his prayers in the synagogue. What he'd felt in his heart! The nearness to God! But now, what do these young Americans know of caring for their tortured mother? What do they care of the *mitzvoth*? Leah! Tell me, what do they care?'

Leah glanced at Barney, and blushed. The gentle grip she

45

had on Mrs Blitz's wrist was abruptly reversed, as Mrs Blitz seized her arm and stared at her in indignation. 'You think of marrying such a *gonif*? You think of taking him away? Oh, no, he has duties! Duties to his mother! You'll see! That young man is wedded already to his faith! Tonight, that young man is going to be married! Not to you, my fine young lady! Oh, no. To his duties! To *me*!'

Riboyne Shel O'lem, thought Barney. *That's why she's wearing the wedding-dress.*

'Mama,' said Barney. 'Can we just eat the dinner, and leave the talk until later?'

Leah said, 'This chopped chicken liver, it's delicious. Do you think I could take the recipe home to Mother?'

Feigel Blitz touched her forehead with her fingertips, as if she were blessing herself. 'Maybe it's your father's fault,' she muttered. 'He was devout, yes, but he cut off the *payess*, tried to make himself American. Americans don't wear *payess*, he said! Have you ever seen an American with side-curls? Two days after we came here, two days off Ellis Island, and he cut them off, and later his beard, too. But the day he cut off the *payess*, I cried all day. Your poor father.'

David put down his fork. 'I *know* you,' he said to Leah, with childish abruptness. 'I met you before.'

Leah looked at Barney. Barney, very slowly, shook his head.

The *Shabbes* feast went on, punctuated only by occasional skirmishes of quirky anger from Feigel Blitz, and empty, tangential comments from David. By the time it was over, Barney was trembling, wound up as tight as a hundred feet of silk lining, too tense to say anything sensible, or even devotional. He left the table, and went straight to his room, where he stood in the darkness with his fists clenched, and his teeth clamped together, and prayed for strength more ardently than he had ever prayed before.

Oh God, King of Heaven, give me strength to survive my mother. Give me faith so that I can be what she wants me to be. Give me peace.

And more than anything else, O Lord, let me know, deep within myself, that I am a real Jew. Let me feel in my bones and my blood that I have inherited my father's beliefs, and the beliefs of his fathers, and of their fathers.

46

There was a light tapping at the door. Barney opened his eyes, and turned around. The tapping came again. 'Barney? It's me, Leah.'

He opened the door. He was sweating. In the dim light that fell along the corridor, he could see her eyes glistening, the shine on her lips. He said, with more gentleness than he had ever spoken to anybody before, 'Leah? What is it?'

'I wanted you to know that it's not your fault,' she whispered. 'The dinner, what your mother said. I know that she's not –'

'The neighbours call her a *meshuggeneh*,' said Barney, baldly. After the performance his mother had given during dinner, he no longer felt so loyal. But he still found it difficult to hold back an unexpected prickling of tears.

Leah touched his hand. 'I understand. That's why I came to say that . . . well, I don't hold it against you. I'm fond of you, Barney. We've always been friends.'

'Yes,' he said, in a hoarse voice.

They stood watching each other in silence for almost a minute. Barney, for one vivid second, could remember sitting beside her under a pushcart on the corner of Hester and Clinton, concealed from the street by the drapes and folds of fabric that hung down from the cart on every side. It had been shady in there, their own private house, and grown-ups had been nothing more than a shuffling parade of disembodied boots and shoes. Leah must have been seven then, or maybe eight. The summer of 1858, when Barney's father, unknown to his family, was being kept alive by Leah's father. Leah had worn an emerald-green dress, and she had smelled of warm child, and perfume. If Barney could ever think of a moment when he had fallen in love with her, it was then.

Leah reached up and touched Barney's cheek. 'Don't let her make you too unhappy,' she said.

He shook his head.

They paused for one more instant, and for the rest of his life Barney never forgot the way she looked then, her head slightly tilted to one side, her lips touched by a smile.

'I love you,' he told her, not so much as a lover would, not trying to tell her anything except that he loved her for being Leah, and for being a friend when he needed one.

47

She smiled a little more widely, and then she went off down the corridor towards the kitchen. Barney could see his mother in there, clearing dishes. He could also see David, leaning awkwardly against the door-frame, munching on a dill pickle. What a Sabbath, he thought, and closed his bedroom door again. In the dark, he cupped his hands over his face, so that it was even darker.

He knew he had friends. He knew he had *meshpocheh* who would help him. But that wasn't really enough. He was only nineteen years old, and to have to keep the tailor's business going, especially with such cranky opposition from Irving and Hyman, and to have to cope with his mother's incessant tantrums, that was almost too much. What was even more distressing was that he had not heard from Joel in six months, not a single letter. He felt as if he were carrying the whole of Blitz's and the whole of his mother's madness by himself, like a sackful of wriggling goats.

Later, in the parlour, by the light of the Sabbath candles, he read aloud from the book of Deuteronomy. 'Thou shalt not sacrifice unto the Lord thy God any bullock, or sheep, wherein is blemish, or any evil-favouredness: for that is an abomination unto the Lord thy God.'

His mother sat opposite, her hands folded in her lap, her eyes peculiarly half-closed, so that Barney could just see them glittering under the lids. David did not even seem to be listening. He was fiddling with the tassels that hung down from the tablecloth and grinning from time to time at Leah. Leah herself was attentive, but obviously uncomfortable. Sometimes, as Barney read, she whispered the words of the *Torah* along with him.

'If there be found among you . . . man or woman . . . who hath gone and served other gods, and worshipped them, either the sun or the moon, or any of the host of heaven, which I have not commanded; then thou shalt bring forth that man or that woman, and shalt stone them with stones, till they die.'

At last, early, they retired to bed. Barney's mother went without a word, without even a blessing. Leah was to sleep in Joel's old room, and David was going to spend the night in a makeshift bed on the sofa. That sofa, sagging and shiny with wear, had been a bed of refuge for more *oyrechs* than Barney could remember. He and Joel used to help their father lug it down the stairs to the back yard to fumigate it with Persian Insect Powder, guaranteed to kill bedbugs, croton bugs, and fleas.

Barney, in his nightshirt, stood by the rain-freckled window of his bedroom and looked out at the back yard, and at the mean tenements all around. Washing-lines were suspended from every kitchen window, and on some of them, heavy with damp, hung sheets and bedcovers. Up above the washing-lines was the night sky, pale with cloud.

He climbed into bed. Beside him, on a small wooden shelf he had put up himself, was the leather-bound *Torah* that his father had given him, along with his prayer-shawl, his *tallis*, on the day of his *Bar Mitzva*. There was also a dim, out-of-focus daguerrotype of Joel, already faded by the sunlight which fell through Barney's bedroom window for only an hour each day.

Quietly, his head on the pillow, he said a prayer. He blessed his mother and hoped that the Lord would see fit, in his mercy, to make her well. He prayed for Joel, wherever he was; and he prayed for himself, for patience, and for wisdom, and for enough strength to carry him through the coming years.

He slept, and dreamed almost straight away of Leah. He dreamed he was running after her along Hester Street, in the direction of the Bowery, shouting at her in a strangely strangled voice to stop. But she kept on running ahead of him, not turning around, mingling with the crowds of midday shoppers, her white dress lost in a kaleidoscope of light and shade. It was a stifling day, the Lower East Side in August. He could hardly breathe, and his body seemed to be drained of energy. He felt as if he were going to collapse into the gutter from sheet weakness.

Then, abruptly, he woke up. His eyes wide, his ears alert. He could hear Leah gasping in the next bedroom – odd, choking gasps, as if she were suffering from asthma, or throwing a fit. But then she moaned, 'No – *no*, David – no!'

Barney ripped back his bedcovers, rolled out of bed, and tugged open his bedroom door. Leah's door was already wide open, and her bedside lamp was still lit, although the wick was guttering so low that Barney couldn't see anything at first but harlequin shadows. Then Leah cried out again, and wrestled around on the bed, and he understood what was happening.

It was David. Childish, ridiculous David. He had flung himself on to Leah's bed, right beside her, one leg across her hips. His borrowed nightshirt had ridden right up, and Barney could see his fat bottom, and a glimpse of his stiff purple penis. He was wrenching at Leah's nightdress with the jerky, insistent movements of a vicious marionette, a rabid Pinocchio. Leah's arms were twisted above her head, caught up in her bodice and lacy sleeves, and she was struggling to break free. Barney saw, with aroused horror, her wide-brimmed nipples, the curve of her thighs.

He caught David by the scruff of his nightshirt, tearing it loudly. Leah screamed, and tried to wriggle out of the way, but David shoved Barney away from him with lunatic strength, and dropped back on top of her, hugging her possessively close. Barney grabbed him again, and managed to heave him off the side of the bed on to the floor.

'You're crazy!' yelled Barney, so harshly that he hurt his throat. 'You're crazy!'

David scrambled crabwise across the rug, his big white bottom up in the air. Barney kicked him, and knocked him against the green-painted bureau. David yipped, clutching his head.

Barney felt a rage so fierce that it filled his lungs like a wind at sea. He dragged David on to his feet, throwing him against the bureau so that he struck his back, and fell to the floor again in a clattering shower of hairbrushes, combs, and hair-pins.

'You're filthy!' Barney screeched at him. 'Filthy and crazy and sick!'

David groped for the bedside table to lift himself up again. His face was white, and there was phlegm swinging from the end of his nose. Barney seized him again, and tried to raise him up on his feet, but the soft worn cotton of his nightshirt tore right down the front, and David collapsed inside it like a conjuring trick.

Barney reached inside the nightshirt and snatched David's

hair, pulling his head clear, and tearing out a whole bloody lump of scalp. There was nothing that could reach Barney now, no control, no reasoning, no sanity. He punched David in the side of the face with his fist, and then right between the eyes. He shook him, and kicked him, and pummelled at him, while David flopped heavily from one side of the floor to the other, squeaking and crying with every punch.

At last, his teeth chattering with shock, Barney stood over David, exhausted. Leah was kneeling up on her bed, her blanket clutched around her, her face as familiar but as ghost-like as the face that appears when you bend over the water of a washbasin.

'Barney –' she said, desperately. '*Barney –*'

Barney heard her, but did not want to answer. He was still bursting with his own anger. 'As if everything else isn't enough,' he breathed at David. 'As if the business isn't enough, as if Irving and Hyman aren't enough. And now you! What am I supposed to do? I'm supposed to look after *you* for the rest of your life? I'm supposed to hold your hand, you foul-minded *golem*? I can't do it! I don't want to do it! You're crazy, you're nothing but a crazy lunatic!'

He leaned against the bureau, breathing in short, frustrated gasps. David was still hunched up on the floor, dabbling at the blood that dripped from his nose, and mewling.

'That lousy business is lousy enough without you!' Barney shouted at him. 'A whole stinking roomful of bad-tempered old men and stupid women! All cloth, and gas, and struggling to keep the whole thing going! My God in Heaven, David, if it wasn't for that madwoman who calls herself my mother, I would have left it years ago! Joel had the right idea, he got out! Well, that's what I should do, and leave the whole whining, crazy, *kvetching* lot of you to choke on your own problems!'

There was that kind of total silence when you feel that someone, somewhere in the world, must have died. David crept blindly over to the bed, coughing, his torn nightshirt decorated with splatters of blood. Leah was crying, her tears shining in the dim light of the burned-down oil lamp, her fingertips pressed against her lips.

'*Madwoman?*' asked a soft, disturbing voice.

51

Barney looked towards the door. In the corridor, still wearing her wedding-dress, stood his mother. Her hands were demurely held together as if she were posing for a wedding-picture. Her hair was dishevelled, and she wore no shoes, but she was smiling.

'Mama?' said Barney. 'Mama, I'm sorry. I didn't mean it. I lost my temper. This – David here was attacking Leah. I saw red. Mama?'

'You'd leave me?' said Mrs Blitz. 'You'd go, like your father went, like Joel went? You'd leave me all alone? Is that what you've wanted to do all along?'

'Mrs Blitz,' put in Leah, her words crowded with tears. 'Mrs Blitz, he didn't mean it.'

David mumbled bloodily, 'Thou wast a prisoner in the land of Egypt.'

'Well, now I know the truth,' said Feigel Blitz. 'Now I know everything. A madwoman he calls me. Mad! And after all our years of marriage! Did you think I was mad the day you married me? Did you look at me when we were dancing together, and think, this girl is crazy? Did you think that all those years ago? What? Jacob – I'm asking you a question!'

The sound of his father's name gave Barney a sensation like being prickled with needles all over. It was scarcely ever mentioned, either by Feigel or by Barney, and even their family friends had grown to learn that the name of Jacob was almost a holy word in the Blitz household, a name that Mrs Blitz did not like to hear mentioned lightly.

'Mama?' Barney said, stepping slowly towards her. 'Mama, it's *me*, Barney.'

'You won't leave me,' she told him, shaking her head with a cramped, sideways motion. 'You won't ever leave me. Not any more.'

She turned, and walked unevenly along the corridor to the kitchen. She closed the door behind her, and turned the key.

Barney let out a breath. 'You'd better go clean up,' he said to David. 'There's a jug of water and a bowl on my dresser.'

David edged out of the room, keeping as far away from Barney as he could. Barney ignored him, and looked instead towards Leah.

'It wouldn't surprise me if you wanted me to take you someplace else,' he said. 'Maybe to Mr and Mrs Feinbaum.'

She said, 'No. I'll be all right. I'm upset, more than anything. He didn't hurt me.' There were still tears in her eyes, and her shoulders were shaking.

'I don't know what to say,' Barney told her. 'I don't know how I can ever make amends.'

'It wasn't your fault, Barney. You weren't to know.'

'That's twice tonight you've had to forgive me.'

'Don't you *want* to be forgiven?' she asked him.

He rubbed slowly at his knuckles. There was a chip of skin flapping up from his fist where he had hit David in the teeth. 'I just wish I was anyplace else but here,' he said. 'Anyplace at all but here.'

'I think I'd like some tea,' said Leah. 'Do you think it would be breaking the Sabbath to make some?'

Barney said, 'No. Not after this. I'll go put the kettle on the range.'

He went back to his room and shrugged on the worn-out maroon robe that had once been his father's. David was over in the corner, carefully bathing his swollen lips with cold water. He did not say anything when Barney came in, but he stopped dabbling in the washbasin, and he waited tensely until Barney had left the room again.

Barney went to the kitchen and tried the door. It was still locked, so he tapped at it. 'Mama? Open up, it's Barney.'

There was no answer. He rapped once more, and called louder, 'Mama! You have to open the door!'

He wondered if maybe she had locked the door behind her and gone out. If so, he and David and Leah were shut in, because ever since their old friend Daniel Lipschitz had enlarged the kitchen for them by bricking up part of the corridor, the only way to the bedrooms was by passing through the kitchen. He pounded on the door again.

'Mama! Listen – I'm not going to leave you! I promise! Just open the door!'

He heard a shuffling noise inside the kitchen. Then a pillowy thump – as if his mother had fallen against the door.

'Mama? Are you okay? Do you hear what I'm telling you?'

53

'*You promise?*' his mother asked, in an indistinct whisper.

'Mama, I promise. I was mad, that was all. David was messing with Leah and I went off my head. Can you understand that, Mama? Mama?'

He waited. He rattled the doorknob impatiently. 'Mama,' he said, 'you're going to have to open this door. I mean it.'

At last, he heard the key slowly turn, and the cheap lock levers click back. He pushed the door, and it opened a few inches, but his mother seemed to be leaning against it.

'Mama, can you step back?' he said. 'What are you doing, Mama? You're leaning on the door. Can you step back?'

His mother made a gargling noise. He realised then that something terrible had taken place, that his mother had done something hideous. He shoved hard against the door, and squeezed himself through. It slammed shut behind him, swung by the listless weight of her body. She stared at him, and laughed at his horror.

She had attacked herself with the kitchen knife. Her forehead was speckled with small triangular wounds where she had attempted to dig the point of the knife into her head. Her cheeks were in bloody slices, and there were ribbons of blood running down her neck. The front of her wedding-dress was a chaos of lace and gore, where she had furiously mutilated her breasts. All around the kitchen there were bloody handprints and bright red splatters.

Barney felt dizzy. The whole kitchen seemed to tilt like a weighing-scale around the fulcrum of his mother's leering face. Then, with an incongruous chuckling sound, she slid sideways to the floor.

'Leah!' called Barney. His voice echoed inside his head. 'Leah, help me!'

David put his head around the door, his chin red with bruises. He blinked at Mrs Blitz, and the splashes of blood, and he said, with the desperation of a child, 'What's happened? Barney, what's happened?'

Barney knelt down beside his mother. Her eyes, masked in blood, turned towards him. She whispered, 'Jacob?'

Barney took her hand. It was sticky with congealing gore, as if it had been painted. 'Feigel . . .' he said. He had never called her by her name before. 'Birdy.'

'You love me, don't you?' she pleaded. 'You won't leave me?'

'No,' he told her. He was crying now. 'No, Feigel, I won't leave you.'

'It's been so long,' she said. Blood was welling out of the side of her mouth now, and on to the linoleum. 'Don't leave me any more. Please, Jacob.'

Her eyes stayed open, but they lost their life. Her arm fell to the floor. Barney looked up, his mouth pursed with grief, and saw Leah standing in the doorway, stiff with fright.

'I've killed her,' said Barney. 'My own mother.'

Leah backed away from the kitchen, her hands raised to her cheeks. She accidentally bumped into David, who was standing in the corridor distraught, biting his nails. She stared at him as if she did not know who he was.

Barney stood up. He wiped the tears away from his eyes, and marked his face with his mother's blood. When Dr Seligman finally arrived, an hour later, he was standing by the kitchen range, his head in his hands, waiting for the kettle to boil.

'Tea?' he asked Dr Seligman. Dr Seligman took off his pince-nez, looked around at the blood, and quickly shook his head.

He found Joel's letters after the funeral. He was sitting on his mother's bed, sorting through her jewellery and her papers, and there they were – three of them, carefully folded away in a scarf.

The first was from Liverpool, England. The Atlantic crossing had been rough, and Joel had been seasick for three days; but now the weather had cleared and he was enjoying himself. He still loved her, and he sent his love to Barney. The Liverpudlians were a curious race of people, who never spoke of walking anywhere, but always 'legging it'.

The next letter was from Capetown. 'Mama, you must be sure to tell Barney what a place this is! What opportunities!' The third letter, more stained and crumpled than the other two, had arrived only two weeks ago from Oranjerivier, South Africa. Joel had invested his seaman's wages in a small farm, and he was working the land. 'Please let Barney come out to join me – I need the help badly, and I know Barney would love it. Don't keep him in the tailor's shop – Moishe can manage just as well. Mama, we'll make our fortune if we can work together out here. This is the real *goldeneh medina*!'

Barney folded up the letters and tucked them back in their envelopes. He sat on the bed for a long time, looking at them, not moving. Outside in the corridor, he heard Leah's mother say, 'Such a *levaya* I wouldn't have given a dog! Did you hear what the rabbi said?'

He had not understood until now how much his mother must have suffered. She had loved his father so much that she had seen his death as deliberate desertion. The Lord would not have made her suffer so much. It must have been Jacob's fault. And so when Joel had left, too, her suspicions had been confirmed. There was some hereditary quirk in the Blitz family which made their young men footloose, and disloyal. Soon, she was going to be left all on her own, useless and unloved.

Barney looked down at his right hand, at the crooked white scar which ran an inch between his thumb and his index finger. Dr Seligman had said nothing at all when Barney had asked him to sew it up, but maybe Dr Seligman had known what was inevitably going to happen. Maybe he should have seen it himself.

There was a hesitant knock at the bedroom door. He said, 'Come in.'

It was Irving and Hyman, embarrassed and dithery. Irving said, 'I guess we've come to say how sorry we are. Such a shock, you know, and your mother such a fine woman. A saint.'

'A saint?' said Barney. There was an embarrassed pause. Hyman, nervous and apologetic, shrugged.

'You're going to keep on the business?' asked Irving. 'Blitz, Tailors?'

'Any reason why I shouldn't?'

'No, not at all. Just asking.'

'That's okay then,' said Barney. 'As long as you're happy. You've always got Sussman's to go to, if you're not.'

'Sussman's,' said Hyman. 'I should *cholilleh* go to Sussman's?'

'Maybe,' said Barney. 'I'm selling my share of the business to Moishe. I'm pulling out.'

Irving frowned. 'You can't do that. This is your father's business.'

'My father's dead, in case you've forgotten. Now my mother's dead, too, and that leaves me with no responsibility to keep the business going whatsoever. I've had enough, Irving. I'm sorry.'

'But you were doing so good.'

'You didn't seem to think so a few days ago. Bespoke, you wanted, not ready-to-wear. Come on, Irving, you mustn't let sentimentality cloud your better judgement. You've been in the tailoring business for forty years. A young upstart like me should tell you what suits to make?'

'We delivered the tunics to the Academy,' said Hyman. 'They said the workmanship was excellent. They'll order again.'

Barney gathered up the letters and the papers on the bed – his mother's identity papers, her birth certificate, the letters from friends and relatives left behind in north Germany.

'That's good news,' he said, without lifting his eyes. 'Too bad you'll be going back to private orders only.'

There was another knock, and Leah looked around the door. Barney stood up, and offered his hand to Irving in the confident manner of a man who wants friendship, but not forgiveness. Irving took it, and gave him a regretful smile.

'I'm sorry to see you go. Blitz's won't be the same, with no Blitz.'

'It'll probably be better,' said Barney.

Irving and Hyman left, and Leah stepped into the room. She stood staring at Barney for a long time before she spoke.

'Moishe Teitelbaum told me you're going to sell up,' she said, gently.

He nodded.

'You're not – well, you're not acting too quickly, because of what happened on Friday night?'

'No,' he said flatly. 'I've been wanting to go for a long time. Ever since Joel left.'

'Are you going to stay here, in New York?'

'For what? For this rundown apartment on Clinton Street? For the sake of my mother's memory?'

'For me?' suggested Leah.

Barney laid his hand on the cold brass bedrail. The bedroom seemed suddenly very confined, and stuffy, and stale. His mother's silver-backed hairbrush lay on the dressing-table, still clotted with her own wiry hair. Unlike many Ashkenazic Jews, Feigel's family had not held with shaving their daughters' hair when they were married. There was nothing in the Bible which decreed that a woman had to wear a *shaytl*, a wig, Feigel's mother had protested, and a scarf was far more becoming.

'I have to go,' said Barney. 'There's nothing to keep me here but bad memories.'

'I love you,' said Leah, boldly.

Barney took her hands. They were small, and cold.

'You think you love me,' he said. 'But who else have you met? All those prissy boys your mother invites around for tea? Anybody would look lovable, compared to them.'

'But,' she said, more firmly, 'I love *you*.'

He kissed her forehead. 'I'm going to have to go. I want to be rich, Leah. I want to be able to come back to New York and buy a mansion on Third Avenue. Give me two years, that's all, and I'll come back and deck you out with gold. That's if you still want me.'

She stroked his cheek with the back of her fingers. 'Mother always says you look like one of those toughs from the Bowery.'

He gripped her wrist. Then he lifted her fingers against his lips, and kissed them. Her eyes glistened with tears.

'You won't forget to come back, will you?' she asked him.

He shook his head.

There was another knock at the door. It was Rabbi Levitz, stocky and fussy, with his thick ginger beard, and his tiny spectacles.

'Come in, rabbi,' said Barney. 'We were only talking about the funeral.'

The rabbi lifted his hands. 'Bless you,' he nodded. 'You make a fine couple.'

Leah turned to go. 'One day, maybe,' she said, softly.

Rabbi Levitz smiled at her as she walked out of the room. 'That was just what I wanted to talk to you about,' he told

Barney. 'Isn't it time you were thinking of marriage? You could certainly do worse than Leah Ginzburg.'

Barney rubbed his eyes. 'I'm tired, rabbi. I've just buried my mother. I don't want to talk about marriage.'

'But you're going away, aren't you? So Moishe tells me.'

'That's right. I was thinking of going to California. But there's a letter here from Joel, from South Africa. He says he's bought a farm there, and he wants me to help him. So, well – I guess I'll go.'

The rabbi held his arm. 'You should take a Jewish bride out with you. Maybe a girl like Leah. You never know what kind of woman you're going to meet in Africa. Maybe a *schwartzeh*.'

Barney couldn't help smiling. 'They have Jewish girls in South Africa, too, rabbi.'

Rabbi Levitz made a deprecatory face. 'Dutch, maybe. But no *landsleit*. No Germans.'

They stood side by side for a while in silence.

'Well,' said Rabbi Levitz. 'I shouldn't take up your time. I just wanted to tell you how sorry I am about your mother. I remember Feigel when she was such a pretty, gay girl. She and your father were my favourite young couple.'

'My mother's in Heaven?' asked Barney. 'Despite ...?'

The rabbi nodded. 'She was possessed by a devil, a *dybbuk*, and she exorcised it the only way she knew how. She pierced her flesh to let it out. Your mother is in Heaven, Barney, with your father. She led a good life.'

'And me?' asked Barney. 'Is there a place in Heaven for me?'

'There shouldn't be?' frowned the rabbi.

'I don't know. Sometimes I feel as if I can't keep a grasp on my faith. Sometimes I feel more like an American than a Jew.'

'You can't be both?'

Barney looked away. 'I've tried. But when I think of my father, and my grandfather, and my great-grandfather ... I feel like I don't belong any more.'

The rabbi grasped Barney's shoulder. 'You belong,' he said, simply. 'You're not the only young man I've talked to who feels the way you do. Your father used to feel it. He cut off his *payess* to make it easier for him to do business with Gentiles, and because he wanted to show that he'd left the past behind him.

It happens with every generation – questioning, doubt, who am I? A German, or a Jew? An American, or a Jew?'

Barney said, 'What, then? What's the answer?'

'The answer is to study the *Torah*, to seek enlightenment in the word of God, and to perform your sacred obligations with a happy heart. That is all.'

'That's enough?'

The rabbi smiled. 'Some of the greatest men in Ashkenazic history have devoted their entire lives to those three tasks, and have still died unsatisfied.'

The small funeral party began to disperse after an hour. Mr and Mrs Ginzburg came into the bedroom to offer Barney their condolences – Mr Ginzburg mournfully shaking Barney's hand, and Mrs Ginzburg tightening her lips and looking scornfully around the shabby apartment like an inquisitive chicken. When all the guests had left, Mrs Kowalski came down from her apartment upstairs to clean up. Mrs Blitz had always looked down on Mrs Kowalski – that ignorant *Poylish opstairsikeh* – but Mrs Kowalski washed up the wine glasses carefully, and swept the kitchen floor, and asked Barney in a motherly way as she wiped her hands on her apron if he wanted 'a bite supper'.

Barney, sitting alone at the kitchen table with a last glass of wine, said, 'No, no thank you. I have to get used to doing things for myself now.'

Mrs Kowalski hung up her apron behind the door. 'You should get a wife,' she told him, with a wide grin. 'What's a man, with no wife?'

Moishe bought out Barney's share in Blitz, Tailors, for $2123, although he was only able to raise $750 of that in cash. The rest was pledged as a mortgage on Moishe's brownstone-fronted house on Suffolk Street, which he owned, and by Moishe's cousin Avrum, who was part-owner of a kosher butcher's in Brooklyn. Barney took $150 straight away to the Inman steamship office on Broadway and bought himself a ticket to Liverpool on the *City of Paris*. Afterwards, he went to Lord & Taylor and kitted himself out with a new lightweight suit, in khaki; two pairs of stout canvas walking boots; shirts; underwear; and thick socks. He also purchased a Colt Shopkeeper's revolver, since Joel had described Cape Colony as 'very wild'.

The evening before he was due to sail, he climbed the stairs to the workroom of Blitz's for the last time. Everybody had gone home, but as he stood in the centre aisle between the workbenches he could imagine them all there, and hear the chatter of the girls, the slicing sound of the scissors, and the thump-thump-thump as Hyman rolled over a bolt of broadcloth. He ran his hand along the worn woodwork, and tried to remember how his father had looked, bent over a pattern, with his black business vest and his dangling gold watch chain, in those days when Barney had been sent along the street by his mother to take him a tray covered by a white napkin. *Latkes*, usually, or cold gefilte fish. His father would sit Barney on his knee while he ate, and say, 'One day, you and me, we're going to be working here side by side.'

The workroom door squeaked open. It was Moishe. He came puffing along to the end of the benches, and handed Barney a small package, wrapped up in brown paper.

'I went round to your apartment,' he said, mopping his forehead. 'Mrs Kowalski told me you'd probably be here.'

'What's this?' asked Barney, holding up the package.

'Open it and see.'

Barney slowly tore open the paper. Inside was a flat cardboard box, and inside that, neatly folded, a new prayer shawl. Barney lifted it out, and laid it carefully over his arm.

'I'm touched,' he said. 'Thank you.'

'It's from all of us. Irving and Hyman too. We want to wish you good luck, but not to forget us.'

'I couldn't forget you. I'm sorry I've let you down.'

'Let us down? How's that? You're young, you have yourself to think about. You have to follow the voice inside of your own head. Your father came to America to seek his fortune. You have to go someplace else.'

Barney wrapped the prayer shawl up again. 'I'm going to miss Clinton Street,' he said, 'for all of its problems.'

Moishe gripped his shoulder affectionately. 'Clinton Street is going to miss you.'

61

It was cold, dry, and windy the next morning, when Barney closed the apartment door behind him and stepped out into the street. He hefted his worn brown leather valise, and walked the length of Clinton Street to the intersection with Hester Street with his head bent, not looking at the sad landscape of his past. On the corner of Hester Street, the wind was so piercing that he had to turn his coat-collar up.

The *City of Paris*, one of the first screw-driven Atlantic steamers, held the blue riband for the fastest crossing from Liverpool to New York, at thirteen and a half knots. But during Barney's voyage, in the first two weeks of November 1868, the ocean was so tumultuous, like a vast encampment of grey army tents which were constantly being raised and then struck, and then raised again, that the steamship rolled and wallowed for six days at less than eight knots. Barney, huddled on the second-class deck in oilskins, had never felt so sick or so battered-about in his whole life, and by the end of the first week he began to believe that he had spent years on this tilting deck, under this barr granite sky, and that he was doomed to churn across the Atlantic for ever. To pass the time, he read magazines, or played cards with an earnest seven-year-old English boy who was never sea-sick and won three games out of four. He prayed, in the cabin he shared with a tall Scotsman, who was all tweed and elbows; and sometimes he and the Scotsman would struggle their way around the deck together, gripping the rails and the ropes, and scurrying in a hilarious *pas-de-deux* from one side of the promenade to the other when the ship heeled over in the waves. The second-class steward cheerfully described their progress as 'labouring, pitching, lurching, and spraying all over'.

It was drizzling when they docked at Liverpool. The *City of Paris* was two days late, and Barney had missed by six hours the sailing of the White Star steamer *Rubric* to Lisbon, and then down the coast of Africa to Cape Colony. In a noisy shed with a corrugated iron roof, he bought himself a ticket instead for the German ship *Weser*, due to sail in four days. Then, lugging his valise, he walked through the wet cobbled streets of Liverpool looking for somewhere to stay.

He felt utterly alone during those four days. He stayed at a small bed-and-breakfast house, run by a massive woman with a blaring laugh and a taste for topping up her cups of cheap bright tea with straight gin. Her husband was away in South America, she told Barney, and she was always glad of comfort. He took 'comfort' at first to mean liquor, but when on the second night she came tapping at his door to ask if he cared to come along to her room and share a nightcap, he was left in little doubt that she was looking for what a coarse friend of his father used to call 'a *yentz*'. For one unbalanced moment, he was almost tempted. It was still raining, he was thousands of miles away from home, and to lie in *anybody's* arms would have been reassuring. But he told himself that God was with him, and so were the best wishes of his friends, and he turned over in his narrow horsehair bed and tried to get to sleep. A steamship's siren blew him a mournful and echoing goodnight.

On the third afternoon, he walked along by the Mersey, watching the gulls swoop over the grey, rain-speckled water. Behind him were the docks, the funnels of coasters and packet ships and Atlantic steamers; and a stolid Victorian skyline of prosperous stone office buildings. Ahead of him was the dismal stretch of the estuary, and, on the far side, the wet green hills of Cheshire.

He thought of his mother, and for some odd reason he began to imagine that she was walking beside him, just one or two paces back, out of his line of sight. He stopped, and turned around, but there was nothing. Only the reflecting cobbles of the quay, and the rainy sky. He said a prayer for her. He wanted to think about her the way she had been before his father died – gentle and smiling. The bloody leer in the kitchen was a picture he would have to discipline himself to forget.

He took his meals at a small Jewish delicatessen close to the docks, Weinmans, where he sat at a sticky marble-topped table surrounded by steamed-up mirrors, and ate fatty salt beef. The proprietor was bustling and unfriendly: Barney could scarcely understand his Liverpudlian Yiddish at all. But on the morning that Barney was due to leave, the proprietor waved him away when he came up to the counter to pay 9d for his breakfast. 'Wherever you're going, you'll need the money,' he said, dismissively. 'Go on, before I change my mind, and good luck.'

The *Weser* was a paddle-steamer of the Bremerhaven

line, and almost twenty years old. Barney was allocated an awkwardly-shaped cabin close to the port paddlewheel housing, which he was to share with a Portuguese wine salesman, who sweated profusely, and gibbered in his sleep, and spent every day staring morosely at the ocean and picking his teeth with a quill. But after a choppy crossing of the Bay of Biscay, and a day's delay at Corunna to repair a broken paddle, the *Weser* began to make a steady seven knots southwards on a calm sea, and each day that dawned through the porthole of Barney's cabin was sunnier, and warmer, and more gilded with promise.

As the paddle-steamer rounded the dim coastline of Sierra Leone, and then followed the Ivory Coast, the Gold Coast, and the Slave Coast, Barney stayed for hours on deck, even during mealtimes, to watch the misty green reaches of West Africa slide slowly past. The sky was streaked with cirrus, but the yellowy-coloured sea, stained with silt from the Niger delta, still sparkled with reflected sunlight.

Off Cape Coast Castle, the *Weser* anchored for a day to take on fresh supplies of water and fruit. There was no harbour here, and everything had to be rowed through huge foaming breakers by native oarsmen. Barney leaned on the *Weser*'s rail and watched for almost the whole afternoon as surfboats came up alongside, and fruit was swung aboard in nets. Up above the scattered rooftops of the town, on the ramparts of a squat, hybrid building that was half castle and half country house, a huge Union Jack flapped idly in the wind. Barney could just catch the mildewed smell of jungle on the air, and the sweetness of overripe fruit.

'Now, *this* is an interesting place,' remarked an Englishman called Hunt, who had joined the *Weser* in Lisbon. Hunt was immaculately smart, quite handsome, but only four feet eleven, so that he looked like a ten-year-old boy in a false beard and a white tropical suit. He had taken to passing occasional remarks to Barney when they were out on deck, and to nodding courteously to him over the dinner table. 'That castle there, Elmina Castle, used to be a great slave emporium. Thousands upon thousands of slaves were sent off to America from there – caught by the Ashanti and brought to the coast with chains round their necks. So you could say that this is where your Civil

War started, couldn't you, if you were to take a long view of things?'

'I guess so,' said Barney, cautiously.

'You *are* an American, aren't you?' Hunt asked him.

'Yes. An American. And a Jew.'

Hunt drew back the lapels of his coat and tucked his thumbs into his neat white vest. 'Well,' he said, with a sharp little laugh that Barney did not really understand. 'I'm sure you're going to play *that* down.'

'Why should I?'

Hunt leaned his elbow on the ship's rail. Behind him, another surf boat was being rowed up to the *Weser's* side, with a cargo of lemons. 'My dear chap, *I* don't mind so much who my chums are, but there are plenty of fellows in Cape Colony who do. You're not English, so they won't worry so much about your school; but they'll certainly give you something of a cold shoulder if they know you're one of the Chosen. They won't treat you as bad as a kaffir, but almost. So if I were you – word of advice – I'd play that side of things down.'

'Why are you telling me this?' asked Barney. He could hardly believe what he was hearing.

'I like you, that's all. You look like a decent sort.'

'Well, maybe I am, but I can't deny my forefathers, just for the sake of socialising with a few bigoted Englishmen.'

Hunt lifted his eyebrows, and let out a stagey little sigh. 'The trouble is, old chap, that those few bigoted Englishmen are the only people out there, apart from the Boers, and *they* talk like ducks, and eat nothing but ham and cheese. There's the blackies, of course, but you wouldn't have much sport if you had nobody but *them* for company.'

'My brother's out there. He says it's a land of great opportunity.'

'So it is! But it all depends on your point of view. Opportunity, certainly. But opportunity for what? I work for the Governor, Sir Philip Woodhouse, and I can tell you on unshakeable authority that Cape Colony is more than a million pounds in debt. There's no wealth there. Oranges, oxen, a few farms, and that's precisely all. Everybody's scratching a living. Why you're going there at all, I can't imagine.'

Barney took out his handkerchief, folded it into a padded square, and wiped the sweat from his face and neck. The green canvas canopy over the second-class promenade deck was supposed to keep it cool, but instead if only served to trap whatever breeze there was, and make it five times hotter. It looked as if the *Weser* was almost ready to leave now. The surfboats had all pulled away, and there was a shudder through the length of the ship as steam was built up.

'I'm looking for a fresh start,' said Barney. 'That's the only reason I came.'

'You'll get *that* all right,' said Hunt. 'But you have to know people. Listen, I can help you, you know. Get you out to Oranjerivier with someone reliable – introduce you to Mr Pelling at the bank. You don't drink, do you, you Jewish chaps?'

'Why?'

'No reason. I was just wondering if you'd like to come down to my cabin for a spot of brandy. Excellent stuff, French. Bought it in Lisbon.'

'Thank you, no,' said Barney.

'Well, how about a game of rummy? Not for money, of course, just for the fun of it.'

'I don't –' Barney hesitated. He didn't like to be rude. Then he said, 'All right. For a half-hour, maybe.'

Hunt stood up straight, and fluffed up his beard with waggling fingers. 'That's excellent. I'm pleased. Why don't you come down in ten minutes or so? It's 23C, starboard side. Knock like this.' He demonstrated a postman's knock on the ship's rail. *Rat-tata-rat-tat – rat-tat!*

Barney watched Hunt strut off along the deck, and then turned back to the ship's rail. The *Weser*'s paddlewheels were beginning to turn over, churning up the sea into a brown froth, and she let out a piercing whistle that echoed flatly from the shoreline. He was thinking deeply, as the *Weser* began to beat her way out to sea, through the Gulf of Guinea, towards her next port-of-call, Port-Gentil, less than one degree south of the Equator, in Gabon. He touched the *yarmulka* on top of his brown curly hair as if he were discovering it for the first time.

After ten minutes, he left the rail and went down through

the varnished doors of the front hatch to C deck, where the second-class passengers were berthed. All the portholes were open, and the ventilators were open, but the humidity down there was suffocating. He rubbed perspiration from his forehead as he walked along the starboard side of the ship, looking for 23C.

He reached it at last, and knocked. Hunt called, 'Come!' and he hesitantly opened the door.

The green canvas blind was drawn across the porthole, so that the tiny cabin was irradiated with a curiously submarine light. The table had been folded down from the wall, and a deck of cards was laid out, as well as a cut-glass decanter of brandy, a carafe of water, and two glasses. Hunt was in the corner, wearing a dark blue bathrobe. He was inspecting himself in the mirror by the porthole, and patting lavender-water on to his cheeks.

'I feel quite faint,' he said, without turning around. 'It's no wonder they call West Africa the White Man's Grave. The heat! And you can get anything here. Portuguese itch, malaria, smallpox, Guinea worm, kraw kraw. You hardly have time to say you hope to God you won't get it, before you've got it.'

He suddenly turned around. His hair was combed flat, and he appeared to have smeared rouge on his cheeks. 'Well, my Chosen friend,' he said, 'What do you think?'

Barney stared at Hunt in disbelief. He had seen effeminate-looking men parading along Broadway, and soon after his Bar Mitzva his father had talked about some of the extraordinary sins of the flesh. But Hunt had transformed himself from a dapper little Englishman into something quite different altogether. A small and sinister clown, with a powdered beard.

'Do you think I look debonair?' demanded Hunt. 'I was a Winchester boy, you know. It wasn't Eton, but it wasn't bad. The flower of pretty youth, innocent and hopeful. The bloom of the British Empire.'

Barney stayed where he was, in the doorway. 'I'm sorry,' he said. 'But I don't think I'd better come in.'

'But you must! The cards are all ready! And I'm sure I can persuade you to try some of my brandy.'

Barney gave a gritty little grin. He was over the shock of

seeing Hunt in his make-up and his robe, and now, in a way that he could not quite understand, he felt sympathy for Hunt, and even warmth; but he knew that nothing would persuade him to enter that green-lit cabin. It would not be fair on Hunt, for one thing; and Hunt was certainly more than Barney was capable of handling – at least, without hurting the man's feelings.

'I don't feel too well,' said Barney. 'I think it must be the heat. Or maybe the fish we had for luncheon.'

'My dear chap, if you don't feel well you ought to lie down. Here – please – you can take my berth.'

Barney raised a hand. 'I'd really rather go back to my own cabin. Thank you all the same.'

Hunt came forward, frowning like a wife who is beginning to suspect that her husband's late business meetings might have been taking place behind the drawn drapes of the St Nicholas Hotel. 'It's very *difficult* out here, you know,' he said, in a sensitive voice. 'One's superiors aren't always very understanding of one's ...'

He hesitated, and then said, 'Predicament,' as if it were the answer to a puzzle which he had been trying to solve all day.

Barney said, 'I think I know what you mean.'

'Yes?' asked Hunt, brightening.

'Well ... maybe not entirely,' said Barney. 'But you have to understand that I'm in a predicament, too. My predicament is that I don't want to upset you, but I can't accept your invitation. I'm sorry.'

Hunt's mouth tightened. His face flickered through a dozen emotions, like a moving-picture machine on a seaside boardwalk. Then, with a flourish, he opened his bathrobe, baring his flat white chest, with a scraggy plume of dark hair on his breastbone, and his soft crimson penis. He stared at Barney with bijou defiance, challenging him to say that he was not impressed and aroused – or at the very least impressed.

Barney could not think of anything else to do but bow his head, and say, 'Excuse me,' and turn away. Hunt said quickly, '*My dear friend* –!' But Barney began walking at a fast pace back along the second-class corridor until he reached the companionway. He climbed up to the promenade deck, and stood for a few minutes in the shade of the awning to collect himself, watching the ochre-coloured sea slide by, and listening to the endless slosh-slosh-slosh of the paddles.

A steward in a tight, sweat-stained tropical jacket came up and asked him almost ferociously if he cared for a glass of lime juice and seltzer. He said, 'No thank you,' and went along to his stuffy little cabin to lie down for an hour or two, and read.

The *Weser* steamed into Table Bay on Thursday, 3 December 1868, just as the sun was nibbling at the edge of Table Mountain. It was summer in the Southern Hemisphere, and even though it was only eight o'clock, the day was already windy and warm. Barney, along with most of the other second-class passengers, was crowded against the rail.

The *Weser* gave a long whistle as she beat her way slowly into the shadow of the massive flat-topped mountain. There were already six or seven ships riding at anchor offshore, including two stately tea-clippers on their way back to England from Bombay. The crew of one of them, with clay pipes and pigtails, watched the *Weser* with casual interest from the foredeck, and whistled shrilly at a pretty young wife who was blushing under her parasol on the first-class promenade.

Once the ship's anchor had plunged into the sea, most of the passengers, chattering and shuffling, filed back to their cabins to finish their packing. Barney, who had already closed his single leather valise, stayed by the rail and took a long, unobstructed look at Capetown.

Under the sheer sandstone ramparts of Table Mountain, which were already shining gold as the sun rose higher in the sky, the houses and churches and offices were clustered amongst glittering green oaks and mulberries. Most of the buildings looked Dutch – flat-fronted and painted white, with neat brown thatched roofs – although Barney could see several new buildings in the heavy, prosperous style of British imperialism, and a seventeenth-century sandstone castle. Two distinctive spires rose above the town – one like a slender wedding-cake, and the other with the plain sharpness of a Dutch Reformed church.

Even though there was a strong smell of salt on the wind, Barney caught an aroma of flowers.

'Well, home again,' said a voice beside him. It was Hunt, in a formal grey suit, smelling of lavender-water.

Barney nodded. He did not really know what to say. He reached into the pocket of his summer suit, freshly-pressed for his arrival by the *Weser*'s Chinese laundryman, and took out a pair of wire-rimmed sunglasses, with tiny black lenses, which he carefully hooked around his ears.

Hunt chuckled nervously, 'You look rather sinister in those. Like a chap I used to know in Kaffraria, who used to shoot Bantus for the sport of it.'

Barney took the sunglasses off.

'You know,' said Hunt, 'I really want to say how sorry I am for what happened the other day. You were frightfully sensitive about it. I mean – quite a few other chaps might have reported me to the captain, or even to the Governor. You were very decent about it.'

Barney looked towards the shore. Already, four or five lighters were being rowed towards the *Weser* through the surf.

'It's nothing,' he said.

'Well, it was appreciated all the same,' said Hunt. 'And if you can ever forgive me for what I did, I really would like to help you. I can arrange for a guide to take you out to Oranjerivier, with a bearer, of course; and I'll introduce you to Mr Hutton at the Standard Bank. It's the very least I can do, considering.'

Barney looked at Hunt for a moment. Then he held out his hand. For the first time since Joel had left him in charge of Blitz's – or maybe as far back as the day when his father had died – he began to feel confident, and self-possessed. He was not quite sure why. Perhaps it was because he had managed to deal with Hunt in a way that he had never been able to deal with his mother, or with Moishe, or with David Stein.

'It says in Genesis, Forgive the trespass of thy brethren,' he told Hunt, simply.

Hunt shok his hand, and then stepped back to show that he did not intend to try any further intimacies without being asked.

'That's excellent, then,' he said. 'I'll find you somewhere to stay tonight, and then tomorrow I'll look for a guide.'

They were rowed ashore within the hour. On the rock-strewn beaches, knee-deep in the foam, black porters were waiting to lift their bags and their trunks out of the lighters and on to a motley assembly of ox-carts, horse-drawn omnibuses, and waggons. A rather shabby brougham from Government House was waiting to collect Hunt, and he enthusiastically offered Barney a ride into the town centre.

'After Portugal, the Cape always strikes me as so *civilised*,' said Hunt, neatly crossing his legs as the brougham jolted them over dry rutted roads. 'It may not have Lisbon's restaurants, or Lisbon's opera, or Lisbon's commercial life. But, by God, you know where you are with people. The order of life is clear-cut, and immutable.'

'I thought you said Cape Colony was very poor,' said Barney.

'Oh, it is,' nodded Hunt. 'And that's what gives life its clarity. No rich Latins of dubious parentage, trying to aspire to white society. No blackies to whom one has to be even the remotest bit polite. There are a few quarrelsome Boers, of course, but most of the really disagreeable ones have trekked out to the Transvaal and the Orange Free State.'

'No Jews?' asked Barney.

Hunt gave him a brief, uncomfortable grimace.

'Not many,' he agreed. 'Not many.'

They rattled their way into Townhall Square, a broad dusty plaza flanked by stately white Dutch façades, some of them supported by Ionic pilllars and decorated with festoons of carved fruit and flowers. The square was thronged with people and animals in almost equal proportions, and an old man with a monkey on a chain was standing not far away from Barney's coach with a Dutch hurdy-gurdy, so that the jostling of oxen and the fluttering of chickens and the constant to-ing and fro-ing of the crowds was set to a strange, droning score.

There were dozens of British soldiers around, in caps and blouson tunics, with their fashionable waxed moustaches and goatee beards; and nearly as many Jack Tars, with muttonchip side-whiskers and wide-brimmed boater hats. Around them, eager for their shillings, swarmed street-sellers with high-pointed straw hats and shoulder-poles laden with everything from sweets to live poultry. And across the square, walking with that swaying dignity that few American Negroes of Barney's acquaintance seemed to have been able to preserve through generations of slavery, Bantu women made their way in their bright headscarves and their flowery Mission-school dresses that may have clothed them from neck to ground in Victorian modesty, but could never suppress the jubilant roll of their hips and the complicated jiggle of their breasts. Almost all of these women seemed to be carrying under their arms a huge bundle of assorted necessities, such as oranges, figs, fish, bunches of greens, and a bored child.

The brougham drew up outside a thatched Dutch building called The Thatch Inn, and the black coachman climbed down to open the door for Barney and extend the steps. Hunt said, 'You find yourself a room here for tonight. Talk to Mr Shearer, he's the proprietor, and tell him you're a guest of Government House. Then tomorrow, at noon, I'll meet you at Clark's Eating House on Adderley Street.'

The coachman carried Barney's valise into the Inn's front doorway, and across the cool black and white tiles of a wide entrance-hall. Then he scurried away. Barney walked up to the mahogany reception desk, above which an array of ill-matched clocks told the time in London, in Moscow, in New York, and The Hague. He stared up at the grimy ormolu clock which told him it was only five o'clock in the morning in New York, and he tried to imagine Clinton Street as it must be now – dark, and freezing, and thick with snow.

The clerk behind the counter was watching him with a composed, monkey-life face. Then, without impatience, he asked Barney 'Yes?'

'Oh, I'm sorry,' said Barney. 'I wanted a room for the night. Just a single room, that's all.'

'That's all your luggage?' asked the clerk, peering over the counter at Barney's valise as if it were a small and unwelcome dog.

Barney shrugged his assent. The clerk scratched his ear with the end of his pen and noisily turned the pages of the hotel register.

'I have an upstairs back. Bit cramped, I'm afraid. Bit hot too, being right under the roof.'

'I *am* a guest of Government House,' ventured Barney.

The clerk stopped scratching and looked at him with an expression that was on the pitying side of sympathy. 'Oh,' he said. 'In that case, I'm going to have to ask you to pay in advance, too.'

'Is Mr Shearer here? The proprietor?'

'Good God, no. Mr Shearer wouldn't stay in Capetown in high summer. He's gone up to Wellington, for his health.'

Reluctantly, Barney paid for his room, and a grinning Bantu in voluminous white trousers showed him up the winding stairs to the upper landing, and along the corridor. Halfway along the corridor hung a colour lithograph of Queen Victoria and Prince Albert, which the Bantu cheerily saluted.

The clerk had been right. Barney's room was tiny, and so hot that he began to sweat as soon as he stepped into it. But it was clean, with whitewashed walls, a wide-boarded yellowwood floor, an iron bed, and a single riempie-thonged chair. He went straight to the window, and opened it, and found he was looking out over a small fenced garden, dense with bougainvillaea, and overshadowed by a tree which he later learned to call a *Huil Boerboonboom*.

Behind the garden, and beyond a scattering of old Cape-Dutch houses, rose the foothills of Table Mountain, and then the mountain itself. Over the clear-cut edge of the mountain, huge white puffy cumulus clouds hung in a sharp blue sky.

Barney sat on the edge of his bed. He said a *broche* for the vivid scenery of Capetown, and a *broche* for his room, and a *broche* for his safe arrival. Then he raised his head, and closed his eyes, and breathed in the scent of flowers and fruit and warmth. He felt as if he had arrived, prematurely, in Paradise.

That evening, he ate alone, in the garden, under the rustling leaves of the *Huil Boerboonboom*, his meal lit by a candle. He was served a curious fried fish which the waiter told him was *snoek*. He drank a fruity Cape wine, and finished his meal with slices of bread spread with *moskonfyt*, a thick grape syrup. From the tables all around him came the scissorlike accents of British farmers, talking about apricot growing, and cattle farming, and

73

the shaky condition of the Colony's economy. A skeletal Scotsman with a brambly red beard was leaning back in his Zandevelt chair and declaring in a loud voice, 'Well – it's my opinion that Sir Philip ought to trek out and find himself another diamond. A few more like the Eureka, and he could at least afford to give Government House a fresh lick of paint.'

One of his companions swallowed a large mouthful of whiskey and shook his head. 'No such luck, McFee. You remember that James Gregory fellow – the one they sent out from Emanuel's in London? Well, he's written a report in this month's *Geological Magazine*, and he says there isn't a single chance of finding diamonds out on the Orange River, or anywhere around. An imposture, he calls it. A South African Bubble.'

'There was the one diamond, though,' pointed out the man called McFee. 'And if there was the one, why shouldn't there be others?'

'It was a fluke,' put in another farmer, dogmatically. 'If you found a sovereign in Riebeeck Square, you wouldn't start digging up the road, would you, to look for more? Gregory says the Eureka was probably dropped by an ostrich.'

'Och, where's your optimism?' said McFee. 'Just think about it. A fellow would only have to find himself one respectable diamond, and he'd be rich for the rest of his life.'

'Are *you* going to trek out to the Orange River and start scrabbling around for one, then?' asked his friend.

McFee raised his glass. 'Not I, Bernard. Too much sweat. And, besides, I wouldn't know what a diamond looked like if I tripped over one.'

Barney lay on his twisted sheet that night, under the shadows of his mosquito net, and thought about what McFee had said. *One respectable diamond. Just one respectable diamond.* Outside, in the hot fragrant darkness, a few of the guests were still drinking and laughing. Someone played an impromptu air on the fiddle for a while. Barney slept, and dreamed of meeting Joel. For some reason, Joel would not look at him, and Barney woke in the small hours of the morning feeling a hair-raising sense of fright.

*

Clark's Eating House was the favourite lunchtime meeting-place for the young shipping agents and bank tellers who worked in the stately white stone buildings of Adderley Street. Clark's did a tolerable beef pie and mashed potatoes, as well as antelope steak, and curried *snoek*. Barney was there ten minutes before Hunt, and he took a table by the window, and asked for a carafe of white wine. All around him sat loud young men with British public-school voices and faces the colour of corned beef. A woven fan flapped steadily overhead, stirring the sweltering air, and vaguely irritating the aspidistras which stood around the eating-house in hideous blue jardinières.

At last Hunt came through the door, wearing a smart white suit and a straw boater. He was tugging along behind him a mournful Boer, whose faded grey linen jacket and worn-out *veld* boots accredited him at a glance as a professional *trekker*.

'Well, you found your way here all right,' smiled Hunt, shaking hands. 'This is your guide, Simon de Koker. Mr de Koker – this is Mr Barney Blitz, from New York.'

Simon de Koker took off his floppy hat and studiously wiped around the sweatband with his table-napkin. He had one of those long, lantern-jawed Boer faces, fringed with whiskers, with tiny sun-bleached eyes, and a mouth that was permanently downturned – whether out of pessimism, or pain, or Calvinist disapproval, it was impossible for Barney to tell. Barney later used to say that when the Lord was fixing on the babies' smiles, He accidentally stuck Simon de Koker's smile on upside-down.

'You want to trek to Oranjerivier?' asked Simon de Koker, in that snipping accent of the Cape Dutch.

'My brother's there. He has a farm.'

'A Jewish fellow, in Oranjerivier, with a farm?'

Barney was pouring Hunt a glass of wine, He paused. 'That's right. His name's Joel Blitz.'

Simon de Koker took a long drink of wine. Then he slowly shook his head. 'I know every farm in Oranjerivier. There's nobody farming out there by the name of Blitz. And no Jews, for sure.'

Barney reached into the pocket of his suit and took out Joel's letter. 'He wrote me and told me. Here it is, look – a sketchmap of how to get there from Oranjerivier itself.'

75

The Boer took the letter and studied it. His nose was beaded with perspiration. Eventually, he handed the letter back and said, 'I know the farm you mean. Derdeheuwel, it's called – third hill. It used to belong to a voortrekker called van Diedrich. Then van Diedrich died, and his daughter sold it. I don't know to whom. But now it's owned by a Portuguese fellow. No question about that. A man called Monsaraz.'

Barney sat back. He felt suddenly, and peculiarly, alone. He had imagined all kinds of difficulties in making a new life for himself in Cape Colony. Joel had written in graphic detail about the heat in the summer and the frosts in the winter, and the thieving Hottentots. But Barney had never thought for a moment that he might not be able to find Joel at all.

'Listen,' said Hunt, 'we ought to order lunch. What will you have, Barney? I can recommend the *snoek*.'

'I had *snoek* for dinner last night,' Barney told him. 'I'll try the antelope steak.'

'Is it *kosher* for Jews to eat antelope?' asked Simon de Koker.

Barney nodded. 'Antelope have cloven hoofs, and chew the cud. I learned that from school. The cooks here may not prepare it according to strict dietary law, but when there's no option, we are allowed to eat some things that are *trayf*. Otherwise the whole world would be populated by starving Jews.'

A Malay waiter came up and took their order. Hunt called for another carafe of wine, and some bread. He sat drinking and chewing for a while, and frowning hard.

'Do you still want to go out to Oranjerivier?' he asked Barney. 'It's all of 700 miles, you know, by horseback or ox-waggon, and that's going to take you the better part of five weeks, maybe longer. It could take you two months. And then, supposing your brother isn't anywhere to be found?'

'What else can I do?' asked Barney. 'I won't be able to find any work here. I'm a tailor. And not even a very good tailor, at that.'

'How much money do you have?' asked Simon de Koker.

'About ninety pounds,' said Barney.

'Well,' said Simon de Koker, dolefully, 'that should last you six or seven months, allowing for the cost of your trip out to

Oranjerivier, and your lodging when you get there. I know a farmer who might rent you a *solder*, a loft.'

'But how do I find my brother?'

Simon de Koker shrugged. 'He's either dead, from malaria, in which case you won't have much trouble finding his grave. Or else he's drunk, and you'll find him at Maloney's Bar, near Dutoitspan, more than likely. Or else he's sold up whatever he's got left, and moved on, in which event you may never see him again. It all depends.'

Barney took a piece of bread, tore it, and began to eat it unbuttered. 'I have to *try* to find him,' he said. 'You can understand that.'

'Of course,' said Hunt. 'But what will you do if he's dead, or gone off without a trace? It's not very hospitable out there, you know. Those that malaria doesn't dispose of, the blackies will.'

'What about diamonds?' asked Barney. 'I heard some fellow yesterday say that if you could find yourself a decent-sized diamond up by the Orange River, you'd be made for life.'

Simon de Koker laughed, although his mouth remained bitterly downturned. Listening to the noise he made was about as pleasant as closing your finger in a doorjamb. 'Diamonds?' he said. 'There was one diamond, the Eureka, and that was found by the Orange River a couple of years ago by a fellow called Schalts van Niekirk. But that was an accident. A twist of fate. It probably came from hundreds of miles away, that diamond, in some animal's paw; or maybe in the crop of an ostrich. They showed it at the Paris Exhibition last year. But you won't find any more, and you'd be a damned fool to try.'

'How much will you charge to take me out to Oranjerivier?' asked Barney.

The food arrived – Hunt's grilled *snoek*, and Simon de Koker's pie. The waiter set Barney's antelope steak in front of him, and asked him if he wanted *moskonfyt* with it. Barney shook his head.

Simon de Koker said, 'I'll take you to Oranjerivier; and find you lodging, for ten pounds, plus feed for the oxen, water at threepence a bucket, and thirty shillings for the bearer.'

'You're a fool to go,' said Hunt, cutting up his fish. 'I could

77

easily get you a job here, with the Cape Bank, or even at Government House.'

Barney sniffed the rare, aromatic smell of antelope meat. In those days, the Great Karoo was thick with antelope.

'Well,' he said, 'I was a fool to give up my business in New York and come all this way to meet my brother. But I think I'd be a greater fool if I didn't make an effort to find him. If you'll guide me, Mr de Koker, I'll go.'

'Oh, I'll guide you,' said Simon de Koker, as he cut up his pie-crust.

Simon de Koker, despite the permanent misery of his expression, turned out to be far more amiable than he had first appeared. He was waiting for Barney outside The Thatch Inn on the morning they were due to leave for Oranjerivier, clad in a red-checked shirt and a huge white hat, and smoking a meerschaum pipe. In the back of his waggon, drawn by a single disconsolate ox, was his own rhinoceros-hide travelling trunk, and a bulging canvas gunny-sack which looked as if it had been stuffed with five small boys.

'No bearer?' asked Barney, as he lifted his valise on to the back of the waggon, and climbed up.

'Not yet,' de Koker told him. 'Just for the sake of convenience, we're travelling as far as Paarl by train.'

The railroad that climbed inland from Capetown to Wellington, a winding distance of sixty-three miles, was Cape Colony's only line, apart from a seven-mile spur which connected Durban, the principal town of Natal, with the coast of the Indian Ocean. No telegraph lines penetrated inland, and all mail and provisions had to be hauled out to the Transvaal and the Orange Free State by ox-waggon. Simon de Koker's gunny-sack was crammed with letters and packages for British and Boer farmers. Some of the letters had been franked over a year ago.

'Those Boer farmers are made of nails,' said Simon de Koker, as he turned the ox-waggon around in the rutted yard of Capetown's Dutch-fronted railroad station. 'Most of them trekked a thousand miles or more, and what they had to endure across those mountains and deserts, well, God only knows. It's going to be bad enough for us, I warn you, but thirty years ago it must have been hell. Even now they're barely scraping a living. But, they're free from the British, and that's their main concern.'

The small steam locomotive laboured up through the sandstone mountains, away from the ocean, under a glaring sky. Simon de Koker sat with his arms tight-folded and his legs crossed, looking out at the trees and brightly-coloured shrubs and rocky *krantzes*, and placidly smoking his pipe. The only other occupants of the carriage were a Dutch girl with huge pale forearms and a blue summer hat the size of a small cartwheel, and an agitated Englishman of about twenty-five, who perspired furiously, and kept fiddling with a selection of large butterfly nets.

Barney asked Simon de Koker, 'Do *you* think I'm a fool, trying to find my brother?'

De Koker shrugged, without taking his pipe out of his mouth. 'If your brother's alive, and you find him, then who can say that you're a fool? But if he's dead, and all his money's gone, and you don't find anything but a gravestone ...'

'I dreamed about him the first night I was here,' said Barney. 'I dreamed he was alive.'

'Well, man,' said de Koker, his face still a study in sadness, 'that might increase his chances.'

Paarl was little more than a small collection of Cape-Dutch cottages and farms in a flowery, upland setting. The air was fresher here, and the scent of summer blooms was carried on a wind that was dry and bracing. It was only a few miles from here, at Wellington, that the proprietor of The Thatch Inn was spending his summer vacation. Barney and Simon de Koker climbed down from the train, and crossed the yard to where an ox-waggon was waiting, tied up to a rail under the shade of a row of mulberry trees. A blackman was asleep in the back of the waggon, his frayed straw hat over his eyes, his long bare legs clustered with flies.

'They've given me Donald again, the bastards,' said Simon de Koker, without any apparent emotion. 'Donald, wake up, you idle Kaffir! Do you know why they call him Donald? His name's Simkwe, really. But some bloody Scotchman paid him to take him across the Great Karoo, and always called him Donald. Whenever Simkwe said, 'Me Simkwe,' that bloody Scotchman said, "You're Donald, Donald, and don't forget it, Donald."'

Donald jerked awake. 'I'm awake, sir!' he shouted.

'I'm pleased to hear it,' said Simon de Koker. 'Go get our bags from the train, and be quick about it.'

'Yes, sir!' Donald exclaimed, and hurried off towards the depot. He was thickset for a blackman, and his skin was the colour of treacle toffee, instead of the intense black of the Bushmen or the Zulus.

'He's a Griqua,' Simon de Koker explained. 'Half Hottentot, and half Boer, and more than half stupid. It's the sun, if you ask me. It's *braaied* his brains.'

'What are we going to do for water, and provisions?' asked Barney.

'That's just where we're going now,' Simon de Koker told him. 'This waggon, and Donald, both belong to a fruit farmer friend of mine, Henk Jeppe. I sent word we were coming a couple of days back, by train. He should have everything ready for us, six pounds the lot.'

Donald came back across the square with Simon de Koker's rhinoceros bag on his head, and the other two pieces of luggage under his arms. 'Mr Henk says you going to Oranjerivier, Mr Simon.'

'That's right, Donald.'

'That's good, Mr Simon. My sister live in Oranjerivier.'

'I thought your sister lived in Hope Town.'

'That's my *other* sister, Mr Simon.'

Donald climbed up on to the waggon, and clicked a loud Xhosa-like click to the oxen. Slowly, their angular haunches going up and down like the bobbins of a sewing-machine, the oxen turned out of the square and along the street.

'Donald has sisters everywhere,' remarked Simon de Koker. 'They're not really sisters, if you know what I mean. But he was brought up by a British missionary, and he learned the art of hypocrisy at an early age. Decorum before truth, you understand.'

Without being asked, Donald drew the waggon up outside

a large *strooidak* church, with an elegant white Dutch façade and a graveyard surrounded by a low whitewashed wall. Simon de Koker eased himself down from the seat, and entered the churchyard through the wrought-iron gates at the front. Barney watched him standing silently amongst the cypress trees, his hat in his hand. After a while, he came back, and climbed up on to the waggon again.

'I used to have a wife,' Simon de Koker said, as the waggon clattered downhill between rows of young cultivated pear trees. 'Seven years ago, that was. I was going to settle down, and start farming. I married her here, in Paarl. That's where she used to live – see that loft house across by the wall there?'

Barney waited for Simon de Koker to tell him more, but the guide seemed to be finished with his explanation. They jiggled around on the ox-waggon's seat in silence until they turned at last into the gateway of a tidy little fruit farm, where chickens clustered in the front yard, and a big blonde woman was hanging up sheets on a washing-line. The hillside all around was planted with rows of apricots and oranges, their leaves rustling in the wind like hushed applause.

Simon de Koker stepped down. 'It was a bird snake,' he said. 'Adaleen's first trip out to the bushveld. We were collecting sticks for the campfire, and she picked it up. Bird snakes look like dried-out branches, you see. Well, it bit her, and there wasn't anything I could do to save her. I brought her back to Paarl only two weeks after we'd left.'

'I'm sorry,' said Barney.

Simon de Koker looked at him expressionlessly. 'You can't be sorry, man. If the people of this country ever stopped to be sorry, then it would never survive, and neither would they.'

Henk Jeppe came up to greet them, a short scarlet-faced man with cropped prickly hair and a handshake that was solid meat. 'How are you keeping, Sy?' he asked Simon de Koker. 'And what's this, a Jewish fellow?'

'Barney Blitz,' said Simon de Koker. 'He's off to Oranjerivier to find his brother.'

'If I were you, man, I'd be careful,' advised Henk Jeppe. 'There's plenty of hard-cooked customers out by the Orange

River who don't take kindly to Jews, or even Catholics, for that matter.'

'I'm an American, Mr Jeppe,' Barney told him. 'And my parents travelled just as far as any of your Boer farmers to get away from persecution. The Boers and the Jews seem to me to have a great deal in common.'

'Well, have it your way, man,' said Henk Jeppe. 'But that's just a friendly word. A hard country breeds hard people. Do you know where your brother is?'

Barney shook his head. 'I'm just going to have to ask around until I find somebody who knows where he went.'

Henk Jeppe glanced at Simon de Koker and said, '*Dit is een krankzinnig idee.*'

'*Misschien,*' shrugged Simon de Koker. '*Dat weten we pas wanneer we het proberen.*'

Barney said to Henk Jeppe, 'You're asking Mr de Koker if I'm crazy?'

Henk Jeppe, embarrassed, raised his hands in a gesture that seemed to mean, 'What can you expect?'

Their waggon was waiting for them in the back yard of Henk Jeppe's farm. It was covered with a hooped canvas top, like a Conestoga waggon, and packed with six barrels of water, two cases of *biltong,* dried apricots, fresh oranges, bacon, cheese, and gunpowder. The four oxen which Henk Jeppe was going to hire them to draw the waggon were lazily swishing at the midday flies in a nearby *kraal.*

'Another word of advice,' Henk Jeppe said to Barney, his beefy hands propped up on his hips. 'Get yourself a decent hat. One with a wide brim. Otherwise you *will* go *krank.*'

That night, Barney and Simon de Koker were guests at the Jeppes' supper table. There was casseroled beef with fresh vegetables, sugar-roasted ham (which Barney politely refused), and little pastry envelopes of cheese and peppers which reminded Barney of his mother's *kreplach.* Under the light of the oil lamps, the long table was lined by Henk Jeppe's three big, ruddy-faced sons, his two well-built daughters, his nephew, his wife's white-haired father, and his taciturn, wrinkle-faced foreman. 'An 'at-home' lantern burned in the dining-room window, to show passers-by that the Jeppes were willing to receive guests.

After dinner, Henk Jeppe read from the Bible, while his family sat around him in respectful silence. Simon de Koker yawned.

'We're off at dawn tomorrow, Barney,' he said, at the foot of the spiral yellowwood staircase, as Barney went up to bed. 'In a couple of days, you're going to get your first look at the Great Karoo.'

Their lonely trek across the Great Karoo had a profound effect on Barney that eventually brought him closer to God, but detached him from his Orthodox background like the silky seed of a South African *stapeliae* flower, which floats away on the wind as soon as the sun opens the seed pod.

The landscape was arid, dusty and endless, with pale broken hill formations on either side of them – the Swartberge to the south-east and the Nieuweveldberge to the north-west – and nothing ahead of them but a flat, heat-misted horizon. The ox-waggon creaked and jolted across the baking plains of silt and volcanic ash for hour after hour, its wheels flattening the scrub and the Bushman grass, and Barney sat under the shade of the canvas cover sleeping or reading or simply staring at the barrels on the other side of the stifling interior. Simon de Koker smoked his pipe and said very little. The pungent smoke was blown away by the wind.

Barney thought about his mother, and his father, and about the words of the *Torah*. The Children of Israel had trekked across the desert like this, seeking the fulfilment of a promise, and they had doubted God again and again. Faced with such limitless tracts of desolate land, whipped by whirlwinds, scorched by the sun, it was natural to doubt. Yet the uncertainty that Barney felt as he crossed the Greak Karoo was not that the Lord did not exist. The evidence of His existence was everywhere – in every range of hills, and every mile of scrub – and if anything, Barney felt nearer to the reality of the Lord out here in the bush than he had in the synagogue on Clinton Street.

What he was beginning to question were the dogmas of his Orthodox upbringing. His childhood studies had prepared him well for a life in the Jewish ghetto of New York's Lower East

Side. But it had left him open and unprepared for the hugeness and drama of the Lord's earthly creation when it was confronted in the raw. The shimmering landscape of the Great Karoo was far more convincing proof to Barney of God's eternal plan than a whole snowstorm of pages out of the *Teitsh-Chumash*. He bagan to feel that if he hearned to live in this country, and to adapt himself to the ways of the people who lived here, he was far more likely to understand God's purpose than if he slavishly recited *schachris*, *mincha*, and *mairev* every day, and kept his nose in the *Talmud*.

Years later, he wrote, 'I was brought up in the ways of a religion that was preoccupied with struggle and survival. Yet, in New York, where was the struggle? We were poor, yes. We had to work hard. But your mother's oven going out on the Sabbath, and spoiling the *kugel*, that's a struggle? For that you have to learn to survive, life or death? In Cape Colony, I saw for the first time what struggle and survival actually meant – and, at that age, the struggle and the survival themselves meant more to me than any religion I had ever been taught.'

On the third day out of Paarl, as their wagon bumped across the *hooyvlakte*, the hay flats which grew from the rich silt around the Ganka River, Barney climbed out on to the waggon's wooden seat wearing a wide buff bush hat. Simon de Koker glanced at him, but did not remark on it.

'There are sheep here,' said Barney. 'Are we close to a township?' He pointed across the flats towards the distant grey dots of a grazing flock.

Simon de Koker knocked his pipe on the waggon's stinkwood brake handle. He had been driving for the past two hours, while Donald slept in the back, his long spidery legs dangling over the tailgate. The desert felt ancient and vast, which it was. Under its layers of deep volcanic ash were compressed the fossils of thousands of prehistoric creatures, 270 million years old; and the previous night, as they gathered sticks for the campfire, Barney had picked up a stone scraper that dated from the times when primitive Bushmen had lived on the Great Karoo.

'We're coming close to Beaufort West,' explained Simon de Koker, in a matter-of-fact voice. 'Those sheep over there are part of Arthur Kinnear's merino flock. You'll see more, as we get closer to town. They make their living from wool around here. Wool, wool, and more wool.'

'It looks too dry for sheep,' commented Barney.

'Oh, you'd be surprised,' Simon de Koker told him. 'There are plenty of underground springs around here. I've come here after a heavy rainstorm, and the green grass has been springing up, and the cosmos flowers, and it looked just like the land of milk and honey. The Hottentot call this land "the Koup", which if you translate it literally means "sheep tail fat". That's how they describe prosperity.'

They travelled on for an hour or two, until they reached a low promontory overlooking the town of Beaufort West. Simon de Koker reined back the oxen, who turned their heads and stared back at him with brown rolling eyes, and let out a chorus of frustrated *meeerrrms*. Through the thorn bushes, at the foot of the rise on which Simon de Koker had drawn the waggon to a stop, the red and brown rooftops of Beaufort West were spread out in a wide valley. Barney could see the lantern-shaped belltower of the town hall, and the grandiose grey stone frontage of the municipal buildings. But he could also make out the modest, well-kept farmhouses and homes amongst the almond, acacia, and cypress trees. Beyond, to the north-east, in the direction of Three Sisters and Victoria West, there was nothing but a hazy skyline.

From where they stood, they could hear faintly the fussing of chickens and the laughter of two men who were thatching a roof nearby. Someone was banging a hammer, and the echo fell flat across the veld, as flat as the shadows of late afternoon.

'You took off your little cap,' said Simon de Koker.

'My *yarmulka*? It wasn't really practical.'

Simon de Koker nodded, as if he understood everything. 'The only practical equipment on the Great Karoo is a good wide hat, a team of healthy oxen, plenty of water, and a good rifle. There are still quite a few lion and leopard around.'

'You don't think that a Bible is necessary equipment?' asked Barney.

Simon de Koker pulled a face. 'If you go in winter, sure. It can get frosty at night, and you can't always find enough wood.

85

A friend of mine burned his Bible page by page, just to keep warm out on Kompasberg one night. The pastor forgave him, because he started at Revelations and worked backwards.'

They spent the night at the home of a sheep farmer called Alf Loubser, who lived in a T-shaped hand-built cottage with a riempie-thonged ceiling. Loubser and Simon de Koker sat outside together on the verandah and drank oily Dutch gin, washed down with lager, while a pressure-lamp hissed on the table, and the last light of the day glowered grudgingly behind the peaks of the Nieuweveldberge. Barney sat a little way away, feeling grimy and exhausted. Loubster's daughter Louise, a shy blonde seventeen-year-old in blue gingham and wooden clogs, kept bringing him glasses of sweet white wine and little home-made zwiebacken.

'You're not happy?' she asked Barney, as she sat cross-legged on a cushion and watched him eat.

'Happy?' he asked her. 'Why shouldn't I be?'

'I don't know. You haven't smiled, or laughed.'

He looked at her. She was pretty, in a *milchedig* Dutch way, with blue eyes and an upturned nose. The pressure-lamp, just behind her, crowned her with glowing, dancing moths.

'I guess I feel a little strange here,' Barney told her. 'A little homesick. It's winter in New York, where I come from. There should be snow.'

It was dark now, and up above the Koup the southern stars were glittering. A dry, hot evening wind was blowing from the north-west, from the Kalahari.

'Do you have a wife?' asked Loubser's daughter.

Barney shook his head.

'I often dream about a husband,' the girl told him.

He reached out and held her hand. She wore a thin silver ring on her third finger, set with an opal.

'Nils Groenewald gave me this ring,' she said. 'He said it should be a keepsake, until he came back. He went to Bloem-fontein to work on a cattle farm. One day, he said, he will have a farm of his own. Then he will come back and marry me.'

Barney said gently, 'You're in love with Nils Groenewald?'

'He's very upright. Very stiff. My friend Attie says he's a real Boer with an upper-case "B". But, I like him, yes.'

Mevrouw Loubser came to the screen door of the farmhouse and called, 'Louise! Come and help me wash the plates! Then you must go to bed!'

Louise stood up, brushed her apron, and then, spontaneously, bent forward and kissed Barney on the forehead.

'Goodnight,' she whispered. Her breath smelled of cloves, from her mother's apple cookies.

Simon de Koker looked around at Barney over his shoulder. His expression gave nothing away, but Barney could guess what he was thinking. On the other side of the table, Alf Loubser was finishing off a mug of his home-brewed pils. He was ruddy and squat, Alf Loubser, and handsome as a well-bred pony. He sensed that something had passed between Simon de Koker and Barney, but he missed the meaning.

'Well,' he said, 'we'd better turn in. I'm up at five tomorrow.'

Barney had been given a small whitewashed room at the side of the house, next to the wood-store, where aromatic cords of pearwood and yellowwood were stacked in readiness for autumn. There was a plain Dutch bed in there, as well as an upturned fruit-box which served as a side-table, a jug of water and a bowl. Barney stripped off his shirt and his trousers and slowly began to lather his body with green household soap.

Outside his shuttered window, a wide-spreading coral-tree flickered in the moonlight.

There was a hesitant knock at his door. He frowned, and said, 'Wait a moment, please,' and reached for his towel. The door opened straight away, and it was Louise. She quickly closed the latch behind her, and stood in the candlelight with her eyes sparkling and her hand held breathlessly on her chest.

'Louise,' said Barney. 'You can't come in here.'

'Why not? I often sleep here, in the summer. Especially when we have guests in the house.'

Barney tugged his towel a little tighter around his waist. 'Come on, Louise – supposing your father finds out you're here?'

'Why should he? You wouldn't tell him, would you? Nils Groenewald never did.'

Barney glanced towards the bed. 'You and Nils ...?'

'I love Nils. I love you, too. Won't you kiss me?'

'Louise, I hardly know you,' Barney protested, but softly.

She came closer and put her arms around his neck. 'Then I shall have to introduce myself to you. My name is Louise Stella Loubser. I am seventeen years old. I live with my mother and my father in the middle of nowhere at all. I used to pretend that I wasn't lonely, when I was younger. I had my dolls to talk to. But now dolls aren't enough.'

Barney whispered, 'I have to move on tomorrow. I may not ever see you again.'

Louise kissed him on the lips. Close to, she felt very soft and arousing. 'That's *why*,' she told him.

She unfastened the top button of her blue gingham dress. Barney looked at her, and felt as if he were drunk or dreaming. He had kissed Naomi Bernstein in a furious collision of closed mouths when he was fifteen; and at the age of seventeen he had walked out with a tall pretty girl from Cherry Street until she had given him up for a *goyish* messenger-boy with a wave of blonde hair like a cockatoo's crest. But he was still a virgin; and even though his father had carefully explained to him the facts that a young man should know and the sacred duty that a young man should remember in his relationships with young ladies, this encounter with Louise was making him feel hot and inexperienced and giddy with need.

She took his wrist and placed his hand gently on her breast. He stared at her, at the half-moons of candlelight that shone under her eyes. Her eyelashes were so fair that they seemed to be sparkling. He leaned forward, slowly, and kissed her.

'Sometimes I ask my dolls to tell me how to be happy,' Louise murmured. 'They never answer me. They never tell me what I should do.'

The second button of her dress, Barney twisted undone himself. Then the third, and the fourth. Louise, open-mouthed, watched Barney's expression with childish but proprietary interest as he slipped his hand under her bodice and cupped her bare breast in his palm. He felt her nipple rise.

'You look so serious,' she said. 'But you're very beautiful. I love your curly hair. You're such a beautiful stranger.'

Barney retreated towards the bed, tugging Louise after him,

and sat down. He wrestled the towel away from his waist, so that it dropped on to the earthenware tiles on the floor. Louise stood over him and bunched up her gingham skirts, raising them high, revealing to Barney the sturdy curves of her white thighs, and the albino blondeness of her pubic hair. His chest tight with anticipation, his mind locked fast with lust, Barney ran his fingers down the sides of her bare legs, and whispered, 'Louise Stella Loubster ...'

She climbed on him, coughing once or twice, her dress tucked under her elbows. Then straight away she started bouncing up and down on him, as if she were churning butter. Her small white fingers clutched the short curly hair at the back of his neck, and she pressed his face forward into the folds of her gingham bodice. Her nipple was pushed right into his eye. She bounced harder and harder, and he felt as if he were being forced to run 500 metres down a dark drainpipe in a crouching position.

'*In Godsnaam*,' Louise panted.

Barney didn't know whether to throw her off his lap or push her down harder. But at last – at last – he was gripped by a spasm that swamped his discomfort, and flodded his guilt and his inexperience, empty kegs on an ebb tide, and in the last shaking moments he gripped Louise Stella Loubser so tight that she cried out, 'Ah! Ah!' for air.

They lay side by side on the bed until the candle was almost burned down. Through the shutters, Barney saw the slotted sky begin to lighten, and he heard the dawn birds twittering on the coral-tree outside. It was morning on the Great Karoo.

Without a word, Louise kissed him, and buttoned up her dress, and left, holding her wooden clogs in her hand as she tiptoed along the duckboards which connected the woodshed with the house. Barney stood by the half-open door and watched her go. One of the geese said, '*monnk*'.

Barney and Simon de Koker set out at six, after a breakfast of cheese and brown bread in mevrouw Loubser's black and white tiled kitchen. Already, Alf Loubser's lunch of boiled mutton and dumplings was simmering on the iron range, fragrant with bay-leaves and rosemary. There was no sign of Louise.

'You'll give my regards to your daughter,' said Barney, as he climbed up on to the ox-waggon. Simon de Koker and Donald were already seated, and Simon de Koker was tamping shag tobacco into his pipe.

Mevrouw Loubser's eyes slanted sideways. She wore a white bonnet, like a woman in a Vermeer painting. Her hands were rough from digging vegetables and bleaching linen and plucking geese.

Simon de Koker snapped his whip in the morning air. Donald grinned widely at nothing in particular. The oxen plodded out of the Loubser's yard and out along Donkin Street, where young pear trees lined the route from Oudtshoorn and the south. The sky was already deep blue, and rich with cumulus clouds.

'How did you find Louise?' asked Simon de Koker, after twenty minutes or so, when they were on the outskirts of town.

'Louise?' asked Barney.

Simon de Koker let out an unexpected giggle. 'She's simple, you know. Touched in the head. Poor old Loubser's been dying for someone to give her a baby so that he can marry her off.'

There was a long silence. Then Barney said, crossly, 'I though she was going to marry someone called Nils Groenewald.'

'Ah, well, that's the story, man,' said Simon de Koker. 'She *was*. But Nils Groenewald trekked up to the Transvaal to make his fortune in cattle farming, and in a week he was killed by a Zulu. Degutted, so they say. And ever since then ...'

Barney stared at Simon de Koker, but said nothing. As they trundled out north-eastwards across the wind-ruffled *hooyvlakte*, they saw Alf Loubser and some of his boys in the distance, gathering in a flock of merino sheep. Simon de Koker waved, and Alf Loubser waved back. Barney tugged the brim of his veld hat further down over his eyes and looked the other way.

In later months, Barney remembered the trek across the veld to Oranjerivier as if it had happened to somebody else. This somebody else had spent six weeks of his life jostling from side to side on the hard wooden seat of the ox-waggon, surrounded by blinding curtains of dust. This somebody else had gone out every evening into the darkness gathering sticks, and then sat exhausted by a popping, crackling campfire, while Donald stirred up a pot of beans and biltong – or, if they'd been lucky with the guns that day – fresh antelope steaks, steaming with blood.

One night, for hour after hideous hour, this somebody else had lain awake under a baobob tree listening to lions roaring – a ravenous, echoing sound like tons of coal being dropped down an empty well. And every day, as the morning winds stirred the Karoo, this somebody else had prayed to arrive in Oranjerivier safely, undevoured by beasts and unbitten by snakes, please God; and to find his brother alive.

They reached Oranjerivier quite suddenly; and for Barney, unexpectedly. One minute they were crossing the veld, their waggon jolting and shaking across stretches of dried grass and windblown sand. The next they were rolling along a grassy track beside a muddy and easy-flowing river.

'There,' said Simon de Koker, nodding along the riverbank. 'That's Oranjerivier.'

Barney stood up on the brakeboard. He had not known what to expect. But here it was – a clustered settlement of twenty or thirty houses and cottages, surrounded by tents, flags, store-houses, *kraals*, and makeshift huts.

'You can take me straight to Derdeheuwel?' asked Barney.

'Whatever you like,' said Simon de Koker.

They drove through an avenue of gossiping willows, and then out past the main settlement of Oranjerivier to a small farm spread across the side of a hill. The farm was fenced around with split rails, and the track which led up to the house was lined with blue poplars and sausage trees. It was past four o'clock, and the shadows of the trees crossed the hard-baked ground like the spokes of a wheel.

Donald drew the ox-waggon up in the farmyard. The place looked dilapidated and deserted. On top of the thatched roof of the house, a rusted weathervane groaned and shuddered in the north-west wind. The white paint was flaking from the stucco façade, and most of the window frames were rotted and

91

grey. A stray cockerel strutted across the yard, stared at them indignantly, and strutted off again.

'There's nobody here,' said Barney.

Simon de Koker jumped down from the waggon and tethered the oxen up to the verandah rail outside the farmhouse. The four dusty beasts stood patiently in the late sunshine, occasionally twirling their tails at the flies. 'You don't know Monsaraz,' Simon de Koker remarked.

While Donald knocked a crust of mouldy meal out of a bucket so that he could bring water for the oxen, Simon de Koker gripped Barney's sleeve and led him along the verandah to the front door. The door was wide open, and the tall Boer dragged Barney straight inside without knocking or shouting or tugging at the tarnished brass bellpull.

The inside of the farmhouse was spectacularly filthy. There was dust and rubbish all over the floors and the rugs, and the hallway was cluttered with pieces of rusty dismantled ploughing machinery, a broken wall clock, two backless chairs, dozens of empty paint-pots, torn-up Portuguese newspapers, a banjo with no strings, two bales of Bushman grass, more wine bottles than Barney could count, and a dim cheval mirror in which both Barney and Simon de Koker found themselves reflected like phantoms of the old voortrekkers, brown and sweaty and smothered in dust. On the veld, their only mirror had been a tiny metal disc which they had used for shaving, and so this was the first time Barney had seen himself properly for over six weeks. He looked thinner and yellower in the face than he had imagined himself, but he looked like an Afrikaner.

There was a clatter from one of the side parlours, and a tall black woman appeared, her hair twisted around in red and blue beads, her eyes bloodshot with gin. She wore a simple white cotton dress which was ragged around the hem and soiled with dirt. She could not have been more than twenty years old, and yet she leaned against the wall scratching at her elbow like an old woman. She sniffed. She did not seem to be able to focus on them.

'Where's Monsaraz?' demanded Simon de Koker. 'Bossman in?'

The woman made a vague gesture and then lurched past

them, disappearing through a door which Barney supposed must lead to the kitchen.

'I hope you're not shocked, man,' said Simon de Koker. 'You'll see plenty worse examples of what civilisation can do to the native races. Mind you, the natives have always been pretty gruesome around here. If a woman had twins, they always used to kill one of them at birth, by stuffing mud in its mouth. And I could tell you some stories about the Zulu.'

Barney glanced at him, and then, without a word, pushed his way into the room from which the black woman had just appeared.

Inside, it was dark. The shutters were closed tight, so that only a few chinks of sunlight penetrated the suffocating heat and the shadows. There was a ripe, overwhelming smell of sweat, sex, and dead flowers. On a brass bed in the corner, fully dressed in a grubby white suit and a Panama hat, with his limp penis hanging from his open fly, lay a sallow young man with a pointed beard.

'You're Monsaraz?' asked Barney. 'You own this place?'

The young man on the bed did not answer.

'I'm looking for my brother,' said Barney. 'Derdeheuwel used to be his. His name's Joel Blitz. Mr de Koker here says you may have bought it from him.'

Monsaraz scratched his face noisily. 'Blitz, was it?' he asked, in a voice that was refined, but slurred by drink. 'I knew his name had to be something Jewish. He told me Barker.'

'Do you know where he is?' asked Barney.

Monsaraz sat up, frowned, and then stood up, tucking himself back in his trousers but not bothering to fasten the buttons. He walked with dragging feet across to a tall mahogany bureau, and poured himself a large gin from the stone bottle which stood beside the mirror on top of it. As he drank, he watched himself, as if for signs of rapid decay.

'Well,' he said, wiping his mouth, 'the truth is that I have no idea. No idea whatsoever. I paid him the money, exchanged the deeds, and off he went. He tried, you know, but he couldn't make the farm pay.'

'It doesn't look like you're doing much better,' remarked Simon de Koker.

'No,' Monsaraz agreed, 'but then I'm not trying.'

Barney said, 'Joel didn't give you any idea where he might be going at all?'

Monsaraz belched. 'He wasn't that kind of a man. Very ... taciturn, he was.'

'That doesn't sound like Joel,' said Barney.

'People change when they live out here,' Monsaraz told him. 'Look at me. I used to be one of my bank's most promising young overseas agents. Now I'm a sod farmer. Well, I'm not even that.'

Simon de Koker said, 'This place stinks.'

Monsaraz poured himself another gin. 'Yes,' he said. 'It stinks of self-pity. Do you want a drink?'

Barney shook his head. 'I want to find my brother, that's all.'

'I wish I could help you,' said Monsaraz. 'But men disappear out here. Sometimes because they want to, sometimes because they don't want to. It's just a little worse than hell.'

'Listen,' said Barney, 'what would you say if I stayed here for a while? Maybe worked the farm for you.'

Monsaraz peered at him. 'What would you want to do that for?'

'I need the work, and I need a place to stay. You have money, don't you?'

Monsaraz looked suspicious, and then waved his arm. 'A little,' he said. 'Do you mean to say you'd want paying as well?'

'If this farm was straightened out, it could make a reasonable living for both of us. You could pay me out of the profits.'

'Well, listen to you,' said Monsaraz, coming up closer. 'The young businessman.'

Simon de Koker pulled a face. 'What do you want to stay here for?' he asked Barney. 'If you want to look for your brother, I could find you a room with the Reitz's. Good and clean. This place is a muckheap.'

'It needn't be for long,' said Barney. 'If other farmers can make a living around here, then so can Mr Monsaraz.'

'I don't know,' said Monsaraz, uncertainly. 'Your brother couldn't make a go of it.'

'I'm not my brother,' Barney told him.

Monsaraz swayed, and shrugged. 'All right, then. If you want to. But don't expect any help from me.'

Barney turned to Simon de Koker. 'I'll pay you now, for bringing me here,' he said. He felt suddenly self-assured, although he was not completely clear what he wanted to do, or why he wanted to stay. 'If it's possible, I'll take Donald off your hands for a while, too, so that he can help me hire some workers. We can afford workers, can we, Mr Monsaraz?'

'As long as their wages don't encroach on the gin budget,' said Monsaraz. He looked pale and rather unsteady, as if he were going to be sick. 'That woman was like a spider,' he added, in a mutter. 'A great black spider.'

Outside, in the yard, Barney gave Simon de Koker seventeen pounds. Simon de Koker beckoned Donald over, and laid his arm around the black man's shoulders.

'You stay here with Mr Blitz, help him find kaffirs to work on this farm,' he said. 'You take care of Mr Blitz, or else next time I come by I chop off your sausage. You got me?'

'Yes, sir,' nodded Donald, grinning widely. 'I like to stay here in Oranjerivier. Very good sisters here, very kind. I stay here long time.'

Barney smiled, and took Simon de Koker's hand. 'Thank you, Mr de Koker. I think you showed me more than the way here. I think you showed me that Cape Colony is a country that you have to fight to live in, or not live in at all.'

Simon de Koker wiped the sweatband of his hat. 'You came here because of a tragedy, didn't you? Someone died? Someone you want to forget?'

Barney nodded.

'Well,' said Simon de Koker, 'don't forget them completely. I never forget my Adaleen. This country should be their memorial.'

He lowered his head, and then raised it again, looking Barney clearly in the eye. His downturned mouth was almost twisted into a smile.

During the autumn, when the wild syringa trees on the bush-veld began to turn to the colour of fresh-minted pennies, the first rumours began to fly around that more diamonds had been found on the Orange River. Barney did not pay them much attention at first. Through January and February of 1869, with

95

Donald fussing and strutting around behind him, he was working from first light until way after dark on the farm at Derdeheuwel.

They employed a dozen kaffirs now, and two half-educated Griquas. One of the Griquas was a second cousin of Nicholas Waterboer, chief of the most numerous of the Griqua tribes, and Barney appointed him foreman. The other Griqua, whose name was Adam Hoovstraten, was tall and lanky like a giraffe, but handy with a saw; and Barney set him to repairing the farmhouse and the stables.

Derdeheuwel had been neglected for years. Barney could see the marks of Joel's first efforts to clear it – a half-tilled field at the back of the farmhouse, and a new chicken-run. But it looked as if Joel had quickly lost heart and given up. There was even a new windmill lying on its side in the barn, still waiting for a well to be bored and for someone to erect it. The second week he was there, Barney borrowed drilling equipment from the farmer across the hill, a hard Englishman called Stubbs with a face like crumpled brown paper, and within five days he had his windmill up and working.

Monsaraz took hardly any interest in the proceedings at all, except occasionally to lean on the verandah with a drink in his hand, watching Barney repairing the cattlesheds. If Barney looked his way, he would raise his glass and call, '*Salut!*' Then he would wander back into the house and lie down in his darkened room with one of his black girls. There were two of them – one he christened Prudence and the other '*A Moça da Fazenda*', which simply meant 'The Village Girl'. He seemed to fornicate with them on and off all day and half of the night, although he never took off his white suit.

Barney was convinced that Monsaraz had thousands of pounds hidden on the farm somewhere. Monsaraz never worked, and never ran short of liquor; and whenever Barney asked for money to buy livestock, he would push an envelope filled with five-pound notes under Barney's bedroom door after dark. By early March, Derdeheuwel was fresh-painted, and stocked with over a hundred head of hardy Scottish cattle, all at Monsaraz' expense. But Barney never asked him where the money came from, or why anyone with what appeared to be bottomless funds should choose to live in near-exile on the Orange River.

Every night, after the cattle had been brought in, Barney would sit in his parlour by the light of an oil-lamp and write letters. He wrote a tender note to Leah, back in New York, and to Moishe. But he also wrote regularly to post-offices and attorneys' offices and local divisional councillors all over north Cape Colony and Griqualand, asking for news of his brother. Not many of his letters were answered. None of them held out any hope that Joel could be found. 'This is a vast and dangerous domain,' wrote an official from the Crown Agents in Hope-town, with Imperial pomposity. 'It is quite conceivable that your brother could have been devoured by a lion.'

In March of 1869, Cape Colony caught diamond fever. Schalk van Niekerk, who had discovered the Eureka diamond four years earlier, came across another stone that had been picked up by a Griqua shepherd boy on a farm near the Orange River. It had come into the possession of a Kaffir witchdoctor, who used it as a magic charm; and van Niekirk had been obliged to pay the man 500 sheep, ten cattle, and a horse for it. But when he sent it down to Capetown for evaluation, it turned out to be a superb white diamond of eighty-five carats, the Star of South Africa, and it was eventually bought by the Earl of Dudley for £25,000. Laying the diamond on the table in front of the Cape Parliament, the Colonial Secretary Sir Robert Southey announced, 'This is the stone, gentlemen, upon which the future of South Africa will be built.'

A correspondent in the *Colesberg Advertiser* asked sarcastic-ally, 'I wonder what that fellow Gregory would say now, if he were here. Perhaps in this instance it was also dropped by an ostrich (?)'

Within weeks, more diamonds were picked up along the banks of the Vaal River a little further north, inside the boundaries of the Orange Free State. The *Cape Argus* carried headlines that screamed *Diamonds! Diamonds! Diamonds!* and by April the tracks from Capetown were crowded with diggers of all nationalities.

The Great Karoo was as dust-blown and as pitiless as ever, and several diggers died on the way, but one reporter said that

97

'they saw in their lively imaginings diamond fields glittering with diamonds like dewdrops in the waving grass or branches of trees along the Vaal River, and covering the highways and by-ways like hoar frost.'

So – regardless of the political independence of the Orange Free State, which had been so bitterly won by the Boers after the Great Trek of 1834, its territory was rapidly invaded by swarms of avaricious prospectors, whose one determination, when they woke up each day, was to be rich before lunch. Soon, every likely stretch of riverbank along the Vaal and the Orange had been staked out as a claim; and latecomers to the diamond fields had to start 'dry diggings' further inland. The Boer farmers around Hopetown and Klipdrift and Pniel found their fences torn down and their trees uprooted, and one by one they gave up the struggle to farm on land that was ravaged again and again by illegal prospecting, and they sold out.

In the early months of the diamond rush, Barney walked along the banks of the Orange River near Derdeheuwel a few times; and occasionally crouched down to sift the gravel through his fingers. But he found nothing that looked remotely like a diamond, and not long after, the tree-lined river banks where he took his evening walks were staked out by diamond diggers. Once or twice, out of curiosity, he went down to watch them sieving mud through kitchen sieves, and separating pebbles with their wooden scrapers. They hardly ever talked to him, though, these bearded men in their cheap work shirts and their clay-stained trousers, except for a suspicious 'good day'. They sat over their wooden rocker-tables for hour after hour, winnowing out the tiniest of diamonds from the huge heaps of mud and gravel which their Kaffir labourers dug out for them. Barney thought that diamond prospecting looked like some kind of fairytale punishment, like spinning a haystack into golden twine.

Soon the pink and white cosmos flowers were blooming on the grasslands, the heralds of winter. It rained mercilessly hard for two weeks, which was good for the farmers. The Afrikaners always said cheerfully, 'The weather looks fine', when the stormclouds started to gather. But the rain was miserable for the diggers, especially when it grew colder, and the tracks and the excavations became rutted and rimed with frost, while the sun shone weak as an opal through the clouds. Still, diggers continued to arrive from Capetown and Durban, in their hundreds, in jolting waggons or on tired horses, and they were always ready to toss up their hats and cheer when they reached the willow-shaded banks of the Vaal, and always ready to pitch their makeshift tents wherever they imagined they could find diamonds.

Some struck it rich almost immediately. One young digger was kneeling in a church to pray, and he found a diamond pressed into the earth floor. One English digger gave up his claim in disgust, having hacked away at it for weeks and found nothing; but the man who took his claim over only had to dig down six inches before he came across a diamond of nearly thirty carats, which he sold for £2500.

Barney found that business at Derdeheuwel farm picked up. Oranjerivier was not so close to the first diamond diggings that its fields were invaded by would-be millionaires, or its fences and barns torn down for firewood. But it was close enough for Barney to be able to send one of his Griquas along each day with a waggonload of milk, eggs, and fresh water, and sell them to the prospectors at prices which improved Derdeheuwel's balance-books dramatically. Milk, 1s 6d the bucket; water, 5d the bucket; eggs, 2d each. Expensive – but where else could the diggers go? Barney even set up a kind of employment agency for kaffir labour, using Donald as a translator and a go-between with the local *dikgôrô*, or native communities; and although he charged £35s 3½d the month for each kaffir, which was a good deal more than anybody else, many of the diggers preferred Barney's labourers to the usual scallywags who hung around the diggings, simply because they were reasonably honest. If any of Barney's kaffirs were tempted to take revenge on their masters for beatings or bad treatment by pocketing or swallowing any of the diamonds they came across, Donald would make sure they were given a first-class thrashing. 'A few teaching smites,' he called it, rather biblically.

'Shortly, the diamonds will all be gone,' said Monsaraz one night, as they sat at the dining-table, eating Donald's *bobotie*. 'Then all these human earthworms will leave us alone.'

99

Barney looked at Monsaraz over the leaning flames of the candelabrum. Monsaraz' face was white from Dutch gin and lack of sun, and there was a sharp muscular spasm beneath his left eye.

'I'd rather they stayed,' said Barney carefully, reaching for his wine. 'They've been very good for the farm. We made fifty-eight pounds profit this month.'

Monsaraz pushed his plate away. 'Why does he always cook this Malayan muck?' he asked, under his breath. He poured himself a tumbler of gin, which he swallowed in three steady gulps.

Barney said, 'Life is going to change around here, Mr Monsaraz. You have to accept it. They found a seven-and-a-half-carat diamond along by the river this morning. Give them a couple of years, these prospectors, and they'll have built themselves a whole city at Oranjerivier, with a townhall, and a courthouse, and a –'

'A courthouse?' bristled Monsaraz. 'You think that's amusing? A courthouse??'

'I simply said that –'

'I suppose that's your Jewish sense of humour? A courthouse? I suppose you think that's funny, to torment me like that?'

'What are you talking about?' asked Barney. 'All I said was that –'

'You know damned well what I'm talking about!' Monsaraz shouted. 'You know *damned well* what I'm talking about!'

He stood up, staggering twice to find his balance. 'You know damned well what I'm talking about,' he repeated. 'Damned well.' Then, with his mouth stretched open and his throat swelling and contracting like a bullfrog, he vomited half-chewed meat and vegetables all the way down the front of his white suit. Barney closed his eyes, and said a prayer.

There were many times during the following two years when Barney felt like leaving Derdeheuwel altogether. But Monsaraz was rarely so offensive again, and the simple fact was that, short of sailing all the way back to New York, Barney had nowhere else to go. He still believed that Joel must be living in Cape Colony or the Orange Free State somewhere, and he took to leaving Donald in charge of the farm and riding in a small horse-drawn surrey as far as Hopetown, Jagersfontein, and even up to Klipdrift. He often loaded the back of the waggon with dried meat, cheese, and dried fruit, which he sold to the diggers he met along the way. Sometimes the diggers paid him in colonial pounds, but more frequently they paid him in small diamonds. As winter flourished into spring, and spring gave way to a harsh, hot summer, Barney got to know the diggers well, and how they worked, and which were the most profitable claims. He also made the acquaintance of some of the diamond buyers who had followed the prospectors out to the diggings.

His favourite buyer was Harold Feinberg, whose office was a small wood and corrugated iron shack not far from the Vaal River at Klipdrift. Feinberg had come out to South Africa from London's East End, leaving his father's cigar-making business because of his health. He was thirty-six years old, round and asthmatic, and always wore a white pith helmet, even indoors. Whenever Barney came by to see him, he would invite him in to the firerce heat of his little back room, and they would sit in riempie armchairs and drink black tea, while Harold Feinberg pushed diamond after diamond across his desk and explained to Barney what the qualities of each one were, and what kind of a price he expected it to fetch.

'This one here, for instance ... seven and three-quarter carats, perfect, but glassy. This one here ... twenty-one carats, but flawed ... you just have to learn what to look for.'

From Harold Feinberg, Barney learned all about illicit diamond buyers ... the men who camped out on the edge of the diamond fields and paid spot cash for diamonds regardless of where they came from, or who brought them in. It was to these unlicensed buyers that most thieving kaffirs brought the diamonds they had pilfered from their masters' claims, and on whom dishonest diggers would offload the stones they had omitted to tell their partners about. But, on the whole, the diamond diggings were quite lawful and orderly. A stern-faced Englishman called Stafford Parker had appointed himself *landdrost* and local governor of the Klipdrift area, and president of the Diggers Protection Association. Drawing on his hair-raising experiences of the violence of the California gold-rush,

Parker made every incoming digger read, sign, and obey a long list of rules and regulations, and he appointed 'magistrates' on daily duty to hear any complaints or disputes. Thieves were punished by flogging, or by being dragged backwards and forwards across the stony bed of the Vaal River a few times behind a galloping horse.

In 1870, Stafford Parker even went as far as declaring the diamond fields to be a Diggers' Republic, of which he was the first president. Barney met him twice – the first time outside Dan Evans' tent at Gong Gong. The local Griqua chief Jan Bloem was there, too, sitting by the campfire on a small folding stool, in the loudest yellow-checked suit that Barney had ever seen. Bloem's umbrella, tightly-rolled, had been stuck into the soft earth beside him.

Stafford Parker turned out to be white-bearded, small, and tanned to the colour of a roasted chicken. He shook Barney fiercely by the hand, and said, 'Digger, are you? No, you can't be. Hands aren't callused enough.'

'I'm a farmer, sir, at Oranjerivier.'

'You don't look like a farmer. You don't *sound* like a farmer.'

'I was in business in New York, originally,' said Barney. 'A tailor.'

Stafford Parker eyed him sharply. 'Tailor, hey? Jewish?'

'Yes, sir.'

'Hmm. Well, make sure you don't get yourself into the diamond-buying business. There are too many kikes in that already.'

Barney coloured. 'Too many what, sir?'

'Kikes,' replied Stafford Parker, in a crisp voice. 'That's what they call you fellows, isn't it?'

'Some people who are too ignorant and abusive to do otherwise call us kikes, yes, sir.'

'That's what I thought,' replied Stafford Parker. 'And I'm afraid to say that by a loyal Englishman's lights, being ignorant of those fellows who crucified Our Lord, or being abusive towards their descendants – well, those failings hardly count as anything but justifiable.'

Stafford Parker had sauntered off, stiff-legged, and Barney had been left taking deep, angry breaths. From across the other side of the campfire, Jan Bloem had been watching the exchange with an interested smile.

'The English have a way of upsetting everybody they meet,' he said, after a moment or two. 'They've been practising it for generations. Henry the Fifth, Sir Walter Raleigh, George the Third, and now Stafford Parker. You must let it roll off you, like the rain off your umbrella.'

Barney had looked at him. The voice that had come from the black man's savage-looking face, with its flat glistening cheeks and its tight-curled beard, had been extraordinarily civilised. Two hooped earrings shone gold under the black man's tall stovepipe hat.

'You must come to my village sometime, and talk about Judaism,' the Griqua went on. 'We Griquas have very strong Christian beliefs, and a great love of religious music. I would be most interested to hear about your points of view on the Bible.'

'Yes,' said Barney. He did not know what else to add. For the first time in over eighteen months, he had been obliged to defend his Jewishness, and it was a disturbing experience, particularly since he had let so much of his observance slide, apart from saying *schachris*, *mincha*, and *mairev* every day, and resting over *Shabbes*. Now, an odd-looking halfcaste actually wanted to discuss the *Talmud*.

'I'll – I'll, er – be back this way in a month or so –' Barney had told him. 'I'll ask my foreman to show me how to get to your village.'

'Well, I'll look forward to that,' said Jan Bloem, and lifted his hat.

Back at Derdeheuwel, as the cosmos flowers flourished again to greet the oncoming winter of 1871, Monsaraz grew steadily gloomier, and drunker, and more introspective. Since Barney had first met him, he appeared to have aged five years, and his hair was already wild with white. He started shouting in the night, long unintelligible tirades; and sometimes he would lock himself in his room for days on end. Other times, thought he would seem quite himself, and he would take dinner with Barney on the verandah if it was warm enough, and restrict himself to a few glasses of pinot chardonnay.

Once, just once, he sent Barney one of his girls. She knocked at his parlour door one evening in June 1871, when Barney was sitting at his desk in the long white cotton robe that Donald had found for him at the kaffir market. It had wide sleeves, this robe, and was printed all around the hem with red shapes like *springbok* horns.

'Master?' said the girl, opening the door. She was small, and handsome, and very black. Her hair was twisted into small pigtails, each of which was decorated with a circle of beads. She wore a simple toga of brown-dyed cotton, under which her big firm breasts swayed with obvious nakedness.

Barney looked up from his writing. He laid down his pen. His eyes were beginning to feel strained these days and he had been thinking of sending to Durban for some spectacles.

'Yes?' he asked her. 'What do you want?'

'Master Mont-harry tell me come.'

Barney stood up. 'I see. Did he give you a message?'

'He say you all alone, master. I come to make you not alone.'

'You mean he sent you to come share my bed?'

The girl nodded.

Barney examined the letter he had been writing. 'Dear Sir, I have for some years been attempting to trace my brother Joel Blitz or Barker, and I wonder ...' He picked up his pen, and snapped it sharply in half, tossing the pieces back on the table.

The black girl stared at him in wonder. '*Efidile*,' she said.

Barney knew what the word meant. 'It has died.' The Bantu believed that household articles were possessed of spirits, and if they broke a plate or a cup, they always said '*efidile*', just as if a man had died.

The next morning, over breakfast, he and Monsarez had a fierce argument. Monsaraz was still drunk from the previous evening, and he kept coughing up blood-streaked phlegm.

'I don't want you to send me any more of your black girls!' Barney shouted at him.

'I was doing you a service!' Monsaraz retaliated. 'God, you're a priggish, ungrateful bastard! I thought you were human enough to want a woman, that's all, and so I sent you one!'

'I'm human,' said Barney. 'But when I find a woman, it will

be a woman of my own choosing. Not one of your disease-ridden rejects!'

'That wasn't a disease-ridden reject!' retorted Monsaraz. He had to stop for almost a minute while he coughed and coughed and coughed. Eventually, he took a mouthful of gin, gargled with it, and spat it on the floor, and he was able to continue. 'That was the girl I call Zanza. She's a Tswana. Incall her Zanza because she plays like a musical instrument. One of those xylophone things they make out of iron.'

'I didn't want her,' said Barney as steadily as he could manage.

'Well, that's all right by me,' Monsaraz told him. 'But it just makes me wonder how you can keep your head screwed on straight. All work and no women. Do you Jews have saints? No? Well, you ought to, because you'll qualify, for sure.'

The same afternoon, Barney rode out to the north-east corner of Derdeheuwel on one of the five horses he had bought in Hopetown. He enjoyed riding, although he did not ride well. Monsaraz said he looked like a side of beef being bounced in a blanket. He reined in his horse on top of a small kopje and looked out over the sloping fields which led back to the white-painted farmhouse. It was a cool, windy day, and he wore a tweed jacket which he had cut down from an overcoat.

Monsaraz, however coarsely he had put it, had been right. He needed a woman. More than that, he needed a wife. Someone who could live with him as a lover, and a friend, and a sharer of secrets and responsibilities. He realised, not for the first time, how painfully lonely he was. He was twenty-two years old, and yet apart from his casual acquaintances among diggers and farmers and diamond-buyers, he was almost completely friendless. He went fishing with Donald sometimes, but Donald's garrulous bursts of that half-Afrikaans dialect that the Griquas spoke, were usually incomprehensible to Barney, and in the end Donald's company became childish and irritating.

He felt inside him enormous warmth towards people, even Monsaraz, and deep reserves of emotional strength. He knew he was good at business, and at organising the farm. Yet there was some greater ambition on the edges of his consciousness which he unable to grasp – an ambition that was as dark and tense as the hour before a summer storm. Only when he clearly understood what this ambition was, would he be able to express his feelings out loud – because until he understood what he wanted out of his life, he would not know who he was or what he was, or what destiny had brought him here.

Most of the local farmers quite liked him, although not many of them could understand his Jewish gentleness, or the comparative sophistication of his New York manners. The Boers were direct people, frank to the point of rudeness; and having trekked 700 miles to escape British domination, they had every right to be. Some called him 'Yid', right to his face; but then genially slapped him on the back until he was winded, and invited him to take a look at their new-born calves. They knew that his farm was neat, and the black fellows seemed to enjoy working for him, and as far as anybody could tell, he was turning a profit. What was more, he was an American Jew, not British.

None of them knew what he felt when he went to bed at night in the narrow yellowwood bed with the carved fruit-and-flowers headboard, exhausted from a day on the farm. None of them knew how often his dreams were visited by his dead father, sorrowful, hard-working, but ultimately ineffectual in that he had never taught his wife or boys to live without him. None of them knew how often he squeezed his hands into fists, and then slowly opened them again, expecting to find his mother's blood in the creases of his palms.

Those who liked him a lot called him 'the Jewish Boer', and he was often invited around to their homesteads for dinner. Pik Du Plooy, whose farm bordered Derdeheuwel to the east was an special friend, a real bread-and cheese Boer with a fiery face and white-blond hair. So was Simon de Klerk, a square little man whose farm on the opposite bank of the Orange River was called *Paddagang*, which meant Frog's Walk. All the same, as much as they liked his company, Barney was still an *Uitlander*, a foreigner, and a Jew; and whenever one of their daughters showed too much obvious admiration of his boxer's good looks, there would be testy silences, or loud and pointed remarks about how tough he was going to find it, poor fellow, to meet a nice Jewish girl all the way out here on the Orange River.

And quite apart from his Jewishness, Barney lived with Monsaraz, and Monsaraz was generally considered to be a devil.

One night, after he had shared a supper of beef dumplings with the Du Plooys, and was driving back to Derdeheuwel in his surrey, he stopped the ponies by the banks of the river, where the willows grew dark, and the fires of the diamond diggers glowed in the night like the encampment of some strange crusade. He sat with his eyes closed, praying for a bolt of lightning from the Lord – not to strike him down, but to illuminate his life, to show him clearly and emphatically what he had to do.

Nothing happened. The Orange River rattled over its rocks; the night breeze blew through the willows like the breathing of sleeping lovers; and the insects sang their monotonous *ihubo*, a song for a thousand voices.

But there were sparkling reflections on the surface of the water from the hidden moon, and Barney thought how much they looked like diamonds.

In the winter and spring of 1871, three completely unrelated events changed Barney's life for ever.

The first was that diamonds were discovered on Vooruitzigt, the estate belonging to two sour-faced Boer brothers, Johannes and Diedrich de Beer, about a mile away from Bultfontein. To begin with, the stones were picked up in the fields, sparsely scattered about. But after two months of only moderately profitable prospecting, a group of diggers, whose distinctive hats had earned them the nickname of the Red Cap Party had the good fortune to throw their black servant Damon out of their camp one night for drunkenness. The following morning, after wandering erratically up and down a small hill nearby known as Colesberg Kopje, Damon came back to them with his hands crammed with rough diamonds – more diamonds of better quality than any of them had ever seen in one place before. The rush was on. Within hours of the news getting out, scores of diggers swarmed to Vooruitzigt, and set about excavating the yellowish diamond-bearing soil with the fury of ants. Colesberg Kopje was promptly renamed 'De Beers New Rush', and a cluster of sheds and tents were erected around the hillock in double-quick time to house the prospectors, the diamond buyers, the gamblers, the attorneys, the tricksters, and the prostitutes. Even Harold Feinberg left his shack at Klipdrift and went up there, too – setting up a fresh office just opposite the London & South African Exploration Company on the muddy stretch of track that served as De Beers New Rush's main street.

Barney recalled afterwards that 'the whole of the countryside was humming with excitement, and there were dozens of stories of incredible fortunes being made overnight.' The De Beer brothers, who had bought their farm ten years previously for fifty pounds, sold out for six thousand, and went to farm elsewhere. They later said, ruefully, that a fairer price might have been six million pounds.

The second event that changed Barney's life was that an English attorney-at-law, Brian Knight, came to De Beers New Rush to set up in business, and brought with him his wife Clemmie and his two daughters, Agnes and Faith.

The third event was that Barney found Joel.

Barney trekked up to see Harold Feinberg at De Beers New Rush in October 1871. He was carrying with him a small leather pouch of uncut diamonds which had been given to him in exchange for fresh milk and eggs by the diggers along the Orange River, and he knew that Harold Feinberg would give him a reasonable price. Apart from that, he needed to get away from Monsaraz for a while. His Portuguese employer was becoming daily more drunken and less rational – breaking windows, collapsing over his meals, and beating the Bantu women who came around to 'jigajig' with him. Only the night before he had left Derdeheuwel, Monsaraz had regaled Barney with a long, sour-breathed story about the time he had locked himself in his room for three days with two Venda girls, aged nine and twelve, and what he had done to them.

Barney took Donald with him to Colesberg Kopje, and left the lanky Adam Hoovstraten in charge of the Kaffirs. Donald relished trips around the countryside, and he would sit self-importantly beside Barney on the wooden seat of their surrey, singing psalms at the top of his voice. Barney had not heard such quavering, off-key singing since Cantor Mittelman in New York. Donald regarded himself these days as Barney's permanent *major-domo* and gentleman's gentleman, and never talked about going back to Paarl.

'Maybe we find you a nice girl in Colesberg,' he said to Barney, as they sat by their evening campfire a few miles north of Ritchie, where the Modder River runs into the Riet. It was a cool, quiet night, and the sky was prickled with stars.

'What makes you think I'm looking for a girl?' asked Barney. He had hung his bush jacket and his riding breeches on a nearby bush, and now he was intently stitching his *veldschoen*, where the upper had come away from the sole.

Donald drew his long frogged coat around his shoulders. He was smoking a pipe, and the aroma of the tobacco mingled with the smells of the night. 'Mr Monsaraz says you look for a girl. But, a fine girl. Not black. Not whore, neither.'

'It's none of Mr Monsaraz' business. Nor yours, for that matter.'

Donald shrugged. 'You say so. But I help you find sister, if you want. I have five good sisters in Oranjerivier, maybe two in Bultfontein.'

'I've seen some of your sisters, Donald. Each one looks uglier than the last.'

'Ugly, maybe,' nodded Donald. 'Yes, ugly! But good for hours! Never get tired!'

Barney reached over for his enamel mug of strong Dutch coffee, and swallowed a mouthful. Tomorrow morning, they would arrive in De Beers New Rush, or 'Kimberley', as it had now been officially named. The British Colonial Secretary had protested that he could neither spell nor pronounce 'Vooruit-zigt' or 'Colesberg Kopje', and he was not even going to try. Moreover, he thought it undignified for Her Majesty's Empire to include any community known as 'De Beers New Rush'. He had therefore taken it upon himself to rechristen the diamond diggings after his favourite foreign administrator, himself.

Barney said, 'What do you make of Monsaraz, Donald. I mean, really?'

Donald's glittering eyes looked back at Barney through the

firelight. 'The Bible says, "Judge not, that ye be not judged." '

'Monsaraz has already judged himself,' replied Barney. 'Whatever he's done, the memory of it is strangling him just as surely as a rope.'

'Well, then,' said Donald, noncommittally. 'If Mr Monsaraz judge himself, we do not have to. Already done.'

'It's the farm that worries me – my own livelihood,' said Barney. 'I've worked for two years of my life straightening that place out. What's going to happen if Monsaraz dies, or decides to sell out to the diggers?'

Donald took a glowing twig from the fire to relight his pipe. 'Mr Monsaraz will not sell. He say to me once – Donald, I come here to Oranjerivier because it is the end of the earth. A secret place. You say to anyone in Portugal, where is Oranjerivier? And they say, no, I don't know that place. Never hear of it, man.'

'People have heard of it now. The diamond rush is world-famous.'

'There you are,' agreed Donald. 'Because of that, Mr Monsaraz is a frightened person. But, he will not try to escape any more. He says he will die on his own *kleinplasie*, his own little farm.'

'I'm glad he's so sentimental about the place that *I've* licked into shape for him.'

Donald did not answer. He had never owned anything himself, and had never aspired to. White acquisitiveness was one of those mysteries of nature, like the extraordinary whims of Rhubega, the weather-god.

Barney lay back on his bedroll. A warm wind began to steal through the grass from the direction of the Modder. North Cape Colony on a spring night was one of the driest, most musical places on the Lord's earth. Dry music through dry grass, like the whistling of Venda herdboys, who could talk to each other over miles of veld by imitating speech patterns as they whistled.

Harold Feinberg was pleased to see him, although depressed about the world price of diamonds. He did not like his office much, either; it was nothing more than a stuffy lean-to with a corrugated iron roof, and a red-haired Irishwoman was annoying him by doing brisk business next door as a prostitute – 'so every ten minutes, the whole place shakes like an earthquake.' Harold offered Barney hot rum and milk, and while Donald went off to find himself a sister, the two of them sat on the step outside the office and talked.

'This diamond mine's even richer than anybody can believe,' said Harold. 'As a matter of fact, I'm doing princely – especially when you consider the world slump in the market. The diggers are bringing me first-quality diamonds out by the bucketful. I mean, literally, by the bucketful. In buckets! I can pick and choose what I want to buy.'

'So how come your office is so seedy?' asked Barney, with a smile.

'I'm supposed to build myself a Gothic building, five stories high, out of mud and straw and corrugated iron?' Harold wanted to know. 'They're sending out bricks and cast-iron balconies and all that kind of thing from Cape Town and Durban. But they won't arrive for a couple of weeks yet. Anyway, the office doesn't matter so much. The most important thing about diamonds is to be where they are. Whether you set up business in a hovel or a palace, that's not important. Be where the diamonds are dug, and you can't fail.'

Barney stirred his rum and milk with a spoon, and drained it down. 'I've been surrounded by diamond mines ever since I came here, but I'm still as poor as I ever was.'

'You're doing well out of the farm, aren't you?'

'Not too bad. But I'm not rich. And what do I get at the end of it? The farm belongs to Monsaraz, not me.'

'Maybe you should buy a holding at the mine.'

'Have you seen the prices they're asking? Well, obviously you have. Three or four thousand pounds. I don't have more than seventy or eighty pounds saved up.'

Harold, under his pith helmet, pulled a deprecatory face. 'You should try to go into partnership. Find someone who wants to dig with you. I mean it, Barney. This mine is once-in-a-lifetime, and when they've dug out all the yellow ground, that's going to be the finish.'

At that moment, a brusque man with a thick moustache and a pointed sun-topi came strutting along the boardwalk, tapping the boards as he came with the ferrule of his cane. Despite the heat, he was dressed in a dark suit, buttoned right up, with a starched white collar and a necktie. As he approached, Barney could see that his eyelashes were as white and spiky as a pig's.

Harold eased himself to his feet, still holding his empty mug. 'Mr Knight, sir. How are you this morning?'

'Offish,' delcared Mr Knight. He took out a handkerchief and loudly blew his nose.

Harold looked suitably sympathetic. 'I can't say that I envy you attorneys, in this scramble.'

'Well, it's not Lincoln's Inn,' replied Mr Knight, his cold eyes staring past Barney across the street. Barney turned and looked in the same direction, and caught sight of two girls in plain ecru sun-dresses standing on the opposite corner, twirling their parasols and talking to a tall young digger in a wide floppy hat.

'This is a young friend of mine from Oranjerivier,' said Harold. 'An American, from New York.'

'Really?' asked Mr Knight, but his attention was patently fixed on the girls across the street. At last, in a sharp voice that carried high above the clatter of a passing ox-cart and the general bustle of a mining town at mid-morning, he called, 'Agnes! Faith!'

The girls turned at once; and when they caught sight of Mr Knight they waved flustered farewells to the digger and came hurrying across the rutted road, their skirts held up out of the dust. They arrived pink-cheeked and breathless and obviously anticipating a telling-off.

'You'll forgive me for one moment, sir,' said Mr Knight, giving Barney the briefest of glances. 'But I have specifically required my daughters not to hob-nob with the diggers and riff-raff of this encampment; and, lo and behold, here they are flaunting my authority right in front of my eyes.'

Barney looked at Mr Knight's daughters first with curiosity and then with undisguised interest. Both of them were very pretty and trim; although the one he took to be Agnes was just a little more petite than her sister, and her fair ringlets were just a little curlier. Both girls had bright china-blue eyes, short straight noses, and squarish jaws. They could have been Swedes rather than Britons. But Agnes had the soft, slightly asymmetric smile that Barney would later have dreams about: the kind of smile that seems to be knowing and innocent both at the same time.

'This is Mr – er –,' said Mr Knight to his mischievous daughters, waving his hand at Barney.

'Barney,' said Barney. Harold Feinberg looked at him in mild surprise, but Barney remembered what Hunt had told him on the deck of the *Weser*. *If I were you, old chap, I'd play that side of things down.*

'Mr Barney, from New York,' said Mr Knight. 'I'm ashamed that his first sight of you should be in the company of a ruffian like that fellow across the street.'

Agnes and Faith both obediently curtseyed in Barney's direction. Barney, who had already taken off his hat, gave them an appreciative nod of his head. He caught Agnes's eye for a second that was as brief as a memory that he could not quite place – a snatch of music, or the sound of bells, or a familiar aroma.

'As a matter of fact, Mr Knight,' Barney said boldly, and somewhat to his own surprise, 'as a matter of fact I can vouch for the good breeding of that fellow across the street. I've done business with him several times – in Capetown, and here. He doesn't usually spread it around, but he's related to British nobility. The Earl of Liverpool, I think.'

Mr Knight squinted back across the street, but the digger had gone. 'Well,' he puffed, confused. 'Nobility, is he? It's surprising what a pass some of these blue-blooded gentlemen have come to.'

'These days, Mr Knight, everybody has to make a living,' put in Harold, gently. He gave Barney an exaggerated wink.

'Yes,' said Mr Knight. 'I suppose you're right. I suppose you are. And since he's nobility, Agnes, I think I can overlook your talking to him, on this occasion at least. But next time, remember to ask my permission; or to mention it to your dear mother.'

'Yes, Papa,' said Agnes, contritely.

'Good, then,' said Mr Knight. He tapped on the boardwalk with his cane as if he were trying to remember something that had escaped him, and brushed at his moustache with the side of his hand.

'Business good, Mr Feinberg?' he asked.

'Tolerable,' nodded Harold.

'So it should be,' said Mr Knight. 'And how about you, Mr –?'

'Barney,' said Barney.

'Well, yes. What's *your* line?'

'I'm a farmer.'

'Farmer, hey? Business good?'

'Tolerable,' said Barney.

Mr Knight fidgeted and puckered his lips. 'Yes. Well, how about joining us for dinner this evening? Is that a distinct possibility? Or is it not?'

Agnes, from the becoming shade of her sun-bonnet, smiled at Barney in obvious entreaty. Faith, seeing what her sister was doing, gave her a dig with her elbow.

'Yes,' said Barney. 'Dinner would be a distinct possibility. I'd be pleased to.'

'Good,' said Mr Knight. 'Eight then, at my place. Mr Feinberg here will tell you where to find us.'

Harold nodded, and smiled, playing the part of the obliging East End Jew. *Anything you say, my boy. Anything you say.* Mr Knight grimaced at him, and then continued his staccato promenade along the boardwalk.

'Well,' said Faith, giving Barney another little curtsey, 'you saved our lives! It seems that we owe you a favour!'

'You were very gallant,' smiled Agnes. 'You know who that *really* is, don't you?'

Barney shook his head. 'I haven't a notion.'

'His name's Jack Westbury. He's a digger, that's all; and not a very successful one so far. He spent all his inheritance on two claims at the Kopje, but so far they haven't turned up anything more than a few small stones that aren't worth anything much at all. But, he's very handsome,' she added, looking at Barney with her head slightly tilted to one side in a way that suggested *he* was handsome, too.

Mr Knight had stopped a few yards along the boardwalk, and had turned on his heel to glare at his daughters again with his piggy little eyes.

'We'd better hurry along,' said Faith, and took her sister's arm. 'But we'll look forward to seeing you at dinner tonight, Mr Barney. Good afternoon.'

Barney raised his hand as the girls hurried along the board-walk after their father, a wave that lingered like a photographic pose. Agnes, he thought. The lamb. A meek name for a very provocative young lady. He watched with amusement as the two sisters bustled past three half-drunken diggers, splendid in their unkept whiskers, their clay-caked trousers, and their hundred-pound velveteen jackets. The diggers stopped, colliding with each other like the boxcars of a shunted train, and stared after the Knight girls as they flounced along, obviously transfixed by every arousing glimpse of their narrow ankles. One of the diggers said something crude in Spanish, and the other two cackled high and silly, like geese.

'What's this "Mr Barney"?' Harold Feinberg asked Barney, gently, as Mr Knight took a daughter on each arm and marched them out of sight round the corner of the ramshackle Dutch Reformed Church.

Barney replaced his hat. 'Sometimes, it doesn't help to be a Jew.'

'Sometimes, in the Orange Free State, it doesn't help to be British. But you wouldn't catch Mr Knight calling himself some damned Boer name like Mr Botha, just for the sake of a dinner invitation.'

'You're misjudging me,' said Barney.

'All right,' shrugged Harold.

Barney turned on him. 'Listen, Harold. I was brought up to be a tailor. Measuring and cutting and delivering bespoke overcoats. That was considered to be a suitable vocation for a Jewish boy. That, or being a rabbi. Well, maybe I'm wrong, and maybe it's terrible of me to deny my background. But since I've left the Lower East Side, I've realised slowly that there's a whole world out here. A world of money, and influence, and class. A world where you can do a whole lot more than take orders for overcoats until you're a hundred years old. It's taken me a long time to build up the courage to say that I'm going to take what this world has to offer me. I've been guilty about my father's memory, and what I did to my mother. But now it's time for me to make something out of myself. To get some respect. And if I have to deny my Jewishness to do it, then I will. Because the day will come when I can stand up and say I'm Jewish, and I'm proud of it, and I'll be too rich and too powerful for anybody to be able to do a damned thing about it.'

Harold Feinberg sat on the stoop, swinging his empty mug by the handle. 'Barney,' he said, 'it makes me sorry to hear you talk like that.'

'I should spend the rest of my life second-class? Is that what you're asking me to do?'

'No!' said Harold Feinberg, fiercely. 'Because to be a Jew, no matter how poor, that's never second-class. We were delivered by the Lord our God out of Egypt. Do you know what that *means*? And you can stand there and tell me you're going to forget about that, forget about your duty to the Lord, at least until you're wealthy enough, and famous enough for them to let you in to all the right *goyish* clubs.'

'You never talked this way before,' said Barney.

'I never had occasion to,' Harold replied.

A man in a white apron walked the length of the dusty street with a wooden tray of honey-cakes on his head, clanging a bell. In the floury white light of noon, he looked like the spectre of a leper.

'I should go, then,' said Barney.

'You be careful of Mr Knight,' warned Harold. 'You may think he's posh, and worth getting to know, but no lawyer brings his wife and his daughters out to a place like this unless he's got a reason. That man practised in London first, until they struck him off. Then he tried to start up a law firm in Capetown, and they soon got wind of his little conjuring-tricks there, and that's why he's *here*. You watch him. He's a lawyer of ill-repute.'

Barney leaned his shoulder against the ironwood upright of Harold's office verandah. 'One day,' he said, 'you'll understand that I'm right.'

Harold looked up at him, and smiled. 'Yes,' he said. 'That's what I'm afraid of.'

In the musty gloom of his corrugated-iron office, with the walls rattling to the commercial ecstasies of the Irishwoman next door, Harold gave Barney £212 for his bag of tiny rough diamonds. Barney knew that £175 of this money had already been spent on new livestock, and on repairing the north wall of the cattle kraal. Monsaraz would take £30 for drink, and women, and laundry, Donald would have to be paid £2, and that would leave Barney with just £5 of his own. He appreciated that this was quite a respectable wage for a month's work: a private soldier in the British Army was still getting only £1 8s od a month, with deductions for extra food. But it was not enough to pay for a diamond-digging claim at Kimberley, or to build the footings of any kind of fortune.

He shook hands with Harold with unusual solemnity, and then walked out into the glare of the street. He wondered for a moment just what Monsaraz would do if he failed to return from Kimberley – if he kept the whole £212 for himself. But Monsaraz was an object lesson in the various ways in which a man could be gradually disassembled, morally and bodily, by self-imposed guilt, and Barney was quite aware that if he walked off with Monsaraz's money, he would be haunted for the rest of his life by memories of that filthy wretched man in his soiled white suit, and that he would hear his whispered obscenities in his ears until he died.

'That little Venda girl cried out only once ... but I hit her with my *sjambok* and she was quiet ... wet all over, shivering, naked, but quiet.'

Harold came to the door just as Barney left – fat-bellied, sad, with his pith helmet pulled down over his ears. 'Listen,' he told Barney. 'I meant what I said.'

'I know,' said Barney, and went back to embrace him. A passing digger paused unsteadily in the street and tried to focus on them through the blurring effects of two bottles of cheap London gin.

'I want you to know that you can always count on me,' said Harold, a little throatily. 'Whatever I've said, I'm always around to help a brother Jew. And, well, whatever you do ... don't stay on that farm too long. You'll never be a Boer.'

Barney was off to find Donald now, so that he could tell him there was no need to pack the trunks nor make the surrey ready until morning. Donald had discovered that Jan Bloem, the Griqua chief, was in Kimberley, to see for himself what riches lay within the boundaries of Griqua territory, and that Bloem had set up camp a little to the west of Colesberg Kopje with his two brothers, his pipe-smoking mother, his servants, and a number of cooks and washerwomen whom Donald regarded as extremely likely candidates for sisterhood.

Barney walked along Kimberley's main street with his hands in the pockets of his riding breeches and his hat pulled low over his eyes. He passed makeshift gambling dens, attorneys' offices, whorehouses, and general merchants. A half-caste girl in a tattered blue dress was leaning in the doorway of one of the shacks, and winked at him as he went by. He smiled back at her, and shook his head.

The Kimberley Mine itself was only a few hundred yards away, across the rough rock-strewn ground. Hundreds of men were digging at a wide, shallow crater with picks, their backs bent under the dusty sky. The sound of all those scores of picks hacking away at the soil was like an extraordinary percussive chorus. For one moment, most of them would seem to be tapping away in unison, but then the chorus would spatter into disarray. There were dozens of tents all around the mine, most of them screened from the wind and the dust by fences of woven grass, and there was a crowd of ox-waggons, too, all loaded up with timber. In the first few weeks of prospecting, the diggers only had to walk across the ground and start excavating where they stood, but some diggers had already sunk their claims ten or twenty feet into the ground, and they needed balks of wood to shore up the sides.

Barney stood for a while and watched the diggers and the kaffirs at work. Wheelbarrows of yellow soil were being propelled to the edge of the mine along the pathways between the claims until they could be emptied out in a heap by a digger's tent, and sorted through for gems. It was hot, strenuous work, but the rewards were worth it. One Dutchman named Smuts had bought a claim in the first two weeks of digging for fifty pounds, and gathered up £20,000 worth of diamonds in less than two months. And only a few feet from the place where Damon had scooped up the first rough diamonds, another digger had picked up a single stone of 175 carats, which had sold for £33,000.

While he was watching, a tall, sad-looking man in a droopy

felt hat and a loose bush-jacket approached Barney from the direction of the mine. He stood a few feet away, his hands on his hips, and grimaced from time to time as if he disapproved of what he saw. Barney glanced at him once or twice, and then said, 'You don't seem impressed.'

The man stared at him. He had a breaky nose and eyebrows as tangled as a bush. 'No,' he said, in a northern British accent which reminded Barney of the people he had met in Liverpool. 'In fact, I think the whole damn mine's a complete bog-up.'

'Excuse me?' asked Barney.

'A bog-up. A pig's dinner. Don't you understand English? They're hacking away there like idiots. Some of them digging five feet down. Some of them twenty. There's no organisation. No co-operation. What's going to happen when they get down a hundred feet?'

'They won't, will they? I mean, the yellow soil will give out way before they get down that far.'

The tall man stared at Barney in exasperation. 'You think the yellow soil is the end of it?'

'I don't know,' said Barney. 'But that's what the diggers say. They only found diamonds in the yellow soil along the Vaal and the Orange. Nowhere else.'

'Well, they're wrong,' said the man. 'Listen, why don't you buy me a drink, and I'll tell you how wrong they are.'

'Is this a touch?' asked Barney. 'I don't mind buying you a drink, but I'd like to know.'

'Not at all,' said the tall man, indignantly. He came closer, and Barney could smell the brandy on his breath. 'My name's Edward Nork. N-o-r-k, as in York. Or fork. I'm a geologist, late of Durham University. I once published a paper in the *Geological Magazine* on extinct volcanoes, and that's precisely why I'm here.'

'Volcanoes?' asked Barney, confused.

Nork took his elbow, and led him back to the main street, and along to a shed whose shingle announced that it was The Paradise Saloon. They went inside, where the atmosphere was thick to within two or three inches of the mud-packed floor with negrohead tobacco smoke, and where diggers in wide straw hats took their midday ease with clay pipes and whiskey.

'What would you like?' Barney asked Nork.

'A half-bottle will be sufficient,' said Nork, sitting himself down on a small keg. 'I've already been treated once this morning, and I do like to be modest in my intake.'

Barney called the saloon-keeper over – an Irishman with a filthy apron and smeary spectacles – and asked for a half-bottle of Jamieson's. When the bottle was brought, Nork carefully poured two or three fingers into his glass, and then proceeded to drink straight from the neck of the bottle itself.

'I like to save a little for when the bottle's empty,' he explained, quite unashamed. Barney shrugged. Nork's alcoholism was not his business.

'Now listen,' said Nork, 'the theory which the diggers hold dear is that only the yellow ground contains diamonds. But, geologically, that doesn't really make sense. If this shallow stratum of yellow ground is the only soil that contains diamonds, how did the diamonds get there, and where did they come from?'

Barney coughed, to clear the tobacco-smoke from his throat, and shook his head.

'Diamonds, my dear fellow, are nothing more nor less than a form of natural carbon, which is one of the world's most common and inexpensive elements,' said Nork. 'But the reason they are so hard, and so bright, and so adamant, is that they are made of carbon which has been subjected to tremendous heat, and tremendous pressure.'

'I see,' said Barney, trying to be affable.

'You *don't* see,' insisted Nork. 'Because there is only one place in the structure of the earth where carbon could have undergone such a conversion, and that is in the throat of a volcano. In the very pipe of volcanic material which rises from the depths of the earth to the surface.'

'Yes?' Barney asked him. He still was not sure what Nork was driving at.

'Don't you *understand*?' Nork said, in exasperation. 'Colesberg Kopje is nothing more nor less than the top of a pipe of volcanic soil which has risen up from the subterranean depths. The soil at the top is yellow simply because it has weathered; and you will find this yellow diamond bearing soil along the

Vaal and the Orange River simply because the river waters have washed it away from the tops of the volcanic pipes and borne it away downstream.'

'You mean that the diamond-bearing soil goes deeper than the yellow ground?' Barney asked Nork, keeping his voice down to a hoarse whisper. 'You're trying to suggest that it just goes down and down and down, and that we may never come to the end of it?'

Nork raised a significant finger. 'Not until you reach the very liquid core of the planet, my boy.'

'But I've seen diggers give up claims after they've got down to the blue bedrock.'

'That's their folly, the result of their ignorance,' smiled Nork. He took a swig from the bottle, and wiped the neck on his sleeve. 'The blue ground lies only sixty or eighty feet down. I know that it *looks* like bedrock; but I can assure you that it isn't. It's diamond-bearing soil, exactly the same as the yellow ground, only it hasn't yet been weathered. I've already christened it Norkite.'

'Norkite?' said Barney. 'I never heard anybody else call it that.'

'Well, you wouldn't have done,' said Nork, petulantly. 'They're all disbelievers, and fools. But you listen to what I've told you. One of these days, when they've dug the Kimberley mine down to the blue ground, and everybody believes they're exhausted, you'll be able to pick up claims for a tenth of what they're really worth – and *then* you'll be able to make a killing.'

Barney narrowed his eyes. 'If you're so sure of this, why are you telling me? Why aren't you keeping it to yourself, and buying up whatever claims you can lay your hands on?'

Nork thought about that, and then sneezed very loudly. 'You don't have a handkerchief, by any chance?' he asked Barney. Barney tossed him over a red rag that he had used earlier that morning for buffing up his shoes. 'I'm sorry, that's all I've got. But you can keep it.'

'It's the dust,' said Nork, 'and I'm not a healthy man. In fact, I'm a drunk, and I'm poor as all hell, and I couldn't even raise one hundredth of the price of a claim, even if I knew that I wasn't going to spend it on whiskey as soon as I'd saved it. Oh – you don't have to look so sorry for me. I don't need sympathy. We – imbibers – know just how deep we have dug our own graves.'

'But why did you tell me?' asked Barney.

Nork pulled a face. 'You remind me of someone I used to know,' he said. 'I don't suppose that sounds like a very convincing motive. But there you were – standing by the mine – and you looked so much like him that I immediately felt warm towards you. Friendly.'

'I *remind* you of someone?' Barney asked him. 'Who?'

Nork waved a dismissive hand. 'A digger. He's here now, at Kimberley. A splendid fellow. Very earnest, very good-humoured. But, well, you know, we fell out. People usually fall out with me after a while. It's Madame Alcohol that does it. I drink too much and say things that I don't mean. I once told him that he was a stingy as a Jew, and he tried to strike me with his pick. And, well ...'

Barney licked his lips. 'This digger ... his name wasn't by any chance Barker, was it? Joel Barker?'

Nork sniffed. 'Barker, no. His name was Havemann. But Joel, yes. Joel Havemann. He has a claim across on the other side of the mine. Number 172.'

Barney stood up at once. He felt breathless, short of oxygen, and the dense tobacco smoke in the saloon did not help. He said to Nork, 'Where can I find you again, if I need you?'

'Find me? Why would you wish to do that?'

'Maybe I want to talk to you some more about diamonds. But right now, I'm going over to 172. I think this man Havemann could be somebody I know.'

'Well ... you could always leave a message for me here,' said Nork. 'Or at any saloon in Kimberley. Or down at Mrs Sperring's whore-emporium. I can't afford the girls, you know, but sometimes Mrs Sperring gives me a bed to sleep on. We're both natives of Leeds, you know. We sit over a bottle of that awful South African cabernet franc and talk about the old times on Crown Street.'

'Okay,' said Barney. He shook Nork's hand, and said, 'Thanks. You may have helped me more than you know.'

'I hope I've helped you more than *you* know,' said Nork. He held up the half-bottle of whiskey, already more than three-quarters empty. 'You wouldn't consider ... before you go ...?'

Barney laid a pound on the barrel-top table. Nork raised his eyebrows at it, and said, 'Whoever you are, sir, you're a gentleman.'

Outside the saloon, Barney walked quickly through the dust and confusion of ox-waggons and donkey-carts around the rim of the mine. As he crossed the pathways through the diggings themselves, he heard German voices, Irish voices, Australians, and Greeks. As the historian James Anthony Froude had remarked on a visit to the diggings, there were 'diggers from America and Australia, German speculators, Fenians, traders, saloon-keepers, professional gamblers, barristers, ex-officers of the Army and Navy, younger sons of good family who have not taken a profession or have been obliged to leave; a marvellous motley assemblage, among whom money flows like water from the amazing productiveness of the mine.'

The mine was almost a mile across, and it was parcelled into more than 1600 claims. Under the determined rule of Stafford Parker, the Diggers' Union had agreed that each claim could be no more than thirty-one feet square – ten times the size of a man's grave – and that no individual digger could own more than two claims. That meant that the chaos of each tiny digging – with kaffirs heaving up buckets of dirt and trundling wheelbarrows around and bringing down great tumbling slides of rock with their picks – was multiplied under the hot afternoon sun more than a thousand times.

Barney heard a cheer a little way away. A kaffir driving a mule-cart had tried to steer his load along the narrow ridge between two deep claims, and the cart and mules had overturned, rolling down a twenty-foot slope and crushing the kaffir underneath one of the wheels and half a ton of rock. Two or three of the diggers were laughing loudly. Accidents were becoming so frequent that they were regarded these days as part of the general amusements.

Barney stopped for a moment, shielding his eyes against the glare. Two other kaffirs were trying to lift the capsized waggon off the man's pelvis, and the man was starting to screech. A gingery-haired digger was storming up and down beside them and shouting, 'Get that damned cart off my claim! Get the damned thing off!'

With another cheer, the cart was rolled further down the slope, dragging the mules with it. A splashy fountain of bright red blood golloped out of the kaffir's mouth.

It took Barney another twenty minutes to reach Claim 172, next to the claim owned by the British Diamond Mining Coy. It was dug down to a depth of about ten feet, and one of its ends was shored up against rockslides with sandbags. But there was nobody working there: only a kaffir in a brown hat and a loincloth sitting on a rock and sorting idly through a heap of dry soil.

'Hey!' called Barney.

The kaffir squinted up at him.

'Where's your bossman?' demanded Barney.

The kaffir shrugged.

'Mr Havemann, your boss. Where is he? He come back?'

The kaffir shook his head again, and went on sorting through the dirt.

Barney waited for a moment – then stroke impatiently down the slope and pushed the kaffir hard on the shoulder.

'I'm talking to you,' he snapped. 'I'm looking for Mr Havemann and I want to know where he is.'

Again, the kaffir looked blank.

'You speak English?' said Barney. 'Afrikaans? What? You speak Bantu?'

'You're wasting your time,' put in a dry voice, from behind him.

Barney turned around. At the top of the ridge which divided Claim 172 from Claim 173 stood a grey-haired suntanned man in a striped shirt and tinted eyeglasses. He came down, his feet sliding sidewise on the loose yellowish soil, and held out his hand.

'My name's Stewart,' he said. 'Have you had trouble with Havemann, too?'

'Barney,' said Barney, introducing himself. 'What do you mean by trouble?'

124

Stewart looked around the claim. 'Whatever he is, or *was*, Havemann was not what you might call your natural-born digger. They caught him yesterday, at last, and well deserved it was too.'

'They caught him? What was he doing?'

'I'm surprised you didn't hear,' said Stewart, still casting his eyes around. 'He'd bribed two or three of the kaffirs from the British Mining Company's claim, next door. Whenever they found a reasonable stone, they were passing it secretly to him, and he was giving them half of whatever he got paid by the IDB boys outside of town. Well, *you* can call it IDB. *I* always call it thieving.'

'He was stealing diamonds?' asked Barney.

Stewart rubbed grit from his eye, and examined it on the end of his finger. 'It's common enough. Stealing's easier than digging. And you can't trust these damned blackies an inch. They swallow more diamonds than they hand over. Last year, in Klipdrift, I caught one of my fellows with two thousand pounds' worth of diamonds pushed up his arse. At least I let him give them back to me the natural way. There was a Dutch digger on the Vaal who caught one of his kaffirs doing that, and he was so wild that he thrust his hand up the fellow's backside and dragged down three feet of intestine. All blood and diamonds. I saw it.'

Barney took off his hat and wiped the sweat from his forehead. 'What's happened to Havemann?' he said.

'Stafford Parker was here, so he dealt with it himself. Questioned the witnesses, everything. Three kaffirs said that Havemann had bribed them, so Stafford Parker ordered him to be staked out.'

'You're joking.'

'Why should I be joking? The man's a thief. What else do you think we ought to do with thieves? Shake them by the hand and buy them a springbok steak dinner at Groot's?'

Riboyne Shel O'lem, thought Barney, with real terror. He knew what staking-out meant. It was the worst of the rough-and-ready punishments that Stafford Parker and his unofficial magistrates meted out on diggers who jumped claims or tried to sell diamonds illegally. Worse than flogging, even worse than being dragged over the bed of the Vaal. Staking-out meant that a man was pegged to the ground without food and water, naked or half-naked, at the mercy of the sun and the wind and the ants.

Staking-out was almost always fatal. And if Joel Havemann was really Joel Blitz, that could mean that Barney's brother was already dead.

Barney tried to swallow, but his throat was constricted and dry. 'I, er, where did they do it?' he asked Stewart.

'Where did they do what?'

'Stake him out. Do you know where they did it?'

Stewart looked at him curiously. 'You want to go and see him? He must have taken *you* for something of a ride.'

'Well, yes, he – he walked out on me once. A long time ago.'

Stewart pointed out towards the south-east corner of the mine. 'They took him out there, as far as I know. About a quarter-mile south of Haarhoff's claim. Ask Haarhoff when you see him, he'll know. He shares part of 190 with a man called Marais.'

'Thank you,' said Barney, in a unsteady voice. 'Can you tell me what's going to happen to this claim?'

'They'll resell it. There won't be any shortage of takers.'

'I see. All right. Thank you again.'

He climbed out of the claim and began to toil his way southwards in the oppressive afternoon heat. He was painfully thirsty now, his tongue sore and swollen, and he stopped by one claim to beg a for a drink. A prickly-headed German digger with a face the colour of raw pork sold him a tin mug of warm brown water for 1s 3d. Barney did not blame him: out here in the middle of the Kimberley Mine, a bucket of water was fetching anything up to 5s 6d. The German watched him drink with fat-embedded eyes, and said, 'I dream of cold beer, myself.'

At the edge of the mine, where the wild scrub still grew, the man called Marais paused in his shovelling for a moment to give Barney directions to the place where he believed Havemann was staked out. He was mournful, and French, and through a mouthful of sausage he told Barney gratuitously that he had once served in the French Foreign Legion. 'It was the same as this, the Legion. All digging.'

Barney reached the place as if he were arriving in one of those small stagey clearings of which the set-designers for grand operas are so fond.

The clearing was screened from the diamond mine by a thicket of thorns, and from the wider horizons of the veld by a row of stubby monkey-orange trees. A solitary Guiqua was standing nearby in a baggy white shirt and home-made cotton breeches, with a Bible under his arm. He raised his head as Barney came stumbling through the thicket, but he turned back almost immediately to the man who was pegged out naked on the ground, as if he were praying for him.

The man on the ground was silent, but not asleep. His wrists and ankles were bound tightly with thongs, and he had been stretched out in the shape of an X. His chest and his legs were already crimson with sunburn, and he was blotched and swollen with hundreds of insect bites. He was full-bearded, and his black hair was grown long, but bearded and disfigured as he was, Barney knew at once that it was his brother.

He stepped closer, treading for some reason with respectful softness through the grass. Now he could see the orange ants which teemed over the man's body in thousands – over his bruised thighs, over his penis, which was already swollen and distorted with bites; over his stomach; and even over his lips. He knelt as close as he could, and whispered, 'Joel?'

Joel, his face alive with ants, stared back at him. He tried to say something, but the ants wriggled into his mouth, and he had to try to spit them out. Barney turned around to the Griqua and asked, 'How long has he been here?'

'One night,' said the Griqua, in a careful Afrikaans accent. He raised the Bible which he had been carrying under his arm. 'I was reading to him. It says in the Bible to comfort the afflicted.'

'You can read?'

'I was schooled by the British missionaries, the same way Jan Bloem was.'

Barney reached into his pocket and took out his clasp-knife. Without a word, he began to cut Joel free. The Griqua stood and watched him for a while and made no effort to help; but when all the thongs were cut, he laid down his Bible in the grass, and assisted Barney in tugging Joel on to his feet. While the Griqua held him steady, Barney slapped the ants from Joel's body, and raked them, jerking and wriggling, out of his hair.

'Where can we take him?' asked Barney. 'None of the people in Kimberley will have him. Not even my friends.'

'This was Mr Stafford Parker's justice, you know,' said the Griqua solemnly. 'He will not let you escape him.'

'The name of Stafford Parker doesn't impress me at all,' retorted Barney. 'And, besides, this happens to be my brother.'

'*Water*,' pleaded Joel, in a thick whisper.

'I'll get you water,' Barney comforted him. 'Let's just get you out of this place first. Do you have any kind of transport?' he asked the Griqua.

'A donkey-cart. It's tied up by the monkey-orange trees.'

'Come on, then,' Barney told him.

Together, Barney and the Griqua half-carried Joel through the grass to the stunted monkey-orange trees, heavy with green and blotchy-orange fruit. The Griqua's cart was small, and the donkey looked at the three of them with misgiving as they approached; but they were able to lift Joel into the back, and cover him with a frayed plaid blanket.

'All right, let's go,' said Barney; and as quickly as they could, they bumped and wheeled their way across the rocky ground towards the north side of Kimberley's collection of shacks. Hardly anybody gave them a second glance, although Joel began to groan loudly for water again when they were passing the end of the main street.

The Griqua encampment was a mile or so beyond Kimberley, a small gathering of neat British Army tents on the long slope of a grassy hillside. The afternoon was already taking on the smoky gold of a north Cape Colony evening as Barney and his Griqua friend rolled through the lines of cooking-fires to the grandest tent of all, a one-time military band marquee which was now the travelling palace of Jan Bloem.

'Wait here,' said the Griqua, reining back the donkey, and

128

swinging himself down from the cart. 'I must first of all tell the chief what has happened. It is his decision whether you can stay here or not.'

Barney climbed down from the cart himself as the Griqua strode over to Jan Bloem's marquee. He lifted the blanket from Joel, and folded it up to make a pillow. Then he walked across to one of the Griqua women who was standing in a plain grey Dutch farmhouse dress, cradling a baby in her arms, and he asked her for water.

The woman called to a girl who sat stirring the black iron cooking pot over the fire. The girl nodded, and stood up, and went to a keg beside the tent. She came up to Barney with a dipper brimming with clear water, and followed him back to the cart.

'Joel, I've brought you water,' said Barney, gently. He raised his brother's head while the Griqua girl held the dipper to his dry, swollen lips. Joel sipped as much as he could, and then sank back on the blanket.

The Griqua girl looked at Barney with wide, dark-brown eyes. Some of the half-caste Dutch-Hottentots were remarkably ugly; but this girl had soft curly hair, the colour of brown chimney-soot, and a pretty, oval face. She wore the same plain grey dress as the woman with the baby; but her body had a natural grace which gave it a simple attractiveness and charm.

'This is your friend?' she asked, in halting English.

'No, my brother. *Broeder*,' Barney explained.

The girl said, 'He should ... get down. Sleep.'

'Is there any place for him to lie? A bed?'

The girl pointed to her tent. 'There ... is good.'

At that moment, in a black opera hat, a monocle, a brown striped racing suit and spats, Jan Bloem appeared from his marquee, with Barney's Griqua friend and two other Griquas behind him.

'Well, well,' he declared. 'It's you again. The kike.'

'I found my brother,' said Barney, with simplicity.

Jan Bloem peered at Joel. 'Yes,' he said. 'Piet Steyn here told me all about it.'

'Can we get him to a bed?' asked Barney. 'He's in real bad shape.'

'He's a thief,' said Jan Bloem, trying to screw his monocle into his left eye.

'Stafford Parker says so,' replied Barney. 'But I know Joel better than Stafford Parker. My brother never stole anything.'

'They were prepared to stake him out. To let him die,' commented Jan Bloem. His monocle dropped out again. 'He must have done something to warrant that kind of punishment. Or don't you think so?'

'I don't know. I just want to get him to bed.'

Jan Bloem linked his arms behind his back and walked around Barney as if he were inspecting a piece of garden statuary. Joel, on the back of the cart, let out a breathy groan. But Bloem ignored him, and continued to pace around Barney with his eyes fixed on him unwaveringly. The smoke from the cooking fires drifted between the tents.

'If I take your brother in – give him succour, as they call it, then in British colonial law I'll be an accessory to his crime. They might try staking me out, too.'

'This is your land. They wouldn't dare. If the British upset you, you might take up with the Boers; and if you did that, they'd lose all these diamond mines to the Orange Free State. No, Mr Bloem. There's no risk of that.'

Jan Bloem abruptly stopped pacing. 'The British are unpredictable,' he said. 'You never know what they're going to do next. Their politics are almost entirely dependent on the opinions of their newspaper readers.'

'My brother may be dying, Mr Bloem. If you won't take him in, then I'll just have to take him elsewhere.'

Donald emerged just then from a tent nearby, followed by a fat middle-aged Griqua woman who was pinning up her hair.

'Mr Blitz!' he called, and came over. 'What happen here, Mr Blitz?'

Barney explained, keeping his gaze steadily and cynically on Jan Bloem. 'The situation is that Joel's dying, but our Griqua chum here is more worried about politics, and the British Colonial Office, and the niceties of law.'

Donald bent over the donkey-cart and examined Joel closely. Then he pointed at Joel with a long finger and asked, 'This is he? This is really your brother?'

130

Barney nodded.

Donald turned on Jan Bloem, still pointing rigidly at Joel, and let fly with a fierce, guttural burst of Griqua. Jan Bloem flushed, and stamped his foot, and shouted back. But then Donald lifted one finger, and pointed upwards, and barked out a whole litany of expletives, until Jan Bloem waved his hand at him to stop.

'I give in,' he told Barney. 'Just tell this mad dog of yours to stop snapping at my ankles.'

'Donald,' cautioned Barney, and Donald felt silent, although he was still twitching with temper.

'This girl here will take care of your brother for you,' said Jan Bloem. 'Her name is Natalia Marneweck. She's a good girl.'

'What about Stafford Parker?' asked Barney. 'And the British authorities?'

'Well, I'll think about them when the time comes,' Jan Bloem told him, although with very little grace. Then he marched back to his tent with his followers in tow, clearing his throat every now and then as if he was on his way to do something extremely important.

'Natalia?' said Barney, turning to the Griqua girl. The girl smiled, and came forward to help Barney and Donald lift Joel down from the back of the cart. Another Griqua man walked across and took the weight of Joel's legs, and between them they carried Joel past the cooking fire and into the tent, where they laid him gently on a pallet of woven grass, covered with a blanket. Joel opened his eyes momentarily in the dim light inside the tent, and gave Barney a small, swollen smile.

Barney stood up. Apart from the pallet, the tent was furnished with nothing more than a brass-bound military chest, which had been spread with a white lace-edged cloth. There was a plain wooden cross standing on it, and a brush and comb.

The girl Natalia said, 'I will help . . . your brother. Go now. Please. It is good he sleeps.'

Barney stayed where he was for a moment, looking down at Joel. For the first time since he had found his brother, he had time to think about New York, and Blitz the tailors, and the long years he had been searching since he had come to South

Africa. He held the back of his hand across his mouth, and the tears ran down his cheeks. Donald hesitated by the tent-flap, and the girl Natalia looked up at him with an expression of such gentleness and sympathy that he could do nothing else but smile at her.

'I'll come back in an hour,' he said, wiping his eyes with his sleeve.

Outside the tent, in the cooler breeze of the early evening, he asked Donald, 'What did you say to Jan Bloem? What made him change his mind?'

Donald shrugged, and turned the other way, across the warm shadowy reaches of the valley. The sun was glowering behind the wild syringa trees, and there was a smell of dry grass in the air.

'Oh, not much. I tell him to remember that Jew people and Griqua people are just one people under the Lord. I tell him to remember his Christian vows. I tell him also a great chief like himself has no dignity if he show fear for the British, or for white-beard Stafford Parker.'

'Is that all?' asked Barney.

Donald still did not turn around. 'Well, maybe I tell him I know of one time when he is not faithful to his wife. Maybe I say that if he does not take in your brother, his wife will find out all about his hanky-panky doublequick.'

Barney said, 'Blackmail?'

'Oh, no sir. Friendly reminder.'

Barney stood for a while with his hands on his hips, admiring the valley. 'You know something, Donald,' he said warmly, 'I think I'm beginning to understand the basic ethics of Christianity.'

Barney considered cancelling his dinner engagement with the Knight family that evening, but by seven o'clock Joel was still immersed in the deepest of sleeps, his eyes as red and swollen as ripe wild figs, and Natalia thought it unlikely that he would wake before morning.

'He won't die, though, will he?' asked Barney, standing over his bruised and slumbering brother.

Natalia shook her head vigorously, so that her curls flew. 'He not die. I promise.'

Barney held her arm for a moment. 'You've been good to him. Thank you.'

Natalia said, 'All Griqua good people.'

'I'm beginning to find that out,' said Barney.

Donald was waiting for him outside, holding the reins of the horses, and idly twitching the carriage-whip at the furry insects which flew aimlessly around him in the evening air. Not far away, beside one of the cooking fires, one of the Griqua men was playing an instrument which sounded as plangent as a Jew's harp, while a sturdy woman in a red wrap-around dress sang loud sallies from the Psalms.

Silently, Barney and Donald sat side by side in the surrey as the horses pulled them over the uneven grassland towards Kimberley. As they crested the rise, they could see out over the diamond mine, where a thousand tiny fires sparkled. There was an aroma of woodsmoke and cooking on the wind.

At last, on the outskirts of the main street, they came to the Knights' house. It was one of the better buildings in town – a white-painted frame bungalow with a long verandah and a shingled roof. There was a small picket fence around its neatly-planted front garden, and the path to the front door had been marked out with white pebbles. Through the open curtains, Barney could see Agnes setting the table, and Faith lighting the oil-lamps.

Donald said, 'What time I come back?'

Barney looked at his watch. 'Make it eleven o'clock. That should be just about right.'

'Just about right for you maybe.'

Barney raised an eyebrow. 'Why, what are you planning on doing?'

Donald gave a wide, checkered grin. 'Jan Bloem tells me new sister arrive today, good fat Hottentot. Jan Bloem says her name is Heavy Mary.'

'I might have known. Well, you can make it eleven-thirty. But no later.'

'You are a good fellow, Mr Blitz.'

As Donald clicked at the horses and drove the surrey away,

Barney walked up the Knights' front path, stepped up on to the verandah, and knocked at the black-painted door. He pretended not to notice the way the lace curtain covering the small window beside the door was hurriedly brushed back into place.

Mr Knight himself opened the front door, although it must have been quite a recent experience for him to have to admit his own guests. He was dressed, as before, in a buttoned-up black coat, and a gates-ajar collar.

'You're very punctual,' he said, in a tone of voice that made Barney wonder whether he considered punctuality a virtue or a slightly shameful peccadillo. 'The girls have been looking forward to seeing you.'

Barney stepped into the living-room. It was furnished with an incongruous collection of expensive mahogany tables, inlaid kingwood tailboys, and atrocious varnished armchairs and sofas. It was the sort of clutter you might expect to see on a refugee's pushcart, a mixture of valuable heirlooms and utter rubbish.

Agnes and Faith were both standing by the green-painted upright boiler, and they curtseyed, with a giggly sparkle in their eyes, as Barney came in.

'I think that I've been looking forward to seeing you two again just as much,' Barney told them. He took off his hat, and his gloves, and Mr Knight relieved him of them, only to juggle with them in embarrassment because there was no hallstand on which they could hang.

'It's been very difficult for us, moving out here to Kimberley,' said Mr Knight. 'We had to leave some of our most precious possessions behind. Apart from our friends, that is, and our social life.' He gave a harsh, high-pitched chuckle. 'And you can't exactly describe the social life out here as scintillating, can you? Not scintillating, by any means.'

'You've enough business here, though?' asked Barney.

Mr Knight at last found a place for Barney's hat, on the left-hand antler of a very sorry-looking stuffed springbok's head. His gloves, he fitted over the right-hand antler. 'Business?' he asked, drawing back his coat tails, and planting his fists on his hips. 'Oh yes, plenty of business. Squabbles over claims, squabbles over diamonds. And quite a few squabbles over women, too.'

A small, pale lady with a face the shape and colour of a blanched almond appeared from the interior of the bungalow. She wore a drab dress of pale green cotton, and dangling earrings of amber cornelian, and when Barney took her hand he felt as if he were trying to save someone with greasy palms from falling over a small cliff.

'M'good woman,' mumbled Mr Knight, abruptly.

'Please to know you,' said Barney.

'Charmed,' said Mrs Knight, in a vague, bright voice. 'The dinner is almost ready.'

Agnes giggled. She was dressed very prettily tonight, in a pink dress of polished cotton with lacy frills at the neck and the cuffs and hem. Faith appeared a little more severe, in grey, with a cameo brooch at her neck, and her hair scraped back from her forehead.

'Mummy's had a very difficult time with the new cook, haven't you, Mummy?' said Agnes.

Mr Knight frowned, but Mrs Knight flapped her hands in amusement and desperation, and said, 'These Malays . . . they can't understand plain English, that's the trouble. I told him to sauté the potatoes, and when I came back, he had simply placed all the *small* potatoes on one side of the drainer, and all the *large* potatoes on the other. "There, missis," he said. "I sort out all the potatoes, just like you say." Isn't it *impossible?*'

'She misses Capetown,' remarked Mr Knight, unnecessarily, as his wife returned to the kitchen to rescue the meal.

They sat down to dinner at last, at an oval table with a wobbly leg. Halfway through the soup, which was thin split-pea with enough pepper in it to make Barney feel as if he were going to sneeze the whole bowlful clear across the cloth, Mr Knight had to get up and wedge a copy of *Good and Great Churchmen* under the offending castor to keep the table level. He was red in the face when he emerged from under the cloth.

'It wasn't always this way,' he intoned, to the world in general. 'There was a time when we owned the finest mahogany dining-table in the entire Colony.'

'Never mind, dear,' his wife soothed him.

135

Faith said, 'Will you be staying until Sunday, Mr Barney?'

Barney was glad of a chance to lay down his spoon and dab at his mouth with his napkin. The napkin was real Irish linen, although rather tired. 'I'm sure I will,' he said. 'I have quite a few days' business in Kimberley.'

'Then you could accompany us to church?' said Faith.

'Faith,' protested her father, gruffly. But Barney could see that the idea did not altogether displease him. It may not have been appropriate for a young woman in England or in Capetown to seek a young man to escort her to church on Sunday, so that they might recite their devotions together, but here in Kimberley it was almost respectable. Better than chattering in the street with diggers, like a common whore. And certainly better than secret liaisons behind the assay office, which he would be unable to inspect either for quality or for moral content.

Mr Knight was sure that both his flirtatious daughters were still virgins, but only just. Another six months in this primitive hurly-burly of miners and prostitutes and thieves, and he would no longer be quite so certain. A daughter's virtue was so fragile, like a protea flower. And he knew, with a kind of quiet desperation, how very attractive to men his daughters were.

'You enjoyed your soup?' asked Mrs Knight, as Agnes got up to clear away the plates. The Knights were obviously very hard up, or else they had servant trouble. But performing the duties of a parlourmaid gave Agnes the opportunity to bend over Barney as she took his bowl, so that he could smell her perfume, and so that he could feel for a moment the young resilience of her breast against his shoulder.

'The soup was delicious,' said Barney. 'I haven't tasted soup like that since I was in New York.'

'I pity New York,' murmured Agnes, as she passed on to collect her father's dish. And she glanced back at Barney and gave him a twinkling smile that was both merry and provocative. Barney found himself blushing, and paying more attention to his breadroll than most people would have considered usual. Faith noticed what had happened, but Mr Knight was too busy propounding a legalistic theory for dividing up the diamond claims, and Mrs Knight was biting her lip and frowning at her husband in a hopeless attempt to follow what he was saying.

'You're a *gentleman* farmer, I suppose?' Mr Knight asked Barney, as Agnes brought to the table a large white tureen brimming with a brown and indiscriminate stew.

Barney gave him a sloping smile. 'I guess so, whatever that's worth in the middle of nowhere at all.'

'Well, it's worth a very great deal, old chap,' said Mr Knight. 'A gentleman farmer can be nominated for membership of the Kimberley Club; whereas any other kind of farmer may not.'

'Is the Kimberley Club so important?'

Mrs Knight tittered abstractedly as she served up the stew, and Mr Knight glared at her. 'Yes,' he said, turning back to Barney. 'It's a little rudimentary at the moment, but then the new building's complete, it'll look like what it was founded to be. A club for gentlemen of social standing; a place where business can be discussed among the select few; an *enclave*, if you like, for those of breeding.'

'You're a member yourself?' asked Barney.

Mr Knight folded his chins into his stiff collar with self-satisfaction. 'Billiards secretary, as a matter of fact.'

'And you're thinking that I might . . .?'

'It would be of considerable advantage to you if you did. It's a question of those *within* the circle, if you see what I mean, and those *without*. And those *without*, well . . . those *without* will never know what it means to be *within*.'

Mrs Knight tittered again, and passed Barney a plate crowded with unlikely-looking pieces of meat. Either she was serving up some completely unknown animal, or else her new cook had no idea of how to cut a brisket up into palatable pieces.

Agnes, her hands prettily clasped in front of her, said, 'Are there really Red Indians in America, Mr Barney? And bears?'

'Both,' nodded Barney, 'but not in New York.'

'So you've never seen any?' Agnes asked. Barney was suddenly conscious of her knee pressing against his under the tablecloth. He looked down at his plate, at the awkward lumps of meat and bone swimming in their pool of greasy gravy, and he wished he had not.

'I saw a Red Indian once,' he said. 'When I was a boy, a Comanche called Eagle Feathers visited New York, and was driven around the streets in a carriage. I was pretty disappointed, though. He wore a top hat and a morning coat, and carried a cane. Not very savage, I'm afraid.'

Mr Knight, sniffed loudly, said, 'Apropos of that – of savages, I mean – I defended a very interesting court-martial once, in Capetown. A chap charged with the theft of silver from the officers' mess at Cape Castle. He was said to have run up some pretty hefty gambling debts which he couldn't pay back. Chatsworth, his name was. Old Harrovian.'

'But not a savage, dear, surely?' asked Mrs Knight, vaguely.

Mr Knight fixed his wife with a look that went beyond mere exasperation. It almost seemed as if he were trying to melt her down by the force of concentrated eyesight.

'This chap,' he went on, still staring at his wife, 'this chap denied the charges completely. And the interesting thing was that the only witness to his alleged theft was a Kaffir cleaner. So after all the evidence had been heard, I stood up before the court-martial and asked them if they considered that kaffirs were more important in the Lord's scheme of things than, say, polo ponies – or *less*. And if they believed, as I did, that a thoroughbred polo pony was more important in the Lord's scheme of things than a Cape Coast blackie, then they would have to come to the conclusion that the only eye-witness in this trial was less than human, and that his so-called testimony was therefore inadmissible. I have to tell you, of course, that we were sitting in front of old Clough-Parker, who used to be an absolute fanatic for polo.'

Barney was stunned. 'And they let him off? Chatsworth, I mean?'

'Of course. Acquitted without hesitation. It shouldn't have come to a hearing, of course, except the colonel in charge of the mess on the night of the alleged theft absolutely hated Chatsworth's guts. Think he believed Chatsworth had been messing around with his wife, something like that. But – and this is the most important thing – old Clough-Parker's decision created something of an interesting precedent ... and the plea that kaffirs can't give admissible evidence in a court of law because

138

they aren't human is still used today, although not as often as it was. It's known as the Polo Pony Precedent.'

Agnes's thigh was now pressing close and warm against Barney's knee, and when he looked at her, she gave him a smile of unmistakable desire. Barney felt excited and confused at the same time. He liked Agnes a great deal; she was pretty, and she stirred up in him the kind of tingling sensations that stayed with him in the morning after an erotic dream. But his experience with girls was limited to his childhood friendship with Leah, and his strenuous defloration by Louise Loubser. He had often stared covertly at the bare breasts of black girls around Oranjerivier, and thought about inviting one of them back to the farm. But in the end he had always been too shy, or too concerned about disease, or too worried that he might end up like Monsaraz, copulating like a fancy-dressed dog.

Faith must have sensed what was going on beneath the table, because she suddenly hissed, '*Agnes*,' as if to reprimand her sister and remind her who had invited Barney to church first.

But quite apart from the Knight girls' coquettish behaviour, Barney had something else on his mind – the possibility of getting Joel acquitted by Stafford Parker's magistrates. If Mr Knight could plead on Joel's behalf, and if the magistrate was prepared to accept the Polo Pony Precedent, them Joel could go free.

'I'll tell you what, Mr Barney,' said Mr Knight, 'if you're interested in becoming a member of the Kimberley Club, I could put your name up. It would stand you in excellent stead, you know.'

'*Billiards*,' said Mrs Knight, scathingly, for no particular reason at all. Barney glanced at her in alarm, but Mr Knight shook his hand to indicate that he should not take any notice.

'We could do with some more gentlemen,' said Mr Knight. 'And gentlemen, of course, includes American gentlemen. We're not xenophobes.' He let out another high, grating laugh, as if he were amazed at his own good humour and tolerance.

Barney reached under the table and held Agnes's knee to keep it still. He was feeling hot and flushed, and inside his best black trousers he had half an erection. 'You don't admit ... half-castes, I suppose?' he asked.

'Half-castes! My dear chap! We don't even admit Wyke-hamists! No, my dear fellow, there isn't a half-caste to be seen. Nor anyone of any of the inferior breeds. No Arabs, no Chinese, no Malays, and no bloody Frenchmen!'

'Jews?' asked Barney.

Mr Knight, with his mouth full of stew, stared at Barney as if he were mad.

'The day they admit a Jew to the Kimberley Club – that'll be the day that I drink five bottles of brandy one after the other and go to seek my place beside the Lord my God. Jews! Mercenary, money-grubbing Jews! What are you thinking about?'

'Actually . . .' said Barney, in a dry voice, 'not all Jews are as grasping as they're made out to be. In fact, one of my very best friends turned out to be a Jew.' The words came out like toads, but he knew he had to say them. 'Jews can be very . . . well, sensitive.'

'Oh, don't misunderstand me,' Mr Knight put in. He chewed for a while, with obvious distaste, and then removed from his mouth a large piece of fawn gristle, corrugated by teethmarks, which he parked prominently on the side of his plate. 'The Jew is a human being, no doubt of it; unlike your kaffir. He has his religion, no matter how perverse many of its tenets may be, and he has his family life. And I've heard people like yourself say that your occasional Jew can be most obliging. No, no, you mustn't get me wrong.'

Barney found it almost impossible to stop himself from pushing back his chair and walking out of Mr Knight's bungalow at once. His brains felt as if they were boiling. But the way that Agnes held his hand close to the warmth of her thigh was somehow soothing as well as erotic, and even more sobering was the thought that Joel's life was still at risk from the magistrates. Mr Knight, with his bristly quiver of well-sharpened bigotry, might well be the only person who could save him.

He had to admit to himself, too, that the idea of becoming a member of the Kimberley Club was something of an attrac-tion. It would establish him as a *bona fide* businessman, and give him the social credentials to start making his way to the top.

Where 'the top' actually was in the hugger-mugger of De Beers New Rush, he was not quite sure. But it had to be better than working Monsaraz' farm for him; and it had to be better than living like the Knights, on thin pulse soup and faded dreams.

'Perhaps you'd consider helping this Jewish friend of mine out of a difficult legal spot,' said Barney.

Mr Knight swallowed wine, and then looked at Barney with great care. 'A difficult legal spot, you say.'

'He's been accused, wrongfully, of theft.'

'Aha! Like our friend Chatsworth.'

'Well, that's right,' said Barney. 'And the similarity doesn't end there. As far as I know, the only witnesses were kaffirs.'

'What was he accused of stealing?' asked Mr Knight. 'Not diamonds, I hope.'

Barney nodded. 'It was said that he bribed kaffirs from the British Diamond Mining Company, whose claim was next to his, to bring him the best of their finds. He then sold them on the IDB market.'

'You're talking about Mr Havemann, aren't you?' put in Faith, in surprise. 'I thought he'd been sentenced, and staked out.'

Barney felt hot. 'You knew him?' he asked.

'Everybody knew him,' said Faith. 'But then, everybody here knows everybody. A very morose man, but quite handsome.'

'That's enough, Faith,' interrupted her father. He put down his knife and said to Barney, 'Is Havemann not dead then?'

'He's alive,' said Barney. 'He's not particularly well, but he's alive.'

'Stafford Parker will have him hunted down like a rogue lion, I promise you that, and probably shot.'

'Stafford Parker is not the law,' retorted Barney.

'No, he isn't, not technically speaking. But he has sufficient power and influence to keep the diamond fields under his own control. And you can't say that his control has been unwelcome. There is very little violence here, everything considered.'

'Nonetheless, he should consider an appeal on Mr Havemann's behalf.'

Mr Knight made a face. 'He may do, if the mood takes him.'

'And will you represent him?'

There was a lengthy pause, during which Mr Knight pursued a few rags of meat around the circumference of his plate with determined abstraction.

'There are many crimes committed around Kimberley, almost daily, which are tolerated by most of the diggers because they do not challenge their fundamental reason for being here. They are here for the diamonds, Mr Barney, and most of them have suffered much, and given up much, and travelled far, all for the sake of diamonds. There is blasphemy here, and prostitution, and drunkenness, and gambling. There is sodomy and there is incest. But all of these are considered to be little more than misdemeanours – diversions, if you like, for men of rough character, and forgivable. The stealing of diamonds, however, is *never* forgiven. To steal diamonds, you see, is to steal a man's life.'

'But will you represent him? Will you try? I have nobody else to turn to.'

'A Jew, and a diamond thief? You're asking a great deal, Mr Barney.'

Barney took a shallow breath. 'I know. And I know that you don't have much of a chance of success. But if you *were* to succeed – think of it. You'd be famous throughout the colony.'

'That's as may be,' replied Mr Knight, unimpressed. 'No – you'll have to give me time to consider it. And of course I'll have to talk to Mr Havemann to get his side of the story. Funny, though – I met him once or twice and I never realised he was Jewish. No side-curls, or anything like that.'

'Jews don't *all* look like Shylock,' said Barney, turning his attention first to Mrs Knight, surprising her in the middle of trying to pick a shred of beef from between her teeth; and then to Agnes, and to Faith. It seemed almost incredible to him that none of them had realised he was Jewish himself, although Agnes had probably mistaken his trembling and his heat for sexual arousal, and partly, of course, it was. His trousers felt tight and crowded, and he could feel the moistness of male juice on his cotton combinations. He had never known a dinner like it. Law, prejudice, desire, and indigestion.

After they had out-stared a mountainous blancmange of goat's milk, flavoured with strong vanilla, they left the table, with a great deal of chair-scraping, and sat around the green-painted upright stove. Mr Knight lit an oval Turkish cigarette, and reclined in his chair with his ankles crossed, twiddling his feet as he spoke. Barney sat on the end of the sofa, and Agnes perched herself on the arm right next to him, so that he could breathe in her perfume, and so that she could wind the curls of his hair around her fingers without her father seeing. She hummed under her breath, a repetitive and melancholy air which would always remind Barney of this evening as long as he lived.

'I'll give you one word of advice,' said Mr Knight, as the cloc, on the wall struck eleven. 'Be careful with whom you associate; because in Kimberley you're known by the company you keep. Everybody's allowed their little entertainments – their black women, and so forth. That's natural. But, socially, you should keep yourself beyond reproach. Now, will you have a glass of tonic wine?'

Donald arrived at eleven-thirty, and looked distinctly white around the mouth. Barney bowed to Mrs Knight, and thanked her for dinner, while Mrs Knight giggled and blushed, and Agnes and Faith clutched each other tight and tried not to laugh. Mr Knight stood by with his 'heavens preserve us' expression.

Barney mounted the surrey and waved to the Knight family, who stood in the lighted doorway of their bungalow like a group posing for a Christmas photograph, waving furiously back at him.

'Enough waving?' asked Donald, raising his whip. But just as Barney was about to say 'more than enough – let's go', Agnes came bustling along the pathway towards him, her skirts held high, flapping something frantically in her hand.

'Your gloves, Mr Barney! You forgot your gloves!'

Barney climbed down from the surrey again. 'I'm grateful,' he told Agnes, as she came up close.

'I hid them,' she whispered. 'I wanted to say goodbye to you alone.'

Barney stared into her wide, glistening eyes. She was very

pretty, and she excited him like no girl he had ever met before. Not even Leah had made him feel this way. This girl was all wispy hair and spicy fragrances and moist, tantalising lips. She was well-mannered, but forward too, and the way she had drawn his hand up the length of her thigh during dinner had been electrifying.

Agnes held out her hand, and Barney sandwiched it between his own hands.

'I don't know what to say to you,' he said.

'I know,' she whispered. 'But it doesn't matter. I was in love with a lieutenant when we lived in Capetown . . . I had to leave him because of Papa's business. But he taught me what it takes to please a man.'

'I want to meet you again,' said Barney.

'Then come to church on Sunday. Be kind to Faith – but make sure you sit close to me.'

Barney was suddenly conscious of how hot the night was; of the tireless chirping of the insects in the bush. He was also conscious that Mr Knight was frowning from the verandah; and that his conversation with Agnes had overrun the time that any normal person would have taken to discuss the matter of mislaid gloves.

'You must go,' he said.

Agnes twinkled her eyes at him. 'I know. But won't Faith be jealous?'

She ran back down the path, and Barney stood watching her for a moment before he climbed back up on to the surrey.

'That woman knows you're Jewish?' asked Donald, flicking the whip, and clicking to the horses.

'What difference does it make?' Barney demanded, loosening his necktie.

Donald grinned at him. 'She not know? You not tell her?'

'No. There was no reason to.'

'You don't think God be angry?'

'Why should He be?'

'God doesn't like to be denied.'

'I wasn't denying God. Listen, Donald, to survive in this country, to make it rich, you have to be white, and Christian, and a gentleman. As it happens, I'm only one of those three

144

things. But if I have to let people assume that I'm the other two
– only *assume*, mind you, without barefaced lying – then I'll do
it.'

'Very good,' said Donald.

'Very good? What's very good?'

'Excuse,' said Donald. 'Very good excuse.'

Joel was awake when he returned to the Griqua encampment
on the hillside. Natalia was crouched by the side of his cot,
feeding him with meat broth. When Barney came into the tent,
Joel held Natalia's wrist, and said, 'That's enough soup, thank
you. Really, that's enough.'

'You must get strength,' said Natalia, lifting the spoon again.

Barney sat down on the end of the bed. 'Do what your nurse
tells you.' He smiled at Joel.

Joel was unshaved, red-eyed, and battered. Each cheekbone
was shiny with purple bruises. 'What's the point in fattening
myself up?' he asked Barney. 'Stafford Parker's going to set the
dogs on me when he finds out that I've escaped.'

'Did they really leave you out there to die?'

Joel lay back. 'The punishment was three days staked out.
If you don't die, it's a goddamned miracle.'

Barney said, 'I only heard what had happened to you by
chance. Nork told me.'

'Nork? That buffoon?'

'He didn't seem like a buffoon to me.'

'He's the laughing-stock of the mine. Him and his theories
about volcanoes. You get *shlimazls* like Nork around every
mine, though. The thieves, and the clingers-on, and the so-
called professors.'

Natalia stood up, and carried the bowl of broth out of the
tent. Barney, brimming with affection, said, 'Joel, it's wonderful to see you. I've been searching for you ever since I got here.
Three years, and here you are.'

'Well, you're a few months too late, little brother,' said Joel.
'If you'd come along earlier, you might have been able to help
me dig my claim, and then maybe I would have come up with
something.'

'Your claim didn't yield any diamonds?'

'A handful. Enough to keep me in food and water and precious little else. While everybody around me was digging up rocks the size of pigeons' eggs, and making a fortune, I was scarcely scratching a living. Why the hell do you think I bribed those *schwarzers* to give me the best stones they found?'

Barney stared at him. 'You mean you really did that?'

'How else was I supposed to live? You haven't dug a claim out there, you don't know what the hell it's like. It's so damned hot you feel like you're frying, and it's nothing but rock and mudslides and breaking your damned back.'

'How did they catch you?' asked Barney.

'One of the kaffirs got too smart. I was paying all of them half of what I got from the IDB boys, but this particular one said he wanted two-thirds, or else he'd go tell his bossman at British Diamonds what I was up to. Well, I should have paid him what he wanted, but I got mad at him, and told him to go to the devil. That's where he went – straight to Stafford Parker. And that's why Stafford Parker staked me out.'

'Listen,' said Barney, 'whether you actually stole those diamonds or not, I've found someone who might be able to help you. A lawyer, by the name of Knight. I told him you were a friend of mine, not my brother, because he's prejudiced against Jews. Yes, I know – but he's not the only one. And he got someone acquitted in Capetown once because the only prosecution witness was a kaffir.'

'Are you serious?' asked Joel. 'If I do so much as poke my nose out of that tent-flap, the Diggers' Association will tear me to tiny pieces. The best thing I can do is wait here until I've got my strength back, and then make a run for the coast.'

'Joel, you can't. What about your diamond claim?'

'They'll confiscate it anyway, and sell it off to the next bidder.'

'But it must have cost you everything you had!'

'It did,' nodded Joel. 'I bought the farm at Derdeheuwel out of the wages I'd saved at sea. Then I sold Derdeheuwel off to that damned Portugee for twice what I paid for it. He was desperate for a place, and rich, too, and I was bored with farming by then. That's when I bought a claim at Klipdrift, and

I did well, there. A good steady supply of diamonds that kept me well-dressed and drunk for over a year. Don't get me wrong, though. I saved a little money, too. So by May this year I had three thousand pounds for a single claim here at Kimberley.'

'Joel,' said Barney, sorrowfully, shaking his head.

'I hope you're not thinking to judge me,' retorted Joel, edgily.

'I should judge you?'

'You sound like it, *schmendrick*.'

'What's happened to you, Joel? You're so bitter.'

Joel rubbed the back of his hand across his unshaven chin. 'Bitter? You think I'm bitter?' He turned his face away. 'Yes,' he said, and his voice was less confident now, less aggressive. 'Yes, well I am bitter.'

'You want to talk about it?'

Joel sniffed. Although he was keeping his face hidden by the blanket, Barney could tell that he was upset.

'I'm such a damned waster,' he said. 'I had hundreds of pounds – thousands – when I was at Klipdrift, and I wasted it all. On drink, on gambling, on horses, on women. I was like a ridiculous child. I saved some, sure. But three thousand out of fifteen thousand isn't much to boast about, is it? Particularly when I gave most of it away to a woman.'

'A woman? What woman?'

Joel looked at Barney, and there were tears running down his blistered cheeks. 'She was a whore, Barney. A common whore. I didn't want to go with whores when I first came here. I tried to think of Mama. Somehow ... in some ridiculous way ... I still thought of myself as Mama's property. Almost her husband. If I went with whores, I'd be letting her down. But one night in Klipdrift I got drunk and I went to a whorehouse, and that's where I met Meg. She was Irish. She had hair like fire. And the first night we spent together, it was like a dream. In the morning, I paid her in diamonds for a whole week; and for that whole week we lay in bed and made love. Or fornicated. Call it whatever you like.'

Natalia came back into the tent with a copper basin filled with warm water, and a rough towel. She knelt down again beside Joel and started to dab his face.

'This Meg ...' said Barney. 'You gave her everything?'

'Almost everything,' Joel told him. 'I had three thousand pounds tied up at the bank, and so I couldn't lay my hands on it, thank God. But I bought her clothes, and jewellery, and whatever she wanted. I was crazy for love. Then one day I came back to my cabin a couple of hours early and found her naked with some German. That was the end of it. For a while, I was mad. I still think of her, and it still hurts me to remember what she did to me.'

There was a moment's silence between them. It had been a long time, and they were almost strangers.

But then Joel said, 'How was Mama, when you left her? Have you kept in touch since you've been out here?'

Barney said, 'You didn't get my letter?'

'Letter?'

'I sent you a letter just before I left New York. It was addressed to you at Derdeheuwel.'

Joel frowned. 'Mama's okay, isn't she? She's not sick?'

Barney took his brother's hand. He wanted to say, she's dead, she's been lying in the Jewish cemetery for years now – all those years in which you've been assuming that she's still alive. All those years in which you've been imagining her in her kitchen on Clinton Street, cooking ghostly meals which she never cooked, lighting every Friday evening those *Shabbes* candles which she never lit.

He wanted to say, she's dead, but the words would not leave his mouth.

Joel said, 'What's wrong? What's the matter? You've heard from her, haven't you? She's written?'

'Joel,' said Barney, in a hoarse voice, 'the reason I left New York was because Mama died.'

'She *died*? You're telling me that Mama *died*?'

Barney nodded.

'*Zeeser Gottenyu*,' whispered Joel. He held his hands together and covered his mouth.

'She, er ... we had one of those crazy arguments. She killed herself in the kitchen. She was going out of her mind, Joel. There was nothing that anybody could do to help her. Ever since *Tateh* died ...'

'Yes,' whispered Joel. 'Ever since *Tateh* died.'

'It wasn't your fault,' said Barney. 'It wasn't mine, either, although sometimes I have bad dreams about it. Sometimes I wake up and I can feel her blood on the palms of my hands. Wet, and sticky. But it's only a dream.'

'How did she do it?' asked Joel. The pupils of his eyes dilated, and he kept glancing sideways, as if he found it difficult to concentrate.

'Knife,' Barney told him, in one single strangulated word.

Joel closed his eyes. 'Knife,' he repeated, sadly. 'Poor Mama.'

They talked, in odd fragmented sentences, for another hour, until Joel began to tire. Barney told Joel everything that had happened to him since he left New York – about Hunt, and Monsaraz, and Stafford Parker, and about his evening with the Knight family. Joel seemed intent on making an immediate break for the Orange Free State, but Barney managed to persuade him that it might be worth talking to Mr Knight about his case, and about the possibility of lodging an appeal.

At two o'clock in the morning, Joel's eyes began to close, and Barney covered his brother with the blanket, and turned to leave the tent.

'Barney?' murmured Joel, sleepily.

'What is it?'

'She never haunted you, did she? I mean Mama?'

Barney said, 'All sons are haunted by their mothers, Joel. It's what motherhood and sonhood are all about. And maybe you and I are more haunted than most.'

Outside, in the grass, Natalia Marneweck was standing with a shawl around her shoulders. The sky above her was thick with showers of stars, as if all the thousands of diamonds from the Kimberley mine had been spilled across the darkness. She turned around as Barney came out of the tent, and walked towards him.

'Your brother is good now?'

'Much better, thank you, thanks to you.'

'I have blankets here, if you want sleep.'

Barney saw that two or three red and white woven blankets had been spread out on the grass to form a bed. He looked around the encampment, and all the tents were in darkness, apart from one or two dying cooking-fires, and a flickering torch outside Jan Bloem's marquee. The wind blew stealthily across the hillside, and raised the hairs on the back of Barney's neck.

Without a word, Barney went across to the blankets, and sat down. He eased off his boots, and set them side by side in the grass. Then he struggled out of his black coat, and folded it up.

'I go stay with my cousin now,' said Natalia. 'That tent, by the fire!'

Barney, unfastening his cufflinks, looked at her. In her white woollen shawl, with her curls blowing across her face, she appeared in the darkness like a heroine from a Victorian story-book, her face and her clasped hands impossibly sweet and pretty.

'Don't go,' he said. He was surprised by his own directness. He smoothed out the blanket beside him and said, 'Stay here with me.'

There was a silence. Natalia stayed where she was, making no move towards him, but making no move away from him, either.

'You think I lie with every man?' she asked him.

'I don't think that at all. I just want you to lie with me.'

She came across, hesitated, and then squatted down beside him. She touched his forehead with the cool fingers of her left hand. 'One day I find another man to lie with,' she said. 'But the Bible says he must be my husband.'

'You think I wouldn't consider marrying you? You're beautiful.'

She leaned forward and kissed his cheek. 'You, too, are beautiful. But I must not.'

She started to get up, but Barney gripped her wrist. 'I want you to stay with me,' he insisted.

Natalia tried to tug herself away, but Barney twisted her arm around and pulled her back on to the blanket. Then he scrambled on top of her, and gripped her between his thighs.

She stared up at him, panting. 'I shall cry out,' she warned.

Barney bent his head, and kissed her. First, she turned her face away, so that he could only kiss her neck and her cheek. But then she turned back again, with a gasp, and he kissed her full on the mouth. She bit his lips, and he tasted the sharp taste of blood, but he kissed her again, and again. She let out a stifled gasp, and pushed up against his chest.

Barney was too strong for her. His wide-shouldered boxer's body was too hard with muscle, too wiry with sinew, and all those months of working on Monsaraz' farm, all those days of chopping down trees and hammering fences, all those sweaty hours of hefting animal feedbags and heaving balks of timber, all gave his passion the physical power it needed to break its way loose.

His inhibitions gave way like an earth dam collapsing in front of a winter flood. His religious ethics fell like drowned fences. His respect for his father and his guilt for his mother were both swirled away. There was nothing inside his head but a thundering torrent of released repressions, of lust and anger and love that had never found any expression. His penis was almost painfully rigid, and already quaked with spasms that blinded him to anything but taking Natalia, and to letting go that tension that Agnes Knight had been tightening up inside him all evening.

He pulled Natalia's shawl away from her shoulders, and wrenched at the bodice of her mission-school dress. The cotton tore away with a noise that reminded him for one jigsaw-puzzled second of the tailor's shop on Clinton Street; but then her heavy brown breast was bared, and he clutched it in his hand, a whole handful of softness, with a hard nipple that protruded between his fingers.

'No,' whispered Natalia, as he squeezed and caressed her bare breast, rolling the nipple between his thumb and his finger. 'No, I must not.'

She fought him, but she fought him silently, digging her fingernails into his shoulder, and wrestling her body between his tight-clenched thighs. Yet every twist of her hips aroused him more, and by the time he had gripped her tight enough to be able to pull at his own buttons; the front of his underwear was already wet with his repeated ejaculations of sperm. He said something inside his mind that approached a prayer.

Frantically, he untangled himself from his combinations, half-standing, half-hopping, to step out of his trousers. Then, naked, he forced himself down on Natalia, and snatched at the hem of her dress.

She rolled over on to her stomach, kicking at him with her heels; but Barney rolled over with her and pulled up her dress at the back, exposing her bottom.

'Natalia,' he panted, through clenched teeth. 'Natalia, please, Natalia ...'

With a muted mewling sound, Natalia tried to wriggle forward on her elbows through the grass. But now Barney seized her thighs, and dragged her back towards him. Forcefully, he parted the cheeks of her bottom with his thumbs, as if he were opening up the twin dusky-coloured halves of a large fruit. Inside the fruit, Natalia's flesh was glistening and pink, and her pungency aroused Barney even more.

He wrestled with her, and jabbed at her with his penis. Twice he struck her thigh, and twice she managed to twist herself away. But then he clutched her shoulders, and grabbed at her curls, and pulled her downwards and backwards so that she was forced to sit in his lap, and so that his hardened penis slipped inside her, deep and urgent and swollen with lust that had been confined too long.

At first, with her back arched, and her muscles as taut and dimpled as a marble by Michaelangelo, Natalia struggled against him. Then, as he thrust into her again and again, his hands grasping her breasts, one breast bare and one breast clothed, she began to struggle *with* him, until he realised by her trembling and gasps and her little birdlike cries that she wanted him, and that she had probably wanted him right from the beginning. This had not been a rape, but a demand from Natalia to show her just how strong he was prepared to be.

Towards the end, crouched together in the grass under that diamond-encrusted sky, they were thrusting together, faster and faster, like runners, or racing horses, and Barney's thighs were anointed with Natalia's slippery juices. They shuddered together, winced together in ecstatic anguish, grappled with each other for one last moment. Then it was over and they fell away from each other and lay apart on the blankets, each of them seeking breath and balance; each of them re-mapping their lives to take account of the cataclysmic landmark that both of them had just reached.

In one violent act of love, two destinies had been irrevocably altered. In five minutes, Barney had realised both his strength and his weakness, and what essential tasks now lay before him.

He grasped Natalia's wrist, and turned to stare at her. Her face glistened with sweat, and she was holding her one bare breast in her hand, absently fondling the nipple with her fingers, touching it lightly, teasing it. Her thighs were still parted, her sex sparkling in the light like diamonds, like some freshly cut-open eatable at a magical picnic under the clouds of the night.

'Do you hate me now?' Barney asked her.

Natalia stared back at him for a moment, and then shook her head.

'I shouldn't have done that,' said Barney. He sat up, and raked his fingers through his hair. 'My God, I shouldn't have done that.'

He started to look around for his discarded underwear, but Natalia sat up, too, and wrapped her arms round him, holding him close, burying her head in the middle of his naked back.

'I am already married,' she said. 'Last year, my husband die. I am so sad without him. I always say – I can never find another man – not like my husband. But you have that same look.'

Barney could feel her soft curls against his bare back, and the feeling was feminine, and reassuring, and warm. He reached one hand behind him, and touched her head gently. 'I could love you, Natalia,' he said, in a tone that almost made it a question, as if he were asking her to tell him that she could love him, too.

'You must call me Mooi Klip,' she said. 'That is what my husband always calls me.'

'Mooi Klip?'

'In Afrikaans, it means "pretty stone". It is what they call the first big diamond.'

He turned around, and kissed her smooth forehead. She

smelled of musky perfume, and Pears soap, and sweat. 'All right, Mooi Klip,' he told her. 'You shall be my pretty stone from now on.'

They slept together in the blankets until the first wan light of dawn, when the birds began to call across the valley, and the grass rustled in the wind. Then, when Barney was still half-asleep, the girl called Mooi Klip folded back her bed and went to light up a cooking-fire, so that by the time the sun came over the eastern horizon, she was able to bring Barney an enamel mug of hot tea and some warm, doughy bread.

Barney sat up on his elbow, sipping the tea and munching the bread, while Mooi Klip knelt beside him and watched him with the pleased, proprietorial interest of a new bride.

Stafford Parker arrived in the Griqua camp at noon, red-faced and white-bearded, and accompanied by his usual entourage of magistrates and diggers and Griqua interpreters. He had not come unheralded: a Griqua boy had run in through the lines of tents about half an hour before, and warned Jan Bloem that he should expect an important visitor. Accordingly, Jan Bloem was standing outside his marquee dressed in his best Sunday suit, while his mother sat not far away in a red plush drawing-room chair which had been a gift from Sir Philip Woodhouse, dressed in an emerald-green promenading gown with a prominent bustle, and smoking a clay pipe.

Barney had spent most of the morning with Joel, who had developed a slight fever, and was thrashing around on his cot in a chilly sweat. But when he heard two or three lookout rifles crackle on the ridge, he knew that Stafford Parker was coming, and he left Joel with Mooi Klip while he opened the tent flap and went outside.

'Well, then, how do you do,' said Stafford Parker, planting himself in front of Jan Bloem with his fists on his hips. It was an aggressive, confident pose, and it reminded Barney of Mr Knight. Barney came closer, so that he was standing only a few feet away from Mrs Bloem's parlour chair, and close enough to smell her Navy Cut tobacco.

'I do very well,' smiled Jan Bloem. 'How do *you* do?'

Stafford Parker reached behind him with a peremptory wiggle of his fingers; and one of his magistrates, a thin man with a particularly knobbly nose and a particularly blue chin, handed him a Bible. Parker held it up. and Barney recognised it at once as the Bible from which his Griqua friend Piet Steyn had been giving Joel 'comfort to the afflicted'. They must have accidentally left it behind on the ground when they cut Joel free from his bonds.

'This *Bible*,' said Stafford Parker, with enunciation so clear that it echoed, like the sound of two housebricks being clapped together, 'this *Bible* was found in an incriminating place.'

'Ah,' smiled Jan Bloem. 'And where would that be?'

'That would be a few hundred yards south of the mine,' Stafford Parker told him. 'At the very spot where a convicted diamond-thief was staked out for a sentence of three days, or death, whichever came the sooner.'

'I see,' Jan Bloem replied, unhelpfully.

'Well, apparently you *don't* see,' snapped Stafford Parker, shaking the Bible as if it were a box of sugar. 'Because the convicted diamond-thief was illegally released, and given refuge, and this Bible was left behind by whoever it was who let him go.'

'You have proof of that,' said Jan Bloem, expressionlessly. He turned to smile at his mother, who was relighting her pipe with a great deal of puffing and sucking and waving of matches.

'What proof do I require?' Stafford Parker demanded. 'Here is the Bible. The Bible is proof in itself.'

'It may have been dropped on another occasion,' Jan Bloem suggested. 'It may have been stolen from its owner, and dropped there as a deliberate red-herring.'

'I don't care for your mission-school English,' growled Stafford Parker. 'And I don't care for your excuses, either. It says in the flyleaf of this Bible that it belongs to Piet Steyn, and Piet Steyn, as everybody in Griqualand is quite aware, is a second cousin of yours. So if the convicted man is anywhere at all, he is here, with you, and with your mother, and all the rest of your cronies.'

'And what if he is?' asked Jan Bloem.

Stafford Parker stared at him with a grim, set, colonial

155

expression. 'If he is here, my good Mr Bloem, then I shall have the right to cause you more trouble than you have ever had to cope with before. I shall have the right to arrest you personally, and your second cousin, and everybody else in this encampment who has given the fugitive any assistance.'

Barney came forward now, and rested his hand on the cresting-rail of Mrs Bloem's chair. The old woman looked up at him curiously, with the face of a benign orang-utan, and nodded with every word he spoke, although she understood no English whatsoever.

'Your fugitive *is* here, Mr Parker,' he said. 'But he is under my care, not Mr Bloem's, and his release was entirely my responsibility. Nobody here is to blame.'

Stafford Parker turned and glared at Barney, and then said loudly, 'I know you. I know your face. I've met you before.'

'My name is Barney Blitz. We met at Gong Gong once. You called me a kike.'

'Aha,' said Stafford Parker brusquely, although Barney could tell that he was embarrassed.

Barney said, 'Your diamond-thief, as you call him, was not far away from death. I rescued him as an act of humanity. I also rescued him because I want to challenge your sentence against him – properly and fairly, in a court of law, and in front of a jury of twelve men.'

'That's absurd,' retorted Stafford Parker, waving his hand dismissively. 'He's already been convicted. His sentence has already been passed. If everybody challenged every sentence I handed down, this place would be chaos.'

'We should arrest you too, you know,' put in the blue-chinned magistrate, in a sharp Lancashire accent.

'Yes, we should,' huffed Stafford Parker, although it was clear that he was not going to try it. The everyday needs of law and order in Kimberley were generally satisfied by the trial and punishment of murder, claim-jumping, and diamond smuggling, those three. Any other offences such as rape, or harbouring a fugitive, or public drunkenness, were usually too complicated and confusing to be worth pursuing.

'You can arrest me if you like,' Barney challenged. 'But that will only make your miscarriage of justice more serious. I have a lawyer who is willing to make representations on Mr Have-

156

mann's behalf, and I think for the sake of your own reputation you should pay us some heed.'

'A lawyer? What lawyer?'

'A lawyer of considerable reputation, and that's all I'm going to say.'

'You're bluffing,' said Stafford Parker. 'You're doing nothing more than playing for time, while Havemann recovers his strength. If I let you appeal, and set a date for a hearing, he'll be scuttling off to the border as soon as he's well enough.'

Barney reached into the pocket of his coat and took out the £212 which Harold Feinberg had paid him for his diamonds. He held the money up, and said, 'There are more than two hundred pounds here. You can keep them as a bond.'

Stafford Parker frowned, while his magistrate leaned forward and whispered something in his ear. Then Parker replied, 'If I take that money, who's to say that you didn't bribe me? And why should I hear an appeal anyway? If I agree to hear an appeal, that would only be admitting that I might have been wrong in the first place.'

'Perhaps you were, through no fault of your own,' said Barney. 'But could you bear to live for the rest of your life with the death of an innocent man on your hands, all because you were too stubborn to listen to an appeal?'

Stafford Parker conferred with his magistrate again. 'I want a good sound jury,' he said. 'No Griquas, or foreigners. And no Americans, either.'

'Very well,' agreed Barney.

Parker was silent for a moment, pouting, while he thought about Barney's suggestion. His magistrate waited with obvious unease. Eventually, he said. 'All right. If you really believe you have a case to be heard, I'll hear it.'

'Do you want the money?' asked Barney.

Stafford Parker shook his head. 'You can keep your bond. I'm a man of my word, and I hope for your sake that you are, too.' He raised one rigid finger. 'Because if you prove to be playing me false, Mr Blitz, I'll have my dogs on you, and my dogs will chase you through thick and thin, through every part of this colony, just to get at your miserable Jewish guts.'

'*Kishkehs*, we call them,' grinned Barney.

Stafford Parker, however, had already turned on his heel and started to march away up the hillside. Only his followers looked over their shoulders at Barney, and Jan Bloem, and the old orang-utan woman sitting amidst the tents in her red drawing-room chair.

Jan Bloem thrust his hands into the pockets of his black Sunday suit, and regarded Barney with interest.

'You're strong today,' he said, pointedly. 'How come you're suddenly so strong?'

Barney shrugged. 'Joel's my brother. I think I've found a purpose at last, a purpose that I didn't have before.'

'Are you in love with somebody?' asked Jan Bloem.

Mrs Bloem cackled, and spat tobacco-coloured saliva into the grass. Barney did not answer, but found it impossible to suppress a smile.

Jan Bloem turned his head and focused his eyes on Natalia Marneweck's tent. 'Rik Marneweck was a close, special friend to me,' he said. 'I swore to him when he died that I would watch out for his widow.'

'I won't hurt her,' said Barney.

Jan Bloem made a face. 'You can't make promises like that. Even Jesus didn't make promises like that.'

Late on Saturday evening, a boy came with a message that a re-trial had been set for Monday afternoon, at three o'clock, and that Stafford Parker had already selected a jury.

'He'll have chosen nothing but Protestant bigots,' protested Joel, sitting up in bed with a blue china bowl of *sosatie* that Mooi Klip had made for him. His eyes were circled with dark shadows, and he was still unshaven, but he was much brighter than before, and he was already talking about ways in which he and Barney could make their fortunes in Zanzibar, growing cloves, or in Madagascar.

'That's precisely what I'd hoped for,' said Barney. He glanced up at Joel and smiled.

'You'd *hoped* for Protestants? One of the most damning points Stafford Parker made against me in my first trial was that I was a Jew. A thief by heritage, he said. I'd tried to hide it, of course. You know what they're like around here. But one of the diggers remembered me from the ship I used to work on; and that was that. Being a Jew was almost enough to have me staked out on its own.'

'Nonetheless,' said Barney, quietly, 'I was hoping for a Protestant jury. They'll have a choice, you see, between believing the evidence of a kaffir, a mere black, and giving some credit to a white man, whether he's Jewish or not. What I'm trying to do here, quite frankly, is play a greater prejudice off against a lesser prejudice.'

Joel scooped up the last of his *sosatie* and set the bowl down beside his cot. 'I always thought you had a good head for business,' he told Barney. There was admiration in his voice, but also a slight seasoning of jealousy. 'Maybe I should have insisted that you came along with me from the start.'

'There was Mama,' said Barney.

Joel rubbed at his eyebrow with his fingertips, as if he were trying to erase a smut of persistent guilt. 'Yes,' he said. 'I hadn't forgotten.'

'You shouldn't blame yourself,' said Barney. 'It wasn't your fault any more than it was my fault.'

'Maybe it wasn't. But you still dreamed about her blood on your hands, didn't you? And *I* still dream about the way she looked that night I walked out on you.'

Mooi Klip came into the tent and picked up the lantern to lower the wick. 'Joel,' she admonished him, 'it's time you sleep.'

'Who needs a mother?' asked Joel, with an ironic smile. 'This girl tells me when to wake up, when to go to sleep, when to wash my teeth. She feeds me and bathes me and treats me like her own.'

Barney stood up. 'You'll be better tomorrow. And by Monday you'll be fighting fit. Fit enough to fight the Diggers' Association, anyway.'

'When are you seeing that lawyer friend of yours?'

'Tomorrow, after church.'

'Church? They let Jews into church?'

'Mr Barney they let into church. Mr Blitz they don't.'

Joel raked his fingers through the stubble of his beard. 'I

hope for your sake they don't find out. They'll kick your backside all the way to Capetown.'

Mooi Klip straightened Joel's blankers, and then joined Barney outside the tent. Barney took her hand, and drew her close to him. He kissed her, and she closed her eyes and kissed him in return, softly, quickly, as if she were tasting *moskonfyt* on his lips.

She said, 'In two days, we go back to Klipdrift.'

'Who's going back to Klipdrift?'

'Jan Bloem, his mother, all of us. He speaks already to the British, and the diggers. Now he goes home.'

Barney touched her cheek with his fingertips. 'And what will you do? Will you go back to Klipdrift along with him?'

'My family is there. My mother, my father, and my brothers.'

'I know. But will you go back?'

Mooi Klip lowered her head. 'Do you want me to?' she asked him.

Barney licked his lips in uncertainty. When he had taken Mooi Klip in the grass, when he had first made love to her, he had not thought for a single second about the complications of starting a liaison with a coloured girl. She was pretty, and she had a gentle way about her that fascinated him, and made him feel like holding her close and protecting her. But this was Cape Colony, and she was a half-caste.

Mooi Klip whispered, 'The Griquas say that anything you know in your heart in the first minute you meet – that knowing will stay good for a whole lifetime.'

Barney looked at her, and then smiled. 'I know. That was one of the little mottoes that Jan Bloem gave me when he realised we were lovers – that, and a few paragraphs out of the Bible.'

'But something is wrong? You smile, but your eyes look hurting.'

She was right. Barney was already feeling pain. It was close to the pain that he had felt for his mother; and to the pain he still felt whenever he renounced his Jewishness; but this time it was more stifling, like the first pangs of a heart seizure. And, in a way, that was exactly what it was.

No matter how delicate and erotic Mooi Klip was, no matter how fine a wife she would make, she was a Griqua, and if he were to marry her, or even have her living in, then he knew that he would be sacrificing any chances he might ever have of making a name and a fortune for himself in Cape Colony business. He had already meet three or four of those unhappy men who had married or shacked up with blacks, and they were invariably disillusioned, defeated, and scraping their living from the fringes of white society. Storekeepers, grooms, or servants. White, but not socially acceptable.

If Barney could court and marry a girl like Agnes Knight, however, and make a friend of her father, then his future would start to look far more promising. A girl like Agnes would give him immediate credentials. It did not matter what legal trickery her father had been involved in when he was practising in Capetown; here in Kimberley he was white, well-spoken, and the billiards secretary of the Kimberley Club. Barney was smitten by Mooi Klip, but he had not been blinded to the fierce reality of Cape Colony's social stratification. Mooi Klip could only bring him poverty and humiliation; Agnes Knight could bring him wealth.

Barney had his mother's passion, but his father's sanity. In him, his parents' differences would rail against each other in perpetuity, even though both of them were dead.

'I shall go, then,' said Mooi Klip, in response to Barney's silence.

'I think I love you,' Barney told her.

'No,' she said.

'Listen – we've only been together for a couple of days,' said Barney. 'It's too sudden for you to ask me to take you along. I don't live a particularly easy life. And now I've got Joel to take care of, too – at least until we've sorted out his legal problems.'

Mooi Klip touched a finger to his lips, indicating that he should not say anything more. But he held her finger in his fist, and moved it away.

'Those aren't excuses. I don't need to make excuses for anything. What I'm trying to tell you is that I think I love you, but I have other things to do. When they're done, I'll come to Klipdrift and find you.'

She searched his face for reassurance that he was telling her the truth. Her eyes were myopic with tears.

'Don't tell me you love me if you don't,' she said. 'I only give myself in all my life to three men. One, a young lover. Then my husband. And now you. You look beautiful when I first see you. Now, I love you – more than you love me. Don't play with me. Don't tell me you love me if you don't.'

'Natalia . . .'

'Mooi Klip.'

Barney held her tight. He lifted his head towards the clouds. 'Mooi Klip,' he repeated, in his gentlest voice. 'I love you, and one day soon I'm going to come to Klipdrift and find you.'

His destiny was shaping itself. He felt as if great and shadowy forces were moving themselves into place, in preparation for his future. And the dreams he had dreamed when he was crossing the Great Karoo began to solidify, and take on flesh.

Kimberley's Anglican church was a little white-painted building of dry timber and corrugated iron at the end of the main street, conveniently located for those who liked to pray for forgiveness as soon as possible after committing their sins right next door to Aunt Olive's Pleasure House, and opposite the Kimberley Bar.

On Sunday mornings, the white Christian élite of the diamond-digging community would assemble in the dusty churchyard in their finest clothes, to parade themselves, and exchange dignified words of greeting to each other, and reassure themselves that God, and England, were both on their side. Although they rarely admitted it, not to themselves and especially not to the Germans and the Boers and the coloureds, it was often difficult out here amongst the flies and sicknesses of a Cape Colony summer to remember that the chapel bells were still pealing across the frost-silvered lawns of Oxford, and that crumpets were still being toasted in front of a hundred thousand British coal fires.

Barney, nervous, arrived early. He stood by the picket fence in his best black suit and a clean dinner shirt which he had borrowed from a reluctant Harold Feinberg. The single church bell was clanking dolefully across the street, and huge cumulus clouds were already mounting the morning sky like castles of thickened cream. It was hot, and Barney felt as if his coat were too tight under the arms.

At last, promenading along the boardwalk at the exact moment which Mr Knight had judged would be late enough to turn everybody's heads and yet not too late to be considered vulgar, came Agnes and Faith, both in severe but well-styled Sunday dresses, followed by Mr and Mrs Knight, arm in arm, with benign and superior smiles.

Barney took off his hat as the two girls entered the church-yard.

'Good morning,' he said, with a small bow. 'You both look charming.'

Mr Knight imperiously turned his head this way and that, to make sure that everybody had an opportunity to notice that he had arrived, and that he had clipped his whiskers. Mrs Knight's smile came in and out like the sun behind the clouds, whenever she remembered where she was, and what her firm instructions were.

'Not such a good turnout this morning,' remarked Mr Knight. 'Where are the Maymans? Bad form, you know, not turning out for communion. It's the one thing that keeps us together, keeps us civilised.'

'I guess you're right,' said Barney. 'Listen, I've seen my Jewish friend again. The one whose case I want you take?'

'Later, dear chap, later,' Mr Knight told him, with a dis-missive wave. 'I'm not so sure it's the kind of case I want to have anything to do with.'

'Stafford Parker's agreed to a re-trial, tomorrow afternoon. He's picking a jury.'

'Is he now?' said Mr Knight, suddenly interested. 'Well, that should be an event-and-a-half.'

'That's what I thought,' said Barney, coaxingly. 'And if you were to defend my friend, and win ... well, then, think what a legal feather in your cap that would be. They'd report it in all the newspapers, and it would probably be heard of in London.'

'Ah, London ...' mused Mr Knight, lifting his chin at the

very thought of it. 'Well, my dear fellow, we'll see. Come back to the house after church, and we'll talk it over. It doesn't allow us much time, though, does it? Monday afternoon.'

'It won't be a case of evidence and fact,' Barney told him. 'It'll be a case of prejudice and fear. That's what you're good at, though, aren't you?'

Mr Knight gave a tight grimace. 'It is one of my specialties, yes, I suppose.'

Faith, impatient to take Barney's arm, said, 'Shall we go in, Papa?' Agnes, who was obviously sulking, stood a few feet away in the shade of a scraggly thornbush, her grey reticule twisted in her hands as if she were surreptitiously choking a chicken. Barney took Faith's arm, and then drew her across to where Agnes was standing, and held out his hand for Agnes's arm as well.

'Neither of you will object if I escort you *both* into church, will you?' he grinned.

Faith stiffened. Barney could feel her arm, which at first had wrapped around his so responsively, become as rigid as a wooden Indian's. But Agnes came forward, all smiles and little curtseys, and whispered, 'Obliged, Mr Barney. Obliged.'

As the last leaden clank of the church bell summoned them inside, the congregation crowded in through the door and took their places on their allotted pews. Inside the church, it was as hot and airless as a Dutch oven. There was an altar, spread with a crochet tablecloth, in front of which stood the Anglican priest, a pimply young curate from Wimbledon who had felt the call to undertake missionary work after a sad and sorry courtship. Beside him at an upright piano sat an elderly English woman with spectacles and a feathery hat.

The pews themselves were fine – solid carved mahogany from St David's in Capetown – dragged across the desert by ox-cart. The Knights sat close to the front, amongst the more illustrious members of the Kimberley Club, and two or three of the richer English prospectors. Between them, they gave off a powerful smell of lavenderwater and mothballs. Barney wedged himself in between Agnes and Faith and hoped that God would forgive him for worshipping Him in such surroundings, and in such unfamiliar words.

They sang hymns – and Barney had never in his life before heard such ragged, mournful singing. Mr Knight was in strong voice, and his quavering baritone held on to the last note of every verse long after the rest of the congregation had fallen silent. Then, they took communion, and like the rest of the assembly Barney shuffled forward to kneel before the altar and partake of the body and blood of Jesus Christ.

He closed his eyes as the communion wafer dissolved on his tongue, but there was no earthquake, nor was his brain vaporised inside his skull. He returned to his seat, and Agnes for one moment laid her small white-gloved hand on his thigh, and smiled to herself.

After communion, the young curate stood before the lectern and gave, in an odd barking voice, like an outraged chow, a mercifully short sermon about the price of redemption. As Barney sat with his leg pressed close to the warmth of Agnes's thigh, some of the words came through to him like an accusation.

'We all know the sad history of man's sin, and its penalty. Sin and death were somehow bound up with each other. It was said of the forbidden fruit, "In the day that thou eatest thereof thou shalt surely die." Man did eat thereof. God loved him still; and yet God was perfectly just, and therefore He must keep to His word, and exact and due penalty!'

Agnes, in her pale grey dress, with its tiny lace collar and its grey silk sash, kept her eyes on her hymnbook. Faith bustled around in her seat as if she were sitting on nettles, and came out from time to time with small explosive sighs. Only Mr Knight's attention was fixed exclusively on the sermon; or at least it appeared to be. Perhaps he was considering his own sins, as well as the sins of the people he had defended. Perhaps he was simply criticising the young curate's staccato delivery.

Back in the sunshine, and the dust, Mr Knight tugged on his gloves and said, 'Sin? You wonder what a raw carrot of a curate can possibly know about sin,' and that was all. He took his wife's bewildered arm and led her out of the churchyard and back along the street. Barney, with Faith huffing alone on one side of him, and Agnes pressing close to him on the other, followed a few yards behind.

At home, over glasses of paralysingly dry sherry, Mr Knight invited Barney to tell him more about Joel's offence, and what had happened out at Jan Bloem's camp. In the end, Mr Knight tented his fingers in front of his face, so that Barney could only see one of his eyes, and regarded him very thoughtfully.

'Jewish, you say, this Havemann? And not called Havemann at all, but Blitz? Well, we'd better keep that quiet. Juries don't care much for aliases. If a man has an alias, it means he has something to hide, and that in itself is an admission of guilt. Not the guilt in question, perhaps; but you know how illogical people can be. Especially diggers. If they were logical, they wouldn't be out here scrabbling in the dirt for dia-monds.'

Barney took a sip of his sherry and then set the glass back on the rickety wine table beside him. 'Do you think you can get him off, that's the question?'

'He admits that he actually stole the diamonds, you say?' Barney nodded.

'Well, of course, he mustn't admit that before a jury,' said Mr Knight. 'In fact, he must be outraged that anyone could suggest such a thing. He must be bursting with righteous indignation. He must look his accusers in the eye and tell them they're liars. But on no account must he call them *Gentile* liars; and on no account must he use any Yiddish expression which might remind the jury that he is a Jew. He must talk of the kaffirs as unreliable mongrels, and the whites as equals. Well – *nearly* equals. He must show that he knows his place in the world, too. He must conduct himself with the manner of, say, a wrongfully accused moneylender.'

Barney looked up. Agnes was coming into the room with a tray of cutlery, ready to lay the table for Sunday lunch. There was an unpleasant smell of boiling vegetables coming from the kitchen. Agnes polished the soup spoons on her apron, and pretended to admire herself in their curved reflections. Barney found himself thinking of her pale thighs, and whether the curls beneath her petticoats were blonde or brown. She was a tease, Agnes, and she stirred him.

'What do you think of that, then?' asked Mr Knight.

'I'm sorry – what do I think of what?' Barney flustered.

'What do you think of declaring a mis-trial on the grounds that nobody can produce any evidence? Nobody white, that is, or even coloured. You could find out for me, if you would, if any of Mr Havemann's accusers are converts to Christianity. Better if they're not. Better if they believe in Unkulunkulu, or Mdali. That's the odd question, of course. Is it possible to save a kaffir's sould if he doesn't have one? Does he acquire a soul, once he's been converted? Very interesting argument altogether. So what do you say, old chap?'

'It sounds fine to me,' said Barney, watching Agnes prancing out of the room.

'Good,' said Mr Knight, and stood up. 'I think we're going to pull this one off, by a short margin. It won't be easy, but I think we're going to pull it off. Oh – and one thing more. I've arranged for you to come round to the club on Wednesday evening, so that you can see what you think of it. See what the members think of you, too. Some of them don't like your Yankees, I'll admit, but you may be lucky.'

'I shall look forward to it,' said Barney.

'Course you will,' nodded Mr Knight. 'And there's something else, too. I can't help noticing that you and Agnes seem to get along rather well.'

Barney felt himself flush. 'We . . . well, I believe we like each other.'

'Good. I'm pleased. There's precious little a girl of Agnes's age can do, out in a God-deserted place like this. I'd be pleased to see her courted by a reasonable chap like yourself. Why don't you come round after the trial tomorrow, and take some dinner? We can play some music, perhaps, and you two can get to know each other better.'

'I'd like that,' Barney assured him.

'Course you would. Now, I'm sorry I can't invite you to stay right now, but the Wilberforces are coming round. You know Kenneth Wilberforce, do you? Well, he's very dull, between you and me, but he's membership secretary, and I have to humour the silly ass from time to time.'

'Father,' said Faith, putting her head around the kitchen door and pointedly ignoring Barney. 'Mama asks if you're ready to carve the meat.'

167

Mr Knight clapped his hands together. 'Meat!' he exclaimed. 'Something for a man to sink his teeth into! I'll see you to-morrow morning, my dear chap, along with Mr Havemann, and we'll make ourselves ready for the trial. Meat! That's what it is, to a fellow like me. Meat and drink!'

Later that Sunday, Joel and Barney and Mooi Klip went for a short walk down the slope of the Griqua encampment. Joel limped along with the help of a roughtly-carved walking-stick which a cousin of Piet Steyn's had made for him. He had shaved, and dressed in a blue checked workshirt and canvas trousers; and although he was still in pain, and short of breath, he was plainly very much better.

They reached a small sandstone outcropping, where Joel eased himself down with his back against the rock, and Barney and Mooi Klip sat beside him.

'You wouldn't think such a beautiful country could turn out so goddamned hard, would you?' said Joel.

'It can be licked,' replied Barney. 'There's nothing on earth that can't be licked, if you tackle it the right way.'

'What have you been doing? Farming!' Joel retorted. 'You don't know what it's like when you're scrabbling in the dirt looking for diamonds. It's hell on earth.'

'I shall soon find out.'

'What are you talking about?'

Barney ran his hand through his brown curls. 'Tomorrow, after the trial, we're going to set up in business together, you and I. Blitz and Blitz, diamond diggers.'

'I shouldn't count on it.'

'Why not? You've got one of the best lawyers in Kimberley.'

'I'm a Jew, Barney, and I'm well known around here. You don't seriously think they're going to let me go? You don't seriously think that Stafford Parker's going to undermine his own prestige by reversing his decision?'

Barney nodded. 'I believe he will. In any case, you'd better hope that he will.'

'This is against my better judgement, you know,' said Joel. 'I should have made a run for Wesselstroom as soon as I was able to move one leg in front of the other.'

'You'll get off,' said Barney, confidently.

Joel looked out across the blue misted valley. 'If I do,' he said, 'then Blitz and Blitz it's going to be. Fifty-fifty, down the middle. Partners. But I don't believe for one single moment that I will.'

After half an hour, Barney and Mooi Klip helped Joel back to the tent. Then they went together to the tent of Mooi Klip's second cousin, who was spending the evening with Jan Bloem, singing hymns and carols and some of the old Hottentot songs from long ago.

Inside, the tent smelled of incense and cooking. There was a wide straw pallet, wrapped in blankets, and a large wicker hamper in which Mooi Klip's cousin carried her belongings. On the blue poplar tent support hung a sad framed portrait of Jesus, surrounded by His cherubim.

Barney stripped off his shirt, and pulled down his trousers. He was already erect with anticipation. Mooi Klip turned her back and unbuttoned her dress with modesty, silhouetted by the small storm lantern which her second cousin had left burning for them.

She stepped out of her dress, and turned. Her shy nakedness made Barney quiver. She was brown-skinned, heavy-breasted, and her stomach had a sensual roundness which reminded Barney of an old French painting he had once seen, as a boy, on a pushcart in New York.

He buried his fingers in her hair, and kissed her. He said, 'You know that I'll come back for you as soon as I can.'

'No,' she said. 'I don't know that. But tonight I do not want to think about it.'

They lay down on the straw pallet side by side and stared closely into each other's eyes, as though each were concealing a cosmic mystery somewhere behind the darkness of their pupils. Barney kissed Mooi Klip's shoulder and it tasted slightly salty and perfumey, and it was like no other taste he had ever come across before.

They made love with the slowness and rhythm of a brass clock, and there were moments when Barney seemed to forget where he was, and what was happening, as if he were sleeping and waking and sleeping again. He could not tell how much time passed. But he remembered opening his eyes again and again to see Mooi Klip with her eyes closed, or looking at him intently, or sleeping, and all the while the storm lantern flickered like a signal from a forgotten past.

Toward midnight, they reached together a peak of almost unbearable sexual intensity, a moment when Barney looked downwards at the curves of their bodies, and saw how deeply he was penetrating her. Then there was a stillness between them, an unquiet peace, that same feeling that all lovers know when their lovemaking is ended. Why did it have to end, and will we ever make love again?

The music from Jan Bloem's marquee abruptly ended. Barney raised himself on his elbow and looked down at Mooi Klip with love and pain and a little fear. He touched her face with his hand, and then he said, 'I guess I'd better go.'

They assembled in the open air, diggers and gamblers and whiskery dignitaries and whores, and for most of that afternoon the clattering and shovelling and shouting of De Beers New Rush was silenced. This was a serious matter: the re-trial of a convicted diamond thief. And whatever the outcome of it, whatever Stafford Parker finally decided, that decision would affect the diamond diggers for years to come.

It was a hot day, intensely still. The horizons rippled and shifted, and heat flowed off the corrugated-iron rooftops like clear syrup. Up above the gathering of diggers, in the cloudless sky, hawks circled and circled as if they were too idle to swoop down on their natural prey, and the moon hung over the western horizon, pale-faced and friendless, an uninvited reminder of the night to come.

A leather-topped desk had been dragged out into the dust for Stafford Parker and his magistrates, and two fumbling kaffirs had propped up over it a wonky canvas shade, with fringes. The body of the court was made up of fifty or sixty chairs, of all shapes and sizes – Windsor chairs, wheelbacks, ladderbacks, and riempie-thong chairs – and Joel and Barney and Mr Knight sat at the side of Stafford Parker's desk on a broken chapel pew. Joel had heavily bandanged his left leg on Mr Knight's specific instructions ('make it appear as if you have suffered enough already') and his stick was propped against the seat.

At two o'clock, everybody was gathered, and Stafford Parker took his place in a high-backed chair to hear Joel's appeal. He tucked his thumbs into the pockets of his light grey vest, and raised his chin so that his white beard was lifted like an oriole's tail, and said, 'This court of the Digger's Republic is now in session.'

There was a murmur throughout the crowd, and Stafford Parker banged a gavel on his desk in protest. 'Let us have order. The Diggers' Protection Association and the Diggers' Republic were founded on the notion of order. Let it prevail today.'

Stafford Parker's blue-chinned magistrate stood up, and said, 'We are considering today an appeal by Mr Joel Havemann, of Claim 172, here at Kimberley Mine, against his sentence last week of staking-out, which was occasioned by his conviction for diamond thieving. Mr Havemann was released from his staking-out by friends – quite illegally – but he is represented here today by Mr Knight – who assures us that Mr Havemann can justify his escape, and also that he can justify his crime.'

There was another flurry of argument and scuffling, and Stafford Parker beat at his desk as if he were trying to flatten a sheet of gold. 'I have decided that this case should be heard,' he cried out, in a strained voice, 'and heard it will be!'

Gradually, the assembly came to order. The jury, who were sitting opposite Joel and Barney on two more pews, were as noisy and disorderly as everybody else, and when Barney looked them over, he could see why. Stafford Parker may have been playing at judicial fairness by allowing Joel's appeal to be heard in public, but he certainly was not taking any chances on the outcome. The twelve good men and true were crimson-faced Anglo-Saxons, all of them – the ill-mannered graduates of some of England's less honoured public schools – the kind of men who became planters and traders and Crown Agents. If Barney had not actually been depending on a jury that was bigoted at heart and crass in intellect, he would have despaired. They sat on their benches as if they were posing for a school photograph – plump with drink, fat-thighed, and smug, and with as little experience of law or life as the First XI of some redbrick boys' academy in Leicester.

'Mr Knight,' said Stafford Parker, donnishly, 'perhaps you would like to make your representations on behalf of your client?'

Mr Knight turned to Barney, smiled like an acid-drop, then gathered his notes and stood up. This morning's briefing had not been particularly successful. Joel had admitted his guilt to Mr Knight straight away, almost aggressively, and when Mr Knight had tried to cajole him into believing that he might have been mistaken, and that the whole affair might have been, well, *imaginary*, old chap – the inevitable result of too much heat and too much cheap whiskey – Joel had called him a *shtunk*, which Mr Knight had not understood, not literally, but which had offended him deeply.

'A *shtunk*,' he had repeated, in his sharp British accent. 'A *shtunk*. So that's what you think of me.'

Barney had taken Joel aside and talked to him earnestly for five minutes, trying to convince him that Mr Knight was his only hope for his release, the only man who could help him to get his diamond claim back from the Diggers' Association, and eventually, grudgingly, Joel had agreed to co-operate. He had made it clear, though, that he did not particularly care for little brother meddling in his life. 'I'm a grown man, Barney. I can manage my own affairs. I got myself into this mess, I should be able to get myself out.'

'So it's your pride that's bothering you?' Barney had asked him.

'Maybe,' Joel had admitted. Then he had spat on the grass. Barney had never seen him spit before.

Now, Mr Knight stepped forward in front of Stafford Parker's desk, his hand tucked behind him so that his coat-tails stuck out like the black plumes of a cockerel. He paused for effect, just like he had in the Kimberley churchyard, and Barney could imagine him stepping in front of juries in England and Capetown with the same theatrical strut. In the High Court in London, his pose may not have seemed particularly original, or impressive; but out here, in front of a motley crowd of diamond diggers, it was magnificent.

'There appears before you now a man who was rescued from out of the very maw of death ... a man who had looked into the eyes of His Maker and then been snatched away. Joel Havemann, a Jew, admittedly – but a very honest and straightforward member of his race, who was convicted by the Diggers' Republic of the theft of several diamonds from the Kimberley Mine. It was said that he bribed kaffirs of the British Diamond Mining Company to pass him stones that he might illegally sell to the shadier buyers who have gathered around the fringes of this rush ... it was said that his own claim was proving barren of diamonds, and that instead he was attempting to make a fortune out of stolen stones...

'But let me ask you these questions!' exclaimed Mr Knight, swivelling around on one heel, and raising a rigid finger. 'Let me ask you if any of you knew Joel Havemann to be rich, to be the kind of man who lavished money on himself and his friends as if it were water! Let me ask you if you knew of any act of dishonesty that Joel Havemann ever committed! Joel Havemann worked a claim, and any of you need only to walk out to that claim to see how deep Joel Havemann has dug, how much strenuous effort he has expended. Does a dishonest man ever bother to work at all? If he intended to make his living by stealing, by dealing with the IDB buyers, then why did he bother to lift a single finger to excavate his claim? Why didn't he just waylay the kaffirs of the British Diamond Company on their way back to their shelters, and relieve them of their ill-gotten diamonds then?'

Now Mr Knight let his chins settle in his collar, and he pouted with offended righteousness. 'Far be it from me to suggest that the British Diamond Mining Company had a covetous eye on Mr Havemann's claim, which was contiguous with theirs, and which barred their way to the acquisition of a whole block of claims. Far be it! And far be it from me to suggest that those kaffirs who gave evidence against my client at his so-called trial last week were guilty of distorting reality. Yet – if you examine a map of the claims on the Kimberley Mine – it does strike you, doesn't it, that Mr Havemann's claim could have been quite an irritation to the British Diamond Mining Company; and it does strike you, doesn't it, that if those

173

kaffirs who were said to have supplied Mr Havemann with diamonds could be bribed by Mr Havemann, then equally they could have been bribed by the British Diamond Mining Company to perjure themselves in the interests of the company's financial expansion.

'Money talks,' said Mr Knight, narrowing his eyes towards the jury. 'And the more money, the less truth.'

Barney, sitting back on his pew, could see that the jury were interested but not totally convinced. One or two of them had folded their arms and clenched their jaws as if to show that no amount of clever argument and cajolery could swerve them from their opinion that Jews were dishonest, and that Joel, being a Jew, was therefore a liar and a thief. It was nearly three o'clock now, and the heat was roraring away like a furnace. In the second and third rows of chairs, the ladies began to wave their fans as furiously as a gathering of clipped piegeons. Barney saw Agnes, and caught her eye, and Agnes smiled at him coyly from the shade of her parasol.

Mr Knight said, 'I am sure that a representative of the British Diamond Mining Company will shortly get to his feet and tell you that my suggestions are utterly unfounded; that the British Diamond Mining Company looked upon Mr Havemann as nothing more than an industrious neighbour, and that even if his claim were standing in their way, they would have accepted the economic and practical problems with equilibrium and stiff upper lips. This representative may not tell you that the British Diamond Mining Company was the first to enter an offer for claim No. 176 upon Mr Havemann's conviction last week – but then, we could not possibly expect him to, could we?'

There was an expostulation of protest from a gentleman in muttonchop sidewhiskers and a tall beige hat who was sitting on the opposite side of the court, but Stafford Parker rapped his gavel again, and the gentleman subsided, and contented himself with industriously wiping his hatband.

'I wish to say one thing more,' said Mr Knight, in a quiet but distinct voice. 'The evidence that was brought against my client was the evidence of kaffirs alone. Ignorant, uneducated, and bewildered servants of the British Diamond Mining Company. Now, when this court first made its decision to convict

174

Mr Havemann, it may understandably have been incensed with what it heard. It may have been in a mood of righteousness and vengeance, which – when you consider how vital the discovery of diamonds is to all of our livelihoods – can be seen to have been fully justified.

'However, because of his ignorance, because of his want of enlightenment, because he was born to be a servant and a subordinate, the kaffir cannot justifiably be held to be a human being ... not in the same Biblical sense as a white man. Does it not say in Psalm 49 that regardless of a man's honour, *if he understandeth not*, then he shall perish like the beasts. Well, the kaffir understandeth not, and therefore, sad for him, he can only be regarded as a beast. A good, obedient beast, maybe, but a beast all the same.

'And there is no court of law in the world, Mr Parker, and gentlemen – there is no court of law in the whole world which can rightly convict a man on the evidence of beasts.'

Mr Knight, with solemn windbaggery, quoted the precedent of the Polo Pony; and Barney could see that Stafford Parker was suitably impressed. Then Mr Knight sat down, and invited anyone in the court to cross-question his client 'to their heart's, and their curiosity's, contentment.'

But Stafford Parker stood up, and banged his gavel, and looked around the assembly with a stare that silenced everyone, and certainly forestalled any questioning.

'Mr Knight,' he said, 'has spoken most eloquently on his client's behalf. He has raised doubts about his client's guilt which, in my opinion, have made the imposition of a sentence of staking-out questionable, to say the least. He is right: your unconverted kaffir is not an intelligent being in the accepted sense of the words. And, therefore, although I am reversing my own decision, and publicly accepting that my earlier judgement may have been incorrect, I direct that this jury find the Jew Joel Havemann to be not guilty of diamond trafficking, and that his claim should be returned to him.'

There was a babbling uproar for a moment, but then Stafford Parker banged everybody into silence again.

'I must set one condition on Joel Havemann's release, however; and that is that he remains under the supervision of his lawyer, or of some other responsible person. Obviously, he strayed from the accepted code of behaviour. How seriously, I am not now prepared to say; or to condemn him for it. He has been sufficiently punished already. But I must require that he is supervised.'

Mr Knight bobbed up from his seat, and said, 'I regret that Mr Havemann is no more than a client of mine, Mr Parker. I don't really think that I can accept responsibility for his future behaviour.'

'Is there anyone who can?' asked Stafford Parker.

Barney hesitated. He had been trying to avoid Stafford Parker's eye since the trial had begun, since Stafford Parker knew him for a Jew. Now, if he stood up and accepted responsibility for his brother, Mr Knight would know him for a Jew, too. And if Mr Knight knew him for a Jew, that would mean the finish of his courtship of Agnes, and the finish of his chances at the Kimberley Club.

'If nobody will vouch for Mr Havemann's future, I can always change my mind,' said Stafford Parker. 'I can always have him flogged, and his claim confiscated.'

Barney raised his eyes. Stafford Parker was smiling straight at him, and now Barney realised what the price of Joel's freedom was going to be. Stafford Parker had not become president of the Diggers' Republic through pomposity or blindness. He had known who Joel was, and why Barney had released him, and now he was demanding that Barney should stand up in front of everybody in Kimberley and declare that he was a Jew.

In the fifth or sixth row, Barney could see Harold Feinberg, in his sun-helmet, and Harold was deliberately looking elsewhere. Maybe Harold had always been right. Maybe he should never have renounced his faith, and his heritage. Maybe the essence of being Jewish was that your destiny was inescapable.

Then, unexpectedly, at the very edge of the crowd, Barney caught sight of Mooi Klip. She was dressed in red, with a red plumed hat, and she was standing next to one of her Griqua cousins, a tall and serious half-caste in a dark funeral suit, and a black floppy necktie. She did not wave to Barney, or give any indication that she had seen him, but appeared to be waiting with great patience for the outcome of the trial.

Barney raised his hand, and then stood up. 'I will vouch for Mr Havemann,' he said.

'I can't hear you,' replied Stafford Parker. 'You'll have to speak up a little.'

'I said, I will vouch for Mr Havemann.'

'You? And who are you? Will you introduce yourself to this court?'

'You know who I am, Mr Parker. We met at Gong Gong.'

'Ah, yes,' said Stafford Parker, 'but this *court* didn't meet you at Gong Gong. Only myself, in my personal capacity.'

Barney took a breath. The sweat was clinging in his eyebrows and running down the back of his shirt. All around him was a confusion of bright pink faces and staring eyes, like a bucket of freshly-caught shrimps. 'I come from Oranjerivier, where I work a dairy farm. Dairy and beef, that is. I've known Mr Havemann for some years. In fact, I knew him in the United States, before either of us came out to the Cape.'

'Aha,' said Stafford Parker. 'So you're fellow Americans?'

'Correct, sir.'

'Do you know anything of Mr Havemann's business reputation in the United States? Was he fair? Honest, was he?'

'Oh yes, sir,' said Barney, wiping sweat away from his mouth.

'And how about his personal life. Reputable, was he? And religious?'

'Very devout, Mr Parker.'

'Well, I accept your opinion,' said Stafford Parker, 'and I'm sure that you'd make a most reliable watchdog. But what guarantee does the court have that you would maintain a continuing interest in Mr Havemann? Can we be sure that you would be willing to maintain your duties as keeper for any reasonable length of time?'

'You have my word,' said Barney, simply.

'Aha,' said Stafford Parker. 'Your word.'

'You don't trust my word?'

'I have no reason not to trust it. On the other hand, I have no reason to trust it, either. There are plenty of men in Kimberley who live their lives very fast and loose.'

'You're trying to corner me, Mr Parker,' said Barney.

Stafford Parker tugged at his beard in satisfaction. 'I'm simply trying to establish your credentials, Mr –'

There was a pause, as suspenseful and heavy in the afternoon heat as a glob of honey on the brink of dripping from a honeycomb. Everybody turned to Barney, including Mr Knight, and waited for him to finish Stafford Parker's sentence for him.

Barney closed his eyes. The salt perspiration stung the pupils, like tears. Then he opened them again, and said, 'Blitz. My real name is Blitz. Mr Havemann's real name is Blitz, also. We are brothers. That, I would have thought, would be enough to quell any doubts about my continuing interest in his welfare.'

There was another burble of conversation, but Stafford Parker quickly brought the court to order.

'Well, then,' he said, 'I believe that I'm happy that Mr Havemann, or Mr Blitz, as we now know him to be, cannot be proved guilty of illicit dealing in diamonds. And I am also happy that he will be supervised in his future prospecting by a close and interested relative of the same religious and ethnological strain. Mr foreman, does the jury have any other opinion on the matter?'

A tall blond Englishman with a noticeable speech impediment stood up and said, 'We, we, we, we're happy to abide by that decision, Mr Parker. We, we, we, we thank Mr Knight for his excellent appeal.'

Stafford Parker walloped his gavel one more time. 'This court is dismissed. Thank you, gentlemen.'

Joel shook Barney by the hand. His face was glittering with sweat. 'My God, Barney, you've actually done it. And you, Mr Knight, thank you. I don't know what I can say.'

Mr Knight stood straight, and replaced his hat on his head with exaggerated care. 'It appears that the result of the appeal was a foregone conclusion,' he said, coldly. 'Mr Parker seemed already to have made up his mind.'

'I don't think so,' said Barney. 'He was very impressed by what you said.'

Mr Knight stared at Barney with disdain. 'I regret that I can't say that the admiration is mutual.'

178

'Mr Knight –' began Barney, but Mr Knight lifted a hand to silence him.

'I can understand why you deceived me,' he snapped. 'You are a Jew, and I am quite aware that many Jews feel envy and frustration which leads them to attempt to break into Christian society. But, the facts remain that you lied to me; that you made improper advances to my daughters while leading them to believe that you were eligible; and that you are a Jew. I do not mix with Jews, my family do not mix with Jews, and I can assure you here and now that there will never ever be a Jewish member of the Kimberley Club.'

Barney said, 'Agnes is fond of me. You can't deny that.'

'You can be fond of a dog until it bites you,' retorted Mr Knight.

'I would like to continue courting her,' Barney insisted.

Mr Knight pulled a sour face. 'It's quite out of the question. Courting? What on earth is the point?'

'Don't you think love is the point?'

'Love? Piffle! Agnes doesn't love you. And neither do you love Agnes. In any case, I forbid it. Now – I must go. I think I've made quite enough of an ass of myself for one day, without compounding the embarrassment.'

'Your fee?' Barney shouted at him, furious, as Mr Knight stalked off.

Without turning round, Mr Knight waved his hand dismissively. 'I want no fee. What I have had to endure from you this afternoon cannot be paid for. Not in money.'

'But you've won!'

Mr Knight stopped, and then walked back a few paces. 'I haven't won, you ninny. Stafford Parker has won. At my expense, and especially at yours.'

Barney watched Mr Knight take Agnes's arm, and tug her away from the court at a brisk march. Agnes did not turn around even once to look at Barney, and there was something about the way in which she held her head that communicated disdain, and rejection. Agnes had rubbed thighs under the dining-table with a Jew; she was not likely to be quick in forgiving herself, nor him.

At last, there was nothing but a disarray of chairs, and a

collapsed awning, and a few kaffirs sweeping up. Barney stood in the descending light of the sun, and took off his hat.

'I'm sorry,' said Joel.

'Hm,' said Barney, shaking his head. 'You've no need to be. It was my choice, to tell them that you were my brother. I'm proud of you, Joel, we'll make our fortune together, in spite of these Christians.'

From the other side of the court, walking slowly and demurely in her red dress, her hands clasped together, came Mooi Klip. She stood a little way away from Barney, her face concealed by the shadow of her hat, and waited.

'Mooi Klip,' said Barney, so quietly that she could scarcely hear him.

She came to him slowly, her hands still clasped in front of her, and then stood in front of him with tears running down her cheeks.

'I understand now,' she said, with such sympathy that Barney had to raise his eyes away from her, up to the blue and empty sky. 'I understand now everything. I'm sorry.'

Barney spent two more days in Kimberley after Joel's acquittal. Then, while Joel re-registered his claim as a fifty-fifty partnership, and cleared the site ready for further digging, Barney took Donald and Mooi Klip back down to Oranjerivier, to deliver Monsaraz his money and tell him that he was quitting Derdeheuwel for good.

There were heavy electric storms in the sky when they drove in their surrey along the banks of the Orange River, and the bush grass rippled like a fractious sea. At last they reached the avenue of poplars which led up to the farm, and Donald relaxed his hold on the reins so that the horses could trot home at their own pace.

'I feel bad things,' said Donald, as they reached the courtyard. Barney stepped down from the surrey and stretched himself, and he had to agree. The farm looked as broken-down and deserted as the first day he and Donald and Simon de Koker had driven up here. There were no horses in the stables; the krall gate was hanging loose; and it looked as if part of the feed store had been damaged by fire.

'I feel ghost,' said Mooi Klip anxiously, staying where she was on the seat of the surrey. She wore a grey travelling-coat, and a feathered hat which Barney had bought her in Kimberley, at Madame Francesca's. Strangely, she looked duskier and more Hottentot when she dressed in very severe European clothes.

Donald led the horses to a hitching-rail beside the stable, and then walked with Barney towards the house. The front door was hanging open, and the screen was lying flat on the boards of the verandah.

'Where are the kaffirs?' Barney wanted to know. 'Where's Adam Hoovstraten?'

Donald inserted two fingers in his mouth and let out a weird, carrying whistle. He waited for a while, but there was no reply. Beyond the farm buildings, on the curve of the nearby hills, the trees stood as if they had been planted on the very brink of the world. Barney said, 'Maybe Monsaraz decided to quit.'

Cautiously, Barney stepped up on to the verandah, and peered in at the front door. Dust and straw had blown into the hallway, and there were dozens of empty wine bottles lying on the carpet. 'Monsaraz?' he called. His voice sounded as flat as somebody calling into a linen cupboard.

With Donald a few steps behind him, he walked along the corridor as far as Monsaraz's bedroom. It was then that the smell first reached him; the stomach-turning odour of death, and it was all that he could do to stay where he was, and not retreat from the farmhouse as fast as possible.

'You smell that?' he asked Donald.

Donald, grey-faced, gave a nod of sickened assent.

Picking up a walking-cane from the floor, Barney pushed the door of Monsaraz's bedroom open a little wider. He did not need to go inside to see what had happened: the blinds that Monsaraz had usually kept drawn tight had been broken away from the window-frame, so that a geometric pattern of daylight fell across the bed.

Monsaraz had been hacked to pieces where he lay. There was blackened blood halfway up the wall behind the bed, and his white bearded face had fallen back at a ridiculous angle from his chest, where his assailant had half-severed his neck. His white suit was stiff with dried gore, and his waistcoat had been slit open so that he could be spectacularly disembowelled. He had been castrated, too – probably first, before any of the other injuries, so that the rutting dog of Derdeheuwel should suffer the greatest agony of all.

'Jealous husband,' remarked Donald, laconically. 'I tell him two or three times to take care.'

'My God,' whispered Barney.

They went outside again, into the breeze. Barney felt as unsteady as if he had been drinking. He grasped the verandah rail for support, and from the seat of the surrey Mooi Klip frowned at him in anxiety.

He walked across the yard. 'He's dead. Murdered. Somebody's cut him into pieces.'

Mooi Klip stared. 'What will you do?'

'I don't know what I can do. I don't know who his relatives are, or anything. I don't even know where he kept his money.'

'But the farm ... is the farm yours now?'

'I'm not sure. We're going to have to go through his papers to see if he left a will.'

Donald came over, stripping off his coat and then rolling up the sleeves of his shirt. 'I will bury him,' he said, firmly.

'You're sure? I don't know whether I could even go back in the house.'

'I was a guide, remember, Mr Blitz. Many times travellers die, and I bury them. I see worse.'

While Donald dragged Monsaraz's remains out of the bedroom, wrapped up in a brown blanket, Barney and Mooi Klip went into the drawing-room where Monsaraz had kept his disorderly array of papers and bills. Mooi Klip picked up a picture of a pretty French actress, torn roughly from a magazine, and said, 'This Monsaraz was lonely?'

'He had plenty of women – but, yes, I guess you could say he was lonely, *alav ha-sholom*.'

They were both silent as they heard the soft bumping sound of Monsaraz's bare feet being pulled along the corridor outside. Then Barney said, 'Why don't you make us some tea? The kitchen's through there.'

He sat down at Monsaraz's desk and began to sort out some of the documents. There were scores of credit and debit notes from the Credit Bank of La Coruna, as well as a heap of scrawly letters and half-finished diary entries in Portuguese. There were some dog-eared copies of a German illustrated magazine showing buxom Black Forest maidens with plaited hair, copulating with donkeys; and a small black book with a silk moiré cover which was thicketed with accounts.

Mooi Klip came back into the room just as Barney was trying to tug open the bottom left-hand drawer, which seemed to be jammed with waste paper. She said, 'Barney,' in a voice which made him look up straight away. Her hand was pressed over her mouth and her eyes were watering as if she felt sick.

She sat down shakily on the dusty sofa while Barney went into the kitchen. She had left three cups and a teapot on the table, and a tipped-over caddy of Lapsang Souchong. Barney looked around, frowning, unable to make out at first what it was that had upset her. Then he peered into the shadows of the scullery, and saw the bloody handle of a machete protruding from the sink.

He walked across the kitchen, quickly at first, but then he slowed, and stopped. Apart from the machete, the sink contained the sloppy remains of Monsaraz's genitals.

Barney went back into the drawing-room. 'I'm sorry,' he told Mooi Klip, tightly. 'I didn't know. I'm really sorry. Do you want a drink? There's bound to be some whiskey around.'

Mooi Klip shook her head. 'I feel better now. It was a shock. I don't know what it is till I look close.'

Outside, they could hear the echoing sound of a pick, as Donald dug a grave for Monsaraz in the hard-baked soil. Barney sat down again, and pulled at the bottom drawer of the desk as hard as he could. At last, with a ripping of paper, it came open, and banged on to the threadbare rug.

'My God,' said Barney, picking up crumpled handfuls of paper.

'What is it?' asked Mooi Klip. 'Is it money?'

'Is it money? British five-pound notes, hundreds of them! Just stuffed into this desk like rubbish. There must be thousands of pounds in here!'

Mooi Klip came over and stood beside him, resting a hand on his shoulder. 'You're rich, then,' she said.

Barney burrowed through the drawer, digging out more and more money. He held some of the notes up to the window, and as far as he could see they all bore watermarks from the Royal Mint, and they were all genuine.

'There must be nine or ten thousand pounds here. Maybe more. It's unbelievable.'

'What will you do with it?' asked Mooi Klip.

Barney smoothed one of the crumpled notes on his knee. He thought for a moment, and then he lowered his head. 'Nothing,' he said. 'It isn't mine.'

'But it *is* yours! Whose can it be, if it isn't yours? Monsaraz is dead!'

'Monsaraz stole it in the first place, or embezzled it. It didn't belong to him any more than it belongs to me. Why do you think a bright young man like that was rotting away in Oranjerivier? He was hiding from the people he robbed.'

'But who will ever know?' asked Mooi Klip. 'Nobody knows this money is here. If they did, they would come to take it. But even the man who killed Monsaraz did not take it.'

Barney let the smoothed-out note flutter down on to the rest of the heap. 'The man who killed Monsaraz was nothing more than a jealous kaffir. And kaffirs aren't even human, remember? The poor man had probably never seen a five-pound note in his whole life before. Apart from that – I expect he ran off as soon as he'd done what he came to do. He wanted blood, not money.'

Mooi Klip frowned. 'You will leave the money here, for somebody else?

Barney reached up and touched her hand. 'I've found something out this week,' he told her. 'I've found out that it's no use pretending that I'm anything else but a Jew.'

She shook her head. 'I don't understand you.'

'I don't understand myself. When I was crossing the Great Karoo, on my way here to Oranjerivier, I made up my mind that I was going to put my religion behind me. I didn't think my beliefs were enough to help me survive in this place. I didn't think the rabbis in New York could possibly know what it was like to think of making your fortune in a country as wild as this one.'

He nudged the drawerful of five-pound notes with his foot. 'I didn't think, either, that anyone could get rich here unless they were a Gentile. How could I make friends with men like Stafford Parker, being a Jew? How could I become a member of the Kimberley Club? How could I court a girl like Agnes Knight?'

Mooi Klip caressed his fingers. She said nothing.

'Well, pretending to be a Gentile doesn't work,' said Barney. 'There isn't any disguise that can hide the fact that you're a Jew. Not masks, not names, not lies. So all I can do now is make the most of it. Make *more* than the most of it. All I can do is make sure that I'm the richest Jew in the colony.'

'But what about the money?' asked Mooi Klip.

Barney sighed. 'I've probably gone too far away from God to make my way back,' he said, 'but this is as far as I go.'

Mooi Klip waited outside while Barney finished going through Monsaraz's desk. At last, at the very bottom of one of the drawers, Barney found the deeds to Derdeheuwel farm and its surrounding acres. He tucked the deeds into his coat, dusted his hands off, and came out to join Mooi Klip and Donald in the courtyard.

'I've found the deeds,' he told them. 'After everything I've done here, I think I'm entitled to keep the farm. I'll rent it out, most likely.'

Donald said, 'If you're willing to wait for your first six months' rent, Mr Blitz, I'll rent it from you. If I can find Adam Hoovstraten again, he and me could work this place well.'

'You mean you want to stay?'

Donald gave a wide, ugly grin. 'I think it's time I stopped all this travelling, Mr Blitz. Travelling makes the soul restless. And I've got some good sisters in Oranjerivier.'

'Make sure they don't have jealous husbands.'

Donald turned around. 'I've laid Mr Monsaraz to rest in back of the kraal, Mr Blitz. You want to say a prayer?'

Barney shook his head. 'Just go bring that drawerful of paper money out of the drawing-room, carry it out here.'

Donald glanced at Mooi Klip. 'Whatever you say, Mr Blitz.'

Together, Barney and Mooi Klip walked slowly around to Monsaraz's grave – a narrow mound of dry earth, with neither cross nor marker to show that the son of Sgr and Sgra Monsaraz had been laid to rest here after a life of fear and misery and drink. Barney took off his hat and stood beside it, while Mooi Klip murmured a short mission-school prayer.

At last, Donald came out with the desk drawer. Five-pound notes fluttered in the wind, and some of them were tumbled away across the farmyard. He set it down at the head of the grave, and then stood back.

Barney knelt down, took out his matches, and struck one. The thin paper money caught alight straight away, and in a few moments the whole drawerful was blazing. One by one, the five-pound notes curled up and charred, and their fiery ashes were carried away on the breeze.

'Let's hope he rests now,' said Barney quietly; and without waiting for Mooi Klip, he walked slowly back to the surrey.

Barney still had the £212 which Harold Feinberg had given him for his diamonds, however, and that money he kept. When he and Mooi Klip arrived back in Kimberley, he spent almost all of it on a two-bedroom wooden shack not far away from the mine, on the eastern side of main street, and on picks and shovels and winching gear, which he bought from the Kimberley Mining Equipment Company. He had seen how deep some of the claims had already been dug, and he reckoned that within four or five weeks, he and Joel were going to have to wind the yellow soil out of their diggings with a rope and a bucket.

He employed six new kaffir labourers, and guaranteed to pay them bonuses for every diamond they found over five karats. They were an odd collection, the kaffirs. One of them had only one hand, but he could flick the handle of his shovel with his stump of a wrist so that each load of dirt landed precisely in his barrow, ten feet away. Another sang all day, in an octave of only five barely distinguishable tones, and on hot afternoons the sound of his droning voice drove Barney almost mad. The leader of the kaffir working-party was the smallest of all of them – a smiling, energetic imp whom Joel called his *shmeck tabac*, his little pinch of snuff.

Harold Feinberg came out to Claim 172 a week after Barney

and Joel had started digging together. He sat on an upturned wheel barrow and gave himself a thorough mopping with a white handkerchief.

'How's it going?' Harold asked, loudly, above the monotonous singing of the kaffir.

Barney, dressed in a loose sweat-stained shirt, baggy trousers and a broad-brimmed panama hat, stood up straight and held the small of his back. He had only been digging for a few days, but he felt as if he had already worked his way halfway through a life-sentence of hard labour.

'You've forgiven me, have you, Harold?' he asked.

'I should forgive you?'

'You made sure you turned the other way whenever I tried to catch your eye during Joel's appeal.'

'Hm,' said Harold, replacing his hat. 'That was when you were a Gentile. Nowadays, I hear that you've behaving like one of our own again, we should be so fortunate.'

'He's in love,' called Joel, from the other side of the claim, where he was directing his *shmeck tabac*'s efforts to pull down an overhang of crumbling rock.

'Ah, yes, I heard about that, too,' said Harold. 'I met Edward Nork two or three days ago, and he told me you'd set up house with that pretty young Griqua girl.'

'Sh's just housekeeping for us, that's all,' said Barney.

'I should doubt it?' asked Harold.

'You should *hok nit kain tchynik*,' said Joel, making his way across the claim in long, scrambling strides, and wiping his hands on a rag.

'These Blitz brothers,' Harold complained, with an expression of mock-despair. 'But tell me, how's business?'

Barney reached into the pocket of his work shirt and produced a handful of small rough diamonds. Harold Feinberg took them carefully into the sweaty folds of his palm, and then lifted the magnifying loupe around his neck so that he could examine them.

'What do you think?' asked Joel.

'Well . . . they're not bad,' said Harold. 'They won't earn you much of a fortune, but they're not bad.'

Barney pointed around to the sides of the claim, which was

already dug down to twenty feet. 'I reckon Joel was unlucky here. The upper debris had collapsed over the edge of the yellow soil, so that the first ten feet he dug didn't contain any diamonds at all. But now we're getting into the real business.'

'Well, I wish you luck,' said Harold. He grimaced at the sound of the kaffirs, singing as they dug. 'You and your *klezmer* both.'

Later that same afternoon, when the shadows from the rim of the mine had already filled their claim with darkness, Joel's impish kaffir came up with a stone of nearly ten karats. He dropped it into Joel's palm as calmly as if it were a large berry he had picked from a tree. Joel prodded it, scratched it with his thumbnail, and then said to Barney in a hoarse voice, 'Look at this, Barney. Come take a look at this.'

Barney laid down his pick. He held the diamond between his finger and his thumb, and he could not help grinning. 'Joel,' he said, 'I do believe the Blitz Brothers Diamond Company is going to show a profit today.'

Every day, they dug at their claim from the first reddish hints of dawn until it was too dark for them to see what they were doing. In August, it rained solidly for a week, and claim after claim collapsed in a series of mudslides, bringing sandbags and shovels and mule-carts down from one level to the next. Three Australians were buried alive, and a German digger was so badly crushed that his partner shot him to put him out of his agony. Some of the early diggers, satisfied with the few thousand pounds' worth of diamonds they had been able to dig out of the yellow ground, gave up, and sold their claims to the highest and most enthusiastic bidder.

By spring, most of the claims had been excavated so deep that the intervening roadways had collapsed, and the yellow soil had to be winched out to the rim of the mine in a series of hide buckets, suspended from never-ending steel cables. Each of these cables was wound around a series of pulleys, which was fixed to one of scores of rickety and elaborate wooden towers, clustering around the mine like pagan fortifications. The soil was offloaded at the towers, and then shovelled on to mule and ox-carts, to be taken away and sorted.

Mooi Klip became an expert at sorting diamonds. She spent

most of her days in a makeshift shelter not far from the edge of the mine, and there she supervised the kaffirs who tipped the broken ground into a heap in front of her, and pounded it with their shovels until it was broken down into manageable pieces. She watched them as they turned the soil in a rotary sieve called a *trommel*, which was Dutch for 'drum', and then banged away at the finer pieces which were left, before sieving them in fine-mesh hand sieves. Finally, she sat over the sorting table, picking through the stones with her delicate fingers. She wore small wire-rimmed spectacles for this close work, and Barney loved to surprise her as she sat working, because he thought she looked so pretty and vulnerable in eyeglasses.

At night, Barney and Joel and Mooi Klip returned to their shack, which they had now extended to include a large parlour and a verandah, and they would eat a supper of beef and beans before sitting around the fireplace, drinking rum and cocoa, and feeling the tension and pains of the day gradually leaving their muscles. Over the fireplace was a melodramatic litho-graph of the wreck of the steamship *San Francisco*, which Joel considered 'sobering'. He said it would always remind him of now nearly his own fortunes had foundered, and how close he had been to death.

But although Joel seemed more cheerful than he had when Barney had first rescued him, he was still visited from time to time by terrible doubts about what he was doing, and by nagging spells of furious dissatisfaction with himself, and with his surroundings, and especially with Barney.

'We should be living in a palace, the money we're making,' he said one evening in September. Barney was bent over the table, examining a heap of rough diamonds under the bright light of a pressure-lamp. Mooi Klip, her curly hair fresh-washed and brushed, was sitting by the fireplace hemming a red flowery dress. Because of the intense white light, the inside of the room looked like a stage-setting for amateur theatricals.

Barney said, 'I'm more interested in investing our money in another claim. By the end of the month, we should be able to put in a bid for Stuart's patch. Harold told me that Stuart was grumbling about the climate, and that he was planning on selling up and going back to Capetown.'

'You want *another* claim?' Joel demanded. 'Don't you think we have enough work to do with one?'

'We can employ more kaffirs.'

'Oh, sure. More kaffirs! But more kaffirs are going to mean more management, and more management is going to mean even harder work. Aren't you ever satisfied?'

Barney laid down his tweezers. 'What's the point of getting involved in any business of any kind if you don't expand? Right now, the Diggers' Committee only allow two claims per man – but that restriction can't last long. And then what do you think is going to happen here at Kimberley? The big companies will gradually swallow up the individual diggers, one by one; and in a year or two, you mark my words, there won't be any one-man outfits left. It won't be economic to dig one claim only. It won't be worth the effort of shoring up the sides, or of moving the soil to the edge of the mine, or of sorting out the gems. The big companies will undercut us, just because they're operating in bulk.'

'So what are we struggling for?' asked Joel. 'Why don't we sell up while the price is still good, and move out of this godforsaken place before we die out of boredom, or frustration, or some unheard-of disease?'

'Joel, we're just beginning. If we can buy up another claim then we can start to build up a big company of our own. The quicker we do it, the better. For God's sake – instead of being swallowed we could do some swallowing ourselves. Hasn't it occurred to you that you and I together could own the whole of that mine out there? The Blitz Brothers?'

'You're crazy. The heat's got to your brain.'

Barney tilted his chair back and looked at Joel steadily. 'Joel,' he said, 'if we don't work in the diamond business, then what business *are* we going to work in? You want to go back to tailoring? Or farming? You want to go back to sea?'

Joel snapped, 'Don't be so damned patronising.'

'I'm not being patronising. I'm simply trying to find out what you want out of life.'

'What the hell for? You're not my father, are you? You're my younger brother, my little Barnabas, my little son of consolation. Well, aren't you? And who followed whom out to South

Africa? Who bought this claim in the first place? So don't sit there raking through my diamonds and try to tell me what I should be doing with my life.'

'Joel, peace,' said Barney, alarmed by his brother's outburst. But Joel was not in the mood for reconciliation. He stood up, came over to the table, and seized a whole handful of rough, glittering diamonds.

'If it hadn't been for me, you never would have laid your hands on one of these stones. Not one! Now you sit there sorting them out like you're the diamond king of Kimberley. And all your plans! Your big dreams about buying more claims! We could own the whole goddamned mine, could we? Just remember who bought this claim in the first place!'

'I didn't ask you to give me a share,' said Barney, trying to curb his temper. 'Now, will you please put those diamonds down. I'm half way through sorting them.'

'Sorting them, shit!' Joel snarled, and threw the diamonds in a sparkling spray all over the room. 'You've dug yourself into my life pretty good, haven't you? Made me a laughing-stock in front of the whole town – the poor stupid kike who couldn't even save himself from being pegged out on the ground. Then you took half of my diamonds. Now I'm living like a lodger in my own home, and working like a kaffir in my own diamond mine, while you spend your time sorting gems and planning your high-faulting plans and fornicating with that *schwartzeh* like some ass-jerking dog.'

Barney punched Joel very hard in the mouth. The crack of Joel's front tooth breaking was so loud that Barney thought for a moment that he had broken his own knuckle. Joel staggered backwards, collided with a wheelback chair, stumbled, and then fell heavily on to the floor. He crouched there, spitting blood, and shaking his head.

Mooi Klip, without a word, quickly put down her sewing and knelt down among the scattered diamonds to hold Joel's head, and offer him her handkerchief for his bleeding lips. Barney felt as if he were bursting with some uncontrollable effervescence, a shaken-up bottle of beer, and he stood with both fists clenched, trembling, trying to hold back his anger, trying to tell himself that Joel was still sick, and still suffering the after-effects of his trial and his appeal, and that he should not have hit him.

Mooi Klip turned to Barney and said, 'Water. His tooth is broken.'

'He shouldn't have said that,' said Barney. 'I don't care what he feels about me, and I don't care what he says. We're brothers, after all. But he should never have said that about you.'

Mooi Klip simply repeated, '*Water.*'

Barney went to the scullery and came back with a blue enamel basin. Mooi Klip soaked her handkerchief, and gently dabbed Joel's mouth. After a while, Joel seemed to recover from the first concussion, and he pushed Mooi Klip's hand away.

Barney squatted down beside Joel and laid a hand on his shoulder. 'Joel, I'm sorry. Are you okay?'

'Never felt better,' mumbled Joel. He tried to pull himself up on to his feet by holding on to the overturned chair, but he lost his balance and fell forward.

'I don't need your help, thanks,' he told Barney, fiercely, as Barney grasped his arm.

'Joel, I've said I'm sorry. We're partners, aren't we? But you can't say things like that about Mooi Klip.'

'She's not a *schwartzeh*, is that what you're trying to tell me?' said Joel, tentatively touching his mouth with his fingertips. 'You're not living in sin, and exhibiting that sin in front of the whole of Kimberley?'

'I don't care about the whole of Kimberley, Joel. The whole of Kimberley can go to hell. And anyway, what's so high and mighty and moral about Kimberley? There are more whores to the acre in Kimberley than anywhere else in the world.'

'So she's a whore, too? Your *schwartzeh*? Is that what you think of her?'

'I didn't say that,' protested Barney.

'You never say anything, you hypocrite,' said Joel, pulling himself on to his feet. 'You just take what you feel belongs to you, and you take it by any means at your disposal. If your mama could see you now.'

'She can't see me, Joel. She's dead. And besides, I'm not

doing anything I'm ashamed of. I love Mooi Klip, and I love you, and if you'd just stop picking on me so often you'd understand just how much.'

Joel sniffed blood. 'You sanctimonious *pisher*.'

Joel went to his bedroom, and slammed the door so hard behind him that it opened again, and he had to close it more quietly and more firmly. Barney stared at the door for a moment or two, and then went down on his knees and gathered up the diamonds, one by one. Mooi Klip sat on the edge of her chair and watched him.

'He is so angry,' she said.

'You're not fooling. The trouble is, I don't know why.'

'Of course you know why,' said Mooi Klip. 'You have hurt his pride. You saved him from trouble, when he couldn't save himself. Now you are making his business work well, when all he could do was steal. You have bought us a house to live in, and you have a woman, too. What does he have? What has he done? You make him feel like a child.'

'I don't mean to,' said Barney, and it was true. He did not. He loved Joel and he looked up to him, too – whether Joel had made a success of his life or not. Had not Joel shown him how to make bows and arrows out of tailor's elastic, during those hot summers on Clinton Street, when they were boys? Had not Joel shown him how to cut a lining, and how to baste a lapel? Had not Joel protected him against those Armenian bullies along Hester Street, on his way to school? And had not Joel, one night in bed, with the rain tapping on the windows, explained in whispery and reverent detail the mysterious anatomy of girls?

But now Joel was so sour and stand-offish that Barney found it almost impossible to explain that just because *he* had a knack for business, and Joel had not, that did not mean that he loved Joel any the less, or that Joel was not making an equal contribution to their success and to their happiness. Barney wanted them all very much to be a family – himself and Joel and Mooi Klip – but Joel was far too jealous of Barney to play.

Barney felt as if every time he tried to keep the Blitz family together, it fell apart in his hands, like the crumbling clay of the Kimberley mine. The family seemed to be plagued by envy, or madness, or sheer bad temper.

He gathered up as many of the scattered diamonds as he could, and then he went back to the table. He did not say anything to Mooi Klip, but smiled at her briefly, to show her that he loved and appreciated her. He had not mentioned Agnes Knight to her again, not since that day in Oranjerivier when they had found Monsaraz dead. He had seen Agnes two weeks ago, though, in the main street in Kimberley, with her nose tilted to the sky, and her parasol twirling, and her pretty little shoes click-clicking along the dusty boardwalk. He had raised his hat to her from across the street, and said, 'Agnes?' in a rather discouraged voice; but she had flounced on, without looking his way, and he had not had the effrontery to follow her.

Agnes represented a lost dream. Agnes was a prickly reminder that he was *persona non grata* in the Kimberley Club, and that Jews were not particularly welcome in any of those dim rooms where billiards were played, and gin slings drunk, and reminiscences shared between chaps called Biffy and Charles about those dear summer days at Harrow, and those long autumn afternoons in Kent.

Mooi Klip, sewing, said, 'Perhaps Joel would be better if he found a wife.'

Barney spread the rough diamonds out on the dark brown velvet tablecloth in front of him. 'I don't know. He used to be so talkative, so friendly. Everything you'd expect from an older brother. But now ...'

Painstakingly, he began to sort out the diamonds again. First, they had to be divided according to colour and clarity. Most of the diamonds, over eighty per cent, were only fit for industrial use, for glass-cutting and engraving tools, and drillbits. These crystals Barney would sell by the sackful to the Capetown Industrial Diamond Company, or to Mr Schultz of Lippert and Company, from Hamburg, who always paid good prices for industrials.

Then, Barney picked through the stones of gem quality – sorting them by size first. The 'smalls' – anything under one carat – went to one side. The larger gems he categorised according to their shapes. Stones, which were unbroken crystals; cleavages, which were fractured crystals; flats, which were thin crystals like fragments of a broken window; and macles, which were twinned stones, and triangular in shape.

Few diggers could sort diamonds as well as Barney – but then he had listened well to what Harold Feinberg had told him – and in turn he had passed on what he knew to Mooi Klip. He had offered several times to teach Joel to sort diamonds, but Joel had waved him away and said that he would leave the 'diffly business' to those who had the patience for it.

But sorting paid off. It meant that Barney knew exactly what he had to sell, and almost exactly what price he could expect for it, down to the last gold franc. It also meant that he learned to tell the difference between a good stone and an excellent stone, between a very spotted crystal and a slightly spotted crystal. Under his magnifying lens, he could detect the kind of flaws or inclusions which could easily be bruted off a stone when it was cut, and which would only reduce the value of a gem by a very small amount; and the flaws which lay nearer the centre of a stone, and which would give a cutter real difficulty.

Sorting by colour was simpler. Most of the browns and the yellows were unpopular, and so they were set aside as industrials, unless they were unusually large, or clear. But greens, or blues, or pinks were much rarer, and could fetch well above the regular price. Reds were so unusual that Barney had never even seen one.

The whites were more difficult to grade. The finest whites were often called 'blue-whites', and when he had first started sorting, Barney had spent hours trying to detect a slight trace of blue in his better gemstones. But he had learned from experience, and from a cynical Harold Feinberg, that 'blue-white' was a romantic diamond-salesman's fiction, rather than an accurate colour grading; and that most of the stones sold to a starry-eyed public as 'blue-white' were not even top grade whites.

Almost all of the whites that Barney and Joel were digging out of claim No. 172 were very faintly yellowish, which meant that as far as colour was concerned, they could only be classified as fourth- or fifth-grade stones. Occasionally, they came up with a fine clear white, but not enough to satisfy Barney that their claim was a good one. And they had yet to find a gem crystal of more than 12·8 carats.

'Have you finished?' asked Mooi Klip, standing behind Barney and gently stroking his cheek.

Barney laid down his loupe and pinched the bridge of his nose. He had been working since dawn, and his eyes were blurring. All he could see in front of him on the dark brown tablecloth was a rainbow jumble of sparkling light.

'Almost,' he told her. 'Do you want to go to bed?'

'I want to talk, too.'

He opened a notebook, and carefully scratched down the number and estimated value of the crystals on the table. 'Seven hundred pounds, if we're lucky. We should clear £2000 this week.'

'All this money,' said Mooi Klip. 'What are you going to do with it?'

Barney stood up, and closed his notebook. 'I'm going to put it into the bank, like I always do. And then, when he's ready, and when *I'm* ready, I'm going to buy up Stuart's claim next door.'

'I heard a kaffir say Stuart's claim is no good. They're down to bedrock.'

'That's what I hear, too, although Stuart says he's selling because of the climate.'

'But why should you want to buy Stuart's claim, if it's worked out?' asked Mooi Klip.

'Because I believe a man called Nork.'

'Nork?' queried Mooi Klip.

'He used to work with Joel. He's a little strange. A little eccentric. But he thinks the bedrock isn't bedrock at all, but something called Norkite. He thinks we'll find as many diamonds in the Norkite as we're finding in the yellow ground.'

'Is that true?'

'I think it's true. I'll lose a lot of money if it isn't.'

Joel's bedroom door opened. Joel stood there, dressed in nothing but his cotton combinations, his dark hair tousled, watching Barney and Mooi Klip with his mouth turned down in a disapproving curve.

'Nork,' he said, 'is a maniac.'

'Well, he's a little over-enthusiastic,' said Barney. 'He drinks a lot, too. But there's nothing wrong with his theory.'

'You're going to throw good money away on a crackpot geological theory? We're living in a two-bedroomed hovel, dressed in dime-store cottons, eating dried beef and beans, and you're going to throw money away on a theory?'

'I'm going to invest money in something that sounds like a pretty good gamble,' said Barney. 'Now, please, don't let's argue again. If you want to discuss it some more, let's talk about it in the morning.'

'Let's talk about it now.'

'Joel – I'm tired – so are you – and so is Mooi Klip.'

'Barney, my little son of consolation, I'm never too tired to talk about my future. Or what you're going to do with our money. Seventeen thousand pounds we've got now, festering away in the London & South African Bank. Seventeen thousand inert, useless, pounds. So we can buy out Stuart's barren claim. How much is that going to cost us? Eight thousand, nine? All right, that leaves us eight or nine thousand spare. What are we going to do with that?'

Barney put his arm around Mooi Klip's shoulders. 'We'll buy more claims, of course, when we can.'

Joel, his eyebrows drawing together like black iron filings drawn by a magnet, said, '*More* barren claims? *More* worked-out land?'

'It's not worked out. Maybe some diggers think it is, but it isn't.'

'Because Edward Nork says it isn't? *Riboyne Shel O'lem*, Barney, the man's crazy in the head! I knew him months before you did. Years! I even believed him myself for a time. But he's a lunatic. They should lock him up.'

'They haven't so far. And I believe him.'

Joel raked his fingers through his greasy, unkempt hair. With his mouth so bruised and swollen he looked like a prize-fighter. 'You won't take my advice, I suppose?' he asked Barney. 'You don't give me credit for knowing these diamonds fields better than you do?'

Barney tied up the last of the gemstones in a washleather bag. He did not answer.

'All right,' said Joel. 'But let me warn you of one thing. If we hit blue ground, and the blue ground turns out to be barren, then I'm going to take my money out of the bank, whatever's left of it, and I'm also going to insist that you buy me out of whatever claims we own at today's price.'

Barney looked at his brother with nothing but regret. He could not stand to see Joel acting this way: it reminded him so much of his mother. 'Very well,' he said hoarsely.

'*Mazel un b'rachah*,' said Joel, his voice sharp with irony. Because to speak these words, 'good luck and blessings,' were the time-honoured way in which diamond dealers sealed their business arrangements. They never drew up written contracts: a man's word was binding enough.

After Joel had gone back to bed, Barney went over to the wooden hutch where they kept their plates and their cutlery, and poured himself a small glass of brandy. He drank it in one mouthful, without looking round once at Mooi Klip, who was standing in their bedroom doorway watching him.

'Come to bed,' she said, quietly. 'This is not the right time for fighting.'

Barney turned down the pressure-lamp and extinguished it. He crossed the room by the shadowy illumination of the candle in their bedroom, and held Mooi Klip's hand.

'I don't want to fight anyway,' he said.

With the door closed behind them, and held by a hasp, Barney unbuttoned Mooi Klip's dress, and pulled it down from her shoulders. Her nipples showed dark through the fine white cotton of her embroidered bodice. He kissed her, and held her cheek close to his, and felt her curly hair between his fingers.

He was tired, and so he made love to her slowly, with his eyes closed. It was warm, between the percale sheets, under their patchwork comforter, and he held her hips up close to him with hands that were callused now, and strong with work. Each time he slid into her he felt it was like sliding into an affectionate dream.

Afterwards, they lay side-by-side in the flickering candle-light with the covers thrown back. Mooi Klip's lips touched Barney's shoulder again and again in the lightest of kisses, and her hand cupped him between his muscular thighs.

'How do you think of me?' she asked him.

'What do you mean?' he grunted. He had nearly fallen asleep.

'I mean how do you *think* of me.'

Barney turned his head. 'I love you. You know that.'

'You don't think of me as your whore.'

'Of course not.'

'But we live together, and we make love, and we are not married.'

'That bothers you?' asked Barney. He sat up and leaned his head on the sawn-oak bedhead. On the opposite side of the room, on a small table, stood Mooi Klip's crucifix. Its shadow dipped and danced in the light of the candle.

'If my family knew, they would be very unhappy,' said Mooi Klip. 'And I think that I am unhappy myself.'

'You're unhappy? You've never said so.'

She looked away, picking at a stray thread at the edge of the comforter. 'It has never been the right time, before. But now I think you have to decide. You cannot live with me, and expect so much of me, and still nurse your dreams of Agnes Knight.'

Barney said shortly, 'You've learned a lot since we've been together, haven't you? And not just fancy English.'

'I've learned that you have a dream, and that your dream is sometimes stronger than you are.'

'Have you learned that I love you?'

'In your way, you do.'

'In my *way*? And what way is that? Don't you realise that one day I'm going to drape you in diamonds?'

Mooi Klip slowly shook her head. 'No,' she said. Her eyes sparkled in the candlelight. 'No, you will never do that.'

'But you want me to marry you?'

'Yes.'

'Would Jan Bloem give us his blessing?'

'I expect so. He does like you, although he finds it hard to admit it.'

Barney swung his legs out of bed, and sat up. 'What I don't understand is why you suddenly want me to marry you now. Is it what Joel said tonight? Is that what made up your mind?'

'A little,' she said. 'But there is something else, more important.'

'What's that?'

She ran her fingers down his back, and the feeling made him shiver. 'I think I'm going to have your baby,' she said.

He met Agnes a week later, by accident. It was one of those dark afternoons when low cloud hung over the veld like soft grey rags; when the horses were restless, and the noise of the picks and the winches from the Big Hole sounded oddly muffled, like grave-robbers working in a country churchyard.

The Knights had ignored Barney and Joel every time they came across them in the street. Kimberley was such a small place that it was impossible to avoid them altogether; but Mr Knight in particular was an expert in the social art of 'cutting', and he had obviously instructed Faith and Agnes to tilt their noses into the air in exactly the same way. The three of them would bustle past like excited guinea-fowl, all upraised beaks and flustering skirts and contemptuous petticoats.

But early on that Friday afternoon, when Barney walked into town to find a replacement diaphragm for one of their pumps, he found Agnes alone. She was standing on the boarded sidewalk in a cream linen dress and a wide cream sunhat with a brown silk *puggaree* tied around it. She looked as if she were thinking, or dreaming; but in any case she did not notice Barney until he was standing beside her, in his wide hat and his shirt with its sleeves tightly rolled up, and his suspenders.

'Agnes,' he said.

She turned, and stared at him wide-eyed.

'Barney!' she said, but then she remembered herself, and stuck her nose up, and closed her eyes.

Barney couldn't help smiling. 'I may be Jewish, Agnes, but I'm not going to bite your ankle.'

'Papa said I mustn't even look at you. Neither must Faith. We're under strict instructions, he said.'

Barney tilted back his hat. 'Do you really hold it against me so much? That I'm Jewish?'

She opened one eye.

'If you cut me, do I not bleed?' Barney quoted.

Agnes said, 'You don't believe in Jesus, do you?'

'Of course I believe in Jesus.'

'Papa said that Jews were almost heathens. Not quite. But almost.'

Barney looked away, across the dusty street. In the far distance, way beyond the trees on the horizon, lightning flickered like the tongue of an asp. 'We could have loved each other,' he said. 'You know that, don't you?'

She twisted the brown silk cord of her parasol around its *faux*-bamboo handle, but said nothing. The dim light gave her face the soft pastel colours of a portrait by Sir Joshua Reynolds; full of fancy and sentimentality and gentle allegory. A dust-devil stirred the chaff in the street, and far off to the north-west the lighning forked again. Unsettled times.

Barney said, 'I shall always hold you dear, you know. I suppose that's all I can say.'

Agnes said, 'I was supposed to buy Mother some ribbon.'

'Well, you'd better go then,' Barney told her. 'But it would be nice if you could at least say goodbye.'

Agnes turned. To Barney's surprise, there was a faint sparkle in the corner of her eye, where a tear had formed. She said, 'I don't even know why Father is so furious, that you're a Jew. You don't even *look* like a Jew; although he says you do, and that he should have guessed all along. "I invited him to eat at my very table!" he keeps shouting. I tried to argue with him, Barney, I promise you that I tried my best. But he won't let me see you. He won't! And Mother can't understand.'

Barney took a step forward, and held her hand. Her tiny fawn glove was decorated with fine Brussels lace. Her hand inside it was as warm as a small animal. He took off his hat, leaned forward, and kissed her cheek, unshaved and sweaty as he was, with dust in the curls of his hair, and grit around his mouth.

She whispered something indistinct, and Barney said, 'What?'

'I love you,' she said. 'Didn't you hear me? I love you. I've dreamed about you, ever since I first met you. Perhaps it's wrong of me, and I ought to feel guilty. But how can anyone feel guilty, when they feel passions as strong as these? Barney, I love you.'

Barney squeezed her hand. 'It's impossible,' he said. 'You know it is.'

Her face collapsed with grief. 'I've tried so hard,' she told him. 'I've tried to do everything that Father thought was best. Faith believes that I should stand up to him, and tell him that I'm going to walk out with you, no matter what. But I can't, Barney. All I can do is keep my love for you alive, inside my heart, and hope that one day everything will change.'

She took her hand away, and found her handkerchief, and wiped her eyes; but somehow that only made her sob even more. Barney gently put his arm around her, and led her to an iron bench outside a grocery store, where he sat her down, and sat beside her.

'I don't know what to say,' he told her. He was telling her the truth. How could be explain that he had given her up for lost on the day of Joel's trial, simply because the prejudice of her father and of all of the British colonial *goyim* seemed utterly impregnable? How could he tell her about Mooi Klip? He knew that his ambitions had deceived him: he had first been attracted to Agnes because she was the right sort of girl for a colonist to marry, pretty and presentable and radiantly Christian. But he was deeply infatuated with her, too; with her face and her figure and the childish wilfulness of her character; and now that he realised that she still wanted him, and still loved him, in spite of his Jewishness, the intense pain of losing her for ever – and it would have to be for ever – was like an amputation. He would think of that word later, for different reasons, but it would always remind him of losing Agnes.

Agnes said, 'I'd better go. Mother will be wondering where I am.'

He said, 'You won't do anything foolish?'

'Foolish? There's nothing foolish that I can do, not here in Kimberley.'

'I'm sorry,' he said, quietly. 'It should all have been different.'

'It wasn't your fault. You had to stand up for your brother. At lease you had the strength to do that.'

He replaced his hat, and tugged the brim straight. 'I'm beginning to wonder whether that was such a good idea.'

Agnes reached out and held his wrist. 'Listen, Barney,' she told him, 'I know you won't believe this, and there will probably be many times in the future when I will give you good reason not to. But I shall always keep a place in my heart for you. You will always be precious to me. Don't forget that, please.'

'I won't be able to forget it,' said Barney.

They parted on the corner of the street, while thunder began to bang in the distance, and the wind got up. As Agnes was about to walk away, Barney held her arm, and kissed her again, on the lips. She was elegant and small, and her mouth tasted of rosewater.

'Barney,' she said. 'I can't. If my father found out ...'

Barney reluctantly let her go. 'Yes,' he said. 'I know. I didn't mean to compromise you.'

Quickly, she was gone. No matter how many times he met her now, he knew that he would never be able to talk to her again the way he had today. Each of them had a new life to seek out; new obligations to fulfil; and they would have to carry them out apart.

She reached the door of the notions store, and opened the door. For a moment she was silhouetted against the patterned glass. A mule stirred its hoofs at the tying-up post not far away, as if it was frightened of what was to come, but powerless to escape.

In October, the short-lived reign of President Stafford Parker of the Diggers' Republic came to an end. Parker abdicated graciously, though, because the diamond fields were now to come under British rule. At the beginning of November, two days before Barney and Mooi Klip were due to be married, the Union Jack was run up over the Big Hole, and the diggers stood around it and gave three cheers, and waved their hats.

The annexation of the richest diamond diggings in the entire world, with a production of £50,000 worth of diamonds a week, had been a masterpiece of British colonial burglary. Although the mines were well within the territory claimed by the Orange Free State, the Boers had neither the money nor the military strength to resist that particular combination of bullying and guile which had won for Britain some of the wealthiest geographic prizes that the globe could offer.

During the years in which the Orange Free State and the Transvaal had been poor, eking their living from the soil, the British had been content to leave them alone. But the discovery of diamonds on such an extraordinary scale could quickly have made the Boers a formidable enemy, and the British Colonial Secretary, Sir Richard Southey, had been growing increasingly worried about the prospect of two wealthy and hostile republics barring British access from the Cape to Central Africa.

'By definition,' he remarked at a dinner party, 'the only safe Boer is a poor Boer.'

The answer to Sir Richard's problems came when he discovered that all of the new diamond mines lay on land that was inhabited by Griquas. Because it had never mattered before now, nobody had ever satisfactorily decided whether the Boers had any right to claim 'Griqualand' as theirs. So, with great pomp and ceremony, it was announced that the Lieutenant-Governor of Natal, Robert Keate, would head a commission to arbitrate on the Griqua's terrotorial rights.

President Jan Brand, the Boer leader of the Orange Free State, protested in vain that a disinterested foreign country should decide the issue. It was a British matter, said Keate, dismissively, and the British could not possibly tolerate foreigners meddling in their affairs.

Keate's final ruling came as no surprise to the unhappy Boers. The Orange Free State, he concluded, had no jurisdiction over 'Griqualand', nor the diamond mines within its boundaries. And within days, the Griqua chieftains Nicholas Waterboer and Jan Bloem had been persuaded by Keate to ask the British to annex 'Griqualand' into Cape Colony. Up went the Union Jack over Kimberley, and into the British economy came an influx of diamonds more than six times greater than the annual production of South Africa's nearest rival, Brazil.

Enraged, President Brand sent a small commando force to Kimberley to try to recapture the diamond fields. But Sir Henry Barkly, the new Governor of the Cape, immediately responded by rushing up a thousand uniformed British soldiers. Angry, bitter, millions of pounds poorer, the Boers were forced to retreat. They had sustained an injury which would fester now for almost thirty years.

Barney and Joel and Mooi Klip went to see the flag being raised. On the far side of the crowd, Barney could make out the tall stovepipe hat of Mr Knight, surrounded by the feathery bonnets of his daughters. He linked arms with Mooi Klip, over-possessively, and led her through the jostling diggers to a small hillock, where she could stand on an overturned wheelbarrow and watch what was happening.

Joel remarked, 'At least we'll get some law and order around here now.'

'*You* talk of law and order?' smiled Mooi Klip.

'Proper law and order. Not barrelhead justice,' retorted Joel.

The flag was jerkily raised to the head of the staff, and a small military band, in white topis and bright red tunics, played *God Save The Queen*, and *Another Little Patch of Red*. Then there were more cheering, and more hat-waving, and most of the diggers streamed off to Dodd's Bar for a stiff drink. Barney lifted Mooi Klip down from her wheelbarrow.

It was then that Edward Nork appeared, walking like a long-bladed pair of scissors, and dragging behind him a diffident but very well-built young man with a round face, prominent ears, and the sort of well-combed wavy hair that always reminded Barney of British public schoolboys.

'These are the chaps!' Nork announced to his new charge. 'These are just the chaps I've been looking for!'

The young man flushed pink. He was wearing white cricket flannels with very baggy knees, and cricketing boots. He nodded to Barney and Joel and Mooi Klip, and said, 'I hope I'm not imposing. I met Mr Nork here by accident, and he insisted on taking me in tow, like a lifeboat.'

'I knew his father!' Nork exclaimed. 'I used to visit Bishop's Stortford on a bicycle, to visit a very clever young lady I once knew, and his father was the local vicar. We used to discuss the geology of the Holy Land together, his father and I.'

'My name's Cecil Rhodes,' said the young man, in a high-pitched, upper-class English accent. 'My father is the Reverend F. W.'

'I'm Barney Blitz,' replied Barney. 'This is my brother Joel, and this is Mrs Blitz-to-be.'

'Well, congratulations,' smiled Cecil Rhodes. 'My father always said that marriage is the closest estate to heaven that a man can enjoy.'

'You have an Anglican motto for every occasion?' asked Joel.

'I was brought up religiously, if that's what you mean,' Cecil Rhodes replied, cautiously, but not apologetically.

'Well, I think we all were,' said Joel. 'But it doesn't take long for the diamond diggings to drum that nonsense out of you. You'd better come and have some lunch. Do you like *frikkadeller*?'

'Do you mind if I bring my things along?' asked Cecil Rhodes. 'I have an ox-waggon tied up over there.'

'Nobody will steal it,' said Joel. 'What's on it? A shovel or two? A bedroll? You can pick diamonds up off the ground around here, so nobody's going to bother with stuff like that. Water, that's the only expensive commodity out here. Water, and women.'

They walked back to the house, where Mooi Klip stoked up the woodburning range and put the meatballs on to fry. Barney offered to help her, especially since she was pregnant, but she waved him away. At the kitchen door, though, she called him back, and gave him a long and lingering kiss.

'This day next week, I will be Mrs Blitz,' she said, warmly.

'And I will be your husband,' Barney grinned. 'So there.'

Joel was pouring out drinks. He was talking even more loudly than usual, and more abrasively. He did not enjoy having guests at the house at the best of times, and Edward Nork was a particular hatred of his, especially since Sir Joshua Field, another British geologist, had declared that the blue flaky 'bedrock' beneath the yellow ground might actually bear even more diamonds than the topsoil. Joel did not take to Cecil Rhodes, either. Rhodes had that brassy English self-assurance that made Joel feel like grinding his teeth. 'They think they own the whole damned world,' he used to complain to Barney.

'That's probably because they do,' Barney had replied, absent-mindedly.

Cecil Rhodes said, 'I'm joing my brother Herbert, as a

matter of fact, at the De Beers mine. Herbert used to farm cotton in Natal, and I took the business over when he left to go diamond-digging. I brought in a fine crop, too, and I would probably have been doing it still if the prices hadn't been so ridiculously low. You could never get rich by growing cotton.'

'Diamond-digging isn't as easy as it looks,' said Joel, handing round glasses of sherry. 'And it's certainly not for children.'

'Well, I'm eighteen,' said Cecil Rhodes, with a smile. 'I expect that's old enough.'

'Can we call you Cecil?' asked Barney, sitting down in his large woven armchair.

'I'd rather you called me Rhodes, if you don't mind. It's what a fellow gets used to at school.'

'You think you're going to strike it rich?' Barney asked him.

'Rich *and* powerful, I rather hope,' said Rhodes, artlessly. 'You see, it's my belief that the British are the first race in the world – with no offence at all to present company – and that the more of the world we inhabit, the better it is for the human race. The absorption of the greater part of the world under British influence would simply mean an end to all wars.'

'I hope you're not including the United States in your would-be empire,' said Joel. He finished his sherry in two or three gulps, and then poured himself another glassful.

'I don't see why not,' said Rhodes. 'We English-speaking peoples should stand together as closely as possible. If there be a God, I think what He would like me to do is paint as much of the world as possible in British red. Including America.'

'I always knew there was more than one God,' said Joel.

Rhodes made a face which indicated that if *that* was going to be the tone of the conversation, then it would be better if they changed the subject altogether.

'But if you're right, there must be more than one God,' Joel persisted. 'Because *we* were chosen of Adoshem, the true God, not the British. You can mock us for being chosen. You always have. But isn't mockery the last resort of the hopelessly envious? We were chosen, and you weren't; and no matter how many soldiers you send scurrying around the world, you can never alter that fact because it is historical and unalterable.'

'I really think you're missing the point,' said Rhodes. 'These

207

days, it is a combination of wealth, power, and benign intention that makes Britain the chosen instrument of the Lord.'

'Benign intention? The Boers think you're the devil, personified.'

Barney put in, more quietly, trying to divert the conversation from religion and race, 'What do you really plan to do here, Rhodes? You sound as if you have something in mind.'

Rhodes looked him right in the eye, sitting up straight in his basketwork armchair as if he were being interviewed by his housemaster. 'What I really plan to do here, Mr Blitz, is make my fortune. From the little I've already seen of the mines, they're utterly chaotic. They need order, and system. They need to be managed on a large-scale, businesslike basis. If I can achieve that, then I'll have achieved what I came here to do.'

'Magnificent words for an eighteen-year-old,' said Joel, sarcastically.

'Sensible, though,' put in Barney. 'I'd better keep my eye on you, young Rhodes, or you'll be playing me at my own game.'

'Regrettably for both of your empire-building ideas, the Board for the Protection of the Diamond Industries still won't allow one man to own more than two claims,' put in Joel. 'And, by God, two is enough for anybody.'

Rhodes stood up, and tugged his cricket-flannels straight. 'I think we'll just have to see about that,' he said. 'And now I believe I've changed my mind about lunching with you, thanks all the same.'

'You're welcome to stay,' said Barney, amused by Rhodes' abruptness.

'Thank you, but I don't believe I will. I think your brother and I may have something of a clash, and I don't want to spoil your *frikkadeller* for you. You'll give my apologies to your charming fiancée.'

'Running off with your tail tucked between your legs?' smiled Joel. 'That isn't the spirit that got the map of Africa painted red.'

'We'll see,' said Rhodes. He nodded with courtesy to Edward Nork, who returned his nod with a waggle of his fingers; and then to Barney. But Barney had suddenly become aware that this seemingly equable young man was gripping the flannel of his trousers to sightly that he had torn the seam. He must have been within a hair's-breadth of completely losing his self-control.

Barney showed Rhodes out on to the verandah. It was a cool, windy day, and plumes of dust were blowing up from the Big Hole.

'Well, it seems that we may find ourselves in competition one day,' said Rhodes, in a rather metallic tone. He held out his hand to show that, between him and Barney at least, there were no awkward feelings.

'Yes – we may,' said Barney. 'In fact, I hope we do.' There was something about Rhodes' directness that unbalanced him. Rhodes seemed to understand the real implications of the wealth of Kimberley without any effort at all, whereas Barney had taken several months to grasp that these mines were so fabulously rich that anyone who managed to control them could control practically the whole of Africa. Barney felt as if he were up against a dedicated opponent at last, and the prospect both excited and scared him.

'If we do find ourselves competing,' Rhodes replied, 'then I can assure you that you're in for one devil of a scrap.' Then be began to walk back towards Kimberley with his trouser-legs flapping in the wind. A little distance away, with Barney still watching him, he stopped, and produced from one of his pockets a tin of cough-lozenges. He popped one into his mouth, and then continued walking, as steadily and confidently as if the whole diamond mine already belonged to him.

The night before Barney's wedding was the most catastrophic night he had ever lived through. The crisis came without any warming at all. All the arrangements had been made with the pimply young curate from Wimbledon to perform the ceremony at Kimberley's Anglican Church, and the banns had been read. Jan Bloem and his mother were expected to arrive from Klipdrift early in the morning, bringing Mooi Klip's family with him. Mooi Klip herself had butchered half an ox to be roasted, and with the help of a young Yorkshirewoman who lived with her husband in the shack next door, she had made dozens of biscuits and candies.

The inside of the house looked as if it had been decorated for Christmas, with plumes of dried grass and flowers, paper streamers, and stars cut from biscuit-tin lids. There were two barrels of wine, a cluster of borrowed mugs and glasses, and a barrel of sherry. The table was carefully set with plates, and Barney had made a special trip down to Walker's Lunch Rooms to borrow twenty knives and twenty forks. Joel, grudgingly, had torn two dozen napkins from a large dust-sheet – not because they could not afford to buy any, but simply because there were none to be had.

Mooi Klip, already glowing with the first stages of pregnancy, her hair shining, her eyes bright, and her breasts tightening the bodices of her dresses, took on an extra glow. A glow of pride, and rediscovered dignity, and plain love.

Just before noon on the day before the wedding, Barney and Joel went into Kimberley to meet a German salesman about pumping equipment. The weather had been wet and unsettled lately, and most of the claims in the Big Hole were so deep now that whenever it rained, they flooded with bright yellow water, and prospecting could sometimes be held up for days. Even pumps did not help much, although they were better than nothing. If the digger in the next claim did not have a pump, the water from his flooded workings would simply gush over into yours. There were 3600 individual claims in the Big Hole, and the British writer Anthony Trollope had said that it looked as if 'some diabolically ingenious architect had contrived a house with 500 rooms, not one of which should be on the same floor, and to and from none of which there should be a pair of stairs or a door or a window.'

The German pump salesman was stout, with hands like *haxe*, the Bavarian pork-knuckles. He sat in a stained-oak booth at Marshall's Restaurant with a large plate of chops and mashed potatoes in front of him, drinking whiskey and entertaining a succession of anxious diggers. By the time Barney and Joel arrived, he had sold all of the six steam-pumps that he had brought with him from Capetown, and was taking orders for six months ahead.

'But, I will buy you a beer as a consolation,' he told them, gaily waving a chop.

Out in the street again, Joel said, 'What do we do now? We've already lost six days through flooding.'

'Maybe I should go over to the De Beers mine, and see if anybody there can lend us a pump,' said Barney. 'Why don't you go back to the claim, and see what you can do to bale it out with buckets?'

'Okay,' said Joel. He hesistated for a moment.

'Is there something wrong?' asked Barney.

Joel took off his hat, dusted it, and then knocked it back into shape. 'I think I ought to say that I'm sorry,' he said.

'Sorry? What for?'

'Sorry for behaving like a mad dog. Sorry for being so vicious to you when you've done nothing but help me. Just – sorry.'

Barney put his arm around his brother's shoulders and held him very close. 'You don't think I understand how you've been feeling? You've been such a *farbissener*! But it doesn't matter. We love you, both of us. Mooi Klip and I. And that's the way it's always going to be.'

Joel sniffed, and wiped tears away from his face. 'I wanted so much to be strong,' he said. 'But I couldn't carry Mama, and I couldn't carry the tailor's business. When I was at sea, I couldn't take that, either. You know what work it is, on a merchant steamer? Two hours sleep, and twenty-two hours' shifting cargo. Then I bought the farm, and I didn't know how the hell to cope with that, either. It was all weeds, and dereliction! I couldn't even scratch the surface. Now, it's the mine. And it's still Mama, too. I can still see the way she looked. I can still hear her voice. Why in God's name wasn't I born to some other woman?'

Barney stood straight, and held Joel's shoulders with both hands. 'How can you talk this way, when you haven't failed at all? You haven't let anybody down – you've done nothing but succeed. You have a share in one of the richest diamond mines in the whole world. You have a brother who loves you, and a sister-in-law who's going to love you, too.'

'Your Mooi Klip thinks I'm crazy and cantankerous.'

'Don't be so crazy and cantankerous. Or course she doesn't.'

Joel smiled, and then took hold of Barney's curls and affectionately shook his head. 'You're right. I've been acting like a fool. Miserable, sour, and mean, for no reason. And that's why I'm saying sorry.'

'All right,' said Barney, gently. 'You're sorry. Now, don't let's anything more about it. It's my wedding tomorrow.'

They shook hands, and gripped each other tightly for a moment. Then Joel said quietly, 'I'll see you later. On your wedding-eve,' and walked off along Kimberley's main street towards the Big Hole. Barney climbed aboard their ox-waggon, snapped the whip, and steered their two oxen slowly out towards the De Beers mine.

It was an unusually chilly and windy afternoon. Dust and dry weeds tumbled across the veld, and Barney had to cover his mouth with his necktie. In the distance, he could see wind-devils dancing, and trees waving at him with wild helplessness, like drowning bathers. The sky to the west, from the Vaal River and the distant Kuruman Heuwells, was devastatingly black.

Despite the wind, he made the De Beers mine in good time. It was at this location that diamonds had first been discovered on Vooruitzigt, and the one-time arable fields were now deeply pitted with trenches and craters. Work had almost been abandoned here for a while when diamonds had been discovered on Colesberg Kopje, but not a bizarre selection of gallows-like winches were swinging the yellow ground out of the deep-dug claims as fast as they were at the Big Hole.

Barney tethered his ox-waggon, and walked to the rim of the mine. He could see that several of the claims, like his own, were deep in vivid yellow water, and that many of the diggers were doing nothing but sitting around, smoking and drinking and waiting for a couple of days of dry windy weather to evaporate the worst of their floods. But one claim, only a few hundred yards from where he was standing, was being diligently emptied by a noisy clattering steam-pump, and the kaffirs there, although they were ankledeep in water, were at least able to continue shovelling the yellow gravel into their buckets.

Barney skirted the edge of the diggings until he reached the tent where the owner of this claim was sitting. As soon as he saw him, Barney knew that he should have saved himself a walk.

It was Rhodes, sitting on a camp-stool in his cricket clothes, reading Plutarch's *Lives* while his kaffirs heaped mountains of sloshy yellow soil all around him.

'Barney Blitz,' said Rhodes, putting down his book. 'This is a great pleasure.'

'How are you doing?' asked Barney, nodding towards Rhodes' claim.

'Well, quite capital so far,' said Rhodes, in his high-pitched voice. 'I average about twenty pounds a day. Do you know I found a diamond of seventeen carats on Saturday, right outside the door of my tent? Just lying there!'

'You should get at least £100 for it,' said Barney.

'Well, that's what I thought,' nodded Rhodes.

'You must be one of the chosen, after all,' said Barney, with a wry smile.

Rhodes held up his book. 'It's all a question of education, you know. A good education, properly applied, is more compelling than a dozen howitzers. Do you what Pliny the Elder once said?'

'Pliny the who?'

'Pliny the Elder. Born, AD 23, died AD 79. And what he said was, *'ex Africa semper aliquid novi'*, which means "there is always something new coming out of Africa." Now, I learned that at school when I was ten, and when my family doctor said I had to go somewhere dry, to help my tuberculosis, I remembered it. So I thought the very best thing I could do was join Herbert in Natal, and aren't I glad that I did?'

'You must be,' said Barney. 'Could I borrow your pump?'

Rhodes laughed, and kicked his heels like a small boy. 'I was wondering when you were going to ask me that.'

'Oh, yes?' said Barney, rather put out.

'Well, you're not the first,' smiled Rhodes. 'About every half-hour, one disconsolate digger or another comes up and asks me if he can borrow my pump.'

'I see.'

'You don't see,' said Rhodes, slipping a grubby white cricket sock between the pages of his book, to mark the place. 'I can't lend you my pump, because I need it. But I can *hire* you a pump.'

'You have a pump to rent?'

'I have two. They're inside the tent. Take your pick. Two pounds a day, if you're interested.'

'Where the hell did you get them?'

Rhodes was terribly pleased with himself, and kept rubbing the back of his neck with glee. 'I bought them from a frightful German, who was on his way to Kimberley. I used the last of the money I had left over from my cotton harvest. Eight cylinder pumps, eighty pounds. Not bad, eh?'

Barney slowly shook his head. 'I thought you said that nobody could make a fortune from growing cotton.'

'Do you want a pump?' asked Rhodes. 'You'd better make up your mind quickly.'

'All right,' said Barney, and took his brown leather wallet out of his crumpled bush-jacket. 'Here's eight pounds, for four days' pumping. But let me tell you this – these eight pounds are the first and last money that I'm ever going to pay you.'

'Quite right too,' said Rhodes, and smiled even more broadly.

Barney and Rhodes lifted the pump between them on to the back of the ox-waggon, and Barney rode back to Kimberley with the pump's discharge pipe rattling monotonously against the waggon's tailgate as a constant nagging reminder of what he had just been compelled to do. He felt relieved that he had found a pump, but depressed that he had been obliged to hire it from Rhodes. He should have had the foresight to buy up pumps himself. Eight pumps, rented at two pounds a day, would have meant sixteen pounds a day, which meant that Rhodes could cover his eighty pounds outlay in a single week.

There were plenty of fierce competitors at Kimberley – men whom Barney had already picked out of the milling mob of diggers as potential empirebuilders. Francis Baring Gould was one. Severe, haughty, he had excellent financial connections in London, and Barney knew that he was pressuring the Board to relax their old rule that one man could own only two claims. Another was Joseph B. Robinson, an unpleasant and gratuitously argumentative man whose nickname, even among his friends, was 'The Buccaneer'. But Barney felt able to cope with men like Gould and Robinson without too much difficulty. He understood what they were seeking out of the diamond mines – wealth and luxury and petty power – and how they intended to get it. Only Rhodes baffled him. Rhodes, for all of his humour, was almost impossible to puzzle out. And yet only Rhodes seemed likely to stand between Barney and his ultimate ambition.

Because now – with a clarity that fired him up like the finest of diamonds – Barney knew what his ambition was. His dream had taken shape, a bright and scintillating mirage rising from the African desert, and it had revealed itself as nothing less than the kingship of the Kimberley diamond mine. He wanted to stand on the North Reef of the Big Hole and look out across that burrowing chaos of intense human industry and know that it was all his.

He wanted to sink his hands into a bucket of diamonds, a whole bucket, and know that they all belonged to him.

The shadows were already sloping across the veld as he reached Kimberley again, and reined in the ox-waggon outside his bungalow. Most of the heavy cloud seemed to have passed over, and the western sky was like a lake of stirred magnolia honey.

Inside the bungalow, all the lamps were lit, and Barney expected that Mooi Klip was making last-minute alterations to the wedding decorations, and fussing over the range. He loved her the way she was at the moment: very feminine and flustered, and quite unlike the capable Griqua girl who had taken charge of Joel so calmly, on the day that Barney had released him. She had not lost her directness or her common-sense, but she had gained a new vulnerability, a new dependence on him, which Barney secretly enjoyed.

He released the oxen from their yoke, and led them around to the small kraal at the back of the house, where he watered them and fed them. Then, tying the kraal gate, he went around to the front door, and tried to push it open.

To his surprise, it was locked. He tried the handle again, but there was no question about it. He could not get in.

'Natalia!' he called. Then he banged at the door with the flat of his hand. 'Natalia, are you there?'

He thought he heard someone inside the bungalow banging at the floor boards, and then there was the clatter of a chair being knocked over. He listened, his ear pressed against the door. There was nothing for a while, until Mooi Klip's voice was suddenly raised in a scream.

'*Natalia!*' yelled Barney, hoarsely, and slammed at the door with his shoulder. It would not budge. It was built of solid imported wood, and it was held on with double brass hinges. '*Natalia!*' he bellowed again, and gripped the sides of the door-frame so that he could kick at it with his veld boots. One of the panels cracked, but the door still refused to give way.

Exploding with fear and adrenalin, Barney ran around to the toolshed at the side of the house, wrenched open the door, and seized a long-handled axe. Then he ran back to the front, and walloped the axe into the side of the doorframe once, twice, and once again. Splinters flew all around him, and each blow jarred the muscles of his arms.

He kicked at the door again, and again, and at last it racketed open. What he saw made him stop where he was, his axe gripped in both hands, his eyes dense with disbelief and fury.

Mooi Klip lay crouched on the rug, her red dress pulled up over her hips, her petticoat torn into shreds. Her naked thights were criss-crossed with scratches, and patterned with bright crimson bruises. She was covering her face with her hands, and sobbing in a high, breathless pitch that scarcely sounded human.

Joel stood stiff and still in the corner of the living-room, his plaid workshirt open to the waist, baring his dark hairy belly, and his canvas trousers unbuttoned. His face was as grave and as odd as Barney had ever seen it. In his hand, upraised, he held the Shopkeeper's revolver which Barney had bought in New York as part of his supplies for the wilds of South Africa. The muzzle was aimed at the ceiling, but the way in which Joel was holding his arm up left Barney in no doubt that he was threatening him with his life.

Scattered across the floor and ground underfoot were cakes and pastries and baskets of plums. Even the three-tiered white wedding cake, a gift from Scheinman's the bakers, had been smashed sideways.

Barney, his brain as tight as an overwound clock, slowly laid down his axe. Then without keeping his eyes off Joel, he moved across the room and knelt down beside Mooi Klip, lifting her head on to his knee. She was shaking and crying, and she would not take her hands away from her face. Barney smoothed down her dress and held her close to him, gently rocking her, and stroking her hair.

'Are you all right?' he asked her. 'Are you hurt bad?'

Joel waved the pistol around carelessly as if he really had not meant to threaten Barney at all. But he did not put it down. He could see by the expression on Barney's face what would happen to him if he did.

'This isn't what it seems,' he said, lightly. He pulled at his left eyelid with his fingertip, as if he were rubbing sleep out of it.

'Isn't it?' asked Barney, in a deadened voice.

'It's, er – well, it started off as fun. That's all it was. Just fun.'

'Did you touch her?' asked Barney. He felt so cold that he couldn't move.

'We didn't do anything. We were just joking. Horseplay. That's all.'

'Did you touch her?' Barney repeated, more loudly.

Joel grinned. He wiped his nose with the back of his gun-hand. 'She was only arranging the table, that's all, and I thought that – if I –'

'*Did you touch her?*' screamed Barney.

Joel shrugged, and glanced sideways across the wreckage of the room as if he were looking for something special. 'Touch? Well, it depends what you mean by touch.'

'Did you assault her is what I mean.'

Joel's eyes darted back towards Barney, and he frowned.

Barney said, 'I'm going to kill you for this. I mean it. I'm going to kill you.'

He laid Mooi Klip carefully on the rug, and stood up. Mooi Klip lay on her side, bunched up self-protectively tight, her hands clasped in front of her mouth and her eyes wide open. She stared at nothing but the broken cakes and the trodden fruit, and she did not stop shaking.

'You said you were sorry, and I believed you,' Barney told Joel, circling around the table. 'I believed you!'

'I *was* sorry,' said Joel, swallowing hard, unable to look Barney in the face. 'I'm sorry now.'

'You're *sorry?*'

Joel's lips tightened, and then he burst out, 'What do you think it's like, living here with you two? Didn't you think of that, when you set up this cozy little household of yours?'

'What the hell are you talking about?'

'I'm talking about *her!*' said Joel, desperately. 'What do you think it's like, living here with her! Seeing her washing and cooking and cleaning everything up. Seeing her kiss you. Don't you think I'm just as capable of falling in love as you are? Or hasn't that ever occurred to you, that your brother Joel could fall in love? Maybe you can't bring yourself to believe that anybody else apart from the great Barney Blitz has any kind of real existence?'

Barney said, in a low-key, unsteady voice, 'She's my bride, Joel. You knew that. You *knew* that! And yet you could still attack her.'

'Attack her?' protested Joel, in an unexpectedly squeaky tone. 'You don't think that I'd stoop so low, do you? She attacked me! Tore her petticoats, begged me to take her before she was married to you. Begged me! Come on, Barney, she's nothing but a *schwartzeh*, and you know what they're like, even the educated ones! They've got morals like monkeys!'

Barney pushed aside the table, with a scraping of wooden feet, and advanced towards Joel with his fists raised. Joel stumbled back two or three paces, coughing, but then he gripped the revolver in both hands and pointed it directly at Barney's face.

'You'd kill me, would you?' Barney said shakily. 'Your own brother?'

'You're angry,' said Joel. 'You don't know what you're doing. I just want you to stay back.'

He edged around the room, keeping the revolver out in front of him. 'I've *told* you I'm sorry,' he repeated. There was a terrible monotony in his voice, like a deaf and backward child. 'I've told you I'm sorry, and I *am* sorry. But it's one of those things. Who can help it? Anyway, it's all over now. I can't turn the clock back. Even if I could, well, what good what it do? I haven't hurt her. She's pregnant already, so I haven't given her a baby. I wouldn't want to. My own brother's bride?'

Barney hesitated, and lowered his fists. Joel began to lower the gun, too, but when Barney made another move towards him, he quickly lifted it again.

'I think you'd better get out of here,' said Barney. 'Because I'm liable to go for you, whether you've got yourself a gun or not.'

'Oh,' said Joel. 'You're forgiving me, are you?'

'Just get out.'

Joel stared at Barney down the barrel of the Shopkeeper's revolver with eyes that seemed as impenetrable as stones. Barney could hardly believe that this wild and frenzied man was actually his own brother. He felt as if he had suddenly found himself in a petrifying nightmare of mirrors and anguish and broken cake.

There was a clattering sound. A few splatters of wet appeared on the floor around Joel's left foot. Joel wavered, but did not look down. His canvas trousers steamed with urine.

The brothers did not speak another word. Joel slowly retreated out of the doorway, almost tripping over Barney's long-handled axe. He crossed the vehandah, groping behind him for the rail, and then disappeared quickly into the evening shadows.

Barney stood motionless for almost a minute. Then he knelt down and gathered Mooi Klip in his arms, and carried her like a new bride into the bedroom, where he laid her carefully down on the patchwork comforter.

'I'm going to heat water for a bath,' he whispered, close to her ear, close to her sooty-brown curls. 'You can wash, and soak yourself, and then we'll clear everything up.'

'Barney,' she said, her chin crumpled with grief.

'Don't cry,' he told her.

'I can't help it. I can't help crying. How can you marry me now?'

Barney kissed her eyelashes, and the tears that clung to them like the raindrops that clung to the silverleaf.

'You're going to have my baby. How can I not marry you?'

She touched his face in the twilight. 'I don't know what happened. He was all right for most of the day. He went to the

219

claim, and came back again. We talked about the wedding. Then he started teasing me, and trying to put his arms around me.'

Barney laid his fingers on her lips, to try to stop her talking, but she wanted to talk, and she took his hand away.

'I said no. I told him no. But he followed me around the room, and around the house, and he kept grabbing me and pulling at my dress. I called out for Janet next door, but she wasn't there, or else she didn't hear me. He wouldn't stop. He wouldn't leave me alone.'

'Mooi Klip,' said Barney, gently.

'Oh, Barney,' she sobbed, and clung to him tight. 'How can I marry you now?'

Barney couldn't speak for a long time. His chest and his throat felt congested with anguish and grief.

'You can marry me,' he managed to say, at last. 'I'll never forgive you if you don't.'

She turned her head away, and he looked down at her dark profile on the white pillow. Her eyes, and the pretty curve of her nose. He wished he were an artist, or a daguerrotypist, because he wanted to remember the way she looked, framed by the pillow, for ever. Mooi Klip, on Tuesday, 14 November 1871, a day of hopes and joys and indescribable pain.

'My mother and father will be here tomorrow,' said Mooi Klip. 'I will go back to Klipdrift with them.'

'Don't be ridiculous. Tomorrow, we're going to be married.'

'We can't. How can we? You have to stay with Joel. Half of the claim is yours. You can't give it up, just for me.'

'I still have the farm.'

Mooi Klip shook her head. 'You want to make your fortune. The claim is the only way. If you give it up because of me, you would never forget and you would never really forgive.'

Barney kissed her. 'You've crazy,' he told her. 'Do you know that? You're absolutely crazy.' But at the same time, the thought of what he and Joel were going to do about their thirty-one square feet of diamond-bearing ground had already passed across the back of his mind like a ghost seen momentarily at the end of a long corridor.

Mooi Klip closed her eyes. Barney said, 'He didn't hurt you, did he? He didn't hurt you inside? I mean, the baby's going to be all right?'

She gave a slight shake of her head. 'He didn't get properly inside me. I fought him all the time. I'm just tired now.'

'I'll heat the water,' Barney told her. He felt compelled to do something ordinary, something that required no thinking at all. Every thought in his head seemed to have been blasted out of him. He stood up and smiled at Mooi Klip with a smile that was meaningless, because it was neither loving nor reassuring. It was the smile of a man who is still suffering from shock, after an accident that has almost proved fatal.

She bathed in the zinc tub in the living-room, amidst the wreckage of her ruined wedding-breakfast. She wanted the water so hot that Barney could scarcely dip his hand in it; and she sat upright, her face expressionless, her hair tied up with a yellow ribbon. She said hardly anything at all, except to ask him to bring her another piece of soap.

Without looking at him, she knelt up in the tub and lathered herself between her legs over and over again, in a monotonous circular motion, until he felt like shouting out, 'It's over – it's all over – you're clean.' But she went on, and after a few minutes he hung the rough towel which he had been holding for her over the back of his chair, and went to the hutch to pour himself a drink.

Later, he made her some tea. She sat up in bed, wrapped in a blanket, and cupped the mug in both hands, like a child. Barney sat beside the bed with a fixed smile on his face until he realised that she was not even looking at him, and then his smile grew even more falser, although he could not think of anything else to do. Should he frown? Or scowl? Should he shout at her to pull herself together? It was supposed to be her wedding-day tomorrow, the day that she going to be happy again, forever.

He held her hand, and although she did not take away, it lay in his grasp like a glove. He said, 'Mooi Klip?' but she did not answer. Her eyes and her thoughts, were somewhere else.

Sometime after one o'clock in the morning, after wedging the broken front door with a chair, Barney wearily undressed and slipped into bed. Mooi Klip was still awake, still sitting up with her eyes open. He put his arm around her but she was so unresponsive that after a few minutes, uncomfortable and embarrassed, he took it away again.

'We're still going to get married tomorrow,' he told her. 'We planned to get married tomorrow, and we will.'

Mooi Klip stared down at her hands lying on the patchwork comforter as if she could not work out whose hands they were.

Barney said, 'You are going to marry me, aren't you?'

'Someday,' she said, and nodded. 'Perhaps someday.'

They were woken up at dawn by someone shouting and banging at the front of the house. Barney threw back the comforter, and staggered naked to the bedroom door, where his cotton nightshirt hung on a cuphook.

'Barney!' a voice called loudly. 'Barney, come quick!'

He negotiated his way across the cake-strewn living-room, and tugged the chair away from the front door. It was bright outside, and still chilly with the dew that settled in the early hours of the night like imaginary diamonds. On the verandah stood Edward Nork, in grubby twill trousers and puttees, and a jacket that looked as if it had once belonged to the fattest man in Cape Colony. Behind him, two kaffirs were waiting with grins as orange as slices of sausage fruit, bearing a woven litter, on which was huddled the body of a man, smothered in blood and yellow mud.

Edward Nork said, 'You're going to have to be calm, now, Barney. It's Joel. There's been rather a bad accident.'

'Joel?' asked Barney. He could not understand what Edward Nork was trying to tell him. Then he looked again at the gory body on the litter, and saw a hand that was unmistakably Joel's hanging from one side. The shirt, although it was torn and basted with mud, was also unmistakably Joel's. Barney crossed the verandah as if he were still asleep, and one of the kaffirs said. 'He not dead, boss. He was screaming out just a while back. Screaming like blue murder.'

'Take him inside,' Barney instructed. But he looked up, and

there in the doorway in her nightgown was Mooi Klip, her face pale, her hands crossed over her breasts.

'Natalia,' said Barney, and she could hear the question in his voice. 'Natalia, it's Joel.'

She did not move, did not speak, but stood in the doorway waiting for Barney to make up his mind what he was going to do.

'He's hurt,' said Barney. 'He could be dying.'

Mooi Klip raised her chin defiantly. 'A funeral?' she asked him.

'I don't know what you mean. Look at him. He needs help.'

'You can have a funeral or a wedding,' said Mooi Klip. 'Not both.'

Edward Nork wound his loose jacket around him in discomfort. He was a geologist, and a drinker. He was always ill-at-ease in family arguments. 'Dwyka tillite does not answer back, nor put one into embarrassing corners,' he had told Barney over dinner, the night that Rhodes had first arrived. 'Neither does whiskey. But wives and children unfortunately do.'

Mooi Klip said, 'I don't care if he's dying or not, Barney. I don't want him here. And if you go to his funeral, I won't ever speak to you again. You won't get anything out of me but silence, for the rest of my life.'

Joel whimpered. Barney looked down at his battered, mud-crusted face, and saw that his lips were blue and that his eyes were rolled up so that the whites were exposed.

'What happened?' Barney asked Edward Nork.

Edward shrugged, as if to say that he knew, but he did not want to talk about it in front of Mooi Klip.

'All right,' said Barney. 'Get him inside.'

Mooi Klip retreated back into the house, and into the bedroom. She closed the door, and as Barney stepped in after her to clear the floor of cake and fruit, he heard her click the hasp into place.

'Down here,' he told the kaffirs. 'And gently, for God's sake.'

The kaffirs laid Joel down on the floor, and then ran off. Edward Nork, pacing around the living-room in embarrassment, said, 'Your wedding today? Looks like the food got a bit of a bashing.'

'It was *supposed* to have been my wedding today,' said Barney.

Edward nodded his head towards the bedroom door. 'Bit of trouble? I've heard some of those Griquas are rather hot-tempered.'

Baney knelt down beside Joel and unbuttoned his shirt. From the lumpy bruises that protruded from Joel's chest, it looked as if four or five of his ribs were broken. Joel groaned, and licked his muddy lips.

'Edward – will you do me a favour?' asked Barney. 'Stoke up the range. There's plenty of fresh firewood in the kitchen. I need some hot water to clean him up.'

'Don't you want to hear what happened?'

'Just get the fire going, please. I've had enough grief for one night.

'Anything you say,' said Edward, and disappeared into the kitchen.

It took over half an hour to get Joel undressed and cleaned up, and laid on his bed. He whimpered and cried constantly, and Barney could feel that apart from his ribs, his left leg was badly smashed. His arms and legs were raw with cuts and abrasions, and the middle finger on his right hand was pulped almost flat.

Between them, with Edward holding his head and Barney tilting up the bottle, they managed to force Joel to drink almost a quarter of a bottle of brandy. He brought up a couple of mouthfuls of vomit, half-digested meat pie, and whiskey, but he kept enough of the brandy down to send him to sleep for a while.

'All right then, what happened?' asked Barney, closing Joel's door behind him. He glanced at Mooi Klip's door, but then looked away again. Edward noticed, though, and gave a wry schoolboy grin.

'We were all at Dodd's Bar,' said Edward. 'None of us were doing very much. Getting drunk, playing billiards, you know. Another entertaining evening in Kimberley. But then Joel came in, and I must say he looked rather mad. Mad in the English sense, if you know what I mean.'

'You mean he was acting crazy.'

'Well, quite so. He had a pistol, which he was waving around, until Harry Munt took it away from him, and locked it in his safe. And I must say that Joel *smelled*, rather. Not too fussy about cleanliness, myself. You can't be, out here, with water so scarce. But he definitely *smelled*.'

Barney lowered his head and stood with his hands clasped at the back of his neck. 'Go on,' he said. 'Do you want a drink?'

'That's rather like asking an ostrich if it wants to fly.'

Barney drained the last of the sherry bottle, and then topped it up with sherry from the cask which had been intended for the wedding. He paused for a moment and stared at the cake, a broken litter of almond paste and white frosting, and crushed silver horseshoes.

'That looks a bit wonky,' said Edward, trying to be conversational.

'Yes,' said Barney, picking up one of the horseshoes and then dropping it again, 'I think that's the word. Wonky.'

Edward took his sherry, and drank half of it straight away. Then, wiping his mouth, he said, 'The trouble really started when that lady from Capetown came in. Well, *lady* isn't quite the word. Whore, is what she was. She was drunk as any of us, but the trouble was that she'd been waiting all night at Madame Lavinia's, and nobody had given her a try. It really wasn't surprising, to tell you the truth. Rather unfortunate boat race. Oh, I'm sorry. That's Cockney rhyming slang for "face"; it always amused me, don't know why. I didn't even go to Oxford or Cambridge. But anyway, there she was – drunk, and red-haired, and very much in the mood for mischief – and she decided to auction herself to the highest bidder.'

Barney poured another drink for himself, but right now his stomach felt too tight for him to swallow it. 'Go on,' he said, dryly.

'Well, this is the ticklish bit,' said Edward. 'There was a Dutch diamond buyer there, and he bid £25, and then £30, and then £100. He was quite out of his mind with Geneva gin, of course. I mean, almost insensible. But Joel seemed determined to bust him. And, in the end, he bid his claim.'

'He did *what*?'

'He bid his claim. All thirty-one square feet of it, in return for a night with madame from down the road.'

'But Joel doesn't *own* the whole claim. We're equal partners, fifty-fifty. He can't sell out without offering me the option to buy his half, any more than I can sell out without offering him the option to buy mine. He can't dispose of the whole claim on his own, and especially not in Dodd's Bar, for some flea-bitten prostitute.'

'That's what I thought,' said Edward. 'And, merry as I was, I told him so.'

'But?' demanded Barney.

'But, old fellow, I'm afraid that Joel has rather outsmarted you. If you can call it smart, of course, to hand over a £5000 diamond claim to a common prostitute, in return for a night of passion that you never had. Joel told me that he had never actually re-registered the claim in your favour at all. The claim is entirely his. So when he put in his bid for this drunken red-haired lady, he was entirely within his rights. And she will be entirely within *her* rights if she tries to enforce her ownership. Which, knowing her, at least from one night at Dodd's Bar, she most certainly will.'

Barney stared at Edward for a long time in silence.

'I'm sorry,' said Edward. 'If only I'd known, I would have told you sooner. But, well –'

'What happened?' asked Barney, harshly and soft. 'How did he get so hurt?'

'There was rather an argument,' said Edward. 'Do you have some more of that excellent sherry, incidentally? Thank you. Good. Anyway, the Dutch diamond buyer declared that he was in love with this lady from Madame Lavinia's, regardless of Joel's winning bid, and hauled her off with him. I must say there was a great deal of amusement at this ... you know the kind of thing. Laughing, and throwing bottles. So Joel led a whole gang of diggers out of Dodd's Bar, and they followed the poor little Dutch fellow all the way to his tent ... and when he was just about to stake his claim, if you understand what I mean ... just as he was settling down with this lady from Madame Lavinia's ... the whole lot of them heaved out his tent-pegs, and whisked away his tent, and there the poor fellow was, caught in the act!'

Barney looked away. He felt tired, and unreal, and Edward's story fell on his consciousness like dead leaves.

'There was something of a fight,' said Edward, almost apologetically. 'The Dutch diamond buyer wasn't much of a pug, but of course Joel was incapably drunk. There was a lot of scuffling, and then Joel fell down the side of the mine, into somebody's claim; and the ground being so wet, it collapsed on top of him. Rocks, winching-gear, everything. It took ten men to dig him out.'

'What about a doctor?' asked Barney.

'We tried Tuter. We sent somebody round to his home.'

'And?'

'He wouldn't come. He *couldn't* come, actually. He was drunk.'

'So my brother's going to die. Is that it?'

Edward had been holding up his empty glass, but now he set it down again, abashed. 'An awful lot of diggers die out here, Barney, It's one of the natural hazards of diamond-mining. There's malaria, dysentery, and cholera. There's women and there's drink. Your brother's quite lucky he won't linger.'

'Lucky?' said Barney. 'Such a *miesse meshina*, and he's lucky?'

'*Comparatively* lucky,' Edward corrected himself.

Barney crossed the room and looked in at Joel's door. Joel was lying just where they had left him, his face the colour of dirty canvas. His teeth were softly and endlessly chattering, and he twitched from time to time in pain. Barney knew only too well what would happen to him if he did not receive professional medical attention right away. Since they had started mining their claim, they had both seen scores of diggers and kaffirs poisoned by gangrene, or felled by blood clots to the brain. He remembered the time an Australian digger had crushed his left hand in the winding gear of his steel cable, and had tried to carry on working with his fingers bandaged up. He had died within two weeks of the foulest infection that Barney had ever seen. There were dozens of graves outside Kimberley, on the veld, and most of the men who lay in them had died for the want of a surgeon.

'There's nothing I can do, then?' asked Barney. 'I just have to wait here and watch him suffer?'

Edward had been helping himself to more sherry. 'I hear that

227

Sir Thomas Sutter is in Durban at the moment, visiting his nephew.'

'Sir Thomas Sutter? Who's he?'

'Only the most eminent surgeon and bonesetter in England, old chap. Barring the Queen's physician, of course. Don't tell me you've never heard of Sutter the Cutter?'

'No, I haven't. But he's no use to Joel, is he, if he's in Durban?'

Edward sighed. 'You could try to get him there. I mean, there's no guarantee that he'd arrive alive, or even in an operable condition. There isn't even any kind of guarantee that Sir Thomas would consent to operate. He's frightfully particular about who he cuts up, and frightfully pricey, too. But ... it may be worth a try.'

Barney closed his eyes. This was supposed to have been the happiest day he had ever woken up to. Now, like his wedding-cake, it lay in pieces. He wished to God that he had been born somewhere else, to someone else, in another day and another age. It would have been better never to have met Mooi Klip at all, rather than meet her and love her and lose her this way. And all because of his ridiculous brother.

'I suppose I should try to get there,' said Barney. 'As long as Joel doesn't suffer too much.'

Edward sat forward in his chair. 'If he does suffer ... well, Harry Munt's still got your gun.'

Shortly after nine o'clock, there was the sharp rapping of a cane on the front door. Barney had been bathing Joel's forehead with a wet cloth, while Edward had gone over to Dr Tuter's place to persuade him to prescribe some painkillers for the journey to Durban. Barney carefully propped Joel's head with a pillow, and went out to see who it was.

Silhouetted against the dazzle of the day, formally dressed in black, his hat straight and his walking-cane tucked under his arm, was Mr Knight.

Barney wiped his hands on a towel. 'Yes?' he asked. 'And what can I do for you?'

'Not much,' said Mr Knight, sharply. 'It's your brother Joel Blitz I've come to see.'

'My brother's seriously ill.'

'Well, I knew that. But all the same I have to serve notice on him. Laws of the land, and all that.'

'Whatever it is, you can tell me.'

'I really have to serve it on your brother.'

Barney rolled down his sleeves with two or three aggressive tugs at his cuffs. 'Either tell me, or get the hell out of here.'

'Very well. I suppose you could be considered to be standing in for him as his legal proxy. The fact of the matter is,' and here he cleared his throat, 'the fact of the matter is that I represent a young lady named Dorothy Evans, or "Dottie", as she is known to her friends. She came to me very early this morning in order to press her ownership of claim No. 172 at the Kimberley Mine which previously belonged in whole to Mr Joel Blitz.'

'I think the young lady must be making a mistake,' said Barney. 'Claim No. 172 belongs to my brother and that's it.'

'Well, you're wrong, I'm afraid. Miss Evans has written proof – written and witnessed – that your brother handed the claim over to her, complete with all mining equipment, at Dodd's Bar at approximately eleven o'clock last night.'

Barney looked at Mr Knight steadily. There was no doubt at all that Mr Knight was enjoying every moment of this. A sweet and legalistic revenge for the way in which Barney had tricked and humiliated himself and his family. 'There is no better situation for a Jew,' Mr Knight had told Dottie Evans that morning, 'than to be wriggling like an insect on the end of a very sharp stick.'

Barney said, 'What written proof? Show me.'

Mr Knight produced a crumpled piece of paper from the breast pocket of his coat, like a children's conjuror. 'A humble piece of paper,' he smiled. 'The label from a bottle of patent bitters, if I'm not mistaken. But the writing on it has all the weight of English law.'

Barney took the paper and read it. In a sloping scrawl, Joel had written the words, 'I Joel Blitz hereby pass all title in my claim No. 172 at Colesberg Kop to Dottie Evans, and all my mining equpt.' That was all. Joel must have been so drunk that he had even stipulated what favours Miss Dottie Evans was supposed to give him in return.

'This is worthless,' said Barney. 'Joel was totally drunk at the time. I have witnesses.'

'Witnesses? A collection of lechers and confirmed alcoholics?'

'Miss Dottie Evans herself is a whore,' Barney reminded him.

Mr Knight raised a beatific hand. 'She *was* a whore. She was, indeed, a whore. But now she has seen the error of her ways, and raised herself from the mire.'

'She can afford to, I suppose, now she has a free diamond mine.'

'Don't be so sour,' grinned Mr Knight, snatching the bitters label back between two grey-gloved fingers.

'I'm not,' said Barney. 'Right now, I haven't time to be sour. My brother is badly hurt and I have to get him to a doctor.'

'Well, I'm sorry,' said Mr Knight. 'I truly am. But – the law is the law.'

He looked around the living-room. 'Wasn't today supposed to be the day you were going to marry that little black girl?' he asked. 'I heard the banns read in church, and I must tell you that I stood up for you when one or two of the congregation started expressing objections. "Why should we allow a Jew and a blackie to get married in an Anglican church?" they asked. But I said, "Is that your spirit of Christian charity? The Griquas are just as much Christians as we are, and with any luck the Jewish fellow will learn the error of his ways."'

'You're right,' said Barney. 'I have learned the error of my ways. And it was you who taught me the lesson. You *momzer*.'

Mr Knight widened his eyes interrogatively.

'It's a name we give to anybody who's clever,' Barney told him. 'You know the type. Wily, smart, that type of person.'

'Well,' said Mr Knight, 'I'm glad you've taken the whole thing so well.'

'*Monzer* also means bastard,' Barney added.

Mr Knight pressed his tongue thoughtfully inside his cheek. Then he said coldly, 'I have to warn you that any attempt by you or your kaffirs to dig in claim No. 172 will be regarded as claim-jumping, and theft, and that if you are caught trespassing

230

on claim No. 172 my client will consider your action as a most serious breach of her digging rights.'

'Get out of my house before I hit you,' said Barney.

Edward came back just as Mr Knight was leaving. He raised his hat to him, and was mildly surprised when the laywer brushed past him without even saying, 'Good day.'

'That was your legal chap, wasn't it?' he asked, emptying his coat pockets of dozens of glass vials of white powder. 'He didn't seem very jolly did he?'

'What are these?' asked Barney, picking up one of the vials and examining it. 'Are these painkillers?'

'Dover's powder, old chap. Ten per cent of opium, to be given in doses of five grains to begin with, up to ten if the pain gets worse. And I'm afraid you owe me eleven pounds for this little lot. Four pounds for the medicine itself, and seven to persuade Dr Tuter to give them to me. Mind you, he's quite addicted to the stuff himself.'

At that moment, the bedroom door opened. Barney turned around, and there stood Mooi Klip, in her pale blue overdress and hat, her gloves held tightly in her hand, her eyes swollen from crying.

Edward said quickly, 'I'll just go and give Joel his first dose. Dr Tuter said to start as soon as possible.'

'Thank you, Edward,' said Barney, his eyes on Mooi Klip.

Mooi Klip stepped out into the living-room. The sun from the open doorway sparkled on the $2\frac{1}{2}$-carat diamond betrothal ring that Harry Feinberg had ordered for Barney from Cape-town, and which Barney had slipped on to Mooi Klip's finger one warm evening when they had been sitting on the verandah outside, under a moon like a tiger's-eye.

She raised her hand and twisted the ring around and around, the way that women do when they feel anxious. She would not look at Barney, but stared sadly at their weeding-breakfast instead.

'I've packed my clothes,' she said.

'You're really going?'

She nodded.

'You know how much I love you, don't you?'

She nodded again.

231

He bit his lip. 'What can I say that will make you stay? Can I say anything?'

'Not now,' she said. 'Right now, you have to look after your brother.'

'I had to bring him in. You understand that, don't you? He's – well, he's probably going to die anyway.'

'I'm sorry,' said Mooi Klip. 'What I said outside, about never speaking to you again – I didn't mean it. I was just –'

'If you didn't mean it, then stay. Please. What do you think I'm going to do without you?'

Mooi Klip slowly shook her head. 'You don't need me now. I won't be anything but a burden. And everything that's happened ... it's spoiled this day for us, and we'd be foolish if we tried to patch it up. I don't want to be married with a broken wedding-cake. I don't want to be married while we're arguing. I want to be married to your properly, in peace, and in love; and to know that we can have nothing but happiness.'

'We *will* be happy.'

She smiled at him. A smile of such sadness and regret; but also a smile of determination. 'Not yet,' she said. 'We're not ready for each other yet, even if we ever were. I love you, Barney. I don't think you even understand how much. You've taught me about the world, and about all kinds of things. But I'm not really what you want, or what you need, am I?'

'You're going back to Klipdrift?' he asked her.

'As soon as my mother and father arrive.'

'And what are you going to tell them? And Jan Bloem?'

'I shall tell them the truth. That's all. The truth isn't difficult to tell. I still love you, and I'm not ashamed of that.'

'What about the baby?' asked Barney.

She laid her hand on her stomach. 'I shall cherish the baby. And when she's born, if we're still not together by then, I shall send someone with a message to you, so that you can come and see her.'

Barney felt as if a dry ball of desert weed had caught in his throat. 'You're so sure it's going to be a girl,' he said, trying hard not to cry.

'Wouldn't you like a pretty little daughter, just like me?'

Barney nodded. Mooi Klip came over to him, and put her arms around his waist, and held him very tight. He could smell that familiar smell of hers, like flowers and spices, and he wound her curls around his fingers the way he had always done, ever since their first night together under the stars at Jan Bloem's encampment. He could not believe that she was going. He could not believe that he might never hold her again. Her hard stomach, still high under her breasts, was pressed between them like the most precious possession they had ever owned. Brighter, and more valuable, than diamonds.

She whispered against his shirt, 'I heard everything that Edward said, about your losing the claim.'

'And Mr Knight?'

She said, 'Yes. I'm so sorry.'

'I guess I can start again.'

'You'll need money for Joel's operation,' she said.

'I've got enough in the bank.'

'You'll need the money in the bank, to buy another claim.'

'I've got the farm, too, at Derdeheuwel. I can always sell that, if I have to.'

Mooi Klip stood away from him, and opened her purse. 'I've been meaning to give you this, anyway. It wasn't really right that I should keep it.'

'What are you talking about?'

Tied tightly in a roll, and tucked into the small pocket at the side of Mooi Klip's purse, were scores of English five-pound notes. Mooi Klip pushed the roll into Barney's shirt pocket, and then kissed him on the lips, quickly, so that he could not make the kiss linger.

He took the money out again. 'Where did you get all this?'

'From Derdeheuwel, the day we buried Monsaraz. I admired your gesture, burning the money, but sometimes I think that women are more practical than men, even if their gestures aren't so admirable.'

'There must be six or seven hundred pounds here.'

'Six hundred and twenty. I've counted it.'

'I should burn it,' said Barney.

'You have your brother to look after.'

'What are *you* going to do for money?'

She smiled. 'My people will look after me now.'

'Aren't I your people?'

She came close again, and touched the unshaved bristles on his cheek. 'You will always be my people,' she told him. 'Oh, Barney, I love you so much.'

Edward coughed politely at the bedroom door. 'He's sleeping again,' he announced. 'But he's only going to get worse, not better. Do you want me to help you make up a bed on the waggon?'

'Yes, please,' said Barney, and turned away from Jooi Klip feeling as if there were nothing inside of him but tears that could not be cried.

Mooi Klip's mother and father arrived at eleven o'clock, all dressed up in their wedding outfits. Jan Bloem was there, too, and two of his favourite cronies, and Piet Steyn. Their shoes were all brightly polished, their hats were brushed, and in their morning-coats and striped trousers they looked, in the sarcastic words of Harry Munt, who had watched them pass from the boardwalk outside of Dodd's Bar, 'like the guests of honour at a gorilla's ball.'

Mooi Klip's mother was small as her daughter, but plump, and she was dressed up in a lemon-yellow day frock with a grey-piped bolero, and a hat that was dancing with huge white ostrich feathers. Her father was tall, handsome, and very black. Neither of them spoke English – only the curious Afrikaans of the Griquas.

There were tears and arguments and explanations as soon as they arrived. It had been enough for Mooi Klip's father that she should live with a man outside of wedlock, and be carrying his child. Now, using a confused Jan Bloem as an occasional interpreter, he started to shout in a loud demanding voice at everybody, including his wife. Barney sat tiredly on the verandah steps, his head in his hands, and waited until everybody had finished squabbling. The waggon had been made ready to carry Joel to Durban, with blankets and pillows and leather straps to keep his broken leg straight, and all Barney wanted to do now was go.

At last, Mooi Klip's father came marching over to Barney, with Jan Bloem beside him, and let out a burst of guttural Afrikaans. There were diamonds of sweat on his shiny black upper lip, and he was as indignant and upright as any father that Barney had ever seen. There was a fresh white orchid in his buttonhole.

Barney understood only one or two words of what he was saying, but the strain of the tirade was inescapable. Jan Bloem said dryly, 'You hear what he's saying, my friend? He's saying you took everything from his daughter, and gave nothing back. He's saying you should be ashamed of what you and your brother have done, and that if it wasn't flying in the face of the Lord, he would turn you inside-out, and use your insides to feed his dogs.'

'Tell him he's quite justified in being so angry,' said Barney.

Jan Bloem translated. Mooi Klip's father listened, and then lifted one quivering finger, and came out with another interminable salvo of explosive rhetoric.

'He's very upset,' explained Jan Bloem. 'He wants to know what you're going to do.'

'I'm going to take my brother to Durban to try to save his life,' said Barney, flatly. 'Then I'm going to come back here to marry his daughter.'

'He doesn't believe you,' said Jan Bloem. 'He says you're a scallywag.'

'Tell him I love Natalia.'

'He says if you love her, how could you treat her so wrongly?'

'Tell him it was all a series of tragic mistakes, and that he doesn't have to keep shouting at me because I think I've suffered enough already. I love his daughter, and for the time being I'm losing her. I love my brother, and he's hurt the only woman I love. Just tell him to look at my face and see what's there.'

There was a long frowning pause from Mooi Klip's father when Jan Bloem had translated these words. Then he leaned forward, his hands on his knees, and stared at Barney's face from only five or six inches away, his jet-black eyes searching Barney's expression as narrowly and as painstakingly as Barney himself ever inspected a rough stone from the mine. At last,

Mooi Klip's father stood straight, and self-importantly brushed a little fluff from the cuff of his coat.

'Well?' asked Barney. 'I'm going to have to go soon, if I'm going to make any distance before dark.'

'He says he still thinks you're a scallywag,' smiled Jan Bloem. 'However, he believes what you say, that you love his daughter. When your brother is well, he says, you must come to speak to him again. But he says he will not easily let you marry her, unless you have proved your good intentions.'

'I see,' said Barney, and attempted a friendly nod towards Mooi Klip's father. The Griqua's face remained impassive, and Barney found himself converting the nod into a stiff-jointed twist of his neck, as if he had been sleeping all night at an odd angle.

'He says one thing more,' said Jan Bloem. 'He says he has brought you a gift, and that he wants you to accept his gift regardless of what has happened today. He says he is not a rich man, but this is a good gift; and he hopes you will accept it.'

'Tell him I'll be delighted,' said Barney, cautiously.

Mooi Klip's father went off to get his gift, and Jan Bloem screwed his monocle into his eye and watched Barney with mischievous anticipation.

'You know why he's insisting that you accept this gift?' he asked Barney.

'Not entirely,' said Barney.

'Well, then, you're not as bright as I thought,' said Jan Bloem. 'He wants you to accept this gift so that you'll feel bound to come back and marry his daughter. And you can't blame him, can you?'

'I don't,' said Barney. 'If I had any control over events, I'd marry his daughter today.'

Jan Bloem gave him a sympathetic smile. 'I spoke to Natalia,' he said. 'You mustn't blame her.'

'I blame myself.'

'That's just as ridiculous. Learn to attribute blame where blame should be attributed. Don't be a martyr. That's my motto.'

'You're full of mottoes.'

'It's better than being wise.'

Mooi Klip's father came around the side of the bungalow, leading behind him on a frayed rope a swaybacked, moth-eaten horse. Barney took one look at the animal and glanced at Jan Bloem in quick, furtive desperation. Jan Bloem kept up his friendly grin, but his monocle dropped out of his eye and swung on its black silk cord. Barney could tell that he was only a sixteenth of an inch away from laughing.

'This is for you,' translated Jan Bloem, while Mooi Klip's father watched him expectantly. 'His name is Alsjeblieft.'

'Alsjeblieft?' asked Barney. 'That means *please*, doesn't it?'

'That's right,' grinned Jan Bloem. 'Every time you want this horse to do anything for you, you have to say Alsjeblieft.'

Mooi Klip's father held out the rope. Barney hesistated for a moment, and then took it. The horse snuffled and whinnied, and swung its head around.

Barney said, 'Please tell Mooi Klip's father that I am delighted by his gift, and that if I had the time I would invite him to have a drink with me. But he obviously understands that I have to go.'

'He understands,' said Jan Bloem. 'He says that this horse used to belong to an old *kopje walloper*, one of the fellows who went around buying up diamonds from the small diggings around Klipdrift and Dutoitspan. It was a good horse, in its day.'

Barney nodded and smiled to Mooi Klip's father. Mooi Klip's father nodded, unsmiling, in return. Then he let out a short, sharp volley of Afrikaans, which he ended up with an emphatic, '*huh!*' as if to say '*so there!*'

'What did he say?' Barney asked Jan Bloem.

'He says you can think what you like about the horse, but he paid £27 10s for it.'

Barney, wearily, smiled again. 'Tell him I'm eternally grateful.'

At last, Mooi Klip's parents were ready to leave, taking their daughter home with them. Mooi Klip sat between her mother and her father, her carpet-bag stowed in the back of the ox-waggon, and she looked as stiff and as pale as marble. Her mother give Barney a small, understanding wave, and Barney guessed what Mooi Klip must have said to her.

'One word,' said Jan Bloem, before he climbed up on to his own waggon.

Barney said, 'What's that? Don't count chickens before the eggs are laid?'

'No, it's not a motto,' said Jan Bloem. He held Barney's arm with one black, well-manicured hand. 'I just want to say that if you care for Natalia, come back as quickly as you can and marry her. But, if you don't, then leave her alone. She's pretty, she'll find someone else in time. One of our own people, more than likely; and whoever it is, they'll look after your baby for you. But don't hurt her any more.'

Barney laid his hand on top of Jan Bloem's. 'Thanks for your advice,' he said, 'but only Natalia and I can decide what we're going to do next. Not you, not her parents. Not anybody.'

'Well,' Jan Bloem told him, 'I wish you the best of luck in any case. What do you say? *Mazel tov*!'

'Say *mazel tov* when I get back from Durban with a healthy brother,' said Barney. The horse Alsjeblieft snorted and tugged at his rope. He could sense that Jan Bloem and Mooi Klip's family were about to set off, and he was feeling anxious about being left behind.

Mooi Klip turned around only once as her father drove their ox-waggon away through the midday dust, and steered around the rim of the Kimberley Mine. Barney thought he saw her mouth the word 'goodbye' but he could not quite be sure. Edward Nork came up and said, 'It'll work out all right, you know. It really must. Do you want me to take care of this dreadful horse while you're gone?'

'I suppose so,' said Barney, eyeing the creature's fraying mane and speckled, fly-bitten hide. 'If you can ride it, by all means ride it. If you can't, then probably the best thing you can do is to eat it.'

Edward looked at the horse reflectively, as if he could imagine it on a dinner-plate, with roasted potatoes and fresh peas. The horse snuffled nervously, and backed away from him on clicking hooves.

*

Not even Barney's voyage out to South Africa and his attempts to find Joel among the mines and settlements of north Cape Colony had been as harsh and as hopeless as his six-week journey to Durban. With Joel strapped in as comfortably as possible on a bed of blankets and pillows, Barney travelled day after day across the vast plains of the Orange Free State, under skies that were dark with sunshine, amidst dust that was as blinding as flour. The odds were almost overwhelming that Joel would die of infection within a matter of days, but when each morning broke across the grasslands and Joel was still alive, still murmuring and whispering and crying with the pain of his injuries, Barney would mount the waggon's seat and snap his whip at the oxen, and they would plod eastwards again, towards a blue hazy horizon which they never seemed to reach.

Joel had hours of lucidity, when he would lie amongst his pillows, his face set in a grimace, talking to Barney in short, agonised sentences about what had happened. Barney kept his back to his brother most of the time, rarely turning around. The Blitz family burden, at this stage in his life, was more than he could bear. He was driving Joel to Durban because he had to drive Joel to Durban, because it was the best hope for Joel's survival, and because Joel was his brother. There were no other reasons.

One Thursday morning, they saw for the first time the distant blue outline of the Drakensberg Mountains, which they would have to cross before descending into Natal, and then making their way down through Colenso and Pieter Maritzburg to Durban. Joel, propped up on his pillows, said, 'We shouldn't go back you know.'

'Because you've lost us our claim?' said Barney.

'Because there's nothing to go back for,' said Joel. 'It's a fool's game, diamond mining. What the hell's the point of it? You dig all day, you break your back, and for what?'

'We could have been rich,' said Barney.

'We could have been old before our time,' retorted Joel.

Barney wiped the back of his neck with a handkerchief. Ahead of him, the oxen plodded steadily foward, their heads down, their thin-bladed haunches rising and falling with every step. 'You can stay in Durban if you want to,' he told Joel. 'But I'm going back. There's all of our money in the London and South African Bank, for one thing.'

Joel brushed a fly away from his face. 'To tell you the truth,' he said, 'we have a little problem with that.'

Barney lowered the reins. 'Problem? What are you talking about? We have seventeen thousand pounds in that bank. What problems?'

Joel looked towards the horizon. 'We owe the bank two thousand pounds'.

Gradually, Barney drew the oxen to a halt. Then he turned on his seat and said, '*What?*'

Joel's face was ghastly with pain. Pursing his lips, he said, 'It doesn't matter. For God's sake, just carry on.'

'I want to know, Joel. What problem? How in God's name can we owe the bank two thousand pounds?'

Joel said, 'I gambled a little. At Dodd's.'

'You gambled? But you didn't gamble seventeen thousand pounds!'

Joel nodded. 'Just get this waggon going, will you? The sooner we get this trip over, the better.'

But Barney was wide-eyed, paralysed. 'You gambled all of those seventeen thousand pounds at Dodd's Bar? All of them? And two thousand more?'

Joel raised a hand beseechingly. 'Barney – will you please get going. I can't take any more of this.'

'*You* can't take any more?' screamed Barney. He jumped down from the driving seat, and advanced on Joel with his face crimson. 'How can you say that? Everything I've worked for, everything I've been counting on! You've wasted everything! All that talk about saving our money, about sticking to one claim only! God, you're crazy! God, you're as crazy as Mama was!'

Joel lay back on his pillows. He eas exhausted with heat and agony. 'All right, so I'm crazy. You got your gun back from Harry Munt. So shoot. Save yourself a journey.'

Barney stood beside the ox-waggon for over a minute, in the relentless heat of the afternoon. The oxen flicked their tails at the flies, and the insects chirruped on the beld, and there was nobody and nothing around for mile upon mile, as far as the settlement of Paul Roux.

He could have taken out his Shopkeeper's pistol and shot Joel in the head, and nobody would ever have known. He could have buried the body in the dust, and returned to Kimberley and told Edward Nork and everybody else at the mine that Joel had died of his injuries. Joel had gambled away all his money, raped his wife-to-be, ruined his wedding, and cheated him out of his claim. What else did he deserve, but death?

Yet Barney remembered his father, sitting by the pale light of the upstairs window at Clinton Street, and the way his father's fingers had turned the first thin page of the Bible, and read, 'What hast thou done? the voice of thy brother's blood crieth unto me from the ground. And now art thou cursed from the earth, which hath opened her mouth to receive thy brother's blood from thy hand. A fugitive and a vagabond shalt thou be in the earth.'

Barney turned his face in the direction of the wind, narrowing his eyes against the grit and the heat. Then he climbed back up on to the waggon, and clicked at the oxen, the same Xhosa click that Donald had taught him, and they continued their trek across the plains of the Orange Free State.

Each night was the same, huddled under blankets by a flickering fire, after a meal of dried meat, dried fruit, and warm water. Each night Barney had to let down the side of the waggon and help Joel to roll off on to the ground, so that he could lie on the dust on his back to empty his bowels. Most nights, Joel screamed out loud as he forced shit through his shattered pelvis; and then he would whimper incessantly as Barney cleaned him up. After that, there would be a gagged-down meal, a heavy dose of ipecacuanha, and a few hours of restless sleep. In the morning, the process would have to be repeated all over again.

Miraculously, though, Joel's crushed leg remained free of serious infection. It began to knit together in an odd crooked shape, and it gave him excruciating pain, so much so that whenever the waggon lurched down a rough slope, he would shriek out to Barney to shoot him at once. But the skin had not been broken, and most of the lacerations had now healed up, and as they approached the Golden Gate, Barney's hopes at last began to rise a little.

The Golden Gate was utterly silent and eerie as Barney's ox-waggon passed through. It was a towering formation of weird and brooding sandstone crags, rising out of the scrub like massive totems. Above the crags, the sky was as dark and unforgiving as always, and the lamb-catching eagles, the *lammargayers*, circled and circled on wings as wide as sailboats. As he wended his way upwards through the mountains, past Mushroom Rock and Brandwag Rock, with their dazzling golden faces, Barney could hear the distant grinding echo of his ox-waggon wheels like a ghostly reminder of voortrekkers from forty years ago. There were other echoes in these mountains, too: of the Bushmen who had lived here in prehistoric times, and had painted the sandstone caves with pictures of plants and bird and long-forgotten rituals. Of the cannibals who had once roamed the valley of the Caledon River, and who had slaughtered and eaten more than 30,000 people.

In breezy silence, Barney passed a dark and distant amphitheatre of basalt cliffs; and then climbed even further through the Drakensberg to Mont-aux-Sources, where the rivers divided, and where he crossed at last into Natal. From Mont-aux-Sources, on that vividly clear afternoon, he could see back into the Orange Free State, and Basutoland, and as far as Utrecht in the Transvall, hazy miles of dust and trees and patches of greenery. Ahead of him, off to his right, he could make out the mountain they called Giant's Castle, where dark clouds gathered, even on a fine day, and lightning flickered incessantly. The black people had named this mountain N'Tabayi Konjwa, the mountain at which you may not point without terrible consequences.

Joel by now was delirious. He sweated and raved and screamed, and sometimes in the night he would let out a hideous inhuman shriek that had Barney sitting up in his blankets, scrabbling for his revolver, his body cold with fright.

But they descended the mountains at last into Natal, following the deep imprints in the rocks that the iron-shod wheels of the huge Boer waggons had left, when they had deserted their newly-established Republic of Natalia in 1842. Jan Bloem had told Barney all about those days, and it was easy for Barney to understand how bitter the Boers felt about the British. Their four-year-old republic had been annexed by the British by force, and the Volksraad, the Boer Parliament, had grimly voted to accept the annexation without fighting back. Almost immediately, the Boer farmers had packed their ox-waggons and trekked back west over the Drakensberg, to the Orange Free State, and the Transvaal.

Five weeks after he had set out from Kimberley, Barney steered his ox-waggon between the shalestone and yellow-wood cottages of Boom Street, in Pieter-Maritzburg, the capital of Natal. It was here, on the banks of the river that the Zulus had called the Mzunduzi, that the Boers had first found what they had believed to be their promised land. Pieter-Maritzburg, named after two voortrekkers called Pieter Retief and Gerrit Maritz, had been established on the floor of a broad, lush valley, over which the shadows of the afternoon clouds passed like memories.

Barney and Joel stayed the night with an elderly Dutch couple who ran a small dairy on the outskirts of town; and while Joel shivered in a cot in an upstairs bedroom, Barney sat wearily at the kitchen table and ate cheese and ham and drank home-made lager. The old Dutchman watched him through tiny spectacles, an unread copy of the *Natal Witness* lying in the table in front of him; but he only spoke when Barney had quite finished, and pushed aside the wooden board from which he had eaten his meal.

'You brought your brother all the way from the diamond fields?'

Barney nodded. 'I didn't have any choice. We don't have any surgeons out there – none that are worth a damn, anyway.'

'He must have suffered, your brother.'

Barney said, 'Yes. He's suffered. and he'll suffer some more before he's through.'

'Is it worth it?' the old Dutchman asked.

Barney looked him straight in the eye. 'Your people fought and died to build this town, and to stay free, and you're asking me if it's worth it?'

The old Dutchman picked up his paper. 'You're right, I

suppose. Do you know that I was there, under the acacia tree, when the Volksraad voted to let the British take over Natalia without recourse to arms. I was standing as near to Andries Pretorius as you're sitting now. I could have reached out and touched him.'

'Yes,' said Barney, tiredly. 'Now, I think I'd better get some sleep. I want to get to Durban tomorrow, if I can.'

'You might make Pinetown. But Durban? It's ninety miles, easily.'

'My brother's dying. I'll make it to Durban.'

After supper, Barney sat in an old rocking-chair on the tiled living-room floor, and dozed. The tiles were patterned with blue flowers, and first he dreamed of fire lilies and watsonia. Then he was riding again across miles of desert, with the oxen hunched doggedly in front of him. He dreamed of the strange pinnacles of sandstone that stood silent guard over the passes between the Orange Free State and Basutoland; and of the wild herds of red hartebeest and Burchell's zebra which fled across the grasslands.

He was woken by a cough. He had half-dreamed that it was a baboon barking in some far-off kloof. But it was the old Dutchman, bending over him with an expression of wrinkled concern. 'Your brother's worse,' he said. 'Do you want us to send for the priest?'

Barney had to stay for two days and two nights in Pieter-Maritzburg, while Joel twisted and shook and babbled in his whitewashed upstairs bedroom. It was December now, and the humidity was exhausting. For the first day, Barney did nothing but sit in the house, resting; but on the second morning he went down to the banks of the Umzinduzi to feel the early breeze blowing off the ruffled water.

The old Dutchman called the local doctor, a whiskery Englishman who rolled up his sleeves to reveal the hairiest arms that Barney had ever come across. But the doctor could no nothing better than to prescribe more Dover's powder to keep Joel's temperature down, and to express the opinion, as he was leaving, that Joel would soon by lying in a casket in Church Street.

On the third morning, however, when Barney went up to Joel's room, Joel was lying on his cot with his eyes open, and a hint of colour in his cheeks, and he managed to raise his hand in a half-mocking greeting.

'How are you feeling?' Barney asked him, drawing up a chair.

'I'm not dead yet, whatever that doctor thinks.'

'You heard him?'

'I couldn't help it. The window was open, and the man had a voice like a French horn.'

'Do you think you're up to travelling on?'

Joel apprehensively rubbed his left thigh. 'How far is it? This leg seems to have stiffened.'

'About eighty, ninety miles. The roads are better, though. So they tell me.'

Joel closed his eyes. 'Just fill me up with that specific, and make me comfortable, and let's go.'

The last few miles of the journey were gruelling. Under his broadbrimmed hat, Barney's face was streaked with dust and sweat, and Joel lay back on his grimy pillows with a face as ghastly as a waxwork. They could not reach Durban by night-fall, even though their waggon was light and almost empty of supplies, since Barney had to keep stopping by the side of the rutted road to bathe Joel's face with water, and dose him up with painkillers. They slept outside Pinetown, under their canvas shelter amidst the racketing noise of cicadas.

It wqs Saturday, 23 December, when they eventually arrived on the outskirts of Durban, like two exhausted survivors from some lost pioneering expedition, and passers-by stared at them in open curiosity as they slowly plodded towards the centre of town.

In spite of the heat, Christmas decorations were everywhere. There were flags flying outside the stores along West Street, and the ironwork uprights of the horse-drawn omnibuses were wound with tinsel. Durban lay under the deep blue lunchtime sky like a small, prosperous British town, with wide streets and smart carriages and buildings as solid as any in Croydon.

Barney asked directions of a red-faced English grocer who was standing outside his store in his striped apron, taking a mid-morning smoke. The grocer pointed out the Natalia Hotel with the stem of his pipe; but had certainly never heard of anyone called Sir Thomas Sutter, or anyone related to anyone called Sir Thomas Sutter. 'Not unless you mean – but no,' he added, looking at Barney's clothes.

'That fellow in the back looks a bit dicky,' he remarked, gratuitously, as Barney whipped the oxen and turned the waggon across the street.

Barney guessed that it was suitably sad and ironic that he should stay with Joel at an hotel called the Natalia. The manager was reluctant at first to admit Joel; but when Barney paid for a suite in advance in English fivepound notes, he whistled sharply to four Kaffirs in white shorts to carry Joel on the hotel stretcher to his room upstairs.

'As long as he doesn't pass away,' the manager explained, noisily rubbing his hands as he watched Barney sign the register. 'It does disturb the guests, you know ... expiry.'

Barney looked around the green marble hotel foyer, with its drawn blinds and its leather armchairs and its obligatory elephant's-foot umbrella stand. After weeks in the mountains, he felt so tired that none of these staid Victorian surroundings seemed real; and the way in which straight-backed women in their long summer skirts came and went across the reflecting floor was like a silent ballet remembered from a dream.

'You don't happen to know a family called Sutter, by any chance?' Barney asked the manager. The manager had finished rubbing his hands and was now smoothing down his black, brilliantined hair.

'Sutter? Not *the* Sutters, presumably?'

'I don't know. Who are *the* Sutters?'

'Well, *the* Sutters own Sutters the shipping line. Second largest shipping line in Port Natal. And certainly the first people you'd think of if you ever wanted to send something up the east coast of Africa, no matter what it was. A parcel, or a parrot, or a piano.'

'Where do they live?' asked Barney.

The manager swivelled the register around and peered at Barney's signature. 'You can't possibly miss it. It's about a mile to the south, towards Umlazi. A large, lemon-coloured place, in its own palm grove. But you'll never get in without an appointment. Or even at *all*, dressed like that.'

246

Barney said, 'You can have your porter empty the Bible box on my waggon. There are two suits in there, and some shirts, and I'd like them sponged down, and pressed. Then you can send a plate of beefsteak and a bottle of mineral waters up to my room.'

'Anything else, Mr Blitz?'

'Yes. Is there a synagogue in Durban?'

The manager stared at him humourlessly for a long time. 'I'll enquire,' he said, and closed the register with a loud snap.

After a bath in a high enamelled bathtub on lion's-claw feet, with hissing hot water supplied by an arrangement of brass pipes like a church organ, Barney towelled himself down, and came back into his bedroom to find his wedding-suit neatly laid out on his bed, and his shirt ironed with so much starch that he had to push his hands down the sleeves with all the force of a Navy icebreaker cutting through Antarctic glaciers.

Under a silver cover, a rather tough beefsteak waited for him, along with a bottle of Ashbourne water, on ice. He sat down on the end of the bed and ate the steak quickly and hungrily. Then he went to the basin to wash his hands, tie up his necktie, and brush his wet hair.

Before he left, he went into the second bedroom to look at Joel. Joel was sleeping now, murmuring as he slept, but quietly, as if he were dreaming complicated and subtle dreams, rather than nightmares of pain and fear and sudden death.

Severe and smart in his dark grey suit, with grey gloves and a grey hat, Barney crossed the foyer of the Natalia Hotel with clicking heels. The half-caste doorman hailed him a hansom cab, and remarked on the closeness of the heat. Two kaffirs were sitting in the street outside, playing jacks in the dust. Barney tipped the doorman a shilling, and mounted the black-and-maroon hansom with the confidence of a man who is perfectly familiar with riding in carriages. The black cab-driver had only taken him to the corner, however, before he was dry-mouthed and sweating, and his hurriedly-chewed steak was sitting on his stomach like chunks of sodden wood.

They drove out of town and up the tree-lined road towards Umlazi. On his left, through the dense undergrowth, Barney could make out the glittering reaches of the Indian Ocean, with two mail steamers making their way towards Port Natal. The air was sickly-sweet with the smell of flowers and decaying subtropical greenery, and the sound of the carriage wheels was swallowed up by the chirruping of insects and the querulous cry of birds.

At last, they came to a small hill, almost unnaturally round, and vividly green. It was fringed with palm trees, and laid out with lawns and pathways that were so neat they were irritating to look at. The lower slopes of the hill were surrounded by black-painted iron railings, each one cast in the shape of a Zulu assegai, and admittance to the estate was only by way of a pair of iron gates, decorated with iron replicas of Zulu shields.

On the crown of the hill stood a fine symmetrical mansion, painted, as the manager of the Natalia Hotel had told Barney, in the palest of lemon yellows. There were small fruiting orange trees in green tubs all the way around the house at precise intervals, and accurately-clipped hedges beneath every window. Peacocks swept their tails around the gardens like clockwork toys.

'This is where you want?' asked the cab driver, turning in his wornout leather seat. 'Khotso?'

Barney sat upright. 'Is that what the house is called?'

'Yes, boss. Everybody know that. This is where you want?'

'I believe so,' said Barney. 'But wait here for me, will you?'

The cab driver reigned his carriage in under the shade of a coral-tree and lit up a clay pipe. Barney climbed down, crossed the road, and approached the gates of Khotso with apprehension. The beefsteak had given him a griping pain in his stomach, and he would much rather have been lying on his bed in the Natalia Hotel, nursing his tiredness and his indigestion, than out here looking for Sir Thomas Sutter.

There was nobody at the gate; but there was a mechanical bell-pull, and Barney tugged at it twice. Then he waited, his back sticky with sweat, to see what would happen.

After a full minute, a small black man appeared, in peach-coloured trousers and a white sash, with a white turban on his head. He walked at an even pace along the precise perspective

248

of the front path, his arms swinging beside him military-style, and Barney could have timed almost to the second the moment when he was due to arrive at the gate.

'Good afternoon, sir,' the black man said at last. 'You wish to leave your card?'

'I wish to see Sir Thomas Sutter, if he's still here.'

'Sir Thomas? Well, sir, he's still here. But I'm afraid it's lunchtime. If you wish to leave your card.'

'Can you please tell him that I'm here, and that it's urgent? I've come all the way from the diamond fields at Kimberley.'

The black man raised his hands. 'With respect, sir, Mrs Sutter doesn't like to have luncheon interrupted. Not for anything. The Zulus attacked the Sutters once, sir, when they were on a picnic, and Mrs Sutter handed round meat sandwiches while the menfolk fought the Zulus off with pistols. So goes the story, sir.'

'I'm prepared to wait. It's a question of life or death.'

'Well, sir,' said the black man, rather regretfully. 'Life or death is one thing. Lunch is another.'

'I'll wait! My brother's dying, and I want Sir Thomas to see him!'

Just then, a girl appeared on the steps by the house – a tall girl, with dark brown ringlets, wearing a rust-coloured satin dress that was richly trimmed with Brussels lace. She hesitated for a moment, her pale hands held up like doves, trying to see what was happening down at the gate; and then she came rustling down the path with her skirts discreetly held above the patterned brick, and her head raised with aloof curiosity.

As she came closer, Barney could see that she was a very tall girl – almost as tall as him, even in her satin slippers. But her figure was in beautiful proportion, with wide shoulders, large breasts, and a narrow waist. Her face was square and strong, with vivid, wide-apart eyes; and if Barney had been asked to guess her nationality he would have said German or Polish rather than British. British women were almost invariably pear-shaped, with sloping shoulders and hips like gun-carriages.

Her voice, though, was as sharp and brittle as any girl from England's southern counties. And when she came up and said, 'What's the mattah, William? What's going on heah?' the black man touched his turban and stepped back as if he had been stung by a sjambok.

'Hello,' said the girl, looking Barney straight in the eye. 'I'm Sara Sutter.'

'I'm pleased to make your acquaintance,' said Barney. 'I'm Barney Blitz.'

'Well, well! Ess-ess and bee-bee! That must be a coincidence! Do you care for palmistry, at all?'

'I'm sorry?'

'Don't be. I'm an enthusiast, myself. Did you want to see Papa?'

'It was Sir Thomas I was looking for, as a matter of fact.'

'Great-Uncle Tee! What on earth do you want with him? He's getting ready for his afternoon nap, I believe! But come in! We can't have you standing outside looking like a lost soul, can we?'

William unlocked the gates, and swung both of them open, although Barney could easily have stepped through one. Sara Sutter looked him up and down, and said, 'You look very *hot*. Perhaps you'd care for a glass of lime-juice? Or perhaps tea?'

They walked up to the house together. Inside the railings of the house called Khotso, everything looked even more precise than it had from the road. Barney had the feeling that even if a snail were to be bold enough to silver the pathway, a black servant would have to come out and scrub the stones until the trail was gone.

'You're an American, I suppose, by your accent?' asked Sara Sutter. 'I can always tell an accent.'

'That's right. From New York, originally. But I live in Kimberley these days. I'm a diamond digger.'

'Are you *rea*-leh? How frightfully exciting! Father will be most interested to meet you, if only I can find him! And so will Great-Uncle Tee. Oh, look! What luck! There he is now!'

As they turned round a corner of the lemon-yellow house, they saw a tall white-bearded man with a belly as magnificent as a pregnant hippopotamus, sitting outside a pair of open French windows on a gilded sofa, smoking a cigar. He was wrapped in a blue and gold Chinese dressing-gown, and on his feet were a pair of white canvas polo boots. A copy of *The*

Times had been dumped in an untidy heap beside him, and was gradually being blown across the lawn by the afternoon wind.

'Great-Uncle Tee!' said Sara Sutter, gripping Barney's arm. 'I've someone to see you! Mr Blitz, from Kimberley!'

Sir Thomas Sutter looked Barney up and down with a single protuberant eye, his other eye closed against the smoke from his cigar. 'Mr Blitz? Well, how do you do! Pardon me if I don't get up, but it's taken me a good twenty minutes to get myself sat down. A heavy lunch, don't you know.'

Barney took off his hat. 'I'm real sorry to intrude like this,' he said. 'But a friend of mine in Kimberley told me that you were taking a vacation here, and I came on the chance that you would still be here when I arrived, and that you might agree to help me.'

Sir Thomas rubbed his beard. 'Jewish, is it, Blitz?'

Barney blinked at him. 'I'm sorry?'

'The name "Blitz". Jewish, is it?'

'Yes, sir. It is. We came from north Germany originally. Then we moved to New York. We used to be tailors, until we sold out and moved here.'

'I see. Well, I admire the Jews. They make excellent doctors. And they make excellent money, too. The Rothschilds are particular friends of mine.'

Barney did not know what to say. He simply shrugged, and lifted his hat slightly, as if he were pleased to hear it, which he was.

'Well,' said Sir Thomas, 'if you've come all the way from Kimberley on the chance that I might still be here, then obviously you want something. Some medical advice, perhaps? Some suggestions about starting a field hospital?'

Barney said, 'I want something, yes. But I'm afraid it's not that philanthropic.'

'You don't want surgery, I hope? I'm on holiday. I've left all my scalpels in London.'

'I'm afraid that's exactly what I do want.'

Sir Thomas puffed at his cigar. 'It's not for you, is it? You look as fit as a fiddle.'

'No, sir. It's my brother Joel. He was involved in a mining

accident out at the Big Hole at Kimberley. His left leg's crushed, and I think his pelvis has been smashed. He broke three, maybe four ribs.'

'I'm sorry to hear it. When did it happen?'

'Around six weeks ago.'

'Six *weeks* ago?'

'It's more than five hundred miles from Kimberley to Durban, sir. I got him here as fast as I could.'

Sir Thomas blew out his cheeks. 'Yes . . . I can see that you did. You managed it in remarkable time, too. But by now I expect that your brother's fractures have knit themselves together again, and I doubt if there is very much that I can do.'

'His hips are still giving him pain, Sir Thomas, and his left leg is twisted right out of shape.'

'The skin isn't broken anywhere? There are no protruding bones?'

'No, sir. There were some cuts and bruises, but they've all healed up now.'

'Well,' said Sir Thomas, 'they sound like simple fractures. And if he's still alive after six weeks of bumping all the way from Kimberley to Durban, then he's probably going to stay alive. Can he walk?'

'No, sir.'

'His leg is distorted, I suppose? That's only to be expected. When the bone is broken, you see, a large clot of blood forms between the broken ends, and this clot gradually turns into what we call a soft callus. After a while, the soft callus attracts lime salts from the system, and these lime salts harden to form a thick ring of bone. Should the broken limbs not be properly reduced and set, however, an even thicker ring of bone than normal can form; and thus an awkward healing is more difficult to rectify.'

Barney said, 'I don't think his pelvis has even set properly. He keeps complaining that it's grating, and that it hurts.'

'That's what we call *crepitus*,' said Sir Thomas. 'If your brother is still feeling that sensation, then his pelvis may have been so badly damaged that it has healed and then re-broken. I couldn't tell without examining him.'

'Will you do it?' asked Barney.

Sir Thomas stared at him. In the gardens, the peacocks let out a long, sad whoop.

'My dear chap,' he said, 'I'm on holiday.'

'I can pay you.'

'I'm sure you can. But there are plenty of other good surgeons in Durban. There's Pieter Botha at the Durban Calvinish Hospital. There's Humphrey Young, in Port Natal. I don't even have the staff, or the facilities.'

'But you're the best,' insisted Barney.

Sara Sutter said, 'I don't know what you're arguing about, Great-Uncle Tee. You've been chafing to get back to work ever since you got here. You'd love to do it, wouldn't you?'

'But it's out of the question,' protested Sir Thomas.

Right then, a tall, straight-backed man in a white dinner-jacket came round the corner and confronted them with surprise.

'What's out of the question?' he said, sharply.

'This is Gerald Sutter, my nephew,' explained Sir Thomas. 'Gerald – this gentleman has simply called by to seek my medical opinion.'

'How do you do,' said Gerald Sutter, tightly, without offering his hand. 'I'm afraid my uncle is on holiday at the moment, and we really prefer it if patients leave him in peace. He's going to have enough of that when he sails back to London.'

'Mr Blitz has impressed me, though,' put in Sir Thomas. 'His brother was hurt in an accident at Kimberley, and he has brought him five hundred miles just to be treated by me.'

'I'm afraid Mr Blitz was being rather over-optimistic,' said Gerald Sutter. 'A man may travel six months to London to ask the Queen for a knighthood, but that doesn't mean that he deserves one.'

'Oh, Papa, you're being pompous,' said Sara. 'This is Natal, not London! And his brother may die!'

'All the same,' Gerald Sutter said, turning with a cold smile to Barney and making a following gesture with his hands that Barney should consider leaving.

'No, no,' put in Sir Thomas. 'The whole thing rather appeals to me. It has a what-might-you-call-it, a *drama* about it. I could give some useful lectures to my students when I get back, particularly on the subject of perseverance. If you can get me a theatre at the Dalitary Hospital, Gerald, I'll do it.'

'Uncle, really,' protested Gerald. Then he turned to Barney. 'My uncle was supposed to be resting. I can't say I'm keen on this at all.'

'I had to try,' Barney told him, simply.

Sara Sutter clapped her hands. 'Great-Uncle Tee is absolutely right! It is dramatic, isn't it? Just like a play! Mr Blitz, you must take some tea. I'm sure Great-Uncle Tee must want to ask you lots of questions.'

Gerald Sutter sighed testily. 'Are you sure this is what you want, Uncle? I can't persuade you to change your mind?'

'Gerald, my dear chap, you've given me the finest holiday of my entire life. Seven months of blissful solitude and contemplative study. I have enjoyed myself no end, and your house is aptly named. But here we have an interesting case of fractures that must be re-broken, and re-reduced, and re-set, in the most colonial of circumstances, and I must say that I would very much like to get my hands on it.'

At last, Gerald Sutter allowed himself a nod of acceptance. 'Very well, Uncle, if it makes you happy. Sara – would you call Umzinto and ask him to bring tea?'

Two black servants brought decorative garden chairs around, and set a table with a pale damask cloth. Then they poured out fragile white cups of tea, with neither cream nor sugar.

'This is the most expensive of the Formosa Oolongs,' remarked Gerald Sutter. 'It's called Peach Blossom, and in London it can fetch anything up to £8 the pound. Her Majesty drinks it, when she can get it. I have it every afternoon, at four.'

'It's excellent,' said Barney. 'I'm afraid we don't have such delicacies out at Kimberley, even those of us who can afford them.'

The next hour passed with such calm and civilisation that Barney began to feel at peace for the first time for months. The sun fell slowly behind the palms, so that their frondy shadows lay across the lawns, and the peacocks gathered round for any crumbs that might be left from the teatable. Sir Thomas talked

254

about the difficulties of good bonesetting, and Gerald talked about fast steamers, and how he could have a packet sent from Port Natal to Delagoa Bay, a distance of 295 miles, in less than forty-one hours.

'All that concerns us now is the Zulus,' said Gerald, crossing his well-creased ducks. 'Mpande is not a well man, and if Mpande dies, we shall be left with Cetewayo, and Cetewayo is one of those black gentlemen who believes in the glorious days of Shaka.'

'And I'm afraid the days of Shaka weren't all that glorious,' added Sir Thomas. 'He had the same interest in human anatomy as I do, but I regret that he didn't have the same skills. He once ordered a hundred pregnant women cut open with spears, just because he was momentarily interested in embryology.'

'Great-Uncle *Tee*,' protested Sara, setting down her cup.

'I do apologise, my dear,' said Sir Thomas. 'I'm always doing that. I forget that the more sanguinary details of medicine make other people squeamish.'

After tea, Sara walked Barney down to the gate. 'I've been greatly encouraged,' said Barney. 'Thank you.'

'I suppose you'll be staying in Durban for a while, until your brother is better?'

'As long as necessary.'

'What about your diamond mines?'

'They'll have to wait.'

Sara smiled. 'You really do strike me as a most straightforward and determined person. I should very much like it if you could come to supper one evening. I shall do what I can to persuade Papa.'

'Your father doesn't object to Jews?'

'Why on earth should he? My mother's mother came from a very aristocratic Jewish family in Russia. You'll have to meet my mother. She's so beautiful, and quite adorable.'

'Qualities which *you* seem to have inherited in full measure,' said Barney.

Sara Sutter made a funny little face, and then giggled. 'I love to be flattered,' she said. 'One gets so few compliments, out heah.'

255

'By the way,' asked Barney, touching the nameplate on the gate, 'what does Khotso mean?'

'It's Basuto for "peace",' said Sara. 'I suppose you would say "shalom."'

Barney took her hand. 'Yes,' he told her. 'I would say shalom.'

Barney spent Christmas Day alone in his suite at the Natalia Hotel. On Sunday morning, Christmas Eve, four black porters from the Durban Military Hospital had arrived with a stretcher and carried Joel away, so that he could be examined and bathed and prepared for his operation. Later that day, a messenger had come round with a letter for Barney written in an almost unintelligible copperplate, and this informed him that Sir Thomas was to operate the day after Boxing Day, Tuesday, and that he had high hopes that Joel would be walking again within two or three months, given that his internal injuries were not too serious. And, by the way, a merry Christmas.

Most of Christmas Day, Barney spent dozing on his bed, or reading. He even read the First Book of Samuel again, from the Bible which The London Missionary Society had left on his bedside table. 'The Lord maketh poor, and maketh rich; he bringeth low, and lifteth up. He raiseth up the poor out of the dust, and lifteth up the beggar from the dunghill, to set them among princes, and to make them inherit the throne of glory.'

At lunchtime, the management sent up on a tray a traditional Christmas lunch, with turkey and sausages and roasted potatoes. There was even a sprig of holly on the side of the plate. Barney ate his meal in silence, sitting on the end of his bed. He had never celebrated Christmas at home, of course, and out at Oranjerivier it had only been marked by Monsaraz getting drunker than usual. But even though it was not a festival that meant anything to him religiously, or in his memories, the whole of Durban was celebrating today, the church bells were ringing out across the rusty corrugated-iron rooftops, and echoing from the forested hills, and he could not help feeling more lonely than ever. He had celebrated Chanukah somewhere in the mountains, by whispering prayers to himself as

256

he lay in his blankets. He was beginning to feel the need of his God again, and of his religion, and he was also beginning to miss Mooi Klip.

On the writing-desk under the window was a dried-up pot of ink, and a small sheaf of writing-paper with the printed heading 'Natalia'. He lifted up a sheet of paper and touched the word with his fingers. Natalia. Then he laid it down again. The Lord bringeth low, and lifteth up. Oh Lord, he prayed, lift me up. Oh Lord, lift me up.

At five o'clock, he decided to go for a walk. Bue he was just crossing the foyer of the hotel when the deputy manager called to him from the registration desk, and held up a small brown-paper parcel.

'For you, Mr Blitz. It was left only a few minutes ago.'

Barney took the parcel across to one of the leather armchairs, sat down, and untied it. Inside the brown paper was a red leather-covered box, and inside the box was a silver penknife, with the initials BB engraved on the side.

A small card was tied to the penknife. It read, 'To Mr Barney Blitz, wishing you the best compliments of the season, Sara Sutter.'

A knife was the most appropriate gift she could have sent him. That Christmas Day, she cut him to the bone.

Joel told him later that the pain he had suffered crossing the Drakensberg mountains had been nothing compared with the pain that Sir Thomas Sutter inflicted. But Sir Thomas Sutter had to break his leg and his hips again, and cut away all the superfluous bone that had formed, and reset everything as best he could. The ribs were all right, since the ribcage had formed a natural splint, but the collarbone had to be re-broken and re-set, and there was a severe rupture of the groin. When Barney was first allowed to visit Joel, on Wednesday evening, Joel was lying in traction, his face white, his senses still blurred by morphine, and all he could say was, 'How's Mama?'

Sir Thomas Sutter was waiting outside with two of his assistants. 'Your brother will live, God willing, and he will walk again; though never without a stick. I must say it was a most

257

interesting and difficult case. It hardly ever happens in England, you see, that a man so seriously injured is brought to surgery so late as six weeks after his accident.'

'I'm very thankful,' said Barney.

'Well, I'm thankful to you for bringing him in,' said Sir Thomas. 'All this has made a very recreational end to my holiday, if you'll forgive me talking about your brother's misfortune as a recreation.'

'That's probably the right word,' Barney told him.

'Well, excellent,' said Sir Thomas. 'And you must come out and have a meal with us this evening. My grand-niece absolutely insists, and so do I. I expect they'll be serving cold turkey again, but as a matter of fact Gerald was so extravagant that he shipped in a turkey the size of an ostrich, and we'll be eating it as curries and croquettes until March, I shouldn't wonder. Well, the family will. I'm sailing back to London the day after New Year's.'

'Do I have time to change?' asked Barney.

'My dear chap, of course. I'll pick you up at the Natalia at six, when I've finished here. There's a frightfully interesting case upstairs, you know. An orderly from the 24th Foot was stepped on by an elephant. It's a miracle he's still alive.'

Barney walked back to the Natalia Hotel between lighted storefronts and decorated restaurants. There was a sea-breeze blowing, and up above him the sky was prickled with stars. A half-caste woman called out to him from the shadow corner of Commercial Street, but he shook his head without even turning her way. He could smell spicy East African food on the wind.

Sir Thomas was wrong: the Sutters did not serve up cold turkey that evening, but noisettes of lamb, and turtle soup, and a whole array of decorative moulds and jellies. Mrs Sutter, Gerald's wife, turned out to be just as beautiful as her daughter had described her – dark-haired, slender, and tall, with an endless white neck, and she immediately made Barney feel at ease by laughing at herself for forgetting what she had ordered the servants to cook that night. 'I was *so* sure that it was going to be fish,' she said, 'that my palate is quite disappointed at the prospect of lamb.'

The interior of Khotso was as pristine as its gardens. The dining-room was laid with a shining floor of polished English oak, and surrounded by mirrors. The drawing-room, to which they withdrew when the meal was finally over, was decorated in blue watered silk, and furnished in elegant turn-of-the-century mahogany. Mrs Sutter sat on a small French sofa, rising from the white satin petals of her evening-gown like the stamens of a flower; and Sara sat next to Barney, her hair drawn back and secured with strings of pearls, her dress as vivid and orange as the coral-tree blossoms which herald the South African spring.

Both Gerald Sutter and Sir Thomas were dressed in starched white shirts and white ties, with tailcoats; and Barney felt distinctly uncomfortable in his day suit, dark and well tailored as it was.

'Uncle is wonderfully pleased with your brother's progress,' smiled Mrs Sutter. 'I must say that we're all delighted.'

'Thought you had something of a nerve, to begin with, said Gerald Sutter. 'But things have worked out rather well, don't you think? Uncle's had something to amuse him; your brother's on the mend; and Sara's found herself a new chum.'

'I was wondering if you'd like to ride tomorrow,' said Sara, touching Barney's sleeve.

'I'm afraid I don't have a horse. Nor riding clothes, either.'

Gerald Sutter grunted in amusement. 'My dear boy, we have something in excess of twenty first-class mounts here, apart from a collection of harmless hacks. You can borrow any of them you have a mind to. And, as for clothes, we must have enough to fit out the whole Zulu army.'

'Yes,' said Sir Thomas. 'It would be nice to see those blackies decently dressed for a change.'

They all laughed, and their servant Umzinto, who was dressed up for the evening in a yellow and white footman's costume, with a white pigtailed wig, leaned forward to pour them all some more coffee.

The following day, Barney and Sara took out a grey and a chestnut, and rode as far as the beach where the Umiazi River flows into the Indian Ocean. It was a humid, misty morning, and as Sara rode ahead of Barney through the sloping shallows, she was silhouetted against the pearly mist, tall and upright on her mare, her riding hat tilted fashionably forwards, her skirts carefully arranged side-saddle. They reined in their horses for a while, and listened to the foaming of the surf, and the occasional whistle of a mail-packet approaching Port Natal through the haze. Then Sara swung herself down into the sea, and led her mare back towards the beach, her cream-coloured skirts trailing in the water. Barney rode after her, and when he reached the beach, he dismounted, too.

'Sometimes this feels like the most distant, remote corner of the whole Empire,' said Sara. Her face was framed by the triangular space between her mare's chest and jaw.

'You're lonely? asked Barney.

Sara looked at him. 'Aren't you?'

They had a chaperone with them, of course – an eLangeni woman who had brought up Sara since she was nine years old. She had stayed at a suitable distance all the way from the house, fat and very black, and perched on a shaggy pony so precariously that Barney had found himself looking back at her every now and then to make sure that she was still mounted. But now, the eLangeni woman found the surf so absorbing that she climbed down from her pony and gave the waves her unshakeable attention.

'This is wrong, you know,' said Sara, in a tone that gave away her feeling that she was glad that it was.

Barney said nothing, but released the reins of his horse and put his arms around her and held her near to him. In her riding-boots, she was almost as tall as he was, but everything about her was feminine and giving and warm. They kissed, and he tasted her perfume. They kissed again. Then he was clutching her so tight, so close to him, that he prayed he would never have to let her go. He closed his eyes and he could hear the ocean seething up the beach; he opened them again and he could see Sara's eyes in close-up, their dark brown irises folded like coral.

'You're so strong,' she said. 'You're weak. I can see you have weaknesses. But you're so strong, too. And that's what makes you so attractive.'

He pressed his forehead against hers, his hands linked behind her slender waist. 'Where can this possibly lead?' he asked her. 'I have to go back to Kimberley soon.'

She gently touched his lips with her finger. 'How can you think about the future? Tomorrow, the Zulus might rise and we'll all be dead. Assegaied in our beds.'

'What makes you think they're going to rise?'

Sara kissed him. 'They must do. It's in their blood. Everybody has to do what their destiny compels them to do.'

He let go of her, and turned away. His horse was tugging at some wild seagrass with its teeth.

'I'm not asking you to love me,' she said.

He nodded. 'I know. But right now, I think I could do with somebody to love.'

It was late February before Joel could walk again. Barney would go to visit him at the Durban Military Hospital every afternoon, and each afternoon Joel would gripe and sweat and swing himself around the ward on his walking-stick, before sitting down next to Barney in a thick sweat, his chest rising and falling with effort, and his hands trembling like an old man.

'I'll walk, just you wait and see.'

'Sir Thomas said you'd always have to carry a stick.'

'You think so? That shows what a *gonif* Sir Thomas is.'

'A *gonif*? And he's fixed you up so well?'

Joel leaned over to Barney and grinned at him. 'One day, my little brother, you're going to learn what life is all about. Life is all about taking, and not trusting. You live it any other way, and you're crazy.'

'I trusted you with our diamond claim.'

'And what happened?' gibbed Joel.

'I don't even know how you can look me in the face after what you did,' said Barney. 'And all that money. You must have been out of your mind.'

'It was the greatest poker game ever. I could have won fifty thousand. *Then* you wouldn't have argued.'

'But you didn't win, did you?' said Barney. 'You lost everything. And you lied. You told me you were going to put that claim fifty-fifty in our joint names. You never even went to the Diggers' Committee to re-register it, did you? You *momzer*.'

'Barney,' protested Joel. 'You're my brother.'

'Sure I'm your brother. And most of the time I wish that I wasn't.'

Joel gave an uneasy laugh. 'Well,' he said, 'I'm not sure that I blame you.'

Barney rubbed his eyes, and sat forward on his bentwood chair with his chin cupped in his hands. 'It's too late now, anyway. We've lost the claim and we've lost all of our savings and that's it. *Mechuleh*. Finished!'

The afternoon light fell across the parquet floor of the hospital ward. In the nearest bed, a British soldier with an amputed leg lay on his bed playing a board game called 'Lord Chelmsford's Revenge'.

Joel said, 'Sometimes I think I'm going mad.'

'For God's sake, you're not going mad.'

'But I *do*, Barney. Sometimes it feels like the whole world's pushing in on me from all sides, and all I can do is try to trick my way out of it, before I get caught. It was like that in Kimberley, when we were living with Mooi Klip. There was you, and her, and this everyday routine of getting up and digging the claim and sorting the stones, and I felt like the whole thing was crushing me to death. Every pound we put into the bank was like another brick in my tomb. Do you understand what I'm saying? The whole thing was crushing me, and the only way to get free was to throw it all away.'

Barney would not look at him. 'I should have let you die,' he said, bitterly. 'The only trouble was, you wouldn't.'

Joel was silent for a while. Then he said, 'No, I didn't die. And I don't intend to.'

He swung himself upright on his sticks, and pivoted himself away down the ward for another agonising exercise walk. Out of the corner of his eye, Barney watched him; and when Joel reached the end of the ward and suddenly cried out, 'Ah! Barney!' Barney was already out of his chair, and hurrying to support him.

He saw Sara two or three times a week. Usually, they went riding, with the Sutter's conveniently ill-sighted chaperone teetering along behind them; but occasionally it thundered, and then they would sit in the morning-room and talk, or play ludo, while the tropical rain clattered against the glass of the French windows, and the stone lions in the garden stared mournfully out across the lawns with drips on their noses.

They kissed as often as they could, and embraced. But there was no doubt that Sara considered herself a young lady of correct upbringing, and that the idea of going to bed with an admirer before marriage was quite out of the question. She was twenty and two months old, and a virgin, and the only reason she had not married before was because of the isolated life she led out at Khotso, wealthy and mannered and bored to distraction, a true daughter of the British Empire. When he talked to Sara, Barney was frequently electrified by her unshakeable certainty that whatever the British did was the work of the Lord, and that the Zulu and the Boer were nothing but clumsy mischief-makers who might one day upset the just and equable Scheme of Things so much that they would have to be Taught A Lesson. That was a phrase Barney heard time and time again since he had come to Cape Colony: they will have to be Taught A Lesson. The British seemed to regard the administration of the world as nothing more than an extension of their public-school geography classes.

For the first time, Barney began to understand the thinking of Cecil Rhodes.

By early March, his sabbatical ended, Sir Thomas Sutter had sailed back to London on the steamship *Agamemnon*, and Joel was limping around with the aid of a single stick. Barney was almost in love with Sara, to the point where he found it hard to go through a day without seeing her, or sending her a message; and when he did see her, and go riding with her, he would return to the Natalia Hotel in a mood that was half satisfaction and half frustration. One evening he came back from Khotso, went into the bathroom, and rubbed himself furiously until semen shot over his hand. He could have gone to a whore, but he did not want to. He did not feel like talking to any other girl but Sara. But he lay back on his bed afterwards feeling empty and resentful, and staring at the geccoes which ran over the ceiling in their own upside-down world where guilt and loneliness were unknown.

Then the money ran out. Sir Thomas Sutter had only charged 150 guineas for his surgery and after-care, but Joel's hospital fees had now topped £200, and the bill for Barney's suite at the Natalia Hotel took care of the rest. Barney had to go to Khotso on the morning of 11 March and tell Sara that he was returning to Kimberley.

It was hot and sunny on the steps outside the house, but in the distance, over the Indian Ocean, blue-black thunderheads had gathered, and lightning was licking at the sea.

Sara said, in a high, breathless voice, 'Shall I see you again! Ever?'

Barney nodded. 'If you want me to, I'll come back. But first I have to go see to my business.'

'Well,' she said, with a difficult smile, 'I suppose I can be brave.'

She walked a little way down the garden path, her hands clasped in front of her, and then she turned and looked at him with complete misery. 'Do you have to?' she asked. 'Do you really have to?'

Barney said, 'I'm sorry.'

'Oh,' she said, and her eyes flooded with tears. 'Oh, Barney.'

He held her hand. 'It couldn't have been any other way. I would have had to go back to Kimberley, no matter what.'

'But I could have come with you.'

'You? In Kimberley? Do you have any idea what it's like there?'

'The only think I know about it is that you're going to be there, and I'm not.'

'It's a madhouse. Rough, dirty, hardly any fresh water. Shortages of food. Nothing but diamond dealers and prostitutes and drunken diggers.'

'But I love you,' she squeaked.

Barney put his arm around her neck and held her face against his shoulder. 'I have to go back, Sara. And that's all. If I don't go back, then I might as well buy myself a ticket to New York, to the Lower East Side, and take up tailoring again. And you wouldn't want to follow me then.'

'Wouldn't I?' she challenged him. Her eyes were blurred with tears.

In the distance, the thunder grumbled aggressively. It sounded like Zulu *impi* rattling their assegais against their shields, and rumbling their warcry, '*uSuthu*! *uSuthu*!'

'Give me time,' Barney pleaded.

She looked up at him. 'You'll give *me* time, too, won't you? You won't go off with anyone else? I don't mind prostitutes. I could stand that. But not another fiancée.'

'Fiancée?'

Sara's cheeks flushed pink. 'I naturally assumed –'

Barney took her hands, and held them between his own hands, tightly and safely and warmly. 'Sara,' he said, 'you're a Sutter. Look at this house, look at your background. You couldn't possibly marry anybody like me. I know you don't care that I'm Jewish, but I'm not even *rich* Jewish. As a matter of fact, I don't even own my own diamond-digging claim, just at the moment.'

'Barney, I don't *care*. What does money matter?'

He lowered his eyes, looked at her hands, and then released them. 'I wish it didn't matter at all. But I'm afraid that it does. Sara, I'm sorry. Maybe I've deceived you a little, just because I've enjoyed your company. No – I'm telling lies now. I've more than enjoyed it. I think I love you. But if we tried to marry ... it wouldn't work. You wouldn't have any horses or any servants or any gowns. I couldn't give you the life that you've been used to. The whole thing would be a mistake.'

Sara said quietly, and with an impeccable accent, 'I see.'

'I'll come back,' said Barney. 'I promise you that. When I've made some money, which by God I'm going to, then I'll come back.'

'And how long will that be?'

'I don't know. I'm starting from scratch.'

She was trying very hard to be offish; but she could not. She looked at Barney with tears sliding down her cheeks and all she could say was, 'Don't make it too long. I might be married to somebody else. And if that happened, and you came back too late, then I couldn't bear it.'

It began to rain, dark spots on the neat pathways of Khotso the size of pennies. English pennies, with the Queen's head on one side, and Britannia on the other. Barney kissed Sara quickly, and her mouth tasted of salt tears and rain.

*

They travelled more slowly back to Kimberley, arriving at the diamond mines in mid-May. The cosmos flowers had bloomed again on the veld, and the weather was cooler. They had ridden for days on the ox-waggon without speaking. Barney had been too preoccupied with thoughts of Sara, whom he had left behind, and Mooi Klip, who by now must have given birth to his child. I have a baby, he thought to himself, and I don't even know if it's a boy or a girl. I don't even know if it was born alive.

I don't even know if Mooi Klip's alive.

They were amazed, both of them, at the depth to which the Big Hole had now been dug. When they drove up to the east reef of the mine, they could see below them a scurrying ants'-nest of hundreds of diggers, all of them swarming over the hollows and hills and burrows with tireless energy, shovelling and hacking and walling up their claims with sandbags. The steel cables which connected each claim to the surface were now on three tiers of pulleys, the top tier bringing out the yellow ground from the claims in the centre of the mine, and the bottom two tiers serving the claims that were nearer to the rim. There were hundreds and hundreds of cables, shining in the afternoon sun like a giant spiderweb.

'We could have been a part of that,' said Barney, more to himself than to Joel. 'We could have been rich by now.'

'But we're not,' said Joel. 'So let's make the best of it.'

Barney cracked his whip, and the oxen trudged the last few yards towards their bungalow. Edward Nork was there, sitting on the verandah in his socks, trying to sew a patch on a pair of work trousers. He had grown a long gingery beard which made him look like a hermit, and he was wearing tiny wire-rimmed eyeglasses.

'The Lord in heaven,' he said, setting down his needlework. 'You came back. And you're better, Joel! I do believe you're better!'

Joel climbed down from the waggon and limped on his stick to the verandah steps. 'I'm not better, Edward. I'm worse. These days, I have to walk with a stick. But I'm still alive, if that's what you mean.'

Barney led the oxen through to the kraal, and Edward followed him. 'I'm afraid I haven't kept the house all that tidy,' he apologised. 'I'm not very methodical when it comes to cleaning.'

Barney said, 'At least you've kept it warm for us.'

With Edward's help, Barney freed the oxen from their harnesses, and then led them over to the trough to drink.

'Is there any feed?' he asked.

'I can get hold of some.'

'Thanks, I reckon these beasts deserve some kind of reward.'

Edward took off his eyeglasses and folded them. He appeared to be embarrassed. 'I heard from Mooi Klip,' he said.

'I was going to ask you if you had. Is she all right?'

'Oh, yes. She's doing very well. It was terrible, what happened between you and Joel.'

Barney said, 'The baby?'

'Oh, she had the baby all right. No trouble at all. It was a boy. She said she was going to call him Pieter.'

'Pieter,' said Barney. 'You mean like Pieter Retief?'

'I don't think so. More like Pieter Steyn. He was the Griqua who was praying for Joel, wasn't he, when you found him staked out?'

Barney nodded. 'She's still at Klipdrift?'

'As far as I know.'

'Well,' said Barney, 'I guess I'd better get over there and see her. And Pieter, too.'

'Congratulations,' smiled Edward Nork. 'You're a father.'

Joel came hobbling around to the kraal on his stick. 'Have you seen the inside of this house?' he demanded. 'It's a pigsty. In fact, it's worse than pigsty. Where the hell are we supposed to sleep?'

'Oh, yes,' said Edward Nork, uncomfortably. 'I'm afraid I had to dispose of some of the furniture.'

'You mean you had to sell our beds to buy yourself drink?' snapped Joel.

'If you like,' said Edward, with a touch of defiance in his voice. 'I didn't think you were ever coming back, to tell you the truth. Nobody did.'

'Do you know what's happened to Claim 172?' asked Barney.

'I heard that it was bought by an Australian. A fellow called McIntyre. He keeps himself to himself, though, and never buys a round of drinks, so I'm not at all sure how he's doing. He's not a millionaire yet, if that's any consolation.'

'I'm not sure that it is,' said Barney.

At that moment, there was a sharp rattling sound from the small stable at the side of the kraal. 'Oh,' said Edward, 'that's Alsjeblieft. I expect he's feeling hungry.'

'You've still got that mangy horse?' asked Barney.

Edward shrugged. 'I've grown rather fond of him, as a matter of fact. He's the only horse who's ever let me ride him. He's so docile, he even takes me home when I'm drunk. I think he'd put me to bed if I let him into the house.'

'Or if we had any beds,' put in Joel, sharply.

'I'll make it up to you,' said Edward. 'Don't you worry, my dear chap. I'll make it up to you.'

They spent the rest of the day sweeping out the bungalow and building up the fire. Then Barney cooked up a mess of beef and beans, and they sat on the floor in the living-room and ate it with their billy-can spoons. They talked for a while about diamonds, and Edward told them that the world market was slumping so badly that many of the Kimberley diggers were already selling up and moving on. Diggers were always searching for quick and easy fortunes, and there were rumours of gold having been discovered in the Transvaal.

The next morning, there was heavy grey cloud cover, and that fine persistent rain the Boers called *motreën* – rain as fine as mist. Barney woke up early, rolling out of the blankets that he had spread on the floor of the bedroom he had once shared with Mooi Klip. He lit the range to cook himself a breakfast of beef hash and eggs, and boiled up the coffee that he and Joel had made themselves the previous night. Then, while Joel was still sleeping, and Edward Nork was snoring away in the living-room in an alcoholic stupor, he opened the front door and went around to the kraal to saddle up Alsjeblieft.

The old horse shivered and snuffled in the rain, but stood there patiently while Barney tightened his girth, and clumsily swung himself aboard. This was not like riding at Khotso, where a black servant was always waiting with a portable step, and one's feet were inserted into the stirrups by the groom. But Barney had learned enough about riding with Sara Sutter to be able to direct Alsjeblieft out of the kraal and out through the early-morning outskirts of Kimberley, and point his nose north-westwards to Klipdrift. Barney had to blink from time to time, to shake the rain out of his eyes but there was a dreary familiarity about the landscape which made him feel at home.

The odd thing was, when Barney tried to ride around the De Beers Mine, where Cecil Rhodes was digging, the horse trotted to the north side of the mine without being bidden. Barney tried to tug his reins in the opposite direction, but he seemed to know exactly where he was going, and when he reached a rain-sodden tent, with pools of water collecting in its canvas sides, he stopped, and stood still, the rain dripping off his patchy hide, as if he expected Barney to dismount. Barney, wonderingly, climbed down.

The tent flap was flung back, and water gurgled on to the mud. A short, bearded digger in a checked shirt and a broad-brimmed hat and no trousers came struggling out into the daylight, snuffling and sniffing.

'I'm sorry,' said Barney. 'I didn't mean to wake you up.'

The digger stared at Barney and then at the horse. 'Screw me if that isn't Alsjeblieft,' he said, in a strong Irish accent.

'That's right,' nodded Barney. 'Alsjeblieft.'

'Well, that's a pity,' said the digger. 'I sell my diamonds to Dan Isaacs these days, ever since old Vandenberg passed over. But how are you, Alsjeblieft?' he asked, paddling his way through the churned-up mud, and rubbing the horse on the nose. 'I've got some sugar-lumps stashed away someplace. I'll find him one.'

'Dan Isaacs give you a good price?' asked Barney.

The digger looked up at him, and then shrugged. 'Good enough. Maybe not as good as old Vandenberg. But they say the market's going down the hill, you know? As long as I make myself enough to keep my body and my soul in the same tent.'

'Whatever Dan Isaacs gives you, I'll top,' said Barney.

The digger frowned uncertainly. 'Have you taken over from old Vandenberg?'

'I may have. I came here on Alsjeblieft, didn't I?'

'Well, sure. But can you pay me ready money?'

'Show me what you've got.'

The digger thought about that, and then nodded. 'All right. But let me put my trousers on first. I don't like to do business when I'm half-dressed.'

Barney waited in the drizzling rain while the digger dressed himself. Then the digger reappeared with a wash-leather bag, which he opened up and spread across the palm of his stubby hand. There were ten or eleven rough diamonds there, none of them less than two and a half carats. 'What would you pay me for these?' he asked.

Barney fished inside his waistcoat pocket for his loupe. He squinted at the stones one by one, and then he said, 'A hundred and fifty. Bearing in mind that we're going through a world slump.'

'All right,' said the digger, 'You're on. That's twenty more than Isaacs would have paid me. Can you pay me ready money?'

'Tomorrow. And that's a promise. I didn't come out here expecting to buy.'

'You came out on Alsjeblieft and you didn't expect to buy? Why, that horse would come out on his *own* and buy.'

Barney patted Alsjeblieft's wet flanks. 'I'm beginning to realise that.'

Barney rode on towards Klipdrift. The rain began to clear, and the sky was rich with white and stately clouds. He arrived on the banks of the Vaal River just as the sun was setting over the Kaap Plato, and the evening was alive with chorusing insects. He stopped at the first digger's hut he came across – a long, English-style cottage with a thatched roof and mud-plastered walls – and asked the woman sitting outside if she knew where he could find the Griquas.

She pointed, dumbly, to the northern part of the settlement. Barney raised his hat and followed her directions. The pale blue sky lay in the ruts of the dark muddy road like fragments of a broken mirror. Somewhere, someone was playing '*Rose of Ireland*' on a harmonica.

The Griqua houses were just like the rest – narrow and thatched and surrounded by mud. But somehow they seemed more permanent. Almost all of them were fenced, and most of them had vegetable gardens, neatly laid out in rows, the way the Boers always did it. One of the gardens even boasted a scarecrow – a sad-looking half-caste effigy with his body stuffed with straw.

He saw Mooi Klip before she saw him. She was walking ahead of him, her bare feet squeezing into the mud, her baby held around her in a sling of Indian cotton. She must have been walking down to the Vaal River to wash, or fetch water. In one hand she carried a large pitcher of terracotta clay. Barney dismounted from his horse, and followed her only two or three paces behind, leading Alsjeblieft by the reins.

Sudden sunshine lit up the houses all around them. Barney said, 'Mooi Klip,' in his softest voice. Mooi Klip hesitated, and then turned, and when she saw Barney all she could do was stand in that muddy street with her hand against her cheek, and stare at him as if he were a dream. A stray cat sprang on to a low mud wall beside her, and watched them both with curiosity.

'Barney,' she said. 'I didn't think I would ever see you again.'

'You called him Pieter,' Barney said, trying to sound steady. 'May I see him?'

Mooi Klip untied the Indian cotton sling, and carefully lifted Pieter out. He was only three weeks old, red and crunched-up and tiny, and his fingers groped at the air as if he were feeling for something that he could never reach. Barney held his hands out, and Mooi Klip let him hold his son for the first time.

'He's so small,' said Barney, breathlessly.

Mooi Klip nodded, and shrugged. Barney held Pieter up against his shoulder, and stroked his soft dark hair, and it was all he could do to stop himself from crying. This was his son, his small baby son, by the woman he loved more than anyone else.

'Joel's fine now,' Barney told Mooi Klip, swallowing the constriction in his throat. 'It hurt him a lot, that trip to Durban. But he survived, and they operated on him. He can walk now, provided he uses a stick.'

Mooi Klip said nothing, but turned away. Barney said, 'It wasn't my fault, Natalia.'

'No,' she said. 'It wasn't your fault. But you didn't really want to marry me, did you?'

'I don't know what you mean.'

'*Barney*,' she chided him, 'you loved me, but I was never right for you, was I? A Griqua girl. When you first met me, I could scarcely speak English. How can you introduce a black savage like me to all of your society friends, or to Agnes Knight?'

'Agnes Knight? She was nothing at all. Look at what you've produced. Pieter Blitz. My first child.'

'Pieter Marneweck.'

'I'm sorry?'

'His name's Pieter Marneweck. Not Blitz. We were never married, were we?'

'But, Natalia, he's my son. And, anyway, can't we marry now? What's to stop us?'

She gently took Pieter out of Barney's arms. The last light of the evening touched her curly hair, and sparkled in her eyes.

'I'm sorry, Barney, it just wouldn't work. There was a time when I thought it could. But you taught me more than English. You taught me that everybody in this world has their place, and that my place isn't beside you.'

'What am I going to do?' asked Barney. His throat felt as if it were coated in dust.

'You can live without me.'

'But how?'

'You've been living without me ever since you took Joel to Durban. And I've been living without you. It's easy. All you have to do is to pretend that pain is something that everybody has to live with, all of the time.'

Barney said, 'What about Pieter?'

'You can see him, whenever you like. I'll always be here.'

Barney lowered his head. 'And what about you?' he said, softly.

'I can manage,' said Mooi Klip.

Barney took a deep breath. 'I want to tell you something,' he said. 'I love you more than anybody else in this whole continent. I love you more than anybody else in this whole world. It's almost unbearable for me to stand here next to you and know that I can't have you. I want to get inside of your mouth and change the words that you're saying to me. For

God's sake, Natalia, how can you be so aloof? Haven't you missed me? Don't you feel anything for me at all? Don't you understand that nothing has any meaning unless you're right beside me to share it?'

'You want me to live with Joel?' asked Mooi Klip, raising an eyebrow.

'Natalia – that will never happen again – I can promise you that.'

'It happened once, and once was more than enough.'

'Natalie –'

She smiled. 'Why don't you call me Mooi Klip? The pretty stone. The glittering diamond you found in the mud, and then cast aside.'

Barney looked up at the evening sky. 'I don't know what to say to you,' he told her, throatily.

'Don't say anything. Not now. Come again when you want to. Perhaps bring a gift for your new son. I am not shutting myself away from you, Barney. I love you still. But the time is not ready yet, and neither are you.'

'I've brought a gift,' said Barney. And he took out of his pocket the wash-leather bag that the digger at the De Beers Mine had given him, crammed with rough diamonds.

Mooi Klip opened the bag carefully and stared at the gems with widened eyes. Then she said, 'No. You will need these. You can't.'

'Take them,' he said. 'One day, they're going to be worth a thousand times more than they are now. You can rely on diamonds to look after you, even when people can't.'

With an awkward heave, he mounted Alsjeblieft again, and raised his hat. 'This is ridiculously formal,' he said. 'I love you, and that's all there is to it.'

Barney tugged at the reins, and Alsjeblieft plodded back along the street between the shacks and the tin-roofed houses and the half-built wooden bungalows. Then, without any kind of urging, the horse turned south, and began to carry him along the banks of the Vaal River towards the nearest digger's settlement, under the willows.

'Do you know something, Alsjebelieft,' said Barney, 'I really believe that you know where you're going.'

The horse kept plodding through the long grass, leaving the twinkling lights of Klipdrift far behind in the Cape Colony night. Barney began to whistle a tune that he heard a street-corner violinist playing in Durban. The tune was called *'Will Ye No Come Back Again?'*

TWO

Edward Nork had left a message for him on the kitchen table. 'Am drunk, but can be found at Dodd's.' Barney read it, turned it over to see if anything was written on the other side, and then crumpled it up. Edward had been drinking so heavily lately that Barney expected to discover him dead one day in a ditch.

He could not entirely blame Edward for his alcoholism. The world price of diamonds had been depressed for years, and life at Kimberley was harsher and more lonely than the profits from a thirty-one foot claim could ever relieve. When the diamond diggers were not being chilled by torrential rain, they were pickled like walnuts by the sun; and the Big Hole was now so deep and treacherous that floods and slides and cave-ins were killing and injuring diggers by ones and twos every day. Hundreds of hopefuls abandoned their claims, either because the work was too hard for the profits they were making; or because they believed they had reached bedrock, and that their ground was all cleaned out. So many left that the restrictions on how many claims one man could own were finally lifted.

It was not difficult for a man to persuade himself that he had reached the bottom of the diamond bearing soil, particularly when he was grimy and exhausted and alone, and he had saved up just enough money to get back to whichever country he had first come from.

That was not to say that the town of Kimberley itself had not improved. Bricks and fancy building materials had reached the town from Durban and the Cape, including a fine collection of cast-iron balconies. The Kimberley Club was now an imposing edifice of red tuck-pointed brick, with iron-pillared verandahs, a mahogany entrance-door with engraved glass panels, and a billiard-room on the second floor, under a skylight. The effect was rather spoiled by the rusting corrugated-iron roof, but in north Cape Colony, shingles were even rarer than diamonds.

There was a new hotel, The Kimberley Palace, and a new whorehouse with private bathrooms and brown velvet drapes with tassels. There were countless new bars; and there was even a rudimentary racetrack, with wooden bleachers, where motley races were run on Saturdays between horses that rarely looked fitter than Alsjeblieft. Most of the bets were laid in rough diamonds, or claim deeds, and Joel went along there whenever he could, although Barney kept a tight check on how much money he took with him. These days, with ill grace, Joel was prepared to let Barney keep the company books, and to allow Barney to be the sole signatory to their bank account.

All in all, though, Kimberley remained a crude and un-civilised male society, where even the smallest luxuries like badger's-hair shaving brushes and scented soap were almost impossible to come by, and where there was very little else to do but drink, gamble, dig the ground, or go to prostitutes. There was a small library on Barkly Street, but most of its books were inspirational stories of Christian derring-do in isolated corners of the British Empire, or bound volumes of scientific periodicals of what Edward called 'exemplary dry-ness'. There was an amateur dramatic society, too, but Barney had been reluctant to join it because he knew that Agnes Knight was a member, and that she was now engaged to be married to its leading male actor, a tall Australian with wavy golden hair and a high nasal whine. His name was Robert Joy.

It was four years since Joel had lost claim No. 172 to Dottie Evans. The claim had been sold three or four times since then, and Dottie Evans herself had been so sick of a social disease that she had left Kimberley and gone to the Cape for her health. Joel still walked with a tilting limp, and his hips gave him pain when the weather was damp, or when the wind was about to change, but otherwise he was much better. He worked for Harold Feinberg most of the time, as a kind of clerk; for Harold had done so well that he had built himself a fine brick-fronted office on the main street, with an upstairs workroom facing the north light, and he now employed a staff of seven, mostly Jews from London's East End.

Barney had been practically pressganged by his horse Alsjeblieft into that occupation known as 'kopje-walloping' – riding from one diamond claim to another, buying up roughs. Every morning at six o'clock sharp, Alsjeblieft started to kick at the rails of the kraal, and would not stop until Barney had saddled him up. There was rarely any need for Barney to direct the horse at all: he would simply trot off on the same rounds that his previous master must have taken since diamonds were first discovered.

The veteran diggers knew Alsjeblieft by sight; and they soon made Barney's acquaintance, too. In a white sun-topi, a belted jacket, and loud check trousers and spats, Barney was welcomed wherever he rode, and he quickly learned to play up to the diggers' expectations of what a good 'kopje-walloper' should be. He brought news, and gossip, and sometimes he brought tobacco, and whiskey, and rude French playing-cards. If a new popular song had reached Kimberley from the Cape, he would learn it, and sing it to every digger he met.

His four years of 'kopje-walloping' did more to strengthen his resolve to be rich, and more to help him through the pain of losing Mooi Klip, than any amount of consolation from Joel, or starry-eyed dreams from Edward. He had lost a would-be wife, and a son. But he came across men who had left everything behind them – their wives, their children, and their homes, just to break their backs in the pits of Kimberley, or De Beers, or wash through gravel on the banks of the Vaal. He met hard men and bitter men; men who scarcely spoke, and men who wanted to talk to him all night. He sat by more camp fires than he could count, and shook more hands than he could ever remember. He learned to be patient, and bright, and above all he learned to be understanding. One digger had talked to him for three hours about his beloved wife Fanny, with whom he had lived in a small redbrick cottage in Streatham, in southern England. It was only later that the digger confessed that he had been found guilty of Fanny's manslaughter, and had only managed to escape to South Africa by a lucky chance.

'You don't know what it is, to love someone, and then to lose them,' he told Barney.

Barney did not argue. He had learned never to argue with the men from whom he bought diamonds. They had to argue enough with their kaffirs, and with the weather, and with the yellow ground from which they were struggling to make their fortunes. All they wanted from Barney were nods of encouragement, and a reasonable price for their stones, and a song or two, and maybe a ounce of British Pluck. They did not want to know that Barney had problems of his own, or that he was the father of a four-year-old child whom he hardly ever saw.

Barney did not pay much for his diamonds: in fact, he gave four or five shillings less than almost any other dealer. But he always paid on time and he was always square, and that was what the diggers liked about him. They felt he was one of them: a small man struggling against the world, and they would often sell him some of their best gems at bargain prices just because he had made them laugh, or brought them an envelope of dubious Egyptian photographs, or sang them two choruses of 'The Flowers of Loch Rannoch'. He was good at Scottish songs, because of his Yiddish accent. The 'Cheery Kopje-Walloper' was a part that Barney had to play as dramatically as Agnes Knight and Robert Joy were to play *Romeo and Juliet* in the Kimberley Dramatic Society's Christmas entertainment at the church hall, except that Barney had to play his part every single day, and with unflagging good humour, through thunderstorms and winds and droughts and days when the flies swarmed as thick as currants in a cake. His ambition depended on it.

During Agnes's play, he sat on a folding chair at the very back of the hall, his head lifted so that he could see over all the hats. Few men in Kimberley were in the habit of taking their hats off indoors, or even when they bathed, and some were known to keep them on even when they visited a prostitute. 'You only take your hat off to a lady, after all.' Barney thought how charming and spun-sugary Agnes looked, in her white diaphanous Juliet dress and her blonde hair plaited into medieval horns. And when she said clearly, 'I, a maid, die maiden-widowed,' he felt so affected that he had to go outside, and take a few deep breaths in the sweltering night air. He had lost her, charming and pretty as she was, and he knew that she would never have him back again. Wrong background, old chap. Sorry. The English had won an Empire by saying 'sorry'.

278

'Bored?' a voice asked him, out of the shadows.

Barney frowned. It was a girl's voice, and it was familiar. 'Faith?' he asked. 'Is that you?'

She emerged from the darkness of the church hall porch into the misty light of the pressure-lamp which hung by the door. She was wearing a pale turquoise evening-dress, and turquoise gloves, and her hair was tied up in dozens of tiny turquoise ribbons. Behind her, the moths plattered against the lamp, and there was a shower of applause from the audience.

'Actually, I came out to look at the stars,' said Faith. 'I've had more of Romeo and Juliet in two months than most people can stomach in a life-time. Agnes has been practising her lines every night since September. But soft! What light at yonder window breaks!'

'Excuse me?'

Faith smiled. 'That's a line from the play. I think I'm even beginning to recite it in my sleep.'

'I'm surprised you're still talking to me,' said Barney. 'You're not worried you might catch something, like a liking for matzo balls, or a chronic inability to work on Saturdays?'

'Jews have never worried me, I'm afraid,' said Faith.

'I see. Only your father and Agnes dislike us, is that it?'

'Agnes doesn't mind Jews either. She was only upset because she thinks you made a fool of her.'

'I guess I did, in a way. It was my own fault. I thought that if everybody took me for a goy, I'd stand a better chance of making a success of my business.'

'Well, you're right, of course,' smiled Faith, rather absently, patting at her ribbons.

'I used to believe I was right,' Barney told her. 'But these days, I don't think it matters a damn if you play billiards at the Kimberley Club or not. As long as you work hard, and make money, who cares?'

Faith nodded. 'I only wish people *didn't* care. But they do. Well, the sort of people that *I* mix with do.'

'The people that *you* mix with don't strike me as particularly pleasant or particularly tolerant or even particularly successful,' said Barney, sharply.

'No, I suppose they wouldn't. Strike you as any of those things, I mean. But ... they all went to the right school. And they all belong to the right club. And they've all seen service in the right regiments. And he who hath fagged at Eton, and been commissioned in the Blues ... yea verily, success and financial ease shall follow him all of his days.'

Barney said, 'It takes an exception to prove a rule.'

'And you're going to be the exception?'

He looked at her. She was a handsome girl, quite broad-shouldered, with a generous figure. He could not understand why she was not married; or perhaps he could. Out of all the English girls he had met since he had come to South Africa, she was the only one with a distinct and uncompromising personality. He knew that she liked botany, and walking, and collecting African artefacts; and maybe all of that was why the gentlemen of Kimberley stayed politely away. They expected from their womenfolk a very special combination of fortitude and subservience, a mixture of durability and feminine fragility. If a women could reload a Lee Enfield under ferocious attack from kaffirs, and still blush furiously at an inadvertent mention of turkey breasts at table; if she could give birth to children in a strooidak hut in 110-degree heat, and still flirt and coo when her husband came home from the diamond office; if she could wield a hammer and nails during the day, and then patiently allow her husband to go out gambling and drinking at night on his own; then a Kimberley man would propose without a moment's hesitation.

Faith was not that kind of a girl, and that was why nobody had asked her.

Barney said, 'I'm going to be rich one day. That's all I can say. And those snobbish friends of yours will tip their hats to me in the street.'

'I hope they do.'

There was a silence between them. The moths pit-pattered on the lamp. From inside the hall, they could hear nothing but the distorted voice of Juliet's nurse, bewailing her charge's death.

'When are they going to be married?' asked Barney.

'Who?'

He nodded towards the church hall doors. 'Those two. Robert and Agnes.'

'Oh, I don't know. They're talking about April.'

'Does she love him?'

Faith smiled at him, and nodded. 'I think so. He's just her type. All wavy hair and no intellect.'

'You sound like you don't approve.'

'Oh, I approve. Anything to keep Agnes entertained.'

Barney laughed. Then he said, seriously, 'Do you think your father would object if I asked you to step out with me? There's a cello recital next week, just after Christmas.'

'Me?' asked Faith. 'No, you can't ask me.'

'Why not?'

'Because.'

'What do you mean, "because"?'

She lowered her eyelashes. 'Because you would probably hurt me, in the end. I asked you to accompany me to church one day, remember? And what happened then? I wasn't hurt much. Please don't think that I was. But if I started to step out with you, then I would undoubtedly and quite ridiculously lose my self-control, and then I would lose you, too, and that would be rather more than I could tolerate.'

Barney reached out and took her hand. There were three strings of pearls around her gloved wrists, and they shone as pale as solidified tears.

'I don't want to hurt you,' he told her. 'All I want to do is take you out to a cello recital.'

She gave a sad, small smile. 'One think leads to another in my life. A cello recital would lead to a symphony; and I can't bear symphonies. They always have such melodramatic endings. They make me cry.'

'Faith –'

'Let's be friends,' she whispered. 'When we meet in the street, let's pass the time of day. Let's have coffee together, when we can. One day perhaps I'll show you my botany book. I have some lovely drawings of acacias.'

'Acacias?' he asked her, as if he could not understand what she meant.

That had been a year and a half ago, and he had only talked to Faith twice since then. Once in the street, when they accidentally met on the boardwalk, and once at a concert, when a stentorious singer called Daniel Napier had bellowed out thirty British patriotic songs, one after the other, without pausing for breath.

Barney liked Faith. He trusted her, and there were many times during those four years of kopje-walloping when he felt he could have proposed to her, and married her, if only Mr Knight would have allowed him. But as time went by, he began to understand that it would have been a mistake, and that Faith's estimation of their probable effect on each other was quite right. He would only have hurt her, in the end. He would only have made her cry.

He saw Mooi Klip once or twice a month, whenever Alsje-blieft decided it was time for them to plod up to Klipdrift. Mooi Klip's mother and father lived in a neat, white-painted strooidak house not far from the bend in the river, among a whole community of Griquas. They were quietly but firmly protective of Mooi Klip, and especially of Pieter, and whenever Barney arrived to see them, they would wait in the background, their arms patiently folded, and Barney could only talk to Mooi Klip in the most stilted way.

Sitting together on those riempie-thonged chairs, close to the shuttered window, Barney asked Mooi Klip time and time again to think of coming back to him, to consider starting again. But each time she would smile at him and shake her head. Even when he suggested buying out Joel, and paying for him to go back to America, Mooi Klip declined to think about marriage.

'I don't understand *why*,' he hissed at her. Her father was sitting in his big yellow-wood chair only three feet away from them.

'Because I am not ready to marry.'

'You were ready before. How can you possibly not be ready now?'

'You know what happened,' said Mooi Klip. Then, softer, 'It changed everything.'

'But I don't understand what's wrong. Is it because you don't love me?'

'No. You know that I love you.'

'Well, I love you, and I can't stand to be without you. So how can you stand to be without me?'

Mooi Klip brushed back her curls. 'Sometimes there are more important things than being together.'

'Like what? I can't think of a single consideration that could possibly be more important than our getting married.'

She looked at him straight. The washed-out afternoon light caught the side of her face, so that she looked like a sepia photograph of herself. But Barney did not even own a picture of her, let alone the real thing.

'It's much more important that you make yourself rich,' she said. '*That* is what is important.'

Barney let out a short, impatient breath. 'Do you really think that money matters to me that much? More than you?'

She nodded. 'It *must* matter.'

'And what about Pieter? I suppose I don't care about him? I suppose I'm not interested in being a father to him?'

'You are his father. Nobody can ever take that away from you, nor from him.'

'But how can I –'

Mooi Klip reached out and touched his cheek, stroking it gently, calming him down. 'You came here to Africa to make your fortune. You must make it. I have learned that I will only stand in your way.'

'You think I care about those narrow-minded Englishmen, and those prejudiced Boers?'

'You will do, when you are wealthy, and you have to do big business with them. What will they way, if you try to take a Griqua wife along to their garden parties, and their banquets? A wife who is as black as their servants? You are Jewish, and that is enough of a difficulty for you. Do not make it worse for yourself by marrying me.'

'Natalia –'

She raised her hand to hush him. 'I can only say that because I love you and because I know that it is best for you.'

They argued like that almost every time they met; but Mooi Klip was patient and adamant. She had been ready to marry him once, but not now. He could see Pieter whenever he wanted, and his fatherhood would never be denied him. But she would not marry him. Not when he shouted at her, and slammed doors; not when he tried to cajole her, or bribe her; not even when he cried.

Little Pieter was all that he could have wanted a son to be. He had his mother's dark curly hair, and dusky complexion, but by the age of four there was no doubt at all that he had inherited his father's chiselled face and big-boned physique. 'The little boxer,' his grandfather called him, which in itself was a courteous acknowledgement of Barney's rights.

Pieter spoke mostly in Griqua-Afrikaans, but Mooi Klip taught him English, too, and insisted that he should always speak English to his father. He only broke into Afrikaans when he was excited, or angry, and then Mooi Klip would smack him on the cheeks with both hands, as if she were playing the cymbals, and tell him not to be rude to his father. Barney told Pieter long stories about his adventures on Alsjeblieft, and on long cool autumn evenings he would sit him up in the old horse's saddle and walk him along the banks of the Vaal, with the sun spreading across the mud flats and the birds flickering up from the distant treeline like handfuls of cloves.

His occasional visits to Klipdrift were days of great calm, and of great joy; and also of bittersweet sadness. But in the extraordinary times that were to come, he would always look back on them as if he were looking through a series of lighted windows at landscapes made tiny by the perspective of the years, each of them rich with warmth, and with happiness, and with precious regret.

He found Edward in the far corner of Dodd's Bar, his head resting on his arms, a collection of smeary whiskey glasses assembled around his elbows. An Irishman in a green Derby hat and a green silk vest was sitting at the upright piano, playing an off-key song about Paddy O'Leary's party, and three other Irishmen had linked arms to dance a shambolic jig across the bare boarded floor. The air was thick with Empire tobacco, from cigarettes and pipes, since only yesterday an ox-waggon had arrived from Capetown with fresh supplies. The diamond diggers smoked what they could get, and sometimes, when the roads were barred all they could get was dried wild syringa leaves.

Barney sat down opposite Edward, seized his hair, and shook his head around to wake him up.

284

'What's the matter?' Edward protested.

'It's me, Barney. You left me a note.'

Edward raised his head and peered at Barney through eyes as bloodshot as garnets.

'A note?'

'That's right. On the kitchen table. You said you were drunk, but I could find you here.'

'Oh, did I? Well, that only goes to show what a foolish fellow I am.'

Barney beckoned the barman, who came across in his blue striped apron and stared at Edward with a face like a leg of pork.

'If you're buying any more for him, then it's up to you to drag him out of here,' he cautioned Barney.

'Just bring me a jug of water,' asked Barney.

'Five shillings,' said the barman.

'Just bring me the water, will you?'

The barman went off, and Edward gave him an inebriated wave. 'Never could stand that fellow,' he said. 'Too censorious.'

'You left me a note,' Barney repeated.

'Oh, yes. I did,' agreed Edward. 'Well quite right, too. Particularly since I've set you back on the road to fame and fortune, prosperity and wealth.'

'I see. And how did you manage that?'

Edward reached into his inside pocket, and then into his side pocket. Eventually, he found what he was looking for in his breast pocket – a sheaf of crumpled claim deeds. He held them up, and gave Barney an unstable grin.

'What are those?' asked Barney, sharply.

'These, my dear chap, are the title deeds for claims No. 203, 202, and 233, as well as half of 201 and half of 232.'

'Did you *steal* them?'

'My dear old fellow, of course I didn't steal them. I *bought* them. And what's more, I bought them on your behalf. Here,' he said, and pushed them across the table. 'They're all yours. Take them. Make the most of them.'

Barney, very slowly and cautiously, picked up the deeds that Edward had laid on the table. He leafed through them, and then put them down again.

'They're genuine,' he said. 'Four genuine claims.'

'Of course they're genuine.'

'But how did you pay for them? They must be worth forty thousand pounds!'

'I gave them an IOU. In your name, of course.'

'You did what? An IOU for forty thousand pounds? How the hell am I going to meet an IOU for forty thousand pounds?'

Edward waved his hand. 'My dear chap – wait. Hold your horses. The claims *are* worth forty thousand pounds, yes. But only in *our* opinion. The chaps who have been mining them have dug right down to the blue Norkite. They're all ready to pack up and go home, simply because they believe that they've reached rock bottom. They were willing to sell for a *very* reduced price.'

Barney stared at him. All he had in the bank was £3211 – the carefully-accrued profits from four years of kopje-walloping. 'How much?' he asked, in a thick whisper.

The barman brought their jug of water, and banged it on the table. He held out his hand ungraciously, and Barney gave him four shillings. He spat on them, and then walked off.

Edward poured himself a large glass with shaking hands.

'Three thousand, one hundred pounds,' he said, triumphantly.

Barney picked the deeds up again. Four claims, right in the centre of the Big Hole. It seemed like a hallucination, the reappearance of his mirage. 'Edward,' he said, 'you're a genius. One day, I'm going to erect a statue to you. In marble, like a Roman emperor, right on the reef of the Kimberley Mine. Edward, you're a *genius*!'

'Well, yes, I know,' said Edward, modestly.

'I must go tell Joel,' Barney said. He could hardly sit still. 'Lord above, this is marvellous!'

'The least you could do is buy me a drink,' remarked Edward.

'I'll buy you a hundred drinks. But first of all I want to go to the bank and draw out enough money to pay off this IOU. I want to know that these claims are actually mine.'

'One small snort of whiskey would do,' said Edward.

Barney snapped his fingers at the barman. 'Bring this gentleman another drink,' he directed. 'And treat him like the genius he is.'

*

286

Joel was dubious at first. He was quite comfortable working in Harold Feinberg's sorting-room, and a pretty young French girl had just come out from Natal to work with Harold on the commercial side. To leave the fine brick building on the main street and go back to the mud and the flies and the days of hard digging did not seem at all attractive, and he argued with Barney for hours before he finally gave in.

'I think those claims are a waste of money, mind you,' he said petulantly, once he had agreed to help Barney dig. 'If Johnson and Kelly have left them, how can they possibly be worth having? Johnson's the meanest man in the whole colony, if not the whole of Africa.'

'I agree with you. But Johnson's selling because he believes that his claims are all worked out.'

'But other diggers have kept on going, and still found diamonds. Surely Johnson knows that.'

'It's a question of soil break-down, that's what Edward says. The blue ground underneath the yellow ground gradually weathers into yellow ground itself when it's been exposed to the air. It's all the same kind of soil. But men like Johnson are usually in too much of a hurry to wait around and see that happen. They think they've reached the end of their claim, and they're only too willing to make a small profit and get out fast.'

Joel sniffed loudly, and tapped his walking-stick on the living-room floor. 'I still think Johnson knows what he's doing. I just hope you won't be too sore about losing four years of hard-earned money.'

'We'll never get anywhere if we don't take a risk.'

'A risk?' mocked Joel. 'Moses took less of a risk when he led the Children of Israel out of Egypt.'

'Moses had God on his side. Maybe we do, too.'

'I'll believe that when a divine Hand reaches out of the clouds and digs out a few cubic yards of soil for me. Get me a drink, will you? There's a bottle of port on the hutch.'

There was a cheerful rap on the bungalow door. Barney, halfway across the room, said, 'Come on in!' and Cecil Rhodes appeared, looking distinctly pleased with himself, in a creased cotton bush-jacket and jodphurs with mud-caked knees.

'What-ho, Blitz!' he said. He set his sun-topi down on the

287

table. 'I hear that you're back in the diamond-digging business again! No more kopje-walloping?'

'Not if I can help it,' said Barney.

'I always heard that you were a splendid walloper. Friendly, affable, and never wasted your time on dud claims.'

'I have my horse to thank for that. Alsjeblieft wouldn't go near an unprofitable claim, even if you filled it to the brim with oats and carrots.'

'How's life at De Beers?' asked Joel, sourly. 'I hear that you and your pals own half rhe claims there these days.'

Rhodes pulled up a chair, and sat down. 'Actually, now that the board have relaxed the rules on ownership, the whole show's going very much better. It was so unprofitable, with all those tiny claims! Now we've consolidated fifteen or sixteen claims together, and that means we can dig them all at the same level, and dig them deeper. We can serve them all with the same cables and buckets, too, and drain them all with one pump.'

'They tell me you're really quite rich these days,' said Joel.

'Wealth doesn't come into it, old boy. What we're doing here is extending the Empire, and making sure that we manage things the British way. Efficiently, profitably, and in the best interests of all.'

Barney brought them both a glass of port. 'Well,' he told Rhodes, 'you once told me that we might have a scrap on our hands. Let's see how we get on.'

'I'm looking forward to it,' said Rhodes, lifting his glass. 'I have to go back to Oxford in the spring. I'm studying for my doctorate in law. But I have a splendid fellow called Charles Rudd who looks after things for me when I'm away.'

'Well, I'm glad for you,' said Joel, finishing his drink in two quick swallows. 'It must be wonderful to be so rich, and surrounded by so many splendid chaps and fellows.'

Rhodes stared at Joel levelly. 'Yes,' he said, after a while. 'It is.'

The following morning, Thursday, Barney and Joel negotiated their way across the uneven, crumbling pathways of the Big Hole to inspect their new property. Edward had been right: the four claims had been dug really deep, right down to the blue ground, which in spite of Edward's constant efforts to

288

christen 'Norkite' was now fairly generally known throughout the digging community as 'Kimberlite'. Joel limped around the claims, morosely kicking the ground with his boot-heel, and prodding it with his stick.

'Seems pretty well worked out to me.'

'That's what Johnson thought. But if Edward's right, this is only the beginning.'

'Edward's a drunk. I don't know why he impresses you so much. You wouldn't have been impressed by a drunk cutter, back at the tailor's shop, would you?'

Barney propped his fists on his hips and looked around. Right beside him, in the next claim, which belonged to the Compagnie Française des Diamants du Cap, a kaffir was loading earth into the buckets which hung from one of the steel cables. Since Barney had last dug here, the cables seemed to have multiplied, and everywhere he looked there were dangling buckets being jerked slowly towards the rim of the mine, and down again. Few cables were wound by hand any more: most of the diggers had set up huge horizontal winding-wheels on the edge of the mine, which were rotated by horses in harness. These wheels were called horse whims, and apart from being more powerful they freed the diggers to attack the soil of the Big Hole with even greater speed and ferocity.

'You really believe we're going to make ourselves rich?' asked Joel, dubiously.

'Why not? Rhodes has. And Rhodes isn't any cleverer than us.'

'He may not be cleverer,' said Joel. 'But he's English, and he's been to the right school.'

Barney walked across the claim and picked up an abandoned shovel. 'By the time we're finished,' he said, 'it won't matter a damn what school anybody's been to. It won't matter if they're Jewish or goyish. There's only one human currency out here, when it really comes down to it, and that's diamonds.'

He thrust the point of the shovel in to the hard blue ground, and dug some out. Then he crumbled it between the palms of his hands, picking out the pebbles and the gravel. He was left with three small diamonds.

'You see?' he said, holding the stones up to the sun. 'One of these is nearly a carat. And the other two are good-quality smalls.'

'What are you waiting for, then?' demanded Joel, with a smile. 'Go get some kaffirs, and let's get started.'

'You're sure?' asked Barney.

Joel made a face. 'You don't *have* to have me, you know,' he told Barney. 'I certainly haven't done you any favours, and I don't suppose I ever will. But we're brothers, aren't we, and I suppose that's a good enough reason for working together.'

'I think so,' said Barney. Then he made his way up the slope towards the edge of the mine, while Joel sat on the handle of the shovel and watched him go.

Diamond-fever caught them both. Every shovelful of blue ground they dug up from their four claims brought more gems, and more profits, and by the end of 1876 they were making more than £2000 a week. In 1877, on his twenty-ninth birthday, Barney reckoned that he was worth more than £75,000, and to celebrate he ordered an architect up from Durban to plan a mansion for himself and Joel on the outskirts of Kimberley, on a small kopje among the trees. He wanted a billiards-room, just like the Kimberley Club, even though he did not have the faintest idea how to play billiards; and a field for playing polo. He also wanted a long curving driveway, so that anyone who came to see him would have plenty of time to be impressed by the gounds and the house and the formal gardens.

He began to dress, at weekends, in well-tailored frock coats which he ordered from Capetown, with dark blue silk facings on the lapels. He also ordered ten smart double-breasted vests, and a dozen white collars, and spotted ties, and tweed trousers. Joel bought himself a small varnished brougham, and a pair of frisky grey horses, and spent his Saturdays trotting up and down Kimberley's main street in his smart white suits, raising his hat to all the girls.

The house began to take shape, and when the foundations were laid, Barney broke a bottle of champagne over its brown Cape bricks and named it Vogel Vlei. Joel, who stood a little way off with a red-haired Scottish girl called Mary, gave him an encouraging wave with his stick.

But even his money could not protect Barney from tragedy and violence. Two days later, without any warning, Alsjeblieft began to shiver and shake and foam at the mouth, and he had to call in Dr Schoeman to give him medication. 'He's old,' Dr Schoeman told him, coming out of the stable and tugging down his sleeves. 'The kindest thing you can do is to put him down.'

Barney said, 'But he did everything. He made my fortune for me.'

'All the more reason to be kind to him,' said Dr Schoeman, his eyes as blue and bulging as those glass marbles which English schoolboys called Sea-Blue Sailors.

'Let's wait and see,' said Barney.

Dr Schoeman shrugged. 'He's only going to suffer. His liver's gone.'

Later than evening, while Joel was laughing in the living-room with Mary, Barney went outside with his Shopkeeper's pistol, fully loaded, and walked around the house to the stable. The insects chirped and chirruped in the scrub all around him, and high above Kimberley the full moon was suspended bright and cold, the temptation of an age yet to come. He hesitated by the kraal gate, and then he went inside, and crossed the kraal towards the stable.

Alsjeblieft was lying on his side in the straw, his eyes wide, panting as he breathed. There were flecks of foam around his mouth. He raised his head slightly as Barney came in.

Barney tugged at his mane. 'How are you feeling?' he asked gently. 'Pretty bad, hunh? You have a *krenk*?' He was conscious of how nearly he sounded like his mother, on those winter days in New York when he had stayed home, in bed, with a snuffle.

Alsjeblieft whinnied, and his throat was thick with fluid. Barney stroked his shoulder, and thought of all the miles and all the days they had travelled together, Alsjeblieft and he, and how Pieter had sat in the old horse's saddle and pretended that he was a soldier, a Life Guard of Her Majesty the Queen.

'I hope you forgive me,' said Barney, and raised the muzzle of his revolver so that it pointed directly between Alsjeblieft's ears. Alsjeblieft seemed to sense that something was wrong, because he shifted on his straw, and almost tried to get up on to his knees.

'Forgive me, *alsjeblieft*,' Barney asked him, and then there was a very loud, flat shot, and the horse collapsed on to his pallet with a sigh that sounded human. Maybe it was a sigh of relief. Barney stood up, with the heavy pistol hanging in his hand, and looked down at the horse with a choking feeling in his chest. Then he left the stable and walked outside, breathing with as much difficulty as a man who has run a quarter of a mile in his veld boots.

Joel came hurrying out with his shirt tail flapping out of his trousers. 'What's the matter? What's all the shooting about?'

Barney nodded towards the stable. 'Alsjeblieft,' he said. 'Dr Schoeman said it was the best thing to do.'

'I see. Well, I'm sorry. I know what that horse meant to you.'

'And to you, too, Joel. Without that old horse, we never could have afforded those four claims.'

Joel clapped his arm around Barney's shoulders. 'You know your trouble, Barney? You're too sentimental. You saved up the money for those claims by working your backside off, and that's all. If you weren't so sentimental, maybe you would have found yourself a decent woman by now.'

'Like Mary?' asked Barney, sarcastically.

'Mary's all right. There's nothing wrong with Mary. And you can take my word for it that she's a genuine redhead.'

Barney irritably twisted himself free from Joel's arm. 'I'm not in the mood, Joel. That's all. I don't forget anybody who's done me a favour, whether it's a human or a horse.'

'Meaning that *I* do? Meaning that I should have to spend the rest of my life being humbly grateful to you for dragging me halfway across the Orange Free State in an ox-waggon, and having me operated on by some halfwitted British surgeon, so that I could have the privilege of walking around like a cripple? God, you're sanctimonious.'

Barney stopped, and seized the front of Joel's shirt. 'Listen,' he breathed, his jaw protruding with aggression, 'one more word out of you and I'll break your other leg.'

Joel pushed him away. 'One day you're going to stop threatening me, young Barney. The trouble with you is, your intellect gives out too early and then all you have to fall back on is your fists. All these fancy clothes, all these pretensions. A mansion you want, called Vogel Vlei? Why don't you call it Knishes?'

292

Barney rubbed the back of his neck, easing his wired-up muscles. 'Just leave it, will you, Joel?'

'Come on, now, you threatened to break my leg. I should leave? Let you walk away forgiven? I shouldn't say my piece about what kind of a hypocritical bastard you've turned out to be? And don't try to say that you're not. You're so damned hypocritical that you keep your little black woman tucked away in Klipdrift, as well as your half-caste son; while at the same time you prance around Kimberley complaining to all those goyish cretins about the kaffirs, and how primitive the Bantu are. You should *realise*, Barney – those goys don't respect you, whatever you say. They think that you're just as untouchable as the blackies. So don't try to match your prejudice with theirs. You'll never win.'

Barney listened to this in silence, and then stopped by the verandah steps. 'You've got me wrong, Joel. All wrong. There's only one thing I want out of life, and that's money. You see that mine out there? I want all of it. Then, I can do or say whatever I want and it won't matter.'

'You can do or say whatever you want right *now*.'

Barney shook his head. 'Not now. But the time will come.'

'When? When you're rich enough? You're pretty rich now.'

'When the whole of that Big Hole belongs to me. That's when.'

Joel gave him a sardonic grin. 'I see. That's when you're going to declare that you were born a Jew, that you've always been a Jew, and that you're always going to go to the synagogue and say your prayers, until they bury you in the ground. But not before then, right?'

'Get out of my way.'

'Or what? You'll hit me? You've got the gun this time. Why don't you shoot me?'

'I should have shot you a long time ago. You've been sicker than Alsjeblieft for years.'

'Oh, come on, now, Barney,' said Joel, hopping towards him on his one good leg. 'Don't tell me you're going to act the outraged little brother? Because of that black woman? Is that it? There are twenty black women at least as good as her down on Main Street right now, and you could have any one of them for two pounds ten. I saved you that day! I saved you from yourself! Why, if you'd been married now –'

Barney raised the Shopkeeper's pistol and fired at Joel point-blank. He deliberately aimed to miss, of course, by more than three feet. But the sharp report of the gun stopped Joel right where he was, wide-eyed, his hands raised up to his chest in the posture of a frightened animal, and when Barney turned around to climb up the verandah steps, he was still standing there, his mouth opening and closing noiselessly, and the echo of the pistol shot was still racketing around the Kimberley kopjes like a shout of hatred that could never be forgotten.

Later that evening, Barney took the small ox-waggon and drove up to the site of Vogel Vlei. It was past ten o'clock, but the moon had not yet set, and the outlines of the foundations could clearly be seen in the darkness. He stood there with his hands in his pockets, the wind blowing his curly hair, and he could imagine for a moment the dinners he would hold here, in the dining-room; and the games of billiards he would play with Kimberley's diamond-dealers; and he could imagine the dances he would arrange on summer evenings, with the rows of French windows open to the lawns, and the waltz music wafting out over the trees.

Then he thought of Mooi Klip, and the moon as it sank was reflected in perfect miniature in the tear that formed in his eye.

By the winter of 1878, Vogel Vlei was almost completed. It was an E-shaped, symmetrical mansion in the English country house style, with a stables for eight horses, a kraal for oxen, and a magnificent gravelled courtyard in front of the main entrance, with a fountain which Barney's architect had bought in Ravenna, Italy, and which had been laboriously carried on ox-waggons across the Great Karoo in sixteen separate pieces. It did not matter that there was not enough water on Barney's estate to make the fountain actually work. He had a fountain, and that was impressive enough on its own.

Mooi Klip allowed Barney to take Pieter down to Kimberley one weekend, to inspect the new house. She declined to come herself, although Barney tried hard to persuade her. She was being cautiously courted these days by a young Griqua farmer, a very tall young man with noticeably Dutch looks about him called Coen Boonzaier. He and Mooi Klip were going to take advantage of Pieter's absence to visit friends along the Vaal River.

Barney took Pieter's hand and led him in through the carved oak doors of Vogel Vlei to the pillared hallway, with its shining parquet floors, and its decorative and its sweeping curved staircase. Pieter was six now, a composed and dignified little boy, and his mother had dressed him in cream and beige union suit, with a brown bonnet. He was tall for his age, with big feet, and he had a very grave way of talking which amused strangers but which Barney always found touching.

As he grew older, Pieter was changing more and more to look like his mother; and Barney would sometimes sit him on his knee and stare at him for minutes on end, remembering the brown wide-apart eyes, the smoky-coloured curls, and the lips which had once parted to kiss him, and to tell him that she would marry him and love him for ever.

'Well, what do you think of the house?' Barney asked Pieter.

'It's fine,' said Pieter.

'Fine? It's magnificent! It's the best house in Kimberley! It's probably the best house in the whole colony!'

Pieter looked around the empty uncarpeted rooms, echoing and bare. So far, Barney had not decided on any drapes or furniture or decorations. He had not been entirely sure what to do. His architect had suggested a few names of decorators in Capetown – the man who had furnished Sir Henry Sarkly's house for him, and the company of designers who had converted the old Quinn house from a model of Georgian serenity into a confusion of Victorian over-indulgence. But Barney had demurred. He had vague and persistent memories of Khotso, and he wanted Vogel Vlei to have the same atmosphere. Elegant, immaculate, but also relaxed.

'Can I go home?' asked Pieter, in his strong Afrikaans accent.

'This *is* your home,' said Barney, laying a hand on his shoulder. 'Well, it's one of your homes, at least.'

'It doesn't feel like home.'

'No, not yet. But it will, I promise you. And I promise you

295

something else. You will always be welcome here, no matter what. You're my son, my only boy, and my first boy, and I want you to remember that, because it's important. If you want to tell people that Barney Blitz is your father, then it's all right by me. In fact, I'll be proud of it. In fact, I'll be more than proud of it.'

'Mama won't marry you,' said Pieter, flatly.

Barney looked down at Pieter, and Pieter was so much like his mother that it gave him a strange sensation of unreality. 'She *says* she won't.'

'Is it because of Uncle Joel?'

'Uncle Joel?' asked Barney, and his voice echoed across the oak flooring. He could see a reflection of himself and Pieter in the long line of French windows opposite, two pale figures in a huge sunlit room. 'Well – I suppose it's partly because of Uncle Joel.'

'She doesn't like him.'

'How do you know? She never told you that.'

Pieter blushed. 'I know. But I just know she doesn't like him.'

'I see.'

They inspected the first floor in silence. The ballroom. The library. The dining-room. The kitchens, with their cold black ranges, and their bare beams. Everywhere they went, there was a sharp smell of newly-cut wood, and plaster.

Upstairs, looking out of the landing window over the few straggling trees which formed the southern border of Vogel Vlei, Pieter said suddenly, 'I love you.'

Barney looked at him cautiously. 'You love me? You really mean that?'

Pieter turned towards him, and Barney could see that his son's eyes were tight with tears, and his mouth was down-turned. 'Mama says you're good. And I know you are. But she cries. Why can't you stay with Mama, instead of going away every time?'

Barney knelt down, and held Pieter tight in his arms. He tangled his fingers into the baby curls at the back of Pieter's neck, and then he said gently, 'Sometimes things happen whether we want them to happen or not. I was going to stay with your mama once, but things went wrong. It wasn't my fault. It wasn't your mama's fault, either. But they did, and now we don't seem to be able to get back together again.'

'Can I ask her?' said Pieter.

'Can you ask her what?'

'Can I ask her to have you back with us, to stay?'

Barney stood up, his hands on his hips, and looked around the deserted living-room. 'You can ask her if she wants to come and live here.'

Pieter looked away.

'You don't want to ask her?' Barney queried. 'Or is it that you don't want to live here yourself?'

Pieter said, 'It's not home. Mama won't think it's home. Your other house is home.'

'The bungalow? But that's just a – well, it's just a bungalow.'

'This isn't home,' insisted Pieter.

'Of course it's home. It's the biggest home in the whole of Kimberley. Come on, Pieter, I haven't even moved in yet. But when I do, then you'll see how friendly it is. I promise you.'

At that moment, Harold Feinberg's voice called, 'Hallooo? Anyone at home?'

'There you are,' Barney told Pieter. 'I told you it was home.'

Harold came squeaking into the living-room on soft black-leather pumps, and took off his sun helmet. He was breathing rather noisily, as if he had walked all the way from his office.

'Home?' he said. 'This place will never be home to anyone, .east of all you.'

'You want to make a bet on that?'

'If you like. I bet you *my* best diamond of the day against *your* best diamond of the day, that on New Year's Day, next year, you won't even be living here.'

'Jewish or Gregorian New Year's Day?'

Harold Feinberg pulled an expression of mock outrage. 'Jewish, of course. Just because *you've* given up your religion, that doesn't mean to say that *I* have.'

Barney laid his hand on Pieter's shoulder. Harold said, 'That boy's growing, you know. I don't know what his mother's feeding him, fertilizer, maybe? – but he's growing.'

'Of course he's growing. He's six years old.'

297

'Your son and heir, huh?' asked Harold.

'That's right.'

'So why don't you marry the mother?'

Barney took a slow breath. 'I would, if she'd have me.'

'No, you wouldn't,' retorted Harold, pacing across the bare floorboards with exaggerated steps. He stopped, silhouetted against the sunlight that flared in from the uncurtained window. 'You wouldn't marry her for *nothing*.'

'What do you know about it?' asked Barney, more cuttingly than he meant to.

'What do I know about it? I'm a diamond dealer. And if you want to know about human nature, I'm your man. Come on, Barney, you've seen it for yourself, when you were out kopje-walloping. Greed, you've seen, haven't you, and despair, and hopelessness, and ridiculous optimism? You've seen all of those.'

'Sure.'

'Well – you may recognise those things in other people – but maybe you don't see them in yourself. When I look at you, do you know what I see?'

'I don't know,' said Barney, brusquely. 'What?'

'I see ambition. That's what I see. I see ambition, and I see one thing more.'

'Oh, yes?'

'I see you burning yourself out before you're forty-five. A young death. Because, believe me, you've already got the kind of house that most people can only dream about, and you're making more money in one week that most English people make in a year. Do you know how much they pay a butler, these days, a fully-trained butler, in an English household? Seventy-five pounds a year. A year! And you're making two thousand pounds in a week.'

'You're not doing too badly yourself, Harold.'

'You think I'm in the business for money? I'm in business for satisfaction. I'm in business because it's good for my digestion. But let me tell you something. You won't ever live here, not happily, anyway; and that poor boy won't ever be your son and heir.'

Barney said, 'What the hell gives you the right to say something like that?'

Harold Feinberg lifted his hands in pretended innocence. 'I say it because it's true.'

'It's true, is it? Well, let me tell you something. This boy is my son, and my heir, and when I die everything that I own will belong to him.'

Harold Feinberg came across to Pieter, and took a half-crown from the pocket of his grey vest. 'You hear that, my boy? he asked. 'Your papa's just bequeathed you everything. His house, his diamonds, his broken heart. They're all going to be yours.'

'Harold,' warned Barney.

Harold stood up straight. 'I'm sorry. I was brought up in Whitechapel. It makes your tongue a little sharper than it should be.'

'You didn't come here to give Pieter a half-crown, did you? Or to spend your afternoon baiting me?'

'No, I didn't. I came to tell you that the Belgian Company right next to yours want to dispose of their claims, provided they can get a reasonable price.'

'Westerlo? Are you sure? But they own eight and a half claims.'

'With your money, you should be able to afford them.'

'What are they asking?'

'Two hundred thousand. Cheap at the price, I can tell you.'

Barney pushed his hands into the pockets of his trousers, and made a face. 'I'd go to one-eighty, but no more.'

'They'd probably accept that. I'd have to talk to them for a while, though.'

'Then talk to them. I'll pay your commission.'

Harold said, 'There's more than commission involved in this. Waterlo have business connections with Ascher and Mendel, in Antwerp.'

'The cutters?'

'That's right. And, believe me, they're the very finest. They specialise in odd-shaped stones . . . getting the best out of a gem that most cutters wouldn't even know what to do with. They cut the Orange Diamond last year, as a seminavette. Seventy-one carats.'

'I remember. But what are you trying to tell me?'

Harold laced his fingers over his camel-coloured vest. 'What

I'm trying to suggest is a three-corner partnership. You mine the diamonds, I market them, and Ascher and Mendel's cut them. Between the three of us, in time, we could control almost every major diamond that Cape Colony can produce.'

Barney eyed Harold thoughtfully. 'You're talking a lot of speculative hot air, Harold,' he said. 'But you're also talking a lot of sense. The only thing that disturbs me is why Waterlo want to sell.'

'They invested too much money in diamonds before the slump. Now they need capital. It's as simple as that. And – let's be truthful – diamonds were never a good investment, were they?'

Barney ruffled Pieter's hair. 'You know what Rhodes said to me once?' he asked Harold. 'As long as women go on falling in love, he said, the future of the diamond industry will be assured. Four million diamond engagement rings are required each year, and that means that four million diamonds are required.'

'Rhodes is a cynic, when it comes to women.'

'I wish I were, sometimes,' said Barney.

'I'm glad you're not,' smiled Harold. 'The day that you're not desperately in love with one lady or another, that's the day I will call for the rabbi.'

Barney linked arms with Harold and led him through to the library. The only piece of furniture in the entire house stood there: a small chipped Pembroke table, clustered with bottles of South African sherry and sweet white wines. There was also a bottle of whiskey.

'Do you want a drink?' asked Barney.

Harold shook his head. He sat on one of the windowsills and watched as Barney poured himself a small measure of Soctch.

'You never used to drink,' he remarked.

'I never used to be a millionaire,' said Barney. 'It's a responsibility, being a millionaire.'

'What do you think of my partnership, then?' asked Harold. 'You want to try?'

'I'm not sure.'

'You're going to have to do *something* dramatic, sooner or later. Have you seen how Rhodes is buying up claims at De

300

Beers? In a few years, he's going to have control of the whole mine. Then he's going to start looking at the Big Hole.'

'He won't find it easy, taking over Kimberley.'

'He will, unless you're strong enough to resist him. And that means buying up as many claims as you can, and controlling the price of diamonds. You won't win out against Rhodes unless you control the price. That's why I think it's worth your forming an alliance with me, and with Ascher and Mendel. If we're clever, we can keep the price of diamonds high when Rhodes wants to buy, and low when he wants to sell.'

Barney poured himself another whiskey. Across on the other side of the library, Pieter was scuffing his foot across the oak parquet flooring to make curving marks, like giant eyebrows, or scimitars, or unsmiling lips.

'Maybe you're right, Harold,' he said, softly. 'Maybe we should get into the cutting side, and the marketing side, and the retail side. After all, it's the retail side that counts.'

'Well, sure,' said Harold. 'It's on the retail side that they make most of the profit. You think *you* make a profit when you sell a rough diamond to me? You think *I* make a profit when I sell a rough diamond to a dealer from Europe? You think *he* makes a profit?' Harold pouted his lips, and shook his head. 'Not a chance. What we make is piffle. The people that make money are the jewellers. They mark up those diamonds a hundred, two hundred, three hundred per cent! And the poor fellow in the street pays two hundred pounds for that glassy stone you sold to me for ten pounds. Then he goes waving it around, telling all his friends what a wonderful investment he's made! A two hundred pound diamond! What an investment! He should try to sell it back to the trade and see what he gets for it. Diamonds are the worst investment since the South Sea Bubble.'

'The South Sea Bubble?' asked Barney.

Harold waved a dismissive hand. 'Take it from me, a bad investment. But for you and me, diamonds could be tremendous – as long as we control the business right from the mines to the shops.'

'And as long as we own enough claims to keep Rhodes out of Kimberley.'

'That goes without saying.'

Barney finished his drink, grimaced at the taste of it, and then held out his hand for Pieter. 'Pieter, *kom*.' He said to Harold, 'I'll talk to you later, when I've had a chance to discuss things with Joel.'

'I thought everything was yours. The claims, the house. What do you have to ask *his* permission for?'

'He's my brother, and he does half of the work, at least. I wouldn't presume to change the whole of his future life without talking it over with him first.'

Harold set his hat on top of his head, and tilted it a few degrees backwards. 'All right. It's your funeral. But don't wait too long. The French people have got their eyes on those claims, too. Let me know yes or no by morning.'

Barney lifted Pieter up in his arms, and said, 'Pieter – say goodbye to your Uncle Harold.'

Harold raised his hat, and leaned forward with his moustache puckered up to give Pieter a kiss on the cheek. 'You're almost a lucky boy,' he told him, and then he gave Barney a brief and sideways smile that was friendly and sad and a little bit sour, all at the same time.

At noon the following day, in the offices of the Board for the Protection of Mining Industries, amidst the aromatic dust of cedar pencil-sharpenings and barathea business suits, Barney was handed in silence the titles to all of the eight and a half claims belonging to the Waterlo Diamond Coy. In return, he passed to the clerk of the board, a bespectacled Englishman with a face as pale as calf's-foot jelly and a disposition to match, a cheque for £18,500 and a few pence. This cheque was duly passed to a short freckly Belgian called Mr Wuustwezel, who waved it in the air in jolly celebration, only to be peered at by the clerk with an expression of dire disapproval.

'This is a solemn trading matter, Mr Wuustwezel, not a carnival.'

'For you, maybe,' smiled Mr Wuustwezel, irrepressibly.

Afterwards, they all gathered at the Kimberley Hotel, where Mr Wuustwezel ordered French champagne and cigars, and where they sat around highly varnished yellow-wood tables, surrounded by smoke, and talked of diamond prices and diamond digging and, most important of all, of Cecil Rhodes.

'Against a man of Rhodes' determination, you will never win,' attested Mr Wuustwezel. 'He will take over every diamond mine in South Africa, simply because he believes it is his divine duty to do so.'

'Just because he's a religious zealot, that doesn't mean he's going to get what he wants,' said Joel, testily.

'Do *you* have such inspiration? Such ambition?' asked Mr Wuustwezel.

Joel eased his mended leg into a more comfortable position, and pulled a face. 'I have a taste for riches, if that's what you mean.'

'I suppose you have to,' put in Edward Nork. 'Morphis is expensive, out here in the back of beyond.'

Joel drained his glass of champagne, and set it down on the table with a sharp click. 'I have pain,' he told Edward. 'Particularly in damp weather, and in the company of idiots.'

'You don't change, do you?' smiled Edward, reaching down beneath his chair to retrieve his bottle of Irish whiskey, and top up his glass.

Barney said, 'We can really start to mine on a large scale now. That's if you don't mind my interrupting your personal vendetta with a little business talk. We can level off our own four claims to the same depth as the Belgian claims, and drain them all with one pump. The Belgians have two horse whims, if I remember, and those two can serve to carry out all of the blue ground from all twelve claims. We'll have three times the mining area and yet our daily expenses will scarcely be increased at all.'

'You'll need more kaffirs,' said Mr Wuustwezel, raising his champagne so that one of his appeared to be grossly magnified through the glass.

'Kaffirs aren't expensive,' said Joel.

'Not your run-of-the-mill kaffirs. But there's one kaffir I recommend you take on in particular. His name's Jack, and he's a Ndebele. He'll cost you twice the price of your usual kaffir, because he's educated, and he knows what's what. He's a good foreman, too. Takes care of all your workers for you, keeps an eye on all the stones they find, and makes sure you don't get trouble.'

'How much did you pay him?' asked Barney.

'Nineteen shillings a month. And when you think this mine's losing fifteen or twenty thousand pounds a week through pilfering, that's a worthwhile investment.'

Joel reached across the table and poured himself some more champagne. 'Nineteen shillings a month?' he asked, wrinkling up his nose. 'Don't you think they'll start getting ideas, if you pay them as much as that?'

'Jack's a Christian, Mr Blitz,' said Mr Wuustwezel, his round face suddenly solemn. 'He's honest, and temperate, and he has no ideas other than to do good work so that he can earn himself good wages.'

'I alwyas suspect fellows who don't drink,' said Joel. 'Even blackies.'

Barney stood up. 'I think it's time we went,' he said. 'We have a great many arrangements to make. And besides, I've decided to go to Durban in two weeks' time to buy furniture and furnishings for Vogel Vlei.'

Joel looked up. 'You didn't tell me that.'

'I've only just decided.'

'I see. I suppose you want to go sniffing around that Sutter girl again.' He turned to Mr Wuustwezel and said, 'My brother is not a man for whores. He likes his relationships to be difficult; even tragic, if possible. He is a man who is aroused by hardship. Girls who simply lie on their backs with their legs in the air just will not do.'

Mr Wuustwezel reached for his grey Derby hat and carefully put it on. 'I think I, too, must be leaving,' he said.

'The party's just started,' protested Joel. 'What about some more champagne?'

'If you want more champagne. I regret that you will have to pay for it yourself,' Mr Wuustwezel told him. 'After all, you are now the part-owner of one of the largest diamond mines in Kimberley, aren't you?'

Barney reached across the table and shook the Belgian's

hand. Mr Wuustwezel said, 'Thank you for everything, Mr Blitz. I hope that you will make much profit out of our mines, and I hope that your problems will not prove too great a burden for you.'

Joel raised his head. 'What problems?' he demanded.

Mr Wuustwezel touched his hat, and walked away across the polished boards of the hotel lounge.

'What problems?' Joel shouted after him. 'What problems?'

Then he turned around and saw the look on Barney's face, and he seized his champagne glass and emptied it in one exaggerated swallow.

Jack, the Ndebele, turned out to be one of the suavest black men that Barney had ever come across. He had tight curly hair, a broad, handsome face, and he wore a gold and ivory earring in his left earlobe. But there his resemblance to his brother kaffirs ended. He spoke almost perfect English, in a Shropshire accent, and he always wore a white collar and a grey morning suit. He was known around the Big Hole as 'Gentleman Jack'; but although his civilised manners would normally have aroused suspicions that he was trying to ape the white man, and pretend that he could be the white man's equal, Jack's devotion to his work and his reputation for honesty were enough to quell the fears of those diggers who liked to make sure, for safety's sake, that they kept their kaffirs overworked and underpaid. 'There is no more dangerous nigger than a nigger who has tasted kindness,' a Boer farmer had once told Barney, back in Oranjerivier. 'You must keep them without hope that they will ever know anything better; because hope is the first ingredient of unrest.'

Jack met Barney the day after the titles to the eight and a half Belgian claims had been handed over, out by the North Reef. It was a cool morning, and Barney was wearing his blue covert coat, and his cap. Work had already started on most of the claims, and the clatter of picks and shovels and the squealing of winding-gear had frightened away the birds which came to pick over the freshly-dug earth whenever the miners were away.

'Good morning, Mr Blitzboss,' said Jack, climbing out of the steepsided claim in his grey suit and rubber galoshes.

'Good morning,' nodded Barney. 'I see no kaffirs here.'

'I'm here, Mr Blitzboss. I've worked here since they first broke ground.'

'I've seen you. And Mr Wuustwezel recommended that I take you on.'

'I was hoping you would, Mr Blitzboss. I am a worker of exemplary character. Excellent references from all my places of employment. Orphan from three years old, Mr Blitzboss, both parents died of the cholera. Taken in by Wallington, an excellent missionary and his family, and taught the exemplary manners of British people. I wear underwear, Mr Blitzboss, clean every week.'

Barney gave him an uneasy smile. 'Good. Well, I'm glad to hear it.'

Jack tugged at his tie, to straighten it. 'Without a necktie, Mr Blitzboss, no man is properly attired. That's what they taught me when I worked for Mr Jones. He sold pianofortes and religious music, sir, and it was my part to sing Psalm 23 at a position of attention while Mr Jones demonstrated the pianoforte from the back of his waggon. Later I got work building houses at Klipdrift, and then mining. Now I am here, if you wish to take me on, sir.'

'Sure I'll take you on. Mr Wuustwezel paid you nineteen shillings the month, didn't he?'

'And fourpence, Mr Blitzboss.'

'What was the fourpence for?'

'A special extra emolument, sir. For keeping Mr Wuustwezel's cook cheerful. You see, if she wasn't kept cheerful, she cooked badly, and Mr Wuustwezel was a stickler for good food. So, three times in each month, he would say to me, "The soup's getting thin, Jack," or "The cutlets are burned again, Jack," and off I went that night to make his cook cheerful. A fine bit Basuto woman, Mr Blitzboss – well, a quarter French, but black like tar. I can tell you that I earned my fourpence.'

'It sounds as if you did,' smiled Barney. 'Perhaps I ought to pay you a pound a month, just to make up for what you'll be missing.'

Gentleman Jack's left eyelid trembled into what was almost a wink. 'A pound will be satisfactory, Mr Blitzboss. You will get excellent work from Jack for a pound.'

'Let me tell you something,' Barney told him. 'In a few days, I'll be leaving Kimberley for a month or two and going to Durban. You've seen my house, I expect – Voegl Vlei? Well, it needs furnishing, and decorating, and I'm going to Durban to find someone to do it for me. When I'm away, my brother Mr Joel Blitz is going to be in charge. So – no matter what he does or says, I want you to make sure you obey his orders and do exactly what he tells you. He's a Blitzboss too.'

'I understand,' said Jack, simply.

'Well, make sure that you do. I don't want to come back from Durban and find there's been trouble.'

'No, sir. You won't find any trouble.'

Barney looked down at the cluster of diamond claims that were now his. There was nearly enough space how to use a steam-shovel, and excavate the rock at three times the speed. The sides of most claims were now collapsing so regularly that more and more debris had to be dug out than ever to reach the diamond-bearing soil. Rhodes had been right. The sooner all these hundreds of individual diggers could be bought out, and their claims amalgamated, the sooner the mine could be prospected by largescale, mechanised methods. Barney determined to order two steam winding-engines while he was in Durban, and more rotary trommels for sorting the soil once it had been dug out.

'I'll leave you in charge, then,' Barney told Gengleman Jack. 'I want this mine working at top speed by eleven o'clock this morning, with the best kaffirs you can find. You can tell them that if they work extra hard, they get extra rations.'

'You think that's a good idea, Mr Blitzboss?'

'What do you mean?'

Jack smiled. 'Mr Wallington always taught me that black men should be satisfied with their lot. They should work hard because it's good for their bodies and their souls, not because a white man has offered them more rations.'

Barney stared at him for a while. 'You really believe that?' he asked.

307

'Mr Wallington said it was so, sir.'

'Well, if you think Mr Wallington was right, how come you're happy to take a pound, instead of nineteen shillings?'

'And fourpence, sir.'

'Yes, and fourpence?'

Jack gave an enigmatic shrug. 'Maybe, Mr Blitzboss, I am ahead of my time.'

'Maybe,' said Barney. 'And maybe you're a damned rascal.'

It took two weeks before the Blitz Brothers Diamond Mining Company was bringing up diamonds in sufficient quantities from their new possessions to be able to show a profit. The sides of the Belgian claims had collapsed, from weeks of neglect filling them with tons of worked-out debris, and Gentleman Jack spent five days clearing it all away. Even so, the claims were dug so deep that frequent cave-ins were unavoidable, and there were some days when they had to shovel out three tons of rock and debris just to extract one ton of diamond-bearing blue ground.

Barney, impatient, had no choice but to wait until the excavations were going smoothly before leaving for Durban. But Joel and Gentleman Jack seemed to get along quite well with each other, which was one comfort; and Edward Nork was devising a way of shoring up the sides of the claim with discarded iron girders which he had rescued from the construction site of the new London & South African Bank; and so by mid-July, Barney was able to take his two best horses, Boitumelo and Moonshine, and load them up for a journey across the plains of the Transvaal and the mountains of Natal.

Mooi Klip was rolling out dough in the kitchen of her parents' house in Klipdrift when Mr Ransome rapped at the door and called, 'Anybody at home?'

Mooi Klip pushed her curls away from her eyes with the back of her hand, leaving a floury white smudge on the dark skin of her forehead. 'Come in,' she said. 'There's only me.'

Mr Ransome came through the open doorway with his hat clutched in his hands the same way a small and timid animal clutches its food. He looked around the kitchen with quick, jerky smiles; and then beamed at Mooi Klip appreciatively.

'What a wonderful sight,' he said. 'Surely this is how God meant a family home to look. The gentle woman in her place, preparing food. The fragrance of baking. And those pies! There is nothing to me more holy than a pie!'

'You can take one if you want to,' said Mooi Klip, amused. 'But they're hot.'

'Well, no, I won't at the moment,' said Mr Ransome. 'But if you have a glass of milk, I would appreciate that. I've been driving around all morning, and I'm feeling quite tired with the heat. It's unseasonably hot, don't you think.'

Mooi Klip wiped her hands on her blue-checked apron, and went across to the dented metal churn in the corner, where her mother kept the goat's milk. She poured out a glassful with a dipper, and set it on the plain oak table. 'You can have a pie if you want to,' she said. 'I won't be cross if you change your mind.'

Mr Ransome eyed the pies thoughtfully. Then he said, 'No, no. I must abstain. I must show some self-control. I do try to perform at least one conscious act of self-control every day.'

Mooi Klip went back to her pastry-rolling. The sun shone in through the open door, and glittered in the dust and the flour, and crossed the white-washed wall of the kitchen in a long triangle. The room was simple, but its simplicity, and the simplicity of Mooi Klip's work, made it curiously restful; so that Mr Ransome found himself saying nothing at all, but leaning back in his riempie chair and watching her through drowsy eyes as she rolled and turned the dough, and cut it into ovals for those small vegetable-filled pasties which the Griqua people called 'little birds'.

It was on days like this that Mr Ransome felt close to his God. He had been educated as a child with pictorial Bibles, in which he had seen the boy Jesus in His father's carpentry shop; and he was still enchanted by sunshine and honest work. If he was ever asked about conscience, or complicated struggles of the spirit, he would smile vaguely and look the other way, his bland face transfigured by thoughts of those crisp and curled-up wood shavings around the Messiah's youthful feet. Oh, to have been there, to have actually been there, and helped Our Lord with his chamfering, and his planing!

Mr Ransome was a missionary; a former curate at St

Augustine's Church, in Kennington, near London, and now the sole propagator of the Word for hundreds of miles around. At the age of twenty-nine, he still looked boyish, with an oval face like one of Mrs Beeton's pie-dishes, and a long pointed nose, and thick brown hair which defied combing. He was wearing his cassock today, as always, and his dog-collar. He believed in the simple smybols of Christian stewardship, especially when he was making the rounds of the Griqua community, whose beliefs were fierce and direct and fundamental. The Griquas combined the earthly magic of the Hottentots with the abrasive simplicity of the Boers, and Mr Ransome often thought (secretly) that they spoke about their religion with even more conviction than he did.

He had been to see Mooi Klip several times since Pieter's birth. He had christened Pieter in the stone font of St Margaret's Chapel, a corrugated-iron building by the banks of the Vaal. He found something noble and yet pathetic in Mooi Klip's predicament, and he had tried to bring her the comfort of companionship and words from the Bible. She had told him about Barney, and about Joel; and about Coen, too; and they had knelt on the brown tiles of the kitchen floor and prayed together several times.

'Mr Ransome – I've been worried,' said Mooi Klip, sifting flour on to the table.

'Worried?' asked Mr Ransome. 'Why?'

'I don't know. I shouldn't worry. But Pieter came back from seeing his father at Kimberley not long ago, and he told me that his father wanted me to think about going to live with him, in his new house.'

Mr Ransome tucked his fingers together. 'Surely that's good news.'

'I don't know. What about Coen?'

'You feel more strongly for Barney than you do for Coen, don't you? At least that's the impression you've always given me. It was only a sorry accident that you didn't marry him.'

Mooi Klip glanced at Mr Ransome and then shook her head. 'It wasn't an accident, Mr Ransome.'

'You still haven't forgiven him?'

'I don't think I could.'

310

Mr Ransome scratched his ankle vigorously. 'I really don't know what to suggest. If you hate Joel so intensely, and if you feel that Barney has betrayed you by sticking up for his brother rather than cleaving to you; and if you are still not sure of your feelings for Coen ... well, then, I can only suggest that you work and pray a little longer, that you seek further guidance from the Lord. It would be very unwise to do anything precipitate, particularly when you have Pieter's happiness to consider, as well as your own.'

Mooi Klip laid down her pastry knife. 'I feel so sad sometimes,' she said, softly. 'I think of Barney, and how things could have been between us. Then I think of Joel, and I can only feel hatred. I know that hatred is not Christian, and that I should try to forgive him. But I will never find happiness with Barney as long as his brother is there.'

'And Coen?'

She lowered her head. 'Coen is good and kind, and I could learn to love him. But I would hate to hurt him, and I think that if I married him, I would.'

Mr Ransome considered what Mooi Klip had said, and drummed his fingers on the table. Then he picked up his glass of goat's milk, and drank half of it. Wiping his mouth, he said, 'How would it be if I spoke to Barney myself? If I were to intercede on your behalf?'

'I don't know whether that would help,' said Mooi Klip.

'Well, it might not,' Mr Ransome admitted, 'but on the other hand it might. You never know. Jesus was always trying the impossible, and succeeding. Think what an impossible task it must have seemed in those days to redeem the sins of the entire world!'

'There's only one person whose sins need to be redeemed to make me happy,' said Mooi Klip.

'Ah yes,' signed Mr Ransome. 'The dreadful Joel Blitz.'

He stood up. He looked across at the pies. 'I have to go to Kimberley at the end of the week,' he said. 'Perhaps I should call on him then.'

'You won't upset him? I don't want him to think that I'm pressing him to take me back.'

'My dear Natalia, I'll be most discreet.'

311

He took her wrist and gave it a confident squeeze. With dabs of flour on her cheeks, and her curly hair brushed back, Mooi Klip looked as pretty as an Italian painting. There was a golden, fragrant aura about her which Mr Ransome found strangely disturbing. It was only the mid-afternoon sunlight in her hair; only the fragrance of a young woman at work; but he found himself glancing covertly at the way that her breasts pressed so tightly against the flowery fabric of her dress, and at that shadowy crevice where her silver crucifix hung, and he knew, he just knew, that his ears had turned bright red.

Mooi Klip smiled at him, and then kissed his cheek. 'You've been such a friend to me,' she said.

He did not know how to answer her. He felt as if there were no words in his vocational vocabulary to describe exactly how he felt. No words to say how attracted he was, or how elated, or how ironic he felt it was that he should have volunteered to go off to see Barney on a mission of reconciliation when all the time he wished that he could have this disturbingly attractive Griqua woman for himself. He felt confident, yes: but also profoundly depressed, and yet excited, too. God, his feelings were so maddening! He did not realise that he was actually in love, nor that he had been for almost two years.

He remembered the moment, though, when he had noticed Mooi Klip as a woman, instead of nothing more than an unfortunate ewe in his Christian flock. He had seen her in the yard outside her parents' *strooidak* house one hot November morning, washing clothes in a wooden butt, rubbing them on a corrugated washboard with kitchen soap. Her hair had been tied back, and the sleeves of her white cotton dress had been buttoned up. He had reined in his small spidery black carriage to wish her good day, and ask how she was; and she had looked up at him, shielding her eyes against the sun, a picture of the tender savage, one dark nipple visible through the wet material of her dress like a kiss through gauze.

Mooi Klip said, 'Why don't you give in to temptation?'

'I beg your pardon?' Mr Ransome blushed.

'Give in to temptation. Have a pie. I'm sure you can practise your self-control on something else.'

Mr Ransome's lips felt dry. He ran his tongue around them,

and then he nodded. 'Yes, you're right. I shouldn't be too ascetic, should I?' He took one of the pies, and held it up in a gesture of appreciation. 'It looks good. I shall save it for my tea.'

She watched him from the kitchen doorway as he walked back to his carriage, where it was tied up to a nearby fence. He turned around twice, and raised his hat to her, and as he climbed up on to his seat, he called back, 'I shall let you know about Barney as soon as I can! I promise!'

Mooi Klip waved and smiled, and then returned to her pastry. Mr Ransome hesitated for a moment, reining back his horse. He felt like jumping down again, striding down the garden path, taking Mooi Klip in his arms and telling her that he was passionately fond of her. But unstead, he said 'gee-up', and flicked his whip, and his horse obediently began to carry him off along the rutted pathway.

'I mustn't,' Mr Ransome whispered to himself, as he reached the outskirts of Klipdrift. 'I am a missionary of God. I mustn't!' And his self-denial that afternoon was more painful than the refusal of a thousand pastries. He munched his pie as he drove, and he cried as he munched, and halfway back to his house he had to stop the carriage and thump his chest, because he was almost choking.

On the night that Barney crossed the border into Natal, five hundred miles away, Joel was sitting in the dining hall of Vogel Vlei, with empty gunpowder boxes for chairs, and a large ship's trunk for a table, playing Pope Joan with Gentleman Jack and an old-time Kimberley character called Champagne Charlie. All around them, scores of candles swayed and dipped, stuck to the polished parquet flooring with their own wax. The three men's voices and laughter echoed from one deserted room to another; and even up the uncarpeted stairs into the upper landings.

Champagne Charlie was a small florid man with a gingery moustache like hanks of a horse's tail. He had earned his nickname in Dutoitspan, in 1874, by scattering broken-up fragments of the bottoms of champagne bottles over a worthless tract of dry farmland, and selling it for £3000 to a guillible

313

diamond digger. He was known as a gambler, too, and an addict of unlikely bets.

Jack eventually threw in his cards, and stood up. 'I believe I've had enough gaming for one evening,' he said. 'Would either of you two gentlemen care for some more port-wine? Mr Blitzboss?'

'I never thought the day would come when I would sit down on a wooden box and play Pope Joan with a kaffir,' cackled Champagne Charlie. 'But he's a smart player, ain't he, Joel? A smart player. And he drinks now, too! It only goes to show that you can teach a monkey a trick or two, if you try hard enough.'

Joel played a queen and a jack, winning 'Intrigue'. He looked tired, and his face was greasy and pale. 'Some monkeys learn quicker than others,' he said, and there was a touch of caustic in his voice.

'Oh, you mustn't let Barney get you down,' said Champagne Charlie. He knew what Joel was talking about. After all, in every saloon and gambling house and brothel in Kimberley, wherever diggers and engineers and diamond dealers met to drink and talk and win money, Joel had tirelessly complained about Barney, about how righteous Barney was, and how super-cilious, and how Barney deliberately kept away from black women just to show off his moral supremacy.

'Barney does a good deal more than get me down,' said Joel. 'Barney makes me wish that one or other of us had never have been born. I wouldn't have minded which. It would have been better for me not to have existed at all than to be obliged to live out this preposterous life with this intolerable brother.'

'He doesn't seem like such a bad fellow to me,' said Jack, bringing over three glasses of port. 'He paid me extra money, right out, and he's always been straight.'

'He wouldn't even let me *die*,' Joel complained. He stared at Champagne Charlie with citric intensity. 'I was hurt, I was going to be carried away to my Creator. I was finally going to be released. But would my wonderful younger brother let me go? Oh, no. He had other plans for me. Six weeks of sheer agony on the back of a waggon. And then six hours of hell in an operating theatre, while my bones were broken and re-set. Now look at me. Worse off than ever, with a stick and a limp, like a cripple. Half-owner of a diamond mine that *I* know and *he* knows I don't even deserve. "What do you think of *our* mine, Joel?" "How shall we decorate *our* house?" When all the time he knows damned well that I did nothing to contribute to either of them. That's the salt he keeps grinding into my open wounds. He knows I hate him, he knows that I deliberately tried to ruin his life, and yet he still forgives me.'

'Ain't you pleased?' asked Champagne Charlie, relighting his cigar. 'I'd be pleased, if I'd done what you'd done, and my brother still forgave me. I'd be downright delighted.'

Joel lurched off his gunpowder box, and kicked it over with a loud slamming noise. Then, leaning on his stick, he stalked around the huge dining-room, weaving in and out of the candles that were stuck to the floor, his face ghastly in the guttering light.

'Being forgiven,' he said, 'is the most terrible punishment of all. I cannot endure it.'

Gentleman Jack, standing tall and black in his grey frock-coat, turned his eyes towards Champagne Charlie, and rolled his lips downwards like a comical mask. Champagne Charlie let out a nervous snicker.

'One day,' said Joel, his voice distorted by the bare walls, 'one day, I dream that Barney will do something to me that requires my forgiveness.'

He paused, breathing hard, the ferrule of his cane vibrating against the hard oak floor, *tip-tip-tip-tip-tip*, his right shoulder hunched and his crooked left leg bent beneath him as if it had been drawn by a child. 'Oh, I dream of that,' he said, under his breath. 'I dream of the moment when he has to come to me and say, "Joel, I'm sorry, please forgive me."'

'And then you can spit in his eye!' cried Champagne Charlie, slapping his thigh.

Joel shot him a quick, triumphant look. 'Oh, no, Charlie! I'd never do that! I'd forgive him! That's what I'd do! I'd forgive him!'

Gentleman Jack finished his port. 'I believe I'm going to get some sleep now,' he said. 'That's if you'll excuse me, Mr Blitzboss. We have an early start tomorrow. A whole lot of earth to move.'

'Don't worry about that,' said Joel. 'Pour yourself another drink.'

Gentleman Jack shrugged. 'Whatever you say, Mr Blitzboss.'

Joel took two or three ungainly steps through the candles. 'You know something Charlie,' he said, thoughtfully, 'I do believe I love Barney. I do believe that, in spite of everything, I love him. He was my father's favourite, you know. Not my mother's. My mother always preferred me. But then I think that all mothers have a special soft spot for their first born. Yet ... in spite of everything, I do believe I love him.'

'He's always been regular with me,' said Champagne Charlie.

'Ah, well,' Joel told him, dismissively, 'that's because you're not his brother. But I do love him. I love him still. The only thing that irks me about him, the only thing that enrages me about him, is that he always believes that he's better than me. He always has. Even though he's always been younger, and always will be. Even though he's always had less experience. He – *assumes* – as if it's a direct gift from Our Lord – he – *assumes* – that he's better. And that's what makes me feel like dragging him down, and breaking everything he believes is precious. Can you understand that? I used to break his toys. I tore pages out of his bar-mitzvah Torah. But it's good for him, you know. He mustn't always believe that he's superior. You know that? He has to understand that he's just as weak and as human and as sinful as the rest of us. Because if he doesn't, you know – are you listening, Charlie? – if he doesn't, he's going to be very, very, seriously hurt.'

Champagne Charlie pursed his lips in discomfort. 'Well,' he said, 'do you want to play some more cards?'

'I feel more like drinking,' said Joel and lifted his empty glass at the end of a stiffly raised arm. Gentleman Jack came across the floor on tapping heels and poured him another port-wine.

'No women tonight?' asked Champagne Charlie.

'I don't know. I'm tired of blackies. I'm tired of those French whores too, that cackling collection of stinking women they brought in from Algeria. Only God knows how many niggers and donkeys *they've* fucked, in their lifetime. I'm tired of everything.'

Champagne Charlie ceaselessly shuffled the cards, his podgy

316

fingers pouring fountains of fluttering pasteboard from one hand to the other, over and over and over. 'I hear that Agnes Knight is playing it a little fast and quick these days.'

'Knight's daughter?'

'The blonde one. The pretty one. The one who married that thick-headed Aussie.'

'Agnes Knight, hey?' asked Joel. 'Yes, I remember her. I thought she was going to leave Kimberley, and go to Capetown.'

'Her husband was thinking of it, but in the end Agnes didn't want to go. The story goes that she was having a little slap-and-tickle with the surface manager of the Beaconsfield Diamond Mining Company. She didn't want to give him up.'

'And her husband didn't suspect?' asked Joel.

'He's an Aussie. Aussies never suspect anything, not until they climb into bed one night, and try to put their arms around their wives, and another fellow's voice says, "Hold on, chum, you've got to wait your turn!"'

Champagne Charlie burst out laughing in deep, breathy gusts, so that his yellow-cheked vest went in and out like the bellows of a home harmonium. Joel, leaning on his cane, allowed himself a dry smile, and waited until Champagne Charlie had finished. Then Joel said, 'Barney used to be struck on Agnes Knight at one time, you know. I believe he would have married her, if he could have done.'

'Knight wouldn't have let his favourite daughter marry a Jew-boy.'

'Well, that was exactly it. That was exactly why they didn't get married. But if she's playing a few games these days, maybe we can cajole her into helping us with Barney.'

Champagne Charlie stopped laughing, and cleared his throat. 'Don't get you, old chap. What do you mean by "helping us with Barney"?'

Joel slashed his cane around in an whistling arc, and lopped the top off one of the candles. Then he hit another one, and another one, until the dining-room began to grow shadowy and dark.

'Have another drink,' said Joel. 'Have another drink. You'll see what I mean when it happens. You'll see!'

*

They sat in the rose drawing-room at Khotso taking tea. Gerald Sutter stood with his back to the fireplace, one hand cocked under his tailcoats, his other hand holding his teacup across his chest as rigidly as if he were the standard-bearer at a military church-parade. His wife sat on a small crinoline chair, looking a little tired from a recent headache, but as elegant as ever in a pewter-grey silk dress, and silk slippers.

Sara, flushed, sat on the sofa next to Barney, her neck wound with pearls, her pale pink dress embroidered with flowers. The rose-coloured upholstery of the furniture and the pink moiré silk on the walls lent her even more lightness and grace. She made Barney, in his best black suit, feel as severe as a mortician.

'*You're* a surprise, you are,' Gerald Sutter told Barney, loudly.

'Isn't he just!' exclaimed Sara. 'I do love surprises!'

Mrs Sutter could not resist smiling, and she lifted her arm towards her husband as if she wanted him to take her hand; although he did not. He was too busy trying to compose a suitable response to Barney's proposal.

'Over the mountains you come,' he said, with a tight wave of his teacup. 'Cool as a cucumber. And, damn me!'

'Gerald,' protested Mrs Sutter, mildly.

'Well, it's true,' argued Gerald Sutter. 'You can't say the fellow's got anything but nerve. Damned, outright nerve!'

'Gerald, my dear, you don't have to curse to convey your feelings.'

'Curse? If I were to say out loud all the curses that came into my head when this fellow knocked at the door and told me that he'd decided to marry Sara, the damned plaster would fall off the damned walls at the sound of it!'

'You know that Sara was engaged to be married last year,' said Mrs Sutter gently, inclining her head towards Barney.

'She told me,' Barney nodded.

'It was so sad. A young boy from the Colonial Office. Tall, and straight. An Eton boy, actually. You wouldn't have thought he had a care in the world, to look at him. Disease strikes so quickly!'

Sara said, 'Really, Mother, I didn't love him. I was heart-broken when he died. But I didn't truly love him.'

'How can you say that?' demanded Gerald Sutter.

'Because it's *true*, Papa. That's how I can say it. He was good-looking and enormously polite. He could ride, and play bridge. He would have made a terribly suitable husband. But I didn't love him, and that was that.'

Gerald Sutter puffed out his cheeks. 'Well,' he said, 'if you didn't love a chap with all of those qualifications, then I don't know what love is.'

His wife touched him again, with gentle fingers. 'Of course you do, my darling. You could hardly stay in the saddle when I married you, and you could never concentrate at bridge. But I still loved you.'

'The point is,' said Gerald, 'does Sara really love Barney? *That* is the point.'

Sara turned towards Barney and took his hand. 'I haven't been able to forget him since I first met him,' she said. 'I fell in love with him then, and I love him still.'

'It's all very irregular,' said Gerald Sutter. 'Especially since he wants to marry you so damned quick.'

'Papa – I'm twenty-four years old. That's quite old enough to make up my mind, and *very* much too old to be still a maid.'

Gerald Sutter looked as if he were going to say something, but then he pouted, and puffed, and jerked his shoulders in mute acceptance. He did not want to have Sara on his hands for the rest of his life, after all. And what if Barney's proposal had been irregular, and sudden, and sprung on the family with all the abruptness of an opening cosmos flower – well, at least the chap had money, and at least he could ride, and at least Sara actually professed to love him.

And who was he, Gerald Sutter, to stand without reason in the way of true love? Especially when it was going to save him the cost of Sara's upkeep.

'Well,' he said, at length, 'very well. I'll agree to it. But against my usual principles.'

Barney leaned across the sofa and kissed Sara's cheek. 'There,' he told her. 'I knew that he'd be reasonable.'

'Reasonable!' exclaimed Gerald Surter, in mock indignation, while Mrs Sutter raised her hands and laughed. 'Damn me! *Reasonable!*'

Barney's proposal of marriage to Sara Sutter had come almost as much as a surprise to Barney as it had to the Sutter family. He had missed her painfully when he had left Durban six years ago to return to Kimberley, and he had often thought about her when he was kopje-walloping on Alsjeblieft. But he had always assumed that Sara would marry, and that somehow he would find a way to get back together with Mooi Klip; and after a year or two those rides by the shores of the Indian Ocean had become little more than restless images in the photograph-album of his mind. Sometimes he had woken in his bungalow and heard the desert wind, and thought it was the sea. Occasionally, a letter had arrived from Durban from a pump company, or a diamond-dealer, and he had thought for a fleeting moment before he opened it that it might be a letter from Sara. But love is unable to survive on memories alone, especially for a busy man, and the flowers that had been ruffled by the wind in the gardens of Khotso had long ago been dried and pressed between the pages of *Pilgrim's Progress*, and forgotten.

It was only when Barney had come to decorating Vogel Vlei that he had thought of Sara again. He had resisted the thought at first. He still believed that Mooi Klip might come back to him, and that there could somehow be a happy life for them together. But his sense of ambition told him that he would ever allow it to happen, not for real, not now. Mooi Klip would be nothing but an embarrassment, when it came to business. It was all right for a chap to have had a bit of black on the side, and quite acceptable to have sired a half-caste son. But to *marry* a darkie – well, that was something different. And from that excuse, it was an easy step to the next excuse, which was that he could not possibly marry Mooi Klip, in case he hurt her.

He had given their love a last chance. He had asked Pieter to tell Mooi Klip that she was welcome at Vogel Vlei. He had waited and waited for an answer. He had even pretended to himself that he needed to stay an extra week in Kimberley to make sure that the digging at the Belgian mines was going properly. But there had been no reply; and the date that he had set himself for leaving Kimberley had eventually arrived, as fresh and windy as any other winter day in north Cape Colony, and he had been obliged by his own pre-arranged plans to go.

He had quite convinced himself when he first set off for Durban that he was going to do nothing more than refresh his memories of the Sutter house, and ask them where they had bought their furniture, and how they had arranged for their drapes and their carpets to be made up. Vogel Vlei's white-washed exterior was a conscious imitation of Khotso, and its rooms were in similar proportions, and all Barney needed now was the upholstery and furnishings that would turn it into an elegant yet friendly country house.

But as he had ridden alone across the vast horizons of the north colony, under skies that dreamed with clouds, he had thought with increasing excitement of Sara, and their days together in the summer of 1872, against a remembered back-ground of loss, and pain, and thundery monsoon clouds. He had been sure that she would have married. She had gone back to England, more than likely, and even as he rode eastwards across the plains of the Orange Free State towards his half-forgotten image of her, she was probably walking her terriers across the green and rounded Downs of Sussex, in her ribboned bonnet and her sensible boots. And yet, he could still think of her.

Barney was richer now than he had ever been in his life before – richer than anyone he had ever known. But Mooi Klip's continual refusals to consider marrying him, and his lonely, ramshackle life at Kimberley, had convinced him that now was the time to find a companion. He needed a wife, desperately; someone he could decorate with diamonds, and adore. Someone he could wake up next to, and with whom he could share his silliest and his most serious desires. He was twenty-eight, and he was wealthy, and he was also Jewish, despite his renunciation of the ideals of his faith. Twenty-eight and not married? he could hear his father saying. What's wrong with the boy? He doesn't like girls?

What had happened with Mooi Klip stayed as a sad and complicated thought at the back of his mind; but what he had looked forward to more and more as he crossed the Drakensberg into Natal had been meeting Sara again. Sara was more than pretty; she was educated, and she was English. She would be an asset to him in the diamond business, as well as a good wife. And if she wasn't there ... well, he would face up to the bitterness of that when he came to it.

She had opened the door, herself. She had looked six years older; more elegant, more self-assured. Her voice had been less clipped, as if she no longer felt the need to assert herself. And she had peered at him myopically for a moment the way a gardener peers at a caper spurge which has unexpectedly seeded itself in another part of the flowerbed.

'Barney,' she had said. '*Barney*.'

He had hesitated on the doorstep, breathless. 'I want you to tell to me something,' he had said, trying to keep the urgency out of his voice. 'I want you to tell me if you're married.'

'No,' she had told him, straight away, puzzled. 'No, I'm not. But don't just *stand* there, come in.'

'Thank God,' he had said. 'Will you marry me?'

She had blinked. 'I'm sorreh?'

'I said, will you marry me? I've just arrived here from Kimberley and I really think that's all I want to know.'

There had been a moment of strange hesitation. 'What will you do if I turn you down?' she had asked him. 'Will you ride straight back again?'

He had shaken his head. 'I shall hammer on the door until you change your mind.'

'Well,' she had told him faintly. 'I'm not sure. I mean yes, probably. But not on the doorstep. You'd better come in.'

They had talked furiously for a while in the hallway, in whispers. Barney had been able to watch himself in a gilded Dutch mirror, and it had reminded him disconcertingly of van Eyck's fifteenth-century portrait of a newly-married couple, all stiffness and piety. At last, Mrs Sutter had appeared, and looked at them as curiously as a peahen, her head on one side, and said, 'If it isn't Mr Blitz!'

Now, over tea, it seemed as if they were actually engaged. It had been less than an hour since he had knocked at the front door, and a purplish calotype of Sara's unfortunate Old Etonian still stood on the maplewood bureau by the window, smiling with brave inanity. Bht she was Barney's now, and they would be married within the month, and Barney's life would take on the style and the peace and the English elegance of Khotso. He had proposed marriage to more than a wife: he had proposed to a home, and a style of life, and parents-in-law who were prosperous and acceptable. If only his mother and father could have seen what a rich *machuten* he was going to have. Who needed the Kimberley Club?

'I've built a house out at Kimberley,' Barney explained to Gerald Sutter. 'I call it Vogel Vlei, which is Afrikaans for "Bird Marsh". It's the grandest house for five hundred miles, and it's all been built with diamonds.'

'Prospecting for diamonds always seemed like rather a *grubby* game to me,' remarked Gerald Sutter, laying down his teacup and patting the pockets of his coat to find his cigarettes. 'All that shovelling, and sorting. And they're an odd lot, aren't they, the diggers? I hope you'll keep Sara well away.'

'Of course. Vogel Vlei is a good mile away from the mine itself.'

'Glad to hear it. Healthy, is it, out there? No cholera?'

'As healthy as anywhere else in Africa.'

'Well, that's not saying much. Have you finished your tea? I think I could do with a snort of whiskey, to tell you the truth. It's not every day your daughter decides to get married. We must talk about a *lobola*, too, although I don't suppose you've much use for ten head of cattle.'

Barney grinned, 'I thought I was supposed to pay *you* the *lobola*, for losing a daughter and a worker.'

'A worker! My great-grandfather's rear quarters! Only if you think that riding and spending money constitute work! That girl pays more for one silly hat than I pay my groom for the whole year, did you know that? Fifteen pounds for a hat, and there's this poor fellow trying to bring up a family on twelve pounds six shillings a year. If it wasn't just, it would be positively scandalous!'

Later, after dinner, Barney sat with Sara on the patio overlooking the sloping lawns of Khotso. Peace, they called this house, and he felt that he might have found it. The diamond business was going well, the world price of gems was rising at last; and here he was with this tall, good-looking girl, about to be married.

'You know, at the Passover *Seder*, Four Questions are asked,' said Barney. 'The first question is, *"Mah nishtana ha-leila ha-zeh mikol ha-laillos?"* and that means, "What makes this night special, compared with any other night?" If I were to ask that question tonight, then I'd know the answer.'

'I was quite resigned to living the rest of my life as a wizened old maid,' said Sara, leaning her dark hair against his shoulder. 'I read my palms, you know, and my heart line was frightfully fragmented. As for my Lower Mars and my Mount of Venus ... well, you only have to see for yourself.'

She opened her hand and held it out to him. Barney took it, and stared at it for a while. Then he bent his head and kissed it. 'I don't know about palmistry,' he told her, hoarsely. 'All I know is that I should have proposed to you when I first met you.'

'I missed you, when you left,' Sara told him. 'I suppose I shouldn't admit it.'

'I missed you, too. I'm not ashamed of that.'

'Then why didn't you come back sooner?'

Barney held the open palm of her hand against his cheek, and kissed that part of her hand which she would have called her Upper Mars. 'There were other things I had to take care of, apart from my diamond claims ... I had old problems ... difficulties that had to be taken care of, one way or another.'

'And are they all taken care of?'

He looked towards the sea. It was too dark to make out anything but the dim white lines of the breakers, but he could hear it and smell it and feel its wind against his face. 'Yes,' he said. 'They're all taken care of.'

'There's good riding at Kimberley, I suppose? And a club?'

'Well, the riding's good. You can gallop flat-out for twenty miles and not see so much as a tree.'

'What about social life?'

'There's a dramatic society. They put on a special play at Christmas.'

'And a club?'

Barney made a face, and nodded. 'Sure, there's a club.'

'Well, that's all right, then. Somewhere to ride, somewhere to meet one's friends. A place to dance, and a house for entertaining in! I look forward to it!'

Barney stood up, and walked across the springy, close-cropped lawn with his hands in his pockets. Sara watched him, her scarf fluttering in the evening breeze. 'You're very handsome, you know,' she told him. He turned around. 'You're very beautiful,' he answered.

From inside the house came the steady, resonant sound of a Beethoven piano concerto, as Mrs Sutter began her practice. Sara left the garden seat and crossed the grass towards Barney and took his hand. In her evening slippers, she did not seem so tall, and she rested her forehead against him so that her hair blew against his face.

'I will love you, and I will be devoted to you,' she said. 'I shall never forget how you came back to rescue me after all these years.'

Gently, and yet not without confidence, Barney placed the outspread fingers of his left hand over her breast. She raised her head, and looked at him questioningly, as if she needed to know whether this was the correct thing to do. But he simply kissed her, twice, and nuzzled his face against hers; and in the shadows of the orange trees he eased down her light silk evening-gown, and then the cotton of her bodice, and held her warm heavy breast in his hand as if it were a prize, its crinkled nipple against his palm between his head line and his line of fortune, and caressed and squeezed it in time to the chords of Beethoven.

Sara closed her sapphire-painted eyelids, her lips slightly parted, and sighed as softly as the wind. Barney kissed her neck, and felt that he desired her and loved her more than anyone; which at that moment, on the lawns of Khotso, may well have been right.

They were married within three weeks, while the bells of St Paul's Church in Durban rang above their heads, and Mrs Sutter scattered rice, and the amateur brass band of the Durban Colonial Office played *The British Grenadiers* five times over, in dogged discord. Later, they went to the Oxford Road synagogue, where they were married again by a rabbi. This time, according to tradition, Mrs Sutter threw barley, and wept twice as copiously. She said she was pleased, though, that Sara had not had her head shaved, and adopted a *shaytl*, or wig. 'My great-grandmother wore one, and all I can remember about it is that it looked like a lopsided loaf of bread.'

In bed on their wedding-night, in the purple velvet-hung guest bedroom at Khotso, they made love in silence, their breath as quiet as the birds that slept in the branches of the coral trees. For a moment, they held each other so tight that Barney did not know if they were one person or two. Then Sara kissed him matter-of-factly on the forehead, and struggled to pull her nightdress down.

'You don't want more?' Barney whispered, kissing her cheeks, and her eyes, and her lips.

She hesitated before answering. Then she said, 'Well, it's all very well, isn't it? But it's not everything.'

Barney stayed where he was for a moment, leaning on his elbows. Sara lay absolutely still, watching him.

'We're married now,' he told her.

'Yes,' she said. 'Isn't it jolly?'

He dipped his head forward and kissed her once more. Then he rolled over on to his back and lay with his hands behind his head, staring up at the dark drapes of the four-poster bed.

She reached over and pressed her lips against his ear. 'I do love you, you know, Barney. I do love you an awful lot.'

He turned and looked at her. 'Yes,' he said. 'I love you, too.'

There was a fragrance of Mansion House pot-pourri in the air, and Sara sneezed.

Early the next morning, Barney woke up and found Sara's face only an inch away from his. Her mouth was open, and she was snoring softly. He looked at her for a long time, at the way her dark hair curled on the broderie-anglaise pillow, at her long shining eyelashes. She was a beautiful girl by anybody's lights, and he touched her cheek with his fingertips as gently as a man touches anything precious.

The French clock on the commode said a quarter to eight.

He eased himself out of bed, and padded naked across the room to the wardrobe, where his clothes had been hung. He struggled into a pair of sharply-creased trousers, and a white shirt, and buttoned up his suspenders. Then he quietly left the room, and tip-toed along the corridor until he reached the stairs.

It was only when he reached the morning-room that he realised that somebody else had been up before him. The French windows were open on to the dewy lawns, and Gerald Sutter was standing by the sundial in a lavish Chinese dressing-gown, smoking a pipe. Barney ventured out after him, and stood a little way away, his slippers stained by the wet grass.

'Up early,' remarked Gerald Sutter, taking his pipe out of his mouth and prodding at the tobacco with his finger.

'I just wanted a little fresh air,' said Barney. 'I think I drank too much champagne yesterday.'

'Well, you're entitled, on your wedding-day. Come to think of it, you're entitled whenever you please.'

'I want to thank you for a marvellous wedding. Well – *two* marvellous weddings.'

'Don't give me any credit for the ceremony at the synagogue. That was all my wife's affair.'

'It was appreciated, all the same.'

'Good. Good show.'

Barney said, 'I just want to tell you that I love Sara very much, and I think we're going to be very happy together.'

'Excellent. I'm glad to hear it.'

'Perhaps you'll come out to Kimberley to visit us soon,' suggested Barney.

Gerald Sutter swung around with his pipe in his mouth and gave Barney the sort of puckered-up look that Englishmen tend to give everybody who says anything nice, but manifestly silly. 'Very decent of you, old chap, but I must say I'm pretty much tied up in Durban. A shipping line to run, don't you know.'

'It's very exciting out there. The Kimberley mine is worth a visit.'

'Well, I suppose it is,' said Gerald Sutter, in a tone that implied that he supposed it *was not*, not for the least moment.

There was an uncomfortable silence between them for almost a minute. Then Barney said, 'Well, I'd better be going back in.'

'Ha, ha,' replied Gerald Sutter, without taking his pipe out of his mouth.

'I'll see you at breakfast, then,' said Barney.

'Good show. Kedgeree today, I wouldn't be surprised.'

'Good,' said Barney, and found himself back inside the house, at the foot of the staircase, suddenly uncertain of what he was doing here. I'm married, he thought to himself. A wealthy, well-heeled, properly married man. I might even have children in a year or so.

A Bantu servant walked past him, bearing a silver dish of steaming kidneys. Barney nodded to the servant without knowing why. For a moment he felt just like the small boy who had hidden under the summertime pushcarts of Hester Street, playing house with Leah Ginzburg.

The breakfast gong sounded, as if it were ringing in the start of his new life.

'Mr Blitzboss!' called Gentleman Jack, when he was still more than a hundred yards away. 'Mr Blitzboss!'

Joel shifted himself around on the woven chair that he had dragged out on to the bungalow's verandah, his face tight with pain. His leg had given him a difficult night, and now he was sitting out in the early sunlight with a bottle of whiskey and two packets of Dover's powders, trying to ease the cramps which crawled up and down his left thighbone like incandescent crabs. His drugs were running low, and that did nothing to improve his temper.

'What are you getting yourself so excited about?' he asked irritably, as Gentleman Jack slid off his dusty horse and tethered it quickly to the rail. 'Can't a man drink his breakfast in peace?'

'Mr Blitzboss – eureka!'

'What are you talking about, you damned black dressed-up monkey?'

'Eureka, Mr Blitzboss. Nothing less! Absolutely eureka!'

Joel ran his fingers through his straggly hair. His years of suffering had turned him grey, and he had a wide bald patch which he usually tried to cover up by brushing his hair straight back. This morning, though, he had not tried to conceal it. He had nobody to impress but himself.

'Just pass me that bottle, will you?' he said, reaching out his hand. 'I haven't slept all night with this damned thighbone of mine. And losing fifty pounds to you at poker hasn't made me feel any better, either.'

'Don't worry about the bottle, sir,' said Gentleman Jack. 'Here – look at this!'

He tugged out of his pocket a greasy leather rag which the kaffirs used to protect their hands when they gripped hold of the steel winding-cable. He laid it on the wicker-topped table, and unfolded it. One flap, two flaps, and there it was. A huge rough stone, still half-embedded in Kimberlite, measuring more than an inch by three-quarters of an inch by an inch. Most of the stone's surface was covered in dull and pitted earth, but at one corner the earth had been knocked off, and the translucent point that emerged from it was immediately recognisable as diamond.

Joel stared at it for a very long time in absolute silence. Gentleman Jack watched him, panting slightly from his hard ride, his expression fixed in an irrepressible grin.

'Give me the bottle,' Joel said at last. Gentleman Jack handed it over, and Joel poured himself a full tumbler of whiskey. He drank two or three mouthfuls, and gagged. Then he set the tumbler down, and continued to stare at the stone on the table as if he expected it to move, or to speak to him, or to disappear in front of his eyes.

'This is a joke,' he declared. 'Edward Nork put you up to this. Edward Nork and Champagne Charlie. This is a melted-down lump of wine bottle, that's what that is, covered in mud.'

'Certainly not, Mr Blitzboss,' said Gentleman Jack, vigorously shaking his head. 'Absolutely not. That stone we found fifteen minutes ago, on the claim No. 202. The kaffir they call Ntsanwisi dug it up with the point of his pick.'

Joel, wincing, leaned forward and examined the stone more narrowly. 'You're sure? You're telling me the truth? Because, by God, if you're not, then I'm going to tie you up by your balls and let the vultures peck your stupid brain out. I'm not in any kind of a mood for jokes.'

'This is no joke, Mr Blitzboss,' Gentleman Jack protested. 'This stone was found just like I've told you.'

At last, cautiously, Joel picked the stone up, and felt the weight of it in his hand. 'This is enormous,' he said. 'It can't be diamond. No diamond comes this big. Have you ever seen a real diamond, this big?'

'Not me, Mr Blitzboss.'

'Give me your knife,' said Joel. He took Jack's penknife, opened it up, and scraped away at the dry Kimberlite on the sides of the stone. Jack continued to grin as little by little. Joel laid bare the dull, ground-glass facets of what looked exactly like a giant diamond. At last, when most of the earth had been picked and worried away, Joel gave the stone a perfunctory rub with the leather cloth, and laid it down on the table again.

Rough and wrinkled as it was, the stone possessed a shine so extraordinary that it made Joel's skin tingle just to look at it. Beneath its surface, it seemed to be harbouring a magical brilliance, a brightness as sharp and dazzling as a star, and whichever way Joel turned it, he caught glimpses of rainbows and scimitars, sequins and teardrops. It was a diamond – inconceivably large, impossibly beautiful, and probably worth more on the open market than everything that Joel had ever owned in his whole life – clothes, books, rings, hats, shoes, horses, and oxen. For more than 100 million years, which was the age of the diamond deposits at Kimberley, this stone had held beneath the ground a living fire, an almost animate light, and for all of those 100 million years it had been waiting for release, waiting for the one spectacular moment when it could stun the eyes of anybody and everybody who looked at it. The dealers gave diamonds names when they were as huge as this one: but Joel could not imagine a name for anything so remote, and so ancient, and so brilliantly cold. It rested eerily on his wickerwork table, this diamond, as if it had silently arrived from another star, and Joel found it impossible to take his eyes away from it.

'It's a diamond,' he whispered. 'It's an enormous, preposterous, incredible diamond.'

'Yes, Mr Blitzboss,' said Gentleman Jack.

'Jack – it's a *diamond*. Do you see the size of it? Do you see the *size* of it, Jack? It must be – what – three hundred and fifty carats. Three hundred and sixty! Look at the size of it! It's like a dream! I can't wake up! Jack, it's incredible!'

Gentleman Jack, uninvited, sat down. He wedged his stubby black fingers together like the dovetailed joints of a mahogany bureau, and stared at Joel with serious and intelligent eyes. 'You know what, Mr Blitzboss? If that stone isn't flawed, it will probably fetch more than half a million pounds. Maybe more. Maybe a million.'

Joel nodded. He groped for the whiskey bottle without taking his eyes off the diamond, and splashed out another glassful, wiping the table with his sleeve. 'Look at it,' he breathed. 'Look at that bastard. Three hundred carats, at least. A fortune! Listen – go get me the scales out of the kitchen. Kitty will show you where they are. Go on, hurry, I want to weigh this bastard!'

While Jack pushed his way into the kitchen to fetch the scales from the Griqua cook Kitty, Joel heaved himself out of his chair, picked up the diamond, and shuffled to the edge of the verandah with it, so that he could hold it up to the sharp morning sunlight. It felt cold to the touch, as a diamond should. He placed it right against his eye, and squinted without focusing into the very depths of it, through the smooth cleaved side where it had probably been broken away from another, larger piece of diamond. Edward Nork had been right about diamonds being formed by the intense heat of subterranean volcanoes: and the devastating force of the eruptions which had driven the diamonds to the surface had often broken and cleaved them. Two large stones of nearly fifty carats each had recently been dug up three hundred yards apart by kaffirs of the British Diamond Mining Company, and it had turned out that they fitted exactly together.

Inside the diamond, Joel saw white light of a strange quality that he had never seen before, even in some of the highest grade gems that they had dug up. It was tinged with the palest of exquisite lilacs, the colour of the morning sky when the last stars begin to fade. It was like a vision of purity, of unalterable truth. He could have stared at that light all day, until the sun set. He felt as if he could somehow transfer his consciousness

331

into the actual interior of the stone – and that it was somewhere he could feel certain, clear of his intentions, strong, wavering, and true. Inside the diamond there was no pain, no drink, no morphia, no self-betrayal. It was a sharp and celestial world in which whiskey and gambling and pubic lice were unknown. Joel felt that to look inside that diamond was to know for a moment what dying was like. There could be nothing deader than the fused carbon of a diamond: nothing harder, nor more sterile. Yet the dealers talked about a diamond's 'fire', about its 'life', and they were right. In the deadest of all gems, the most vivacious of all reflections danced. In a diamond like this, all of his dreams could be resurrected; all of his confusions and his humiliations could be forgotten. This diamond was *certainly* incarnate, and he knew as he turned it, and turned it, and turned it, that it had to be his.

Not Barney's. Not even half Barney's. But *his*.

Gentleman Jack came out with the weighing-scale, a brass balance with an agate fulcrum, and set it on the table. He produced the small brass weights from his pockets, and set them out in a neat line. Joel lowered the diamond and came over to the table with it clenched tight in his hand.

'Feel that,' he said at last, dropping the stone directly into Gentleman Jack's outstretched palm.

'It's warm,' said Gentleman Jack.

'That's right. And that's one of the ways you can tell if it's a real diamond. It should be cold when you first pick it up, but it should quickly warm up when you hold it.'

'You learned something from Mr Nork, then,' said Gentleman Jack, a little archly.

'Don't talk to me about Nork,' retorted Joel. 'Balance the scale, and let's see how much this bastard weighs.'

It took them a few minutes to adjust the balance and weigh the diamond in the small curved pan. The scales were hardly accurate: Kitty usually used them for weighing out spices and herbs for cooking. But an approximation was all that Joel needed to satisfy his excitement. And when Gentleman Jack carefully lowered on the tiny brass weight that tipped the scales at more than two and a half ounces, Joel knew for certain that at 142 carats to the ounce, the diamond must be well over 350 carats.

He stood straight, his hands on his hips, and looked at Gentleman Jack triumphantly. 'Half a million?' he said. 'Three-quarters of a million, easily. Maybe a million.'

'Yes, Mr Blitzboss. That's right.'

Joel picked the stone out of the scales and walked along the length of the verandah, juggling it in his hand. 'Mind you,' he said, 'it won't be worth selling it here, in Kimberley. We'll obviously have to take it to Capetown. Maybe to Antwerp, or Amsterdam, to have it cut. If you have it cut first, you can ask twice the price.'

'Ascher and Mendel will do it, Mr Blitzboss. Mr Barney made a special arrangement.'

Joel inclined his head towards the eastern horizon, where the twisted branches of a camelthorn tree still clawed at the early sun. 'I wasn't actually thinking of Ascher and Mendel.'

'They're one of the best, Mr Blitzboss.'

'You're a Ndebele, Jack. What do you know from diamond cutters?'

'I know the business. Mr Blitzboss. I know Ascher and Mendel by name. Good cutters, that's what everyone says. Absolutely excellent with difficult stones.'

Joel gnawed at the side of his lip. Then he said, 'This Ntsanwisi. Can you trust him?'

'What do you mean, sir?'

'Can you *trust* him, that's what I mean. Don't you understand plain English?'

'Better than most white men understand plain Ndebele, sir.'

Joel limped back down the verandah. 'What I'm trying to ask you is, will he talk about this diamond? Will he spread it around?'

Gentleman Jack closed his eyes, and almost imperceptibiliy shook his head.

'You're sure about that?' Joel demanded.

'Yes, Mr Blitzboss. Ntsanwisi will never give you trouble. Maybe you should pay him money. Five, six pounds. But he will never talk about this diamond again if you tell him not to.'

'All right. And what about you?'

Gentleman Jack looked up warily. 'Me, sir?'

'Yes, you.'

'I don't understand, sir.'

Joel held the huge diamond up between his finger and his thumb, turning it in the sunlight so that it shone in soft prismatic colours. 'If you don't understand, Jack, let me put it clearly for you. This diamond is mine. It was found when Mr Barney was away, and that makes it mine.'

'Mr Barney is half owner, sir.'

'Maybe. But when this diamond was discovered, who was in charge? Me. And there's a little saying that goes, "Finders keepers, losers weepers". Or, "What the eye don't see, the heart don't grieve over."'

'Mr Blitzboss?'

'Don't act dumb,' snapped Joel. 'We're going to take this stone to Europe, under some pretext or other, and we're going to have it cut. Then we're going to put it on the market at a million pounds and make ourselves rich. And if that doesn't make any sense to you, then you're a damn sight more stupid than you look.'

Gentleman Jack clicked his knuckles, one by one. His handsome black face was expressionless.

'You taught me many things, Mr Blitzboss. Drinking, Pope Joan. All those things you taught me.'

Joel nodded. 'That's right. That's perfectly right.'

'Well, Mr Blitzboss,' said Gentleman Jack, 'the trouble is that I was brought up by good missionary people. They always said to me, be honest. Don't cheat. Don't lie. Don't consume the alcoholic spirits. Don't fornicate.'

Joel narrowed one eye suspiciously.

'I didn't always stay pure,' Gentleman Jack went on. 'I liked fornicating. I liked it very much. So, lots of times, I fornicated. No matter what it said in the Bible, I enjoyed it, and the women I took, they seemed like they enjoyed it, too. One Venda woman I know, she only likes it when church choirs sing, so when you fornicate, you have to take her to the back of the chapel, and hide in a bush. But that can't be wrong. Fornicating for joy, and listening to God's music.'

'What are you getting at?' Joel wanted to know.

'Only one thing, sir. This diamond mine is righteously half belonging to Mr Barney, even if he's in Durban. And not to tell him that we have found this stone – well, sir, it seems to me like stealing.'

334

Joel said, 'Hmmph,' and rubbed his left thigh with his hand. His face was fixed in a sour, abstracted mask.

'I fornicate, Mr Blitzboss,' said Gentleman Jack. 'I drink, too, and play cards, ever since I come to work for you. But diamond-stealing – never. No diamond-stealing, sir. Don't ask me.'

Joel picked up his cane, and poked it towards Jack's chest, two or three emphatic prods. 'I'm not asking you, Jack. I'm telling you.'

'It's not right, sir. God's punishment.'

'You think God cares about one single piece of rock? God doesn't cafe about rock. All His rocks are the same to him, granite or salt or diamond. Only men give them value. Look at this,' said Joel, and raised the diamond in the palm of his right hand. 'I could throw this diamond out into the bush, and you could never find it again. How much would it be worth then? Nothing. Nothing at all. And that's the point I'm trying to get into your thick woolly head. This diamond is valuable only because Ntsanwisi found it, and because you brought it to me, and because I know how to market it. Mr Barney didn't give it any value. What did he do? He wasn't even here. This diamond is ours because it's ours, and that's all there is to it.'

Gentleman Jack said slowly, 'You're going to take the whole thing? You're going to have it cut, and you're going to sell it, and you're never going to tell Mr Barney what happened?'

'You're a perceptive man,' smiled Joel. 'I like perceptive men.'

Gentleman Jack lowered his head. 'Supposing *I* tell Mr Barney about it?'

Joel stared at him coldly. 'You wouldn't.'

'But, supposing I did.'

'You're a kaffir,' said Joel. 'You have no rights, no legal standing, no soul. You may speak pretty fancy English, and you may dress up like a Capetown dandy, but that's as far as it goes. Inside of that tailored vest you're nothing but a primitive savage, and nobody's going to credit your word for one single moment, not even if you swear to God that you're going to cut your throat. But I'll tell you one thing. If Barney gets to hear about this diamond, and he gets to hear about it through you,

335

then cutting your throat is going to be one thing you'll wish that you'd done.'

Gentleman Jack stared at Joel wide-eyed. Then he let out a breath of resignation, and looked away, and smeared at his mouth with his hand.

'You got that straight?' asked Joel.

'Straight?'

'You understand what you have to do?'

'I know,' said Gentleman Jack. 'I have to go back to work and I have to keep my mouth closed.'

Joel held up the diamond again, angling it this way and that in the rapidly brightening sunshine. 'You have to do more than keep your mouth closed. You have to tell yourself that you never saw this stone before in your whole life.'

'I want my share, Mr Blitzboss.'

'Your share? Your share of what?'

Gentleman Jack's expression remained unaltered – polite, subservient, restrained – but there was a barely perceptible tightening of his stance, a tension in the set of his shoulders.

'My share of the diamond, Mr Blitzboss. You know that.'

Joel dropped the diamond carefully into the pocket of his shirt. Then he looked at Gentleman Jack with the steadiest of impudent gazes and said, 'What diamond?'

'Come on, now, Mr Blitzboss. I got proof. Ntsanwisi will say he found that diamond.'

'You call that proof? What Ntsanwisi found was nothing but a worthless lump of Kimberlite and quarts.'

'Mr Blitzboss, I warn you, I want my share.'

Joel limped around the table, and then grinned. 'Of course you'll get your share. You think I'm going to cheat you? You brought me the diamond, I'll pay you. I'll pay you for keeping quiet, too. How does five hundred pounds sound?'

'Seven hundred and fifty, Mr Blitzboss.'

'Five hundred and that's it.'

Gentleman Jack slowly nodded his head. His ivory earring flashed in the sunlight. 'All right, Mr Blitzboss. Five hundred. But you have to pay me now.'

'I'll pay you when I sell the diamond.'

'No, Mr Blitzboss. Now. Otherwise, I tell the happy tidings

to Mr Barney Blitzboss, when he comes back. Good news! I'll say. The Lord has smiled on you. A giant diamond!'

'All right,' said Joel, easing himself back into his chair. 'I'll pay you when I go to the bank. You want a drink?'

'I don't really think I've got anything to celebrate, Mr Blitzboss.'

Just then, Kitty the Griqua cook came out to see if there were any dishes or glasses to collect up. She was a plump, friendly woman, a widow who had lost her husband and her two children from cholera more than six years ago, and who had worked as a servant in white people's households ever since. She had come to cook and clean for Barney and Joel after her previous employer, Mr Oliver Peters of the British Diamond Mining Company, had hurried home to England to take care of his paralysed mother in Eastbourne. Joel hated her with considerable vigour, more for her Christian hymns than her pot-roasts, although he hated her pot-roasts, too.

'I hear you talking about diamonds, sir?' she said, tidying up the wickerwork table. Her head was tied up in a tight green scarf, and she wore a simple Empire-line dress in dyed green percale.

'I'm always talking about diamonds,' said Joel, loudly and slowly, as if he were addressing a backward child. 'They're my business.'

Unabashed, Kitty grinned at him with her gappy teeth, and let out a wheezing laugh. 'I know that, sir. Diamonds are your business all right, sir. But they're not your *principal* business.' She held up the half-empty whiskey bottle, and shook it so that it sloshed. 'This here, this is your *principal* business.'

'Don't be so damned impertinent,' Joel told her, but without obvious anger. 'Go and make me some poached eggs before I kick your fat bottom out of this house for good and all. You hear me? And make sure they don't come out like bullets, the way they usually do.'

'Whatever you say, Mr Blitz,' smiled Kitty. 'I expect you've got yourself a whole lot of diamond business to talk over.'

Joel scowled. He would have dismissed Kitty months ago if the decision had been his. He would not even have hired her. But Kitty was a distant friend of Mooi Klip's family, and

Barney liked to have her around because her Griqua accent reminded him of Mooi Klip, and she could remember the days when Mooi Klip had been a small girl, and because he liked to think that whatever happened, Mooi Klip was not irrevocably lost to him, or too far away.

Joel thought Barney was showing all the signs of being soft in the head. One day, Barney would suffocate himself in the self-propagating kapok of his own sentimentality, and it would serve him right. Barney did not seem to be able to see that his skills at business and his showy determination to lick Cecil Rhodes at his own game were nothing more than superficial tricks and varnish. Underneath it all, he was still a dewy-eyed Clinton Street Jew-boy, all bread-and-*shmaltz*, and hugging your *mama*, and hot plates of *tsimmes* on Sabbath eve. He had ambition, sure; but his ambition would always be limited by his boyhood. The Lower East Side was not easily forgotten, even out on the plains of Cape Colony. The kaffirs' candles, as they dug during the long-drawn-out evenings, would always remind Barney of *menorah*, glittering in the darkness of New York.

Gentleman Jack said, 'I'll go back to the Hole, then.' It was more of a question than a statement.

'Sure, go back,' said Joel. 'I'll see you later on. After luncheon, maybe.'

'Are you going to want lunch today, Mr Joel?' asked Kitty, turning back, and keeping the screen door open with her foot.

'Maybe a meat pasty, or some cheese,' said Joel.

'There's some cold beef, Mr Joel. You could have that, with pickles.'

Joel looked up. 'Whatever you like. Now, will you let me get on with this diamond-talk that you think so little of?'

Kitty inclined her head, so that her double-chin rolled out like a shiny bratwurst. 'You know that the Griqua people say, Mr Joel, about where those diamonds came from?'

'No, Kitty, I don't.'

'Well, whenever I hear any of those diggers squabbling about who owns a diamond, who it actually belongs to, I think of the old Griqua story; and that story says that a long time ago there was pain and sorrow and hunger in this land, and so some kindly spirit brought a basketful of diamonds down from

338

Heaven, and decided he was going to scatter them all over the land hereabouts, to make people happy. So this spirit came flying across the Vaal River, throwing out diamonds, until he reached Colesberg Kopje, at the place they call Kimberley; and in those days there were plenty of tall camelthorn trees at Colesberg Kopje. The spirit caught his foot in the branches of the camelthorn trees, and dropped all of his diamonds in one place, right there on the hill, and that's where the white people found them.'

'Yes,' said Joel, testily. 'It's a very pretty story.'

'It sets me to thinking, though,' Kitty interrupted him. 'I think to myself, if it was *really* a spirit who scattered those diamonds, then which man can rightfully say that any of those diamonds belongs to him? They were a gift from Heaven to the people on earth, and I believe they really belong to all of us, don't you?'

Joel tapped his fingers on the table. Gentleman Jack glanced at him, uncertain of what he was thinking, and bit his lip.

'People have had all kinds of misconceptions about diamonds for hundreds of years,' Joel said at last. 'In India, they still believe that diamonds grow like crystals, and that every twenty years they're going to be able to dig up a fresh crop. Even here, it wasn't too long ago that some people thought they might be solidified dewdrops, congealed by the rays which emanated from a particular conjunction of the stars.

'The truth is, though, that diamonds aren't any of those things. They're nothing more than lumps of carbon which have been heated up by volcanoes; and they're lying around on the ground for anyone to claim as their own. They're not magic, and they're not mysterious. They're just lumps of carbon. And now I'd really appreciate it if you went in and cooked my eggs for me. And don't use too much vinegar.'

'Anything you say, sir,' nodded Kitty, and went inside. The screen door banged shut behind her.

Joel lay back in his chair and looked at Gentleman Jack with his eyes as neutral as pebbles, his hand crooked in front of his mouth.

'You know what I think, Jack?' he said.

'What's that, Mr Blitzboss?'

339

'I think it's a mistake to educate the blacks. I think it's the beginning of the end, when you educate the blacks. They're happier when they're ignorant, and living the life of savages. They used to sing *ihubo*. What do they sing how? Dreary Anglican hymns. You mark my words, Gentleman Jack, nothing but strife will come out of educating the blacks.'

'She's not a bad woman,' said Gentleman Jack, nodding towards the bungalow.

'You don't think so? She's inquisitive, that's what I don't like about her. And what was all that stuff about spirits and diamonds, and who they belong to?'

'I don't know, sir.'

'You think she overheard us?'

Gentleman Jack shrugged.

Joel monotonously stroked his bald patch, over and over again, and stared at a knothole in the verandah floor, through which he could see the sunshine glittering on the dust and the chaff beneath.

Then he placed his hand on his breast pocket, where the diamond nestled already warm with the heat of his body; and he smiled at Gentleman Jack with widening amusement.

'How soon should I leave for Capetown?' he asked. 'Next week, maybe? Edward Nork can take over the mine until Barney comes back, can't he? Edward's drunk, most of the time, but he knows what he's doing.'

'What would you say was your reason for going?' Gentleman Jack wanted to know. 'Just remember – if *you* get caught with this diamond, then *I* get caught too – and you know what they'll do to me.'

'I would say I was going to buy pumps,' suggested Joel.

'Pumps? You wouldn't have to go to Capetown for pumps. Mr Rhodes has plenty of pumps at De Beers.'

'Then I would say that I was going to find myself a wife.'

'A *wife*, Mr Blitzboss?'

Joel caught the tone in Gentleman Jack's voice, and laughed. 'Yes,' he said, softly. 'We all have to think of getting married at some time or another, don't we?'

*

The train of ox-waggons which brought Barney home to Kimberley with 54 chairs, 18 tables, 16 beds, a mile and a quarter of carpet, 23 Persian rugs, 31 paintings, 11 wardrobes, two miles of curtain fabrics, as well as an assortment of clocks, bureaux, sofas, birdcages, and tallboys, was generally considered by all who saw it pass, Boers and Basutos and diggers alike, to be one of the greatest spectacles of 1878.

The *Colesberg Advertiser* described its arrival in Kimberley as 'the nearest we have ever seen in this town to the visit of a travelling circus', and its slow procession towards Vogel Vlei was accompanied by dancing barefoot black boys, jeering layabouts, and two Irish prostitutes who were eager to make the acquaintance of the drivers.

The waggons brought more than furniture, though. They also brought Barney's new bride, sitting ahead of the train in her polished brougham, shaded by a tasselled parasol of cream silk, tall and straight-backed and more composed than any woman that Kimberley had ever encountered. 'The new Mrs Barney Blitz is a ravishing beauty!' exclaimed the *Advertiser's* social column. 'She is Junoesque; she is feminine perfection incarnate! We *eagerly* await the privilege of her acquaintance!'

While the drivers and the porters unloaded the waggons, Barney showed Sara in silence through the rooms of Vogel Vlei. Their footsteps echoed from dining-room to morning-room, from kitchen to stairs, from landing to landing, until they reached the main bedroom suite.

Barney sat on the wide windowsill in his smart dove-grey suit, took off his hat, and watched Sara twirl around the polished wooden floor.

'Well?' he asked her, setting his hat down beside him.

'Barney, it's going to be entrancing! *Far* more entrancing than Khotso.'

'I'm glad,' he said. 'I knew you'd like it.'

She swept over towards him, her arms outstretched, and then she kissed him on the tip of the nose. 'It's wonderful,' she whispered. 'It's like a dream. Wait until Nareez sees this beautiful room you've given us!'

'I think Nareez is too busy unpacking,' said Barney.

'Unpacking? Where?'

'In her own room, of course. Now, what would you say to a cold bottle of that French champagne, and some antelope pie?'

Sara was frowning. 'Nareez is my *amah*,' she said. 'Nareez brought me up from the cradle, from the day I was born.'

'Yes?' said Barney, puzzled.

Sara moved Barney's hat and sat down on the windowsill beside him, spreading her skirts of her pale-blue travelling dress. Her plumed bonnet had such a wide brim that it almost touched Barney's forehead, and he had to lean back a little to talk to her.

'There's nothing wrong, is there?' he asked her. 'The way you talked about Nareez just then, I got the feeling –'

Sara's expression gave nothing away. She blinked twice – two feminine, exaggerated blinks – the pupils of her wide-set eyes as dusty-brown and dewy as the undersides of mushrooms in those first cold moments of morning. But she allowed Barney's sentence to remain in the air unfinished, and un-answered, and when he inclined his head to one side, trying to show her that he expected some kind of response, she simply pursed her lips and continued to stare at him like the innocent, coequettish heroine of a bad amateur play.

Barney attempted a smile, but he found it difficult. The whole trek from Durban to Kimberley had been difficult. It had thundered all through Natal, and their slow processional climb up the foothills of the Drakensberg had been constantly halted by mudslides and broken traces and collapsing axles. One Sunday afternoon, under a sky like splintered slate, they had found their way through the mountains blocked by a huge slanting landslip; and in torrential rain they had been obliged to dismantle the ox-waggons in the way the old voortrekkers had done, and 'toboggan' the hulls down the slippery rocks until they could rejoin the road. All through the journey Sara had been composed and English and almost completely un-approachable. She had slept in one of the furniture-waggons with her Bengali *amah* Nareez, a small woman with a ruby in her left nostril who drenched herself in musk and swaddled herself in crimson silk, and who insisted on setting up her spirit stove every evening, no matter where she was, to stir up rancid *bhuna ghosth*, and to fry *parathas*. Nareez may have smelled like *brinjal bhaji* soaked in cologne, but Sara adored her, and treated her as if she were her own sister, or even her mother. And during all of those weeks it had taken to cross the mountains of Basutoland and the plains of the Orange Free State; even on those nights which had been heralded by the most gorgeous and romantic of sunsets, with the clouds on fire and the syringa trees blazing with scarlet light, Barney had never been allowed near Sara's 'travelling apartments' as she called them, and had never even seen her in her underwear. When he knocked on the tailboard of her waggon one morning, when the dew lay on the bushgrass like diamonds, he was greeted only by an indignant Nareez, who poked her head out of the canvas and cried out, 'Go away! Ladies' quarters only! No Peeping Toms!'

Barney had hoped that once they arrived at Vogel Vlei, he would be able to curtail Nareez's influence, and to assert his authority as Sara's husband and lover. He had planned weeks ago that Nareez should be assigned the smallest bedroom in the east wing of the house, which looked towards Kimberley and the Big Hole. The main bedroom suite took up most of the upper floor of the west wing, and faced out over the scrubby acreage which was Vogel Vlei's garden.

'If you don't tell me what's wrong,' said Barney, 'I can't possibly put it right.'

'I thought you would have *known* what was wrong,' said Sara.

'I'm not a mind-reader. Maybe you should have married a mind-reader.'

'There's no need to be ridiculous; nor offensive, either. I was simply saying that I expected more sensitivity from you, and perhaps a little more *savoir-faire*.'

'I don't happen to know what *savoir-faire* is. I'm American, not German.'

'*Savoir-faire* is French, as a matter of fact, and it means knowing how to do things properly.'

Barney lifted his hands in resigned acceptance, and let them drop back to his knees again. 'Okay, I don't have any *savoir-faire*. Now, what in particular makes you say that?'

343

'Well, the bedroom,' said Sara. 'The arrangements. I'm a lady, after all, and yet you seem to expect me to spend my entire life in your personal presence.'

Barney looked at her for a moment, and then said, 'Yes, I do. Isn't that the whole point of getting married?'

'But *Barneh*,' she said, clasping her hands together like an exasperated little girl, and exaggerating her English county accent so much that, for the very first time, it made Barney wince to hear it. 'A lady has to do so many private and intimate things ... things that she can't possibly do in front of her husband. I mean, good Lord, you don't expect to see me at my toilet, do you, or dressing? A woman should be the perfect mystery ... that's what mother always said ... she should appear as a vision of prettiness without ever giving away the little secrets which made her so. And, besides, it's *embarrassing*.'

'You're *embarrassed* I should see you dressing?'

Sara blushed, and lowered her head so that the brim of her hat obscured her face. Barney cupped her chin in his hand, and raised her face towards him again, frowning into her eyes in disbelief.

'How can you be embarrassed, if we're married?'

'Barney, my darling, that's part of being a lady.'

'But you've never said anything before. You weren't embarrassed on our wedding-night.'

'I didn't undress in front of you on my wedding-night. And, in any case, I *was* embarrassed.'

'You *were* embarrassed? Embarrassed by what?'

She turned her head away from his hand, and presented him with a profile that was as classic as a sculpture by Donatello, and equally cold.

'I can't talk about it,' she said. 'It isn't proper.'

'Between husband and wife, it isn't proper to talk about love? Between husband and wife, it isn't proper to talk about sex? If it isn't proper between husband and wife, then when *is* it proper?'

Sara licked her lips with the tip of her tongue, as if the actual words that came out of her mouth were distasteful to her. 'Men discuss it in clubs, and in the polo changing-rooms.'

Barney, was so stupefied that he felt as if someone had

punched all the breath out of him. He stood up, and walked across the bedroom floor, and then turned around on his heel and came back to the window again.

'In clubs? And in the polo changing rooms? Is that what your mother told you?'

'Barney, my mother brought me up to be a complete lady. To ride and to sew, to speak French and to play the piano, and to run a household. She also instructed me in marriage, and what any normal husband would expect from me. She wasn't a prude. Her lessons did include the duty of sexual intimacy, and in some detail.'

'Sara,' said Barney, gently, but with great intensity, 'sex isn't a duty. It's a pleasure, and the best way there is of showing somebody that you truly love them. It's one of the greatest joys of marriage.'

'You seem to have forgotten that sex is mainly for the purpose of bearing children. I *will* have your children, Barney. I won't fail you that way. Nor, I hope, in any other way.'

'Sara – I don't think you will. But you have to understand that I don't only want to see you when you're dressed up, or when you're bathed and ready for bed. I want to see you the way you really are. I want to see you night and day, whether your hair is combed or uncombed, whether you're wearing evening-gowns or underwear, with or without powder, in or out of make-up.'

Sara tittered, but without much amusement. 'That's nonsense,' she said. 'My parents never shared a bedroom. How could *we* possibly share a bedroom?'

'We shared a bedroom at Khotso.'

'That was our honeymoon. Of course we shared a bedroom on our *honeymoon*. But now we're talking about normal life.'

'*Normal*?' expostulated Barney. 'You call it *normal*, a man tip-toeing down the corridor with his slippers in his hand, every time he wants to make love to his own wife?'

'But, Barney, we *can't* share a bedroom. What about Nareez?'

'Nareez? What in hell does Nareez have to do with it? I married *you*, not Nareez!'

'Nareez is my *amah*, Barney. She bathes me, and dresses me, and does my hair. She brings me water in the night if I'm thirsty. She sits up and talks to me if I can't sleep. She rubs

345

my forehead if I've got a headache. It can't possibly work out, the three of us in one bedroom. It's just not the thing.'

Barney stared at her. 'Oh,' he said, flatly. 'It's not the thing. Why didn't you tell me in the first place? If I'd only realised that it wasn't the thing, that would have saved us all of this squabbling. For the love of God, Sara, what are you talking about? This is our bedroom, yours and mine – husband and wife. Do you seriously think I built this bedroom so that you could share it with some fat greasy Indian woman, while I sleep in another bed, in another room, without even the consolation of being able to hold you and kiss you whenever I so desire? The thing! If sleeping apart is the thing in England, then I'm not surprised they're all so damned eccentric!'

'The English are *not* eccentric and Nareez is *not* fat and greasy! How dare you!'

'I dare because it's true, and I dare because you're talking like a middle-aged spinster, instead of a passionate young wife. And I dare most of all because I love you, and I'm not going to sleep without you.'

Sara sat rigidly upright, not moving. The sun had moved around the house so that it was shining through the window in which she sat; and her hair with highlights of red and bronze. But the brightness of the light behind her also concentrated the shadows on her face, so that her eyes, already dark with tiredness and displeasure, grew darker still.

When she next spoke, she was back to her airy patronising again. 'You will realise, Barney, when you've had longer to acquaint yourself with the habits of society, that there is a time and a place for everything. Passion included.'

'What a smart girl you are,' Barney told her, his arms hanging by his sides as if he were exhausted to the point of collapse.

'There are times when affection can be properly expressed, and times when it is better held in check. There should be just as much etiquette between man and wife, after all, as there is between friends or strangers.'

'Did your mother tell you that, or did you read it in one of those twopenny books on manners?'

'Barney! You're being so unpleasant!'

346

Barney loosened his necktie and dragged it out from under his collar. Then he wound it around his fists like a garotte. 'I seem to remember a time on the lawn at Khotso when you weren't so worried about etiquette,' he said.

Sara said, 'You're very bad-mannered, to remind me of that, especially now that I'm so upset. But just because I believe in doing everything the proper way, that doesn't mean that I don't love you, or that my feelings towards you aren't passionate.'

Barney glanced at her. 'Well, then,' he said, 'if that's the way you truly feel about me, Nareez can stay where she is, in the east wing, and you and I will share this bedroom. If you like, I'll have a bell installed so that you can call Nareez if you really need her. But you might remember that *I* can fetch water, just as competently as Nareez; and that *I* can talk to you, when you can't sleep, and without a Bengali accent, too; and that *I* can rub your poor aching head if you're suffering from the neuralgia, just as soothingly.'

'And what about my toilette?'

'We have a private dressing-room, and a private bathroom. You can close the doors of both, if you really don't want me to see you in your corset-cover and your hairpins.'

'I don't wear a –' Sara began, with indignation, but then she realised that the subject was indelicate, and she angrily got to her feet, and stamped. 'You're impossible! Why are you insisting on being so impossible? Why do you have to be so piggish about telling everybody where they might sleep, and where they mightn't?'

Barney came over to the window and held Sara's arms, so tightly that she gave a little cry. 'Barney!' she begged him.

He smiled at her, but there was no softness in his voice at all. 'I'm being impossible because I have a right to be. This is *my* house, and you are *my* wife, and like any good bride, Jewish or Christian, you are going to do what *I* tell you.'

'And if I defy you?'

He kissed her, first on the cheek, then on the lips. His kisses were quick, and light, but they betrayed his urgency. 'You won't defy me,' he told her. 'You love me too much.'

He tried to kiss her more deeply, on the mouth, but she plucked her face abruptly away and said, 'No!'

347

The echo of that 'No!' was heard in ten rooms at once, and even downstairs, where four kaffirs were sweating and grunting as they carried in through the front doors the huge solid-mahogany marriage bed.

Joel appeared, unshaven, hurriedly dressed in a pair of grubby twill trousers and a mud-splattered shirt. 'I didn't know you were going to come back so soon,' he said breathlessly, limping after Barney across the hallway. 'I didn't expect you back until the middle of next month, at least.'

Barney directed a kaffir to carry a gilded French chair into the dining-room. 'Neither did we. But the way the weather was, we decided to set out as soon as we'd gathered the bulk of the furniture together, in case we were caught by the rains. We still need more furniture, of course, but this will get us started. At least we'll be able to entertain.'

'I wish you'd sent a message on ahead of you,' Joel complained. 'I've decided to leave for Capetown on Monday.'

'Capetown? What for? I need you here.'

'Well, I know you do.'

'Then stay. You don't really need to go to Capetown, do you? The journey will half kill you, in the middle of summer. Besides. I'm having a special dinner next Wednesday night, and you *must* come to that. Even Rhodes is invited.'

Joel snapped his fingers at another kaffir who was carrying a chair on top of his head into the day-room. The kaffir set the chair down on the floor, and Joel perched himself on the edge of it, his aching back kept straight, his weight supported on his cane. 'The truth is, Barney, I'm going to to try to find myself a companion, among other things.'

'But you've got plenty of friends here in Kimberley. And servants. And by the way, we're going to have to train up a butler, no question about it. Maybe we can find a digger with domestic experience. And Kitty's going to need some more kitchen staff, now that we're moving in properly.'

'As long as their principal qualification is that they don't know how to cook pot-roast, then I quite agree with you,' said Joel. 'But to go back to what I was saying – I'm going to look for a wife.'

Barney had been beckoning frantically to a lone kaffir who was wandering around with a bronze statue of a dancing cherub, looking for somewhere to put it down. But now he turned around and stared at Joel, and said, 'A *wife?*' as if Joel had suddenly announced that he was *geshmat*. 'You want a wife? With all the girls here in Kimberley?'

'Girls are girls, Barney. What I need now is somebody who's going to look after me. I'm getting older, my leg and my hip give me agony most of the time. I want somebody to share the rest of my life. That's all. A true companion.'

'There's nobody here in Kimberley?'

'The decent girls are married; and none of the indecent girls are Jewish. Besides, I don't want a wife who's had as many diggers shovelling away at her as the Big Hole. I want somebody quiet, don't you know. Respectable. *Zaftig.*'

Barney said, 'You're really serious? You want a wife?'

'Why do you sound so surprised?'

'I'm not surprised. I guess I'm just pleased. And in any case, that'll make two of us.'

Joel's expression altered with such subtlety that only someone who knew him very well could have detected the difference. But the lines in his face, which had bitten deeper into his skin since his accident, like acid into a steel engraving, grew straighter, and tenser, and more pronounced. It was as if he had aged five years in the time it took for the sun to brighten as it came out from behind a cloud; or a *lammergayer* to wheel on the wind.

'What happened in Durban?' he asked, with corrosive quietness.

Barney had not expected him to react so sharply. 'What happened? Can't you guess what happened?'

'Tell me what happened. I want to hear you say it.'

'Well . . .' said Barney, defensively. 'What happened was, I got married.

'You got married? You just went to Durban and got married?'

'Have you any objections?' snapped Barney.

'I don't know. It's done. What's to object about? It was that Sutter girl, I suppose. You've been having polluted dreams about her ever since you visited Natal the first time. Either her, or some nigger.'

349

Barney retorted furiously, 'What the hell gives you the right to say something like that? I *did* marry Sara, as a matter of fact. She's my wife. And if you've got anything smart to say about it, you'd better be ready to have your other leg broken.'

'Or to be shot at,' said Joel, dryly.

'She's a beautiful, gentle girl,' said Barney.

'Sure. And she's a *shikseh*.'

'After all the whores you've paid for, you can say that?'

Joel pulled a face. 'At least I didn't marry any of them, did I?'

Barney slowly rubbed his cheeks with his hands. 'All right, Joel,' he said. 'Let's stop arguing about it, shall we? Whatever you say, it's not going to change the fact that Miss Sara Sutter is now Mrs Sara Blitz, and that you have yourself a new sister-in-law. Neither is anything you say going to divert me from asking you to join us on Wednesday night for our celebration dinner.'

'I've arranged to leave on Monday, with Henk van der Westhuizen.'

'Why can't you leave next Friday? You could go with Harold Feinberg, when he takes his diamonds down.'

Joel looked around at two kaffirs carrying a ponderous carved wardrobe through the polished hallway, like two black ants shouldering a matchbox a hundred times their size. 'Well,' he said, uneasily, 'I just think I'd prefer to go with Henk, that's all.'

'What difference are three days going to make?' asked Barney. 'You're going to catch a wife, not a train.'

'I don't know,' said Joel.

'Well, I do,' Barney told him, slapping his shoulder. Joel closed his eyes in pain. 'I know that you're going to stay and have a really good time. Look – here's Sara now.'

Sara came down the curved stairway in a pale green day dress and pearls. On her left breast she wore a darker green ostrich plume, and an array of diamonds, an engagement present from Barney. Her dark hair was fashionably plaited, and arrayed with turquoise combs. Barney went across to meet her at the foot of the stairs, and take her arm. 'Come and say hello to Joel,' he said. 'You haven't seen him since he was in hospital.'

Joel painfully forced himself to stand, and took Sara's hand. He dropped his head forward and kissed her fingers, and then he turned her hand around, palm upwards, and traced the tip of his finger lightly along her line of health, her line of heart, and her line of life. She watched him with a little curiosity, a little pity, and a little repulsion. He looked more twisted and haggard these days, and he smelled of stale whiskey. But he still had a little of his old charm about him, and he was still able to flatter a woman with his old sense of fancy.

'You have a long and wealthy life ahead of you, I see,' he told her.

'I didn't know you read palms,' she said.

'I don't,' smiled Joel. 'But I like stroking any pretty woman's hand, and I'm not so stupid that I can't tell that any woman who marries into one of the largest diamond companies in Kimberley is going to be ridiculously rich for the rest of her life.'

'You're teasing me,' said Sara. 'Barney, your brother is teasing me.'

'Yes,' Barney told her, with enthusiasm.

'You're coming to our celebration dinner, of course?' Sara asked Joel.

Joel's eyes flickered sideways, towards Barney. Barney responded by looking sideways at Sara.

'Well,' said Joel, clearing his throat, 'I was thinking of leaving for Capetown on Monday.'

'That's quite out of the question,' smiled Sara. 'You must come along on Wednesday night, and dress yourself up like the nob I'm sure you can be, and make 'a speech, too, telling everybody that we're married!'

'I'd really like to –' Joel began, but Sara shushed him.

'That's quite settled then,' she interrupted him. 'Now do come and help me re-arrange some of these pictures upstairs, Barney, my darling. I must have mixed and moved them around twenty times, and they still don't look quite right!'

Joel looked at Barney appealingly, but Barney simply shrugged. And at that moment, Nareez came downstairs, slip-slopping in her silk mules, and frowned at Joel so contemptuously, in his scruffy shirt and dirty trousers, that he raised his stick to Barney, said '*shalom*', and hobbled out of Vogel Vlei as quickly as he had hurried in.

'*Shalom*,' called Barney.

'Is that another devil?' asked Nareez, in her dense Bengali accent.

'That's my brother,' Barney told her.

'That's what I said,' replied Nareez, folding her arms. 'Now, Miss Sara, time for your oils.'

'I thought we were going to re-arrange the paintings,' said Barney.

Sara blew him a little kiss. 'Soft skin has to come first, my darling. And Nareez is *marvellous* when it comes to massage. Anyway, I'm very tired, and I think it will calm me down. Nareez will massage you, too, if you care for it.'

Barney shook his head. 'I think I'd rather go out and be trampled by elephants, thank you. What time will you be down?'

'For tea, of course. I'll tell that cook of yours to have it ready on the back terrace. Now, you will take care, my love, won't you, and you won't work too hard.'

'Come along now, Miss Sara,' said Nareez, taking Sara's arm. Behind Sara's back, Barney gave the *amah* a teeth-gritting scowl that made her gather up the hem of her sari and shuffle up the uncarpeted stairs as fast as she could, all bangles and chiffon and big bustling bottom.

Barney was sitting in the day-room in his green dressing-gown reading a three-month-old copy of the London *Morning Post* when Gentleman Jack knocked at the door. It was the day after their arrival back at Kimberley, and Sara was still asleep, her hair in curl-papers, her lashes prettily closed. Barney had come down early for a cup of tea and a dish of Kitty's chicken livers and onions; and now he was relaxing with a second cup of tea, a basket of fruit, and some stale news from England.

'Jack,' he said, affably, as Gentleman Jack ventured into the room. 'It's good to see you. How are things at the mine?'

'Excellent, Mr Blitzboss, thank you. Absolutely excellent. Since you went away, the average week is three thousand, seven hundred pounds. And some good fine gemstones, sir. One was twenty-three carats.'

'That's good news, Jack. How did you get on with Mr Joel?'

'No trouble, sir. Very fine. A most amenable relationship, I must say.'

'Well, that's a relief, anyway. Do you want a cup of tea? Kitty has some brewed in the kitchen.'

'No, sir. I just came by to say welcome back.'

'That's very good of you. I'm pleased to be back. Did we get those new steam-engines yet, for the winding-gear?'

'Two arrived, sir. One damaged. But I believe we can have the first one running in two days.'

'Good, fine.'

Barney went back to his newspaper, but after a minute or so he became aware that Gentleman Jack was still standing there, in his grey morning-coat and his muddy shoes, and that he was rotating the brim of his hat around and around in his hands as if he had something to say.

'Yes?' asked Barney, lowering his paper again. 'Was there anything else?'

Gentleman Jack let out a short hiss of breath, like a man who is irritated with himself. 'The truth is, Mr Blitzboss, I am not very sure.'

'You're not *sure*? What is it that you're not sure about?'

'Well, sir, it's to do with diamonds, and God, sir. And who is it who owns a diamond, once it's found.'

'That's easy,' said Barney. 'A diamond belongs, in law, to the man on whose claim it's discovered.'

'No matter who finds it, sir?'

'Of course.'

There was another awkward silence, and then Gentleman Jack said, 'If a man owns a diamond-mine, sir; and there's a diamond lying in the ground in that diamond-mine, and he never digs it up, then who does it belong to then, sir?'

'Jack – whether a man decides to dig up his diamonds or not – they're still his.'

'Even if he doesn't know that he owns them, sir?'

Barney set aside his *Morning Post* and stood up. He walked across to the doorway where Gentleman Jack was standing, his hands plunged deep into his dressing-gown pockets, and he

353

stared intently into Gentleman Jack's face. The Ndebele was almost six inches taller than Barney, but he shied back, and gave Barney a foolish, apprehensive grin.

'What's happened, Jack?' Barney asked, quietly.

'Nothing, Mr Blitzboss. Everything is absolutely fine. I was just seeking clarification, sir. Legal clarification, you understand, and moral clarification. That's all, sir. It says in Deuteronomy, sir, that the law requires perfect obedience. And to obey the law, you have to know it.'

'You're sure nothing's happened? You seem like you're unhappy about something.'

'Everything's absolutely top notch, sir.'

Barney stared at Gentleman Jack for a moment, and then went back and picked up his newspaper. 'You know something, Jack, I spent the larger part of my childhood years, and most of my time as a young man, not knowing what it was that I wanted from myself, nor out of my life, nor the people around me. These days, I'm making a great deal of money, and I know exactly what I want to do, and how I want to do it.'

He folded the newspaper with careful, exaggerated gestures. Then he said, without looking up, 'I want to own the entire Kimberley diamond mine, personally. I want to be a member of the Kimberley Club – not because it will help me to get on, but because I'm going to be so wealthy and so powerful that they won't have any option but to admit me. I want to lead a happy married life, with lots of children. And I want to find my religion again, which I lost when I came out here to Cape Colony, and which seems to have been eluding me lately, like a ghost.'

'Yes, sir,' said Gentleman Jack.

Barney sat down again. 'How about you, Jack?' he asked him. 'Do you know what you want out of your life?'

Jack examined his hat as if he expected to find the answer to Barney's question written on the grey silk hatband. 'I just want to be a good foreman, sir. That's all.'

'You're sure?'

'It's the most that a black man can hope for, Mr Blitzboss.'

'It's more than most black men can hope for. A whole lot more.'

354

'I know that, sir.'

'All right, then. As long as you understand. Now, you'd better get back to the mine and get those winding-engines repaired.'

'Yes, sir. Oh – and, sir. There's a gentleman waiting for you outside, sir, in the hall. Mr Ransome, he says his name is.'

'A white man?'

'Yes, sir.'

'Why didn't you tell me before? You mean to tell me you've kept a white man waiting all the time you've been engaging me in this ridiculous conversation about legal clarification?'

'I'm sorry, Mr Blitzboss.'

Barney tightened his mouth in annoyance. 'You're lucky I don't sack you on the spot,' he told Jack. 'Go out there at once, and ask Mr Ransome to come through. And apologise for keeping him waiting. Do you happen to know what he wants?'

'He didn't say, sir. But he's a reverend, sir. The white collar, and the black dress, sir.'

'Very well. Now, go get him.'

'Yes, sir. And thank you.'

After a minute or two, there was a timorous knock at the door-post. Barney said, 'Come in!' and a small shabby man in a clerical cassock stepped into the room, and removed his hat in a visible cloud of dust.

'Mr Blitz?' he asked, in a voice as uncontrolled as that of a pubescent boy.

'That's right. Mr Barney Blitz. And you must be Mr Ransome. I'm sorry my foreman kept you waiting. I had no idea you were out there.'

'I, ah, well – it doesn't matter. Waiting always gives one an opportunity to meditate, don't you think? Really – you must excuse my dust. It was such a dry day, and I rode over from Klipdrift rather *hurriedly*.'

'Sit down,' Barney told him. 'Would you like some tea?'

'That's most kind. My throat feels like the Sinai desert must have done, to the Children of Israel.' He said 'the Children of Israel' with noticeable emphasis.

Barney lifted his head. 'Are you trying to tell me something, Mr Ransome?'

Mr Ransome blushed. 'Please – really. I didn't mean any offence. I was simply trying to delineate our differences, as it were. I mean, me being an Anglican, as it were, and you, well, being Jewish.'

'That requires delineation?' asked Barney, sharply.

'I'm not very sure. I just thought I ought to stake out the ground before I told you why I came here.'

Barney tinkled the brass handbell for more tea. Then he folded his arms across his chest and inspected Mr Ransome with undisguised directness. Mr Ransome picked at a stray thread on the arm of his chair until he realised with some embarrassment that he was pulling apart his host's furniture fabric in front of his eyes; and then he sat up straight, his fists clenched, and let out an involuntary whinny that reminded Barney of Alsjeblieft on a cold July morning.

'I've actually come here to talk to you about Natalia Marneweck,' said Mr Ransome. 'I'm not sure why, not entirely. I personally think that she's better off without you, if you'll forgive my saying so. But in six years she hasn't forgotten you, not completely, in spite of having tried. And before she marries her new fiancé, whom I understand you know of, Coen Boonzaier, I thought it worth taking the trouble to ask you if you still harboured any ... well, *affectionate* feelings towards her.'

'Is this a joke, Mr Ransome?' asked Barney. 'Because if it is, it's in pretty poor taste.'

'A joke?' said Mr Ransome. His ears were very red in the morning sun light, with a tracery of crimson veins. 'Why on earth should I perpetrate a joke, especially of such a nature, and especially on you, whom I scarcely know?'

'You tell me.'

'Mr Blitz,' protested Mr Ransome, 'I *revere* Miss Marneweck. She is not only a young woman of considerable personal beauty, but a character of extraordinary fortitude, gentleness, and religious purity. By most, she is considered to be a fallen woman, particularly since she has conceived and borne a child out of wedlock. But even though she may have fallen, she has risen again, by virtue of her simplicity, her straightforwardness and her love of God.'

Barney pulled reflectively at the skin of his cheek. He

356

thought, for one kaleidoscopic moment, of all those days he had spent with Mooi Klip in the bungalow; of their nights together in that squeaking brass bed; of their kisses and their whispers and their walks along the dry tracks of Kimberley on those evenings when the sun was magnified by the day's heat and inflamed by the day's dust. He thought of their wedding-cake, and of all those days of happiness when Mooi Klip had been busying herself to marry him. He thought of the wedding-breakfast, smashed on the bungalow floor, and he thought of Joel.

'Mrs Marneweck loved me once, Mr Ransome,' said Barney. 'But I spent six hopeless years trying to persuade her that *I* still loved *her*, and that we ought to get married; and every time she turned me down. I admit that she was hurt by me and my brother, Mr Ransome – hurt very badly. But she hurt me, too. And that's why I was so suspicious when you asked me if I still felt any affection for her.'

'You still love her?' Mr Ransome asked, throatily.

Barney went across to the window, and stared out at the rough uncultivated ground of Vogel Vlei's gardens. One day there would be flowerbeds here, and gravel paths, and orange trees. One day there would be neatly-clipped topiary to amuse the children. One day there would be children. He turned around to Mr Ransome, and said distinctly, 'Yes. I still love her. I will probably love her for the rest of my life. But I'm married now. I married more than two months ago, when I was in Durban.'

Mr Ransome's mouth opened and closed silently, and he looked around at the day-room as if he expected to see a thunderoulsy vengeful wife materialising out of the upholstery or bursting out of the drapes. 'You're married?' he squeaked and growled, in his breaking voice. 'I had no idea. I don't know what to say.'

'It's not your fault,' Barney told him. He wished, unconditionally, that the painful tightness that was congesting his chest would go away. He also wished more than anything that he had never found out that Mooi Klip still loved him. *She still loved him* – after everything she had said, after all those arguments and all those rebuffs, after all those visits and all. *She* still loved him, after all these years. He felt raw all over, flayed. This stuttering clergyman might just as well have come into the room and lashed him with wire, until he bled.

He loved Sara, he knew it. But the love he felt for Sara was part of the love he felt for his own career, and his own future. Sara would help him get into the Kimberley Club. Sara would act as the perfect hostess, the wife who knew that 'don't you know' was fashionably pronounced 'don't-chi-know', and that nobody of any breeding said 'doin'' or 'thinkin'' as if they had 'g' on the end. She was also quite aware without having to be told that soup was never helped twice, that gentlemen who called at lunchtime and were invited to join the meal should always take their hat and their cane in to the dining-room, and that a visiting card must be *exactly* three inches by one-and-one-half inches, and printed in italics.

She was almost beautiful, too. Her face was well-boned, and her body was trim from all those years of riding. Her hair was soft. Her eyes were extraordinary. Her nipples were like azalea peatals that had fallen into bowls of cream.

Sara was everything a rich diamond-miner could want; except that she was not Mooi Klip.

Mr Ransome said, unhappily, 'I think I'd better leave. I'm sorry that I came.'

'What will you tell Natalia?' asked Barney.

'Simply that you're married. You wouldn't want me to say that you still love her, would you?'

'No,' said Barney, 'I suppose not.'

'It wouldn't be proper,' Mr Ransome insisted. 'After all, whatever your emotions, you have now made a lifelong commitment to your new wife.'

'Thank you, I'm aware of that,' said Barney.

'I'll go, then,' flustered Mr Ransome. 'My horse could do with a drink.'

'I'll have one of the blackies take it round to the trough for you.'

'Thank you. And, well, I'm very sorry to have troubled you this way. I thought that my errand was all for the best; but as it turned out, it was all for the worst. I'm sorry.'

Barney showed Mr Ransome to the door; but, as he opened

it wider, he thought he heard the squeak of a sandal on the polished hall floor outside. He looked quickly around to see if there was anyone there, but the hall was deserted. All he could detect was the faintest aroma of musk, and curry, and sweat.

'Nareez?' he queried. His voice echoed across the hallway. Mr Ransome gave him an uncomprehending smile. 'There doesn't seem to be anybody there, Mr Blitz.'

'No,' said Barney. 'But perhaps when there isn't anybody there, that's the time to start worrying.'

One of the servants came across the hall, a thin-legged Malay with spectacles so thick that they made his eyes look like two freshly-opened oysters. 'You were ringing, Mr Blitz? More tea?'

Barney turned to Mr Ransome, but Mr Ransome gave a modest little shake of his head, and raised his hand in an unconsciously Jesus-like gesture of polite refusal. 'I think it would be better all around if I just went quietly back to Klipdrift, don't you?'

That night, when Barney came back to Vogel Vlei from a long meeting with Harold Feinberg, frayed and tired, he found the bedroom door locked against him. He shook the handle once or twice, and then knocked.

'Sara? It's Barney! Come and open the door!'

There was no answer, so he knocked again, and rattled the handle more furiously. 'Sara! Please! What's going on?'

He listened for nearly a minute, but still there was no response. He shook the handle again, and finished up by giving the bottom of the door a thunderous kick with the toe of his veld boot. 'Sara! You must be in there! Open up at once! You're not still sulking about sharing a bedroom, are you? Sara?'

He stood in the darkness outside the door and waited. Whatever the reason, Sara was plainly not going to answer, nor was she going to open up. Still, there was a spare key to the bedroom in the butler's pantry downstairs, and since the workmen had not yet been around to fit sliding bolts to any of the doors, he would be able to open the bedroom up without any trouble. Tired and angry, he stamped downstairs again, crossed the hall, and pushed his way into the kitchen.

359

Kitty was still there, slicing beef for tomorrow's breakfast. So was Gentleman Jack and their new groom John Gcumisa, a laconic, woolly-haired Zulu who had originally cared for Jan Brand's horses in Bloemfontein. The two blacks put down their teacups and stood to uneasy attention when Barney walked in, and nodded to him in bashful deference. 'Good evening, Mr Blitzboss, sir.'

'I want the key to the master bedroom suite,' said Barney.

Kitty laid down her knife, wiped her hands on her apron, and went into the butler's pantry to find it. Barney waited in the middle of the blue and white tiled kitchen floor, his shoulder muscles crowded with tension, while Gentleman Jack and John Gcumisa stood silently staring at him, their tea steaming in white enamel mugs, and all the paraphernalia of the private evening which Barney had so suddenly interrupted lying on the table all around them: buttons, thread, playing-cards, matches, and a blue paper packet of tobacco.

'Here,' said Kitty, laying the key in Barney's hand. Barney looked at it, and then squeezed it in between tightly closed fingers.

'Everything's all right, Mr Blitz?' asked Kitty, although she posed the question in such an oblique tone that anybody else would have thought it was a statement of simple fact.

'Thank you, Kitty,' said Barney. 'Just – get on with what you have to do. You too, Jack.'

'Yes, sir, Mr Blitzboss.'

As Barney went to the door, Kitty said, gently, 'I saw the Reverend Ransome this morning, Mr Blitz. I used to know him, when he first came to Klipdrift.'

'Yes?'

Kitty kept her head down, wrapped in its black and red scarf. Her gold hoop earrings swung in the lamplight. 'He didn't tell no tales, sir. But he explained to me why he came here. And he said he was very sorry that things worked out the way they did.'

Barney laid his hand on Kitty's shoulder. 'I think I understand what you're trying to tell me,' he said. 'But you know that I'll appreciate it more if you keep it to yourself.'

'Yes, sir, I know that.'

Barney climbed the curved stairs to the upper landing again, holding the key to the bedroom door so tightly that it made a scarlet impression on his palm. Before he tried to open the door he looked down at his hand and thought: what would a palmist make of this? The key line? The line that showed which doors would open and which would close? Which doors would bring happiness and which would bring tears?

The worst part of it was, he already suspected why Sara was refusing to let him in. If Nareez had overheard his conversation this morning with Mr Ransome, there was no question at all that she would have told Sara all about it. And if Sara had believed that he still loved a Griqua woman, a woman who had given birth to his only child, her English sense of moral indignation would already have been stirred beyond any hope of reasonable recovery. Sara had been brought up, like all good colonial girls, to be a brick in times of native attack or malaria, but a swooner and a locker of doors in times of marital difficulty.

'Sara!' Barney shouted. 'I've got a key and I'm coming in!'

He unlocked the door, and pushed it. Sara had wedged one of the bedroom chairs under the handle but not firmly enough; and Barney had only to tussle against it with his shoulder, grunting, and the chair fell away. Then he threw the door wide, and burst in.

Sara was sitting up in bed, the sheets clutched to her breasts, her eyes wide with hysterical indignation and fright. Next to her sat Nareez, her hair wound up into a calico mobcap, equally wide-eyed, and equally frightened.

'You've no right!' shrilled Sara.

'No *right*?' Barney demanded. 'I built this house out of my own sweat and blood. And you're trying to tell me that I have no *right*?'

'Not after what Nareez heard you saying today, no. You brought me heah under the falsest of pretences. You gave me to believe that you loved me. You lied to me. You tricked me. And I believed you.'

'Oh, sure,' said Barney. 'It was all a practical joke. I travelled more than five hundred miles to Durban, and more than five hundred miles back, just to get a cheap laugh. You stun me

361

sometimes, Sara. You stun me! Yesterday, you were arguing against our sleeping together. Today, you're convinced that I was lying to you when I said that I loved you. What do you want? What do you want me to say? I thought I said it all already in the church, and in the temple. I said I wanted you for my wife, if you can remember, that I was going to love you and cherish you from this day forth. Cherish! What a promise that is! And now you're trying to tell me that you don't believe me? That you don't think I actually meant it?'

Sara, her voice shaky, said, 'You told that clergyman that you were still in love with a woman called Natalia.'

'Who told you that?' snapped Barney.

'Well,' said Sara, petulantly, 'Nareez.'

'Nareez,' Barney nodded. 'The *kibitzer* from Bengal.'

'She wanted to *protect* me, that's all,' Sara protested. 'You can't possibly blame her for that. She was passing the day-room, so she told me, and she couldn't help overhearing.'

Barney walked around the bed until he was only inches away from Nareez. The *amah* pulled the bedspread right up to her chin, and stared at him in hypnotised alarm.

'I did know a woman called Natalia,' said Barney, much more quietly, 'and, a very long time ago, I did love her. Didn't *you* have other loves? How about your old Etonian?'

Sara looked across at him sharply, but then she flinched, and looked away. 'I wasn't to know that you would come back for me, was I? And I certainly wasn't to know that poor Trevor would die.'

'No, quite,' said Barney. 'But just like it was for you with Trevor, that's the way it was for me with Natalia. Everything else you've heard about it is gossip. Eavesdropping, maliciously misreported.'

'You can't say that!' babbled Nareez. 'What you are saying is slander! What I heard was quite by accident, from open door. If you do not closet yourself in secrecy, then you must expect people to listen. This is open house.'

'You think it's an open house, do you?' Barney demanded. 'You think you can wander where you please, listening in to private conversations, and meddling in other people's marriages?'

'Miss Sara is not other people. Miss Sara is my charge.'

'Don't interrupt me, you fat Indian *shtunk*. Just get out of my bed and don't let me catch you in here again.'

'Barney, this is awful!' Sara exclaimed. 'Poor Nareez was only –'

'Get the hell out of my bed!' Barney bellowed. 'Get your big fat smelly carcass out of my bed!'

Nareez, incensed, threw back the covers, picked up her lopsided silk slippers, and pushed past Barney to the door. 'You haven't heard the very last of this, you devil!' she cried, wagging her finger at him. 'You certainly haven't heard the last! I know what I heard in the day-room! I know what you said, about loving that girl! Well, Miss Sara is my charge! Ever since birth I have nursed Miss Sara, and not you nor anybody will hurt her! I'll see to that!'

Barney took a deep breath. 'I want you to leave my bedroom, Nareez,' he said, in a voice that trembled like a telegraph wire under gradually increasing tension. 'I want you to leave my bedroom and I don't want you ever – *ever* – to set foot in here again. And there's something else, before you go. I never want you to call Mrs Blitz "Miss Sara" again. Her name, to you, is Mrs Blitz. And – wait – there's one thing more. I want you to go downstairs and tell Kitty to come up here and change the sheets. Tell her they were inadvertently soiled.'

Nareez glared at Barney with hatred. In her mob cap and her voluminous nightgown, with her long black braid hanging down her back, Barney thought that she looked like an enraged caliph out of the Arabian nights. She slammed the door behind her, and left Barney and Sara alone.

Barney walked across to the bureau, unfastening his gold and diamond cufflinks.

'You're undressing?' asked Sara, rather shrilly.

'You prefer me to get into bed with my clothes on?'

'I prefer you not to get into bed at all.'

Barney made a deliberately patient performance of putting his cufflinks and collar-stud back in their red velvet box, and closing the drawer of the bureau. He could see Sara in the mirror, sitting upright in bed with her arms crossed over her breasts. The oil-lamp beside the bed lit her face in an odd way, and made her look different. She could have been her own sister; or a stand-in from the theatre.

'If you must know, Sara,' said Barney, enunciating his words with exaggerated care, 'I am extremely tired. I have been talking business most of the evening with Harold, and all I want to do right now is get into bed and sleep.'

'Nareez was right, wasn't she?' asked Sara.

'Right about what? Nareez is never right about anything. She's a fussy, jealous, stupid, greedy, superstitious harridan.'

'How can you say such a thing?'

'I can say it because it's self-evident. Ever since we've been married, she's done nothing but interfere. She's always trying to make me look as if I'm some kind of lustful monster, intent on ruining your virtue. And the worst of it is, you let her.'

'I have to listen to her, Barney. She's my *amah*. She loves me.'

'Only children have *amahs*, Sara. You're quite old enough to look after yourself, without the help of some ignorant *platke-macher*. If I had anything to do with it at all, I'd pack up her bags and send her back to Durban on the next waggon. *Biryani* and all.'

Sara watched Barney as he unbuttoned his underwear with an expression that he could not quite understand. It was more concerned than remote, and yet Barney was not at all certain if the concern she was feeling was for herself, or for Nareez, or for him. There was also an almost imperceptible tightening of the muscles around her eyes that reminded him of the way a young child looks when she anticipates a smack.

As he stepped out of his drawers and stood in front of her naked, it suddenly occurred to him that she might be afraid of him. Not afraid that he would hit her, or abuse her. But simply afraid of his ambition, and his Jewishness, and his growing self-assurance in a world which, to her, was unfamiliar and uncomfortable.

He was partly right. Sara came from a family that had brought her up in the traditional English colonial manner, and while she had been excited at the thought of marrying a man who had trekked five hundred miles to find her, and of living in a grand mansion on the brink of a diamond mine, she was quickly discovering that her romantic fantasy had betrayed her. Life in Kimberley with Barney Blitz was not going to be anything but difficult, isolated, and deprived. Barney was rich, all right, but what on earth was the use of being rich when there were no luxuries to be bought, no theatres to go to, no smart parties, no hunts, and none of the feverish social intrigue that made colonial life so absorbing. What was life without five o'clock tea, and supper dances, and the regular arrival on one of Papa's steamers of the season's modes from London? How could she survive without coddled eggs, and opera? And how she missed those evening chats with her mother, over hot chocolate and mint cake!

Her feeling of alienation from her new surroundings made her feel alienated from Barney, too. Watching him talk to heavyweight diamond dealers like Harold Feinberg and wild-eyed geologists like Edward Nork, seeing him barking out orders to the thirty mud-caked kaffirs who dug with picks and shovels at the Blitz Brothers' diamond claims, all this placed him in a strange and rough environment which Sara felt she could never possibly enter.

And what was more, as he stood naked in front of her, watching her with an expression which, to her, was just as incomprehensible as her expression was to him, there was the most significant symbol of his strangeness. His penis, with its bare, plum-coloured glans; the seal of God.

'I think I'd rather sleep alone tonight,' said Sara. 'Please . . . if you don't mind too much.'

'You still believe that Nareez was right?' Barney asked her.

'I don't know. I'm confused. I just want to lie here on my own and work it out for myself.'

Barney sat down on the edge of the bed. Sara, keeping the covers tight under her arm, turned away from him.

'Sara, there's something wrong between us, isn't there?' asked Barney, his voice as soft as the shadows that surrounded them.

'What could possibly be wrong?'

'I don't know. That's what I want to find out. I'm beginning to believe that perhaps you don't love me any more. Sometimes I find myself thinking that maybe you never loved me at all.'

Sara whispered, 'Do *you* love *me*?'

'Of course I do. You know it.'

'And you're sure you don't love anybody else? No girls called Natalia?'

Barney laid his hand on her shoulder, but she resisted his attempt to pull her towards him. 'You're my wife, Sara, that's the most important thing.'

'Is it? None of the colonial staff seemed to let their wives get in their way when they went chasing black women in Durban.'

'I'm not like that. And, in any case, I love you.'

She sat up in bed and looked at him intensely. 'Are you sure? You love me, and me alone?'

'Would I lie to you?'

'Make an oath,' she told him. 'Swear to me on the Bible that you love only me.'

Barney lifted his hand and touched her hair. 'Do you have to ask me to swear on the Bible to know whether I love you or not?'

'If you really do love me, it'll be easy.'

The bedroom seemed suddenly airless to Barney, and sweltering hot. He could still smell *jeera* on the sheets, too, from that Bengali woman. He stood up, and went to the window to open the white-painted shutters out wider.

'I took a solemn oath in church, and in the synagogue,' he told Sara. 'I'm not going to go through the rest of my married life being forced into reaffirming it. I love you, and that's all you need to know.'

'I see,' said Sara, with unexpected crispness, as if she had just been told by a servant that he had taken two sacks of brown sugar home without permission. 'In that case, Nareez wasn't mistaken.'

'For God's sake!' Barney flared up. 'How much longer am I going to have to live under the regime of that sow of an *amah* of yours?'

Sara thrashed her way out of the bed-covers, went to the wardrobe, and took down her long white robe with a rattle of clothes-hangers.

'What are you doing?' Barney shouted. 'Just because I happen to object to having my marriage messed around by some –'

366

'It's nothing to *do* with that,' Sara burst out, going to the door and opening it as furiously as Nareez had slammed it. 'It's all to do with love, and trust, and taking care of me. You don't have the first idea, do you, how strange and horrible this place seems to me. I'm miserable already, and I've only been here two days. You haven't done anything to comfort me, or make me feel at home. You've done nothing but shout at me, and shout at Nareez. Well, I think your behaviour has been utterly beastly and I'm not going to stay with you one moment longer!'

'Sara –'

'I won't listen! You're hateful!' And with that, she ran off down the corridor on bare feet, mewling like a self-pitying ghost.

Barney stood still for a moment, staring at the open door. Then he walked over with a tired sigh and closed it. For the first time in a long time, he felt like a drink. He sat down on the end of the bed, his chin propped on his hands, and wondered abstractedly how Mooi Klip was, and how much Pieter had grown since he had been away.

He slept on Sara's side of the bed, but he still slept badly. At five o'clock he woke up after dreaming a dream about Gentleman Jack tracking mud all over his new rugs, and climbed stiffly out of bed. He knelt in front of the window, while the incandescent rim of the sun came edging over his window-ledge from the other side of the world, and he said *schachris*, the morning prayer, with more entreaty in his voice than he had ever said it before.

He was given the first hint by Harold Feinberg, two days later, early on Friday afternoon. They had met for three hours with the unctuous, stiff-collared lawyers of the Rose Innes Diamond Mining Company, negotiating the purchase of six more claims. Normally, Joel would have joined in the negotiations, too, but it was one of those odd days when the barometric pressure drops, and the skies of north Cape Colony grow soft and grey, and fretful dust-storms whip up on the veld. On days like these, Joel would retreat to his private suite of rooms at the back of Vogel Vlei, and lie on his bed with the drapes drawn, his whole existence decaying with pain.

367

On days like these, not even whiskey and morphia would help. The cramp in his bones seemed to attack him like a wild beast. When he heard that a kaffir had been attacked and mauled by a lioness, he simply laughed. 'I've been eaten by lions a hundred times over.'

Harold had looked tired during the meeting. He was several stones overweight these days, and he had been complaining that his heart had been slow-dancing like an elephant in a Hungarian ballet. 'It's the work,' he complained, although Joel thought it had much more to do with the pretty young French girl from Natal, the girl he had once fancied himself, and who had recently been seen on Harold's arm on Kimberley's main street, and sharing supper with him at the Woodhouse Restaurant.

By three o'clock, Barney had come to an arrangement with the Rose Innes lawyers that Blitz Brothers would purchase four of their claims for £75,000, and take out a two-week option on the remaining two. The lawyers offered handshakes that were as reticent and scaly as turkey claws, and then left. Harold went to the rolltop desk in the corner of his office, took out a bottle of brandy, and poured himself a large glassful.

'You want some? Just to celebrate?' he asked Barney.

Barney, standing by the window, shook his head. Below him, in the street, he had just caught sight of Agnes Joy, *née* Knight, in the company of two tall young diggers. He recognised the diggers as Hugh Johnson and David Mackie, the successful young owners of the Cape Star Diamond Company. Apart from Barney himself, Johnson and Mackie were two of the richest men in town. Agnes threw her head back in silent laughter, and Barney saw Mackie give her a quick, saucy squeeze.

Harold joined Barney at the window, sipping his brandy. 'That's Agnes, isn't it?' he asked, and Barney nodded. 'She ought to be more circumspect, that girl. She's getting herself a reputation.'

'What for? Walking along the street laughing?'

'You know what I mean. I shall never know why she married that thick Australian from the drama club. He couldn't even act.'

Barney said, 'I guess I'd better be going home. Sara was planning on an early supper tonight.'

'How's she settling down?'

'Not too bad. It's a little rougher here than she expected, but I guess she'll get used to it.'

Harold gestured towards the window, with its view of brick façades and corrugated-iron rooftops and chimneys. 'In five years' time, she won't even recognise the place. It'll look like the West End of London. Do you remember what it was like when you first came here? That terrible old shack I used to work in, with the Irish whore next door? Those were the rough days!'

Barney took his hat from the hatstand, and brushed the top of it with his sleeve. 'I'm pretty satisfied with the Rose Innes arrangement,' he said, 'But I want to start pushing the Octahedron Company as soon as I can. We've got the capital; it's about time we started building up some momentum. We've been too slow lately, don't you think? I know I've been away, but Rhodes has already bought up a third of the De Beers mine, one way or another, and I'm damned if I'm going to let him outstrip me.'

'I heard that Rhodes has teamed up with Alfred Beit,' remarked Harold.

'Alfred Beit? Didn't he work for Lippert & Company, in Hamburg?'

'He used to. But then they made him a partner of Jules Porges, and as everybody knows, they're the wealthiest diamond merchants in the whole world, bar none. He's a genius. You think I'm a genius? Beit can remember almost every stone he's ever handled. One of Duncan's men tried to sell him some stolen gems, and he recognised them straight away as the same gems that had passed through his hands seven years ago.'

Barney raised his eyebrows. 'So we're in for some stiff competition, then?'

'From Beit, sure. Beit once told me that his only aim in life was to own every single diamond mine in Africa.'

'Looks like he and Rhodes are going to get on well.'

Harold accompanied Barney downstairs to the front door of the office, so that he could lock up. On the way down, he said off-handedly, 'By the way, did you hear about the giant diamond yet?'

369

Barney opened the front door of the office, and the noises of the hot afternoon came in – waggons, and laughter, and the distant *shuggg-shuggg-shuggg* of steam-powered winding-gear. A Bantu was sitting on the boardwalk outside blowing a soft, monotonous tune out of an instrument like an ocarina. 'Giant diamond?' asked Barney, shaking his head. 'What is it, a leg-pull?'

Harold leaned against the door, sweating. He loosened his tie to take some of the pressure off his throat. 'I'm not sure,' he said, 'I heard a garbled kind of a story from one of the kaffirs who works out at Isaacs' claim. All he said was, 'Boss, how much a gemstone worth as big as this?'' and he made a circle with his finger and his thumb, like this, so that the tip of his finger and the tip of his thumb just touched.'

'Diamonds don't come that big,' said Barney. 'Not here in South Africa, anyway.'

'Why not?' said Harold. 'There was the Koh-i-Noor, wasn't there – one hundred and eight carats. And the French Blue, sixty-seven carats. And, I forgot – the Florentine was one hundred and thirty-seven carats.'

'Sure, but all of those diamonds were Indian, weren't they? And a diamond as big as your kaffir tried to describe would be twice the size of any of those – twice the size of the Florentine. It's just a fairy-story, Harold, that's all. You know what the kaffirs are like when they've been at the whiskey.'

'I don't know,' said Harold, 'he didn't *seem* to be drunk, and he didn't seem to be trying to spin me any kind of yarn. He just said, "How much a gemstone worth as big as this?" and when I told him it would depend on who you could find to buy such a stone, rather than the current market price of diamonds, he said, "Difficult to sell, then, boss?" and I said, "Yes, of course," I mean – if he was seriously talking about a diamond in excess of three hundred carats, then my own guess is that you could ask over a million pounds for it. Perhaps more, if you could persuade a government to buy it.'

Barney swung the door backwards and forwards, feeling the draught against his face. There was something about this tale of a giant diamond that irritated his consciousness in the same way that grit can irritate a clam. There was something about

370

it which seemed to make other feelings that he had been having since he returned from Durban fit uneasily into place.

'What else did this kaffir say?' he asked Harold. 'Did he say that he'd actually *seen* a diamond as big as the one he was talking about?'

'No,' said Harold. 'But I can't think why he asked me, unless he had. And where could he have seen it? That was the question I asked myself.'

'Isaacs only borders on to three other claims. Francis and Company, the Griqualand Diamond Mining Company, and mine. So, we've got a choice of four.'

'Yours included,' said Harold.

'Yes,' agreed Barney, 'mine included.'

'What worries me is the implications of someone discovering a stone that size,' Harold said, patting his forehead with his bunched-up handkerchief. 'They might get themselves a million pounds, personally, but you know what effect it'll have on the market, don't you? The diggers will start producing twice as fast as usual, all trying to dig up the big one, and the market's going to be flooded again, just like it was in '74. It's taken us almost four years to get the prices up from '74, and if they go down again, well, a lot of diamond dealers are going to be ruined.'

Barney laid a hand on Harold's shoulder. 'I shouldn't worry. It's probably on ly a wild rumour. Maybe somebody dug up a hefty piece of quartz.'

'I don't know,' said Harold. 'I just don't know. But keep it to yourself, won't you? An imaginary diamond can cause almost as much of a panic as a real diamond.'

'Well – you can console yourself with one thing,' said Barney. 'What we did this afternoon, buying up most of Rose Innes, that's a step in the right direction. One day, you'll have just two or three diamond companies controlling the whole of South African mining, and then we can fix the prices as high as the public will pay.'

Harold held his hand over his chest. He was short of breath now, and he was sweating so much that his face looked as if it had been basted in honey. 'I don't suppose I shall live to see it.'

'Are you all right?' Barney asked him, frowning.

Harold nodded. 'Too much work,' he said, and each word was an abrupt gasp. 'You get along now. I'll see you on Wednesday, for your celebration dinner.'

Barney stood in the doorway until Harold had climbed heavily back up the stairs to his office. Then he stepped out into the dull, humid afternoon, adjusted his hat, and walked slowly along the boardwalk to the sidestreet where his carriage was waiting. His new black driver, Michael, was sitting up on the box in shirtsleeves, ragged trousers, and a formal black opera hat. The staff uniforms had yet to be ordered from Capetown.

'Back to Vogel Vlei, boss?' asked Michael, twitching his whip.

Barney said absent-mindedly, 'Yes.' Then, 'Michael?'

'Yessir, boss?'

'Has anyone spoken to you lately about a diamond?'

Michael whistled at the horses, and they wheeled edgily around in a semi-circle. 'Diamond, boss? One diamond special, boss?'

'That's right. One diamond special.'

'Well, boss, I did hear something.'

Barney sat back in his seat, his legs crossed, trying to appear relaxed. 'What did you hear, Michael? Did someone tell you about a giant diamond? Big as an eagle's egg?'

'You heard it too, boss.'

'Was that all you heard? You don't know who found it, or where?'

'No, sir, boss. But what I did hear was that someone was paying money to keep the story quiet.'

'And you don't know who that "someone" was?'

Michael drove the horses out along Main Street until they cleared the last of the offices and houses and lean-to stores. The day was as dull as a photograph. 'If I knew who that "someone" was, boss, I'd be round to his door myself, asking for hush-me-up money. Not that you don't pay me good, boss. You pay goodest in Kimberley.'

Barney did not answer. He was trying to remember something that someone had said to him during the past two or three days. A word, a fragmented phrase. A feeling that something

372

extraordinary had happened, and that he was being deliberately kept in the dark about it.

Joel was out of bed when Barney returned to Vogel Vlei, but still in a difficult temper. He had ordered tea once and then sent it all back because it was cold, and because there were not any spongecakes. Now he was sprawled on the couch with his left leg propped up on heaps of cushions, drinking whiskey out of the neck of the bottle and humming to himself in an oddly threatening way.

Barney came into the drawing-room and crossed the Indian carpet to the open French windows without even glancing at Joel. In the middle distance, like a scene from one of those perpetually enchanted landscapes by Claude Lorraine, two kaffirs worked at the stony ground with hoes, levelling the wide area which Barney eventually hoped to use as a paddock. There was a dry, aromatic smell in the air; a smell which, years later, would always remind Barney of Africa. The sun gilded the dusty furrows, and flashed on the blades of the kaffirs' uplifted hoes, and Barney could hear the men talking from almost a quarter of a mile away.

'Your lady wife is preparing her hair for supper,' announced Joel, in a blotchy voice. 'No!' he giggled. 'That's wrong! She is *not* preparing her hair for supper – that is, she is not preparing her hair for us to *eat* for supper – she is – preparing her hair – in *time* for supper.'

Barney closed the French windows and locked them. 'How much have you drunk?' he asked, flatly.

'In proportion to the intoxicating effect of the Dover's powders I have consumed, scarcely anything. This is only my second bottle, as a matter of fact, and I puked up most of the first.'

'Give it to me,' said Barney, holding out his hand.

Joel clutched the bottle to his chest, and slowly and emphatically shook his head. 'Not on your life, little brother.'

'All right,' agreed Barney. 'But if you want to go on drinking, to back to your room. I don't want you lying here, making an exhibition of yourself.'

373

'Exhibition? Me?' protested Joel.

'Just get upstairs,' Barney told him.

'Oh, you can talk about exhibitions. You're a fine one! As if the whole household doesn't know that you kicked Nareez out of your bedroom the other night, and that you and Sara haven't slept together more than once since you've been back! Exhibitions! You can talk about exhibitions!'

'Just get out,' snapped Barney.

'I'm going,' Joel cautioned him. 'I'm on my way. But if I were you, I'd really try to keep my personal life a little quieter. I would, really! It's not good for staff spirit, you know, all this argy-bargy upstairs.'

'Get out of here before I kick you out,' Barney ordered him.

Unsteadily, hobbling and hopping from one piece of furniture to the next, clutching at the moulding on top of the cream-painted dado for support, Joel made his way to the stairs. Barney followed a few paces behind him.

'You're a fool, you know,' gasped Joel, at the foot of the stairs. 'The most contemptible fool I've ever come across.'

Then, gripping the bannister rail, hand-over-hand, Joel began his agonising climb to the second-floor landing. Barney, tight-mouthed with anger and frustration and sheer despair, stood at the bottom of the stairs and watched him, not moving, not once attempting to help. The terrible part of it was that he *wanted* to help, he *wanted* to run up those five or six stairs and take Joel's arm; he wanted to show that in spite of everything they were still brothers, borne by the same mother, *alevasholem*, and raised in the same tenement on Clinton Street. But Joel at last had reached the upper landing, and was leaning over the bannisters with a face as grotesque as a dried-clay gargoyle.

'You hear me, *gonif*!' he shouted. 'You should keep your marital failures to yourself!' And with that, he shuffled and stumbled back to his bedroom, colliding with the brassbound linen-chest as he went.

Barney mounted the first stair, intent on following him; but then he stopped himself, and lowered his head, and turned back. He had followed Joel too many times after too many arguments, and he knew only too well how illogical and fierce his brother could be when he was drunk and drugged. Even if

374

Barney did succeed in calming him down, and settling all of their differences, Joel would usually have forgotten by the following morning what they had talked about, and he would sit at the breakfast-table white-faced and incommunicative, eating nothing but dry toast, painfully attempting to overcome both severe morphia withdrawal and a pounding hangover. Dr Truter, who came to examine Joel every two or three weeks with his untidy brown leather bag and his green-corroded stethoscope, had whispered to Barney on several occasions that it was 'an Act of God' that Joel was still alive.

As Barney crossed the hallway on his way back to the sitting-room, Michael came walking quickly towards him on slapping slippers, and said, 'Mr Blitz, sir?'

'What is it, Michael?'

'Someone to see you, boss. In the kitchen.'

'In the *kitchen*? What do you mean, in the kitchen? Who is it?'

Michael hesitated, and then glanced cautiously up the stairs. 'An old friend, sir,' he said, in a confidential tone.

'An old –?' began Barney, but then he looked at Michael's meaningful expression, and he realised who it was. At least, he *thought* he realised who it was. 'Lead the way,' he said, brusquely. Michael turned immediately and slip-slapped back towards the servants' quarters. 'One of those funny days, boss,' he remarked.

'Yes,' said Barney, without even hearing him.

She was waiting for him at the far end of the cluttered kitchen table, posed on a spare bentwood chair as if she were having her portrait painted. The dull daylight shone through the lacy curtains behind her and blurred the outline of her severe black travelling-coat and her small fashionable hat, so that Barney felt as if he were seeing her through tears.

'Natalia,' he said, walking forward and taking her hands. He kissed her fingers, and then he bent down and kissed her cheek, which was still just as soft, and perfumed with that same elusive musk.

'Well,' she said bravely, 'I hear that you're married.'

'Yes,' he told her. He cleared aside a tin cheese-grater and half of a red cabbage, and perched himself on the edge of the kitchen table. 'I was married in Durban, to an English girl.'

'Kitty told me.'

Barney looked up at Kitty, who was ostentatiously keeping herself busy by scouring the baking-trays and clattering the milk pans. He smiled, and then turned back to Mooi Klip. He thought she looked tired. There were dark shadows under her eyes, and she seemed to have lost weight.

'You can't keep a secret long if you tell it to Kitty,' Barney confessed. 'But how are you? Did you just arrive from Klip-drift?'

'This afternoon. One of the diggers had to come over here for equipment, pumps and shovels, and he gave me a ride.'

'And Pieter?'

'He's staying with Mama and Papa.'

'He's well?'

'He's wonderful. He's starting to read.'

'You're a good mother, Natalia.'

There was a moment's silence. Mooi Klip twisted the diamond engagement ring on her finger around and around and around, and did her best to keep up a collected smile. But Barney had lived with her long enough to know how unsettled she felt, and that she had something else to tell him. So he sat on the edge of the table and waited for her to come to the point. His father would have said abruptly, 'What's the *tachlis*, my friend?' – 'Let's get down to the nitty-gritty.' For Barney, it was enough just to wait.

'I had a visit from Mr Ransome yesterday,' said Mooi Klip, at last. 'That was right after he came back from talking to you.'

'You knew he was coming here? I mean, before he came?'

Mooi Klip nodded. The sun caught the curls on the top of her head, and made them shine like the shavings of lathe-cut copper. 'It was his idea, to begin with. But I didn't do anything to stop him. I didn't know you were married, you see. Neither of us did. If I had – well, I don't know what difference it would have made.'

'I didn't think you loved me,' said Barney, quietly.

'I *didn't*,' she said. 'Not for quite a long time. I was frightened of you, believe it or not, and I was frightened of Joel, and

376

I was also frightened by the things you used to say. You used to talk of owning the whole of Kimberley. That was too much for me. Too heady. Do you know how rich a man would be, if he owned the whole of Kimberley? He would be like a god. I used to lie awake, thinking about that. If you became as rich as that, I would have had to meet princes and maharajahs and even kings. We would have had to hold banquets! An uneducated Griqua women like me would have done nothing but shame you.'

'I don't know how you can talk like that,' said Barney, standing up, and walking around to the back of her chair. 'I loved you that day when I was going to marry you, and I love you still. You could have faced up to princes and maharajahs as well as anybody. In any case, don't talk to me about maharajahs. It's closed season for Indians in this house, right at the moment.'

'Kitty told me about Nareez.'

'Well, you'd better believe what she says,' grinned Barney. 'Nareez is a human curry. Better out of your system than in.'

'I still wasn't right for you, Barney, was I?' said Mooi Klip, in the gentlest of voices. 'At least, you didn't think I was. I know you loved me, and I believe you when you say that you still love me, even today. But you didn't try too hard to get me back, did you? That was what I was afraid of, that was why I always chased you away. You were always willing to admit defeat a little too early; you were never willing to come back and back and back until I didn't have any choice at all but to say that I was going to be your wife.'

Barney blew out his cheeks. 'I tried as hard as I knew how. How can you say I didn't try?'

Mooi Klip turned around in her chair and took Barney's hands. Her eyes were dry of tears, but there was a look of such hopelessness and regret on her face that Barney felt as if he wanted to vaporise everything around him, dissolve Vogel Vlei, and return to those months in the bungalow when there was nothing but laughter and lovemaking and evenings around the fire. The months before Joel's rape, and Sara Sutter.

'I just came down here to make sure that you really *were* married,' said Mooi Klip. 'Well – I knew that it had to be true

377

if Mr Ransome had told me. But I wanted to say goodbye, too. I shall probably marry Coen Boonzaier, I suppose, and spend the rest of my life in a *strooidak* farmhouse, speaking Afrikaans and baking soda bread.'

'I promised I would drape you with diamonds, didn't I?' said Barney, sadly.

She ran the tip of her finger across the four bruised hills of his knuckles. 'Don't worry about keeping promises. Promises are only a way of saying that you love somebody, and that you want to give them everything. Lovers don't expect their promises to come true.'

'Natalia . . .' said Barney, but Mooi Klip rose from her chair, and took hold of his arms, and shook her head to show him that she did not want him to say any more.

'You're married now. You love your wife. Don't spoil everything.'

Barney could not look at her. It was only now, seeing her here, that he realised what a catastrophic mistake he had made. He felt as if the walls of the house were slowly collapsing in on him; as if every second of every minute for the rest of his life had now become a claustrophobic burden. He had married Sara with such confidence and happiness, and he knew that it had been the right thing to do. Sara had been a little 'mature' for marriage, but unquestionably pretty, and still a good colonial 'catch'. She would guide him and grace him through countless business receptions and dinners and political soirées, her big breasts rising from her low-cut evening-gowns with patriotic buoyancy, her hair fussily plaited with ribbons and clips and pearls, and her voice as sharp and cultured as the diamonds on which her fortune depended. She and Barney would make love, once or twice, in tolerant breathlessness, and she would probably be fertile enough to bear him a son, and a daughter, and a second son with a penchant for breaking windows. They would travel widely, on steamers, in separate staterooms, and reach a wealthy and honourable old age, white-haired, forgetful, and eccentric, their memories of Africa fogged by time and distance and their own preposterous anecdotes. It had been the right thing to do; to marry Sara; for Queen and Empire and personal fortune.

The only agony was: he loved Mooi Klip.

'What I told Mr Ransome ... that was all true, you know,' he told her 'I still love you. I would still have you back.'

'You can't. Think of your wife.'

'Natalia, I don't know what to say. I just didn't believe that you felt anything for me any more. I was lonely. You don't even know how lonely. And, well, I thought that I loved her.'

He found that his throat was blocked with rising grief, and that he could not even tell Mooi Klip how much he wanted her. But he held her close to him, and through the linen of her travelling-suit he felt the body that he had loved on so many nights, and which had once been swollen with his own baby. A body that the laws of marriage and adultery now decreed that he should no longer touch. Lord, he could remember her naked shoulders, and the dark twin moles on either side of her spine. He could remember the way her neck felt, under her hair, when he stroked her. He could remember her nipples, wide and brown, and the softness of her breasts. He could feel in the palms of his hands the ghostly and half-forgotten sensation of her whole body, in the same way that an amputee can feel a ghostly image of his lost leg.

He could remember lying next to her in bed, their foreheads touching, doing nothing at all but talking for hours. He could remember teaching her the English for 'passion' and 'heady' and 'adorable'.

He had lost it all now, and he felt as shattered as if somebody close to him had died.

'I'd better go,' said Mooi Klip. 'I can't do you any good here. But I will write to you, and tell you how I am; and you can see Pieter whenever you want. He misses you.'

'I miss him,' said Barney, with tears in his eyes.

'Ssh,' whispered Mooi Klip, touching his tears with her fingertips. 'You are a rich, successful, proud, well-married man. Don't let your servants see that you are human, too.'

He gave her an unhappy smile. 'I guess you're right. Well, you *are* right. There's no use crying over – mismatched marriages – is there?'

'There's one thing more,' Mooi Klip told him, her voice so soft that he could scarcely hear her.

379

'What's that?'

'It's to do with diamonds. Kitty told me, but she wanted me to make sure that she wouldn't be punished, or sacked.'

'What is it?' asked Barney.

'First you must promise that you won't be angry with Kitty.'

Barney dropped his head down in resignation. 'Okay, if it's really necessary. I promise.'

'Kitty says that Gentleman Jack found a huge diamond on your property. It happened while you were away in Durban. But this diamond is so big that Kitty says it looks like the sun. As bright as the sun, she said.'

Barney looked up, startled. 'She's actually *seen* it?' he said, louder than he meant to. 'She's *seen* it, and it's *mine*?'

'You've heard about it?' asked Mooi Klip.

'Well, sure I've heard about it. Harold Feinberg told me this afternoon. I was probably the last to know, though. It sounds as if every diamond trader and every digger and every gossipy kaffir in Kimberley has been talking about it.'

'Kitty said that Gentleman Jack brought it along to the bungalow, a few days before you came back. He showed it to Joel, and Joel told Gentleman Jack to borrow Kitty's kitchen scales, so that he could weigh it.'

Barney glanced towards Kitty, but Kitty was scrubbing a tea-towel on her corrugated scrubbing-board with almost maniacal violence, determined not to hear what was being said about her at any price at all.

'Did Kitty hear Joel say how much the diamond weighed?' asked Barney. He felt extraordinarily light-headed, and his voice seemed to echo flatly inside his ears. So the giant diamond was more than a drunken kaffir's fantasy: it was real. And what was more incredible about the whole story, the diamond was *his*. Or it would have been his, if Joel had not taken charge of it.

Mooi Klip turned to Kitty and asked her something in Afrikaans. Without looking around, Kitty said, 'Twee en 'n half ons.'

'Two and a half ounces,' said Mooi Klip. 'They were careless enough to leave the weight on the scales when they brought them back into the kitchen.'

Barney made a quick calculation. Then, awed, he mouthed to Mooi Klip, 'Two and a half ounces is *three hundred fifty-five carats*. Do you know how much a stone like that could be *worth?*'

Mooi Klip shook her head. 'I don't care what it's worth. It's *your* fortune, Barney. It's all yours. But when Kitty told me, I couldn't resist passing it on. It isn't very often that you get the chance to take your revenge on somebody who's done you wrong; and I do think that Joel deserves everything he's going to get.'

'God, I should have married you the first day I set eyes on you,' said Barney.

She reached up and kissed him. 'Don't say any more. Please.'

'But this diamond –' he said, spreading out his hands. 'Why didn't Kitty tell me as soon as I got back? Or Gentleman Jack?'

'They're servants,' said Mooi Klip. 'All they want to do is get through the day without problems. They don't want trouble. Even when it's not their fault, they know they might lose their jobs. So, they say nothing. Anyway – who are they to tell tales on Mr Joel Blitzboss, really? They're employed to do what they're told, that's all. And Mr Joel Blitzboss told them to keep their mouths shut. He probably even paid them, too.'

Barney paced across the kitchen, and them smacked his fist into the palm of his hand. 'It all makes sense now! Joel wanted to leave for Capetown on the first possible waggon. Gentleman Jack wanted to know all about the legal rights of ownership of diamonds. It all makes complete sense! They found a giant diamond, and Joel decided to keep it a secret!'

Mooi Klip watched Barney with cautious respect. 'You won't hurt him, will you, Barney?'

'Who, Joel? I'll break his back!'

'Barney – don't even think of it. That's not the way you are. Why do you think I still love you? I know that you honour your loyalties, that's why. I want Joel to lose that diamond, but I don't want you to hurt him.'

Barney looked at Mooi Klip, and then abruptly pulled over a chair, and sat down. 'I'm broken apart,' he told her. 'Lord God, I'm broken apart.'

Mooi Klip knelt on the floor beside him, and grasped his hands tightly. 'I know,' she said, gently. 'I know you're upset. But try to be strong. Remember I love you, and that Pieter loves you. Remember who you are.'

Barney looked at her wryly. 'I'm a tailor, that's all. Blitz, Tailors, of Clinton Street, New York.'

'No,' she said, 'not to me. To me, you're Barney Blitz, the grand diamond millionaire. And you're Barney Blitz, the gentle lover, too. Think of both of those things when you talk to Joel. Remember that you're both of them; the strong and the sensitive. Then you won't think of hurting him. Only *pitying* him, for everything he's done.'

The kitchen door opened suddenly, and Gentleman Jack walked in. When he saw Barney and Mooi Klip together, he hesistated for a moment; and when Kitty flashed him a quick and cautionary look, he retreated towards the pantry.

'Jack,' said Barney, without looking around.

'Yessir, Mr Blitzboss?' said Jack, freezing in alarm, like a partygoer caught in a game of 'statues'.

'Jack, a funny thing has happened.'

'What's that, Mr Blitzboss?'

'Well,' said Barney, sitting up straight in his chair, but still keeping his head turned away from Gentleman Jack, 'it turns out that somebody has found a diamond on my property – a quite considerable diamond.'

'Mr Blitzboss?'

'You don't have to act stupid, Jack, You can save that for the Kimberley Dramatic Society. I understand that they're sorely in need of a black individual for their Christmas production of *Robinson Crusoe*.'

Gentleman Jack said nothing, but stood up sheepish and straight, and placed his hat on the draining-board.

'I'm not the kind of man who likes to punish people for innocent mistakes, Jack,' Barney continued. 'I believe that everybody's entitled to an error or two. I make them myself.' (And here Mooi Klip squeezed his hand.) 'But when it comes to stealing, that's different; and all I can say about people who steal is that they're breaking the eighth commandment which was given to Moses by the Lord Our God.'

'Yes, sir,' said Gentleman Jack, tentatively.

'So – when it turns out that somebody has found a diamond on my property – a quite considerable diamond – and when I haven't yet had any sight of that diamond, regardless of the fact that I've been back here at Vogel Vlei for more than a day or two – well, I can only assume that whoever found that diamond is hiding it from me.'

'I'd say that, yes, sir,' said Gentleman Jack.

'I didn't ask for your comments, or what you'd say,' said Barney, coldly. 'All I'm asking you to do is to pass it on to whoever is hiding my diamond from me that I intend to search this house from attic to basement, even if it means tearing up the floorboards, and that I'm going to unearth that diamond no matter what.'

'I don't know who took it, sir, I promise,' said Gentleman Jack.

Barney suddenly turned around and stared at him. 'I know you've been paid to keep your mouth shut, Jack, and I know that you're worried about your job. But let me tell you this: I have enough evidence to implicate you in the disappearance of this diamond, and if you don't co-operate by flushing it out for me, than I'm going to pass you over to the soldiers and have you hanged from a camelthorn tree, frock coat or not.'

Gentleman Jack reached for his hat, and smirked in terror. 'Whatever you say, boss.'

'That's right,' said Barney. 'Whatever I say.'

There was a frigid pause, and then Gentleman Jack tugged open the kitchen door, and rushed out.

When he was gone, Mooi Klip stood up, and kissed Barney's forehead. 'I have to be going, too.'

'At night?'

'I'm staying with some Griqua people in Kimberley, then I'm going back to Klipdrift tomorrow.'

'I'll come up to see you soon. I promise.'

'Don't make promises, Barney. Just think about the love we used to have, and the child we gave birth to, and that will be enough.'

'Natalia, don't go.'

'I have to, Barney.'

'Don't. Stay with me here, tonight.'

She shook her head. 'Our stars may have said that we should have been happy together; my almanac says that we should. But stars aren't everything. Time is more important, isn't it, and circumstance.'

'You've learned some long words.'

'Mr Ransome taught me. He said, "It's a question of circumstance."'

'Yes,' said Barney, reaching out for Mooi Klip's hand. 'I guess that Mr Ransome is right.'

Mooi Klip kissed him again, with great tenderness. '*Ek het jou lief*, Barney, *wat ookal gebeur*.'

Joel was almost asleep when there was a furtive scrabbling at the door of his bedroom. He opened one eye, and listened. The room was filled with a warm and dusky radiance as the sun set over the veld, and there was a noisy chorus of birds outside on the trees. The scrabbling was repeated, and then a stage whisper said, 'Mr Blitzboss, it's me, Jack. You have to open the door, Mt Blitzboss.'

'Jack?' said Joel. 'What in hell do you want? I'm trying to sleep.'

'I'm sorry, Mr Blitzboss; but it's urgent.'

'Come in, then, it isn't locked.'

Gentleman Jack opened the door, and stepped into the room in one long-legged stride, quickly closing the door behind him. 'Mr Blitzboss, we have absolute problems now.'

'What problems? Pass me that glass of water, will you?'

Jack handed over the water, and then stood beside Joel's bed flustered and fidgety while Joel drank. When he was finished, Joel handed him the empty glass.

'Now, what's so urgent that you have to wake me up?' Joel wanted to know.

'It's the diamond, Mr Blitzboss. Mr Barney's found out.'

'Found out what? What are you talking about? He's found out that someone discovered it, or that we've got it?'

'He's found out everything, sir. He knows when it was picked up, and how much it weighs, and he knows that you probably have it hidden, sir.'

384

Joel pulled himself upright in bed. 'Who told him? Who the devil told him? Was it you? I'll cut your worthless black ears off, if it was you!'

'Not me, sir. That Griqua girl Natalia Marneweck. She was here this afternoon, sir, talking to Mr Barney.'

'Of course, damn,' breathed Joel. 'She's a cousin of Kitty's, isn't she? Or something like that. That damned Natalia. What was she doing here anyway? Didn't she know that Barney was married?'

'I don't know, sir.'

'Well, she probably did,' said Joel. 'That's probably made Barney seem all the more attractive. She was always one of those snooty *schwarzehs* who only want what they can't get.'

Joel swung off the bed, reached for his stick, and then walked across to the ugly rosewood bureau at the side of his room. He fished a small brass key out of his vest pocket, and opened the second drawer down. Inside, wrapped in a blue silk scarf, lay the huge 350-carat diamond. Gentleman Jack looked at it nervously.

'Mr Barney said he was going to search the house, sir. Top to bottom. Rip up the floorboards, he said.'

Joel picked up the diamond and clutched it tightly in his hand. He had held it like this over and over again in the past few days, since Gentleman Jack had brought it from the mine. Sometimes, when the pain in his hips and legs had kept him awake nights, he had sat in his straight-backed armchair by the window with the diamond cupped in both hands, feeling with a kind of silent passion the way it absorbed his warmth. It was *his* diamond, and nobody else could have it. Nobody else could understand the mysterious grandeur of its incredible size, or the glittering dreams that were secretly crystallised within its depths. Joel had kissed it, and licked it, and held it against his heart. He had even caressed his penis with it, his eyes closed, his mind aroused with fantasies of riches and beautiful women.

'We're going to have to say that Kitty was lying,' said Joel.

'Lying, sir? But what would she lie for?'

'Just to get her own back, that's what for. She never liked me. We're going to have to say that she heard rumours about someone in Kimberley digging up a giant diamond, and that

385

she thought she'd get me into trouble by saying it was me. We're going to have to deny everything – deny it completely.'

'But what if Mr Barney searches the house, Mr Blitzboss? That's a big diamond, difficult to hide.'

'There are plenty of places where he'd never find it, Jack. I could bury it in the garden.'

'They're hoeing the garden right now, Mr Blitzboss. Some-one would see you; or maybe they'd even dig it up. And, anyway – how are you going to be sure that you can recover it in time to take it to Capetown with you? Mr Barney's going to be absolutely suspicious, sir, especially when you leave. You're going to have to be careful he doesn't insist on searching your luggage.'

'He doesn't have any right to search me, or my luggage.'

Gentleman Jack said warningly, 'I don't think Mr Barney's going to be too concerned about that, sir. He knows there's a fancy diamond around, sir, and he knows that it rightly belongs to him, and this time I don't think you're going to be able to put him off.'

'A *choleria* on him.'

'Sir,' said Gentleman Jack, 'you have to do something, sir. Maybe you should hand the diamond over, and say it was all a mistake. If Mr Barney finds that diamond hidden, sir, he's going to have me hung.'

'Don't be ridiculous. My brother doesn't have the guts to hang anybody.'

'Please,' persisted Gentleman Jack. 'I have people who depend on me, sir. And even if Mr Barney doesn't have me hung, sir, or flogged, I'll never be able to find good work again, sir.'

'You should have thought about that when you were so insistent about getting your share of the tainted proceeds,' Joel retorted. 'You make me sick, you mission-school niggers, you really do. It takes more than a white collar and a tailored grey coat to turn a four-legged animal into a man. I should know, I used to be a tailor myself. So you speak like a white man, and know your letters, and believe in Jesus Christ? I could train a dog to do the same, Jack, and at least a dog wouldn't come whining back to be sick on my rug, the way that you have, just because the meat got a little too rich for it.'

He held up the gleaming diamond in front of Gentleman Jack's wide-eyed face.

'Jack,' he said, 'this is *my* diamond. That's all I'm going to say. And if you breathe one word to Mr Barney about where it is, or where it's going, or if you even so much as admit that it *exists*, then God help me I'm going to murder you, and I mean it.'

Gentleman Jack gave an involuntary shiver. 'Mr Blitzboss,' he began, 'I really wish you'd –'

Joel whipped the diamond away, and clenched it in his fist, close to his chest. 'Don't say anything,' he warned. 'Don't appeal to my better nature, because until I've got this diamond out of Kimberley and safely on its way to Capetown, I can't afford to have one. Now, get out of here.'

Gentleman Jack backed away to the door. He opened it an inch or two, peered through to make sure that nobody was about, and then slipped away on tip-toe. Joel closed the door behind him, and turned the key.

The trouble was, Gentleman Jack was right. He could not hide the diamond inside the house, because no matter how clever he was, there was always a chance that Barney might actually find it; and if Barney found it, and took it away from him, Joel was not at all sure if he was going to be able to survive, physically or emotionally. The diamond promised endless luxury for the rest of his life; all the drugs he needed; all the comfort he craved; and freedom from Barney for ever. To lose it now would be unbearable. He might just as well blow his brains out and have done with it.

He sat down in his armchair and held the diamond up in front of him. A new life, made out of fused carbon. Fiery and vivid and endlessly tantalising, like a glimpse of the future seen through an elaborate arrangement of rainbow prisms.

He could not swallow it, like the kaffirs swallowed roughs out on the claims. It it did not choke him, or lodge permanently in his stomach, he would excrete it out within a day, and he would have to keep on swallowing it, again and again, until next Thursday, just before he left for Capetown. The very thought of it made him gag. He opened his mouth wide and tried to get the diamond inside, but it was impossible. It wedged against his teeth, and he knew that it would never go down his throat,

387

not without suffocating him, or tearing his larynx to shreds.

He could push it up inside his anus, he supposed, but that was another kaffir hiding-place that was too well known, and if Barney was really convinced that he was concealing it somewhere, Joel did not doubt that he would try a forcible body search.

Joel stood up, and went to the mirror. He stared at his reflection as if he expected it to tell him what to do. But what ideas could anyone give him – let alone this tired, pain-racked man in the shadowy room beyond his bureau? He was alone, as long as he wanted to keep this diamond for himself. Friendless, loveless, and running from both his brother and the law. He stared at his unsmiling image and wondered what it was that had brought him here, to this final fatal collision of temperament and greed.

The answer was probably his mother, whose problems were long since over but he could not think about her any more. There comes a time in everybody's life when resentment finally crumbles and flakes away. A sort of forgiveness by default.

Downstairs, Joel could hear voices, and clattering footsteps across the hall. Barney must be starting his search already, turning the house upside-down in a bustle of righteous possessiveness. God, that he should have been born into such a family. God, that he should have been born at all.

He looked towards the half-open bathroom door, and then a thought occurred to him. He remembered an evening about two years ago, when Barney had invited Harold Feinberg around to the bungalow for dinner, and the stories that Harold had afterwards told about the lurid histories of several famous Indian diamonds. One of the stories had concerned the discovery of the Regent diamond, a huge 410-carat rough, in the Parteal Mine on the Kistna River, in 1701. It had been picked up by a slave, who had smuggled it out of the mine, and had then made his way to the coast, where he had tried to buy his passage out of India by offering half the value of the stone to a British sea-captain.

It did not matter that the slave had been murdered by the sea-captain and his body flung overboard. What did matter was the way in which the slave had smuggled the diamond out of the Parteal Mine. He had inflicted a deep wound in his own leg, and tucked the diamond into his flesh.

Joel turned back to the mirror, and his reflection turned to meet him. He had a limp already, from his bone-setting, so if he limped a little more, who would notice? especially if he said that his leg was playing him up. He always wore his left leg strapped in bandages, so a few more bandages would not attract any undue attention.

My God, if he carried the diamond in his leg, then he could openly challenge Barney to search him all over, up his backside, anywhere he felt like it. You can even degrade yourself by combing through my shit, little brother. You won't find what you're looking for.

He stood quite still for a moment, drumming his fingers on the rosewood veneer of the bureau. Then, taking his stick, he limped into the bathroom, where his cut-throat razor lay neatly on the shelf under the looking-glass, next to his shaving-brush. He picked the razor up, and opened it. He would have to strop the blade until it was sharper than ever, and sterilise it by passing it through a flame. He would have to have bandages ready, and a towel for the blood, and plenty of whiskey. He took a shallow breath, and made his way back into the bedroom.

Outside his door, he could hear Michael and some of the other kaffirs running up and down the stairs, and Barney's voice ordering them loudly to search the attic. Barney must have guessed that the diamond was in here, in Joel's room, but he had to go through this whole showy performance just to frighten Joel into handing the diamond over voluntarily. That would be the ultimate humiliation for Joel: to have stolen the chance of a wealthy future, and to be obliged to surrender it like a small boy who had misbehaved himself.

'Whiskey,' Joel whispered to himself. He went across to his night-cabinet, and took out a full bottle of Scotch. He wrenched out the cork, and swallowed three or four mouthfulls straight from the neck. Then he set the bottle carefully upright, and began to unbutton his trousers.

His preparations were careful and over-elaborate. This was partly because he refused to be rushed by the melodramatic searching noises that Barney was making all over the house; and

389

partly because he was afraid of what he was going to have to do. But, after ten minutes or so, he was sitting on the end of the bed, with his china washbasin on the floor beneath his leg, and his trousers off, all prepared to begin his operation.

He suddenly realised that he had left the diamond on top of the bureau, and he had to hop over and get it. Once he had dug a hole out of his leg large enough to take it, he probably would not have the strength or the inclination to hobble around the room looking for it. He took another large swig of straight whiskey, and decided he was ready.

There was a crisp knock at the door.

'Who is it?' he asked, his razor poised above the white hairy skin of his left thigh.

'It's Barney.'

'Go away, I'm tired. I'm trying to sleep. Go and annoy your wife for a change, instead of me.'

'I want to talk to you.'

'Well, you can't. We've said enough already.'

'This isn't about that argument we had earlier. That's forgotten. This is about something different.'

Joel paused. Then he said, 'Whatever it is, it can wait. I'm tired, and I'm drunk, and I don't want to talk about anything.'

'It won't take more than a minute or two, I promise.'

Joel looked down at the huge rough diamond lying on the bed. His hand, still holding the razor poised a quarter of an inch above the skin of his thigh, began to tremble. 'We can talk about it later. Right now, I'm not in a very amenable mood. Now, go away.'

He could hear Barney shuffling outside the door, and he closed his eyes in utter tension. Make him go away, O Lord, Make him go away.

Eventually, though, Barney said, 'All right. I'll come back in an hour or two, when you've slept off that whiskey. But I'm going to talk to you then, Joel, I promise you, even if I have to break your door down to do it.'

'I always told you that you were too violent,' said Joel.

Barney did not answer, but stayed outside the door for a moment before walking off down the landing, to the head of

390

the stairs. 'By the way,' he called, in a challenging voice, 'we're having an early supper tonight, so we'll expect you down at seven.'

Joel did not answer, but waited until he heard Barney go down the stairs, and start talking to the kaffirs who were milling around in the hallway. It sounded like a circus down there, all shouting and whistling and shuffling feet. Joel smiled wryly, and cut into his thigh with the razor before he had fully realised what he doing.

The razor was very sharp, so it sliced through the muscle and the fat without any trouble. It hardly hurt, but what made him shudder was the way the blade seemed to stick to his flesh, as if it wanted to carry on cutting him, all the way up; and the way the muscle of his thigh opened up like a bleeding and expressionless mouth. He laid the razor with trembling fingers on one of his hand-towels, pressed a handkerchief against his thigh to stem the bleeding, and quickly reached for his bottle of whiskey.

'Oh, my God,' he said to himself, trying not to look down at his leg. Then he guzzled at the bottle until his stomach burned with liquor.

Gradually, he lifted the handkerchief away to see if the wound was deep enough to lodge the diamond inside. There was so much blood that it was difficult to say; so he was obliged to press the diamond against his sliced-open skin, and force it into the raw flesh as far as it would go. He bit his lips in anguish as he saw that only about a third of the diamond could actually be concealed inside his first incision. He would have to cut deeper.

His next cut was shaky and uncontrolled, and he had to take the razor away and take five or six steadying breaths before he could bring himself to continue.

'You've started it,' he told himself, angrily, 'you might as well finish it. You hear me? You're going to have a scar anyway, so you might as well make it a useful scar.'

Watching his own hand with horrified fascination, as if it belonged to somebody else, Joel saw the razor cut right into the wound until the tip of it touched his bare bone. Then the razor sliced quickly from side to side, cutting out pale and blood-stained pieces of muscle, until there was a huge and massively bloody hole.

He dropped the razor on the floor. He was juddering and shaking now, like a man in the throes of a fit. Blood was running down his leg in uncontrollable streams, and into the china washbasin. He bundled up one of the hand-towels into a large padded bandage, and held it on top of the wound as hard as he could. It suddenly occurred to him that he was going to bleed to death, and that Barney would break the door down in an hour or so to find him lying on the floor as white as a *kosher* calf, and the diamond on the end of the bed.

Pursing his mouth in pain, he grasped the whiskey bottle again, and swallowed a large mouthful. The rest of it he was going to use to clean out the wound. He lifted away the soaking red towel, and splashed scotch all over his thigh, letting it run right into the blood.

That was the only time he actually cried out loud. He felt as if his leg was actually alight, as if the bone itself were burning. But within a minute or two, the pain had died down to a deep, excruciating numbness and he was able to open his eyes and look around him and realise that only a very short time had elapsed since Barney had come knocking at his door, and that nobody would be suspicious about what he was doing, not yet.

Now he picked up the diamond, rubbed it all over in whiskey to clean it, and pushed in into his raw flesh. It created a lumpy bulge in his leg, but he tightly wrapped a hand-towel around it, and then bound the wound together with bandages.

He sat for more than ten minutes without moving, trying to cope with the shock of what he had done to himself, and with the extraordinary sensation of having the huge diamond buried in his thigh. He thought for a while that he was going to go mad; that he might have gone mad already. But gradually his hysteria subsided, and he was able slowly to gather up the bloody towels and the basin, and clean the blade of his razor.

Unsteadily, cursing as he went, he lurched into the bathroom and replaced the basin on top of the marble-topped toilet stand, and dumped the towels into the tub. He caught sight of his face in the bathroom mirror, and it seemed no different than before:

no greyer, no more agonised, but no less ridiculous, either. He ran the taps so that he could rinse the blood out of the towels before they were too badly stained. He could always tell the servants that he had suffered a severe nose-bleed. He drank so much that he had them regularly.

Then he dragged his throbbing leg back into the bedroom, to take another bottle of scotch out of his night-stand, and drink almost a third of it without taking a breath. Half of it came gushing back up out of his nostrils.

Downstairs, he could hear laughter, as the servants searched through the coats and boots in the hall-cupboard. To think that there was still something in this world worth laughing about. To think that there was still something in this world worth living for. He jumped and shuffled across to his wardrobe, and opened it. He would have to dress himself for supper tonight: he did not want any of the servants to see the bloody bandages on his thigh. He wondered if he had the courage to be able to sit through the entire meal with the diamond buried in his leg, eating soup and game and sweet puddings, and pretending to listen to Sara's inane conversation about the gels she had known in Durban. He wondered if he were going to be sick.

The bedroom began to tilt sideways, and he had to sit down abruptly to stop himself from falling.

When Sara came down for supper, she looked like a European princess. She wore a dress of pale cobalt-blue silk, and her dark hair was tied up with three strings of Indian Ocean pearls. Her bodice was cut surprisingly low, so that her breasts were bared right to the pink tinge at the edge of her nipples, and an emerald and diamond cross rested in her cleavage as if to suggest that here was buried treasure. Her perfume was rich and intoxicating, civet-oils and vetiver and verdigris, and her lips were painted red.

Barney, in his tailcoat and black tie, put down his drink and stood up as she came into the drawing-room, and held out his arms. She came across to him willingly, and kissed him.

'You look beautiful tonight,' he told her, with undisguised admiration.

393

'Don't I always look beautiful?'

'Of course you do. But especially beautiful tonight.'

She kissed him again, and then raised a blue-gloved hand to wipe the lip-colour away from his cheek. 'I wanted to dress up for you. I think it's the only way I can think of to tell you that I'm sorry.'

'You don't have to be sorry. If anybody should apologise, it's me. I behaved like a gorilla.'

Sara sat down on the sofa and spread out her gown. The edges were embroidered with silk braid, in a slightly darker blue, and dozens of seedpearls, stitched on like flowers. Her feet were bare, which Barney found unexpectedly provocative.

'I think I expected too much from you,' she said. 'I certainly expected too much from Kimberley. It was rather a shock for a girl like me to find that there was no formal social life, except among a very few people from the London exploration companies; and that there was hardly anybody whom one might ask for five o'clock tea.'

'There will be, sooner than you think,' said Barney, with his back to the fluted marble fireplace. 'Harold Feinberg says that the town is going to grow as big and as sophisticated as London's West End, in a year or two. They you'll have a social life that anybody in Durban can envy.'

'I'm sure you're right,' Sara smiled. 'But whatever happens, I always want to be your adoring wife. I'm sorry for all our silly arguments, and Nareez has asked me to say that she's sorry, too, She knows that I've been afraid. This is rather a wild place, after all! And she's only been trying to protect me. She's protected me all her life.'

Barney took Sara's hand, and pressed it against his cheek. He looked her straight in the eyes, and the oppression that he had been feeling ever since he had talked to Mooi Klip began to lift. Perhaps Sara was going to turn out to be a happy choice for a wife after all. Perhaps all these wrangles had been caused by nothing more than home-sickness and belated wedding-night nerves.

'We might retire after supper,' Sara suggested, blushing slightly. Barney leaned over and kissed her, first her forehead, then her cheeks, then her lips.

'I shan't have any lip-colour left,' she whispered.

'Can you think of a better way of losing it?'

Just then, their new manservant Horace came in, wearing ill-fitting knee breeches and a draped brown riding-coat. He offered them sweet sherry from a silver tray, and then retreated from the room backwards on squeaking boots.

'I think Horace has heard about royalty,' said Sara. 'He always bows whenever he sees me, and he never turns his back on me, ever. It's rather quaint, isn't it? But I hate to disillusion him.'

They drank a silent toast to each other, and Barney said a *broche* in his mind for Sara's beauty, and also for her new warmth. It was going to take months of difficulty and pain for him to forget all about the love he felt for Mooi Klip, but if Sara was going to be as gentle and as alluring as this, he was going to find it far less harrowing.

'There's been an awful fuss in the house tonight,' remarked Sara. 'I asked Nareez what was going on, but she said she didn't know, not exactly. She said she thought it was some kind of a *search*, though. I couldn't think what on earth we could have lost that could have set off such a disturbance.'

'Ah,' said Barney, running his hand through his curly hair, 'that's rather a long story.'

'Well, I'd love to hear it, especially since it's turning my own house on its roof.'

Barney could not think why he felt reluctant to tell Sara all about it; but somehow he did not quite trust her enough. There was no particular reason why she should not know. In fact, she had every right to. But he found himself hesitating and hedging, and telling her almost nothing.

'The truth is, 'he said,' that I've lost something valuable. At least, I *hope* it's been lost, and that it hasn't been stolen. But I've organised a search for it, as openly as possible, in the hope that if anybody's hiding it, they'll feel constrained to hand it back; or, if it's really lost, and not stolen, that it will soon be turned up.'

Sara looked around the room as if she were appealing to an equally baffled audience. 'Really, my darling, you should have been a colonial governor. I don't think I've heard anybody make such a long speech and say quite so little since Papa invited Sir Henry Barkly to dinner. To begin with, you haven't told me what this valuable thing is, or how you lost it, or whether it's worth stealing.'

'Well ...' said Barney, but at that very moment Joel appeared in the doorway, crisply dressed in a boiled white shirt and tailcoats, but frighteningly haggard. Barney felt his heart beat a slow bump as Joel stared at him, leaning heavily over his cane, obviously waiting for him to finish what he was saying.

'Don't let me interrupt you,' said Joel, hoarsely. 'I'm just as interested as Sara in what this valuable thing might be. After all, how can we help you look for it if we don't know what it is?'

'Well, quite right,' said Sara. 'You *do* seem to be playing games, my darling.'

'Have a drink,' Barney told Joel. 'You look as if you need one.'

Joel heaved himself awkwardly across the room towards the nearest armchair, and sat down. 'Thank you,' he grimaced. 'My leg's been giving me sheer hell today. The weather, I suppose. Down goes the mercury, and I'm done for.'

'Is it a letter?' asked Sara.

'Is what a letter?' frowned Barney.

'This lost or stolen thing! This valuable property that everybody's looking for! Letters are always valuable, aren't they, in love stories, especially when they're passionate, and incriminating.'

'Well, it's not a letter,' smiled Barney, giving Sara an amused nod of his head. 'I'm not very good at writing letters, either passionate or incriminating – or even readable, for that matter.'

'Is it a piece of jewellery, perhaps?' Sara proposed. 'A tie-pin, or a pair of cuff-links?'

'Or a clip?' put in Joel, very softly. The English-Afrikaans pun was not lost on Barney, and he fixed his gaze on his brother very steadily.

'You're nearly right, Sara,' he said, in a flat voice. 'The truth is that it's a diamond. Not just an ordinary diamond, either. But a diamond of unusual size. A real monster, from what I hear.'

'But how exciting! Has someone stolen it?'

Barney gave Sara a wry smile. 'I don't know, to be honest.

I can't prove anything at all until I find it. It was supposed to have been dug up on one of my claims while I was away in Durban. But even though there's been a lot of rumour and gossip about it, nobody has yet admitted that it actually exists, and nobody has yet admitted that they have it ih their possession.'

'It's just another one of those kaffir yarns, I expect,' said Joel, with a smile that was more teeth and muscle than anything else. 'They're always making up stories like that, just to keep the white boss hustling and bustling around like a dog after his own tail. One of them told me that he knew where King Solomon's treasure was hidden. Fifty metres deep, he told me, through solid bedrock. I would have had him flogged to death, if I could have caught him.'

'But this is a diamond, Joel,' said Barney, suddenly serious. 'This is a giant-sized diamond, anything up to 400 carats, and it was supposed to have been found on our claim.'

Joel shook his head, and let out a dry laugh. 'When you were away in Durban, little brother, I was in charge here. And let me tell you something, my supervision of what goes on in this mine is always ten times as strict as yours. If they so much as spit on the ground, those kaffirs, they get cuffed; and if I ever caught any one of them stealing, then God help me I'd strangle him with my bare hands.'

'What you're trying to tell me is that you don't believe this monstrous diamond actually exists? You think it's all a story?'

Joel looked up at Barney keenly. 'It may exist, Barney, but if it does, I haven't seen it. Don't tell me you don't believe me – because what do you think I would have done if I *had* seen it? I would have turned it over to you, wouldn't I? as soon as you got back from Durban? I'm not a diamond thief, whatever else you care to call me. And I'm your brother, too.'

'I'm glad you said that,' Barney replied. 'Because while you're down here, your room is being searched. I've even told them to cut open your cakes of soap.'

Sara was shocked. She said, '*Barney*! I can scarcely believe it!'

'All right,' put in Barney, calmly, 'you can scarcely believe it. But I've heard enough about this mythical diamond today to think that it's worth looking for it; and the first place that I've been looking is inside this house. We're talking about a gemstone that could be worth more than a million pounds here, Sara; and when you start talking about a million pounds, I don't think you can talk about loyalty in the same breath. Family loyalty, servant loyalty, any kind of loyalty. Most people have their morals, sure; and most people have a sense of duty and honesty and good old shoulder-to-shoulder comradeship; but a million pounds is more than most people's honesty is worth. A million pounds is enough to convince most people that it's time to forget about their duty, and their friends, and even the people they love. A million pounds is even enough to persuade most people to forget about their God.'

There was a momentary silence. Joel made a painful face at Sara, and shrugged, as if to say that *he* might not believe me, but I know *you* do.

'Maybe you think I'm crazy,' said Barney. 'Maybe you think that it's just as wicked to suspect your own family of theft as it is for them to steal. Well, maybe you're right. But let me tell you this: when there's a million pounds at stake, I'm as greedy and determined as anyone else, particularly when I know that it's *my* million pounds, and that it's being taken from under my nose.'

'So, you're accusing me of taking a giant-sized diamond, are you?' asked Joel. 'You're accusing me of stealing the largest gemstone that anybody has ever dug up at Kimberley – in fact, one of the largest gemstones that has ever been heard of in the history of the whole world?'

'I didn't say that,' said Barney, in a level voice.

'You didn't have to,' Joel retorted. 'It's enough that you ordered your black monkeys to look through my room. And to cut up my *soap*? You're as mad as Mama.'

'What would you have done?' demanded Barney.

'If *I* had suspected *you* of stealing some fictitious diamond – and by God, Barney, I emphasise *fictitious* – I would at least have had the decency to *ask* you first. I mean, you'll make sure they look through my underwear, won't you? And through all of my personal possessions? My letters, and my pictures of Papa and Mama? You'll make sure that they desecrate what little dignity I have left?'

Barney set down his drink on the small inlaid wine-table beside him. 'I'm sorry, Joel,' he said, quietly. 'But that's always been the difference between you and me.'

'What has? What are you talking about?'

'I'm talking about bluster, that's what I'm talking about. Hot air. You've been appealing to my conscience ever since you could talk; and now you're always appealing to justice, and to God, and to the tides of fortune, and to whatever comes into your head. But you've never actually gotten anything done, have you? You never cultivated the farm at Derdeheuwel. You lost all your money at Klipdrift. You got yourself accused of stealing diamonds at Kimberley. It's no use appealing to the powers that be, Joel, because there's only one reason you're sitting in this drawing-room in evening-dress waiting for a well-cooked supper, and that reason is me.'

'Is that my cue to pack my bags and leave you?' asked Joel, whitefaced and fierce.

'No, it isn't,' said Barney, plainly. 'But it's certainly a cue for you to tell me whatever you know about this diamond, don't you think, and to stop playing ridiculous charades?'

'Charades!' shouted Joel, although his shout was strained and weak, and thick with phlegm. 'You're the one who's playing charades! You spring this story about a monster diamond on me, the very first time I've ever heard such a thing in my whole life, and then you immediately accuse me of having stolen it! It's madness! And then you accuse me of playing charades!'

Sara turned to Barney appealingly. 'Don't you think we ought to drop the subject, darling! I don't want a row just before supper.'

Barney continued to stare at Joel with an expression of deep distrust. 'I just want a straight answer, that's all. There *is* a diamond, I know it. Harold Feinberg told me; and so did one or two other people who ought to know what they're talking about. And if Joel doesn't know anything about it, then I can only say that his memory is proving as inconstant as his loyalty.'

At that moment, Michael came to the open doorway of the drawing-room and gave Barney a quick shake of his head.

'Aha,' said Joel, shifting himself in his chair to make himself more comfortable, 'I suppose that means I've been vindicated.'

'It means they didn't find the diamond in your room, that's all,' said Barney.

'*Diamond*,' mocked Joel, with a sharp laugh. 'If you ask me, Barney, you've been out here in Kimberley far too long. You're getting the fever.'

'There *is* a diamond,' insisted Barney. 'It weighs more than 350 carats, and I'll bet money that it's somewhere in this house.'

'Do you want to reveal the identity of your informant?' asked Joel, raising an eyebrow.

Barney glanced towards Sara. He had already been given enough trouble by Nareez over his continuing affection for Mooi Klip. If Joel provoked Sara's suspicions even more by telling her that Mooi Klip had been round to the house this evening, it would take more than a day or two to persuade Sara that his affair was all over, and that Mooi Klip had returned to Klipdrift for good, to marry a farmer, and rear chickens. Without taking his eyes off Joel, he said quietly, 'All right. Let's forget about diamonds for the rest of the evening. Let's talk about love instead.'

'Love!' sputtered Joel.

'I think it's a very good subject,' enthused Sara. 'Dryden said that love is the noblest frailty of the mind.'

'Yes,' said Joel, 'and Phineas Fletcher said that love is like linen. The more you change it, the sweeter it is.'

Sara did not know what to reply to that; and Barney was too furious with Joel to say anything; so when Horace walked solemnly into the very centre of the drawing-room and rang a little hand-held gong for supper, both of them were more than ready to go through.

'Can I take you in?' Joel asked Sara, heaving himself to his feet, and offering her his uptilted elbow. Sara looked back at Barney, to see what he thought about it, but Barney simply made a face that meant 'go ahead'.

Neither Barney nor Sara could have guessed at the agony that Joel went through, just to walk the length of the hallway to the dining-room. He did not falter once, or cry out; but by the time they reached the dining-room door his face was deep grey, like a victim of angina, and he was crowned with sweat. When he took his place between them at the dining-table, he appeared to be unable to speak, and he shuddered from time to time so violently that he displaced his knives and forks.

'Are you all right?' Barney asked him, gravely.

'What?' said Joel.

'I asked you if you were all right. You look like death.'

Joel opened his linen napkin with fingers as clenched as claws. 'Of course I'm all right. It's the weather, that's all. It gives me a little twinge, now and again.'

'Well, as long as you're sure,' said Barney. 'We don't mind excusing you from the table, if you'd rather have your supper upstairs.'

'Wouldn't that interrupt your searching?' asked Joel, acidly.

'Joel,' said Sara, in a gentle voice. 'You really mustn't take everything so much to heart.'

'Oh, no,' said Joel, with a jerky smile. 'I forgot.'

It was a light supper of liver pâté, toast, and roasted fowl. Horace crept solemnly around the table and poured them chilled Austrian hock, which had been a gift to Harold Feinberg from a diamond dealer in Vienna. Sara talked about Fanny Brewbaker, a débutante she had known in Durban, and how Fanny had attempted to elope with a chump called Watkins, and how she had finished up dangling from the branches of a sausage tree, instead of in Watkins' arms.

Joel forked his food listlessly from one side of his plate to the other, saying nothing at all, and eating scarcely anything. Barney looked at him once or twice expectantly, but he would not even raise his head. What Barney did not know was that the walk from the drawing-room to the dining-room had opened Joel's wound, and that Jowl was bleeding thickly into his left sock.

Before the coffee, Joel stood up, dropped his napkin, and said, 'You'll have to excuse me. I've had a bad day.'

'Wouldn't you care for a brandy before you go up?' asked Sara. 'I'm sure that you and Barney could settle all your differences over a drink.'

Joel leaned against the table to support himself. 'Thank you,' he told her, 'you're very kind. But you know what brothers are. Arguing one minute; and the best of friends the next. I'm sure that Barney didn't mean what he said.'

'You look bad,' said Barney, 'you'd better go lie down.'

'It's nothing much,' Joel told him. 'Fatigue, I think, more than anything.'

Horace brought him his cane, and he made his way slowly to the dining-room door. 'I'm sorry you didn't find your imaginary diamond,' he said, without looking around. 'It would have been wonderful if it had been true.'

'Yes, wouldn't it,' said Barney, without any inflection in his voice at all.

'Goodnight, then,' said Joel, and painfully made his way upstairs.

'He seems very *ill*,' remarked Sara, when he had gone.

Barney peeled himself an orange. 'I think it's the morphia, and the whiskey. He's going to kill himself unless he's careful.'

'He's not a bad man, you know, underneath.'

'I never said that he was.'

'No, I know you didn't,' said Sara, 'but you give him such a difficult time sometimes. He's very much gentler than you, you know. If you ask me, he'd be better off as a painter, or perhaps a musician. He doesn't have the head for all this diamond-digging and all this business. He thinks he ought to, just because *you* have. But he doesn't, at all; and I wonder if that's what makes him so unhappy.'

Barney chewed orange, and carefully spat out the pips into his hand, practising that social legerdemain that he had seen in Capetown and Durban. 'What makes Joel unhappy is his inability to face up to his own shortcomings. He lives in a world of utter fantasy – a world in which he thinks that he's rich, and successful, and unfailingly attractive to women. The simple truth is that he's not, and that he's never done anything to make him that way. He's not capable of it.'

'But you still love him, don't you?' said Sara, reaching out her hand across the damask tablecloth, and touching Barney's wrist. 'I wouldn't want you to fall out with him.'

'I don't know,' Barney told her. 'I used to believe that he and I would always be together, and always love each other, no matter what. Now, with this diamond business –'

'You really believe that there *is* a diamond, and that Joel has it?'

Barney nodded.

'Can I ask you how you found out?'

Barney looked at Sara for a moment, and then reached for some grapes. 'One of the blackies told me. That's all.'

'And you believe the word of a blackie against the word of your own brother?'

Barney did not answer that question, but continued to pluck grapes from the stem which he held in his hand, and eat them as methodically as if he were saying a silent rhyme to himself – she loves me, she loves me not, she loves me, she loves me not.

That night, when he climbed into bed, Sara was naked except for a small lace bodice, and she held out her arms for him almost immediately. He kissed her, and her mouth pressed as hungrily against his lips as if she were devouring a pomegranate. Her sharp-nailed fingers ran down the length of his spine, and around his bottom, and at last cupped his balls with threatening delicacy, caressing them most of the time with infinite care, but now and then squeezing them tightly, which made him gasp.

She opened her thighs for him without question, and guided him towards her parted lips. He felt as if the inside of his head were crackling with electricity, like one of those windy frightening mornings on the Drakensberg. Her desire for him was so unexpected and so aggressive that he was aroused more than at any time he could ever remember in his whole life. To be attacked in bed by a slut was one thing; to be savaged by a girl who was proper enough never to say 'mantelpiece' and to consider that name-cards at a dinner-table were rather 'low' was quite another. She gasped his name over and over again, until he shivered, and reached a climax of three distinct and intensive ejaculations. Yet she wanted more; and as he rolled over on to his back, she rolled on top of him, and gripped him with sticky hands, and whispered words in his ear which even an Australian digger might have coughed at.

'Barney,' she cooed, 'we must be the most marvellous lovers that ever were.'

Barney said nothing. He was too intoxicated by her eager submissiveness and her lewd whispers. It seemed like a dream in which even the most buried of all erotic desires had suddenly become possible. He turned her on to her stomach on the bed, and she raised her bottom urgently towards him, her thighs stretched as wide apart as she could. Barney pushed himself into her, gripping the soft flesh of her hips, until he could push no deeper. He felt extraordinary, dreaming, praying, or drunk.

He did not hear the door open one single inch. Nor did he see Sara, her dark hair spread wildly over the pillow, her face flushed, turn her head towards the doorway and stare with eyes that were incongruously calm and thoughtful at her Indian *amah* Nareez, who stood in the darkness of the hallway like one of the ancient and mystical Rakshasas, the night-stalkers.

Sara lay awake until dawn, listening to Barney breathing and murmuring in his sleep. She felt ashamed of herself, in one way for her lustful lovemaking; but in another way she felt far more settled, and more decided about the course which her life was now going to have to follow. She was sure, particularly now that the tensions of her body had been spent, that she did not really love Barney at all, not in the way in which her mother had loved her father, or in which she believed a woman ought to adore and respect her spouse.

Barney had attracted Sara right from the very first day she had met him. He had a beautiful slow masculinity about him which she still found disturbing. She had often watched his profile in the gilded evening sun and been unable to take her eyes away. But he did not understand her at all, nor did he have any real grasp of what was important to her, and why. Because of that, he plainly saw her abrupt changes of mood as unpredictable and unsettling swings in her character, whereas in truth everything that Sara did and said conformed to the great logic of the British colonial daughter.

It was not Barney's fault. He didn't have any experience at all of the ordered and ritualistic society of the English Abroad. He was an American, and a Jew, and so he was doubly handicapped in his comprehension of God, Queen and Country; of the Raj-like protocol of what to wear, and how to behave, and where to be, at what particular season; of the extraordinary complexities of visiting, and why it was so desperately embarrassing actually to come face to face with the person at whose house you were leaving your visiting-card.

Barney would never know what a *burra mem* was (a phrase that Sara's mother, a true *burra mem*, had fondly borrowed from India); and he would never be able to penetrate the mind of a girl who had been brought up in a world of clubs and polo and flannel underwear and formal picnics, a world of native servants and annual gymkhanas; a world where the rivalry between the Collector's wife and the Colonel's wife could have a whole city quivering for weeks; and where a man who was forgetful enough to put on a solar topee after sundown was generally considered to be guilty of ghastly bad form.

Sara had been swept away by Barney's dramatic proposal, and impressed by his wealth. She had felt passionate about him, too, and still did, although not so completely. After all, it was not only protocol and charm that characterised upper-class English ladies in the colonies, it was also that fierce Hot Weather carnality which had led one old hand to describe their lives as a perfect circle of tea-parties, durbas, picnics, and adultery. In one way, it was only the strictness of their self-imposed etiquette which kept their isolated and outdated world from collapsing into a stew of drunkenness, moral breakdowns, and despair. It was not done to take a drink before the sun went down, nor to continue to drink after dinner. Neither was it done to fornicate so brazenly that anyone (especially one's husband) actually Knew. Conforming rigidly to what was done saved many of the Empire's finest ladies from coming catastrophically undone.

But out here in Kimberley, none of this mannered society in which Sara had been raised existed at all, moral or immoral; and although she had believed at first that she could survive without it, she had quickly discovered that she could not, and it was a severe handicap to the possible success of their marriage that Barney was unable even to imagine what it was that she missed.

But – Sara had decided – she was not going to mope over it. The greatest quality of the *burra mem*, apart from her exact social tone and her overwhelming feminine instincts, was her resilience under Trying Conditions. She would do her best to be a good wife to Barney; she would love him whenever she felt she could; she would seek his body when she needed it. But she could never lose sight of her ambition to be socially glittering, the belle of South Africa, and she would take whatever opportunities to achieve her ambition that offered themselves to her.

She began to feel inside, still half-developed, a capability for ruthlessness that would have given Barney nightmares, had he guessed that it was there. This was the only child that she would bear him.

Joel stayed in his bedroom throughout *Shabbes*, and through most of Sunday. He kept the door locked and asked only for a little chicken broth to be left outside on the landing. Barney went upstairs to speak to him two or three times, but until late on Sunday Joel refused to let him in.

When he finally did open the door, Barney found that the room was gloomy, with all the drapes drawn tight, and that there was an unpleasant smell around, as if Joel had not been washing. Joel was wearing his dark blue bathrobe, and sitting in his upright armchair, reading a book about country houses in New York State and Long Island.

'Are you all right?' Barney asked him. 'Do you want me to open the window?'

Joel shrugged, as if to say that he did not mind one way or the other. Barney drew back one of the drapes, and pushed open the window that overlooked the back of the house. A cool flow of fresh air flowed into the room, and ruffled an untidy sheaf of paper that had been strewn across Joel's desk. Barney picked one of the papers up and saw that it was covered in sketches of a large imposing house, with a pillared portico and formal gardens.

'Are you thinking up more ideas for laying out Vogel Vlei?' he asked. 'I'm glad that you're interested.'

Joel said nothing, but leaned forward to pluck the paper out of Barney's hand, and tuck it down the side of his armchair. Barney stared at him for a minute or so, and then sat on the end of the bed with his hands clasped in front of him, the way a parent addresses himself to a schoolboy who has just been

406

caught behind the orangery, doing something embarrassing.

'Joel,' he said, 'I believe you found a diamond, and I also believe that you still have it hidden someplace.'

'You do, hunh?' said Joel, turning the page of his book.

'Joel – listen, we're fifty-fifty partners in this diamond-mining business, aren't we? If you *have* found a diamond, and it's really worth a million pounds, then you'll still get five hundred thousand. You're going to turn up your nose at five hundred thousand?'

Joel closed his book, and looked back at Barney challengingly. 'What diamond?' he demanded.

'The diamond that Harold told me about, and that Mooi Klip told me about, and that Gentleman Jack is too damned frightened to tell me about. You know damned *well* what diamond!'

'Did you find such a diamond, when you searched the house? Under the floorboards, maybe? In the soap? Why don't you look up my ass, and see if I'm hiding it there?'

'If I don't find it by the time you leave for Capetown, I intend to. And don't think I'm joking.'

'God forbid I should ever think you're joking, Barney. God forbid! Trying to get humour out of you is like cupping a corpse.'

Barney stood up. 'I want that diamond, Joel. That's all I'm going to say.'

'Diamond, diamond, diamond! You're driving me mad with your *tsutcheppenish* about this diamond!'

Resignedly, Barney left Joel's bedroom, closing the door behind him with quiet emphasis. Click. That's it. If that's the way you want it. Then he went quickly downstairs and called Michael to make the carriage ready: he was going to Kimberley to talk to Harold.

Harold was sitting on the verandah of his bungalow, rocking backwards and forwards in a cane rocker, and dozing. His French assistant, slim-wristed and pretty in a Parisian way, with plaited hair and unplucked eyebrows, was embroidering a cushion, and she called out to Barney as he stepped down from his carriage, '*Bonjour*, Monsieur Bleats!'

'This is unexpected,' said Harold, waving Barney towards a

small wicker armchair. 'What brings you *chez* Feinberg on a day like this? Would you care for a drink? Or a cup of tea? How about a *latke*?'

'I've come to pick those brains of yours,' Barney told him, crossing his legs to reveal his loud yellow and red Shetland socks. 'You know that huge diamond we were talking about the other day?'

'Yes?' asked Harold, suspiciously.

'Well, just supposing it was real, okay? And just supposing that a fellow was trying to smuggle it out of Kimberley, and off to the coast. And just supposing this fellow was under pretty close scrutiny, so he couldn't simply carry it in his pocket, or hidden in his luggage. Now, what do you think he might do?'

Harold rocked backwards and forwards and thought about the matter carefully. Then he said, 'First of all, there are plenty of traditional hiding-places which you could rule out straight away, because of the sheer size of this stone. It's as big as that, right – as big as the gap between a finger and a thunb, and that's *big*. So you couldn't swallow it, and you couldn't hide it in your hair. You might be able to tape it under your armpit, but of course that would lay you open to immediate discovery, if you were stripped. The Mogul emperor Mohammed Shah hid the Koh-i-Noor for fifty-eight days in the folds of his turban after he was conquered by the Persian shah Nadir, in 1739. But a harem girl gave Mohammed's secret away; and the next time Nadir invited him to a feast, Nadir insisted that they observe the age-old custom of exchanging turbans. Mohammed couldn't refuse, could he? So Nadir rushed back to his tent, and unwound the turban, and there it was. "It's a mountain of light," he said, and that's what they've called it ever since. "Koh-i-noor." '

'That's all very interesting,' said Barney, 'but nobody in Kimberley wears a turban. Nobody that I know of.'

'I'm going through all the hiding-places I can think of,' protested Harold. 'You want hiding-places, I'll tell you hiding-places.'

'All right, go on. Where else do you think someone could hide a diamond?'

'Well, when it passed to the Afghan princes, the Koh-i-noor

was hidden for *years* in the plaster of Shah Zaman's cell wall, when he was imprisoned and blinded by his brother Shuja.'

'That's a possibility – buried in a plaster wall.'

'It could be,' said Harold, 'except that this fellow you're asking about, he's trying to get it out of Kimberley, right, to sell it? He's not really interested in hiding it away for a year or two.'

'That's right,' nodded Barney.

'The Regent diamond, which Marie Antoinette used to wear in a black velvet hat, *that* was hidden in a hole in a beam in somebody's garret, after it was taken from the treasury during the French Revolution. Have you tried beams?'

'I've taken up floorboards.'

'Well, try beams. Try anything that you can dig a hole in. A mattress, perhaps; or a pillow.'

The French girl came up, and said, 'Would you like some tea, Monsieur Bleats? I will make some, if you like.'

'I'd like that,' said Barney.

Harold said, 'Remember the story I told you about the way the Regent was first discovered, and how it was smuggled out of the Parteal Mine?'

Barney's attention had been briefly distracted by a tall Hottentot girl passing with a clay pot balanced on top of her head, and a baby hanging between her breasts in a loose scarf. 'What did you say?' he asked Harold. 'The Parteal Mine?'

'That's right. A slave came across the Regent diamond on the Kistna River, and cut a hole in his leg so that he could smuggle it out without being detected. A little extreme, wasn't it? But a slave like that would have a lot to gain and nothing to lose.'

'I remember you telling us about that,' nodded Barney. 'I remember Joel remarking that a man would have to be mad to do a thing like that.'

Barney was about to say something else, but then he paused, thinking. Joel had heard that story, too; and if Joel had been thinking of ways to smuggle the diamond out of Kimberley, wouldn't that story have crossed his mind? Joel limped already, from his old fractures. Supposing he wanted the diamond so much that he was prepared to –

That would account for his sudden worsening on Friday night, wouldn't it? And the way in which he had kept himself locked away in his room for the past twenty-four hours? And if he had actually mimicked that poor desperate slave at Parteal – if he had actually dug a hole in his leg that was deep enough to accommodate a 350-carat diamond, wouldn't that also account for the strange stench in his room – the stench of dried-out blood and infected bandages?

'*Riboyne Shel O'lem,*' he said, under his breath.

'What did you say?' asked Harold.

'Nothing. But I have a terrible feeling that I know where I can find that diamond.'

Barney sat staring into space while the French girl brought tea. The cups were Minton, gold and green, and the tea was purest Darjeeling. Harold's fortunes were improving these days, and he was thinking of opening another office at Bultfontein. He did badly want an heir, though: and perhaps that was why he was being so attentive to this girl whom Edward Nork called 'Harry's little froggy'.

'If you do find the diamond,' said Harold, carefully, 'why don't you come and tell me first. We don't want to upset the market, do we? It wouldn't be good for anyone, least of all you. I'm too old and too sick to take another downturn in world prices. I want to leave something behind me, a thriving business. Feinberg and Son.'

'Or Daughter,' suggested Barney.

'If that's what God wills. But, excuse me.'

While Harold went inside to the lavatory, Barney talked for a while to his 'froggy'. Her name was Annette, he learned, and she had been educated in music in Paris, but when she was only sixteen she had run away and lived with an extraordinary eccentric in Navarre, the man who had first fired her interest in precious stones. He had taken her on a voyage to Capetown; but halfway there he had suddenly and for no accountable reason thrown himself overboard. She had been left in Capetown with hardly any money, and nothing but a small talent for playing the piccolo. In despair, she had taken a job as a maid; but later she had found employment as an assistant for a large Capetown diamond dealer, and she had made it her business to learn whatever she could about diamonds.

410

'Do you think that you and Harold will ever have children?' Barney asked her. 'It means a lot to him, you know, having someone to pass his business down to.'

The girl slowly shook her head. 'I know Harold wants children, but a child would kill me. Maybe not really kill, but destroy my liberty. I will never have children, you can be sure of that.'

Barney shrugged. No girl that he had ever come across had been quite so sure that she would not conceive, although he knew that Dr Tuter had a reputation for providing cheap, ir erratic, abortions.

'Each month, I push diamonds into *ma matrice*,' whispered the girl. 'Five gemstones, one carat each. They are enough to keep me from conceiving.'

Barney opened his mouth to answer her, but at that moment Harold reappeared with his shirt tail protruding from his unbuttoned trousers. He sat down with a smile, and picked up his cup of tea. 'Let's drink a toast in good Indian tea,' he said. 'Let's wish you wealth and happiness, and let's look forward to the day when I can invite you to a circumcision.'

The French girl looked at Barney and smiled; and Barney knew for Harold's sake that he would never give her secret away. He doubted, quite honestly, whether the practice of pushing diamonds into her womb would have any effect on her ability to conceive. Diamonds had always been attributed with the oddest of medicinal properties: the Hindus had crushed them up and drunk them, to give them strength, while the czar Ivan the Terrible had been quite sure that they were deadly poison. All Barney knew was that Harold's heart was unsteady, and that if he found out that he was being deceived, the unhappiness of it could kill him.

'What are you going to do about this monster diamond?' asked Harold, when they had finished their tea.

'Right now, nothing,' said Barney. 'If I'm right about it – if it really is where I think it is – then I believe that it will make itself known soon enough.'

'You sound peculiarly vengeful,' said Harold, laying his hand on the French girl's arm with proprietorial absent-mindedness.

Barney gave him a tight smile. 'Tell me about Ascher and

Mendel, in Antwerp,' he asked him. 'Do you think they'd be up to cutting a 350-carat diamond?'

By six o'clock on Wednesday evening, Vogel Vlei was all decorated and lit for the Blitz's first party. Twenty hired kaffirs lined the driveway with smoky torches to guide the carriages around to the front of the house, and Michael stood at the door in a footman's costume which Barney had borrowed from the Kimberley Dramatic Society. Inside the hallway, all the lamps were lit, and the floor had been polished until it seemed as if the guests were walking through to the drawing-room on the utterly still meniscus of a lake. There were black waiters with wide white grins and white gloves, and a string quintet of five doleful Boers whom Barney had first met in his kopje-walloping days in Dutoitspan. There was champagne, and South African wine, and there were more handsome women that Kimberley had ever seen together in one place at one time, at least since the French whorehouse had opened on Kopje Street. The talk was of diamonds, and of last year's British annexation of the bankrupt state of Transvaal, and of Cetewayo, the Zulu king. The accents were English, Dutch, Afrikaans, and Australian, and the laughter was very loud: it was not often that Kimberley saw such a grand occasion, and most of the less illustrious guests were effervescent with delight that they had been invited at all.

There were some conspicuous absentees: gentlemen and ladies whom Sara had particularly invited, and who had courteously but firmly declined. Sara had only been here a week, and she was not yet aware that the 'billiards-room chaps' of the Kimberley Club did not accept social invitations from Jews, or coloureds, or anyone else whose accent and background weren't quite up to the expected mark, don't-chi-know. She was not yet aware that Barney was not actually a member of the club, nor that it was only her own stainless social grace that had led most of her middle-class English guests to accept her invitation and shake out their old-fashioned tailcoats for the sake of one of the Chosen.

There were some eminent guests, though – mostly diamond

dealers. Cecil Rhodes had come over, and before the buffet dinner he stood stiff and wavy-haired in one corner of the fireplace, tugging intermittently at his starched white cuffs and trying to make silly conversation with a tiny woman in a fringed dress whose laughter would have peeled a Jerusalem artichoke at ten feet. Barney knew how uncomfortable Rhodes felt with women – he had seen him in their earlier days together, escorting girls around the reverberating wooden floor of the Kimberley Dance Palace, his back straight and his chin held so high that he looked as if he were composing a patriotic sonnet as he danced, or thinking about diving off a cliff. Rhodes had always chosen the plainest women to dance with, and once he had fulfilled the duties on his card he had always rushed immediately home.

Alfred Beit was there, dark and shy, casting an expert financier's eye over Barney's house and possessions. Sir Joseph Robinson, now Mayor of Kimberley, put in a brief and disagreeable appearance just after eight, because he obviously felt it was his civic duty to drink three glasses of Barney's champagne and eat five of his smoked antelope canapés and not talk to anyone, except to grunt, and blow crumbs off his straggling moustache. Francis Baring Gould had almost turned down his invitation, but changed his mind at the last moment, and arrived with a saucy young Dutch girl who was not his wife. Edward Nork was there, making a considerable effort not to drink too much champagne too early, in the company of the brightest new star at the dramatic society, a soft-faced young girl called Fanny Bees. Harold Feinberg came, proudly escorting his French girl.

Sara was delighted. This was not quite Durban; but then Durban was not quite Capetown; and Capetown was not quite London. It was far more glittery and social than she had expected, though, and she went bright-eyed from guest to guest, as tall and elegant as a swan in her white satin dress, trimmed with white feathers, and she received their compliments and their congratulations with joy. Barney watched her, smiling, and nodded his head to Edward Nork to point out how happy she was.

By eight-thirty, there was still no sign of Joel, even when the

413

guests went through to the buffet. Joel had emerged from his room from time to time during the past two days, but he had been thinner and sicker and less steady on his feet than Barney had ever seen him – even when he had been recovering from Sir Thomas Sutter's surgery in Durban. He spoke as if his mouth were always dry, and his eyes appeared to roam around the room in search of something that he might have forgotten. He had shaved only once in three days, and there was a sickly odour about him which made even Nareez wrinkle up her nose as he passed.

Barney knew what was wrong; or at least he had a pretty good idea. And he had throught seriously about ending Joel's agony by telling him what he suspected. But Joel's destiny was his own. Joel had decided to live his life this particular way, and he had come to this self-imposed Purgatory of his own free will. Over the years, he had hurt Barney too often and too cruelly for Barney to want to relieve his suffering now.

Barney had no intention of remitting his pain.

Gentleman Jack had seen how calm Barney had suddenly become, and how he had stopped searching for the diamond, and Barney's calmness frightened him so much that since Sunday he had made any excuse to avoid him, particularly when Barney made his regular morning visit to the diamond mine. Barney said nothing: he would decide how to punish Gentleman Jack when the diamond at last came to light.

During the buffet, Harold Feinberg came over and said, 'I believe this is the best party I've ever been to. And what a charming hostess Sara has turned out to be.'

'Thank you, Harold,' said Barney, taking a chicken roll from the table, and popping it into his mouth. 'I'm delighted that so many people came. Even if they did come out of curiosity, and nothing else.'

'You've, er – you've found the diamond yet?' asked Harold, glancing around to make sure that nobody could overhear them.

'I have some ideas,' Barney told him, offhandedly, with a smile that was deliberately vague.

'What ideas? You mean you know where it is?'

'I think so.'

414

'So what are you going to do?' asked Harold. 'Barney, listen, this is important.'

'Of course it's important,' said Barney.

Just then, through the open double doors of the dining-room, at the turn of the staircase, Barney saw the tip of Joel's cane, and then Joel's feet, in shiny black kid evening shoes. Step by step, Joel made his way down to the hallway, and Barney watched him with detached pity and with sharp regret; but not with sadness. What Joel was suffering now was entirely his own fault.

Harold said, 'This could turn the whole industry on its back. You know that, don't you? And it won't help you, either, when you're trying to buy up so many claims, all around you. The price will shoot up like a skyrocket.'

Barney did not once take his eyes off Joel, as his brother made painful progress through the hall and into the dining-room. Harold turned around once or twice to try to discover what Barney was looking at; but it did not occur to him that Barney was reserving all of his concentration for his own brother.

Joel looked like a corpse which at the very last minute had refused to be buried, and which had heaved itself out of the casket, and back to the banquet. His whole body appeared to have dislocated itself, and he dragged himself along by means of a complicated ritual with his cane, which involved shifts of grip and tilts of balance. He was only thirty-four, but he could have been a man of seventy.

'You'll promise to tell me, won't you,' said Harold. 'You won't go off half-cock and take the diamond straight to Cape-town?'

'Harold, I'll *tell* you,' Barney soothed him. 'Now go back to the party and enjoy yourself. You worry too much about things that haven't even happened yet.'

As Harold left, Sara came over and took Barney's arm, and kissed him. 'It's wonderful,' she said. 'Everybody's so kind. I don't know why Kimberley alarmed me so much, when I first came here.'

'It's a hard place,' said Barney. 'But the people here are only people, that's all.'

'I met that *nice* Mrs Forsyth,' Sara enthused. 'She was telling me about the monthly ladies' evening they have up at the Kimberley Club. I'd love you to take me to one! I'm sure I could outshine all of them!'

'Maybe next month,' said Barney.

'But you must! If we're going to live here, we must socialise. Particularly now that you're going to be a millionaire!'

Barney took his eyes off Joel for a moment, and stared at Sara in bewilderment. 'Who said I was going to be a millionaire? I'm nothing like a millionaire! I only wish that I was.'

Sara looked flustered; like someone who has made a scene with a stranger in a restaurant in the belief that the stranger was trying to walk off with their coat, and then discovered that it was not their coat, after all – that it had a different label, and unfamiliar gloves in the pocket, and that it even *smelled* like somebody else's. 'The diamond will make you a millionaire, won't it? That's what you said it was worth.'

'Sara, I don't *have* any diamond. If it exists, it's still hidden. You know that as well as I do.'

'But you know where it is. Or don't you?'

'Who *told* you that I know where it is?'

'Nareez. She was talking to that kaffir called Gentleman Jack.'

Barney slowly turned back to keep an eye on Joel. Joel was leaning against one of the buffet tables now, with a small private *kraal* of champagne glasses, downing drink after drink in steady succession, and muttering to himself.

'What else did Nareez tell you?' Barney asked Sara.

'Nothing. She just said that Gentleman Jack was worried, because you'd stopped searching for the diamond; and if you'd stopped searching for it, you must have discovered where it is.'

'Quite an efficient spy you have, in Nareez.'

'It's not spying, in my own house! How can it be? You should have told me yourself!'

'Yes,' said Barney, 'maybe I should.'

'Of course you should! You've so secretive, and then you wonder why I behave so defensively. It will be wonderful if you're a millionaire! Think of all the horses we'll be able to buy! We'll be able to travel to Capetown, and to London, and we'll be able to dress ourselves in all the latest fashions!'

'Sara,' Barney told her, patiently, 'even if we do find the diamond, and even if we do sell it for anything like a million pounds, it's going to take months for the money to come through; and then I'll probably invest the larger part of it in more diamond claims.'

'Of course you won't,' Sara teased him. 'Don't you have enough diamond claims as it is?'

'I want to own the whole of the Kimberley Mine personally,' Barney replied, in a flat voice. 'That's all I'm interested in.'

'That's a fine thing to say to your wife at your wedding celebration party.'

Barney took her hand, and squeezed it. 'Come on, you know I didn't mean it like that. I'm just a little preoccupied this evening, that's all.'

'With fond memories of Natalia Marneweck, I suppose?'

'Of course not! What the hell is that supposed to mean?'

Sara's expression went through as many changes as the drawings in a children's flicker-book. 'You *do* have fond memories of her, don't you?'

'Why shouldn't I? Any less than you have fond memories of Trevor, or of any other gentleman friends you've known?'

'At least I don't continue to meet my gentlemen friends in secret, in the servants' quarters of my new husband's house.'

'What are you saying?' Barney demanded, trying to keep his voice down. He was still holding Sara's hand, but now he was clutching it so tight that she wrestled to get it free.

'I'm saying nothing, except what is true. Nareez happened to go to the kitchen to bring me warm milk, when she saw you talking to Natalia Marneweck. She heard everything you said, and she told me that it sounded most affectionate.'

Barney looked at Sara for a long time, the muscles around his mouth bunched as if he were considering hitting her, or walking out. But then he said quietly, 'Why didn't you tell me before, that you knew?'

'I suppose I was afraid to. In any case, Nareez said that if you were going to be a millionaire, I should be careful. I should be nice to you, and try to make you forget Natalia.'

'Are you really that naïve? Or is this some kind of ridiculous prank? Whatever I felt about Natalia, I'm married to you; and, believe it or not, I want our marriage to be happy. That's all I can say about it. I didn't want to tell you about Natalia coming here because I thought it would only upset you. Nothing happened – except she went back to Klipdrift to marry some farmer. *Adonai El Rachum Ve-Chanum*, did Nareez really listen in to all that? So you knew about the diamond right from the beginning? And you thought I was going to be a millionaire? And that's why you –'

Sara blushed fiercely, and at last succeeded in tugging her hand away.

'Sara?' whispered Barney, intensely. 'Is that why you turned so passionate? Is that it? Because Nareez told you to make me forget about Natalia, in case you lost your share of my million pounds?'

'Don't,' pleaded Sara, mortified.

'Don't *what*? Don't try to get the truth out of you? Are you trying to tell me that all of your passion is faked? That you've been prostituting yourself for this diamond?'

'I'm your wife,' hissed Sara. 'How can you possibly dare to call me such a thing?'

Barney stood with his arms by his sides and looked at Sara with a feeling inside him like dropping off a mountain. 'I suppose I can call you such things because they appear to be true.'

'You're such a stickler for truth, aren't you? You're so noble, and so right, and so compassionate. The trouble with you, my deah, is that your compassion is like a curse. You're so indomitably strong that you crush everybody around you, without understanding your own strength. Did you ever think for a moment, my love, what your ambition *does* to people? You want to own the whole of the Kimberley Mine, and the terrible thing about it is that you will. Nareez understands what you're like, and she was trying very hard to save me from being crushed underneath your charity, and your sense of duty, and the guilt you feel because you married me. But why feel guilty? We probably don't love each othah; but nor do *thousands* of married couples, any more than we do. I'm just as responsible for what happened as you are. You excited me, the way you came to

418

claim me. I'd just lost a fiancé, and I was bored to tears with living at home. I rushed into the wedding as eagerly as you did. Perhaps I've been cold to you sometimes, and unpleasant. Perhaps I've been stiff. Well, I'm that kind of a girl, I suppose, although not always. I've got a fractured life-line, that's the trouble. One day I feel that I'm fond of you, other days you get on my nerves so much that I can scarcely bring myself to speak to you. But, for God's sake, Barneh – don't pity me, and don't blame yourself, and don't try to make everything all right. If you do that, you'll bury me alive, the same way that you've buried your brother alive, and the same way that you've buried Natalia Marneweck alive. You don't realise what a powerful man you are, Barney – not for one second. You're like a landslide – a high-principled landslide that won't be diverted because of its conscience and its responsibilities and its un-wavering, impossible ambition.'

Barney opened his mouth and then closed it again without saying anything. He still felt as if he were dropping off that mountain, suspended weightless in empty space for that long vertiginous moment before the ground below begins to expand like a rapidly-rising load and suddenly slams into you.

'This isn't the place to talk like this,' he told Sara, at last.

'I know,' she agreed. 'But it had to be said.'

He nodded, distraught, off-balance.

'Do you think we can –?' He couldn't find the words. He said instead, 'I'm sorry.'

'No sorrow,' warned Sara. 'Now, I'm going to circulate. I feel rather shaky, as a matter of fact. I need some light conversation to settle me down.'

'Just answer me one question,' said Barney, taking her hand again, but gently this time. 'Were you really so afraid that I'd make a million, and that you wouldn't get a share of it? Afraid enough to –'

Sara thought for a moment, and then gave an ambiguous nod that did not quite seem to mean that she *had* been afraid; but that being afraid was the nearest way she could think of to describe it.

'Then why –' Barney began, but at that moment there was a high-pitched scream, and a smashing of dishes, and a chiming of fallen tureen-covers, and Joel rolled over on to the floor with a ten-foot linen tablecloth wrapped around him, bringing down apples and plums and knives and forks and half-sliced hams. A yellow Gouda cheese rolled across the dining-room and disappeared behind the velvet drapes as if somebody had sent it off on an errand.

'He collapsed!' cried Fanny Bees, the actress, who had been standing close by. 'He swayed like a tree, and then he simply collapsed!'

The quintet music died away in a straggle of discordant notes as Barney knelt down beside Joel and tugged away his necktie. Joel was blue around the mouth, but still breathing, and his left hand kept twitching and trembling from the muscular effort of leaning on his stick. He opened his eyes for a moment and peered at Barney like a man straining to see down a well.

Barney looked up at the gathered guests. 'Somebody help me carry him through to the drawing-room. We can lie him down on the couch.'

'Don't touch me,' breathed Joel. 'Whatever you do, don't touch me.'

'Joel,' insisted Barney, 'we can't leave you lying here.'

'Don't you think you've hurt me enough already, you *putz*?'

Barney untwisted the tablecloth and wrenched it from underneath Joel's back. 'Just keep your filthy language to yourself,' he said, his voice shaking with anger and emotion. He felt as if he could punch Joel and embrace him, both at the same time. God, what he must have suffered, to bring him to this!

A stocky red-haired diamond-buyer called Nathan Golden squatted down on his haunches and offered, 'All right, Barney. I'll take his arms.'

'Don't you lay one finger on me,' cautioned Joel.

Barney reached down and grasped Joel's ankles. 'You can say whatever you like, Joel – you can't stay here on the dining-room floor, surrounded by fruit. You're sick, and we're going to carry you through to the drawing-room. Now – you got him, Nathan?'

Nathan forced his thick-fingered hands under Joel's armpits, and half-hoisted him off the floor. 'Barney!' shouted Joel. Then, in a screech that paralysed everybody in the whole dining-room, and sent cold prickles dancing all over Barney's back, *'Barney! For the love of God! Barney!'*

Wide-eyed, terrified, the veins bulging on his forehead, Nathan Golden stared at Barney in mute alarm. Barney looked down, and Joel's face had the appearance of a rubber carnival mask that had been pulled mercilessly inside-out. Joel was in such agony that he could not speak any more, could not do anything at all but lie on the floor and pray that Nathan and Barney would not try to pick him up again.

Barney said to Nathan, 'Put him down, gently.' Then, to Sara, 'Bring me some cushions, will you, to prop up his head – and, Horace, go find me some sharp scissors from the kitchen, quickly, and some towels.'

Sara brought two or three silk-xovered cushions and lifted Joel's head on to them carefully. Joel was almost unconscious now, and saliva was running from the corner of his mouth. Every now and then, though, his whole body would jerk with a muscular spasm, and his eyes would flicker open and stare at Barney with that strange inhuman neutrality that you only ever see in the eyes of the nearly-dying or the just-born.

Horace came at a bow-legged run, and handed Barney the scissors they used for clipping chickens' wings and parcel-string. The party guests stood in utter silence as Barney took hold of the cuff of Joel's left trouser-leg, and sliced it all the way up to the crotch. Some of the ladies turned away, but most of them stayed where they were, fascinated by the sight of Joel's circumcised penis, and by a sense of impending horror. These were not Capetown ladies.

The fabric of Joel's trouser-leg was already stuck to his thigh by a crust of blood and dried lymph. When Barney tried cautiously to pull it away, Joel crammed his hand into his mouth and uttered a single gargling sound. He kept his hand between his teeth: he obviously understood that there was worse to come. Barney picked up one of the towels that Horace had brought from the kitchen, and tucked it under Joel's thigh before trying to peel the trousers back any further. Then he said to Nathan Golden, 'Whiskey. Bring me a whole bottle of whiskey.'

Everybody waited like a collection of well-dressed tailors'

dummies while Nathan went over to the liquor cabinet on squeaky shoes and came back with a bottle of scotch. Barney said, 'Pour it down his throat. Get him as drunk as you can,' and Nathan hesitantly held the neck of the bottle to Joel's lips. Barney snapped, 'I want him *drunk*, for God's sake, not merry,' and reached over to press the bottle roughly against Joel's teeth, tipping it upright so that the liquor gushed down Joel's throat, and all over his shirt front. Joel coughed, and made a loud retching noise, but he managed to keep most of the whiskey down.

Then, with a single unhesitating tug, Barney pulled away Joel's trouser-leg, along with a makeshift bandage made of torn linen, and revealed his wound. There was a cry of '*Oh!*' throughout the whole room, and almost all of the remaining ladies retreated from the dining-room with their faces as white as the walls. One or two of the men stepped back, too, particularly when the stench of gangrene rose from Joel's leg, and they saw the hideous extent of what Joel had done to himself.

Halfway up Joel's thigh, there was a moist and gaping wound, swollen, tinged with green, and clustered with watery blisters. The wound was weeping effusively, and the smell of rot was almost more than Barney could stand. Out of the wound protruded the pointed corner of what looked like a large fragment of glass.

With the points of the scissors, Barney touched the edges of the wound and the piece of glass. Surprisingly, Joel scarcely flinched. The flesh that formed the fishlike lips of his self-inflicted incision was dead, and the pain that he felt came mostly from the reddened area further around, where the gangrene was just beginning to attack.

Barney had suspected for days what Joel had done, but the reality of it shocked him so much that he found himself unable to speak, or to do anything but lay down the scissors on the towel, and kneel in front of Joel with his head bowed and his eyes closed.

Rhodes said, 'I'll send a boy to bring Dr Tuter.'

Barney raised his eyes. 'Thanks. I don't think I can handle this on my own.'

'Is that what I think it is? asked Rhodes, nodding towards the wound.

'You've heard the rumours, too,' said Barney.

'They make jokes about the bush-telegraph,' Rhodes said, 'but if you keep your ear to the ground you can get to know almost everything. My kaffirs have been all of a-twitter for weeks about a giant diamond that was found on the Jewfella's claim at Kimberley.'

'It seems like the Jewfella was just about the last person to know,' said Barney.

'That scarcely matters,' smiled Rhodes. 'He who laughs last, don't you know. And there it is, it's all yours, if you care to dig it out.'

'Joel is my brother,' said Barney.

'Haven't you heard Harold's wonderful stories about brothers who blinded other brothers and locked them away for the rest of their miserable lives, simply for the sake of diamonds?'

Barney nodded. 'I guess I have.'

'Well, there you are,' said Rhodes. 'There in front of you is the living proof of what men will do for the sake of a large lump of crystallised carbon. Not only to each other, but to themselves.'

Barney knelt in silence for a minute or two, with Rhodes watching him with the very slightest smile on his face – the kind of smile that would have had him caned for smirking, if he were still a schoolboy. Then Barney picked up the scissors again, gripped Joel's leg just below the knee to steady it, and slowly inserted the points in between the lump of glass and the bleb-smothered edge of Joel's skin. Joel was practically unconscious now, and as Barney thrust deeper into the soft, dead flesh, Joel did nothing but whistle softly between partly-closed teeth.

At last, the huge stone dropped out on to the towel. Barney took his handkerchief out of his breast pocket, and disgustedly wrapped it up. Rhodes gave a small grunt that could have been amusement, or irony, or simply relief that it was all over.

Barney stood up. Dr Tuter was walking unsteadily through the doorway, led by the sleeve by a small barefoot Hottentot boy. Dr Tuter blinked at Barney as if he did not quite recognise him.

Over in the corner, Sara was standing with her hands clasped in tension, her face set like plaster. Not far away, in an emerald green sari, stood Nareez. Barney held the handkerchief up, not in triumph but in that ordinary human gesture that means, here it is, I've found it.

Rhodes said, 'Well done,' with unexpected smugness, and pushed his way back through the crowd of guests with his hands in his pockets, to rejoin Alfred Beit, and to help himself to more champagne.

Mr Ransome was sweeping his small back yard when Mooi Klip walked up to his fence in a wide summer bonnet, a basket of okra and purple kale under her arm, and stood watching him in the dusty, dappled sunlight. He propped his broom against the wall, and wiped the sweat from his forehead with the back of his arm. 'Natalia! It's good to see you.'

Mooi Klip smiled. 'I've been meaning to come to talk to you for days,' she said.

Mr Ransome opened the gate, and ushered her in. 'I try to keep the place tidy, but there are so many other things to do, so many souls still to be converted. Mind you, I think we're going to find it easier to bring all of South Africa into the Christian fold when the new Governor has done his stuff.'

'I didn't even know there was a new Governor,' said Mooi Klip. 'That just shows how ignorant I am.'

'There isn't any particular reason why you should have known,' Mr Ransome replied. 'But do come in and have some tea. I had some excellent Keenun sent up from the Cape.'

He led her across the overgrown verandah of his bungalow, under a tangle of creepers and bougainvillaea, and in through the open door to his modest sitting-room, which had been furnished strictly according to a Church of England budget. There was a clutter of dark, cheap chairs, and a mock-Jacobean sofa with sagging cushions. Twine-bound bundles of mission-ary Bibles and hymn books were stacked up untidily against the side of the bureau, which itself was surmounted by a tea-stained doily, a wooden cross, and a tin of Huntley & Palmers' Albany biscuits.

The only personal touch in the whole room was a water-colour of a redbrick suburban street, planted with trees. 'That's a view of my home,' said Mr Ransome. 'My mother painted it when she was recovering from the scarlatina.'

Mooi Klip laid down her basket, and sat on the sofa. The sun lined her profile in light, and poured two careful measures of shadow into the hollows of her collarbone. Mr Ransome looked at her with his hands slightly raised as if he had been going to say something emphatic, but had completely forgotten what it was.

'I've come about Coen,' said Mooi Klip.

'You want to fix a day, I suppose?' asked Mr Ransome. 'Well, let me get my diary, and let me put on the kettle. I gave Elretha the day off to visit her cousin. Very family-minded, Elretha. A good Christian.'

'I've decided not to marry Coen,' said Mooi Klip.

Mr Ransome stared at her. 'You've decided *not* to marry him? But, my dear Natalia, why? Has something gone terribly wrong?'

She looked up, and gave Mr Ransome a small, brave smile. 'We decided it together. He's a good man, and he's gentle like a lamb, but he's not for me. Barney did so much to bring me out, to show me what I could make of myself. If I married Coen, I'd be nothing but a farmer's wife; and I'd probably never speak English again for the rest of my life, except to you.'

Mr Ransome sat down next to Mooi Klip and took her hand. 'My dear, there is no *shame* in being a farmer's wife. It is one of the holiest of occupations, farming. It says in Proverbs that "he who tilleth his land shall be satisfied with bread: but he, or in this case she, who followeth vain persons is void of understanding."'

Mooi Klip turned and frowned at him. 'I'm not sure that I know what that means,' she said.

Mr Ransome's face, inspired by his recitation from the Bible, gradually subsided, until he was frowning too. 'I'm not sure that I do, either.' He stood up. 'I'd better make some tea. You'll feel – calmer – after some tea.'

'I'm calm now,' she said.

'Well, excellent,' said Mr Ransome. 'But what are you going to do? Have you thought about that? Here you are with a six-year-old son, unmarried, and having to depend entirely on your parents. Surely the life you are living now is even more imprisoning then being a farmer's wife would have been: and it will grow even more burdensome to you when your parents grow old.'

Mooi Klip said nothing, but brushed out her flowery skirt with her hands.

'I don't usually say this to young women,' Mr Ransome went on, in a more cautious tone. 'You see – the official line is that it is most desirable for at least one daughter to remain at home, unmarried, to care for the parents in their dotage. That is what the bishop approves of. But, in your case, I think things are different.'

'Why should they be?' asked Mooi Klip.

'My dear girl, they are different because *you* are different. You are a Griqua, a living symbol of this country's oneness under God, the mixing of the black and the white races. Did you know that one of the very first Christian marriages ever solemnised at the Cape in the seventeehth century was between a Hottentot woman and a white employee of the Dutch East India Company? You are an inheritor of that wonderful tradition, the acceptability of one race to another. And apart from that, you are beautiful; and for you to let your beauty wither away unseen in your parents' house for the rest of your life would be a criminal waste of God's bounty.'

'I'm still not sure what you're trying to say,' said Mooi Klip, gently.

Mr Ransome clapped his hand to the back of his neck in exasperation, as if he were swatting a mosquito. 'I'm trying to say, Natalia – I'm trying to say that you are a most exceptional young lady. I'm trying to explain to you that you ought to be married. Your son needs a father, after all. And you need to express, in the fullest proportion, your beautiful and intelligent womanhood.'

He stopped, and licked his lips. 'I hope I haven't embarrassed you.'

Mooi Klip shook her head. 'I'm not embarrassed by compliments. I'm very pleased for them. But why are you so angry? I've never seen you like this, not even when you're preaching. You don't have to be angry about me. I can find a way to live my life happily, you know that.'

'I'm angry because you've been so badly treated,' said Mr Ransome. 'It seems to me that your Barney didn't know a good thing when he saw one. To give you a child like that, and to throw you on the rubbish heap!'

Mooi Klip looked aside. 'Mr Ransome,' she said, 'that kind of sad affair happens all the time. It hurt me. It *still* hurts me, after all these years. Perhaps it wouldn't if I didn't have Pieter to remind me. But we can't cry over spilled milk. We can't be angry just because a man has done to a woman what men have been doing to women since Adam and Eve.'

Mr Ransome lowered his head, and when he spoke his words were very indistinct. 'It's never happened before to somebody I love.'

The small sitting-room was silent. Outside the open door, the leaves on the creepers rustled in a breeze that was as gentle as a secret whisper. The bar of sunlight which had been illuminating the crucifix on the bureau gradually crept across to the tin of Albany biscuits.

Mr Ransome looked up. Mooi Klip was gazing at him in the pose of a dark-skinned madonna. Her bonnet formed a halo.

'The new governor's name is Sir Bartle Frere,' said Mr Ransome, abruptly, loudly, in a violent change of subject. 'He's an old India hand, the bishop tells me. They've given him the job of gathering together all these ill-assorted colonies and native kingdoms and individual Boer states, and forming a single dominion, subject to the British Crown. And to British religion, of course.'

'What did you say?' asked Mooi Klip.

'I said, "subject to British religion, of course," ' Mr Ransome stammered, stepping backwards and stumbling over a heap of Bibles, scattering them all over the floor.

'No, before that. Before you started telling me about the new governor.'

'I didn't say anything. Did you hear me say something?'

427

'Mr Ransome, you're a man of God. You shouldn't tell tales.'

Mr Ransome hiked up his cassock, and got down on his hands and knees to pick up the Bibles. 'I said something out of turn, that's all. I promised my mother years and years ago, when I first entered the church, that I would abstain, that I would keep myself pure, and so what I might have said was quite improper of me, and I would prefer it if you would kindly forget I ever opened my mouth. My mouth was given to me in order that I should sing the praises of the Lord: not for making indecent proposals.'

'You said you loved me,' persisted Mooi Klip.

'Then I was quite out of order. Please forgive me.' Mr Ransome had disappeared behind the sofa now, and all Mooi Klip could see were his black worn-out shoes and his black laddered socks.

'Mr Ransome —' said Mooi Klip. 'Do you have to ask forgiveness for loving someone? Didn't you always tell me that love is the mainstay of the Christian religion?'

Mr Ransome scuffled and snuffled for a moment, and then emerged from behind the sofa red-eyed, with tears sliding down each cheek.

'Mr Ransome, what on earth is the matter?' asked Mooi Klip, reaching her hands out for him. 'Why are you crying?'

'I'm crying because I'm unhappy,' he said. 'I'm sorry, it's quite ridiculous. I shouldn't have said anything at all, and then none of this would have happened. You won't tell anyone, though, will you? If it gets back to the bishop ... I mean, they chose me for Klipdrift because of my self-avowed celibacy. They thought it was advisable to send out somebody chaste ... as a sort of example.'

Mooi Klip smiled. 'An example of what? Of an unhappy man? Of a man who believes in marriage but doesn't practise it?'

Mr Ransome stood up, and poked around under his cassock to find a handkerchief. He blew his nose, and wiped his eyes, and then he said, 'I'm sorry. I can't tell you how sorry I am.'

'Stop telling me you're sorry. I was fond of you long before I met Coen Boonzaier. I liked you the day you first came to

Klipdrift. You always seemed like a breath of the outside world. We can be friends, can't we?'

Mr Ransome cleared his throat. 'Of course. Yes. I mean, we always were, weren't we?' He put the Bibles back against the bureau, and came around to sit down beside Mooi Klip, leaning forward, with his knee clasped in his hands. 'I'm surprised to hear you thought so well of me.'

'Why? You're good-looking. You know all kinds of interesting things. I always thought that if you hadn't been a priest, you would have made a perfect husband.'

'Natalia . . . you really mustn't speak this way. I'm – well, I'm susceptible.'

'I don't know that word.'

'It means that you affect me, in a physical manner.'

Mooi Klip stared at him seriously. She was so feminine and soft and pretty that Mr Ransome could hardly bear to look at the way her chest rose and fell as she breathed. He knew this was all absurd. He was being tempted by the flesh. But the trouble was that Mooi Klip was so direct and innocent in the way she spoke to him, so frank in the profession of her affection, that he found it impossible to believe that what he was feeling was the work of Satan. He closed his eyes, but all he could think of was that moment when he had seen the dark shade of Mooi Klip's nipple through her gauzy blouse; and of the native women he had seen by the Vaal River, their big breasts bare and their Hottentot bottoms protruding through the brightly-coloured wraps they wore around their waists; and of the curious time when he had happened to glance down a side-alley in Klipdrift and seen an astonishingly beautiful long-haired girl of no more than thirteen or fourteen, a half-caste, quite naked except for a chain around her ankle. He had dreamed of that girl afterwards, as he had dreamed of Mooi Klip, and her slanting eyes had followed him unblinking down a thousand wretched and sweaty struggles with his chastity.

'Perhaps I'd better go,' said Mooi Klip, softly.

'I haven't made the tea yet,' said Mr Ransome, awkwardly standing up.

'You don't have to trouble,' Mooi Klip told him. She stood

up, too, and picked up her basket of vegetables. 'I really just came to tell you about Coen.'

'Yes,' said Mr Ransome. 'Well, I'm sorry that you decided not to go ahead with your marriage plans. I, er, I . . . I can only give you consolation from the Bible. As it says in Ecclesiastes, "Sorrow is better than laughter: for by the sadness of the countenance the heart is made better!" '

Mooi Klip stared at Mr Ransome for a moment or two, and then giggled. Mr Ransome laughed too, in an odd staccato way that made Mooi Klip giggle even more. She reached up and kissed his cheek, and said, 'You've consoled me already. I think you're a very fine missionary, Mr Ransome.'

'You ought to call me Hugh.'

'That is your name? Hugh? What does it mean?'

'I'm not honestly sure. My mother knows. She's good on things like that. You know, folklore, history. She embroiders rather well, too. She sent me a whole set of embroidered antimacassars for my birthday, I –' he looked around his cheap and crowded little sitting-room, 'I really haven't had time to put them out yet.'

'You talk of your mother,' said Mooi Klip. 'Why don't you tell me about yourself?'

'There's not a lot to tell, actually.'

'Why don't I make us a picnic, for you and me, and on Friday we can go along to Blaauwkopje and talk? My mother will look after Pieter.'

Hugh Ransome looked at Mooi Klip carefully, and smoothed back his hair. 'I should say no,' he told her. His voice seemed suddenly more mature, quieter. 'Do you really want me to come?'

Mooi Klip nodded. 'I want to hear all of your life, from the day you were born.'

'I'm afraid that the life of a man who has never known a single woman is not very interesting listening.'

'You never know,' said Mooi Klip, and turned around to go. A mongrel dog was barking loudly in the next-door yard.

'Natalia!' said Hugh Ransome, hastily.

'What is it?'

'It's – well, it's nothing, really. I just wanted to say "Natalia". I think the name is as beautiful as the girl.'

'Thank you, Hugh,' said Mooi Klip, and walked out across the verandah into the brilliant early-afternoon sunshine, as if she were a dissolving vision. Hugh Ransome stayed still in the middle of his sitting-room for a long time, embracing himself in his own arms; and then he felt the need to sit down.

'"Discretion shall preserve thee, understanding shall keep thee,"' he recited, under his breath. '"Wisdom shall deliver thee from the strange woman, even from the stranger which flattereth with her words; that thou mayest walk in the way of good men, and keep the paths of the righteous."'

He stared at the worn-out rug on the floor, and thought again of Mooi Klip with her sun-hat halo. 'Damn wisdom, and damn discretion,' he said, and then sat up straight and looked quickly around, to make sure that nobody had heard him.

Barney was working in the library at Vogel Vlei when Horace rapped at the doors and put his black face around it at an alarming sideways angle, with only his eyes showing. Barney looked up from his papers and said, 'What is it, Horace?' without even remarking on the servant's odd posture. He was used to Horace, after six months of living at Vogel Vlei. Horace was entirely individual. He had once tried to warm up a visitor's bed by coaxing a black nanny-goat to lie under the blankets until it was time for the visitor to retire.

'A gentleman from Capetown to see you,' said Horace. 'He presents his card.'

'Very well, then,' said Barney, 'where is it?'

Horace's head disappeared like a badly stage-managed Oriental conjuring trick. Then his right hand emerged, holding the card between two fingers.

'Bring it here, will you, Horace?' asked Barney. 'My eyes are reasonably good, but I can't read a visiting card from fifty feet away.'

Horace withdrew the card, and then remained in hiding behind the door. 'Come on, man, I don't have all day,' Barney demanded.

'I can't, boss.'

'You can't? Why not?'

'My uniform trousers, boss, have torn badly.'

'Then just read me the name on the card.'

'Can't read, boss.'

Barney threw down his pen in impatience, stalked across the library floor and plucked the card out of Horace's hand. It read 'William Hunt, Trade Attaché, Government House, Cape-town.'

'It's me!' exclaimed a sharp voice, and Horace stood back against the door to admit the diminutive Hunt; still bearded, though now touched with wiry silver hairs, still immaculately dressed in a greyish-lavender suit, and still smelling strongly of French cologne. 'My dear Barney, it's such a pleasure to see you! After all this time!'

Barney grasped Hunt's hand, and shook it. 'I'm amazed,' he said. 'What can bring a city fellow like you all the way out to Kimberley? Listen – you must have a drink. Horace – bring us two glasses of schnapps, will you.'

Horace, with his back pressed to the open door, said, 'Now, sir?'

'Yes, Horace, now.'

Horace awkwardly shuffled around, and then hurried off across the hallway as quickly as he could, grabbing behind him for the errant triangular flap of fabric that had torn from his trousers. Hunt watched him go with a look of almost professorial interest, and even took out a pair of wire-rimmed spectacles.

'Fine brown bum your man's got,' he remarked.

'He's something of a clown; but he's good-natured,' said Barney. 'And I see that *you* haven't changed.'

'Would that I could, my dear chap. The truth is that all the new fellows that Sir Bartle has brought in from India are rather a supercilious lot; or, if they aren't supercilious, they're spotty. I'm not sure which I can tolerate the least – haughtiness or hives. Each of them has their own disagreeable poison.'

Hunt walked over to a large brown leather armchair by the fireplace, and sat himself down as if he had lived at Vogel Vlei for most of his life. He leaned his cane against the hearth and tugged off his gloves, one finger at a time, and flopped them over the arm of the chair. 'I've been hearing some very interesting stories about you,' he told Barney. 'They say you're almost a millionaire these days.'

Barney walked around his wide partners' desk and cleared away some of the papers he had been working on. He was entering the final negotiations for buying seven more claims, two of them crucial diggings right in the centre of the Kimberley pipe. Apart from the fact that both claims had been yielding scores of high-quality diamonds every single week since they had first been excavated, they stood right between Blitz Brothers and the French company which owned most of the claims on the Big Hole's southern side. Their owner was asking £360,000, and Barney was doing everything he could to persuade him to bring down his price. Barney was a millionaire, all right, but only on paper.

The trouble was, everybody in town now knew that Barney owned a 350-carat diamond, and even in the local dry goods stores his servants were being charged twice the going price for any supplies that were ordered for Vogel Vlei. Barney was finding that his liquidity was dwindling fast, just when he had the most need of it. He could have stepped up diamond production, but he was anxious not to stir up the whole of the Kimberley mine into a furious burst of digging, in case they flooded the market again and brought the world price down. Whenever he was asked about the monster diamond in public, he said again and again that it was one of a kind, a freak, and that the chances of anyone finding another one of that size were practically nil. Harold Feinberg during the summer of 1878 and 1879 lived on heart flutters, patent antacids, and the dogged sexuality of his little froggy girl. Barney could not even mention the diamond to him without him turning white.

'Owning one fancy diamond doesn't actually make me the richest man in the world,' said Barney.

'No, I understand that, of course,' said Hunt, 'And so does Sir Bartle.'

'Sir Bartle's taking a personal interest in me? I thought Sir Bartle was busy being friendly to the Zulus.'

'Well, he's *not*, actually,' said Hunt, 'and that's part of the reason I'm here. We're in a spot of bother with the Zulus, as a matter of fact. You know how they were always haggling with the Boers over their borders with the Transvaal ... Well, Sir Bartle set up a commission last year to settle the matter, and – rather bad luck – the commission actually found in favour of the Zulus. Bit embarrassing, really, what. But Sir Bartle's trying to sort the whole thing out by insisting that he will only ratify Zululand's border if Cetewayo disbands his army.'

Barney listened to that, and then pulled a face. 'I don't know much about Zulus, but from what I hear of Cetewayo, that's about the last thing he'll do. How can he disband his army and still stay independent? The Boers will have him for breakfast.'

'Between you and me, old chap, you're quite right. But that's just what Sir Bartle's counting on, Cetewayo saying no. And unless Cetewayo disperses his army within a week, Sir Bartle's going to send Lord Chelmsford and two thousand soldiers into Zululand to teach him a considerable lesson. That way, Sir Bartle can keep his promise to honour his commission's findings, *and* crush the Zulus, both at the same time.'

Barney rubbed his eyes. He had been working late almost every night for the past three weeks, and he felt exhausted. 'You Colonial Office monkeys really enjoy this kind of thing, don't you?' he asked. 'But where do I come into it? I know as much about Zulus as everyone else around here, and that's nothing at all.'

Horace came into the library with two glasses of schnapps, and a jug of water. He was wearing his usual black tailcoat, but this time, underneath it, he wore bright yellow riding breeches. Hunt gave him an amused, provocative look which perplexed Horace completely. He turned to Barney for reassurance, and Barney waved him out of the room with a grin.

'It's your diamond we're interested in,' Hunt told Barney. 'It's already been written about in the London papers, of course; but I must say that you kept the press very short of detail. The *Morning Post* said nothing more than that they had heard a "rumour" that a particularly large gemstone had been dug up at Kimberley, and that it was "estimated" to weigh in excess of three hundred carats.'

'I'm not announcing anything else until I'm ready,' said Barney. 'It's taken us years to build up this diamond industry the way it is today, people like Rhodes and Gould and me. The

434

very worst thing that could happen to us now is an old-style diamond rush, and a collapse of diamond prices on the world market.'

'Well, you're right, of course,' said Hunt. 'But I must say that Sir Bartle came up with an excellent idea in his bathtub the other day. He suggested that he should announce the discovery of your diamond right away, in a really dramatic fashion, all champagne and trumpets and God Save The Queen – and that he should then arrange for a special presentation of the diamond to Her Majesty in London. He suggested that you might think of christening the stone the Victoria Star, in her honour.'

'And what would be the point of that?' asked Barney.

Hunt raised a finger. 'The point, my dear chap, is that the attention of Her Majesty and Her Majesty's ministers of State would be diverted long enough by this patriotic charade to allow Sir Bartle to overwhelm the Zulus and capture Cetewayo before anyone in the Government could start squeaking about fair play, and cricket, and all that nonsense.'

Barney sat back in the buttoned armchair behind his desk, and looked at Hunt thoughtfully. Barney had changed a great deal since Hunt had first met him on the deck of the *Weser*, and Hunt, who was sensitive to men, had already been alerted by the flamboyant style of Barney's well-cut tweed suit and by his careful but abrasive mannerisms that Barney was now stronger, and much more aware of his personal power, and that he was going to be far more difficult to handle than the peaky-faced Jewish emigrant whom he had tried to seduce off the coast of equatorial Africa.

What Hunt did not know, although he sensed it, was that Barney had lost at last those youthful sympathies which had made him so gentle and so spontaneous in New York and during his first years at the Cape. He had abandoned his unquestioning devotion to his brother, and to the memory of his mother; and he had grown wise to the papier-mâché *hauteur* of the British colonial classes. Barney had become less pliable, but also more perceptive, and he had begun to organise his business and his household on his own terms and very rarely on anybody else's.

435

All those nights of guilt and all those splattered visions of his mother's blood had long since faded away. Now, he slept dreamlessly next to a well-bred woman who had agreed to say what she was told, and lift her nightdress when she was required, and to smile and be pretty whenever it was called for. In return, he was faithful to her, and he brought her diamond bracelets and necklaces by the handful. Nareez came and went on shuffling silk slippers, and scowled at him whenever she passed him on the landing, but Nareez no longer upset him, because there was no longer any weakness in him for Nareez to pick at. He had come to terms with an attractive woman whom he did not love, and who did not love him in return. He had bought nearly a third of the Big Hole at Kimberley. And to crown it all he owned one of the largest rough diamonds ever found anywhere since the recorded beginning of diamond mining.

'The Victoria Star, huh?' said Barney. 'I'm an American, why should I consent to my diamond being called the Victoria Star?'

'We're friendly, aren't we, Americans and British?' said Hunt.

'I don't know,' Barney told him. 'Are we? Wasn't it Queen Victoria's grandfather who fought against us so bloodily only a hundred years ago?'

Hunt smirked. 'You're pulling my leg. You're German Jewish. You couldn't care a less about George III. Besides the Queen's mostly German herself. As one Kraut to another, you should be glad to give her the Star.'

'*Give?*' asked Barney, ignoring the gibe about his nationality.

'I don't mean *give* in that sense, my dear chap. There will of course be the matter of reasonable payment.'

'By whom?'

'By a consortium of British businessmen who are quite anxious to see South Africa organised into one profitable and easily-administered dominion, and to see that Zululand is All Sir Garnet as soon as possible.'

'All Sir what?'

'Oh, sorry, old chap. Fashionable expression in the colonial service. After Sir Garnet Wolseley, who crushed the Ashanti in '73. It means "shipshape!"'

'You British have a jolly phrase for everything, don't you?' said Barney. 'What's your expression for get the hell out of my house?'

Hunt made a *moue*. 'I think "bugger off" should do nicely for that.'

'Good. Then bugger off.'

Hunt sighed. 'You really don't understand, do you? I'm here to offer you almost anything, within reason, provided you sell us the diamond and make a big splash about how you found it, and how proud you are to hand it over to Her Majesty.'

'I haven't had the diamond valued yet,' said Barney. 'My dealer's still doing tests on it.'

'What have your tests discovered so far? Is it flawed? Is it coloured? I mean, I've really come up here on something of a blind man's errand. It may not be worth handing over to Her Majesty at all.'

'It's an exceptionally fine lilac-coloured stone of exactly 356 carats and two points. There are no flaws. That's all I'm prepared to tell you.'

Hunt tipped back his schnapps glass, and took out his handkerchief to wipe his mouth. 'I'm empowered to offer you £750,000, in gold and notes.'

Barney said, 'It may be worth more, it may be worth less. I can't tell until we've finished our tests. Besides, I don't think I'm particularly keen on the idea of using the diamond simply to take the public's attention away from one of your squalid native wars.'

'Steady on,' said Hunt. 'You can hardly call the spread of the British Empire squalid. Everywhere that Britain rules, there is justice, freedom, stern fair play, and so much gin and adultery that those who aren't down on their knees are flat on their backs.'

Barney gave Hunt a wry smile of amusement. But then he said, 'I'm not selling. Not yet. I want to see this stone through every single stage of its cutting and its marketing, and I want to see that it's bought for the right person for the right reasons. The Victoria Star? You must be joking.'

'I can offer you a million,' said Hunt, with a grin.

437

'Just like that? Sight unseen?'

'Subject to proper examination, of course. But if the stone turns out to be what you claim it to be, a flawless rough of 356·2 carats, then we won't have any difficulties, will we? It will be *worth* a million.'

'I'm not selling,' said Barney.

'A million, two hundred thousand,' said Hunt. 'That's my absolute limit!'

'I just told you that I'm not selling.'

'Then you're a fool, my dear chap. Where else in the world would you get nearly one and a quarter million pounds in gold and notes, even for a flawless 350-carat diamond? This is the best offer you're ever going to get, and I can promise you that if you don't take it now, you'll spend the rest of your natural life regretting it.'

Barney reached across the green leather top of his desk, and picked up a small brass bell with an imp's face on it. He tinkled the bell between his finger and his thumb, keeping his attention unwaveringly on Hunt.

'I'm not selling,' he repeated.

Hunt sat where he was for a second, drumming his fingertips tautly on the arm of the chair. Then he stood up as quickly as an unfolded clasp-knife, picked up his cane and his gloves, and said, 'Very well. If you're not going to sell, then you're not going to sell. It's been nice talking to you again.'

Horace opened the door, and said, 'Yes, boss?'

'You can show Mr Hunt to his carriage now, Horace.'

'Yes, boss. This way, Mr Hunt, sir.'

'Oh, Barney –' said Hunt, as he reached the door. 'There was one more thing I forgot tò ask you.'

'What's that?'

'Your brother Joel ... well, I gather you must have located him, from what the report in the *Colesberg Advertiser* said.'

'Yes, I did.'

'They mentioned that he wasn't well.'

'He's not. He had some kind of infection. He lost his left leg.'

'I'm sorry to hear that,' said Hunt. 'Does he still live here, with you?'

'He has a suite of rooms upstairs. He keeps himself pretty

well secluded these days, though. He plays a lot of chess. I hardly see him from one week to the next.'

Hunt thought about that, still smiling, and then he said, 'There was some suggestion, you know, that your brother found the stone first, and that he tried to keep it hidden from you.'

'Was there?' asked Barney.

'Well, that's the way the chaps over at De Beers tell the story. It could all be nonsense, of course.'

'Then I expect that it is nonsense,' said Barney, in a level voice. 'Now if you'll excuse me, I'm very busy. Are you staying in Kimberley long?'

'A week or two. Just long enough to justify my scandalous expenses.'

'You must come to dinner, then. I'll speak to Sara about it.'

'My dear chap,' said Hunt. 'You were always a gentleman. I'm most obliged.'

After Hunt had left, Barney stood behind his desk, looking tall and grave in the diffuse oval of light that shone from his green-shaded lamp. He felt disturbed by dozens of inexpressible questions – questions about himself, about his happiness, and about his dim, grotesque world of manipulation and money into which his ownership of the huge lilac diamond was beginning to draw him. He remembered the rich people he had seen in New York, in their sleep top hats and their astrakhan-collared coats, sitting back on the seats of their phaetons with immaculately-groomed whiskers and faces as neutral as minor gods. Now he knew why they looked the way they did. They were groomed because they were rich, and could afford to keep servants; but the neutrality of their expression came from the uncertainty they felt that they deserved any of this attention and equally from their determination not to show it. Barney remembered thinking years ago that it must be wonderful to be wealthy: but the truth was, now that he actually *was* wealthy, in this stately library lined with thousands of unread books, that he felt off-balance and unsettled, and that his need for love and for family friendship was still as demanding as ever.

He had no urge to return to Clinton Street, and the Lower East Side. He still preferred to be a diamond magnate, rather than a bespoke tailor. But he was beginning to feel again that excruciating loneliness that he had felt when he first crossed the Atlantic Ocean to Liverpool, and he realised that, apart from those months he had spent with Mooi Klip, it had never once left him.

He left his desk, and walked across the library to the steel and cement Union safe which was installed under one of the bookshelves. He took out his keys, and unlocked the double doors. There, on the top shelf, wrapped up in soft gazelle-skin, was the diamond. He took it out, and carried it back to the lamplight, where he opened up the leather, and let the stone lie exposed and shining, an embodiment of pure fact.

Several merchants had already approached him with offers for the diamond. Most of them had been acting on behalf of governments or wealthy collectors. The Russian court had been showing particularly enthusiastic interest, and had twice sent the Belgian dealers Leopold & Wavers around to see him with offers that were cautiously close to a million. But Harold Feinberg had advised caution. The diamond was so rare and enormous that it would be a political influence as well as a spectacular piece of personal property. It had been discovered on ground that the British were quite sure was theirs, and there had already been letters in *The Times* asking when the diamond was going to be seen in the country of its ownership. It would not help Blitz Brothers with the Board for the Protection of Mining Industries, nor with Government House, if Barney were to let the diamond go to the Czar, or to the Prussians, or worst of all, to the Dutch. There were too many Boer sympathisers among Amsterdam's diamond merchants who might be tempted to restore it to the Orange Free State on a lease-land basis as a symbol of Boer independence, and what the Boer republic considered to be its rightful title to the diamond mines.

Barney had kept the diamond in his safe ever since his wedding-celebration party, although he had allowed Harold to come around to test it and inspect it. Harold had spent all day with it, only stopping for ten minutes to drink a cup of coffee and eat a plateful of beef sandwiches, and even then he had continued to stare at the diamond as if he were bewitched. At four o'clock, Barney had finished his paperwork and come into the conservatory to watch.

440

'I'm almost finished,' Harold had told him. 'It has a few tiny inclusions on one side, but those will be lost when they cleave it. It's a remarkable diamond. Just remarkable. I wish my old father could have seen it. It would have brought tears to his eyes.'

'What tests have you made?' Barney had asked him. 'You're sure that it's a diamond? I mean, one hundred per cent sure?'

'No question about it,' Harold had said. 'I tested it for hardness, by scratching another diamond with it. Also a sapphire. That's not a test you should ever do with a polished diamond, because you can damage the edges. But there wasn't any doubt about this one.'

'I thought the standard test was to hit the diamond with a hammer,' Barney had remarked.

'They used to. But the trouble is, diamonds are brittle, as well as hard, and you could end up with more than a handful of smashed pieces. I know a couple of East End merchants who used to encourage diggers to test if their stones were genuine or not by banging them with a hammer, and when the stones were all broken up, and the diggers went away disappointed, all the merchants had to do was to scoop up the bits and sell them as industrials, or pointers, for shopgirls' engagement-rings. They made themselves a small fortune.'

Barney had picked up the diamond and turned it over. 'What other tests have you done?'

'Surface tension, although it's difficult to get an accurate result with an uncut rough. If you leave a drop of water on the table of a diamond, it will stay there much longer than on any other kind of stone. And then there's conductivity. You've already noticed how quickly this diamond warms up and cools down when you hold it in your hand, or leave it alone on the desk.'

'What's it worth?' Barney had asked him. 'Do you have any idea?'

Harold had rolled down his sleeves and looked at Barney tiredly. 'This diamond is worth as much as anyone in the world will pay for it. If I were you, I wouldn't take less than a million pounds, in gold.'

Now, in the library, Barney sat with his head in his hands staring at the diamond and thinking. It was the most fabulous

441

possession he had ever owned, clear and bright and so uncompromising that it was almost holy. If all the laws and truths of the *Torah* could be crystallised into an object that could be held in one hand, this is what they would look like. It was so enormous that it was worth far more than money. In fact, it was so enormous that Barney knew that it would be impossible to own it for very long: the financial and political claims that the outside world were making on it were too strong.

But for the time being, and especially while he felt as lonely as he did, he found the diamond strangely consoling. He could stare at it for an hour at a time, turning it this way and that way to catch the different lights in the lilac-pink depths of its brilliant interior. For Joel, the diamond had represented dreams of luxury and riches and women. For Barney, it was more like a statement from God that He did exist, that here in the shape of a giant crystal was the adamant and irrefutable evidence, and that Barney had not been forgotten, for all of his desertions, for all of his doubts, and for all of his unsaid prayers.

Under his breath, alone in his grand library, Barney recited the words of the *Kol Nidre*, the prayer that is recited on the eve of Yom Kippur. Then he turned down the wick of his desk-lamp so low that the massive diamond in front of him gleamed with an unearthly pink light. He did not cry. It was far too late for tears. And, besides, he had on his desk the most incredible symbol of man's greed and God's ingenuity that the world had ever seen.

At nine o'clock, Barney went upstairs to see Joel. It was a reluctant duty, because ever since the wedding-party the two brothers had scarcely been able to speak to each other: Joel because of his shame at having been caught, and his chagrin at not having got away with the diamond after suffering so much, and Barney because he no longer trusted Joel to tell him the truth.

Sara was in Joel's bedroom when Barney knocked on the door. She was sitting on the end of the bed playing cards with him, for mint bon-bons. As usual, she was fashionably dressed, in a steel-grey satin tea-gown, with a diamond corsage garland strung beneath her breasts, and her hair was plaited and combed and studded with diamond clasps. All of her diamonds were presents from Barney: the corsage garland, which was valued at more than £22,500, Barney had given her the week after she had discovered that he was not a member of the Kimberley Club, and that being Jewish he probably never would be.

Joel was looking almost rudely healthy. Since Dr Tuter had sawed off his left leg on the evening of the party, an operation in which both surgeon and patient had been almost incapably drunk, he was far fitter and more optimistic than he had ever been before. Dr Tuter had treated his amputation with boric acid ointment, which had prevented the further spread of gangrene, and Joel had slowly but steadily recovered. Once the pain of the operation had faded, Joel had found that the nagging agonies of his reset left leg had left him for ever; and although his hip still felt uncomfortable on stormy days, he slept better, and ate better, and even teased the florid-faced English nurse Betty whom Barney had brought in from Capetown that a lone-legged man could do things to a girl that a two-legged man would find impossible. The kaffir servants, of course, found that it was now far easier to distinguish between their two employers in their conversation. Their orders these days came either from 'Mr One-Leg Blitzboss' or 'Mr Two-Leg Blitzboss.'

'I came to see how you were,' said Barney, standing uncomfortably at the door.

'He's losing badly at farmer's joy, if that's any indication of his health, said Sara.

'I see,' said Barney, with one of those smiles that came and went as quickly as a trick.

'I enjoy losing to your lovely wife,' said Joel, handing Sara three more mints. 'I like to see her excited, for a change.'

'Do you.'

Barney went to the window and drew back the drapes with one hand. Outside, the sky was as balck as plums, with only a single streak of red to show where the sun had gone.

'You're not pensive again, are you, my deah?' asked Sara, shuffling the cards between sharp pink fingernails.

'Mmh?' asked Barney, turning around.

443

'I said, "you're not pensive again, are you?" You seem to spend all your time these days in a brown study.' She dealt from the bottom of the deck, as rapidly and as efficiently as only an English colonial daughter knows how.

'Either a brown study or a diamond-studded library,' chuckled Joel; and Sara caught his eye and laughed.

'I've had an offer for the diamond from a consortium of English colonial businessmen,' said Barney.

'I hope they offered more than those awful Belgians.'

'They did. They said they could put up a million-two.'

Joel looked up – first at Barney and then at Sara. 'That's a lot of money,' he said. 'Even *half* of it is a lot of money.'

'Are you going to sell?' asked Sara. 'Joel, my darling – you *can't* do that. That's cheating.'

'I enjoy cheating,' said Joel. 'Cheating is almost as good as drinking.'

Sara collected two more bon-bons from him. 'Cheating is only enjoyable if it's undetectable, or if it's only discovered when it's far too late.'

'I'm, uh, thinking about it,' put in Barney. 'The offer, I mean. The trouble is, they want the stone for political reasons as well as financial ones. Sir Bartle Frere is intent on invading Zululand, apparently, and he wants to present the stone to Queen Victoria at the same time, to damp down any unpleasant reactions he might get from the cabinet.'

'What a *chozzer!*' Joel remarked. 'Do you know what his nickname is? "Sir Bottled Beer!"'

'Do you have to use language like that?' asked Barney irritably. 'This is a house, not a pigsty.'

Sara tittered. 'I *adore* it when Joel speaks Yiddish. The words are so absolutely expressive. He taught me what *pisher* meant, this morning.'

'Kimberley's a rough place,' said Barney, 'there's no need for either of you to make it any rougher.'

'Oh, Barney,' protested Sara. 'You're getting so stuffy these days!'

'I'm not stuffy, Sara,' Barney retorted. 'I just don't happen to like the sound of a woman using foul language, that's all. Especially when it's a woman who seems to regard herself as a doyenne of society.'

'My *dear* Barney,' said Sara, slapping down her cards, 'I couldn't regard myself as a doyenne of society in this ramshackle little town even if I *wanted* to, since my beloved husband doesn't happen to belong to the only half-decent club for hundreds and hundreds of miles. The only party I have ever given was utterly ruined by his insistence on tearing open his brother's gangrenous leg in front of all of my guests, and in any case I can't afford to give any more parties because he's invested all of his money in those ridiculous diamond mines and he won't sell the only worthwhile asset he's got, which is that stupid oversized diamond.'

'I'm going to sell it, but I'm not going to sell it for the wrong reasons!' snapped Barney. 'And nobody is going to *pressure* me into selling it, either! I'll sell it when I want to, and to *whom* I want to, and at the right price!'

'By the time you get around to selling it, you'll have worn it down to a half-pointer, just by staring at it!' said Sara.

'You don't even understand, do you?' Barney demanded. 'I suppose you want the blood of Cetewayo's Zulus all over your hands, just because you need a few thousand pounds for dresses, and for parties? They're thinking of sending two thousand troops in, and you know what that's going to mean? Well, you obviously don't – a massacre!'

Sara stood up, her fists clenched and her face distorted in utter fury. 'How *dare* you say that to me! How *dare* you! Do you think I'm going to put up with year after year of this obscenely boring place with no money and no social life and no friends, just for the sake of a handful of black savages? And what other excuse are you going to find for keeping me short of money, after the Zulus? The Hottentots, or the Xhosa? You've got to sell the diamond, and that's all there is to it!'

'I'm not selling,' said Barney, quietly.

'They'll send the troops into Zululand anyway,' said Joel, placidly gathering up the scattered cards and mint bon-bons on his quilted bedcover. 'Whether you sell the diamond or not, there's still going to be a massacre.'

'At least I won't be part of it,' Barney declared.

'Listen, Barney,' Joel told him, 'every diamond that was ever dug out of the ground has blood on it. It's the way that diamonds are. This diamond has blood on it already – mine. You don't

445

think a few hundred dead Zulus are going to make any difference?'

'That's the way that people have talked for centuries about the Jews,' said Barney, and his throat was thick with suppressed emotion. 'What does it matter? A few hundred dead Jews aren't going to make any difference! Well, let me tell you something, Joel. I don't know very much about the Zulus, but I do know that they're proud and that they're independent and that they have a culture and a social life of their own. I also happen to know that Cetewayo has tried to keep the peace with the British. But what we're talking about here is betrayal – deliberate betrayal – and deceit – and murder. And the Governor wants to use my diamond to lend his reputation a little spurious lustre, at a time when his reputation is going to be pretty well completely drowned in blood. You can think what you like. You can think I'm stuffy, and you can think that I'm ridiculous. But I'm not allowing that diamond to go to London as the Victoria Star.'

Sara's nostrils flared, like a mare, but she kept her peace. She sat down on the bed again, her back straight, and reached for Joel's hand. 'If you're absolutely determined that you're not going to sell it, then the least you can do to amuse me is to let me hold another party. Perhaps this time you'll be able to resist the temptation to tear Joel's trousers off, and display his stump to all of our guests.'

'I think I can manage that,' said Barney. 'How about the last day of January?'

'I don't suppose anybody will come,' said Sara. 'Not after the last fiasco.'

'Tell them that I'm going to put the diamond on open view,' said Barney. 'Then they'll come.'

'You mean you'd actually let other people ogle your precious diamond, *breathe* on it, just for my sake?' asked Sara, sarcastically.

'Sara,' said Barney, 'I'm doing my best to please you. Do you understand?'

Sara held her breath for a second, and then let it out. 'Yes, my dear,' she nodded. 'I'm terribleh sorreh.' Her over-emphasised accent betrayed the boredom she felt, and the contempt in which any experienced Africa hand would have held a chap who was soft on the natives. Bit of a square peg, don't-chi-know.

446

Barney waited in the bedroom for a moment longer, but by the way in which Joel and Sara sat like children who were impatient for an adult to leave so that they could carry on with their game, he knew that he was not welcome. He said, 'I'll go down and tell Kitty to make us a light supper.'

'I'm not eating,' said Sara.

Barney looked at her, and then at Joel. He had seen that smug expression on Joel's face before. 'In that case, you'll just have to sit there and watch me, won't you?' he said. 'I'll have Horace ring the gong when it's ready.'

He left the bedroom, leaving the door slightly open behind him. At the far end of the landing, in the shadows, he saw Nareez. The Indian *amah* had slipped away before he could say anything, but her perfume lingered on the stairs like an unsettling memory.

'I never thought that clergymen could cook,' said Mooi Klip, sitting back in the cheap varnished armchair by the frosted-glass oil-lamp.

'It wasn't much, I'm afraid,' said Hugh. 'Boiled beef and onion dumplings is really about my limit. Would you care for some tea, to follow it? Or coffee?'

'Later,' said Mooi Klip. 'Come and sit next to me. You've worked so hard to make everything nice.'

'I was a bit worried about the onion dumplings,' Hugh told her, frowning back at the remains of their dinner on the small dining-table. 'I've only made them for myself before, and of course when you're cooking for yourself you don't worry too much if things turn out rather odd. They weren't *odd*, were they?'

'No,' smiled Mooi Klip, taking his hand. 'They weren't odd at all.'

Hugh looked pleased, and dragged across one of the dining-chairs so that he could sit beside her. They had a special closeness now, Hugh and Mooi Klip. They had gone out on picnics together with Pieter, sitting on top of the small hay-coloured hills around the valley at the Vaal River, while clouds puffed past them like the steam from unseen trains, and the air had grown so hot that they had been unable to do anything but stay under their wide parasol and watch each other perspiring. They had gone to a fancy-dress dance run by the Presbyterians. They had walked hand-in-hand, and talked, and once they had gone all the way out to see Coen Boonzaier on his farm, and he had been quite friendly and cheerful, and offered Hugh a suck at his pipe.

Hugh had declined, but with a smile.

Now, with Elretha gone for the night, Hugh had invited Mooi Klip around for one of his home-cooked dinners, and he had decorated the table with wild flowers, and carefully set out his mother's antimacassars as napkins.

Mooi Klip said, 'Will you stay here for the rest of your life? In Griqualand, I mean?'

'It depends on my bishop, rather,' said Hugh. 'But I wouldn't have thought that he would have made me stay here for ever. I would love to take you back to England with me, and Pieter too. Kennington can be very pleasant, you know, in the summer. And I'm sure mother would adore you.'

Mooi Klip looked at Hugh fondly. She reached out to touch his face, to show him how affectionate she felt towards him; but he caught her hand first, and squeezed it tight. Rather too tight: she said, '*Ow*,' and he hastily let go.

'I'm afraid I'm not very good at this,' said Hugh. 'But when I say that I want to take you back to England with me, well, the truth is that I do. The truth is, Natalia, that I've been thinking about this for weeks now, and I want most desperately to marry you, to make you my wife. The truth is, that I love you most awfully.'

Mooi Klip did not appear to be at all surprised. She simply smiled at him, and said, 'Hugh ... you have always been good to me.'

'It's my job,' he said, flustered. 'It's my job to be good to people. It's what I get paid for.'

Mooi Klip shook her head. 'How could your stipend cover all of the affection that you have shown me, and all the understanding that you have given me, and how fatherly you have been to Pieter? It can't. Not twenty years of your stipend could do that. What you have been to me, Hugh, nobody could ever have saved up enough money to pay for.'

'Stipend, eh?' remarked Hugh, furiously scratching at his leg. 'That shows you've been walking out with a clerical fellow!'

448

'Hugh,' said Mooi Klip, 'I want to be honest with you. I don't ever want to lie to you.'

'Well, no, of course,' said Hugh. 'You can't possibly have any kind of a marriage if you lie, if you're not completely straight. Quite right.'

'Barney Blitz will always remain as the man I loved the most,' Mooi Klip told him, with infinite gentleness. 'It happened that way, I don't know why. Each of us brought out the best in each other. Barney made me feel like a woman, but he also made me feel strong. He protected me, but he didn't keep me on a chain. He was jealous, but he gave me freedom. He was a warm lover and a good friend.'

'I see,' said Hugh, white.

Mooi Klip reached out for Hugh again now, and held his right hand between both of hers. 'What I want you to know, Hugh, is that neither time nor the love of anybody else can ever make me forget what Barney was to me. It is a fact of what I am. I can never forget. But I am sensible enough and feminine enough to know that I can never have him back, and that I cannot live without a man beside me for ever. I love you, Hugh. Not the same way that I loved Barney. But I love your friendship, and how gentle you are, and I love to see Pieter playing with you and calling you by your name. If you can take me as I am, knowing that I still have a deep-buried love for someone else, then I promise you that I will always be a good wife to you, and that I will love you and care for you and honour you. If you really want me to marry you, Hugh, then all I can say is yes.'

Hugh was so overcome that the tears sprang into his eyes, and he was incapable of saying anything. He stood up, and then he sat down again. Then he went across the room, and let out a peculiar noise, like a sneeze and a sob mixed up.

'I'm so delighted,' he said. 'I'm so delighted I could cry.'

Mooi Klip smiled. 'You look as if you're crying already.'

'What?' he said, a little fiercely, wiping his eyes. 'Why should I cry when you've just made me feel so happy? Natalia! I can scarcely believe it! My dear Natalia, I love you so much!'

Mooi Klip stood up, and Hugh took her into his arms. 'I feel quite extraordinary,' he said. 'But I feel as if God approves! In

449

fact, I'm sure He does! I can serve Him equally well as your husband as I could as a single man. In fact, I can probably serve him better.'

He kissed Mooi Klip, at first with great tenderness, so that the sound of their lips was as moist and as quiet as the opening wings of a newly-formed butterfly. But then he held her tight, as close as he possibly could, and he was trembling with the excitement of her. They kissed again and again, saying nothing, their eyes closed, and Mooi Klip lifted her hands like a blind girl to touch his face, to feel his hair and his cheeks and the curve of his lashes.

At last, Hugh opened his eyes, and looked at her. 'There is a great deal that you are going to have to teach me,' he told her, in an unsteady voice. 'I am a knowledgeable man, in my way; but I am also an innocent one.'

She did not speak, but took his wrist and led him towards the door. He hesitated at first, with a questioning expression on his face, but then she said, 'Come,' so warmly and so softly that he followed her.

The bedroom was crowded with shadows. An engraved-glass lamp burned low on the chiffonier beside the bed, its flame dipping from time to time in the slight draught that blew from the slightly-open window. The bed itself was as plain as a bed could be: unvarnished oak, dovetailed and pegged, and spread with a patchwork comforter of paisleys and chintzes and dimity. On the wall above the head of the bed was a lurid lithographo of the Garden of Gethsemane. Hugh turned to Mooi Klip in obvious indecision, his voice breathless. 'You are the first woman who has ever been in here, apart from Elretha.'

'You're afraid?' asked Mooi Klip.

'I wouldn't be telling the truth if I said that I wasn't. And I'm not at all sure that we shouldn't wait until we're married. It's really wrong, you know, to –' He stopped, and then 'Well,' he said, in a very low voice, 'it's technically fornication.'

'Are you committed to me?' Mooi Klip whispered.

'You *know* I am,' said Hugh.

'I am committed to you, too. I wouldn't have come here tonight if I hadn't been, because I knew that you were thinking of asking me to marry you. If I hadn't have been committed to you the thought of going to bed with you wouldn't even have entered my mind.'

'I know,' Hugh worried, 'I know. But it still seems so sinful.'

Mooi Klip lowered her eyes. 'We'll wait, then, if that's what you feel we ought to do. You are a man of God, after all.'

She went to the bedroom door and opened it again. Hugh stayed where he was, his face bursting with pent-up emotion, his fists squeezed tight. Just as she was turning away towards the sitting-room, he shouted out, '*No!*'

Mooi Klip looked back at him. In a gentler, less controlled voice, he said, 'No. I don't want to wait, however sinful it might be. I will just have to ask for God's understanding of how much I love you. Do you hear me? I don't want to wait. I can't, a moment longer.'

Slowly, Mooi Klip came towards him and took both of his hands. 'Is there a word for how you feel?' she asked him.

'A word?' he frowned.

'That's how I learn, by asking people how they feel.'

Hugh laughed, rather desperately. 'Well, I can only think of one word, and that's turbulent. I am the original turbulent priest.'

They kissed again, a slow kiss that seemed to Hugh to take whole hours, hours in which pictures from old postcard albums appeared and faded in his mind; the Oval at Kennington, the horse-drawn buses clustered around Piccadilly Circus; the divinity school at Caterham; and then the views of West Africa and the Cape of Good Hope; and the grass huts; and the heat-distorted deserts; and the naked Hottentot women with gold bangles around their arms. The nude child in the alleyway.

Mooi Klip let him go, and then sat down on the bed. 'Come on,' she said, 'it will be beautiful. Come on.'

Clearing his throat as if he were just about to begin a sermon, Hugh stepped forward and started to unbutton her dress at the back. Mooi Klip sat still and graceful while he lowered the dress down to her waist, and while he bent forward to kiss her shoulders. 'What do I do now?' he asked her, anxiously. 'I'm not very good when it comes to women's clothes.'

'Here,' she smiled, and held up the pale blue silk ribbons of her white cotton bodice. Hugh cautiously tugged them, and her bodice slipped down to one side, baring her breast.

'Oh my God,' said Hugh, and reached out to touch her with shaking fingers. Her nipple knurled and stiffened, and she touched his cheek in return, and kissed him.

Together, clumsily but lovingly, they took off their clothes. Soon Hugh was lying on his back on the comforter, his face and hands red from the sun, his body white, while Mooi Klip knelt beside him, stoking the dark crucifix of hair on his chest, and humming to him one of those haunting and repetitive Griqua songs that you can never remember and never forget. 'Their music is like a sad cry on the wind,' Hugh Ransome told the Bishop of Bath, years later.

'I love you,' said Hugh, intensely. 'I can't even begin to describe to you how much.'

Mooi Klip pressed her finger to her lips. In silence, he watched her hand as it coursed through the thicker hair on his stomach, and at last clasped the stiffness of his erection. She stroked him tantalisingly, up and down his virgin penis. Then she rose up on her knees, her large breasts swaying, and mounted him, sitting down on him as slowly as she could, so that he could feel very single tenth of an inch of himself as he was gradually deflowered.

'Natalia,' he breathed. 'Oh Christ Jesus, Natalia ...'

He climaxed almost straight away, but she stayed where she was, smoothing his chest with her hands, touching his nipples, kissing him, soothing him, until he began to uncurl himself again, and rise.

They made love three times before the chiming clock in the sitting-room told them that it was ten o'clock, and time for Mooi Klip to leave. She climbed off the bed, and took her dress from the back of the bedroom chair, and quickly buttoned herself up. Hugh lay where he was, his hands laced behind his head, watching her unwaveringly, as if he were quite convinced that she would vanish through the whitewashed wall, like a ghost.

She leaned over the bed and kissed his forehead. 'I hope you're at peace,' she murmured.

He kissed her back. 'I'm at peace with myself, and I'm at peace with you, and I'm at peace with God. Only God could have given me such ecstasy as that. Only God could have

452

brought you here. Natalia, you are the most wonderful thing that has ever happened to me.'

'Shall I come round tomorrow?'

'I'll come round to you. I promised Pieter that I'd try to finish that kite.'

'What about the wedding?' she asked.

'I shall have to write to the bishop, of course. But there is no reason at all why we shouldn't be married by the end of February. I'll receive an increased stipend, too, you know. Not a fortune, by anybody's standards, but enough to keep us both in moderate comfort.'

'As long as we have enough of your boiled beef and onion dumplings, I shan't mind,' smiled Mooi Klip.

Hugh wrapped himself up in his comforter like a very white-skinned visiting sheikh, and escorted Mooi Klip to the door. She said, 'Don't come out on to the verandah. You know how much people gossip in Klipdrift. I wouldn't want to spoil your reputation.'

'You'll be safe walking home?'

'Of course. Goodnight, Hugh. My love.'

He gave her one last kiss. 'I think I shall sleep better tonight than I have for twenty-nine years.'

Hunt was at his most waspish when he came around for dinner on Thursday evening: he told a complicated and decidedly off-colour story about a diplomat in Capetown who had attended a reception for the French Ambassador dressed as Marie Antoinette, with two wriggling black monkeys crammed down the front of his borrowed gown for a bosom. Barney found Hunt inexpressibly irritating, and he sat at the head of the dining-table petulantly toying with his chicken casserole and wishing that he had never invited him. But Joel, who had swung his way downstairs on his crutches like a human pendulum, and who was now sitting opposite Hunt with his stump firmly wedged against the table-leg, thought Hunt was perfect, and kept calling him his 'pitseleh', his little baby. Sara appeared to enjoy Hunt's company, too, although from the way she looked at Barney whenever she laughed, her eyes sparkling and hard,

453

Barney felt pretty sure that she was exaggerating her amusement just to annoy him.

'The funniest thing that I've ever seen in all of my years in the colonial service was Sir Bottled Beer trying to lower the flag on the back lawn of Government House, and tugging at all the wrong strings,' said Hunt. 'The flag became so hopelessly entangled at the top of the mast that they had to send a kaffir shinning all the way up to the button with a pair of scissors, so that he could cut it free. Poor old Sir Bottle went storming inside and wouldn't come out of his office for a week.'

'You *do* sound as if you have an amusing life,' said Sara. 'I'm absolutely dying to go to Capetown, but of course we're so busy here, aren't we, Barney?'

'Desperately busy,' put in Joel. 'We have to supervise the sunrise and the sunset, and we have to count all the shovels at the end of the day in case any of the kaffirs have tried to smuggle them home in their loincloths; and then we have to decorate this mausoleum of a house in case anybody more important than a member of the Board for the Protection of Mining Industries decides to pay us a visit. It's a full life, *pitseleh*, I can assure you.'

Hunt, with a mouthful of grapes, glanced mischievously along the table to where Barney was sitting, and giggled. 'They're teasing you, Barney. But I can't say I blame them. You're not the same chap you used to be, when I first met you. You were hopeful, then, weren't you? Hopeful and happy. Or as near to happy as anybody can ever be when they're Jewish and penniless at the same time. It's this diamond. It's made you morose. I've heard they do that, you know. They're really rather depressing stones, when all's been said and done.'

'And I suppose the only way to shake off this moroseness is to sell it to you?' asked Barney, finishing off his glass of wine.

'Of course,' said Hunt, winking at Joel. 'You'd be a million pounds better off, and you'd be rid of whatever baleful influence that stone has been having on you. Where's your sense of fun, old boy? You've been chasing that same forkful of food around and around your plate for the past twenty minutes, and you look about as cheerful as a choirmaster in a nunnery.'

Sara said airily, 'It's no use trying to persuade him. He's

454

quite determined to handle this diamond on his own, even if it makes him no money whatsoever. It's his upbringing, I suppose. Poverty affects different people in different ways; but it's evidently made Barney a hoarder. You know, like those old tramps you see with paper parcels packed with rubbish and pieces of string.'

Joel honked like a wild goose with hilarity, and almost lost his balance, tipping a salt-cellar all over the tablecloth. 'Sara has her husband summed up to a T, doesn't she? Oh, Sara! Oh, God, my poor aching *kishkas*! She'll kill me!'

Barney stood up, and tossed down his crumpled napkin.

'Not staying for the brandy?' asked Sara, sharply.

Barney shook his head. 'I'm afraid you'll have to excuse me. I'm going to be obliged to spend the rest of the evening in the library, finishing off some paperwork. We're making a bid for those three Quadrant claims next week, and I still have all the surveys to go through, as well as Harold's reports on their gem samples.'

'It's all right, Barney, *bubeleh*,' grinned Joel. 'I'm sure we can find some way of entertaining ourselves while you're gone. How about some brandy, William, and a game of cards? Sara?'

Sara was watching Barney through the dazzling flames of the silver candelabra, and there was an expression on her face which he had never seen before. He thought at first that she was smiling at him, smiling at the way she had teased him this evening, and he smiled back. But then, narrowing his eyes against the glare, he realised that she was looking at him with *unfamiliarity*, as if she could not quite decide who he was, and where she could remember him from. It was the expression of a woman who no longer feels any affection for her husband at all; a woman who looks at the man at the head of her table, and beside her in her bed, and sees only a stranger. Barney knew that their marriage was formal and remote these days, but until now he had not realised just how much of an outsider he had become in his own house. He looked at Joel, who was lifting his glass in a mocking toast to Hunt; and then he looked back at Sara, and all he could do was push his chair back under the table and walk out of the room.

Once inside the library, with the doors closed behind him,

455

he stood for a long time with his hand held to his mouth, thinking. He had been able to cope with Sara and Joel separately; when Joel had been irascible and alone, and Sara had been aloof and alone. But now they had formed a relationship from which he was being increasingly excluded, a relationship of shared dissatisfactions; of mutually-felt isolation and inadequacy, particularly in the face of Barney's success. He had thought they looked like children, the other night, when he had seen them playing cards, and in a way they were behaving like children, too, keeping secrets from him, stopping in mid-conversation when he came into the room, exchanging glances and smiles. He did not think that they were in love. Love was not what they needed from each other. But he did believe that they were able to share their fears and their uncertainties with each other, far more intimately than they could with him.

During the slow summer months of Joel's recovery, while Barney had been digging and supervising out at the diamond claims for ten to twelve hours a day, and then coming back to eat a hurried supper before working three hours longer with Harold Feinberg, Sara and Joel had been playing whist together, either in Joel's bedroom suite, when his leg was hurting him, or out on the patio, in the sparkling shade of the newly-planted cherry trees. Sometimes they had argued, and if Barney had been at home he had lifted his head from his paperwork in the library to hear Sara snapping at Joel with the accents of a cultured poodle, and he had smiled, and gone back to his surveys. But a man and a woman only argue with such persistence when they are trying to get closer to each other, trying to tease out the real sensitivities behind the prickly manners and the aggressive charades.

On some evenings, sweating with heat and pain and frustration, Joel had talked to Sara about his boyhood on the Lower East Side, and about the way his *papa* had always favoured Barney, giving him rides on his shoulders and sitting him on his knee. He had told her about his *mama*, too, and how she had suffocated him not only with affection but with more and more responsibility, until he had felt that it was impossible for him to breathe. He told Sara about things that he had done and

456

things that he had failed to. He told her secrets that he had never confessed to Barney. He told her what Meg his red-haired lady mistress had done for him, and why he had paid her so much money not to stop.

Sara, in her turn, told Joel all about her stilted upbringing; about her erratic mother and her laconic father. She told him about a life that had always seemed elegant and attractive on the surface, but which had at last proved to be empty of meaning.

And so both of them sat together in the vast, empty rooms of Vogel Vlei, one with a brother to whom he owed everything, including his life and his disfigurement; and the other with a husband who kept her in fine gowns and beautiful diamonds and endless discontentment.

Barney turned up the wick of the oil-lamp, and went to the safe. He hesitated for a moment, but then he unlocked it, and took out the diamond. It lay in the darkness, the diamond, its light unlit; but when Barney laid it down on his desk, on a sheet of white paper, it sent out flares of brilliant iridescence all around it.

'I'm going to name you,' he said. 'No gemstone as magnificent as you are should go without a name.'

He picked the stone up, and clasped his fingers around it, as if he were holding a human heart. 'I name you the Natalia Star.'

It was more than five minutes before he put the diamond down again, and sat at his desk, and then he kept staring at it. He knew that he had just put his deepest and most painful feelings into words; but he did not want to think about it any more. His sense of loss was too complicated and too complete.

He worked for a little over an hour, studying the Quadrant surveys and writing a long letter to Ascher & Mendel in Antwerp, asking them to send a representative to Capetown to discuss the cutting of the Natalia Star. On an impulse, he also wrote to Leah Ginzburg in New York, telling her that he was working hard, and that he was married 'to a very charming English girl from Natal'. Somehow he felt that if he told Leah about his marriage, it would improve things. His life with Sara was not *that* difficult, was it? They still kissed. They still made

457

love. They talked over breakfast. What more could there be to any marriage?

He glanced at the diamond again, and remembered for one brilliant moment a night in the bungalow with Mooi Klip when she had whispered '*I love you, I love you, I love you,*' over and over again.

At last, he laid down his pen, lowered his lamp, and stretched. He was about to return the Natalia Star to the safe, when it occurred to him that it might be amusing to tantalise Hunt with it, and so he wrapped it up in its leather cloth and took it through to the drawing-room.

Sara and Hunt and Joel had just finished a three-handed game of cards, and they were laughing over another of Hunt's outrageous stories – this one about a new recruit to the colonial service who had been served up on his first morning in Africa a boiled ostrich egg, and told that it was frightfully bad form not to finish it. They all went quiet when Barney walked in, and Joel reached over to the bell-rope to call Horace to bring them some more brandy.

'Have you finished, my dear?' asked Sara. Her cheeks were flushed from drinking and laughing.

Barney nodded. 'Just about. I'll have to get up early tomorrow and write two or three more letters before I go to the mine.'

'You poor overworked darling. To think that all we can do is sit here and amuse ourselves while you have to go out and support us. But never mind, it's *Shabbes* the day after tomorrow, and you'll be able to put your feet up.'

'You celebrate the Jewish sabbath out here in Kimberley?' asked Hunt, lifting an eyebrow.

'The sabbath is the sabbath whether you're in Kimberley or Potter's Bar,' said Barney. 'I didn't use to observe it, when I first came here; but life is different now. I have time to remember my background, and my God.'

'He usually has at least five minutes to say a few prayers in between the mine and the library,' said Joel. 'He can say *shachris* while he's shaving; *mincha* in between mouthfuls of lunch; and *mairev* while he's washing his teeth before he goes to bed. Then he's just got time to say *Shema* while the kaffirs reload the mechanical *trommel* with more blue ground; and his Silent Devotions he can recite whenever the whims break down.'

'I didn't know you were so devotedly Orthodox,' said Hunt.

Barney sat down. 'I'm not. I think I forgot about God altogether when I first came to the Cape. My religion didn't seem to be enough to carry me through. But now I'm trying to get back to Him; and the only way I can do that is through prayer. Jews are great prayers, William. They believe that their whole life is a running conversation with the Lord. And why shouldn't I pray, when I've seen such evidence that He really exists.'

With that, Barney opened his hand, and held up the diamond. Joel, on the sofa, turned immediately away, as if Barney had slapped his face. But Hunt stood up, stunned, and stared at the stone as if it had materialised by some kind of magical trick.

'My God,' he said. 'I had no idea.'

Barney continued to hold it up, and Hunt approached it with his eyes wide. When he was close enough, he said, 'May I?' and picked it up carefully from Barney's palm.

'I have never seen anything like this in my life,' Hunt said. hoarsely. 'It makes me feel ridiculous. I mean – I can absolutely see why it has restored your faith in God. My dear chap.'

'I should take a good look at it,' said Joel. 'You won't see it again, ever. Old Shylock here is going to keep it locked up in his coffers until he dies, if you ask me.'

Hunt held the stone up to the lamplight, and rainbows curved across his face. 'It's astonishing. I really don't blame you for wanting to keep it. Look at those colours!'

Sara said, 'I keep telling Barney that it's too beautiful for us to lock away; but he won't listen, will you, my dear? I think the whole world should be able to admire it. But, oh no. Barney wants it for himself. He wants it in his safe, where it's worth nothing at all.'

'This stone has a destiny,' said Barney, holding out his hand for Hunt to give it back to him. 'I just want to make sure that it's the right destiny.'

Hunt turned the diamond around in his fingers one more

time, and then dropped it back into Barney's hand. 'You can't control destiny, old fellow. When you're dead, which you will be one day, that stone will pursue its course through history according to greed, and finance, and politics, and human passion, and you won't be able to do a damned thing about it. So what does it matter to you, its destiny? I'll give you a million-three.'

'I'm not selling,' said Barney.

'A million-four, and that's how confident I am that my backers will like what they see.'

'You're wasting your time, William,' said Joel, his eyes still turned away from the diamond. 'Barney is never tempted by money, only by the chance of proving his ineffable superiority. We used to have a name for people like him back in New York, but I won't repeat it here.'

Hunt looked covetously at the diamond as Barney wrapped it up in its leather cloth again. 'I'm staying in Kimberley for another day or two,' he said. 'Why don't you think it over? A million-four, in gold and securities.'

'There's nothing to discuss,' Barney told him, quietly and firmly. 'Now have some more brandy. Sara, do you know if Kitty made any more of those Dutch sugar cookies? Perhaps William would like a sugar cookie.

Hunt sat down again. 'I just hope you realise what a difficult time Sir Bartle is going to give Blitz Brothers mining company after this. I wouldn't be surprised if he makes moves in court to have your licences revoked.'

'No,' smiled Barney, 'that wouldn't surprise me, either.'

Later that night, as they lay in bed, with the dim moonlight transfiguring their rooms into ice, Sara said, 'Will you *really* not sell?'

Barney had been dropping into sleep, and it took him a moment or two to understand that she had said something. 'What?' he asked her, blurrily.

'The diamond. Will you really not sell it to Hunt?'

'I've told you. I don't want to sell it to anybody until it's cut. That way, it will be worth even more.'

'But we're so short of money. And life is so tedious here. Don't you understand how bored and unhappy I am?'

'Sara,' sighed Barney, 'I don't want to start that argument all over again. I've already written to Ascher & Mendel, the diamond-cutters in Antwerp. In six months or so, we should be able to send the diamond to Europe, and have it cut. Maybe we'll take it to Belgium ourselves. Wouldn't you like to do that?'

'We could go anywhere we *liked* if we sold the diamond to Hunt. And Belgium's such a dreary place anyway. Besides, there's the whole question of patriotism. This *is* a British colony, and any really spectacular riches that are found here ought to go to the Queen, simply as a matter of courtesy. If you don't sell the diamond to Hunt, and allow him to call it the Victoria Star – well, that's a snub to the British throne.'

Barney propped himself up on one elbow and punched his pillow back into shape. 'For one thing, Sara, I'm an American, and I don't feel the slightest obligation to the Queen. And for another thing, I don't trust any of these colonial wheeler-dealers, nor their motives, nor their so-called "gold and securities." '

'Oh, you're so suspicious. Why on earth don't you just sell the diamond and have done with it?'

Barney did not answer, but wrestled himself into a more comfortable position in bed and closed his eyes. He had three letters to write to Quadrant's lawyers in the morning, and if he was going to get them done, he would have to wake up at five o'clock. Digging at the mine started at six, and he wanted to be there early. His kaffirs were finally going to excavate their two newest claims down to the level of all the rest of the Blitz Brothers diggings; and, with luck, Barney would now have sufficient space to bring in a steam-shovel. That would speed up the mine's rate of production more than ten times.

He did not know that Sara lay next to him for the rest of the night without sleeping. Nor did he know when he left the bedroom in the morning, and leaned over the bed to kiss her forehead, that she was still awake. Most poignantly of all, though, he was completely unaware that he would never kiss her again.

He was out at the mine with his foreman, eating a cheese pastry and drinking a mug of black tea, when he first realised that the key to his safe was missing from his key-ring. It was a grillingly hot afternoon, and when they sat down to eat their luch at an old scratched kitchen table, with upended toolboxes for chairs, Barney took off his vest, and hung it on a nearly shovel handle.

'I shouldn't leave your keys in there,' said the foreman. 'We've got some light-fingered kaffirs these days. Jackdaws, I call 'em. They take anything as long as it shines.'

Barney unfastened his key-chain from his buttonhole and dropped the keys on to the table. Then he sat down and opened up the paper bag that Kitty had given him after breakfast to take to the diggings. The foreman, a short squat Australian with forearms like sides of beef, was already munching his way through a doorstep sandwich of sausage and mustard, mostly mustard.

'I saw Gentleman Jack late yesterday,' said the foreman, with his mouth full. 'He was sitting outside of Dodd's Bar, on the boardwalk, and he was pissed out of his mind. You know that fancy grey suit of his? It had holes in the knees and holes in the elbows, and it was so darn filthy it stunk.' He reached over and took a generous swallow of tawny-coloured tea, to wash his bread and sausage down. 'I'm darned if I know why you never handed that nigger over to the Board, and had him hung.'

'It wasn't entirely his fault, that's why,' said Barney. 'And besides, he won't ever get work in the diamond fields again, not from anybody.'

'Stafford Parker would have had him castrated.'

'Maybe he would. But I'm not Stafford Parker.'

He glanced down at his keys, and pushed them a little way across the table because the sun was being reflected by the oval brass name-tag and was getting into his eyes. The keys sprawled apart on the ring, and it was then that he saw the safe-key was missing. He set down his mug with a frown, and picked the keyring up, sorting through it key by key to make sure that he was not mistaken.

'Something wrong?' asked the foreman.

Barney jingled the keys in his hand. 'I'm not sure. Listen, I have to go back to the house for a while. Will you make sure they don't bring that side wall down when they start digging out the last of the debris? I don't want half of Tennent's claim collapsing into ours.'

'Sure. Aren't you going to finish your lunch?'

'You have it, if you're hungry. Now, where's Michael?'

He did not know what to think or what to feel as Michael drove him briskly back over the stony roadway to Vogel Vlei. He took his key-ring out again and again, and searched the pockets of his vest, but the safe key was indisputably gone. And not just lost, either. The key-ring was made out of sturdy steel and Barney practically broke a fingernail every time he tried to twist a key on or off it. The safe key had been taken deliberately, and since he wore the key-ring all day long, it must have been taken at night, when he was asleep.

It could not have been Hunt, because Hunt did not know where he kept his keys at night, under his socks in the drawer of his bureau. It could not have been Joel, either, because Joel could only walk with crutches, and he could not have swung his way into Barney's bedroom without waking him up, no matter how deep Barney had been sleeping.

He did not want to think of the other alternative, but there was no way in which he could stop his mind from turning it over. He closed his eyes as the carriage jostled its way up the tree-lined driveway that led to Vogel Vlei, and all he could see were pictures of Sara. Sara smiling, Sara frowning, Sara sad. The large white house stood silent and dazzling in the heat of the afternoon, and after Michael had turned the horses in front of the main door, and applied the brake, there was no sound at all except for the distant *pick-pick-pick* of the kaffirs who were preparing the gardens.

'You going back to the mine, Mr Blitzboss?' asked Michael.

'I don't know,' said Barney. 'Give the horses a drink, but don't unharness them yet.'

'Yes, sir.'

Barney tried to restrain himself from running as he walked through the open front doors of the house and across the hallway. As he reached the library door, Horace came out of the door to the servants' quarters, and frantically waved. 'Mr Two-Leg! Mr Two-Leg!'

'What is it, Horace?'

'They all gone, Mr Two-Leg. I'm sorry, sir. I told them they should wait. But they said, not to worry, old chap. They said maybe you could catch up with them later. Maybe not.'

'Gone? Who's gone?'

'Mr Hunt, sir; and Mr One-Leg; and the missis; and the *amah*.'

Barney gripped Horace's sleeve for a moment. 'Wait there,' he told him, and pushed open the library door. He crossed quickly to the safe, and tugged at the handle. The heavy door opened on its thick oily hinges to reveal what Barney already knew. The Natalia Star was gone. In its place was propped a letter, addressed to 'Barney Blitz' and marked 'Private' in Sara's schoolgirl handwriting; all loops and curlicues and self-indulgent whorls.

With unsteady hands, Barney took the letter out of the safe and opened it. On a single sheet of fresh notepaper, printed with the letterhead 'Vogel, Vlei, Kimberley, Cape Colony', Sara had written '*Vincit Qui Patitur*, Love Sara.'

Horace was still waiting by the door, nervously scuffing his feet on the marble. Barney called to him, 'What time did they leave? Early?'

'Just about one hour after you went to the mine, sir. They took the landau, sir, and six horses – four in harness, two running behind. They said they were going to Klipdrift for a day or two, to show Mr Hunt the diggings. I asked them if I should tell you where they were, sir; and they said certainly. "Certainly, old chap," they said, sir. "Off to Klipdrift to show Mr Hunt the diggings."'

'Is that all? They didn't say anything else?'

'No, sir, Mr Two-Leg. But they were in high spirits, sir.'

'Yes,' said Barney. 'I expect they probably were.'

He felt shocked, and cold, even though the library windows were all closed to keep the flies out, and the air was stifling. He stood where he was for a moment, by the open safe, with Sara's note in his hand, and then he walked around his desk, opened the top left-hand drawer, and took out the Shopkeeper's revolver with which he had almost shot Joel once before. Lord God, he should have done. Then he would never have married

464

Sara, and he would have been rid of Joel for ever. He released the catch on the revolver's chamber so that it fell open, took out his single box of cartridges, and loaded up with five rounds. He doubted if he was actually going to shoot any of them. He could not imagine killing Hunt, or Nareez or even Joel; and he certainly could not think of shooting Sara. But the simple action of loading the gun made him feel that he was doing something positive to get his diamond back.

'Horace,' he said, beckoning. Horace came over to the desk and stood to attention. 'I want you to pack me a saddlebag. Pack it as quick as you can. I want a couple of clean shirts, shaving tackle, socks, underwear. Roll me up a pair of blankets, too. And tell Kitty to pack me another saddlebag with bread, and *biltong*, and beans.'

'I understand, Mr Two-Leg.'

'I'm going to be away for at least a day,' said Barney, 'maybe two. Make sure you lock the house properly at night. Don't allow any trespassers in nor kopje-wallopers, nor tinkers. You got that? If anybody wants to knows where I am, tell them I had to go to Oranjerivier, in a hurry. All right?'

'Yes, sir.'

'Right. Then get a move on. They're only five or six hours ahead, and none of them know the roads really well. I should catch them at Modderivier.'

'Mr Two-Leg? I thought they were going to Klipdrift, sir? Different way.'

Barney shook his head. 'There's only one way those four are headed, and that's directly to Capetown. Tell Michael to saddle up Jupiter, if they haven't already taken him. I want to get going as soon as I can.'

In half an hour, the chestnut horse was saddled and ready, and Barney had changed into a khaki veld-jacket, riding-breeches, and wide-brimmed hat. Michael, who was holding the horse's bridle, said, 'You want me to come with you, Mr Blitzboss?'

Barney said, 'No thanks. What I'm going to say and do to those four people when I catch up with them, I'm going to do on my own, with no witnesses. Besides, I'll ride faster by myself.'

'God take care of you, Mr Blitzboss.'

465

Barney clicked to his horse, and it trotted down the driveway between the trees to the road. His black servants stood watching Barney go; and they walked across the hot gravel back to the house, saying nothing. It did not occur to them that there was nobody in this huge classical mansion now except them, that there was nobody to call 'boss'. Horace solemnly closed the front doors behind them, and locked them.

He rode south-west across the scrubby veld, and the wind plucked the dust from every step that Jupiter took, and blew it westward. The sun was beginning to sink now, and the landscape was taking on a grainy, inflated appearance, like a coke furnace seen through a muslin curtain. In the distance, on the western horizon, pale gazelles fled through the camelthorn trees, ghosts of their own forthcoming extinction.

They would have needed supplies, he thought. They could not have considered crossing three hundred miles of veld and desert in a horse-drawn landau, two women and a cripple and a pint-sized city-dweller like Hunt, not without water and food and not without a guide. Of course, Hunt had probably brought a guide with him when he came up from Capetown, and there were plenty of shiftless Afrikaners around Kimberley who would have been willing to take them across the Great Karoo for a few pound notes and a drink. But a guide meant one extra person for the horses to pull, and wheels that were going to get bogged down when they forded rivers, or whenever they crossed tracts of soft sand.

There were too many of them, and they were too in-experienced; and if they believed that Barney had swallowed their story and ridden across to Klipdrift to catch up with them, they may not even be hurrying. If he did not overtake them at Modderivier, about twenty miles to the south-west, then he would certainly stop them before they got to Belmont. He thought about what he would say and do when he confronted them, and even rehearsed it all in his head. He knew that Sara would give him the most difficulty. By stealing the Natalia Star from him she had virtually declared herself divorced.

And what made it worse for her, although she was unaware

of it, was the fact that she had taken the stone that Barney had named after the woman he felt he really loved.

Just before darkness, when the sun had dipped below the distant mountains, but the sky was still suffused with a pale bluish half-light, Barney reached a small farm settlement, no more than a whitewashed house with a corrugated-iron roof, and a cluster of barns and huts and straw-strewn *kraals*. He dismounted, and led Jupiter to the drinking-trough by the fence. There were mosquitoes in the air, and the last light in the sky was reflected in broken ripples in the trough as Jupiter lapped up his water.

Across the farmyard, a door opened, and Barney saw the orange glow of lamplight. A voice called, 'Who's there?'

'I stopped to water my horse,' Barney called back. 'I'm on my way to Modderivier.'

'Do you want a drink yourself?' The voice was distinctly Afrikaans.

'Thanks. I'll just tie up the horse and I'll be right over.'

Inside the farmhouse, at a plain wooden supper-table, sat a family of ten – a sun-wrinkled Boer farmer, his sturdy wife, and a collection of eight girls and boys, all blond-haired, and all alike as skittles, with angular cheekbones and snubbed-up noses. The wife took a blue Delft plate down from the high yellow-wood dresser, and ladled out Barney a generous helping of game stew, with floury potatoes. The farmer himself brought out a bottle of johannisboombeer brandy, and filled up a small thick-rimmed glass with it.

'This is very generous of you,' said Barney. 'I was expecting to have to eat my supper on horseback.'

'Bad for the guts, man,' said the farmer. 'My old father always used to say that you could do anything standing up except eat.' He reached across the table to shake Barney's hand. 'My name's Marais Brink, by the way, and this is my wife Elsa, and these are all the little Brinks. Well, not so little these days. Barend, my eldest, is twenty next month. Marietjie is three.'

'I'm looking for four, maybe five people,' Barney said, tearing off a piece of bread. 'They were headed this way in a four-in-hand, with two spare horses running behind.'

Marais Brink forked a large chunk of meat into his mouth,

and Barney had to wait patiently for an answer while he thoroughly chewed it, and took a sip of brandy, and then cleared his throat.

'There's been nobody like that past this way, man. Not today. It was today they were supposed to come by?'

'This morning, maybe eleven or twelve o'clock. They would have been hard to miss.'

'I'll ask my foreman, but I was out in the yard myself all morning, repairing a plough. I wouldn't have missed a rig like that.'

'This is just about the only way they can come, isn't it, right past the front of your farm?'

'Well, that's right,' nodded Marais Brink. 'They can't come around the back of the farm, not in a carriage, because of the ditches. And they can't go far beyond the track in the other direction, because it's all trees, and stones, and after that there's the river. Everything comes past the front here, man. I don't miss a thing.'

Elsa Brink offered Barney another spoonful of stew, but he raised his hand and said, 'Thanks, really. But no thanks. I don't have much of an appetite. Not while I'm still chasing after those people.'

'They took something from you?' asked Elsa Brink, clapping the lid back on the stewpot.

'You could say that.'

'Well, times are difficult, man,' said Marais Brink. 'There's been more thievery than I can ever remember. There was a time when you could leave your horses out at night; but not these days. I had a mule taken about a month ago. As if life isn't difficult enough already.'

Barney stared at him. Then the farmer's words at last sank in, and he blinked, and nodded. 'You're right. It's very difficult.'

After supper, the Brinks invited him to stay; and he sat preoccupied on a riempie chair by the fire, drinking johannisboombeer brandy, while the children sang songs, and the eldest boy Barend played the fiddle. He thought of the tenement on Clinton Street, and of Leib Ginzberg practising his *mazel tov* dances upstairs. He thought of Leah and Moishe, and the thumping of wooden buckets outside the Brink farmhouse

468

sounded so much like the thumping of bolts of cloth on the cutting tables at Blitz, Tailors, that Barney had to make himself sit up straight, and remind himself where he was. Thousands of miles away from the Lower East Side, in the middle of the night, in a small Boer farmhouse in Africa, with everything lost. His wife, his brother, the woman he loved; and the largest diamond ever discovered on the whole sub-continent.

There was something else, too. Tonight was *Shabbes* eve. He turned to Marais Brink, and said, 'Would you mind if I recited something? We call it the *Kiddush*. It's a kind of a prayer for the sabbath.'

'You're Jewish?' asked Elsa Brink.

Barney nodded. 'A Jew from America, a long way from home.'

'It's not unusual for a Jew, is it, to be a long way from home?' asked Marais Brink. 'You go ahead and say your prayers. We both have the same God.'

Later, as Barney lay sleepless in a hard wooden cot in one of the outhouses, with the waning moon watching him sadly through the uncurtained window, he repeated the words that he had spoken, the words that began the *Kiddush*, and he tried to take comfort from them. 'Thus the heavens and the earth were finished, and all the host of them. And on the seventh day God ended his work which he had made; and he rested ...'

But Barney found that rest was impossible. The moon sank behind a bank of early-morning clouds, and the sky began to lighten again, and on the other side of the farmyard a cockerel began to crow. He climbed off the cot, and went to the window, unshaven and exhausted.

If they had not gone to Capetown, where had they gone? Not to Klipdrift, surely; there was nothing for them there, and no escape to the coast. Not east, to the Orange Free State, or across the mountains to Natal. What would be the point of that? No point at all, unless Sara thought her father could help them to escape from South Africa with the diamond or sell it on the IDB black market. But they wouldn't be able to sell it for anything like a million pounds on the black market, not a diamond as huge and as distinctive as the Natalia Star; and Hunt's consortium of British businessmen, if they had ever

469

actually existed, had apparently only been interested in putting up a million-four if they could be sure that the gem was going to be presented to Her Majesty as the Victoria Star.

So where had Hunt and Joel and Sara gone with the stone, and why? There were plenty of unscrupulous merchants and collectors who would pay anything up to £300,000 for it, credentials or not. But it would only take Harold Feinberg a month or two to alert the newspapers and the diamond trade all over the world that the Natalia Stone had gone missing, and anybody who wanted to resell it would either have to choose their client with great care, or else cut the stone up into twenty or thirty anonymous and far smaller diamonds, to be marketed separately. Either way, Sara and Joel would receive only a fraction of the money they might have been able to ask if they had been able to sell the diamond legitimately.

There were always buyers for diamonds of dubious background, but the stones had to be sold and re-sold before they acquired a new respectability. After he had killed the slave who had taken the Regent diamond from the Parteal mine, the British sea-captain who had promised to give him passage out of India had later sold the stone to the Indian diamond merchant Jaurchund for only £1000. Jaurchund had been obliged to put it around discreetly that he had 'exceptionally large diamonds for sale'; and when he was approached by Thomas Pitt, the grandfather of William Pitt and the governor of Fort St George, close to Madras, Jaurchund had been easily beaten down from his asking price of £80,000 to less than £20,000. Pitt sent the Regent to England to be cut into a flawless $140\frac{1}{2}$-carat brilliant, and sold it in 1717 to the Regent of France, the Duke of Orleans, for £135,000; but that did not help the slave, or the sea-captain, or Jaurchund, and Hunt and Sara and Joel were in the same position as the sea-captain.

But however little they were paid for it, and however alert the merchants were, the Natalia Star could still be lost to Barney for ever. As Hunt had reminded him, a large diamond has its own destiny; and unless Barney could very quickly intervene in the destiny of the Natalia Star, it would be out of his reach – cut, sold, mounted, and locked away in some private collection on the other side of the world. Barney thought about the stories he had told the newspapers about the Natalia Star being one of a kind, a once-in-a-lifetime discovery, and the ironic part about it is was that he had been right. It was. He might acquire the whole of the Kimberley mine, and excavate it as deep as it was possible to dig, and never find another diamond as huge as or perfect again.

He felt as if his wife and his brother had taken not only his diamond but his reason for staying in Africa, his reason for battling against Rhodes, his reason for trying to rediscover his religion, and his God. The Natalia Star may have embodied absolute truth, but it seemed to Barney as if absolute truth could too easily be slipped into a thief's pocket, and carried off.

In the morning, he breakfasted with the Brink family at six o'clock, and left them a five-pound note tucked into the blue milk jug on their dresser. Then he rode slowly back to Kimberley, and to Vogel Vlei, where his servants were awaiting his return with domestic patience. Somebody else was awaiting his return, too; and with a game-rifle.

It was Alf Loubser, the sheep-farmer from Beaufort West, looking as fierce as he possibly could. He had drawn his eighteen-ox waggon up outside the front doors of Vogel Vlei in a wide curve of horns and yokes and reins and idly-flopping tails, and he was sitting in the driving-seat with his long-barrelled gun resting across his knees. Beside him, in a gingham dress and a poke bonnet, her hands demurely clasped in her lap, was Louise, his daughter, the girl who had taken Barney's virginity all those years ago on that warm starry night on the Koup.

Barney climbed down from Jupiter wearily, and walked across to the ox-waggon leading the horse on a loose rein. 'It's Alf Loubser, isn't it?' he asked, taking off his hat and shielding his eyes from the sun with his hand. 'And that's Louise. My, you've grown, haven't you, Louise?'

'She's not as grown now as she was after you visited our farm,' commented Alf Loubser, harshly.

Barney stopped where he was, and squinted up at Loubser

awkwardly. The sun was right behind Loubser's head, shining through the canvas top of the waggon, and it blotted out the taut, narrow-eyed expression on the farmer's face.

'I'm not sure what you're saying,' said Barney.

'You're not? I'll suppose you're going to deny it, are you?'

'If I knew what I was supposed to be denying, then maybe I would. Listen, why don't I ask my boys to feed and water your beasts, and then you can come inside and talk this all over in a civilised way, whatever, it is. Did you come all the way from Beaufort?'

'Leg by leg. I have cousins in Hopetown, I was visiting them, too.'

'Well, come along inside. You look like you could use some refreshment, and I know that *I* could. Let me help you down, Louise.'

Alf Loubser reared up the muzzle of his rifle. 'She doesn't need any of your help, man. Leave her alone.'

'I was only trying to be friendly.'

'Well, we don't need friendship like yours. Friendship like yours, we can do without.'

Michael came out of the stables and took Jupiter's reins and Barney told him to fetch four or five of the boys to look after Alf Loubser's oxen. When they were pulling a full-sized eighteen-foot waggon, oxen could manage to plod only at an average of five miles a day, and they usually needed a day's rest after a long haul. It was just as tiring for the driver: a full waggon and its team could stretch 120 feet from the first oxen to the last wheel, and it could easily and frequently be halted by mud or sand or rough ground.

'It's a hell of a place you've got here,' said Alf Loubser, as his team were released from their yokes and led around to the side of the house to graze and drink.

Barney looked around at the dung-strewn driveway. 'You haven't done much to improve it, though, have you?'

'Although he was trying to be fierce, Alf Loubser could not help laughing. 'Don't you know that gravel needs fertilising, man, just like anything else?'

'One day, the Afrikaner sense of humour will penetrate my thick Jewish skull,' said Barney. 'Come along inside. Oh – and you can leave your gun with Horace.'

Alf Loubser frowned at Horace, who was standing attentively by the door and then turned back to Barney. 'I can't leave my gun with him, man. He's one of your boys.'

'You mean you came here with the intention of shooting me?'

'Why shouldn't I shoot you, the way you left Louise? You see this poor girl, three months after you left her belly was out here, and nine months after you left she gave birth to a baby girl.'

Barney looked first at Alf Loubser, with his red sweating face and his eyes as pale as a bleached blue workshirt; and then at Louise, who was still pretty in a white, transparent kind of a way, but who had not improved in the years since he had slept with her. Her figure was slipping under that cheap gingham frock, and there were purplish circles under her eyes. Her snkles were thickening, too, and there were dark blue veins in her legs. In a year or two, she would look like any other hard-worked Dutch farm woman on the Koup.

'The baby was yours, Barney,' she said. 'I didn't go to bed with anybody else for a month before, or a month after.'

'Give Horace the gun,' said Barney. 'I'm not going to talk about this while you're waving a loaded game-rifle at me.'

Reluctantly, Alf Loubser handed the rifle over, and Horace took it with a solemn nod of his head. 'Come inside,' said Barney. 'I'll have some tea and cold meat sent up. Are you hungry?'

'*I'm* hungry,' said Louise, but her father shushed her, and gave her a glare.

Barney led the two of them into the drawing-room. To Barney, it seemed silent and inhospitable without Sara; but Alf Loubser and Louise looked around it in awe, at the blue moiré-silk on the walls, at the ormolu clock with its flying cherubs, and the spindly-elegant French furniture. Barney went to the windows and opened them wide so that a warm breeze could blow in from the back of the house.

'So, you're trying to tell me that I'm a father, are you?' he asked.

'There's no question,' said Alf Loubser. 'She even looks like you. Dark, with curly hair.'

'How old is she?'

'Nearly nine. She's a pretty young girl, too, and clever.'

473

Barney stared across the fields towards the trees. 'Was it really nine years ago? I don't know whether it seems longer or shorter.'

'We call her Heloise,' Alf Loubser told him, not without pride. 'Me and my wife, we've been raising her like our own daughter. Everybody in Beaufort believes she is. She'll be a good worker!'

'Did you bring a picture of her?'

'A picture?'

'Well, how do I know that she actually exists, unless I see a picture?'

Alf Loubser pouted out his lower lip. 'What do you mean, how do you know that she exists? Of course she exists! I kissed her myself in Beaufort, not two months ago!'

'That's scarcely proof. The kiss will have dried by now.'

Louise touched her father's arm, and said, 'You have the birth certificate. It's in the Bible box, on the waggon.'

'All right,' said Barney. 'I'll have Horace bring it in.'

'No, you don't,' put in Alf Loubser. 'That blackie of yours could just as easily take it and burn it, and then you'd say that we didn't have any kind of a claim at all. Louise – you get it.'

Louise left them, and Barney indicated to Alf Loubser that he could sit down. The sheep-farmer squatted awkwardly on the very brim of a small gilded chair, his thighs wide apart, and folded his arms over his chest.

'I suppose you've come here for money,' said Barney.

'Well,' said Alf Loubser, most of his ferocity abated. 'I wouldn't have pursued you for it normally. I know that Louise has had a man or two, although not so many these days, and I suppose babies are one of the risks. But I do believe that Heloise is yours, and now she's growing up the child needs clothes, and shoes, and we're trying to give her some schooling. So, when Somon de Koker said that you'd found that ruddy great diamond, well ... you can't blame me, can you, for thinking that it was worth asking for a small contribution?'

Barney rubbed his eyes. 'I see. So I've got my old friend Simon de Koker to thank for this, have I? When did you last see him?'

'Two months ago, just about. But that was the first time for

474

years. He hasn't worked as a guide since '70, or maybe '71 at the latest.'

'What's he doing now?'

Alf Loubser pressed to his lips a stubby finger, stained with sheep-dip. 'Hush-hush, man. Mustn't say.'

'Something secret?'

Alf Loubser shifted his chair an inch or two closer, and leaned his cropped head forward confidentially. 'Between you and me, man, he's a secret agent. Would you believe that? He works for the old Pretorius government people in the Transvaal. Trying to overthrow the British, you see, and restore the independent Boer republic. But don't tell anyone I told you.'

Barney shook his head. 'I won't tell a soul. But what was he doing all the way down in Beaufort, when he's working as a secret agent in the Transvaal.'

'Don't ask me! What he does, that's hush-hush. He won't even tell you what colour hat he's wearing these days. All I can tell you is that he came past the farm two months ago, and he had a little English fellow with him – a little mannikin, not much taller than Heloise, but smart-looking, a good suit, if you know what I mean. They were on their way to Kimberley, they said, to see about some business, and that was all.'

Horace came in, and Barney ordered tea. 'I thought you said that Simon de Koker told you about my diamond?' he asked Alf Loubser.

Alf Loubser shrugged defensively. 'They were downstairs in the kitchen, talking till twelve o'clock at night. I went down to see if they wanted anything, that's all.'

'And you accidentally overheard what they were waying?' said Barney, raising an eyebrow.

'It's my house!' protested Alf Loubser.

'Of course it is,' agreed Barney. 'You had every right to listen. So, tell me, what did you hear them saying?'

'They didn't say much. Simon de Koker was worried about the weather. But then the little English fellow mentioned your name, and said something about this diamond you'd found, and how much it was worth. He didn't say anything else about it, and after a while they went to bed. But in the morning I talked to the pastor at the church, and he said he'd read in the newspaper about the diamond, so I knew that what the little fellow had said must be true. I talked it over with *mevrouw* Loubser, and we thought I ought to pay you a visit in Kimberley and ask for something to help bring up Heloise.'

Barney stood up, and walked to the open French windows. Then he stepped right out on to the patio, with Alf Loubser watching him uncomfortably from inside the drawing-room.

'You won't tell anybody that I told you?' Alf Loubser called out, anxiously. 'Some of these Boer snipers, they're very promiscuous with a gun!'

Barney shook his head, although he did not know if Alf Loubser could see him or not. He was thinking too hard about what the sheep-farmer had just told him. If Alf Loubser had seen Hunt in the company of Simon de Koker, and Simon de Koker was now an agent for the Boer resistance in the Transvaal, then it was highly unlikely that Hunt was still working for Government House in Capetown, as he had claimed he was. All those stories about Sir Bartle Frere tangling up the Union Jack on the lawns and raw young diplomats being forced to choke down whole ostrich eggs were almost certainly fictitious, dashes of invention that Hunt had put in to add believability to his story about wanting the diamond as a glittering diversion from the Zulu war. He had probably hoped that they would irritate Barney, at the same time.

Now that Barney could think about it more logically, the odds against Hunt still being employed by the colonial service were slight. After all, there had been several changes of Governor since Barney had first met him, and Hunt had probably lost his job years ago, when Sir Philip Woodhouse had returned to England. Apart from that, his homosexuality would always have made his career in the foreign service precarious: especially since most of the public school chaps who staffed Government House were very dull, and straightforward, and were not the sort of chaps who cared to be caught inside some other chap's mosquito-net with their ducks around their ankles.

Barney had no proof of it, but it seemed more than likely that the Natalia Star had been acquired for the Boers – either as a provocative symbol of their independence, and their rights in West Griqualand; or as a means of financing an armed rebellion

476

against the British – or both. Perhaps Hunt had never intended to pay for the diamond at all. Perhaps the 'consortium of businessmen' was all invention, too; and he had come to Vogel Vlei with his extravagant offers of 'a million-four' simply in order to find out how difficult it was going to be to steal the diamond out of Barney's safe. If that was so, Hunt must have found Sara's discontent and Joel's simmering anger to be gifts from Heaven.

Louise came back into the drawing-room with the birth certificate. She offered it to her father, but he indicated with a wave of his hand that she should take it outside to Barney.

Barney took it and read it while Louise stood by his side, occasionally pushing her wind-blown hair out of her eyes. It announced simply that a female child had been born to Louise Stella Loubser at Beaufort West, and that the child had been baptised in the Kleine Kerk in the names of Helois Petra Loubser. Barney folded the paper up again and handed it back.

'Do you really think the child was mine?' he asked Louise.

'I always hoped it was,' she told him.

He looked at her for a while, so young and pale and unsmiling – a girl who lived in a world that was mostly fairy-stories and simple dreams. She had remembered him after all these years, although she probably saw him as somebody quite different from the broad-shouldered diamond digger that he really was. She was the kind of girl who saw stars even on cloudy nights, and who could make a prince out of a kopje-walloper.

'I'll give you some money,' Barney told her. 'I can't admit that the child is mine. My lawyers would burst a blood-vessel. But I'll give you a hundred pounds a year for five years to take care of her clothes and her schooling, and that's just because I like you.'

Louise gave a vague, pretty smile. 'I look at Heloise sometimes and I can remember your face exactly,' she said.

'You'll take care of her?' Barney asked her.

Louise nodded, and then reached on tiptoe and kissed him on the cheek.

Alf Loubser came outside, his hands firmly pushed into his pockets. 'You've seen the certificate? What do you think?'

'I've already told Louise that I'll give her some money. Not much, because even a birth certificate isn't convincing proof that the baby was mine. But enough to make sure that you can educate her, and keep her well fed.'

Alf Loubser scanned the grounds of Vogel Vlei, his eyes wrinkled against the bright sunlight. 'I came up here feeling angry,' he said. 'Well, I'm sorry. You've behaved like a gentleman. I thought I was going to have to frighten you into helping Heloise. But it wasn't necessary. I feel like a bit of a pig, and I just hope that you'll shake my hand on it.'

He took one hand out of his pocket, and held it out. Barney shook it, and then smiled. 'Why don't you stay here the night?' he asked. 'There are plenty of empty rooms.'

'You live in this huge place all by yourself? No children?'

Barney shook his head. 'You know what children are like. They have a way of growing up, and leaving you.'

He took Louise Stella Loubser's arm, and escorted her back into the drawing-room, where Horace had spread a crisp pink cloth on the side-table and was laying out plates of cold tongue, and cold salt beef, and potato salad. Alf Loubser rubbed his hands hungrily, and gave Barney a wink of approval. Neither he nor Louise knew how desolate Barney felt, just at that moment, nor how much he appreciated their simple, unaffected company. Louise leaned her white-blonde hair against his shoulder and Barney touched it the way a child touches anything irresistibly silky.

Later that evening, while Alf Loubser and Louise were having their supper in the small parlour at the back of the house, Barney held a meeting with Harold Feinberg and Edward Nork in the library. Harold was not feeling at all well: his little froggy girl had been upsetting him by threatening to take another lover, and with the discovery of two new pipes at Dorstfontein, the market price of diamonds was looking what Harold always called 'distinctly tremulous'. The sooner the South African diamond industry became a monopoly, Harold grumbled, the better it would be for all of them. Then they could turn the flow of diamonds on and off like a tap, and control the price down to the last farthing.

Edward Nork was somewhere between yesterday's hangover

and tonight's bender, and he kept blinking and coughing and wiping his spectacles on his shirt, and excusing himself to go to the lavatory.

'Sara's out this evening?' asked Harold. 'What is it, crochet circle? Drama group?'

Barney took off his coat and hung it over the back of his chair. 'That's the whole reason I've asked you to come here.'

'What is?' Edward frowned. 'You want *us* to take up crochet, too?'

Harold coughed, clearing a barrowload of phlegm from his throat. He looked pale and unhealthy these days, as if part of him had already started to die. Barney was not at all surprised that his French girl was thinking of taking another lover, although it would not be easy for her to find anyone who could so regularly supply her with her favourite contraceptives.

'You're thinking of selling the diamond, is that it?' he asked. 'Leopold and Wavers have finally come up with an offer that you can't resist? You have that kind of look on your face.'

'Really, Harold, I don't know why you're so nervous about Barney selling this stone,' Edward put in. 'He's got to dispose of it sooner or later, and *later* is going to be just as bad for diamond prices as *sooner*. You should be pleased that he's going to sell it through Feinberg, and that you're going to get a healthy commission. Supposing he took it to Manny Greene?'

Harold slapped his hand on the leather arm of his chair; the same chair in which, only a few days before, Hunt had sat with his legs prissily crossed and proposed a purchase by his 'consortium of British businessmen'. He snapped crossly, 'It's the wrong time to sell. And, besides, I think Barney's original idea of having the diamond cut first, before we put it out to auction, is much better. It will give all of us experience of handling a big stone, all the way along the line; and it will increase our profit three hundred per cent. And don't talk to me about Manny Greene, that *shnorrer*.'

'You're so *cautious*,' Edward retorted. 'If Barney doesn't act quickly on the offers that Leopold and Wavers and all the rest of them have already tabled, he might end up with a stone that's worth three times as much that nobody's actually prepared to buy.'

'Why don't you stick to your geology?' Harold barked at him.

479

'What do you know from diamond dealing? Most of the time you're *shikker*.'

Edward sighed, and took off his spectacles to prod at his eyeballs with his middle finger, as if he were testing plums to see how ripe they were. 'You Jews exasperate me,' he said, with his eyes still tightly closed. 'A chap only has to disagree with you, and you break out into a rash of incomprehensibility.'

'*Shikker* means drunk,' said Barney, in a quiet voice. 'And, in any case, there isn't any future in you two arguing.'

'What do you mean?' said Edward. 'We always argue. It's good for your livers.'

'There you are,' said Harold. 'I'm talking world diamond prices, and he's talking offals.'

Barney said, 'It doesn't matter any more. The diamond's gone. It's been stolen.'

There was a curious silence, interspersed only by Harold's laboured breathing. Edward put on his glasses again and peered at Barney like Galileo trying to distinguish through his foggy seventeenth-century telescope whether the planet Saturn had rings around it, or ears; and hoping for the sake of his sanity that the evidence would not favour ears.

'It's been *stolen*? My dear chap! But how? Didn't you have it locked in your safe? I can't believe it!'

Harold said nothing, but let his chin drop forward on to his chest. His breathing sounded as harsh as the old harmonium bellows in the *strooidak* church in Klipdrift.

'I had a visit from someone I used to know in the colonial service at Capetown,' said Barney. 'He made me an offer for the diamond, saying that the British wanted to present it to the Queen. What I didn't know *then*, but what I've found out *now*, is that he probably no longer works for the colonial service, and hasn't done so for years. He's working in co-operation with a Boer scout called Simon de Koker, who apparently acts as a secret agent for the resistance in the Transvaal.'

Harold raised his head, his eyes protuberant with shock and shortness of breath.

'It's gone to the Boers? The diamond's gone to the Boers?'

'I suspect so,' Barney told him.

'Pitiful God, I can't believe what you're telling me,' said

Harold. 'You know what's going to happen if the Boers lay their hands on it? Either they'll hold it to ransom, and ask for their independence back. Or else they'll sell it to the Russians and buy themselves enough rifles and enough ammunition to push the British out of the diamond fields and back to the Orange River.'

Barney shrugged. 'I know that, Harold. Although I still don't know for sure that it *was* the Boers. There isn't any firm evidence one way or the other. But it seems to me to be the most likely thing that's happened. The Boers would have more to gain than anybody else by stealing it, and more to lose if it were cut and sold abroad.'

'How did they . . .?' asked Edward, nodding towards the safe.

'I'm afraid to say that Sara gave them the key,' said Barney. 'She's gone with them, along with Joel, and Sara's *amah*.'

'Motley sort of a crew,' remarked Edward.

'Motley or not, they've got the Natalia Star, and I don't know where they've gone.'

Harold said, 'I think I'm going to have to trouble you for a glass of water.'

Barney rang the bell for Horace, while Harold loosened his tie and sat in the armchair mopping his forehead and gasping.

'So, you called it the Natalia Star,' smiled Edward. 'Is that one of the reasons why Sara was so keen to help them?'

Barney looked down, and re-arranged some of the pens and pencils on his desk. 'Let's just say that our marriage hadn't been running particularly smoothly. But I was still shocked when I found out what she'd done.'

'When did this happen?' asked Harold.

'Yesterday morning, while I was working at the mine. I didn't find out that my key had been stolen until early afternoon; and then I made a complete fool of myself and chased them along the Hopetown road, thinking they'd made a run for the Cape. There wasn't any sign of them.'

'From what you've said about this Simon de Koker, it's far more likely that they've headed for the Transvaal,' said Edward.

Horace came in, and Barney asked for a glass of water for Harold and a cup of strong coffee for himself. Edward said that he would 'make do' with the whiskey decanter on the library table.

When Horace had gone, Harold said slowly, 'The most important thing of all is to prevent the bastards from cutting it. Once it's cut, you'll have no chance of proving that it's yours. In the rough, we can identify it. I've got photographs of it from all sides; and drawings; and a plaster-cast.'

'They won't have any great difficulty getting it cut, though, will they?' said Barney. 'There must be a dozen good cutters in Amsterdam who would do it for them, no questions asked.'

'Well, you're right,' sighed Harold. 'But it could take anything up to eighteen months to cut a stone as big as yours – the Natalia Star, if that's what you've really decided to call it. And until they've bruted off all the rough surfaces, we've still got a remote chance of proving that it's yours.'

'That's if it actually goes to Amsterdam; and that's if we can find it once it's there. They could just as easily sell it in the rough to the Russian court; or the Austrians; or send it over to America.'

Harold drank his water, and then patted his mouth with his handkerchief. 'The only way we're going to dind out where it's gone is if I put out feelers in the trade. One thing's for sure: they won't take it to a second-rate cutter. They're going to have to go to the best, and that narrows their options considerably. There are only three cutters I can think of who could do it justice – Josef Van Steenwijk, who works for Coster's, in Amsterdam; Levi Baumgold, at Annen's, also in Amsterdam; and Itzik Yussel, who's the head cutter at Roosendaal's in Antwerp.'

Barney leaned back in his chair and sipped disconsolately at his coffee. 'They might keep the diamond for years before they send it out for cutting. They might sell it as a rough, and not bother to have it cut at all.'

'Well,' said Harold, 'there's always a chance of that ... in which case, you'll never see the diamond again. But I'm crediting anyone who has the nerve to steal the continent's biggest diamond from out under the nose of its owner with the intelligence to make as much money out of it as they can. As a rough, it's too easily identifiable, and too difficult to sell and re-sell.

Remember that Thomas Pitt did with the Regent ... he sent it straight to London to be cut, so that nobody else could claim it was theirs. For my money, that diamond is going to be smuggled to Amsterdam or Antwerp within the month.'

Edward Nork had helped himself to a generous glassful of whiskey, and he noisily stoppered the decanter before coming back across the room and standing by Barney's desk, his spectacles propped up on his forehead, his shaggy eyebrows tangled in thought.

'What you're going to have to do is send copies of Harold's drawings to all the major diamond-merchants, explaining that the diamond is stolen. That won't stop anybody really unscrupulous, but it might frighten some of the more respectable houses off. Cheers!'

He swallowed whiskey, and then coughed until he was grey in the face.

'All right,' said Barney. 'If that's the best we can do, let's do it. I can tell you something though: I would rather have lost that diamond down a hole in the ground than lose it to those people.'

'I know,' Harold told him, understandingly. 'But that's the way it is with diamonds. They bring out all of your most possessive and jealous feelings, no matter how much you try to resist them. They make you stlightly mad. And why not? Carat for carat, they're worth more than almost anything you can think of. Nearly twice as much as emeralds. A hundred times more than gold.'

'They're not worth anything at all if you've lost them,' put in Edward, with an exaggeratedly rueful face, and hiccupped.

Barney's guesses about Hunt and Simon de Koker had been mostly accurate, although Hunt had actually resigned from the colonial service only two months ago, the day after de Koker had approached him in an hotel restaurant on Adderley Street and suggested that he might care to help him lay his hands on the Natalia Star. De Koker had not particularly wanted to involve Hunt in a secret Boer mission, but he had needed someone who could get himself admitted to Vogel Vlei without arousing suspicion. He had also been worried that Barney might already have heard that he was working as an agent for the Boers, and might have him arrested by the British as soon as he turned up on the doorstep.

Hunt, for his part, had been more than eager for a little excitement, and a little peril, and the chance to play the starring rôle in a domestic and criminal double-cross. Once inside Vogel Vlei, he had been delighted by Barney's dogmatic insistence that the stone was not for sale at any price – particularly since he had only £36 0s 2d in his Capetown bank account, which fell somewhat short of 'a million-four'. But he had particularly relished Sara, bored and irritated and bourgeois, and he had tried to exploit her frustrations for all he was worth by telling her how beautiful she was, and yet how neglected she was, an English rose flowering unseen and unappreciated in this day and dusty tailing of the Empire. Joel had been easy to recruit: his resentment of Barney was so intense that in Hunt's words 'it could have burned holes in the carpet'.

After they had stolen the stone, though, they had not headed for the Transvaal, as Barney and Harold had supposed, and they had never intended to. De Koker's instructions from Swartplaas, the farm on the Witwatersrand that the Boers were using as a resistance headquarters, were to take the diamond out of the country as quickly as possible, from the port of Lourenço Marques, where a Dutch steamship would be waiting in the third week of March. Their journey to the coast would be difficult and possibly dangerous, but de Koker had arranged for a small escort of Boer volunteers to meet them at Wesselstroom and guide them through the Drakensberg pass to New Scotland, as far as Lake Chrissie, where they would turn eastwards again and follow the course of the Impellus River into Portuguese territory, and then down to the sea.

To begin with, to put Barney off the trail, they had headed northwards out of Kimberley on the track that would have taken them up along the valley of the Vaal towards Klerksdorp, and right into the heart of the Transvaal. But after a few miles they had turned directly eastwards across open country; and spent their first night camping by a smoky fire on the open veld, not far from the settlement of Boshof. When morning came, they had started off early, and made for Bloemfontein, the capital of the Orange Free State. It took them two days to get there, travelling as rapidly as they could; but when they arrived there they rested for another two days, so that Sara could bathe and buy herself two or three new dresses to travel in, and Joel could stock up on the medication he needed, Dover's powder and boric ointment. Simon de Koker exchanged their elegant but impractical landau for a horse-drawn waggon, which he stocked with beef and ham and smoked cheese, and eight kegs of water.

Edward had been right about them: they were a motley band, and from the very beginning of their uncomfortable flight across the Orange Free State there were violent disagreements about who should sit where, and who was in charge, and most crucial of all, who the Natalia Star now belonged to. Sara, who had taken the key from Barney's bureau, and had actually removed the stone from the safe, was quite sure that the diamond was now hers. Simon de Koker said that if the diamond was now hers, then why was he bothering to drive her all the way across southern Africa? The diamond was now the property of the true government of the Transvaal, the Boers, and it would be cut and auctioned in Amsterdam for the sole purpose of financing a Boer campaign against the British oppressors. Joel claimed that the diamond was fifty per cent his, since the mine in which it had been found was fifty per cent his. Hunt argued that the stone should be sold in the rough, as quickly as possible, and the proceeds divided four ways, with a few hundred pounds for Nareez. Nareez was suffering from heatstroke, and said nothing at all, but chewed coriander seeds, and stared at the mirages of lakes and rivers that shimmered on the horizon as if they were visions of the Ganges at Rājshāhi, on the hot days of her childhood.

What none of them knew, as they toiled their way towards the foothills of the Drakensberg, was that Sir Bartle Frere's invasion of Zululand had already started, and that only two hundred miles to the east of them, Lord Chelmsford was advancing towards the Zulu capital of Ulundi with three columns of regular soldiers and volunteers. On 11 January, the week before Sara and Hunt had stolen the diamond, Lord

Chelmsford's central column had forded the Buffalo River at Rorke's Drift and on 20 January, a few miles further on, he had established a new camp in the shadow of the odd sphinx-shaped mountain known as Isandhlwana.

On 22 January, the Wednesday after Sara and Hunt and Joel had stolen the Natalia Star, and when they were a day east from Bloemfontein, twenty thousand Zulu warriors attacked Lord Chelmsford's camp and slaughtered nearly 1400 soldiers and Natal native recruits, leaving the sloping hillside littered with burned-out tents, looted waggons, and stiffened bodies. The six companies of the 2nd Warwickshire regiment died to the last man, and the broken ground down to the Buffalo River was splattered with the blood of grooms, cooks, waggon drivers, and bandsmen, all of whom had tried to escape when the Zulu *impi* broke through the front lines of soldiers. On the same day, the British mission station and hospital at Rorke's Drift was successfully defended against 4000 Zulus by only 104 British soldiers. But Lord Chelmsford had been obliged to withdraw, and call for reinforcements, and to re-assess his previous contempt for Cetewayo's army.

It thundered for three solid days when Hunt and Sara and Joel crossed the Drakensberg mountains, great dark barrages of bumbling noise, with rain so harsh and torrential that it stung their faces. The horses shied and reared, and their hooves kept slipping on the wet rock. Six or seven times in every mile they managed to cover, their waggon wheels would lodge in a groove or a gully, and Simon de Koker and Hunt would have to lever the wheels free with shovel-handles, or push the waggon out with their backs. Joel, cursing and complaining, would have to be lifted out into the storm by Sara and Nareez, to lighten the load, and the three of them would be obliged to sit on a nearby boulder like drowned cats while the waggon was heaved back on to the track again.

'Every now and then, one is given a severe lesson in life that one should have been content with what one had,' Sara remarked, with a drip on the end of her nose, on the day they reached the highest point in the Drakensberg. She was sitting by the side of the road with a khaki canvas kitbag upturned on her head, her waterproof cape drawn around her shoulders, her white leather boots hopelessly muddied and stained with water. The rain was sloping across the pass in sheets of bitterly-cold spray, and the waggon had got jammed again, this time in one of the old narrow tracks that had been gouged out of the rock by the heavy ox-waggons of the Boer *voortrekkers*.

'*Content?*' asked Joel. 'How could you ever have been content with Barney? Even this is better than sitting in that tomb of a house, trying to remember what human dignity was.'

'Do you think you've found your dignity now?' asked Sara, tartly.

Joel looked down at himself. Under his wide wet bush-hat, which was drooping down on all sides, he was dressed in a muddy brown overcoat and frayed grey trousers. He had wound a blanket around his waist to keep his hips warm and the stump of his left leg dry; and inserted his right foot into a leather saddle-pouch to prevent the rain from running into his shoe.

'At least I'm free,' said Joel, although he did not sound very convinced, even of that.

Sara took out a sopping handkerchief and wiped her face. 'I'd give up any amount of freedom for a hot bath.'

'We've got the diamond,' said Joel. 'In a month, we'll all be well on our way to Amsterdam. Then, when it's cut and sold, and we get our share, we'll be rich enough to do whatever we like. By this time next year, we won't have any worries about anything, *helevai*.'

Sara stared at him for a while, the raindrops clustered on her eyelashes. 'Do you really think I'm going to share the diamond with the Boers?'

Joel looked back at her warily. 'What do you mean?'

'Exactly what I say. I didn't take the diamond for the sake of the independence of the Transvaal, I can tell you that. I don't care for Boers one bit. They're crude, and they're uneducated, and they spend all of their time smoking pipes and eating dreadful varieties of cheese. Just look at that Simon de Koker. He smells like a mule, and I shouldn't think he's combed that beard of his for weeks.'

Joel picked up a pebble, and juggled it in the palm of his

hand. Only a few yards away, Simon de Koker was trying to wrestle the iron rim of the waggon wheel out of the rock with a crowbar, and there was a grinding noise of metal against wet sandstone. Hunt, almost purple in the face, was trying to push the waggon forward.

'He won't let you run off with it,' said Joel. 'He didn't travel all the way to Capetown and back, and then across to Lourenço Marques, just to watch you wave him goodbye.'

'*He* may be going to Lourenço Marques, but *I'm* not,' said Sara, emphatically.

Joel tossed the pebble up, and caught it again. 'Where are *you* going?' he asked, in a bland voice.

'You'll betray me, if I tell you. You'll probably betray me anyway.'

'Why should I betray you?' asked Joel, trying to sound surprised.

'You betrayed your own brother.'

Joel sniffed. 'Is that what you call it?'

'What do *you* call it?'

'I call it survival, most of the time. Sometimes I call it justice.'

Simon de Koker snapped his whip at the horses, and, 'Yip! Yip! Yip! Come on now, pull up! Pull up, you bunch of bonebags!'

'I don't think insulting them is going to help,' Joel called loudly, over the cold clattering of the rain. Simon de Koker looked around and gave him a flat, sour stare. Joel grinned back at him, and said, 'Don't mind me. What do I know from horses?'

As the team of horses strained at their harnesses, their hooves skidding and sliding and their flanks steaming with rain, Sara said quietly: 'A million-pound diamond for one would be ideal. A million-pound diamond between two would be almost as good. But a million-pound diamond between four? It's just not enough. Particularly when I suspect that our smelly Boer friend has no intention of giving us anything more than a token reward for our troubles. He's a political zealot, and political zealots are usually even more untrustworthy than common criminals. So Papa said, anyway.'

Joel kept on juggling his pebble, until at last he reached his arm back and tossed it away down the track, back towards the Orange Free State. 'You're going to have to think of a way of getting rid of him, then, aren't you? And Hunt.'

'Hunt won't be at all difficult. He's like a child. It's de Koker that's going to be a problem.'

'What are you thinking of doing? Knocking him on the head with a bottle, and tying him up, and leaving him for the *lemmergayers?*'

Sara's lips were blue from cold. 'We're going to have to kill him,' she said. 'He knows the land far better than we do. If we don't kill him, he's bound to get free, and come hot in pursuit. Anyway, for all we know, he's planning to do the same thing to us. If you were he, would *you* drive a whole waggon-load of cripples and women all the way to Lourenço Marques, when you could make it in half the time on your own? He's probably waiting for nothing less than a convenient place in the mountains, so that he can cut the horses' traces and push us all over a precipice.'

'Your sense of the melodramatic is over-developed, to say the least,' said Joel. 'And less of the "cripples", if you don't mind.'

'If you weren't a cripple you could deal with him yourself,' Sara retorted. 'As it is, it'll have to be me.'

'What are you going to do?' asked Joel, with hopeless jocularity, 'get Nareez to hug him to death?'

'Nareez is my companion,' Sara reminded him, sharply. 'She didn't ask to be dragged halfway across Africa, and she's been very brave.' She hesitated, and then she said, 'I'm going to shoot him.'

'What with? You don't even have a pistol.'

'De Koker has a rifle. That will do.'

'He sleeps with it. He carries it around all day. When do you think he's going to give you the chance to take it away from him?'

'We'll see,' said Sara.

There was a distant mumble of thunder, and lightning illuminated the sky behind the mountains like the scenery of a cheap opera. After a few minutes' pause, the rain began to fall even more heavily than before, and water foamed down the rutted track and sprayed around the wheels of the waggon.

Simon de Koker called, 'Yip! Yip! Yip!' and at last the waggon's back wheels reared out of the rutted track, and the whole rig rolled forwards six or seven feet, its wet canvas top wobbling on its frame.

'There's just one problem,' Joel whispered to Sara, as Simon de Koker and Nareez came across to help him back over the tailboard. 'If we kill de Koker, how do we find our way to wherever we're going?'

'The road's easy from here,' said Sara; and then realising that Simon de Koker had overheard her, she smiled, 'Isn't it, Mr de Koker? Quite easy?'

Simon de Koker picked Joel up as roughly as if he were a broken scarecrow, and with Nareez holding his one remaining leg, which made Joel tilt unnervingly sideways, they carried him over to the back of the waggon.

'The road to Lourenço Marques from here is very difficult,' Simon de Koker said. 'I don't even know it very well myself – which is why we pick up extra guides at Wesselstroom. On purpose, we're not going the easy way. If the British catch us, and take the diamond, it will be years and years before we can afford to fight for our independence again.'

'It's easy to get to Durban from here, though, isn't it?'

'Durban?' asked de Koker, suspiciously, beckoning to Hunt to let down the tailboard.

'I used to live there,' said Sara, smiling as attractively as she could with a wet canvas kitbag on her head.

Simon de Koker grunted, and rolled Joel into the back of the waggon. Hunt, his wet hair stuck to his face, the shoulders of his coat stained dark with damp, locked up the tailboard and said, 'Let's see how far we can get before we have to do this all over again.'

They drove in silence for another four miles, crossing into Natal and descending into the Sand River Valley towards Ladysmith. The rain at last began to ease off, and dissolve into a fine grey fog, which gave the mountainous landscape the silent and eerie quality of another world. Simon de Koker sat up in front of the waggon, driving, with Nareez sitting beside him in her Indian shawl. Joel lay in the back, his head resting against a flour sack, snoring. Hunt and Sara faced each other across the waist, saying nothing, but continually addressing each other with their eyes. Hunt would give Sara a provocative, questioning look; and she would either stare at him with feigned disinterest, or turn away.

'When are you thinking of getting rid of ...?' Hunt asked her, as they rumbled noisily down an incline beside the Klip River.

Sara frowned, but Hunt vigorously nodded his head towards Simon de Koker's hunched-up back.

'I don't know what you're talking about,' said Sara.

'Of course you know what I'm talking about,' Hunt replied, with a teasing smile. 'Tomorrow morning, we turn north, to Ladysmith, and then to the Wakkerstroom, and then in three weeks we should be in Lourenço Marques. This is where the road divides. This way, Lourenço Marques; that way, Durban. Come on, Mrs Blitz, I've seen your mind ticking like a carriage-clock. All those cogs going round, all those jewelled mountings! I've seen you muttering to Joel, too. You're not going to let the Boers get away with your precious diamond, are you? Especially when they're going to use it to fight the British. De Koker may have judged your perfidy exactly; but he's forgotten about your patriotism. A fine colonial lady like you. Capetown's teeming with them; so I should know.'

The noise of the metal-rimmed tyres was just loud enough to prevent Simon de Koker from hearing what Hunt was saying; all his years in the colonial service had given Hunt a particular talent for gossiping about people only two or three feet away from where they were standing, without arousing their suspicions. He liked to call it the 'embassy murmur'.

Sara glanced at Joel, sleeping with his cheek pressed into a sausage-like fold, and his mouth hanging open. 'I *have* been considering alternatives,' she said.

'Of course. Just like de Koker must have been, too.'

Sara pressed her hand over the gazelle-skin bag which was now hanging around her neck, tied to her gold and diamond necklace. 'He's going to have to kill me first. Surely he knows that.'

'I'm quite certain he does. I'm not really sure why he hasn't killed all of us already.'

'I think I know,' said Sara. 'He's one of these men who needs a moral justification for everything he does. It's quite common among Calvinists, and political enthusiasts. They can't act unless they believe that they've been wronged. They're stern people, the Boers – very stern, but also very religious. And that's why Simon de Koker won't try to get us out of the way until *we* make the first move.'

'Well,' said Hunt, pursing his lips, 'it's an interesting theory.'

'I only hope that it's a theory that works,' replied Sara. 'And I hope that when we *do* make the first move, we make it effectively enough for Mr de Koker to be rendered incapable of retaliation.'

'Um, what do you have in mind, in particular?' asked Hunt, with a smile.

Sara looked towards Joel, still snoring on his flour sack. 'That's what *he* wanted to know.'

That night, they drew their waggon off the main road and tied up their horses by a stand of evergreens. It was still foggy, and when they lit their campfire to make tea and cook up a pan of salted beef and beans, the flames were blurred by a smudgy orange halo. They were ten miles short of Ladysmith, and the turning which would take them north to Newcastle and Wesselstroom, and eventually to New Scotland and Lourenço Marques, but the horses were exhausted and shivering, and Joel had been bawling complaints to Simon de Koker for almost an hour about his leg. At last, taciturn and reluctant, Simon de Koker had said, 'We halt here,' and jammed back the waggon's ironwood brake-handle.

They hardly spoke over their meal. They were all exhausted and cold; and since they had crossed the summit of the Drakensberg a noticeable feeling of mutual suspicion had settled amongst them. Simon de Koker sat well away from the rest, his rifle propped against a sapling close beside him, humourlessly stripping the skin from a *weinwurst* with his clasp-knife.

At last, Joel said, 'I'm tired out. Nareez – will you get me my blankets?'

The *amah* made a show of finishing her tin plateful of beans before getting up and bringing Joel's bedding. She considered herself nobody's servant, except Sara's; and even to Sara she was more of a mother than a hired woman. Hunt went to find his own bedroll, and made himself an elaborate little tent under the branches of the trees with the canvas flap which usually covered the boxes and barrels that hung from the sides of the waggon's hull. It was not long before only Sara and Simon de Koker were left by themselves, sitting ten feet apart from each other on opposite sides of the campfire in wary silence. The fire crackled and spat in the damp air, and all around them there was nothing but slowly settling silver, like the particles on a photographic plate, until Sara began to feel that this was the only existence there was, here in this suffocating and unfocused world of fog, and unseen mountains, and ghostly trees.

'I think soon that I will take charge of the diamond,' said Simon de Koker, without looking up.

Sara raised an eyebrow. 'You think so?'

'*Jaha*. It's for safety. A woman shouldn't carry anything so valuable.'

'I think I'm quite capable of looking after it myself, thank you,' said Sara. 'I was brought up in Natal, after all. I know my way around.'

'Well ... that's what I'm worried about,' said Simon de Koker, cutting off another piece of sausage, and pushing it into his mouth from the blade of his knife.

'You're worried that I'm going to run off with the diamond, all on my own?'

Simon de Koker chewed methodically, and then he said, 'It crossed my mind. Don't tell me it didn't cross yours.'

'Of course it did. But then we all went into this little affair together, didn't we? Each of us is equally culpable. Each of us will equally profit. I expect you're going to ask for rather a large percentage of the proceeds for the resistance in the Transvall, but then I can't say I blame you. The British have always been pigheaded about the Boers, and I'm sure that you're not going to give them any more than they deserve.'

493

Simon de Koker watched Sara carefully, his eye glittering orange in the firelight. 'I thought you were a strong British patriot,' he said.

Sara smiled at him. 'I'm afraid that profit comes before patriotism. It always has done in my family. My father is Gerald Sutter the shipper; you've probably heard of him.'

Simon de Koker nodded.

'The truth is, Mr de Koker, that you're a very brave man,' said Sara. She waited a moment or two for that remark to have its full effect, and then she added, 'You're brave because you're risking your life to overthrow a tyranny; and no matter whose tyranny it is – you have a moral and religious right to struggle against it. For once, I'm on the side of the Boers.'

'Are there many English people feel like you?' asked Simon de Koker, warily.

'Some. Mostly the old-time Africa hands – those who have seen for themselves how hard the Boers have had to struggle for their independence. We're not all insensitive, you know. We admire what you're doing, and we know that one day you'll be successful.'

'Hm,' said Simon de Koker, trying to sound suspicious, but clearly pleased.

Sara stood up, and walked around the campfire, so that she was standing only two or three feet away from Simon de Koker, her face softened and blurred by the fog, and by the shadows from the dying flames.

'Unless you've been ignoring me on purpose, you will have seen that I am a woman of great passion,' Sara told him.

'Yes,' said Simon de Koker. He closed his clasp-knife, and then realised that his hands were greasy with *weinwurst*. He wiped them assiduously on the wet grass while Sara came two or three steps closer, and gathered up her skirts so that she could kneel down beside him.

'You mustn't be afraid of me,' she said. 'This is one of those things that happens in war, and during great adventures. Men and women meet in desperate circumstances, and they take whatever they can from each other; not caring about their responsibilities, not caring about the future. You are a Boer agent, and I am an English lady. I should be taking care of my

494

husband, and thinking of my propriety. You should be guard-
ing me, and keeping me prisoner, and not listening to any of
this. You should be thinking of the Transvaal.'

'The Transvaal?' frowned Simon de Koker, as if he could not
understand what she was saying. He was hypnotised by her
perfume, and her femininity, and the way that she spoke so
suggestively in such a glacial English accent. The last woman
he had slept with had been a big, black, broad-bottomed Kaffir
girl in Dutoitspan, in the back room of Maloney's Bar, and that
had been well over three months ago.

Sara reach out and tugged gently at Simon de Koker's fringe
of a beard. 'Ask me no questions,' she whispered. 'Don't expect
anything – least of all that this will ever happen again. I will
always deny it, to my dying breath. But go to the waggon now,
and lay out the blankets; and in a while I will come and join
you.'

Simon de Koker slowly, hesitantly, reached up and held her
wrist. His fingernails were embedded with crescents of black
dirt, and both he and Sara glanced simultaneously at the
contrast between the pale, blue-veined skin of Sara's arm and
the grimy calluses of Simon de Koker's fingers; but then Sara
laid her other hand over Simon's hand, and said *sshh*, as if to
reassure him.

'You're a hero,' she said. 'And there never was a hero, not
a real hereo, with clean hands.'

Simon de Koker said thickly, 'When this is over – tonight
– you will let me have the diamond?'

Sara's eyes were wide and sincere. 'If you can prove you
trust me ... then I can show you just how much I trust you
in return ...'

'The diamond, though?'

'Anything,' she murmured. 'Anything at all.'

Simon de Koker looked round at the huddled blankets all
around the fire, where the others were sleeping, or trying to
sleep. Then he eased himself up, collected his rifle, and stood
for a moment in the fog, still indecisive.

'Just a few minutes,' said Sara; and to encourage him, she
lifted her gold neck-chain, so that he could glimpse the leather
bag in which she kept the diamond. He nodded, and walked

across to the waggon, a tall spindly shadow in the fog, with a wide-brimmed hat.

Sara waited five or six minutes, watching the fire sparkle and subside. Then she lifted the diamond from around her neck, and took it across to where Nareez was already sleeping, and tucked it in between Nareez's blankets. Carefully, she stepped over Joel, and tiptoed towards the waggon.

Simon de Koker was waiting for her, on the blanket bed that he had made up on the floor of the waggon, in between the biscuit-boxes and the kegs of water. As he sucked at his pipe, and the dottle glowed, she saw his sweaty bearded face and the flat herringbone pattern of his ribs, decorated with a pattern of moles and stray curly hairs. He had hung his hat from one of the hooks at the side of the waggon cover; and beside him, as close to his naked body as he could comfortably wedge it, was his Mauser rifle, greasy and dark.

'You took your time,' he smiled.

'I wanted to make sure they were all asleep.'

He took his pipe out of his mouth, and knocked it on one of the water kegs. 'That lot, they fall asleep as soon as they look at a blanket. They're just tenderfeet. I've buried more people like that on the Great Karoo than you could count on ten fingers and ten toes.'

Sara unclasped her cape, and folded it up. Then she began to unbutton her blue flowered dress. Simon de Koker noisily cleared his throat. 'You're not frightened, are you?' asked Sara.

'Frightened?' grinned Simon de Koker, and his Afrikaans accent was so strong that he pronounced it, *'frartened?'*

'I'd understand, if you were,' said Sara. 'We're so different, you and I. It's not just a question of two people sharing the same blankets. It's like two enemies, in the same bed.'

'I'm not your enemy,' said Simon de Koker.

She leaned forward, the front of her dress unbuttoned to reveal her white camisole, and kissed him on the forehead. 'I'm not your enemy, either. And I hope that God forgives us.'

Simon de Koker watched her in silence as she lifted her dress over her head, and then stood up under the blue-willow hoops of the waggon to step out of her underwear. Only the dim flickering light from the campfire, shining through the linseed-treated twill of the waggon cover, limned for him the curve of her body, and showed him for one fleeting second the complicated swaying of her bare breasts.

He threw back the blanket as she climbed on top of him, and reached up for her with both hands. He felt the wiriness of her pubic hair against his thigh.

'Simon . . .' she breathed in his ear. 'You mustn't ever think that this shouldn't have happened. It was fate. I saw it in your hand, in the lines of your palm, when you first took up the traces of Barney's carriage. I saw a broken life-line.'

Simon de Koker kissed her cheek, and then her mouth, and then said, 'What?'

'Your life-line,' she said. She kept on kissing him, little kisses all over his forehead and cheeks that teased him at first, but very quickly irritated him. 'A broken life-line almost always means sickness, you know, or bereavement. Sometimes it means an accident.'

'You're a strange lady,' Simon de Koker breathed. He touched her shoulder, and ran his fingertips down her arm.

She sat up; and in the darkness Simon de Koker thought that she was preparing herself to sit on top of him, and he craned his neck to see. But there was nothing but a dull rattling sound, and then a rapid series of sharp metallic clicks, like castanets. At the very same instant that his mind registered that she had been dragging his rifle towards her, lifting it, and releasing the safety-catch, she pulled the trigger, and with a deafening bang she blew half of his stomach across the waist of the waggon.

Outside, Joel shouted, 'What's happened? *Sara*! What the hell's going on in there? *Sara*!' and Hunt wrestled his way out of his blankets and came scampering around the campfire to see what was going on. He threw open the waggon-cover to see Sara crouched naked, except for her muddy white stockings, with Simon de Koker's rifle under her arm; and Simon de Koker lying back on the floor of the waggon with his eyes wide open and his body plastered in blood.

'Oh my God, it's murder,' said Hunt. 'Oh my God.'

Simon de Koker looked up at Sara with an expression of surprise. His lips moved silently for a while, but then he managed to speak. 'You've shot me,' he said.

Sara was incapable of saying anything. She had been quite

sure that if she shot him, he would die, with a small round puncture as his only wound. She had been totally unprepared for the violent ripple of shock that had shaken his belly like a tent in a storm, and the bucketful of red paint that had splashed over him from nowhere. And he was still alive, and talking to her!

'You've shot my guts art,' Simon de Koker told her, in a liquid whisper. He breathed out through his nose, and a bubble of blood came out of his nostril.

'I – I –' she began, but she was trembling too much to say any more. She felt freezing cold, and when she covered her breasts with her arm, the nipples were as tough and tight as buttons.

'You've got to finish the job,' said Simon de Koker. 'I'm not going to die like this. Not bleeding my guts art.'

'I don't know what to do,' Sara told him, in a hot colliding rush of words. 'Oh my God, I'm sorry. I don't know what to *do*.'

Simon de Koker slowly turned towards his coat, which he had left on top of the salt-barrel. 'In the left-hand pocket, you'll find some more shells,' he told her. 'Take one out, that's it, and I'll tell you what to do next.'

In the gloom, Sara dropped his coat on to the floor, and two or three of the shells rolled away between the boxes of provisions. But she managed to catch one of them, and clutch it in her hand, and sit up straight again, facing Simon de Koker with a feeling of such anguish and shame that she could not do anything but hold it up, and blurt, 'Here.'

Simon de Koker nodded. It took him a few moments to catch enough air in his lungs to be able to say anything. Then he whispered, 'Pull back the bolt on top of the rifle ... to eject the empty ... Then insert the new cartridge ... that's right ... wait, I can't see you very well ... Then push the bolt back in again ... The action of pulling back the bolt ... will have ... the action of pulling ... will have cocked it again.'

Sara's arms seemed to have lost all of their co-ordination. She felt as if she were trying to load the rifle with wooden butter-pats. But at last she managed to jiggle home the bolt, and lift the muzzle again, and say to Simon de Koker in the most haunted of voices, 'It's done.'

With the deliberate slowness of someone who feels very tired, or melancholic, Simon de Koker reached up with one blood-spattered hand and guided the rifle towards his mouth. He closed his lips around it, and then turned his eyes towards Sara, neither pitifully nor appealingly, but in simple resignation at what had to be done. Sara could hardly see him through the tears which suddenly sparkled and danced in front of her eyes.

Hunt said, '*Sara –*!' and that was all she needed. A word to break the spell of her own horror. A word to remind her that she could not sit here a fraction of a second longer, undressed, in the company of a hideously wounded man. She tugged at the trigger, and Simon de Koker's face vanished as abruptly as a china pot knocked off the top of a wall. She did not even hear the bang this time.

Hunt had blankets ready for her as she stepped down from the waggon. There was blood on her knees where she had been crouching down, and she was shaking as uncontrollably as an epileptic. Hunt glanced into the darkness of the waggon cover, and then followed her across to the fire. 'More wood,' he said to Nareez. 'Let's get this fire burning up really decently, shall we? And brandy.'

Joel was sitting up in his bedroll, his face strained and white. 'He's dead?' he asked. It was an irrelevant question, but he had to hear the answer.

Hunt said, in a citric voice, 'A casualty of war. It was quite monstrous, anyway, the idea of selling that marvellous diamond to pay for arms and ammunition, especially since they were going to be used against the British. We must have some principles, mustn't we? *Some* sense of honour, and love of the country that gave us our birthright.'

'*Shah!*' Joel told him, venomously. 'Sara – are you all right?'

Sara lifted her head up and down like a marionette. 'It's the shock,' chipped in Hunt. 'A little brandy, a little sleep, and she'll be perfectly all right.'

Nareez had ignored Hunt's orders to go for more firewood, but she came across with a half-bottle of Napoleon brandy, which she poured into an enamel mug and placed carefully between Sara's shivering fingers. 'You drink now,' she cooed,

499

gently, stroking Sara's hair. 'Don't think about anything at all. Just drink.'

'Well, I think she deserves congratulation,' said Hunt, with his hands perched on his hips, like a dapper little school boy admiring a cracking good innings at house cricket. 'She said she was going to knock the fellow for six, and she did. I think she's an absolute brick.'

'For the love of God, who is understanding and merciful, will you please stop behaving as if this is the snooker-room at Government House?' Joel pleaded. 'Go get some wood. That would be useful. The *amah*'s not going to do it.'

Hunt sighed, misunderstood but unabashed, and started circling around in search of logs. 'Always thought Indians were rather keen on this kind of thing,' he mumbled to himself, as he disappeared behind the line of tethered horses.

Sara finished her brandy, and then threw her head back, and closed her eyes, and stayed silent and still for two or three minutes, the fog prickling her face as it was slowly and wetly precipitated across the valley of the Sand River. Joel looked questioningly at Nareez, but Nareez gave him a little shake of her hand as if to say that he should not worry. A dog barked, somewhere far off in the darkness; or perhaps it was an ape.

Sara opened her eyes. Joel watched her a moment longer, and then said, 'I didn't think you'd do it.'

Sara lowered her head, and ran her fingers into her hair. 'I had to,' she said.

'The world needs more women like you.'

She turned to him, and made a bitter face. 'Does it? Or is it just that men like you need more women like me?'

'You're being unfair to both of us,' said Joel.

'And you don't know what you're saying. If there were more women in the world like me, then I don't think you would care for the world very much, and neither would I. You see only what you want to see, don't you, when you look at me? You never see the struggle that goes on beneath the lace and the jewellery.'

'Struggle?' said Joel. 'Why should you ever have to struggle?'

Sara stood up, keeping her blanket wrapped tightly around her. 'I have to struggle because I'm strong. At least, I could have been strong, if my background and my upbringing had allowed me to be. Can you imagine what it's like, to be born into a wealthy colonial family? Well, I don't suppose you can. It's the most privileged, marvellously idle life you can think of. I loved every minute of it, and I'd be lying if I said that I hadn't. I liked the riding, I liked the parties, I liked the gossip. And it was just as well that I did; because if I chafed against the life, like some women do, then I probably would have ended up mad.'

She was quiet for a little while, and then she said, more gently, 'I had freedom, of course, and money, and whatever dresses I wanted. But it was not considered proper for me to express a political opinion; or to show interest in anybody whose station was below mine; or to be too "enthusiastic". I was quite amazed that my parents consented to my marrying Barney; but then he did own diamond mines, and he had travelled halfway across Africa to find me; and he was Jewish. Mama found him rather romantic.'

Joel rubbed the back of his neck. 'Yes, I suppose you could say that," he mused, with obvious sarcasm, 'He *is* rather romantic. I don't know what else he is, but he *is* rather romantic.'

Sara drew a deep breath, and looked back towards the waggon. 'Anyway,' she said, 'my strength finally overcame my upbringing, and look how violent it turned out to be.'

Joel held up the gazelle-skin bag, dangling on the end of her gold chain. 'You won't forget the whole reason you did it, will you? You left it in Nareez's blankets.'

Sara came over and took the pouch, and hung it around her neck again. 'Thank you,' she said. 'I think you're the only one who really understands what I feel.'

Joel smiled at her, and kissed her cheek.

It was left to Hunt to drag Simon de Koker's stiffened body out of the waggon at first light, and bury him in a shallow depression by the stand of trees. He was still panting and perspiring as Sara and he stood by the grave and said a prayer for Simon de Koker's departed soul. Nareez was busy swilling blood from the planks of the waggon's floor; and Joel was sitting by the ashes of the campfire, trying to shave in icy cold water.

They had decided by default rather than by general consent to make straight for Durban, where Sara believed that her father could help them market the diamond, perhaps to one of his Indian or Persian business friends; and where Hunt could board a steamer for England and for anonymity. Sara was sure that Barney would eventually discover that she was back with her parents, but by that time the diamond would be long gone, and Gerald Sutter's lawyers would be quite capable of dealing with any infamous suggestions that Barney might level against Sara that she had taken the Natalia Star. She had left him because he had wrongfully deceived her about his social status in Kimberley, and because he had been intolerably cruel to her. He had been an ogre, and a Jewish ogre at that. Now he was showing his obsessive cruelty even more openly, by accusing her of stealing a valuable diamond!

This was their plan, anyway. At least, it was mostly Sara's and Hunt's plan. Joel had not yet completely decided what he was going to do; or if he had, he was not telling any of the others what it was. He remained smiling but uncommunicative as they heaved him up on to the freshly-scrubbed waggon, harnessed the horses, and prepared to head eastwards through the morning fog.

'I must say it's all gone rather well,' remarked Hunt, brightly. 'But I pity those poor Boer chaps at Wesselstroom. They're going to have a frightfully long wait if they're expecting *us* to turn up in a day or two!'

'I pity de Koker,' said Sara, baldly; and Hunt could not think of a reply to that. He grimaced like a disgruntled child, and stayed quiet for the next half an hour.

By mid-afternoon, they had reached Colenso, where they stopped to water and feed the horses, and to buy smoked bacon and bran from one of the small farmhouses there. There were a few British Army tents pitched five or six hundred yards away on the banks of one of the tributaries of the Tugela River, among the scrub and the trees, and a cooking-fire was sending up a lazy spiral of smoke into the fog. After he had brought out a thick side of bacon for them on his shoulder, the farmer told them about the massacre at Isandhlwana, only fifty miles or so to the north-east, and about the defence of Rorke's Drift. He was a red, grizzled little Afrikaner, who had decided in 1842 that the trek back across the mountains to the Transvaal was too much for him. He gave bacon and fresh eggs to the British soldiers, and in return they left his farm and his daughters grudgingly alone.

'So,' said Hunt, as they sat around the waggon by the roadside, and ate a scrappy lunch of biscuits and bacon, 'it seems as if Sir Bottled Beer finally went ahead and made a right royal mess of things!'

'They'll crush the Zulu in the end, though, won't they?' asked Sara.

'Of course,' said Hunt. 'The Zulu are terribly fierce, but they don't have any idea of what they're up against; or even why they're up against it. They only have one tactic, too: the "chest and horns", and even Lord Chelmsford should know how to cope with that. God knows what went wrong at this Isandhlwana place, but you can bet your boots that Sir Bottle will want his revenge. I wouldn't be sitting in the royal kraal at Ulundi now for all the tea in China. Not me!'

'Talking of tea,' said Sara, quietly, 'we seem to have run completely out.'

'Didn't that farmer have any?' asked Hunt.

Nareez said, 'I forgot to ask him. I'm sorry. I'll go back and see.'

Sara stood up, rather quickly. 'It's all right. I feel like a ride. I'll go down and ask those soldiers. They're bound to have some. The British Army survives on tea.'

She untethered one of the spare horses from the back of the waggon, threw a blanket over its back, and mounted it. 'I won't be a minute!' she called, and rode off down the rocky slope at the side of the road towards the Army encampment. Her horse slipped and hesitated, but eventually made its way down to level ground.

'Well,' said Joel, 'there she goes.'

Hunt frowned at him. 'What's that supposed to mean, precisely?'

'It means, there she goes. That's the last we'll see of her. Isn't that right, Nareez?'

Nareez looked cross. 'She went to fetch tea. That's all.'

'Oh, she went to fetch tea, did she? Well, you watch her. She's going to skirt right around those Army tents, and ride parallel to the road until she gets two or three miles further east; and then she's going to rejoin the road again and ride like all hell until she's so far ahead of us that we can't catch up, not with a waggon.'

'That's not right!' protested Nareez. 'She will not betray you!'

Joel shook his head. 'She's been thinking about it all day. I've been watching her face, and I could tell. First of all, with Simon de Koker dead, it seemed like a good idea to take the diamond to Durban and split it three ways. But then she probably began to think, why split it at all? I killed de Koker, I did all the dirty work, why should I share the diamond with anybody? Especially with a nancy-boy like Hunt, and a cripple like Joel. And they won't hurt Nareez, those two, so she can meet up with me later.'

'I am telling you, Mr Blitz, she went for tea!' said Nareez.

Joel lifted himself up a little, and then pointed down the valley of the Tugela. Sara had already passed the military encampment; and through the fog they could hear the soldiers whistling at her. Now she was following the course of the tributary north-eastwards, with her horse stepping carefully over the rocks, and she was almost invisible in the greyness, a disappearing ghost.

Joel grinned. 'There you are, Nareez, she's gone, just like you knew she would. All that ridiculous play-acting about tea! "I'm sorry, Mrs Sara, I'll go back and see if there's any tea." "Oh no, Nareez, I'll just get on my horse and trot down to get some from the soldiers. The British Army thrives on tea!" Tea! You women make me choke.'

Nareez said, 'It is rightfully hers, the diamond. It is a small thing, to compensate her for the suffering she has been through.'

'What suffering?' Joel demanded. 'A few boring months at Kimberley? And Barney never mistreated her, did he? Whatever you say about Barney, he always behaved like a gentleman, and a husband, whenever Sara would let him. He didn't love her. That was plain enough. But he didn't make her suffer.'

'I like to hear brothers standing up for each other,' said

Hunt, prissily. Joel ignored him, and twisted himself over sideways, so that he could dig his hand deep into his overcoat pocket. Grunting, he tugged at the lining, until at last he was able to withdraw his fist and sit up straight again.

'She may think she deserves all kinds of things, your charge and mistress,' said Joel. 'But what she thinks she deserves and what she's actually got are two different things. Look.'

He opened his hand, and there on his palm was the Natalia Star, shining dully in the dull afternoon light.

Hunt, in delight, applauded. 'Joel, you're a positive genius! I thought the diamond was around her neck!'

'What she has around her neck is a stone I picked up near Mont aux Sources, when we were crossing the Drakensberg. Every time the waggon was held up, I sorted through the pebbles beside the road until I found one that was almost the same size and shape as the diamond. Yesterday night, when she shot de Koker, she left the pouch in Nareez's blankets; thinking that I was asleep. I took out the diamond, and substituted the stone. A rock for a rock.'

Nareez clenched her fists. 'You are a teef! You are a terrible teef!'

Joel laughed in her face. 'I'm not as much of a thief as Sara; or as any of you. This diamond is legally half mine, in any case. I shall share some of the proceeds with you both, for helping me get to Durban; but I warn you that if you try to betray me to the authorities, you won't get very far. I shall simply say that you kidnapped me, and tried to steal the diamond which rightfully belongs to me and my brother. At the very worst, I shall be forced to share the diamond fifty-fifty with Barney. At the very best, you will both be hung for abduction and theft.'

'I suppose there's a Yiddish word for this kind of ruse,' said Hunt, cuttingly.

Joel held up the diamond, and a single piercing star of refracted light caught Hunt's eye. 'We call it a *chachma*,' said Joel. 'A wily trick.'

Nareez, who was looking the other way, spat noisily on to the ground.

*

505

Even in bright sunlight, the valleys formed by the tributaries of the Tugela River can be hopelessly misleading. In unrelenting fog, they are an endless nightmare of twists and turns and blind alleys, a Chinese puzzle in different shades of grey.

Sara knew that the tributary of the Tugela which flowed north-eastwards from Colenso joined the main river about fifteen miles downstream from Ladysmith; and that if she followed the main river about thirty miles further, she would cross the Newcastle-to-Durban road at Tugela Ferry. All she would have to do then would be to ride hard through Ugg and Greytown, following the road for two or three days until she reached Durban.

She had chosen to ride by a completely different road in case her horse went lame, and Joel was able to catch up with her; or in case they sent Hunt riding on ahead.

What had seemed like a simple escape in principle, though, became more and more confusing and frightening as the day went on. For some reason, around the tiny settlement o Stendal, she began to believe that she had lost her way; and after she had taken a short cut across the brow of a foggy kopje between one tributary and another, she mistook the Tugela River itself for the tributary that ran into the Tugela from Empangueni. She forded the Tugela on her horse, and continued to ride north-eastwards, wet and shivering, when she should have been riding south-eastwards.

Later in the afternoon, the fog began to clear, and the sun came out, wan and yellow at first, but then brightly enough to finish the day with long shadows and a pottery-blue sky, and birdsong. Sara felt better, and stopped to rest her horse and drink from a small stream. She had no food or bottled water with her: she had been counting on finding the Greytown road before dark, and stopping for supper at a farmhouse or an Army encampment.

Now, with the landscape thick with shadows, she made her most foolish mistake. She decided to keep on riding until it was too dark to go on. Refolding the horse's blanket, she mounted up again, and keeping the fading light of the sun on her left, and slightly behind her, she continued north-east. The heavy pouch around her neck walloped regularly against her breastbone as she rode.

There was still a chance for her to find her way: but she crossed a tributary that joined the Tugela from the north-west, believing it to be the Tugela, and carried on riding north-east by the light of the thumbnail moon, trying desperately to find the tributary that she had just forded. Exhausted, hungry, and panicky, she crossed the Newcastle-to-Durban road in the darkness, without realising it.

She was last seen alive on the following morning, a considerable distance away, through the binoculars of a scouting party of the 17th Lancers. They could do nothing else but return to their encampment with a dismayed report that a European woman had been seen riding at the gallop through the bushy ravines close to the Buffalo River, a few miles south-east of Rorke's Drift. She had appeared to have no weapons, no provisions, and no guide; and either she had not heard the three rifle shots that the scouts had fired into the air to attract her attention, or else she had ignored them.

Five days later, scouts of the Natal Native Contingent found the body of a brown-haired white woman by the side of the waggon road which led south-eastwards from Isandhlwana to the Inkanhlda Bush. She had been disembowelled by assegais, the short stabbing spears of the Zulu warriors, and badly mutilated. Around her neck was an empty leather pouch; and in her right hand, clenched so tightly that the scouts had been unable to remove it before they buried her, had been a large jagged pebble. A label in her riding-dress had identified her as Sara Sutter, of Durban.

Joel, Hunt and Nareez arrived in Durban on a humid, irritating day when it seemed as if the only thing worth doing was having a bath and then getting gradually drunk on gin-and-bitters on a cool verandah somewhere. At first, Joel was reluctant to let Nareez go; but when Hunt pointed out that all the *amah* wanted to do was scurry off back to Khotso and rejoin her mistress, who had probably arrived there by now, tearful and tired and not one penny the richer, Joel at last agreed to pay for a hackney carriage to take her out there, and good riddance.

Joel's sense of irony did not leave him, even though he had escaped with the diamond as far as Durban. Remembering his first visit here, with a crushed pelvis and broken legs, he booked rooms for himself and Hunt at the Natalia Hotel, signing his name 'Blitz' on the register with an aggressive flourish. If Barney ever followed him here, the evidence that he had come and gone would be bombastically obvious. He swung his way upstairs on his crutches, and was able at last to lie back on a soft bed, with his shoes off, and close his eyes; while the jumbled sounds of street-peddlers and trotting horses and carriage-wheels wafted in through the slats of his half-open jalousie like noises from a half-forgotten dream.

Joel slept, and then woke. There was a salty taste in his mouth, and he had dribbled a little on to the pillow. He heaved himself up into a sitting position, and then dragged the cheap linen coaster off the bedside table, so that he could wipe his mouth with it, and mop his forehead. He sat still for a while, thinking about Barney, and Sara, and the diamond, and then he seized his crutches from beside the bed, and hopped his way over to the bathroom, so that he could draw himself a deep tubful of hot water.

The bath was running, and steam was drifting idly out of the open window, when there was a sharp knock at the door. Joel said warily, 'Yes?'

'Mr Blitz?' asked an unfamiliar voice.

'Who is that?' Joel demanded.

'It's the manager, Mr Blitz. Charles Pope. Would you mind if I had a word with you, just for a moment?'

'Come on in,' said Joel.

The manager unlocked the door with his pass-key, and stepped into the room with the stiff, mannered movements of an old soldier. He was a short round-headed man, with a clipped moustache, and cheeks that were bright with broken veins, both from sun and brandy. He stood to attention in his black suit and his boiled shirt and his startlingly-elevated white tie, and faced Joel with flustered boldness.

'I saw your name in the register, Mr Blitz, and I was alarmed.'

Joel was sitting on the side of the bed, leaning on his crutches. 'Alarmed?' he asked, with a grin of surprise. 'Why?'

'Well, sir, it's an inheritance, sir; some years old; but an inheritance that I can't really afford to ignore. Not for my own sake, sir; nor for the sake of my family.'

'Why don't you get to the point?' asked Joel.

'Well, sir, the point is that before I took over the management of this hotel, sir – that was when I retired from the Army, sir, Royal Engineers –'

'Yes, yes,' said Joel, impatiently.

'Well, sir, the point is that someone called Mr Blitz stayed here before, some years ago.'

'That's right. It was me, and my brother Barney. What of it?'

Charles Pope clenched his bright yellow false teeth together and managed to look even more embarrassed than he had before. 'It was the way you settled the bill, sir, apparently.'

'You mean we didn't settle it? You're asking for money?'

'Oh, no, sir. The bill was settled quite satisfactory. Well, as far as I know, anyway. The difficulty was that it was paid in five-pound notes of awkward origin, sir.'

'Forged?'

'No, sir, not forged. But one was later passed in change to a particular gentleman from the Durban commercial community, sir, when he came to dine here one evening, or at least that's what I'm told. And this particular gentleman from the commercial community was able to identify the serial numbers on the note, for the reason that he was making concerted efforts to trace a certain quantity of notes that had gone missing, so to speak, from a merchant bank in Portugal.'

Joel nodded towards the bathroom. 'Would you mind turning those taps off? I'd hate to flood your lovely hotel.'

Charles Pope went next door, and turned off the water. When he returned, he said, 'You do follow my drift, don't you?'

'I'm not sure that I do. You're trying to tell me that the money we used to pay our hotel bill, nearly eight years ago, was stolen?'

'That's the drift of it, yes.'

Joel shook his head dismissively. 'You're going to have a difficult time proving it, my friend. And anyway, the bank has probably written the money off by now.'

Charles Pope clapped his hands together, louder than he had

obviously meant to. 'That's the problem, sir! The *bank* probably has. But the gentlemen who were looking for the money most certainly have not. They are gentlemen of unusual persistence.'

'I think you'd better tell me about this straight,' said Joel.

'Well...' said Charles Pope, 'I can only give it to you second-hand, because when you first stayed here, I was still manager of the old Muharrik Hotel in Cairo. But the manager who was here at the time, he told me that a bank in La Coruna, in Portugal, had been swindled some years ago of hundreds of thousands of pounds. It had been done by a whole gang of people, this swindle. Accountants, lawyers, bank officials, registrars. It cost the bank every last penny it had, and it almost brought down the Portuguese government.'

'So what does any of this have to do with me?' asked Joel.

Charles Pope pulled a series of rubbery faces, as if he could not quite decide which expression suited this explanation the best. But then he said, 'It has practically everything to do with you, sir; because the five-pound notes with which you paid your hotel bill were part of the haul of notes which were taken from the bank during this swindle. And the only way in which you could possibly have acquired them was from the one man in the whole gang of swindlers who double-crossed his associates and disappeared with everything, at the crucial moment. Six of the gang were caught and sent to gaol for life. Two more were shot while trying to escape from police custody. There were eight more, who are now living under false names in different parts of the world. Five of them run an export business in Lourenço Marques, in the Portuguese Territory; and one of them acts as an agent for his colleagues here in Durban. It was he who came to the hotel for dinner just after you and your brother had stayed here, and identified one of the stolen notes.'

'Well, this is all very interesting,' said Joel. 'But you have no form proof whatsoever of what you are saying, and for all I know you are lying through those artificial teeth of yours just to frighten me. I don't know anything at all about any stolen money, or any Portuguese swindlers, or anything at all. I'm an ignoramus, and you can't hold a man responsible for that.'

510

'Mr Blitz,' said Charles Pope, patiently, 'you and your brother paid over hundreds of pounds to this hotel, all in the same five-pound notes. Mr Salgadas will be most interested to know that you are here.'

Joel thought about this for a moment, blowing his cheeks in and out reflectively. 'I suppose you're going to tell him that I'm here? Is that it?'

'It would be my duty, sir. For the sake of my family. If Mr Salgadas were to find out that you had visited, sir, and that I had omitted to inform him ...'

'I see,' said Joel. 'It's extortion, is it? How much do you want?'

Charles Pope made a self-deprecatory face. 'Five hundred pounds, sir, should do it easily. Five hundred pounds for two weeks of silence, that's a fair rate.'

'How much does that work out per minute?' Joel demanded.

Charles Pope pressed one finger against his forehead and closed his eyes. 'Almost sixpence, sir,' he said, after a while, and then exposed all of his grotesquely artificial teeth in a wide grin. 'I used to be an accountant, sir, before I went into the hotel trade.'

Joel gathered up his crutches, and swung himself across to the window. 'Open these shutters for me, will you?' he told Pope, and Pope came across and unlatched them for him, so that he could look out over the tiled and corrugated-iron rooftops.

'I'll tell you what,' said Joel, 'I'll make a deal with you. But the problem is that you're going to have to take me on trust.'

Charles Pope took out a handkerchief, and solemnly stared at Joel while he explored the inside of his nose.

'The man who double-crossed the Portuguese swindle gang was called Monsaraz,' said Joel. 'I knew him very well. In fact, I used to run a farm with him out at Oranjerivier, in the north colony. The problem was, he was dying of lung disease. Consumption, probably, that he'd picked up in Portugal. You know what a filthy lot they are there.'

Charles Pope scrutinised his handkerchief. Then he said, 'Go on. I'm listening.'

Joel smiled. 'Before Monsaraz died, he entrusted all of his swindled money to me, and to my brother Barney. He told us to send most of it out of the country, back to Portugal, for his relatives. We disguised it as parcels of dried fruit. In return, he gave us fifty thousand pounds each. You might be interested to know that I invested most of mine in the Sutter Shipping Company, and that I have today almost seventy thousand pounds, just lying in the bank, waiting to be spent.'

Charles Pope said huskily, 'What are you proposing? You're not proposing that I should get myself involved in this, too?'

'I'm not proposing anything of the kind. I'm simply trying to put it to you that if Mr Salgadas were to get hold of the wrong end of the stick – if Mr Salgadas were to take his revenge on somebody in the sincere belief that he was finally getting even for the Monsaraz double-cross, even though that somebody may not be exactly the *right* somebody, then all of my problems would be over; and yours would be over, too, because I would pay you twenty thousand pounds in untraceable banknotes to help me.'

Outside, in the streets of Durban, a water-seller was calling out his high-pitched song in a voice that reminded Joel strangely of the way in which Simon de Koker had encouraged his horses. 'Yip! Yip! Yip!' Beside him, Charles Pope slowly stuffed his handkerchief back into the pocket of his tight hotel-manager's trousers and frowned at the far corner of the room, as if he expected a prompt-card to appear there, and tell him what to do.

After a long ruminative silence, he said, 'What do you mean when you say "that somebody may not exactly be the *right* somebody?"'

The following morning, at eight, Hunt was taking breakfast in the dining-room of the Natalia Hotel – toast and Oxford marmalade, with the morning newspaper propped up against the silver marmalade pot – when two men in off-white tropical suits and dark moustaches hurried through the swing doors, hustled a waitress to one side, and produced revolvers.

Hunt did not even see them. He was too engrossed in a

gossipy paragraph in the paper about Lieutenant Kenneth Ogilvy of the 2/24th, and how he had delayed his engagement to Miss Patricia Penrose, of Marianhill. He was still munching toast when the two men rushed up to his table, went down on to one knee, and aimed their revolvers at his face. Unlike Lieutenant Ogilvy they looked as if they were about to propose.

There were five shots, four more than necessary, and a lot of blue smoke, and broken glass, and blood. Then the men hurried out again. One of them even raised his hat in apology to the waitress he had jostled on the way in. Nobody screamed, or cried out, or even moved. Hunt bent over his newspaper, as if he were examining it from only a quarter of an inch away, and then he flopped back his head and rolled on to the floor.

At the same time, on board the London cargo ship *Wallasey*, which was two miles out from Port Natal off Umlazi, and still visible from the front lawn of Khotso, Joel was drinking whiskey from a flask, and leaning against the windy rail like a seasoned one-legged mariner.

The first mate passed him by, and said, 'Fine morning, sir. Make sure you don't fall in.'

Joel gave him a vague smile, and screwed the top back on his flask again. He had other things on his mind, apart from the sharpness of the morning and the smoothness of the sea. He was thinking of Hunt; and of Sara; and of Charles Pope. It was the thought of Charles Pope that he savoured in particular – and how Pope must have knocked on the door of his room with a tray of tea and a morning paper, only to find that his bed was unslept in, and that even his single bedroom slipper had gone.

The extortionist gets what the extortionist deserves, he thought; and that's nothing.

Barney did not get to hear of Sara's death until 5 July, the day after Lord Chelmsford had advanced on the Zulu capital of Ulundi with an impenetrable square of British troops, mowing down 1000 natives with rifles and Garling guns, and finally setting a torch to the royal kraal.

The letter from Gerald Sutter had been sent mistakenly to

Oranjerivier, and from the brown circles on the envelope it looked as if someone had left it on their mantelshelf for a week or two, and rested their tea-cups on it. It had been re-addressed twice, once to Colesberg and then to Kimberley.

Barney opened it in the drawing-room where he was having coffee with Harold. They had been working since seven o'clock on a deal to buy out three important claims from the Standard Diamond Mining Company, and he was still wearing his blue silk bathrobe. There were papers all over the floor, and even papers propped up against the coffee-pot. Harold had just taken out his tobacco-pouch to light his first pipe of the day.

'It's from Durban,' said Barney, turning the envelope over. On the back flap, embossed into the vellum paper, was the crest of the Sutter family, a ship flanked by pelicans. He tore the envelope open with his thumb, and opened the letter. He was silent for two whole minutes while he read it.

'Is that news about Sara?' asked Harold, thumbing tobacco into his pipe.

Barney folded the letter up, and laid it carefully on the birdcage coffee-tray, on top of all the other papers. It had been a sorrowful letter, perplexed, and gentle. Nareez had arrived at Khotso to say that she and Sara had been on their way to visit the Sutters in the company of a Boer guide and a friend of Barney's. There had been trouble on the way, and the guide had accidentally been killed. Sara had ridden off on her own to get help, and had never been seen alive again.

Three days after Nareez had reached Knotso, the Sutters had advised the British Army garrison that Sara was missing in the area between Colenso and Tugela Ferry. The Army had made enquiries, and ten days later had turned up the report from the Natal Native Contingent that they had buried the mutilated body of a white woman not far south of Isandhlwana.

'I cannot think that she did not die without dignity, or grace, or without opening her heart to the God who understands the Essential Rightness of being English,' wrote her father.

'Are you all right?' Harold asked Barney.

Barney nodded. 'That was from Sara's father,' he said, with a catch in his voice. He cleared his throat. 'She's dead. Or, at least, they found a body who answered to her description.'

514

'What happened? Oh, Barney, I'm so sorry.'

'Here,' said Barney, and handed Harold the letter to read. Harold put on his bifocals, and scanned it carefully, his lips moving as he read, his hand trembling slightly. 'This is a shock,' he said, at last, putting the letter down. 'I don't know what to say to you.'

'You don't have to say anything,' Barney told him. 'I think I began to get over my love for Sara the day after we came back here to Kimberley. I don't think either of us ever found out what it was that we actually wanted from each other. We were better off apart. I'm just sorry that we had to part the way we did, and I'm sorry that she's dead.'

Harold folded up his spectacles and sat back. 'It seems as if they were making for the east coast after all,' he said. 'And from what Mr Sutter says in his letter, it seems as if your friend what-was-his-name, the Boer, was also unfortunate enough not to survive the journey.'

Barney was pouring them each a small brandy from the drinks table by the window. 'You make that sound as if his death wasn't accidental.'

'My dear friend,' wheezed Harold, 'when you have lived in proximity to diamonds for as long as I have, you get to know that they are very dangerous stones to be near; and the nearer you are to them, the more dangerous it is. A stone like the Natalia Star has around it a circle of influence, if you like, and as soon as you step into this circle you are at risk. You remember you told me that you felt the Natalia Star was evidence of God's existence? Well, not everybody feels the same way about diamonds as you do. Not many people are so spiritual about them. But everybody invests them with equally extraordinary importance. And for something that is as important as the physical evidence of the power of God, people will kill.'

Barney handed Harold his brandy, and murmured, '*Mazel tov*,' under his breath. Harold sipped a little, and then put his glass down, and said, 'The question is, if two of the people who stole the Natalia Star are now dead, what has happened to the others? We know about Nareez, of course, but where are Joel and Hunt?'

'Most important of all,' said Barney, 'where is the diamond?'

'Well – there are several possibilities,' Harold told him. 'If Sara was murdered by Zulus, then the diamond could have been taken by the natives and given to Cetewayo.'

'That sounds a bit far-fetched,' Barney remarked.

'Maybe it does, but the history of large diamonds is always far-fetched. I'm more inclined to think that Joel and Hunt still have the stone, but if Sara *was* carrying it, and if it *has* gone to Cetewayo, then we may not be so unlucky after all. I heard from the post office this morning that the Zulu Empire may not last very much longer. The British forces surround Ulundi on three sides, and so the diamond might soon be recovered. We ought to write to Lord Chelmsford's chiefs of staff, and put in a claim, in case the British Army find it in Ulundi.'

'Well,' said Barney, 'if you really think it's worthwhile.'

'Of course it's worthwhile. We're talking a million pounds. Even more, if we can say that the diamond once belonged to Cetewayo. We shouldn't ignore any possibility, no matter how unlikely it seems.'

Barney was quiet for a moment. Then he looked at Harold, and said, 'I'm sorry. I wasn't really listening.'

'It doesn't matter,' Harold told him. 'You've had a bad shock, unpleasant news. Perhaps it's better if I go.'

'I'd rather you stayed,' said Barney. 'I want to settle this Standard Diamond Company purchase.'

'Let's leave it for today,' said Harold. 'The Big Hole will still be there tomorrow morning.'

'No, we'll settle it now. I might have lost my wife, and my brother may be missing, but I've still got my business. How much do you think they'll take for 170 and 160?'

'Barney . . .' protested Harold, spreading his hands wide.

'Don't mother me, Harold,' snapped Barney. 'I've been through just about enough.'

'All right, you want to finish the Standard Diamond Company business, then we'll finish the Standard Diamond Company business. And no mothering. I suggest you try to pay them £27,500 each, for 170 and 169, and £20,000 for 168.'

'That's less than we paid Stewart.'

'That's right. I'm trying to save you money.'

Barney walked across to the fireplace with his hands in his dressing-gown pockets. 'You know something, Harold?' he said. 'I thought I had everything, with Sara, and the diamond, and this house. I thought that I'd almost made it. Now, it's all gone, except the house, and what's the use of a house with nobody in it but yourself? And you know something, for all of the struggle, for all of the arguments, none of it really meant anything.'

Harold took his pocket-watch out of his vest pocket and went through an exaggerated performance of winding it and holding it up to his ear.

Barney said, 'You'd rather listen to your watch ticking, than me complaining about my unfortunate fate?'

'I'd rather not tell you what I think, that's all.'

'So tell me.'

Harold turned around in his chair. 'You really want to know?'

Barney looked back at him, just as sharply, and then looked away. 'Not really. I know it already. I should have tried harder with Natalia. I should have been less forgiving to Joel. I should have realised that only God blesses unions, not English society.'

Harold nodded, his double-chins going in and out like an accordion.

'But damn it, Harold,' said Barney, 'it's bad enough being Jewish. It's bad enough being an outsider because of your race and your religion, without marooning yourself twenty miles out from the rest of the human race because you've married a *schwarzeh*!'

'You still think about her, don't you?' asked Harold. 'After all these years, you still think about her.'

Barney turned his back to Harold and rested his head against the mantelshelf. 'She's got my only son,' he said.

'But more than that,' put in Harold, gently.

'Yes,' said Barney. 'More than that, I still love her.'

He lifted his head and looked at himself in the looking-glass above the fireplace. His short and unhappy marriage to Sara had aged him. There were three or four grey hairs around his ears, and his eyes had a dullness about them which only somebody else who had been through the same kind of loveless struggle would recognise. He thought of Sara and he felt like crying for her, although he found it impossible to squeeze out any tears. He hoped, desperately, that she had not suffered too horribly. And he hoped too, that wherever she was, she would be able to forgive him for being the wrong man at the wrong time, trespassing in a society for which only his diamond mines had given him any right of entry at all: not his class, or his race, or even his ambitions.

Harold held out his glass. 'Give me some more brandy,' he demanded. 'And have another one yourself. You should drink. It's sad, but you're a free man again. Did you think of that?'

A week later, Cecil Rhodes came around to the house and brought Barney a bottle of single malt whiskey and a letter of condolence edged with black. He had put on weight, and his fair wavy hair had receded a little, but he was sunburned and healthy, and he was wearing a putty-coloured suit that was well-tailored to fit his rather broad-bottomed proportions. Barney was still in the habit of assessing people's wealth and personality by the clothes they wore, and from Rhodes's suit he gathered that he was doing very well these days, and that he was gaining confidence and skill.

'I was *frightfully* upset to hear about Sara,' said Rhodes, pacing around the library, and tugging out books now and again to inspect their bindings, and peer at their titles. 'I say – you've got Appelbo's *Complete Gemology* here – no wonder you're so knowledgeable about gemstones. Oh – the pages aren't cut.'

'I'm, uh, having a memorial service soon,' said Barney, taking the book from him, and pushing it back into its place. 'I hope you'll be able to find the time to come.'

'Of course, my dear chap,' said Rhodes. 'Business isn't quite so hectic just at the moment. Did you know that we now own more than fifty per cent of the De Beers mine? Next year, I believe that we're going to set up our own company, the De Beers Diamond Mining Company Limited; at least that's what Alfred Beit has in mind. In a year or two, the whole of the mine should be run as a monopoly, with all of the advantages that a monopoly can afford us.'

518

Barney went back to his desk. 'I suppose then you'll start turning your avaricious eyes towards the Big Hole'.

'Well,' said Rhodes, 'you have to admit that it's in a bit of a jolly old shambles.'

'We're sorting it out,' Barney told him. 'When I first came here, there were 1600 separate claims. Now the whole mine is owned by twelve companies; with just one or two stubborn individuals clinging on around the reefs.'

'Twelve are still far too many,' Rhodes replied, shaking his head like a bullock trying to shake away a fly. 'You're down to six hundred feet deep in places; with flooding, and collapses, and mudslides. You need to excavate the entire mine as one, under the auspices of one company.'

'I agree with you,' said Barney. 'Well, I agree with you that the mine should be owned by one company. I think our opinions only differ about whose company that should be.'

Rhodes picked up his hat. 'Britain, one day, shall control the whole of Africa and her wealth. That was my avowed intention when I came here and it remains my avowed intention. However, let's not talk diamonds any more. I have to go, and I want to tell you how cut up I was about your late wife.'

'Thank you,' said Barney. 'I appreciate your coming.'

Just as Rhodes was about to leave, Horace knocked at the library door, and popped his head into the room. 'Excuse me, Mr Two-Leg, sir.'

'Mr *Two*-Leg?' frowned Rhodes.

Barney gave him a fleeting smile. 'My brother has one leg. Or *had*.'

'You mean he's lost the other one as well?'

'No. He's gone missing, that's all. We're not at all sure of his whereabouts.'

'My dear chap, I had no idea. What a dreadfully trying time you must be having.'

Barney looked down at the papers on his desk, and said, 'Yes,' with as much patience as he could manage. Rhodes could see that he was outstaying his welcome, so he called, 'Cheery-bye. I'll see my own way out. Drop me a line when you've arranged the memorial service.'

Barney gave him an absent-minded wave, and he left. Horace piped up, 'It's a lady for you, sir. Mrs Agnes Joy.'

'Agnes? Is she alone?'

'Yes, sir. Excepting her coachman, of course. He's in the kitchen having a smoke, sir.'

'Oh, he's having a smoke, is he? He must have been pretty sure that his mistress was going to be staying.'

'I don't know, Mr Two-Leg,' said Horace. 'I wouldn't presume.'

'All right, Horace,' Barney told him. 'Show Mrs Joy through to the drawing-room.'

Agnes was sitting on one of the small gilded French chairs when he came into the room, her chin proudly uptilted, her blonde curls tucked up under a severe but fashionable little hat. Because the weather was turning colder now, she wore a blue riding-coat, and buttoned-up boots, and in her hand she held a pair of pale blue gloves. She turned her head towards him as he came in, and smiled the kind of smile that makes an innocent man wonder what he's done to deserve it, and a guilty man feel worried about what he might do next.

'Agnes!' said Barney, coming across the room and taking her hand. 'This is the most happy surprise I've had for weeks.'

'I'm sorry I took so long in coming,' she said, her voice a little throatier than he remembered it. 'But I didn't hear about your wife until last week, and today was the first day that I was able to get away. Robert's gone to Hopetown for a day or two, to talk to somebody about a job.'

'Would you care for a sherry?' asked Barney.

'I'd adore one,' she said. 'A very *sweet* one, if you have any in stock. I don't eat candies, but I do adore very sweet sherry.'

Barney sat down opposite her. 'How have you been?' he asked her. 'I've seen you around Kimberley from time to time. How's Faith? And your family? You haven't decided to have any children yet.'

Agnes pouted. 'Robert wants children, of course. All Australians do. There are so *few* Australians, compared with the size of Australia, that they believe they have an historical duty to increase their numbers as rapidly as possible. But the truth is that I had an infection when I was a little girl, a sort of scarlet-fever, I think; and that the doctor said then that it would be very unlikely that I would ever be able to bear children.'

'And Robert doesn't know?'

'Why should I disillusion him, poor dear? He's very handsome, you know, but he's not particularly passionate; and if you ask me the only thing that ever arouses him is the thought of making me pregnant. So for my own sake it wouldn't be very wise to tell him that he never will.'

Horace came in, and Barney asked him to bring him another brandy, and a glass of oloroso for Agnes. 'How's Faith?' he asked, trying to change the subject from the sexual shortcomings of Robert Joy to something a little more general.

'Oh, she's well, although she's more old-maidish by the minute. She thinks I should have left Robert *years* ago. In fact, she thinks I was an absolute idiot for marrying him. She's quite right, of course. Robert has no money at all, and he's such a fool. Father's grown tired of telling me that I would have been better off marrying you, for all that you're Jewish. He calls you the "Chosen Chump" for some reason that I can't really work out. "You should have told me to mind my own business and married the Chosen Chump," he keeps telling me. "At least he owns half of Kimberley. That Robert of yours doesn't own half a share in a lavatory seat." Actually, do you know, I think Father's going rather, you know, what do you call it, addled.'

'I see,' said Barney. .Well, maybe your father's right. Maybe we should have married. But he didn't exactly make it easy for us, did he? Or even possible.'

'You can't tell him that, not now. He has a most selective memory. He still doesn't like Jews, of course. But in view of his own rather wobbly financial situation, and in view of who's holding most of the purse-strings in the diamond business, he's prepared to make exceptions. Do you know that he even acts for Yosel & Farber?'

'Well, *they're* pretty Jewish,' smiled Barney.

Agnes smiled back at him. Age and experience, if anything, had emphasised the fine Nordic shape of her face, and taken a touch of colour out of her eyes, so that they looked paler, and more translucent, like opals. She was prettier than Barney remembered her, probably because he had tried to persuade himself when Mr Knight had broken up their flowering relationship that she was not really so attractive after all; that she was just another watery English girl with nothing to recommend her but an accent that could splinter your best glassware.

'I was surprised by your letter, though,' said Agnes. 'I don't know whether you were just feeling upset with your wife at the time, or whether you'd seen me in Kimberley with Robert or somebody else and you thought about the life we might have had together . . .'

Barney was staring at her with such a baffled expression that she trailed off. 'The *letter*,' she repeated. 'The one you sent me two or three months ago. That was the whole reason I said I was such a long time in coming. I wasn't sure if you meant it.'

'You weren't sure if I . . .'

Agnes opened her small blue-eyed crocodile purse, rummaged around amongst the rouge and the rice-powder, and at last produced a crumpled letter written on Vogel Vlei note paper.

'Read it to me,' said Barney.

'You don't remember what you said?'

'Just read it to me!'

Agnes fussily closed her purse, straightened out the letter, and then read it out loud to Barney in a clipped, precise voice that was not at all suited to the flowery passion of the text. 'My dearest darling Agnes, I am writing to tell you that my desire for you has still not waned, and that if you can ever find a way to come to see me again, to bring your lips closer to mine so that I may once more press their rosebud beauty with my own lips (she hesitated and stumbled over this part) then I shall be more than fulfilled! Let us forget the differences of our past . . . let us cast aside any thought that both of us have entered into vows with people whose company we sought because of loneliness, and because of confusion. Come to Vogel Vlei on the evening of 26 January, if you can. My wife will be away, and I am sure that you can find a believable excuse to make to your husband. Yours as always, Barney.'

Barney held out his hand for the letter and Agnes gave it to him, her forehead peaked into a tiny frown. Barney only had to glance at it to recognise the handwriting as Joel's; and it only took him a few ticks of the ormolu clock on the mantelshelf to realise why Joel had written it.

All through his convalescence, Joel had been trying to play Sara off against Barney, to stir her discontentment into out-and-out dislike. When he had been crippled and bedbound alienating Sara had been the only means at Joel's disposal of getting his revenge for the loss of the Natalia Star; and his only possible hope of winning the diamond back again. He had still legally owned fifty per cent of the diamond: perhaps he had thought that if he could persuade Sara to divorce Barney on the grounds of cruelty or unfaithfulness, he might also be able to convince Barney that to give Sara the other fifty per cent of the diamond in full settlement would be cheaper than having to assign her a large proportion of the earnings from his diamond mines. Then, Joel would have been left with nothing more difficult than the problem of cajoling her share of the stone out of Sara, and that probably would not have taken him too long. Perhaps he would have told her that the market price of large gemstones had drastically dropped, and offered her a title in one of Blitz Brothers' claims instead. Claim No. 176, perhaps, which was the smallest and the poorest of all of them.

This letter to Agnes must have been part of his ploy. Joel had obviously hoped that Agnes would turn up on the doorstep of Vogel Vlei, dressed in her most provocative gown, on the night of Sara's birthday celebrations, 26 January. One more nail in the coffin of a stillborn marriage.

'I didn't write this,' said Barney, tearing the letter in half.

'I don't understand you,' said Agnes.

'I said, I didn't write it. I didn't invite you here, not on 26 January nor any other day.'

'But that's why I came!'

Barney reached out and took her hands. 'I know. And I'm glad that you had the poise and the consideration not to come before you heard that Sara was dead. You're much more of a lady than any of those gossipy stuck-up *yentas* at the Kimberley Club, with their social mornings and their ladies' nights.'

Agnes asked quietly, 'If you didn't write it, who did?'

523

'Joel, my brother. It was a kind of a nasty joke.'

Agnes stared down at their hands for a long time. Each of them was wearing a wedding-band. 'I suppose you want me to go, then?' she said.

'Agnes –'

'I can't very well stay, can I, when I've thrust myself on a man who hasn't even invited me? I don't even go out with diggers unless they ask me first. I'm not a fallen woman. Not quite, anyway. I still read the *Morning Post*, and pour my milk into my tea last.'

Barney lowered his head. 'Agnes, I'd like you to stay.'

'You're just saying that to preserve my dignity.'

'I think I've been through too much to start worrying about dignity, either yours or mine.'

'Dear Barney,' she said, lightly kissing his eyebrows, and the bridge of his nose. 'I was so fond of you. I wish Daddy hadn't made such a fuss about your being Jewish.'

Barney kissed her back, at the side of the mouth, and then softly on the lips. 'I suppose everybody has to cling on to something. I cling on to my ambitions, and your father clings on to the Kimberley Club, and the important of being English.'

Agnes looked him straight in the eye. 'I ought to go,' she whispered.

Doesn't your husband know how discontented you are?' asked Barney. 'Doesn't he know that you walk out with other men?'

'I tell him lies. I don't know if he believes them or not.'

'I don't know how you can stand it.'

Agnes smiled sadly. 'I can stand it because I can't think what else to do.'

Barney held the pieces of letter up, and then let them fall again. 'I almost wish that I *had* written this letter myself.'

Little by little, Agnes released her hands from Barney's; and then stood up. She touched the top of his hair, and bent forward to kiss him again on the forehead. 'I can't take any more heartbreaks, Barney. I made up my mind at Christmas that I would try to stay faithful to Robert; not because I'm so very concerned about hurting him, but because I can't bear any more of these casual attachments myself. In the past six years,

I think I must have fallen in love a dozen times. But each time my love has come to nothing, and each time I've ended up with nobody. I was infatuated with you when I first met you. I suppose you've been a little dream of mine ever since. But I can't stay with you. I couldn't bear the pain of being hurt again, and especially by you.'

Barney looked up at her. Her face was so concerned and so pretty; and in the shafts of sunlight that fell across the drawing-room she looked like an angelic showgirl, a poised and erotic equestrienne, the soiled but beautiful star from a travelling carnival. Perhaps she could never give all of herself to anyone, not even to him; and perhaps that was why she would always be frustrated and unhappy. But the love of a girl who asked no questions about the past or the future, a girl whose sexual appetite was demanding and immediate, and who played no tortuous games of etiquette and manners, – the love of a girl like that might be just what Barney needed. It might also be short-lived. He could not tell. But as Agnes stood before him in her riding-coat that afternoon, he knew that he was going to ask her to stay with him; for the simple reason that he had nobody else.

'Stay,' he told her.

She did not answer him for almost a minute, watching him with her pale and reflective eyes. 'If I stay, I'm going to have to ask you for a commitment. I warn you now.'

Barney held out his hand for her. 'Stay,' he repeated.

They made love that night with a ferocity that, at times, frightened them both. Quite naked, they clawed and plunged and thrashed, kissing until their lips were swollen and raw; tearing and tugging at each other as if their passions could only be satisfied by vandalising the flesh that inflamed them. Barney remembered for years later an instant when Agnes was underneath him, her head thrown back on the pillow, and how his fingers were clutching her breast so savagely that she screamed at him to stop, but not to stop, and how she held her own hand over his to prevent him from releasing his grip.

The next morning, he opened one eye and looked across the twisted sheets. The carriage-clock beside the bed said six-thirty. The sky was light, but the sun was not yet up, and the bushveld was oddly silent. Agnes had already gone. She had left a note downstairs in the library in writing that was as pretty as she was. It said, 'I will not hold you to any commitment. Love, Agnes.'

Barney quickly dressed, and called Michael to bring the carriage out. When it was ready, he climbed aboard, and sat back on the button-backed leather upholstery.

'Where to, boss?' Michael asked him.

Barney stayed upright in his seat, his morning hat tilted at a slight angle, his cane held rigidly in front of him. As the sun rose, the carriage was silhouetted against the golden haze that shone through the camel thorn trees; an essay in spindly wheels, calligraphic springs, and elegant horses. They could have been posing for an eighteenth-century painting.

'Boss?' Michael asked, turning around on his seat.

Barney took off his hat. 'I don't think I'm going anywhere this morning, Michael, thank you. I'm sorry to have put you to all this trouble.'

'No trouble, boss,' said Michael, and climbed down from his perch once again, to open up the small curved carriage door, and let Barney alight.

On the last day of August 1879, the steam-vessel *Mulhausen* docked at Antwerp, in Belgium, under a humid grey sky. The bells were ringing dolorously from Our Lady's cathedral, and flocks of gulls were keening and crying as they circled around the spires and rooftops and flat-fronted façades of the city, and then sloped out over the wide silvery reaches of the river Schelde.

Joel was all ready to disembark as the *Mulhausen* noisily reversed its screws and nudged up to the grey-cobbled Noorderterras. He was wearing a soft grey hat, a light grey cape, and a rather old-fashioned day suit which he had bought in Dieppe when he had changed ships. His leather valise was packed with two spare shirts, some cotton underwear, a bottle of whiskey, and his single right-footed slipper. He had grown a dark beard, and a full moustache, and if it had not been for his missing left leg, even Barney would probably have passed him by without recognising him.

He had been careful to make his journey from South Africa to Antwerp as misleading as possible to anyone who might be following him. He knew that Barney would soon have learned from Nareez that he had managed to reach Durban, and from then it would have been relatively easy for Barney to discover what ship he had sailed on: even though he had bought his ticket in the name of 'Leonard Matthews'. Only two ships had been sailing from Durban to Europe that day: and one of those had been headed for South Wales.

The *Wallesey* had docked at Lisbon, where Joel had disembarked and bought a fresh ticket to Dieppe under the name of 'Henry Lester'. He had then left the ship for good at Dieppe, and stayed for a week at a small pension off the Rue de Varengeville, in a gloomy high-ceilinged front room with a blotchy cheval mirror and a creaking bed, and a view through dingy lace curtains of the Épicerie Auffay, and a wrought-iron bench where stout old ladies with long black dresses would sit and gabble all afternoon.

Joel had taken two hundred pounds in cash with him when he had left Kimberley, but he was already running short. He had his own company chequebook, but the problem was that if he drew out any money, Barney would eventually be able to trace his whereabouts. He had tried to persuade the shiny-headed manager of the Crédit Seine-Maritime to give him a hundred pounds on his passport and his identity papers alone; but after a long whispery discussion with his chief clerk, the manager had smiled and shook his head. Joel had been forced to write a cheque and hope that Barney did not think of looking through the company bank statements for a few months.

Now he had arrived in Antwerp, on a close and silent Sunday, with the uncut Natalia Star wrapped up in green tissue-paper in his coat pocket, one of the wealthiest men in the city, and one of the most isolated. A shabby carriage with a patched leather hood carried him on clattering and grating wheels across the wide square of the Grote Markt in front of the Town Hall, and all around him people walked on their way to Mass, heads bowed, in scarves and clogs, and from the dusty energetic rawness of Kimberley Joel felt as if he had entered a stale and colourless world of widows and seagulls and narrow flat-fronted buildings, a world in which reality seemed to be affirmed only by greyness and solidity, and through which human beings hurried as indefinitely as shadows.

'You want cheap hotel?' the Flemish cab-driver asked him, drawing up the carriage in a street not far from the Town Hall, The street was only wide enough for one carriage to drive down it at a time, and it smelled sharply of sewage and Javanese tobacco and cooked meat.

Joel looked up at the flaking doorway and the sign which announced that here was the Grand Hotel Putte. 'This will do,' he said. 'You can give me a hand with my bag.'

The Grand Hotel Putte was dark and elderly; a building of panelled landings and windowsills where dead bluebottles lay undisturbed amongst the dust. A plump young Flemish girl in a white apron and white cap showed Joel to his room on the top floor. She smelled of ripe underarms and carbolic soap. Joel opened the window and stared out over the steeply-pitched roof tops while she turned down the bed.

'English?' she asked him, standing by the door.

Joel gave her an uneven smile. 'That's right, English. Here's a franc for your trouble.'

She took the money and dropped it into the pocket of her apron. She was trying to think of a word, and Joel found that he could not turn away until she managed to remember it.

Eventually, she said: '*Je lijkt zo eenzaam. Heb je geen vrienden hier?*'

He shook his head. 'I'm sorry, I don't understand you.'

She waited a little longer, and then she managed to blurt out, 'My – name – is – called – Anna.'

'Good,' said Joel. He couldn't think of anything else to say. Anna hesitated for a little while longer, and then left the room, leaving the door slightly ajar behind her. Joel swung himself across on his crutches and banged it shut. Then, breathing heavily, he struggled back to the bed and sat down. After a minute or so, he opened his valise, and took out his bottle of whiskey. There was no mug in the room, so he drank straight from the neck, tilting the bottle back until he almost choked himself.

The travelling was over: now he was going to have to find someone who could cut the diamond for him, secretly but perfectly. It takes a whole variety of extraordinary skills to cut a diamond, and a stone the size and value of the Natalia Star called for the very finest cleavers, cutters, blockers and brilliandeers, as well as all the facilities that only a major diamond-cutting company could provide. It would be almost impossible to conceal the diamond's whereabouts for very long, and Joel knew that the risk of Barney finding out where it was being cut was dangerously high. But the risk was worth running: if he tried to sell the Natalia Star in the rough, he would probably make no more than £300,000 – maybe less. If he had it cut, however, and then gave it a 'legitimate' history by selling it and re-selling it through any agent or private individual who was interested in earning themselves a commission, he could sell it off for four or five times that amount, or as much as anyone was prepared to bid for it.

He had a list of names, some of which he had taken from Harold Feinberg's files; others which he knew simply by reputation. The cleaver would be the most important figure in the whole cutting operation. It would be the cleaver who would study the stone to decide where the planes of cleavage lay, the lines along which the diamond would be split, and on the skill with which he eventually cleaved it would depend the whole value of the finished gem. The cleavers were the élite of the diamond business, and many of them were driven to the diamond district each morning in their own carriages, and owned fine houses in the centre of the city. The undisputed best in Antwerp was Itzik Yussel, of Rosendaal's; but Joel was reluctant to approach him because he was the first and obvious choice. He had heard that a younger cleaver called Frederick Goldin was beginning to make an impression in the industry with his remarkable talents for saving as much carat weight as possible while shaping his diamonds to a 'make' of almost ideal proportions.

What Joel did not know was whether Goldin would be willing to cut a rough diamond of 350 carats without asking where it came from.

That evening, as the cathedral bells rang again, he lay on his bed and finished off his bottle of whiskey. From where he was lying, he could see a kite-shaped piece of sky, in between the dormer window and the roof of the building next door, and as he watched it, it gradually darkened, until it was black. The air was soft and warm and slightly sour, and riddled with mosquitoes, which bred in the marshy flatlands around the wide curves of the Schelde.

At ten o'clock, there was a gentle knocking at his door. He said slurrily, 'Come in,' and Anna appeared, in a black dress with a white lace collar, her wispy mouse-coloured hair pinned up with jet brooches and pins. She held up a brown glass bottle, and indicated by mime that he should rub it on his arms and his body. Then she circled her finger around in the air and made a buzzing noise.

'Ah,' said Joel, in a thick voice. 'Mosquito repellent.'

Without a word, she came and knelt down beside the bed, tugging back Joel's sheets and blanket. Joel watched her blurrily as she lifted his nightshirt, and unstoppered the bottle. He said, 'What are you doing?' but she did not answer.

Her hands were pudgy but firm, and she applied the lotion to his chest and his stomach as busily as if she were waxing a table. The lotion was cold, and smelled of camphor. She rubbed it on his back, and around his buttocks, and down his leg. He began to feel a tight, tingling sensation between his thighs, but he could not make up his mind if she really wanted to touch him there or not. He opened his eyes wide and stared at her; and she stared back at him, young and ruddy, with glistening drops of perspiration clinging to the blonde hairs on her upper lip.

Just as matter-of-factly as she had massaged the lotion on to the rest of his body, she held him in her fist like a broom-handle, and rubbed him up and down. It was only a matter of seconds before he snorted out loud, and anointed the shoulder of her dress. She stood up, corked her bottle of lotion, and looked down at him with a face that was too plump and expressionless for him to be able to read. She could not have been much older than seventeen.

'Anna,' he said. It was partly a question.

'Sleep,' she told him.

'But why? Why did you do that?'

She looked sideways. She probably did not understand him. Then she went to the window and closed it.

'Sleep,' she said.

Hours later, he woke up, awkwardly tangled in his sheets and smelling so strongly of camphor that he was practically sick. He had been dreaming about Kimberley, and the Big Hole, and the night he had fallen and broken his leg and his pelvis. It was hot and claustrophobic; so hot that he thought for a moment that he was back in Africa; but then he reached out and grasped the edge of the bedside table, and he remembered where he was.

For the first time in a very long time, he said a prayer.

They met at last in Frederick Goldin's workshop on the third floor of de Pecq's, an airy room with high windows facing northwards across the rooftops of the Antwerp diamond district. It was the third week in September, and it had taken Joel all of that time since he had arrived in Antwerp to arrange for an interview. For the first week, he had done nothing but visit the cafés and the restaurants most frequently patronised by diamond merchants, sitting in a corner by himself with a glass of cassis and a plate of stuffed veal, and listening to all of their talk about market prices, and quality, and make, and cut. Most of the dealers were Orthodox Jews, and they huddled around their tables in their *shtreimels*, their black broad-brimmed hats, with the *payess* or side-curls which most young New York Jews had long since cut off. It was an odd but reassuring feeling for Joel, to be back amongst his own people after so long in South Africa; and for the first day or two he had felt like interrupting the merchants' murmured conversations to take them by the hand and tell them how good it was to see them.

Deals in the diamond business were always arranged by

531

understandings; by word-of-mouth; with no written contracts. Hundreds of thousands of francs would be committed to the purchase of a parcel of diamonds without any paperwork at all, and with nothing to regulate the sale except the integrity of the merchants themselves. That murmuring that Joel enjoyed so much was the means by which a glittering torrent of diamonds passed from the traders to the merchants to the cutters, and then to the retailers.

At last, during the second week of his stay, Joel had got into conversation with an English-speaking dealer called Joseph Mandlebaum, a small pot-bellied man in his late forties, bespectacled, with the appearance of a Jewish gnome. From the way Mandlebaum had spoken, it had seemed to Joel that he was more of a wheeler-dealer than many of his colleagues in the Antwerp diamond business: he spent almost half of his time in London, in Hatton Garden, and he regularly sold diamonds to American dealers.

'If you happened to have a very large diamond that you wanted to have cut, very privately, who would be your best man?' Joel had asked him, as they had sat in a booth in a café called Boom's.

Mandlebaum had been sipping tea out of a glass, blowing on the surface to cool it, but he had paused with his cheeks still inflated, and then set down his glass, and looked at Joel through the tiny lenses of his spectacles with slitty-eyed sharpness.

'What do you mean when you say "very large"?'

'I don't know. This is only supposition. But, say, three hundred carats plus.'

Mandlebaum had stared down at his tea. 'That's a big diamond. Where would you find a diamond like that?'

Joel had sat back on his hard wooden seat. 'I don't think you're hearing me right. What I was asking was, where could you get such a stone cut *very privately*, and *very privately* would presuppose that nobody would ask such a question like, where would you find a diamond like that?'

'Umh,' Mandlebaum had said, also sitting back.

'I would presume that whoever arranged such a cutting would expect a fairly large commission, wouldn't you?' Joel had asked. 'And I would also presume that they would get it, without any argument.'

'You'd have to go one of the finest cutters,' Mandlebaum had said, reflectively. 'Someone like Yussels, or Steinberg, or maybe Frederick Goldin. To take a three-hundred carat diamond anywhere else would be – well, if you'll pardon the expression, criminal.'

Joel had grinned. 'I understand. But tell me, out of those three cutters you've just mentioned, which of them would be most likely to take on the job without asking any questions or spreading the word around? I mean, just out of interest?'

'Frederick Goldin, no doubt about it,' Mandlebaum had said. 'All he cares about is what he cuts. A stone like that, he'll see as a challenge, a step forward in his career. He's very jealous of Yussels, you see. He thinks of himself as some kind of prodigy. He believes he can keep more of the original weight of a diamond than Yussels, while still matching Yussels' make.'

Joel had nodded. 'You know him well, Goldin?'

'As well as anybody.'

'All right, then. Why don't you ask him the same question that I've asked you? Just out of interest.'

Mandlebaum had sipped some more tea, cautiously. 'Also as a matter of interest, perhaps I should tell you that a reward of one per cent is being offered throughout the trade for a very sizeable South African diamond of 350 carats known as the Natalia Star.'

Joel looked Mandlebaum calmly in the eye. 'I'm offering a commission of two per cent,' he said. And that was why, a little over a week later, he was helped into Frederick Goldin's work-shop, hopping on one crutch, and given a ladderback chair to sit on beside the well-worn bench where Frederick Goldin himself was studying a parcel of diamonds through his 10 × loupe.

'Mr Deacon,' said Mandlebaum, introducing Joel, and then stood back with his thumbs tucked into the tight pockets of his black best.

Frederick Goldin laid down his loupe, wrapped up the parcel of diamonds, and then turned to face Joel with a lean, rather dog-like face. He was tall, with frizzy gingery hair, and a complexion as freckly as bread-and-sultana pudding. His wrists seemed to be so loosely articulated that his large hands flapped this way and that like slapsticks.

'So,' he said, 'you're Mr Deacon, the man with the very large diamond.'

Joel coughed. 'Correction. I'm the man who's interested in knowing whether you might want to cut a very large diamond, and that's all.'

'You don't have to play word games,' said Frederick Goldin. 'I know what you want, and why you're here. You want a huge stone cut as near to perfection as possible, but instead of having to endure the usual publicity that accompanies such an event, you want it done silently.'

Joel said nothing. However much Goldin committed himself, Joel preferred to wait until he was absolutely sure of Goldin's trustworthiness before he admitted that he actually had the stone in Antwerp with him.

'All I can say to you is that you have not only come to the right man, you have come to the *only* man,' said Goldin. 'You could have gone to Itzik Yussels, and he probably could have done you a fair job, but sooner or later he would have let the cat out of the bag. He is a vain and pompous old man, and he would not be able to resist telling the world how wonderfully he had cut your stone.'

'And you?' asked Joel, quietly. 'You're not vain at all?'

'Of course I'm vain. Anybody who possesses as much talent as I do will always be vain. But I am an outsider in the diamond industry. They do not care for my methods; and they do not care for the way in which I challenge their traditional ways. I have spoken out for years against the second-rate cuts they impose on some of the beautiful gems that pass through their hands. There is a famous cut, a twelve-facet cut called the Antwerp Rose. Most of the cutters here won't hear a word against it; it is Antwerp's own, after all. But it is one of the dullest and most lifeless cuts of all, a cut that not even a topaz deserves.'

'Hmm,' said Joel, 'that's all very well. But what guarantee could you give that you wouldn't change your mind – that once you'd cut the stone, and made a really beautiful job of it, you wouldn't be tempted to win some professional kudos by letting it slip that you'd been responsible?'

Frederick Goldin leaned forward over his worktable. 'Mr Deacon,' he said, 'let us speak quite frankly. I believe that the diamond you have brought here to Antwerp for cutting is the diamond that went missing earlier this year from the Blitz Brothers mine in Kimberley – the diamond they now call the Natalia Star. De Pecq's have had at least two letters about it, one with a sketch showing approximately what the diamond looks like. The letters warn that the diamond will probably be in the possession of Mr Joel Blitz, whse most noticeable feature is that he has only one leg.'

Joel rubbed his chin, slowly and thoughtfully. 'All right,' he replied, 'if you know that much, then answer me one question and one question ohly. Will you cut the diamond, and will you cut it in complete secrecy?'

'That's two questions.'

'If you don't cut it in secrecy, then you don't get to cut it at all.'

Frederick Goldin stood straight. He looked across at Joseph Mandlebaum, who simply shrugged.

'It will be a considerable risk,' said Goldin.

'Not that much of a risk,' Joel told him. 'Fifty per cent of the diamond already belongs legally to me.'

'You want me to cut half of it only?' joked Goldin.

'I want you to say yes or no – will you cut it for me or won't you?'

There was a moment when Joel genuinely feared that Frederick Goldin was going to turn him down; when the diamond cleaver's face seemed to be collecting itself into an expression of regretful refusal. But then Goldin looked a little more whimsical, and mischievous, and then he nodded, and kept on nodding.

'Very well,' he said. 'If anybody finds out what I am doing, it will probably shock the industry to its very roots. But it is the kind of diamond that every cleaver wants to get his hands on before he dies. A diamond that only occurs once in a lifetime. I say yes.' ·

Without another word, Joel reached into his coat pocket and took out the package of green tissue paper. He set it on Goldin's work-table, and sat back.

Goldin stared at the package as nervously as if it contained a live snake. But then he reached forward with his long loose fingers, and tweaked the tissue open. At last, the Natalia Star lay exposed, brilliant and jagged; and next to the five- and ten-carat diamonds that were scattered on Goldin's table, it looked improbably huge.

Goldin sat down. 'Why didn't you show me this diamond the moment you walked in?' he asked. 'It has a morality all of its own.'

Joel smiled self-deprecatingly, and glanced at Joseph Mandlebaum in amusement. But Joseph Mandlebaum had his eyes on the diamond, and his mouth open and Joel had the feeling that he would have had to let off firecrackers to divert his attention away from it.

Frederick Goldin picked the diamond up and turned it one way, and then the other. 'This will have to be my sole occupation for the next two years,' he breathed. 'But what an occupation!'

'Won't de Pecq's get suspicious if you don't turn out your regular number of gemstones?' asked Joel.

Frederick Goldin said, 'No. Not at all. In any case, I will still be able to carry out two-thirds of my routine cleaving. They give me a free hand, you see; partly because I am so talented, and partly because I am so obnoxious to them. Besides it will take me six or seven months just to study this diamond and mark it out for cutting.'

'And two years before it's finished?' asked Joel.

'Maybe a little less. But cutting a stone like this can never be hurried. It is a question of *exact* degrees, *exact* angles, and inspired cleaving. Properly cleaved and cut, this diamond should yield one stupendous gemstone and anything up to five others, all of extraordinary size.'

Frederick Goldin went to the window, and held the diamond up in his hand as if it were a piece of the moon. 'To feel the weight of this diamond in my hand is a privilege in itself,' he said. 'I have never, ever, seen anything like it. I doubt if I ever shall again.'

Joel spent the rest of the day with Goldin, while the cleaver explained how he would study the diamond and determine which way its cleavage planes ran so that he could split it. No matter how talented the cleaver might be, he told Joel, there

536

was always a danger that an invisible stress point inside the diamond would cause it to split the wrong way, and ruin it. But if the cleaving was successful, the stone would then be bruted into outline shape by rubbing another rough diamond up against it – a process which also required remarkable skill. Then, the stone would go for grinding or blocking. The blocker would mount it in a metal arm called a tang, and press it against a revolving wheel dressed with olive oil and diamond dust, gradually grinding down the flat top of the diamond, the table. After that, the blocker would grind the crown facets that slope from the side of the table to the middle of the diamond, the girdle. He would then turn the diamond over and grind the pavilion facets below the girdle; and finish up by grinding the culet facet at the base of the diamond, which had to be precisely parallel to the table.

At last, the diamond would be passed to the brilliandeer, who would cut all the remaining facets. Even on a straightforward emerald cut, there would be fifty-eight of them, and each of them would be checked to within fractions of a degree by eye, lining up edges precisely with other edges, and with reflections of edges.

That evening, Frederick Goldin took Joel for dinner at a French restaurant on Consciencestraat called L'Écstase. They talked nothing but diamonds, and drank four bottles of Chateau Hauteville between them. When Joel finally got back to the Grand Hotel Putte, Anna's father had to heave him upstairs, puffing garlic in his face with every stair.

Just before dawn, when the kite-shaped pieces of sky was already light, Joel's door opened and Anna came in, in her billowy white nightdress. Without being asked, without saying anything, she lifted the nightdress over her puppy-fat hips, and climbed on top of Joel with all the weight of an authentic Rubens.

By February of the following year, Barney controlled almost all of the Kimberley Mine with the exception of the L-shaped cluster of claims owned by the French Company; and, on the whole, he began to feel content. He felt he needed a rest, too, and to socialise more. He had been working so hard on modernising his mining equipment and buying up his competitors that he had not entertained anybody for dinner at Vogel Vlei for months; and he had neglected his visits to Klipdrift for nearly a year. Pieter must have grown beyond recognition.

Barney's friendship with Harold had grown offhand and unsatisfactory, although their increasing estrangement was not entirely Barney's fault. Harold was so ill with his hearing complaint these days that it was all he could do to climb the stairs to his office, and he frequently went home early. There were no more late-night business meetings, and no more five a.m. starts. Everything was done briefly and breathlessly in Harold's office, with the minimum of banter. Negotiate, sign, pay, and go.

Barney had seen Agnes now and again, once with her husband, and once in the company of a brawny young Australian, and he thought about her over and over until the inside of his head felt like a *trommel*. There was something about Agnes which stirred up a part of his personality which Mooi Klip had never touched; an inexplicable desire for sexual suffering and actual pain. He wondered if he harboured a secret need to be punished for his arrogance, but somehow that explanation did not seem to correspond with the excitement he felt when he remembered how Agnes had dug her sharp fingernails into the flesh of his buttocks. Nor did it correspond with his arousing recollection of hurting Agnes in return. He alarmed himself when he thought too deeply about that, and he made himself change the subject.

He thought about that Natalia Star more than anything else. He could close his eyes and remember it exactly: its soft and magical colour, its irresistible brilliance. It had been a symbol of his deepest love, and Joel had taken it from him, in just the same way that he had taken the first Natalia.

To have lost the Natalia Star was, inexplicably, to have lost his direction.

He left Edward Nork in charge of the mine one Thursday morning early in March and rode over to Klipdrift on his horse Jupiter. It was a dazzling day, with only a few clouds clinging to the far horizon, and Barney felt unusually good-humoured.

It had been nearly a year now since Sara had died and his official period of mourning was almost over. He had licked the Big Hole into good shape, so that his combined claims were bringing in more than £75,000 a week. Suddenly the years of work and argument and discontent seemed to be coming to an end, and he could look forward to travelling, and parties, and amusements. Vogel Vlei was almost finished, although he had missed Sara's good taste when he was decorating the guest bedrooms; and in Edward Nork's words the parlour looked like 'the anteroom to Lucrezia Borgia's outhouse'.

Barney reached Klipdrift a little after four o'clock, and rode around to Mooi Klip's house feeling sweaty and tired. He dismounted by her front gate, and to his surprise she was standing by the door, in a summer coat and a bonnet decorated with flowers, and carrying a parasol. Beside her, dark-eyed and solemn, with that short chiselled nose and wedge-shaped forehead that distinguished him as Barney's son, stood Pieter. Around them was a collection of chests and trunks, all locked and labelled.

'Natalia,' said Barney, tying Jupiter up to the gatepost.

She stared at him, her face flushed pink by the late sunlight which shone through her parasol.

'Barney ... why have you come?'

He opened the gate, and walked towards her across the yard. 'What do you mean, why have I come? I came to see Pieter, of course, I came to see you.'

Mooi Klip appeared to be partially paralysed, unable to move or speak properly. 'But *today*,' she said. 'Of all days, you had to come today?'

'What do you mean?' asked Barney. 'You're leaving Klipdrift? You're moving?'

'I sent you a letter,' she said.

'I didn't see any letter.'

'I only sent it today.'

He stepped up close to her, and looked around at all the trunks. 'You were only going to tell me you were leaving after you'd gone?'

She lowered her parasol. 'Do you think I could have had the strength to tell you any other way?'

Barney reached out and held her white-gloved wrist. 'Is this

Natalia Marneweck talking?' he asked her. 'The bold Natalia Marneweck?'

She raised her eyes. They were as dark as an owl's. 'No,' she said. 'This is Natalia Ransome.'

There was a very long silence. Barney released Natalia's wrist and stood with both hands clasped together in front of his mouth, the way the Bantu herdboys held their hands when there were whistling through reeds. Pieter clasped Natalia's sleeve uncertainly, seeking reassurance that everything was all right, but all Natalia could do was touch his hand.

'You married him, then,' said Barney.

Mooi Klip nodded. 'He's very kind,' she said, with a catch in her throat.

'Yes,' smiled Barney. 'That's what I thought about him, when he came to call on me.'

The sun was gradually nibbling at the tops of the trees on the far side of the Vaal River, and on the opposite bank Barney could see a diamond prospector bent over the slow golden shallows, dredging up yellow ground in a bucket. It seemed a hundred years ago that he had walked along the Orange River, and watched the diggers sorting soil on their rocker-tables.

He crouched down, and held out his arms for Pieter. 'How's my favourite son?' he asked. 'I'm sorry it's been so long.'

Mooi Klip coaxed Pieter forward. 'It's been a long time for all of us,' she said. 'The truth is, we're going to England.'

Barney was holding Pieter's hand. The boy seemed so gentle and serious, the same way that Barney had been when he was young. He looked up at Mooi Klip and said, 'England? For how long?'

She pursed her lips, and he knew then that she was going for ever.

'His church has sent him, I suppose?' he asked, and Mooi Klip nodded.

Barney stood up, resting his hand on Pieter's shoulder. Pieter obviously wanted to go back to his mother's side; but there was something about the way in which his mother was looking at him that made him stay where he was.

'I heard about your wife from the newspaper,' said Mooi

Klip. 'I was so sorry for you, but I knew that I couldn't come to see you. I would have to leave that to you. I thought sometimes that you might come. I even prepared myself for what I was going to say to Hugh. But you didn't come, and I had to honour my promises, and think of Pieter as well as myself; and so I married Hugh, in Hopetown, and now we're going to England.'

Barney touched Pieter's hair, and his thin childish neck, and his cheeks, and then let him go back to his mother. 'I left it too late, then,' he said, with less assurance than he'd meant to.

Mooi Klip could not take her eyes off him; any more than Barney had been able to take his eyes off the Natalia Star. The tears slid down her cheeks, and she had to hold her hand over her mouth to suppress her sobs. Barney could do nothing but look at those brown lambent eyes and think of the past, of all those days of love, and of all of those days of loneliness, and it seemed to him now that the past ten years had ruffled by like the leaves of a calendar, page after page after page, a whirlwind of white paper, and that nothing was left on this gilded March evening but regret.

'Kiss me once,' he asked Natalia. 'Kiss me once, the way you used to.'

And in the doorway of that whitewashed *strooidak* house in Klipdrift, they held each other for the very last time, and kissed like they always should have done, while the evening birds rustled up from the river, and the day began to fade.

On Wednesday, 14 July 1880, Harold Feinbert toppled down the stairs of his office on Kimberley's main street, as stiffly as a scarecrow. He died three hours later, in his own bungalow, in his own bed. Barney was at his bedside, and read for him as he died his favourite psalm, number 84, a psalm for the sons of Korah.

'How amiable are thy tabernacles, O Lord of hosts! My soul longeth, yea, even fainteth for the courts of the Lord: my heart and my flesh crieth out for the living God.

'For a day in thy courts is better than a thousand. I had rather be a doorkeeper in the house of my God, than to dwell in the tents of wickedness. For the Lord God is a sun and shield: the Lord will give grace and glory: no good thing will He withhold from them that walk uprightly.

'O Lord of hosts, blessed is the man that trusteth in thee.'

Barney sat by Harold for almost an hour after he died, the Bible open on his knees. It was still morning, a few minutes before noon, and the sunlight shone through the blind in parallel stripes. A stray dog barked and barked, and yet Harold could not hear it. The silver hairs in Harold's ears still curled around his lobes; his nose was still as proud and fleshy and Jewish as always; his hands looked as if they were about to move at any moment. But he was dead, and he would never speak again.

Barney cried no tears for Harold, but he knew that Harold would understand. He simply stood by the window and looked out across the street and wondered on Harold's behalf why a God who was supposed to be such a model of humility should invest his children with so much ambition.

A week and one day later, a small spiky-haired boy in clogs came around to the Grand Hotel Putte and asked to speak to Joel. When Joel came out of the hotel dining-room, wiping sauce from his mouth with his napkin, the boy handed him a note. Joel gave him ten centimes and shooed him away. Then he swung himself back to his table, where his poached lemon sole was growing cold, and tore open the envelope with his butter-knife.

The note read: 'I am ready to cleave the diamond. I expect you by noon. Respectfully, Frederick Goldin.'

Joel finished his breakfast slowly, mopping up the last of his hollandaise sauce with torn-off pieces of breadroll. After his coffee, he asked for a schnapps, which he stared at for five minutes, and then drank with a flourish. Anna, who served as a waitress at mealtimes, dragged out his table for him so that he could haul himself out on his crutches, and make his way upstairs. She said, 'You're all right?', and he nodded at her.

He dressed with care, tying his necktie in a large butterfly bow. Afterwards, he felt so tense that he had to sit on the bed and pour himself a brandy from the bottle that he kept in his bedside table. He had been living on his own in Antwerp for a year now, so short of money that he had scarcely been able to afford to eat, waiting with badly-controlled impatience for Frederick Goldin to finish his preliminary studies of the Natalia Star and begin cutting.

Anna knocked on the door, and looked in on him. 'That was not bad news?' she asked.

'No,' said Joel. 'It was very good news. News that I've been waiting to hear for a long time.'

'You will have money soon? Father is worried about your bill.'

Joel drained his brandy glass. 'Father will just have to be patient for a little while longer. But don't let him fret. When I do settle up, I'll pay him twice over, plus interest.'

Anna came across and took his hands. 'I don't know if I feel frightened of you or sorry for you,' she said, in Flemish.

Joel grunted. 'I'd rather you didn't feel either way. I'd rather you just felt affectionate.'

She kissed him. 'You can *wish* me to feel anything; but how I will really feel, that will be private, inside of me.'

'Anna,' said Joel, quietly.

Before directing the cab driver to take him to de Pecq's, Joel asked him to stop at the small synagogue on Pelikaan straat. He was thinking of offering a prayer before he went to see the diamond being cleaved. But when the cab actually drew up outside, Joel changed his mind. All he could depend on now was his own luck, the flukes and chances of his own destiny. He rapped his crutch against the side of the cab and told the driver to carry on.

Usually, the cleaving of a huge diamond would have been a well-publicised and well-attended event, and the workshop would have been jostling with dignitaries and journalists and artists. But when Joel arrived in Frederick Goldin's rooms a few minutes after twelve, Frederick Goldin and Joseph Mandlebaum and two assistants were the only people there. Outside the windows, the sky was relentlessly grey. Joel stood in the doorway for a moment, and then one of Goldin's assistants brought forward a chair for him, while the other closed the door behind him and, on Goldin's instructions, locked it.

The Natalia Star had been placed into a little wooden cup called a dop, and set there firmly with a cement of brickdust, shellac, and rosin, so that only the angle to be cleaved off was exposed. Goldin had already cut a small notch or kerf in the top of the Star with another diamond, and had wedged the dop into a tapered hole in his workbench. All he had to do now was slot a knife blade into the kerf, tap the blade with an iron rod, and the diamond would split along its cleavage plane. At least, it was supposed to.

'I intend to cut the diamond into an emerald-shaped stone of about 160 carats,' said Goldin. 'Then there will be three other major stones – a square emerald, a briolette, and a baguette.'

'You're only going to be able to get a 160-carat diamond out of a 350-carat rough?' frowned Joel.

'Believe me,' Frederick Goldin told him, 'that's a greater saving of weight than Yussels could manage out of the same stone. The Regent is only 140·5 carats, out of a rough of 410 carats. Weight is important, but not if it detracts from a diamond's brilliance. What I will give you out of this stone will almost be a miracle. So remember that.'

'Very well then,' said Joel. 'You'd better get on with it.'

Frederick Goldin rolled up his shirtsleeves, and dragged over a stool to sit down at his workbench. He positioned the long rectangular metal knife-blade in the kerf, resting it between his thumb and his index finger. It seemed to take him over half an hour to position the blade to his complete satisfaction, and Joel began to feel stiff and uncomfortable, and to wish that he had stayed at the Grand Hotel Putte instead of coming here to watch. To have to sit utterly still and silent while his whole future was put at crucial risk in front of his eyes was almost more than he could bear. He would have done anything for a drink. He wished he had brought his flask with him. But now Frederick Goldin was ready for the first cleaving, and the workroom was crowded with tension.

'This first blow will decide exactly how much of the weight of this diamond I shall be able to recover, and exactly how valuable the finished Natalia Star will be,' said Goldin, matter-of-factly. 'You can understand that the slightest error on my part, the slightest miscalculation, could result in the loss of thousands of francs of value. So, I will have to be careful, won't I?'

Without any further preliminaries, he tapped the iron rod on to the back of the knife-blade in a way that appeared to Joel to be absurdly casual. The rough fragment of diamond which was protruding from the cleaver's cement dropped neatly on to the workbench.

Joseph Mandlebaum let out a noisy sigh of relief. The two assistants gave Frederick Goldin a short burst of spontaneous applause. Frederick Goldin looked at Joel and grinned in pride.

'Is that all?' asked Joel.

Goldin's narrow face gradually cleared of self-satisfaction, like clouds moving away in front of a cold easterly wind. 'What do you mean, "is that all"?' he asked Joel.

'It took you nearly a year to get yourself ready to do that? Just one tap?'

'You're playing a joke on me,' said Goldin. His two assistants laughed, but not very happily.

'You think so?' Joel demanded. 'I'm beginning to wonder who's playing the joke around here, you or me. It took you nearly a year to cut one piece off the side of that diamond; how long is it going to take you to finish it?'

'Mr Blitz, with the greatest respect, you know that such a cutting just can't be hurried. That is why you brought the rough to me in the first place. To have it cut perfectly, not hastily. Now you're trying to tell me that I'm too slow?'

Joel took a breath. 'When I first brought you the Natalia Star, I had a little money left. Now, I don't have anything. I'm broke; and as you can probably understand, that makes a difference.'

'You really don't have money?' asked Joseph Mandlebaum. 'But you own half of the world's largest diamond-mine.'

'Sure I do. I'm a wealthy man. Except that as soon as I start drawing money out of my accounts with the Capetown banks, my brother is going to be able to locate me within a matter of weeks.'

Frederick Goldin looked across at Joseph Mandlebaum and

made a face. 'Maybe between us we could advance you a few thousand francs,' he suggested. 'Just enough for you to live on until I finish the diamond.'

Joel said sourly, 'That's just marvellous, isn't it? The poverty-strucken millionaire. When I first looked at that diamond, I saw dreams of incredible riches. Now look at me.'

Goldin held up the cleaved-off fragment of the Natalia Star. 'When this diamond is polished, my friend, you won't be poverty stricken any longer. You will be a king in your own right. You know that, don't you? And that is why you must give me the time that I need to do this job to perfection.'

Joel reached for his crutches. 'Come on, Mandlebaum,' he said. 'I believe you can start advancing me money by buying me a drink.'

On the morning of February 1881, Boer guerrillas shot and killed ninety-three British soldiers in a surprise attack on the crest of Majuba Hill, in the Transvaal. There were only a handful of them, but they abruptly and successfully halted a full-scale British advance through Laing's Nek to relieve British garrisons trapped in the Transvaal by a recent Boer uprising. The action was described by the British C-in-C as 'a rout almost unparalleled in the long annals of our Army.'

The Boers wept openly as they fired at the fleeing backs of the Gordon Highlanders and Northamptons; but by August they had won from the negotiations which followed Majuba a concession which they fervently hoped would be a first step towards fresh independence. The British government agreed to reconginse Paul Kruger and his advisers as the legitimate leaders of the Boers, and to let them administer the Transvaal independently – although they were still to be subordinate to what was vaguely described as 'British suzerainty'.

The Treaty of Pretoria which guaranteed these concessions sent nervous ripples through the diamond industry – as any signs of Boer independence always did. The prime target for any act of Boer aggression against the British would obviously be the diamond fileds at Kimberley, especially since the Orange Free Staters still bitterly resented their annexation.

For Barney, however, Majuba Hill had an immediate and startling effect. When the news reached Kimberley the following day over the new cable link, it was reported that among the 133 wounded was a young Australian naval rating named James McPherson. McPherson, as it turned out, was a cousin by marriage to Agnes Knight's husband, Robert Joy, and in their boyhood in Sydney they had been inseparable and loving friends, 'Bob and Jim.' After a week of indecision, Robert Joy decided with almost violent immediacy to travel to Durban, where James McPherson was in the military hospital, with the declared intention of bringing him back to Kimberley to recuperate.

Two months later, in April, Agnes received a telegraphic message from Natal saying that Robert had decided to take his wounded cousin straight back to Australia. His cousin had lost his right eye and the use of his left arm, and Robert wanted to take care of him. It was 'unlikely' that he would return. 'Kimberley is not really for me and I suppose neither are you really, my dear,' part of his message had read. 'You may seek annulment on grounds of desertion and keep whatever I have left behind. I am sure you will be much happier with somebody else; after all, you always were happier in other men's arms.'

Mr Knight was outraged that his daughter's honour should have been impugned over the open telegraph, but Agnes soon calmed him down. She was glad to be rid of Robert so painlessly, although she discovered that before he had set sail for Sydney he had drawn the last remaining three hundred and sixty pounds out of their bank, and left her with a few coppers.

It may have been for that reason that she arrived on the front doorstep of Vogel Vlei on a hot shimmering afternoon just before Christmas, 1881, in a wide white sun-bonnet and a white layered dress of silks and Brussels lace, and asked Horace if she might speak to Barney.

Barney came to the door himself, still carrying the copy of the Capetown newspaper he had been reading. He was wearing a pure silk shirt and a fawn-coloured vest and trousers that had been tailored for him in London. His dark brown silk necktie was held in place with a 22-carat diamond stickpin.

'Agnes?' he asked her. 'Won't you come in?'

Through the white veil of her hat she looked as if she might have been crying. She said, 'Only if you want me to.'

'Why shouldn't I want you to?'

'You know why. I've never been a faithful person.'

He folded his paper up, and smiled. 'I don't know whether I've ever been looking for a faithful person.'

'You heard about Robert?' she said.

He nodded. 'It was the talk of Kimberley for a whole month. I don't think I could have avoided hearing about it.'

In the distance, a farmcart trundled through the heat, and even from a quarter of a mile away, Barney could hear its iron-rimmed wheels on the road. Agnes said, 'The marriage won't be annulled for another six months, at least. But I couldn't wait to ask you.'

Barney lowered his head. He knew what she was going to say; and he knew, too, that it was what he wanted. But somehow on this warm and restless day, with the air like liquid mirrors, the words seemed to be magnified beyond any sensible meaning. Too obvious, and too overblown, and years too late. Yet what else could he do? Live alone in his decorated palace for another silent decade, in his fashionable suits and his opulent jewellery, eating alone in a dining-room that could have seated a hundred? He had been a prisoner of his own life when he was poor, and living in New York; but in Vogel Vlei he would be just as trapped, just as isolated, even though he was rich.

He said to Anges, 'Come back when they tell you your marriage is over. I'll be here.'

'Are you sure?' she asked him, her voice so soft that he could hardly hear her.

He nodded. Then he reached out for her hand, and held it against his cheek. 'Something tells me that we were made for each other,' he told her.

It was snowing when Joel laboriously mounted the stairs of Frederick Goldin's workshop in the last week of February 1882. Outside, he could see the grey flakes whirling down on to the rooftops of Antwerp, and transforming the whole city into an encampment of white.

548

It was today, Wednesday, that Frederick Goldin had promised him that the Natalia Star would finally be ready.

Joel had seen the diamond through every stage of its cleaving and grinding and polishing. The last time he had examined it, only two weeks ago, it had already appeared to be finished. A brilliant, flashing lozenge of pure light. But Goldin had told him that one of Antwerp's most talented brilliandeers was going to spend a final few days bringing it up to a perfect shine. To Goldin, everything had to be 'perfection'.

'I can never show the diamond to anybody, and claim credit for it, so my reputation is not at stake,' he had told Joel. 'But, I must satisfy my own pride.'

Joel knocked on the door of the workshop, and one of Goldin's assistants let him in. The light in the room was grey and unearthly, and from up here the view of the city seemed even more unreal. Even the rigging on the ships that were moored along the slate-coloured curve of the River Schelde had snared the snow, so that they looked like ghostly vessels from a nightmare.

Frederick Goldin was cleaving a small canary-yellow diamond in his dop; and Joel had to wait until he had halved the stone before he could approach him.

'Well?' Joel said, peeling off his damp leather gloves, and forcing them into his coat pocket.

Goldin looked at him for a long time. 'Well, what?' he asked, at last.

Joel cleared his throat. 'Where's the diamond?' he said. 'Is it completely finished?'

Goldin sat up straight on his stool and looked this way and that in obvious bafflement. 'I don't think I know what you're talking about.'

'What do you mean, you don't think you know what I'm talking about? I want to see the diamond!'

'I don't know what diamond you mean,' Goldin protested.

'The Natalia Star,' whispered Joel. 'What else do you think I mean?'

Goldin stood up. 'There's no such diamond,' he said.

'What the devil are you playing at?' Joel snapped. 'The Natalia Star. Three hundred and fifty carats of lilac-pink diamond. You've been cutting it for the past two years!'

Frederick Goldin turned towards one of his assistants, and the assistant shook his head.

'I've been in the diamond business long enough to know every major diamond,' said Goldin. 'It's my profession to know them. But I have never seen or heard of a diamond called the Natalia Star.'

'I brought it here myself,' Joel told him. 'It's my diamond and I want to know where it is.'

'You say *you* brought the diamond? It's yours?'

'You know damn well I did! By God, Goldin, I'm going to have you thrown in to jail for this! Where the hell is my diamond?'

'I'm sorry. You never brought me any diamond of any description,' smiled Goldin. 'And as for your threats of jail . . . well, if you can prove that I took such a diamond from you, then obviously I will have to be arrested, and perhaps tried. But where is your proof? Where are your documents of provenance? What have you got on paper to say that the diamond ever existed, or that even if it did, it was yours?'

Joel closed his eyes, and swayed a little on his crutches. 'I don't think I can believe what I'm hearing,' he said. 'I'm going to count to ten, and when I'm finished, I want you to show me my diamond. Because if you don't . . .'

'If I don't, what? You will strike me with your crutch?'

Joel opened his eyes again and stared at Frederick Goldin hauntedly. 'I went through agony and exile for that diamond, Goldin. I've suffered for that diamond for years. Don't think you're going to be able to take it away from me, because you're not.'

Goldin thought about that, and then smiled again. 'There was never any diamond, Mr Blitz. Come on, you're a sick man. You must have imagined it. You drink, don't you? Maybe it was something you hallucinated.'

'I'll kill you,' said Joel.

'No, you won't,' Goldin told him. 'You have no reason to.'

'I have plenty of reason. A perfect emerald-cut diamond of 158·4 carats, that's reason enough. The Natalia Star. It existed because I saw it. It shines like no other gemstone on the whole of this earth. It's mine, Goldin, and if you don't give it to me then I swear to you that you will die.'

'You're over-wrought,' said Goldin. 'Perhaps you'd like to sit down and drink a glass of water. Gilbert, would you bring Mr Blitz a glass of water?'

'I want my diamond,' repeated Joel.

Goldin shook his head. 'There was never any diamond,' he said. 'It was a dream.'

Joel stood on his crutches in silence while one of the assistants brought him a chair and a glass of water. He ignored both of them; although the assistant remained where he was, holding out the glass, one hand on the back of the chair, solicitous and still. Joel stared at the snow as it fell on Antwerp, on Jezusstraat and Twaalfmaandenstraat and the Oude Koornmarkt, on the Gothic spire of the cathedral, on the statues of Rubens and Quinten Matsys, on the Vlaeykensgang and into the river. He felt as if time had suspended itself, as if nothing else was ever going to happen, because the key to his future had disappeared as briefly and as completely as a star winking out behind a distant rooftop, a star by which he had desperately hoped to steer himself, but which had proved to be a false star, a wandering star, and a star too bright.

Agnes said, 'You know, my darling, I should have married you at the very first.'

Barney was bent over his desk, almost crouched over it, reading through a packet of letters that had arrived that morning from Kimberley. The light that strained into the drawing-room was autumnal and brown, and yet at four o'clock it seemed too early to call the servants to light the lamps.

'Hmh?' he said, as he pencilled a note into the margin of one letter. Then, looking up, he said, 'Well . . . that's a strange thing to tell me.'

Agnes smiled at him. She had been sitting contentedly for most of the afternoon in the small blue crinoline chair by the fireplace, tatting. The folds of her smock and her overdress revealed that she was heavily pregnant, and her face had that roundness and that light moustache of fine blonde hair that betrayed a woman whose body is enriching itself for that final moment of birth. Their second child was expected in ten days, perhaps sooner.

Barney put down his letter and stood up. It was five years since Joel had lost the Natalia Star to Frederick Goldin, five years and four months, and during that time Barney had worked more furiously than ever. Agnes thought he looked old, and very tired, but there was nothing she could do to woo him away from his desk and his diamonds. She tried to accept his work in the same spirit that she might have accepted the constant presence in their home of a crippled uncle: with patience, and endurance, and as much charm as she could. After all, Barney was very thoughtful, and very loving to her, and he adored their first child, David, as if he were a cherub.

'I don't give you much of a life, do I?' asked Barney. He touched the curls of hair that strayed over her ears. 'I'm surprised that you haven't asked me why I married you at all; not why I didn't marry you earlier.'

'You have to do what's right for you,' said Agnes.

Barney leaned forward and kissed her, first on the hairline, and then on the forehead, and then on the lips. The sound of their lips parting, in the stillness of that afternoon room, sounded like a mayfly falling on a still pool somewhere.

'Other married people see even less of each other,' said Agnes. 'I think we should just be happy for what we have.'

Barney looked at her for a while, and then kissed her once more to release himself from her loving but unwavering gaze. He went to the window behind his desk and stared out at the leaf-cluttered garden. They had been in London for three weeks now and already it was beginning to depress him. The heavy skies, the whirling leaves, the grey-shouldered buildings. London was a city of weight and law and majesty, but at the same time it was one of the most melancholy cities on God's earth. To be sad in New York could be maddening, maniacal, or even elegaic. But to be sad in London was to feel the shackles of history closing around one's ankles, shackles that one had to drag around from Regent Street to Hatton Garden, from Hatton Garden to Barnes, like the chains which Marley's ghost had forged for himself in *A Christmas Carol*.

Barney knew that he had very little to feel sad about. He had lost Joel, of course; and he had lost Sara. He had lost Mooi Klip, and he had lost the Natalia Star. But in April 1882, only three months after Joel had been tricked out of his diamond by Frederick Goldin, he and Agnes had been married, drawn together again by the same feelings that had first attracted them. She was fair-haired, and pretty, and coquettish, and for Barney she had all the temptingly unreliable qualities that so many Jewish girls lacked. He, to her, had been individualistic, even odd, even obsessed. But he was handsome, gentle, and he could touch her sensitivities in a way that no other man had been able to before. Perhaps it was the sense of fate that he carried around with him, of great events, even of doom, that attracted her. She always suspected that one day he would kill himself, and that he would never tell her why. There was a side of his mind that was always concealed from her – sometimes under the lock-and-key of direct refusal, at other times hidden beneath the dusty drapery of evasiveness and silence.

They loved each other, certainly, although it was impossible for either of them to tell quite how much. Not as much as they might have done if they had married when they first met. There had been too many painful encounters with too many other people since then. Not as much as they might have done if the Natalia Star had never been discovered, and if it hadn't burned its image into Barney's consciousness like the sun on his unprotected eyes.

They had married in Capetown in April 1882, first at the synagogue and then at the Anglican church. It had showered that day, and the quicksilver puddles had trapped the petals that their guests had thrown, and pasted them on to the wheels of their carriage. They had spent their honeymoon in Paarl, in a quiet and private *strooidak* house with an enclosed courtyard, and for the first two weeks they had talked and kissed and made love like two delirious young lovers. Barney could still remember the feeling of those warm afternoons on the old Dutch bed, under the thatched roof, with the windows open on to the flowering garden, and the distant clouds lazing their way across the mountains. He could remember the clock ticking in the corridor, the only sound in the silence after they had made love, and he could remember thinking that things could never be the way they were again.

The diamond business was too demanding, and Barney

wanted it to be too demanding. To reflect was to reflect on Joel, and the Natalia Star, and the dark and mesmerizing woman for whom the Natalia Star had been named. During the last days of their honeymoon, Barney began to have nightmares about his mother, about blood, and knives, and the old days on Clinton Street.

Once Barney and Agnes had returned to Vogel Vlei, Barney had worked harder than ever before. He would often rise before dawn, and have to bend over the washbasin and retch because his stomach was nauseous from lack of sleep. Most nights, he would return well after dark, too tired to do anything but eat a frugal supper of bread and stew, and then take a bath, and collapse into bed. Agnes had lain next to him, listening to him breathing, listening to him stirring and murmuring as nightmares raced through his brain, and she had often felt that she might spontaneously break down and cry out of frustrated passion.

There was a time, at a dinner party in Capetown, when Agnes had caught the eye of a handsome and straightbacked young British ordnance officer. They had danced twice, and at the end of the second dance, the officer had asked her if he could meet her again. She had been tempted, God knows, but she had refused, and kissed him once on the cheek as a consolation.

Agnes's married life had improved, however, after the birth of their first child, David, in 1884. Not long afterwards, Cecil Rhodes had introduced to Barney the son of an old schoolfriend of his, a smart and personable young man called Lance Pollock. Despite his public-school drawl, and his liking for loud cricket blazers and straw boaters and a monocle, Pollock was an astute and extremely hard young businessman, and he took over many of Barney's administrative chores and paperwork – apart from supervising at the mine. He was very harsh with the blacks. When he visited the mine, he always took a George Taylor riding-crop with him, and he never hesitated to use it. Barney always said that he would not trust Pollock with a single point; but Pollock was glib, and quick, and mercilessly efficient, and when Barney found that Pollock's management of the mine enabled him to spend whole days with Agnes and their tawny-haired baby boy, and even to take his first vacation, he began to rely on him more and more.

By the fall of 1887, Barney's accountants informed him politely that he was one of the wealthiest men in the British Empire. Together, he and Agnes had bought this huge country house in Barnes, along by the Thames; and another house on Fifth Avenue, in New York, cater-corner from Mrs Astor's house at Number 350. The demands of the diamond business took Mr and Mrs Blitz away from Vogel Vlei more and more often; until the popular name for it at Kimberley became 'the Ghost House'.

With his riches, came fame. Barney and Agnes Blitz were invited to all of the best parties, and were photographed with Vanderbilts and Huntingtons and even at Mount McGregor, with the dying President Grant. Agnes dressed in silks and velvets and lace, and for their third wedding anniversary Barney gave her a 120-carat diamond necklace. They financed one of New York's most memorable productions of *La Traviata*, with Gisella Fini. They met the Queen of England, and presented her with a Kimberley diamond cut as a teardrop, a silent crystalline memorial to her grief for Albert. They sailed from America to Europe and back again six times, and each of their sailings was noted in the London *Times* and in *The New York Times*. Some of their more lavish weekend parties in Barnes were described, in breathless detail, in the popular magazines bought by housemaids and governesses.

Agnes adored the parties and the riches and the unceasing attention she received. She was slightly sensitive about Barney's Jewishness; but he was never maudlin about his upbringing, and he never once took her back to see Clinton Street. He never went back himself. Clinton Street was the bottomless treacherous pool where his nightmare dwelt. It was a grave, rather than a memory. And besides that, it reminded him too much of Joel.

Agnes said, 'Would you like some tea now? Or would you rather wait?'

'We could have it now,' said Barney. 'These letters are giving me a headache.'

Agnes went across to the bell-pull to ring for the maid, but before she could do so, the door opened and their footman Edwards appeared. 'There's a gentleman outside to see you, sir. Mr Cecil Rhodes.'

'Rhodes? Here?' asked Barney, in surprise.

Agnes glanced at him quickly; as if to say, what's wrong? But Barney said, 'Show him in. Please. And tell Harriet to bring us tea.'

Rhodes strode confidently into the drawing-room. He was looking browner and plumper than before, and his grey Savile Row suit seemed to be too tight all around, especially across the front buttons, but he was in excellent humour, and he pumped Barney's hand with enthusiasm.

'Barney, my dear chap! And Agnes! How good to see you! I'm so sorry I descended without an invitation, but I'm only in London for two or three days, and time presseth. I hope I'm not interrupting anything crucial?'

'I'm just trying to catch up with my correspondence,' said Barney. 'I've always been a terrible letter-writer.'

'Well,' said Rhodes, drawing back the front of his coat and thrusting his hands into the pockets of his trousers, 'the reason I'm here is to save both of us a great deal of letter-writing. The fact is that I've put in a bid for the French Company, and if all goes well we're going to be neighbours in the Big Hole.'

Barney looked at Rhodes cautiously, but said nothing. Up until now, he had been quite content to share the Big Hole with the French Company simply because it would have cost him well over a million to buy them up, and because he had felt sure that they were far too expensive for anyone else to take over. The French Company had been peaceful and non-acquisitive, but if Rhodes took them over, Barney knew that it would only be a matter of months before Rhodes began to put pressure on *him*, too. For Rhodes, only complete control of South Africa's diamond industry would ever be enough. He had demonstrated that by the way he had voraciously acquired the whole of the De Beers mine, and he never stopped talking about a diamond monopoly to control prices of precious stones throughout the world.

Barney however, was emotionally tired. He had no dreams left, except to watch his children grow up happily. He had achieved wealth and success beyond anything he ever could have imagined in Clinton Street; and in doing so, he had lost everything that had ever fired his heart. With Mooi Klip, he

had briefly experienced the vividness and strangeness of unconditional love. With Joel, he had just as briefly experienced
unconditional hatred. With Sara, he had felt pride, humiliation,
frustration, inadequacy and loss. He did not believe that he
would ever feel emotions as turbulent as these again.

Nor did he believe that, for all the digging at the Big Hole,
he would ever own another Natalia Star.

Rhodes stood with his hands in his pockets, his head slightly
inclined to one side, waiting for Barney to say something.
Agnes said, 'Would you like some tea, Cecil? I've just asked for
some.'

'Well, yes. Capital,' said Rhodes. 'Although I'm afraid I've
been overeating lately. Do you mind if I sit down?'

'I'm sorry,' said Barney. 'Go ahead.'

'The fact is,' Rhodes went on, as if he had been interrupted
in the flow of a long financial monologue, 'the fact is that
N. M. Rothschild's have put up a million, and that I myself
have put up £400,000; and that the French Company seem
more than interested. Well, you know as well as I do that
they're losing interest in the diamond market. They don't have
sufficient influence to be able to control it, the way you and I
can. They're bound to sell, sooner or later.'

Barney went to the window again. A black and white cat was
walking along the back wall of the garden. He said, 'It looks
like rain again. It does nothing but rain here. I feel as if I'm
drowning, sometimes.'

'You ought to come back to Kimberley,' said Rhodes.

'What for?' asked Barney. 'To be sacrificed on the altar of
British imperialism?'

Rhodes laughed, and turned to Agnes. 'He *will* rib me, you
know. He's always been a ribber.'

Barney attempted a smile. 'Whatever you bid for the French
Company,' he said, 'I'll outbid you. I can promise you that.'

'I'm surprised,' said Rhodes. His voice abruptly lost its
humour. 'I thought you'd be rather bucked. After all, you and
I, we've been in it right from the beginning, haven't we?'

'Yes,' said Barney, 'and that's why I know you so well. And
that's why, whatever you bid for the French Company, I'll
outbid you.'

'You can't bid more than two million,' said Rhodes, suspiciously.

Barney sat down, and crossed his legs. He wished that he did not feel so weary, and so used-up. But he drummed his fingers on the arm of the chair, and smiled again, and said, 'I can bid whatever you bid, and more.'

The maid, Harriet, a pale girl with a face that always reminded Barney in its indistinctness of someone who had inadvertently moved during the taking of a daguerrotype portrait, brought in currant scones and Darjeeling tea. The steam rose in the afternoon light like the hair of a drowning woman. Rhodes smiled, and cuddled his stomach, and took two scones, which he spread with butter and greengage jam.

Eventually, Rhodes said, 'You can go on bidding *ad infinitum*, old chap, but we shall have it in the end.'

'You think so?' asked Barney.

'Sure of it,' Rhodes nodded. 'Absolutely sure of it.'

Barney stared at the small cluster of bubbles that circled in the centre of his cup of tea. 'It seems to me that you've come here with a proposition,' he said. 'You seem to have that air about you.'

'Well, that's true,' said Rhodes. He glanced at Agnes, and gave her a smile that was intended to be winning. Agnes patted the back of her upswept hair, and nervously looked towards Barney.

Barney said dryly, 'You'd better tell me what it is.'

'Barney,' Agnes protested. 'It's tea-time.'

'Cecil didn't come here to eat scones and drink tea,' said Barney. 'He came to talk business, and I think we'd better know what it is.'

'It's very simple,' said Rhodes. 'My suggestion is that you allow me to bid for the French company at my original price of £1,400,000, which I am quite confident they will accept. I will then immediately resell the French Company to *you* for just £300,000, plus a one-fifth share of Blitz Brothers.'

'You want only a fifth share in Blitz Brothers? And you'll let me buy the French Company from you?'

Rhodes nodded. 'You've overestimated my greed, I think. You've also overestimated how much of a monopoly I'm after.

As long as you and I control the price of diamonds between us, then what difference does it make? I just want the French Company to be out of it. They'be been over-producing for years, and keeping the price down. What this business needs is careful control, and I'm sure that between us, you and I can exert it.'

Barney sipped his tea, and then set the cup down on the table. 'I'd have to talk to my accountants.'

'Of course,' said Rhodes. 'But in principle?'

Barney thought for a moment, and then nodded. 'In principle,' he said, 'it seems to make sense.'

Agnes caught the mood of relief from Rhodes, and the mood of cautious optimism from Barney. She leaned forward and said, 'Would you care for another scone, Mr Rhodes?'

Rhodes hesitated, and then took one. Barney watched him in silence as he pushed in into his mouth, devouring it in two or three bites, and then sucked the butter from his fingers with noisy relish.

'It's getting dark,' said Barney. 'I think, Agnes, you'd better instruct the servants to light the lamps.'

It was nearly six months before Barney saw Rhodes again, and by that time the Blitzes had left London and returned to South Africa. They were breakfasting at their bedroom balcony at Vogel Vlei one morning in April when one of their sixty black servants brought Barney a sealed envelope embossed with the seal of the De Beers Mining Company.

'It's from Rhodes,' said Barney, when Agnes raised her head. She had been embroidering a sun-bonnet for Naomi, their daughter, who had been born after twenty-three agonising hours of labour in early December last year. Agnes had sworn to God that after Naomi she would never have any more children. Not one. The pain and the humiliation had been too much.

Barney opened the letter. He knew what it would contain. Rhodes wanted to meet him that evening at the Kimberley Club, to talk over business. What Rhodes *really* wanted to do, as Barney was quite aware, was to ask Barney to sell out.

559

Since Barney had signed, late last year, the agreements that gave De Beers control of one-fifth of Blitz Brothers, Cecil had been working furiously to acquire even more Blitz shares. Rhodes had promised Barney's shareholders a glittering future, a future of diamonds and gold, and he was prepared to pay anything up to £40 for a £15-share to demonstrate his confidence.

At first, only a handful of shareholders had deserted Barney. But when Rhodes had increased his price to £45, and then at last to £50, there had been a mad scramble to sell out, and to take as much as possible before the price dropped again. By March, it was clear that despite Barney's protests, now Rhodes owned a substantial proportion of Blitz Brothers mining – a proportion that was large enough for him to be able to call on Barney by messenger and have him drive all the way along Kimberley's rutted high street at six o'clock in the evening to discuss what they were going to do about it.

Barney felt hot, and there was a red rash under his collar, and by the time the carriage drew up outside the clubhouse, he felt so irritable that he almost wished that somebody would accidentally trip him up, or poke him with their umbrella, so that he would have some justification for punching them very hard. As it was, he had to be content with squeezing the palms of his hands really tightly, and controlling his breathing.

The black coachman said, 'You want me to wait here, Mr Two-Leg?'

Barney said hoarsely, 'Yes,' and climbed the steps to the front door. The verandah below his feet was spread with a fine Indian carpet, and as he approached the entrance he was intercepted by a Persian doorman in a watered silk jacket and an amber silk turban.

'Mr Blitz, sir, pleased to welcome you. Mr Rhodes is waiting for you upstairs.'

His slippers squeaking on the polished floors, the Persian led Barney through the lobby to the main stairs, and then up to a small private room where Cecil Rhodes was sitting in a casual linen jacket, reading *The Field* and idly sipping a tall glass of brandy and seltzer. The shutters were wide open, because the Kimberley Club, for all its exclusiveness and all of its grandeur, still had nothing more than a corrugated-iron roof, and at this time of year it grew beastly hot.

'Ah, Barney,' said Rhodes, without getting up. 'My dear chap. Do sit yourself down. Would you care for a drink?'

'Tea,' said Barney.

'I can recommend the rum and hot milk,' said Rhodes.

'Very well then, I'll have one of those,' Barney assented.

The Persian squeaked off again, and Rhodes and Barney were left alone. Rhodes lifted his glass and tinkled the ice in it reflectively. 'Well,' he said, 'we've been having quite a struggle, haven't we, you and I?'

'I shall outbid you in the end,' said Barney.

'Perhaps you will,' Rhodes told him. 'But outbidding is not necessarily the crucial factor in this little skirmish. You can offer your shareholders whatever you like, in terms of pound notes. But I can offer them something far more valuable. I can offer them a monopoly of the diamond business, and the control of diamond prices on the world market; and that, my dear Barney, will make them rich beyond anything *you* could ever hope to offer them.'

Barney stared back at Rhodes, but said nothing. He was thinking of the day when Rhodes had first arrived in South Africa, like a plump and eager schoolboy, with his books and his cough lozenges.

'I shall win the day, you know,' said Rhodes. 'I have the historic tide of the British Empire behind me. I would annex the planets if I could. I have often dreamed of that. I shall win the day because I am on the side of *right*.'

'Well, that's your opinion,' said Barney. 'But, meanwhile, I'm not going to sell.'

'I knew you'd be stubborn,' smiled Rhodes. 'That's why I asked you to come here in person. I want to make you an offer which will make all this far easier for you to swallow. I mean, you must accept that a monopoly will protect all of our interests. At the moment, while we're still in competition, we're each of us vulnerable to the quantity of diamonds that the other decides to unload on the market. If I were to release next month all of the roughs that I have in Amsterdam and London, the price would drop through the floor. You'd be ruined; and it would take even me several months to recover.'

'I hope that isn't a threat,' said Barney.

'You know it isn't,' said Rhodes. 'Look, here's your rum and milk. I always find rum and milk excellent when I'm hungry, and my spirits are low.'

Barney took his drink from the black steward in the high-buttoned white jacket who had brought it up for him; and sipped it once before setting it down on the small brass table between them.

'What's your proposition?' he said.

Rhodes smiled. 'I may be misjudging you,' he said, 'but I don't think so.' And with that remark, he reached into the pocket of his white linen jacket, and produced a small envelope of dark blue tissue paper. 'Here,' he said, handing it across the table to Barney. 'Unwrap it. See what you think.'

Barney hesitated, but then took the tissue-paper package, and weighed it cautiously in the palm of his hand.

'Open it,' urged Rhodes.

Barney slowly unwrapped the tissue. He knew, with an intuition which made him tremble, what the package contained. It could not be, and yet he knew that it *must* be – otherwise Rhodes would never have offered it to him. It was the one single object on earth to which he was utterly susceptible.

At last, all the tissue was folded back; and there, in Barney's fingers, was a huge lilac-pink emerald-cut diamond, of at least 150 carats. It snapped at the evening light which bathed the room, as fiercely as a small dog, and turned the light into lances of orange flame.

Rhodes watched Barney's face with amusement. 'You recognise it?' he asked.

Barney nodded. 'It's been cut, of course. But there's no question about the colour. It's the Natalia Star.'

'These days, it's called the Rio Diamond.'

'Where did you get it?'

'It's only on loan,' said Rhodes. 'At the moment it belongs to the South American Diamond Company, and it was supposed to have been discovered four years ago in Brazil.'

'It's the Natalia Star,' whispered Barney.

'That's what I thought, when I first saw it,' Rhodes agreed. 'It *has* to be. There aren't any records of a diamond of any size being discovered in Brazil, not for years. It's 158·4 carats, and if you calculate what it must have weighed in the rough, you come out with a figure very close to the weight of the Natalia Star. I'm not frightfully enthusiastic about emerald cuts, but whoever did this one was a genius. In fact, there are only two people who could have done it. Only *one*, actually, and that's Frederick Goldin, at de Pecq's, in Antwerp.'

Barney held the diamond up to the last ray of blood-red sunshine; and the facets of the diamond split the blood into light and fire. '*Natalia*,' he said, scarcely moving his lips.

Rhodes watched him, in satisfaction. 'I had my agent in Antwerp talk to Goldin,' he said. 'Of course, Goldin denied that he had ever seen such a stone. But Goldin is living in a new house in a well-to-do district these days, and there are rumours in the trade that he made the money from a huge black-market stone.'

Barney said, 'Is this stone for sale?'

'You're rushing me,' said Rhodes. 'I was going to tell you that my agent undertook further investigations, and took around to de Pecq's a picture which I had sent him. It was *this* picture, from the *Cape Courier*.'

He handed Barney a small yellowed piece of paper. On it, was a blurred newsprint photograph of a frowning man, and the caption underneath read, '*Mr Joel Blitz, of Kimberley*.'

Rhodes said, 'A man who looked like this – a one-legged man who looked like this – visited de Pecq's several times during 1881 and 1882.'

Barney allowed his hands to close over the Rio Diamond, tightly and possessively. 'Then this stone is mine,' he said.

'You can't prove it,' said Rhodes. 'The South American Company have all the papers of provenance.'

'Then how much is it?'

'They're going to auction it. It's expected to fetch two million.'

'Pounds?'

Rhodes nodded.

Barney understood at last the circle through which his destiny had turned. It was a destiny which he himself had determined, or, at least, which his passions had determined.

His life had revolved around this stone, the Natalia Star, and around the woman from whom he had named it, Natalia Marneweck, Mooi Klip. The stone was the symbol of the woman, and the woman was the symbol of the stone, and both were symbolic of Barney's hopes, and beliefs, and of his understanding of life and God. At last, with this diamond in his hand, he saw the pattern of his existence, as regular and as symmetrical as a well-cut diamond. The only trouble was, it was all too late. He had lost almost everything out of which the pattern was formed. The understanding was nothing without the substance.

'How much will you pay me for the Blitz Brothers mine?' Barney asked Rhodes.

'One million six hundred thousand,' said Rhodes, calmly. 'As well as which, you can have a life governorship in De Beers mines; you will always be guaranteed the largest individual shareholding; and you can become a full member of the Kimberley Club.'

'One million six hundred thousand?' asked Barney.

'The price of that stone,' Rhodes told him, with a self-satisfied smile. 'The South American Company have already agreed to sell it to me for that price, if I want it. All you have to do is say yes, and the stone's yours.'

Barney took the stone to the balcony, and held it up again, a star to the early stars.

'And you can guarantee my election to the club?'

Rhodes inclined his head, as if to say, you only have to ask.

Barney knew that he was going to agree. There was no point in fighting for ambitions which had already died; for affections which had already faded; for prizes which had already been won, and spent, and tarnished. And somehow, the thought that he would be able to come down here to the Kimberley Club every evening for a drink – a simple social pleasure from which his Jewish background had always excluded him – that seemed more of a temptation than anything.

Barney looked at the diamond in his hand. 'Very well,' he said. 'I don't think I can stand in the way of history any longer.'

Rhodes said, 'Have another rum and milk.'

*

She was hanging up the bunting for St Julian's Summer Fair when Mrs Cross came over and said that there was a gentleman waiting for her outside. She gave the end of her line of flags to Miss Hornchurch, and climbed as elegantly as she could down from the platform, her skirts and her petticoats raised just a little to reveal her white canvas summer boots, tiny and tightly-laced.

'He's in the lobby, Mrs Ransome,' said Mrs Cross. Mrs Cross was looking hot, and the fruit and feathers on her hat were in their usual disarray. 'Not an Englishman, though. A *colonist*, I'd say.'

Natalia crossed the floor of the village hall until she reached the lobby doors. There was a small window of hammered glass in each of them, and before she opened them, she tried to peer through one of the windows to see who this unexpected gentleman might be. Not far away, at the top of his ladder, Mrs Unsworth was singing '*The Old Hundredth*': 'All people that on earth do dwell ... Sing to the Lord with cheerful voice ...'

Natalia could just distinguish a dark and distorted figure through the glass, but she could not be sure who it was. So she opened the doors, and confronted the 'gentleman' with a polite nod of her head. 'Good afternoon, sir. Mrs Cross said you were asking for me.'

The man stood straight, his hands by his sides. He was wearing a grey morning-coat, and a wing-collar. He did not appear to have a hat; or, if he did, he had left it outside in his carriage.

He said, '*Mooi Klip*.'

Her heart bumped against her ribs. She stared at him in surprise and shock. And yet it was him. It was. He was older, and his hair was greyer, and he seemed to have put on more weight. But it was Barney Blitz, as handsome and solid as a prizefighter; as real as daylight.

She could not speak; neither could she move. But her mouth tightened with happiness and grief, and her eyes filled up with tears.

'Barney?' she asked. 'Is it really you?'

'Natalia,' he said, softly, and that was all it was necessary for him to say.

565

They walked together, arm in arm, up the sun-dappled suburban avenue. Once or twice, Barney had to step off the pavement to allow nurses to come by with baby-carriages, fringed and embroidered and protected by parasols. There was a dusty smell of lime trees and dried horse manure, the smell of transpontine London, south of the river, in the late 1880s, when Chiswick was still a village and people still moved out to Notting Hill for the fields and the fresh air.

Natalia said, 'Are you here for long?'

'I own a house at Barnes,' he told her. 'I've been here for a week, but I have to sail for New York on Friday.'

'I read about you in Hugh's newspapers,' she said. 'You're quite a socialite now.'

'Not really.'

He looked at her in the hazy sunlight. The extraordinary thing was that in spite of the brown summer dress she wore, and her veil, and her bonnet, she was still Natalia Marneweck, still as dark and as beautiful as that day when he had brought Joel into the Griqua encampment for help and rest. The years in between might have fled. But they had not: and now he was Agnes's husband, and she was Hugh's, and all the nights they had shared in Kimberley were nothing more than a remembered taste of sweetness; a taste of flowers and honey that could never quite be recaptured.

She said, 'Why did you come?'

'To make sure that you were happy.'

'Well ...' she said, turning her face away. 'I'm happy.'

'Are you sure?'

'Yes, Barney.'

They had tea at a corner café, behind layers of net curtains, while outside the horses clip-clopped along the streets with drays and carriages. Barney did not even taste his tea. It seemed to be scalding hot and nothing else. But he remembered for years afterward the flypaper which hung from the ceiling, and the dead flies which clung to it.

At last, Natalia said, 'I have to go back. I can't leave Miss Hornchurch to do everything. It's our summer fair on Saturday.'

'I wish I could come,' said Barney, with a rueful smile. He